Bridgeport Public Library
1200 Johnson Avenue
Brid--   / 26330

HELEN

London Calling

F
CAR

Copyright © Helen Carey 2018.

All rights reserved.

The right of Helen Carey to be identified as the author of this work has been asserted by her in accordance with the Copyright Designs and Patents Act 1988

No part of this publication may be reproduced, stored in a retrieval system, or transmitted in any form or by any means without the prior permission in writing of the publisher. Nor be otherwise circulated in any form or binding or cover other than that in which it is published and without a similar condition being imposed on the subsequent purchaser.

All characters and events in this publication, other than those clearly in the public domain, are fictitious and any resemblance to real persons, living or dead, is purely coincidental.

First published in Great Britain in 2016 by Headline Publishing Group
This edition published in 2018 by Cambria Publishing.

ISBN 978-1-9996129-5-5

In memory of my uncle, Basil Beazley, who died during the invasion of Sicily in 1943

Prologue

12 December 1942

With considerable relief, Molly Coogan pulled her cloak round her, checked that her nurse's cap was pinned on securely, ran down the last few stairs and crossed the dimly lit lobby towards the heavily sandbagged doors.

Her hand was already on the handle when she heard someone speak behind her.

'I wouldn't go out there if I was you.'

The voice was portentous, almost gleeful in its gloomy menace, and Molly turned to see one of the hospital porters pinning a poster up on the wall next to the empty reception desk.

'That sounds ominous,' she said. 'Why not?'

It struck her suddenly that the whole lobby was unusually empty. Visiting hour was long past, but there were normally a few staff coming and going. She knew it wasn't an air raid. Even in the depths of the Wilhelmina septic wards she would have heard the sirens. She had heard them often enough. And the planes that followed.

Much of south London had been smashed to smithereens by Nazi bombs over the last couple of years. But the Wilhelmina Hospital had been built to withstand the Zeppelin raids of the Great War. It was proving equally effective against the Luftwaffe, despite its proximity to tempting targets like the Clapham Junction rail interchange and the Battersea Power Station.

In her darker moments Molly sometimes wished that the Wilhelmina would suffer a direct hit and put everyone out of their misery. Throbbing and humming gently, insulated from the real world by its emergency generators, it was like some sinister old submarine. And she hated it. She hated the boarded windows, the hushed gloom, the ghastly competing scents of sepsis and iodine, the dogmatic senior nurses and the smug, complacent doctors. Most of all she hated the constant presence of death.

She didn't know how much more she could take. Even tonight … She stopped and shook her head.

'Why not?' she asked again. 'What's going on outside?'

'Fog,' the porter said.

1

He took a spare drawing pin out from between his teeth and stood back to admire his handiwork. Even in the muted light, Molly could see that it was a picture of Winston Churchill.

'Fog?' Molly repeated. 'I'm not scared of a bit of fog.'

But then she hesitated. It was an excuse not to go up to the Flag and Garter. A legitimate excuse. She could go back to the nurses' home instead, crawl into bed and block out the day, block out the thought of a young girl dying of septic infection only ten days after pricking her finger on a rose bush.

'That's easy to say, but it's a right old pea-souper tonight,' the porter said. 'Just like the old days.'

Molly felt torn. She was dog tired. But she had promised her friend Katy Frazer that she would help up at the pub.

'You can't see your hand in front of your face,' the porter added.

Wondering what other platitudes he would come out with, Molly took a step forward to read the slogan under Winston Churchill's face. *We will go forward together.*

That was all very well for him, Molly thought. Going forward for old Winnie probably meant being tucked up in front of a log fire somewhere nice and safe with a big fat cigar in his hand and a map of the world on his lap. But for her it meant struggling up to Lavender Road to spend the evening behind the bar in a noisy, smoky pub.

She nodded an unenthusiastic good night to the porter and pushed out through the heavy doors. She had to go. It was her last chance to give Katy a hand. She was back on nights again tomorrow, and by next weekend, fingers crossed, she would be at the maternity hospital in Croydon, starting midwifery training.

It wasn't much of a change. There'd still be scrubbing and cleaning and starchy old ward sisters to contend with. But at least she would be ushering life into the world rather than out of it. And if nothing else, it would get her away from the Wilhelmina, from London, from Lavender Road. And from Katy and her lovely Canadian husband Ward Frazer.

She would try to make a fresh start. It would be a wrench. A terrible wrench. But she knew it had to be done. For the sake of her sanity.

Chapter One

As soon as Molly emerged on to St John's Hill, she realised that the porter had been right. The fog was indeed so thick that she really couldn't see her hand in front of her face. She took two steps forward and immediately felt unbalanced, disorientated. She couldn't even see the ground she stood on. There was no traffic, no noise at all.

She took her torch out of her pocket. But all it illuminated was a thick yellow circle ahead of her, more like custard than pea soup. Or the beige-grey batter of hospital toad in the hole. Molly smiled grimly. Trapped in the impenetrable fog, she felt a bit like a toad in a hole herself right now.

Once again she hesitated. She used to love going up to help Katy at the pub. She and Katy had been probationer nurses together at the Wilhelmina at the beginning of the war. Katy had left nursing when she got married, but her continuing friendship had been the one thing that had kept Molly going over the last couple of years. But now everything had changed. Katy's husband had come home, and—

Molly spun round. For a moment she thought she had heard something. A tapping noise. Behind her. It came again. Tap, tap, tap, then silence, and then tap, tap, tap.

It was getting louder, faster, nearer.

Molly's eyes stung as she peered through the sulphurous gloom, trying to see what it was. Muffled gunshots? A ticking bomb of some sort? She wondered if she should panic, run away, shout for help. Her hand clenched involuntarily on the heavy torch.

But before she could do anything, something swiped her on the ankle. Even as she screamed, she realised what it was. A blind man tapping down the road with a white stick.

As he lurched back, she caught his arm to steady him. 'I'm so sorry,' she stammered. 'But you made me jump. It's really foggy, and I didn't see you coming.'

'I didn't see you either,' he said. 'That's why I've got the stick. I'm blind. The fog don't make any difference to me.'

'Well it makes a difference to me,' Molly said. 'I'm meant to be helping out at the Flag and Garter in Lavender Road. I go there so often, I thought I'd be able to find my way blindfold, but ...' She stopped abruptly, groaning inwardly. She tried so hard not to, but she always somehow managed to say the wrong thing. Sister Parkes was constantly telling her off for her impudence. The other nurses thought it was hilarious. She often caught them sniggering in the sluice room when she'd queried an instruction or asked a question out of turn.

But the man didn't seem to mind. 'Well I *can* see my way blindfold,' he said. 'I'll walk you to Lavender Road if you want. I'm going that way. Here, take my arm.'

Apart from the scuff of their footsteps and the intermittent tap, tap, tap of the stick, they walked down the hill in silence. Instinctively Molly felt herself picking her feet up higher than usual, her spare arm stretched out in front of her like a sleepwalker. The last thing she needed was a black eye from bumping into a lamp post.

The blind man's arm was strong and his step was confident, but it was an unnerving, almost mystical sensation marching along through a blanket of muffled darkness. Molly was just wondering rather fancifully if she had somehow stepped into another dimension when he slowed and said, 'Watch out, kerb coming up.'

'Thanks,' she said. 'Where are we? By the library?'

'That's right.' He seemed pleased that she had worked it out. As they stepped up on to the opposite kerb, he asked her how long she had been nursing.

'How did you know I was a nurse?' Molly asked in surprise.

'Well, you were standing right outside the hospital, wearing a nurse's uniform. What else could you be?'

'How do you know I'm in uniform?'

'I can hear it rustling under your cloak.'

'And I probably stink of iodine.'

Her companion chuckled. 'That too.'

Molly's grimace was lost in the darkness. 'Just over two years,' she said. 'And I've hated every minute of it. I knew I would.'

'Why did you go into it, then?'

She hesitated. She didn't like to talk about it. But something about the ghostly darkness and the anonymity of her escort made her want to tell him. She'd probably never see him again anyway. And he'd certainly never see her.

'A bomb fell on our block of flats,' she said. 'One evening in 1940. Everyone except me was killed.'

'So you lost your whole family that night?'

'They were my adopted family,' she said. 'At least that's what I called them. They took me in when I was about ten. I was in an orphanage before

4

that.' She was conscious of a slight constriction in her throat and went on quickly. 'So I had to do something. I'd always been good at biology at school. Nursing seemed as good a job as anything else. And it came with accommodation.'

The man didn't respond immediately, so they walked on in silence. 'What terrible times we live in,' he said at last. 'What an extraordinary girl you must be.' He tightened his grip on her arm. 'We are crossing the road here, so mind your step.'

'I'm not at all extraordinary,' Molly said, stumbling over the gutter. 'All the other people I know do amazing things.' She thought of Katy reopening her father's pub after it had been bombed in the Blitz. Katy's posh friend Helen de Burrel working as a secret agent in France. Even that flouncy bit Jen Carter was beginning to make a success for herself on the stage. And as for Ward Frazer, what he'd been through didn't bear thinking about. 'I'm just stuck here doing the same thing day after day.'

'But you're a nurse,' the blind man said. 'That's useful. Ah,' he added, tapping his cane on the wall. 'I reckon this must be Lavender Road now.'

'I'm not useful,' Molly said as they turned the corner together, still arm in arm. 'I'm always getting told off. And I'm on one of the septic wards. Nearly everyone dies there.'

'But at least they have you to care for them.'

'I don't want to care for them,' Molly said. 'I want to cure them.'

'Then you should have been a doctor.'

Molly laughed. 'If only.'

'Things are going to change,' the man said. He spoke quietly, but his voice carried a strange kind of conviction.

'What do you mean?' Molly blinked in the darkness. She wished she could see his face. 'What things?'

He was silent for a moment, as if he was reluctant to answer. 'It's strange,' he said at last. 'But since I lost my sight, I can see more than I used to be able to. Or maybe *sense* is a better word. And I can sense that your life is about to enter a new phase.' He paused. 'A more testing phase.'

'Well, I have been offered a place on a midwifery course at Croydon.'

'And have you accepted?'

'Yes, I'm just waiting for Matron to authorise it.'

His pace slowed, as though he was going to make some observation. But he didn't. He just squeezed her arm slightly. 'Well then,' he said. 'I wish you luck. And courage.'

'Thank you. But Croydon.' Molly sighed. 'It's hardly groundbreaking, is it? I don't think I'm going to need much courage there.'

He chuckled appreciatively but didn't answer. A moment later he stopped and released her arm. 'Your moment will come, my dear. Believe me. Your moment will come.'

He patted her on the shoulder and turned around, and with three taps of his stick he was gone, into the fog, back the way they had come, leaving her shivering outside the pub, wondering if she had somehow imagined the whole encounter.

Joyce Carter gritted her teeth and thrust her hand into the weeds growing along the side of the Anderson shelter. Touching something cold and hard, she gave a grunt of satisfaction. But it was only an empty bottle. She sat back on her heels and inspected it in the foggy glow of her shrouded torch. A beer bottle. Probably one of her husband Stanley's, discarded as he lurched into the shelter, half cut, during one of the endless Blitz raids.

She remembered those nights only too well, his beery breath as he ranted about the bloody government or the bloody Germans. She also remembered the dread of catching that awful randy look in his eye in the light of the lantern. And the impact of his fist if she didn't comply.

Well, Stanley's beer-drinking days were over now. Well and truly over. Even now, two weeks after she had received the notification of his death from the governor of the prison where he had been incarcerated, she could hardly believe it. A burst appendix.

If she'd ever thought about Stanley dying, she would have guessed it would be in a late-night drunken fall into the river, or from an unlucky punch in a pub brawl. Once, one particularly bad time, she had even held a gun on him, wishing she had the courage to put a bullet through him.

But no, it was a burst appendix that had done for him in the end. And that was that. He was gone, and she was free.

Unfortunately, so was her new pet tortoise.

Previously when she had let the tortoise out of his box, he had just wandered about aimlessly before coming back for his food. But this time he hadn't come back.

She had been keeping an eye out for him ever since she had got home from the café, sure he would be lured in by the winter cabbage leaves Mrs Rutherford had picked from her veg patch especially for him. Mrs Rutherford lived in one of the big houses at the top end of Lavender Road. The end that overlooked Clapham Common. The Rutherfords had a sizeable garden and Celia Rutherford had thrown herself enthusiastically into the Dig for Victory campaign. Somewhat to Joyce's surprise, considering her well-to-do background, she had also thrown herself enthusiastically into the local café that she and Joyce now ran together.

As the wife of the owner of the local brewery, Mrs Rutherford had never previously done a day's work in her life, apart from a bit of service on the WVS tea van during the Blitz. Oddly enough, it was that experience that had given her the idea of opening a café. She claimed that it was a way for her to do something towards the war effort, but Joyce suspected that it was because she wanted to prove to her old-fashioned, autocratic husband Greville that women could be just as successful in business as men. Either way, Joyce was grateful. She had always had a dream of running a little café, and now Celia Rutherford had made that dream come true. Joyce certainly wasn't going to rock the boat by asking questions. Mrs Rutherford was far too superior to discuss anything of a personal nature. But she also had a good heart, and it had been kind of her to offer up some of her precious cabbage leaves.

Not that Monty, the tortoise, seemed to care. Joyce had laid them out temptingly by the back door, but so far there was no sign of him, and she didn't want to leave him out in the cold all night.

Joyce didn't know much about tortoises, but she knew they didn't like the cold. And now she was getting worried. She'd always fancied having a tortoise, so she'd been quite overcome when Mr Lorenz had presented her with one as a gift to celebrate the first year of running the café. Where he had got a tortoise from right in the middle of a war, God only knew. But he had. And now, just a week later, she had lost it.

Joyce rubbed her hands against the cold. Mr Lorenz was the local pawnbroker. Stanley had ranted on about him and all. Mr Lorenz was Jewish, and Stanley didn't like Jews. He'd always suspected Lorenz of having a soft spot for her. Joyce'd thought he felt sorry for her, and was just being kind sneaking her some sugar, or the odd Guinness, to help her over a bad patch. But it turned out that Stanley had been right. Mr Lorenz did have a soft spot for her. And secretly she had a bit of a soft spot for him too. Who cared if he was Jewish? He was a nice man, kind and generous, but—

'What on earth are you doing?'

Joyce swung round to see her daughter, Jen, silhouetted in the kitchen doorway. In certain lights Jen's auburn hair took on a fiery reddish hue, which some might say matched her unpredictable temper, but tonight the combination of the light spilling out of the kitchen and the yellow fog made her fancy Veronica Lake-style perm look unnervingly like a golden halo.

'For goodness' sake shut the door,' Joyce snapped. 'I don't want some busybody reporting us.'

'There won't be any raids tonight,' Jen retorted. 'The fog is so thick the Nazi pilots wouldn't be able to see their arses from their elbows.'

'That won't stop us getting fined.'

'OK, OK, keep your hair on,' Jen said. But instead of going back indoors, she stepped out into the yard and closed the door behind her. 'So what are you doing out here? Seems an odd time of night to be weeding the back yard. Not that it doesn't need doing, of course ...'

Joyce gritted her teeth. When did Jen think she had time to do the weeding when she was working her knuckles to the bone in the café from dawn to dusk? She bit back an irritable retort. Nobody had the power to wind her up like Jen did. What with her arty-farty theatrical ways and her ridiculous pride, anyone would think she was already a famous actress, not just a two-bit singer in a back-street revue. But when Jen had moved back home two weeks ago, after undergoing a small throat operation, Joyce had determined that she would try not to rise to her taunts.

'I was looking for Monty,' she said. 'The tortoise. He's disappeared.'

'He must be here somewhere,' Jen said. 'He's hardly going to scale the back wall, is he? Not unless he's found a rope. Or maybe he thinks he's a prisoner of war and he's decided to dig a tunnel.'

'It's not funny,' Joyce said.

'It is funny,' Jen said. 'Just the thought of old Lorenz giving you a tortoise as a love token is funny. I wonder why he didn't think of roses.'

For a moment Joyce felt herself bristle, but then her lips twitched. Well it *was* funny. Jen was right.

'I tell you what, though,' Jen said. 'He probably *has* dug a tunnel. Isn't that what they do? Like bears. Dig a hole and go to sleep for the winter?' She gave a gurgle of laughter. 'He's probably halfway to Australia by now.'

And sure enough, by dint of groping their way around the garden and shining the torch on every possible patch of ground, they did indeed find the tortoise, asleep in a nest of old leaves.

'Ha,' Jen said smugly as Joyce gently dug him out and carried him into the house. 'You see. I'm not just a pretty face!'

'No, you're a right smart-arse as well,' Joyce retorted.

'Maybe.' Jen picked up her coat and turned away along the passage towards the front door. 'But old Monty has got his head screwed on too. With any luck, by the time he wakes up the war will be over.'

'Pity that bugger Hitler doesn't hibernate and all,' Joyce called after her, and was gratified to hear Jen laugh as she opened the door.

'I'm just going over to the pub for half an hour,' she called back. 'I'll be back for supper.'

As she tucked the tortoise up in his box under one of Pete's old jumpers, Joyce found herself thinking that maybe it wouldn't be so bad having Jen back home after all. It might even be a bit of fun. She'd have been all on her own otherwise. Her two youngest children, Angie and Paul, were still down in Devon on a farm where they'd lived since being evacuated at the beginning of the war, and her other sons were all away. Pete had gone off on a training course for the navy, Mick was already in the merchant marine, and Bob, her eldest, was stuck in a POW camp somewhere in North Africa.

Joyce couldn't imagine Bob tunnelling out. Not like Jen's old school friend Katy's husband, that nice Ward Frazer over the road. Ward had escaped from a POW camp in Germany and had only recently arrived home after being on the run in Nazi Europe for months on end.

Joyce smiled to herself. No, with her children all accounted for, the café going well, the tortoise nicely tucked up in his box and Stanley nicely tucked up in his grave, for once in her life she had nothing to worry about.

The Flag and Garter was busy and the cloud of cigarette smoke inside was almost as thick as the fog outside. Against the background of Glenn Miller thumping out some swing on the radio was a cacophony of men's voices discussing the latest war news: the valiant Russian resistance at Stalingrad, General Montgomery's recent successes in North Africa. Someone else was telling a rather rude joke involving Hitler, Mussolini and a plate of sauerkraut.

As Molly disentangled herself from the heavy blackout curtain inside the door, she saw Katy and Ward Frazer standing together behind the bar, laughing at the punchline, and suddenly wished she hadn't come.

Bracing herself, she responded to Katy's quick wave, took off her cloak and started to weave her way across the room.

She had only advanced a few steps when there was a commotion behind her. The door flew open and the blackout curtain billowed wildly as a small boy launched himself into the pub, slipped on some wet sawdust and nose-dived on to the floor at Molly's feet. Barefoot, clad only in a thin pair of pyjamas, his curly fair hair tousled from the damp air outside, he made a pitiful little figure.

Recognising him as George, the adopted son of Pam and Alan Nelson, Molly reached down to help him up. But she was too late. The boy was already scrambling to his feet, barging on through the bar towards his father.

Unbalanced by the unexpected onslaught, Alan staggered back a pace, spilling his beer. 'George,' he said. 'For goodness' sake, what's happened?'

'Mum says Helen de Burrel is dead!' George wailed.

In the stunned silence that followed, Molly saw Alan's head turn instinctively towards Katy behind the bar. She saw the colour leave Katy's cheeks as she turned blindly to Ward. She saw the sudden tension on Ward

9

Frazer's handsome face as the laughter died out of his grey eyes. She also saw the steadying hand that he put on Katy's shoulder as he stepped out from behind the bar, wincing slightly as he inadvertently put too much weight on his injured leg.

Before he had been injured and captured in France, Ward Frazer had been working as an undercover agent for the Special Operations Executive, the SOE. Helen de Burrel was part of the same organisation. It was all very hush-hush, of course, but inevitably some details had become common knowledge among their friends.

Molly knew, for example, that Ward had met Helen de Burrel at some fancy party at the beginning of the war. When he had discovered that Helen spoke fluent French, he had recruited her as a research assistant in the London office. It was Helen who had told Katy that Ward had been captured by the Germans when his drop-off plane crash-landed, and during the subsequent traumatic months of his incarceration and escape she and Katy had become very close.

But three weeks ago, while Ward was still away, the SOE had sent Helen on a top-secret assignment to blow up the ships in Toulon harbour to prevent them falling into German hands. Molly obviously didn't know all the details, but it seemed the operation had been successful. The BBC had announced that the ships had been scuttled, many with their captains still on board. But nobody knew what had happened to Helen. For the last two weeks her friends had been getting increasingly concerned. Not least the Nelsons. Helen had been lodging in their house when she was selected for the mission, and she and eight-year-old George had formed a close bond. When he had inadvertently discovered where she was going, and why, his affection had turned into downright adulation.

'It's not true, is it? It can't be true.' George was crying now, his face pressed into Alan's stomach. His nose was bleeding, and the mixture of tears and blood was rapidly staining Alan's shirt red.

'Hey, George, tell us what happened.' It was Ward who spoke, firmly, calmly, crouching painfully beside the boy. 'Did someone come to the house? Was there a telegram?'

George shook his head, smearing even more blood on Alan's clothes.

'So what did happen? What did your mum say?' Ward asked.

'She said we had to be strong because Helen might be dead,' George whimpered.

The relief was palpable. Even people who didn't know what he was talking about seemed to relax and turn back to their drinks. Molly saw Ward glance back at Katy, and her heart twisted.

'Well, she's right,' Ward said to George. 'We do have to be strong. Like

Katy was strong about me when I was missing. She didn't hear anything about me for months and months. But I wasn't dead. And just because we don't know what has happened to Helen, it doesn't mean she's dead either.'

George thought about it, then sniffed disconsolately. 'But it does mean she can't take me to see the elephant.'

Ward looked somewhat taken aback at this unexpected turn in the conversation and glanced up at Alan for clarification. Catching Katy's eye, Molly bit back a smile. 'Is there any ice?' she whispered. 'It might help stop the bleeding.'

Katy nodded. She scooped some ice out of the cold box under the bar, wrapped it in a tea towel and pushed it across the counter.

Tentatively Molly offered the ice pack to Ward. But he didn't take it. 'Aha,' he said to George instead. 'Look. Here's Nurse Coogan come to make you better, in her sexy uniform and everything.'

Molly felt herself blush. How could he be so mean as to tease her like that? In front of everyone? But then it got even worse. As she leaned forward quickly to hide her hot face, two Kirby grips pinged out of her hair, her cap fell off and a strand of hair escaped from her severe hospital bun and flopped down over her eyes. Molly was self-conscious about her lank, shapeless dark hair at the best of times, but now she wished the floor would open up and swallow her whole.

Ignoring Ward Frazer, she thrust the ice pack into George's small hands. 'Here,' she said. 'Hold this on your nose for a minute. It will stop the bleeding.'

It did. But it took quite a while. And by the time she had mopped him up as best she could, with a flannel and a bowl of water Katy had brought her, the atmosphere in the pub had returned to normal.

And then Jen Carter walked in.

'Good God!' she said, catching sight of Alan's bloodstained shirt. 'Have you been in a fight?' Noticing Molly's dishevelment, and the nurse's cap still lying on the floor, she laughed delightedly. 'Not over Molly Coogan, surely? What were you doing, Alan? Protecting her virtue from Ward Frazer's amorous advances?'

Mortified, Molly picked up the bowl of bloody water, only just resisting the urge to throw it straight into Jen's pretty face, and escaped into the small kitchen.

Katy followed her in. 'Don't take any notice of Jen,' she murmured, as Molly tried to tidy her hair. 'She's only being stupid. You know what she's like.' Molly didn't reply. 'Oh no,' Katy added after a moment. 'You've got blood on your uniform. Let me wash it off for you. I don't want you getting into trouble with Sister Parkes.'

11

Squeezing out the cloth, Katy started dabbing Molly's dress. 'Thanks so much for coming tonight,' she said. 'Everyone says the fog is really thick. I'm surprised you could find your way.'

After a moment's hesitation, Molly told her about the blind man. 'He said that being blind made him see things,' she said. 'Things that other people can't see.'

'Sounds like he was completely bonkers,' a sarcastic voice remarked behind them. Jen was leaning against the door frame. 'Sorry to interrupt this cosy domestic scene,' she said. 'But Ward has gone over the road to tell Pam that George is OK. And there's someone waiting at the bar.'

'He wasn't at all bonkers,' Molly said, drying her hands. 'He was nice.'

'So what could he *see* about you?' Jen asked sceptically.

'He said my moment would come.'

'Your moment?' Jen raised her neatly plucked eyebrows. 'What moment?'

'I don't know,' Molly said. She wished she had just kept her stupid mouth shut. She might have known Jen would take the mickey. 'He didn't say. Maybe I'll save someone's life, or—'

She was interrupted by an impatient voice from the bar. 'Oi, any chance of getting a drink around here?'

Jen laughed delightedly. 'I think your moment has come sooner than you thought,' she said. 'That old bugger will have a coronary if he doesn't get served soon. You'd better go and save *his* life.'

As Molly went back to the bar, she heard Jen's voice behind her. 'Talk about the blind leading the blind.' And Katy's voice shushing her, telling her not to be so mean.

Molly was encouraging the customer to put his change into the Spitfire Fund collecting tin on the counter when Alan Nelson came up to the bar with George in tow.

They were both still somewhat bloodstained, but at least George was looking a bit more cheerful. Molly smiled at him. 'Are you feeling better now?'

'Yes, but I still want to go and see the baby elephant,' he said. 'I've never seen an elephant.'

'Nor have I actually,' Molly said. 'Well, not a real live one anyway.

George looked surprised. Then suddenly his angelic little face brightened. 'Will *you* take me, Molly? We could see it together.'

Oh no, Molly thought. What have I done now? She glanced at Alan Nelson. 'Where exactly is this elephant?'

'It's up in town,' he said. 'In Oxford Street. At John Lewis's.'

'But John Lewis's is completely bombed out.'

'The Ministry of Food are using the site to put on a Christmas potato fair,' Alan said. He rolled his eyes. 'And they've advertised an elephant on opening day.'

'There's a magician too,' George put in. 'He's called Mr Trickster. Oh go on, Molly, pleeease?'

Molly felt herself weakening. She had always felt an affinity with George. Like her, he had lost his entire family in the early years of the war. His only stroke of good fortune was that Pam and Alan Nelson had been prepared to take him in and subsequently adopt him. 'When is the opening day?' she asked.

'Tomorrow,' George responded eagerly.

'I expect Nurse Coogan is on duty,' Alan said sternly.

'Actually, I'm starting nights tomorrow, so I am free during the day, but …' She stopped awkwardly, suddenly wondering if Alan didn't want George to go.

But Alan was smiling. 'You'd be doing us a huge favour,' he said. 'I can't go because I'm on Home Guard duty. And Pam can't go because of the new baby.' Then, lowering his voice, 'And it might take his mind off this awful Helen de Burrel business.'

Chapter Two

It was still dark when Katy Frazer woke the next morning. She lay, heart hammering, caught in the tail end of some unremembered but alarming dream. Wondering what had woken her, she raised her head and listened. But there was no sound from the baby's room. Malcolm was obviously asleep. As was Ward. She could sense him there beside her, the warmth of him, and the low, slow rhythm of his breathing.

Ward Frazer. Her husband. She wished it was light so she could look at him. She wanted to study him, to examine every feature of his face, his body. But she wanted to do it methodically, impartially, at her leisure, which was impossible when he was awake. Because when he was awake, she was distracted by who he was, his smile, his eyes, his very aliveness.

Lowering herself back on the pillow, she berated herself for being stupid. Looking at Ward wouldn't make her know him any better. Looking at him would only make her wonder anew at the miracle that had not only made this wonderful man want to marry her in the first place, but had also brought him back to her after months of almost unbearable anxiety.

Oddly, having him back hadn't taken that anxiety away. It had just refocused it. Now, instead of worrying whether he was even alive, she was worried about the leg he had broken when the plane taking him on that last fateful mission – the mission so important that he had been recalled from their honeymoon – had crashed, and which his German captors had failed to deal with properly. She could hardly bear to think of the pain he must have endured. She knew it still hurt now, even though he denied it.

He wanted to get rid of the limp. He wanted to have the bones reset. But that was a risk. Any surgical intervention was a risk. The danger of septicaemia setting in was all too real. Even during her short period as a probationer nurse at the oh-so-hygiene-conscious Wilhelmina, Katy had seen countless people die after the simplest of operations. Once a wound got infected and that infection got into the bloodstream, there was nothing anyone could do. And it wasn't just poor people in old-fashioned hospitals that suffered. Septicaemia was no respecter of class. She had read somewhere that General Montgomery's wife had died after an insect bite went septic. They said it was his broken heart that made him so ruthless in battle.

And there was another worry too. If Ward did have the bones reset successfully, then he would go back on active service. He hadn't said it, but Katy knew that was what he wanted. Even now, after all he had been through, he didn't want to sit on the sidelines. He didn't want to be on sick leave, or rehabilitation leave, or whatever they called it. He wanted to go on fighting the war. Whether or not he stayed in the SOE, he wanted to see Hitler and his beastly Nazi regime defeated. Well, who didn't? There was no doubt that the Nazis needed defeating. But it didn't have to be Ward Frazer who did it. Surely he had already done enough.

She moved restlessly in the bed. Suddenly she felt angry. Angry with him and angry with herself. She had been mad to fall in love with someone like Ward. She had sentenced herself to a life of anxiety. A man like him was never going to settle down to family life, to running a pub, to a normal, comfortable existence. He would always want to be in the thick of things, always looking for adventure, and she would be left behind with little Malcolm, missing him, worrying about him, worrying about a future without him, worrying about how to keep the show on the road.

And surely it wouldn't take long for Ward to get bored with her, bored of her stay-at-home ways, bored of her mousy looks and nervous disposition. Because however much he claimed to love her now, surely sooner or later he would find someone more glamorous, more lively, more suited to his derring-do lifestyle.

And that person wouldn't be hard to find. Because everyone liked him. Well, everyone except Molly Coogan, of course. But Molly was so awkward and shy. She had never been good with men.

Another worry was Ward's family in Canada. And his friends. Presumably, sooner or later, Katy was going to have to meet them, and would see them wondering why, of all the women available to him, he had chosen to marry her. What if—

She froze as Ward turned over. A draught of cold air ran down the bed between them. 'Why are you awake?' he murmured.

'I'm not awake,' Katy said.

'You are,' he said. He reached over to pull her into his arms. 'And you're fretting about something. You're all tense and cross.'

'I'm not,' she said.

'Tell me,' he said.

But she couldn't. How could she? She could feel the heat of him against her now, that lovely long, strong body cradling her, his fingers moving in a rhythmic caress down her spine. Already her anxieties were fading into a languorous sense of contentment. I'm in his thrall, she thought in desperation. I can't think straight in his presence, let alone in his arms.

'Are you worrying about Helen? After what George said last night?'

Honesty compelled her to shake her head. She *was* worried about Helen de Burrel, of course. Desperately worried. But she hadn't given up hope. Wartime communications were notoriously difficult even at the best of times, and virtually impossible from within enemy-held territory. And Helen was resourceful. Even if she had lost radio contact with the SOE due to the rapid German occupation of southern France, surely she would find a way to get back in touch via one of their underground networks.

'What is it, then?' he murmured against her hair.

'What do you mean?'

'If it isn't Helen, what is it? What are you worrying about?'

Katy groaned inwardly. As well as everything else, he was so astute. So alert to her mood. And unbearably irresistible. She suddenly recalled the moment when he had first kissed her, under the mistletoe in the entrance of the Wilhelmina Hospital. Even at the thought of it, her heart accelerated wildly.

'Mistletoe,' she said suddenly. 'We haven't got any mistletoe.'

'*Mistletoe*? You were lying awake worrying about mistletoe?'

She giggled and snuggled closer to him, feeling the steady beat of his heart against her face. 'Well, no, but ...'

'But what?'

'But we do need some. And some holly.'

He didn't respond at once, and she thought he was going to quiz her further. Then he adjusted his own position in the bed. She felt sudden heat course through her body.

'I'll go see if I can find some later today,' he said, and she could hear the smile in his voice. 'But don't forget we're married now, sweetheart, we don't need the excuse of mistletoe any more ...'

Joyce had already got the urns on when Mrs Rutherford bustled into the café the following morning.

'From the garden,' she said, dumping a box of vegetables on the counter.

Joyce inspected the contents of the box with interest. 'What do you think about a nice hotpot for a change?' she suggested. 'I'll make some dumpling floaters and we can get a few old bones from Mr Dove, the butcher, to give it some flavour?'

Celia Rutherford shrugged off her coat and hung it on the peg on the back of the door. 'You're a marvel, Mrs Carter,' she said. 'You ought to be on the wireless after Mr Middleton's gardening programme, then you could tell everyone what to do with all his wonderful produce!'

'I could certainly tell *him* what to do with his wonderful produce,' Joyce said acidly. 'Especially his enormous parsnips. But I don't think the BBC would allow it.'

Mrs Rutherford gave a shocked snort of amusement as she tied on her apron. 'I should think not,' she said. 'Oh, and I asked in Arding and Hobbs about a new kettle. But apparently there's a three-year waiting list for kettles, and five years for cutlery.'

Joyce had measured out some egg powder for an omelette. Now she whisked it into milk and poured the mixture into a frying pan. 'Then we'll have to use a saucepan as a back-up, unless Mr Lorenz can get us one,' she said. 'Or perhaps I should ask young Aaref Hoch. He can sometimes lay his hands on things.'

Celia Rutherford paused in her attempt to light the grill. 'Not black market, Mrs Carter?'

'Needs must where the devil drives, Mrs Rutherford,' Joyce replied.

She knew Mrs Rutherford disapproved of Aaref Hoch, the young Jewish refugee. And it wasn't entirely due to his somewhat nefarious entrepreneurial activities. It was because he'd always had a bit of an eye for her daughter, Louise. Miss Fancy-Pants Louise Rutherford had always been trouble, and even though she now had a nice young husband of her own in the Royal Navy, it hadn't stopped her flirting with Aaref Hoch while he was away.

'I'd rather you asked Mr Lorenz,' Mrs Rutherford said now. She glanced slyly at Joyce. 'I'm sure he would bend over backwards to get you a kettle if he knew you needed one.'

'Well I don't know about that,' Joyce said. She fussed about with the frying pan to hide her sudden flush. 'But we are going out together next week.'

'Oh?' The grill flared suddenly and Mrs Rutherford jumped back with well-practised timing. 'A date with Mr Lorenz?'

'No, not a date,' Joyce said firmly. 'It's only to see Jen's show. She's organised it to thank him for paying for her throat operation. I don't know if I ought to go really, but—'

'Goodness me, why not?' Celia Rutherford interrupted in her brisk, no-nonsense way. 'You are a free agent now. There's nothing to stop you letting your hair down and having a bit of fun.'

Joyce ran a knife round the edge of the omelette and flipped it neatly out on to a plate. She looked at it with satisfaction. She's right, she thought. For the first time in a long while, I haven't got any responsibilities, not pressing ones anyway. Maybe I can have a bit of fun.

*

17

It was only a couple of hours later when the bell on the door clanged and the post girl came in.

'Letter for you, Mrs Carter,' she said. 'I thought you'd be here.'

Joyce wiped her hands on her apron. 'A letter? For me?' She suddenly had an awful thought that it would be from the prison to say that it had all been a terrible mistake and Stanley wasn't dead after all.

But the address was handwritten and the postmark was Devon.

The only person she knew in Devon was Mrs Baxter, who had the farm where Angie and Paul were evacuees. But Mrs Baxter had never written before. Nor, come to think of it, had Angie or Paul.

Nervously she tore open the envelope and drew out a sheet of flimsy war paper.

12th December 1943

Dear Mrs Carter,

I'm sorry to write out of the blue, but we think it's best if your Angie comes back to you in London. In other circumstances we'd be happy to keep her because she's a good girl, but we have prisoners of war working on the farm now. They are nice boys but when all's said and done they are the enemy and I'm worried that they are taking too much interest in Angie. We can't supervise them all the time, so if it's all right with you, I'll send her back in time for Christmas.

With kind regards.

Yours sincerely,

Betty Baxter

PS Hope you are keeping well. It sounds from the paper as if the bombing in London isn't so bad now that blighter Hitler has turned his attention to Russia.

Joyce stared at the letter blankly. She couldn't quite believe it. Little Angie was coming home.

She had only seen her younger daughter once in the three years she had been away. That was two years ago. Angie must still have been thirteen then, a rosy-cheeked schoolgirl, shy, but childishly eager to show Joyce around the farm. How on earth was the poor child going to cope with being back in war-torn London? She would probably be overwhelmed after living such a peaceful life in the country. For a second Joyce was conscious of a guilty flicker of dismay. So much for her new-found freedom. But then she shook her head. Angie wouldn't be any trouble. She had always been a good little thing. It would be nice to have her home again.

Molly and George's trip to the Christmas potato fair in Oxford Street was a big success. The previous night's fog had lifted and George's sunny good humour had been fully restored at the prospect of the treat in store.

The bombed-out, gutted carcass of the John Lewis department store had been transformed by the Ministry of Food into a bower of greenery with tents and stalls. Hordes of people had turned up to explore the various excitements on offer. There was an off-ration sweet stall, a mocked-up allotment, a merry-go-round, and several stands demonstrating the different ways you could cook potatoes. There was even a fortune-teller dressed all in black called Romany Rose who occupied a fake-looking gypsy caravan.

After her encounter with the prophetic blind man the previous evening, Molly was tempted to visit Romany Rose. But conscious that the much-vaunted baby elephant and the magic show were George's priority, she set out to track them down first. Thankfully they were both easy to find.

Comet, the baby elephant, was already causing considerable hilarity by blowing water from a bucket all over his keeper. But despite his antics, Molly thought he looked sad. She wondered if he minded being laughed at, and couldn't help thinking he would be much happier living in the wilds of Africa.

The magician, 'The Amazing Mr Trickster', proved to be a skilled showman, the only downside being that, because of his popularity, and the fact that his show was free, his tent was crammed with a huge number of grubby, down-at-heel children all trying to get as close as they could to the stage.

Everyone was pretty down-at-heel these days, of course. Three years of war had taken their toll on people as well as buildings. But most of the children at the potato fair looked as though they had spent the war living in the gutter. Or if not the gutter, then certainly in tube stations or bomb shelters.

In due course, dragged forward by George every time anyone left, Molly found herself perched in the front row on a narrow bench next to an unsavoury youth with pustulating red spots on his face. Crammed in on her other side, George was craning forward eagerly, utterly transfixed by Mr Trickster's tricks. Molly was pretty transfixed herself, her enjoyment only tempered by the fug of unwashed bodies and the worrying thought that Mr Trickster might feel tempted to summon her up on stage as a stooge.

Eventually the fear of being invited to be sawn in half began to outweigh the fascination of Mr Trickster's sleight of hand, and she whispered to George that she would wait for him outside.

Almost before she had stood up, two more children surged forward. Barely taking his eyes off the magician, George obligingly moved along next to the spotty youth to make room for them. Rather unnerved that Mr Trickster had caught her eye, winked, and given her a little regretful wave goodbye, Molly hastily made her way out of the tent.

Guessing she would be in for a long wait, she wandered across to inspect the gypsy caravan.

At once Romany Rose popped her head out of the door. 'Do come in,' she said.

Molly glanced back at Mr Twister's tent. 'I can't. I'm waiting for someone and I don't want to miss him.'

'Then wait here and I'll fetch the crystal ball,' Romany Rose said and disappeared into her caravan.

Molly had never actually seen a crystal ball and was disappointed when Romany Rose brought out what looked like a plain glass ball about the size of a grapefruit. Patting the step beside her for Molly to sit down, she balanced the ball in her voluminous skirt and peered into it intently.

'You have suffered much and you have lost people you love,' she said.

For a moment Molly was impressed, then she reminded herself that there was probably hardly anyone left in London who hadn't lost someone they loved.

When Romany Rose spoke again, her voice had changed into a kind of eerie sing-song. 'You are troubled. In love and in life. You are hoping for change.'

Aren't we all? Molly thought. 'Mm,' she said, non-committally. The extraordinary fake ululating voice made her want to laugh. Close up, she could see that Romany Rose had nicely manicured fingernails, and she was wearing what smelled like rather expensive perfume. She was clearly no more a gypsy than Molly was.

'You will soon be going on a journey.'

'Well, I am hoping to go to Croydon.'

'I don't think we are talking about Croydon, dear,' Romany Rose said in her normal voice. 'We are talking about a journey to far-distant lands.'

Molly giggled and Romany Rose looked up, affronted. 'Well if you don't want to know ...'

'No, no, please go on,' Molly said. 'I'm really interested.'

Romany Rose glared at her and then returned her gaze to the ball. 'I see fear, darkness, hardship and danger.'

Molly shivered. 'Are you sure it's not a tall, dark, handsome stranger?' she suggested hopefully. 'It sounds almost the same.'

'Quite sure,' Romany Rose snapped. 'But wait.' She put on her sing-song voice again. 'There is a man. A tall, strong man. A foreigner, but not a stranger.'

'Oh well, he'll do,' Molly said, stifling another giggle. 'Where can I find him?'

Romany Rose looked up from the ball. She had gone rather pale. 'I don't know,' she said. 'But if you can find him, he'll be your salvation.'

Molly frowned and was about to question her further, but was interrupted by a piercing squeak on the tannoy followed by an announcement that the Minister of Food, Lord Woolton, had arrived and was about to make a speech. Already people were streaming out of Mr Trickster's tent. Hastily handing over the required sixpence halfpenny to Romany Rose, Molly hurried across to intercept George before he disappeared into the crowds.

After the excitement of Mr Trickster and Romany Rose, Lord Woolton's speech about the difficulties of importing enough wheat with so many merchant ships being sunk by Nazi submarines was a bit of an anticlimax. But Molly and George dutifully signed the book pledging that, as a gift to Britain's gallant sailors, they would in future eat more potatoes and less bread.

Then, armed with a small paper cone of aniseed balls, two blackjacks and a bag of potatoes for Pam, they emerged back on to Oxford Street.

As they waited for the bus opposite bomb-scarred Selfridges, George turned to Molly, eyes shining. 'That was brilliant, wasn't it?' he said.

'It was,' she said.

It had, indeed, been one of the best days Molly had had for a long time. She would think of it as a final, happy farewell to London. Surely this evening Matron would sign her transfer papers. Then she would be gone, and all her troubles would be behind her.

Katy was polishing glasses ready for the evening opening when Louise came into the pub, straight off her Saturday shift at the factory in Clapham where she worked.

'I'm exhausted,' Louise exclaimed. 'I turned out a hundred and forty bolts today, which is a record for me, and certainly more than any of the men ever manage. I need a strong drink to celebrate.'

Katy smiled. She was amused by Louise's pride in her factory job. She just wished she took as much pride in her marriage.

Perching on a bar stool, Louise took a slug of the whisky Katy handed her and looked around the empty bar. 'Where's Ward?'

'He's taken Malcolm off up to Wimbledon Common to try and find some mistletoe,' Katy said. She glanced at the grandfather clock behind the bar. It was the first time Ward had taken the baby out on his own, and they'd been gone an awfully long time.

'Hm.' Louise tapped an oil-stained finger against her lips. 'Ward Frazer and mistletoe,' she murmured. 'Is that a wise combination? You'll have every woman in Clapham in here queuing up for a kiss if you're not careful.'

'Nonsense,' Katy said.

Louise swirled the liquid in her glass. 'Aha,' she said. 'There speaks a happily married woman.'

Katy was about to start lifting the glasses carefully up on to the shelf. Glasses were very hard to come by these days, and she didn't want to break any unnecessarily. But something in Louise's voice made her pause. 'You're a happily married woman too, Louise,' she said. 'Or at least you certainly seemed to be when Jack was on leave.'

Louise flapped her hand. 'Of course I love Jack. But I miss him so much when he's away at sea. It's so dull without him.'

Katy turned back to her glasses. She had been without Ward for nearly two years, not just two short weeks. If anyone knew what missing someone was like, she did. What was more, she knew perfectly well that Louise had been to the pictures with Aaref Hoch the previous evening.

She told herself that it was nothing to do with her if Louise was messing around with other men. But she knew that if it all went wrong, as things connected with Louise so often did, she would be the one picking up the bits. It didn't help that Louise and Aaref now lived in the same building. When Louise had got married to the handsome young naval officer Jack Delmaine, she had been determined to move out of her parents' house, even though Jack would be away at sea most of the time. But the only place she had been able to afford was the little attic apartment at the top of the house that Aaref and his younger brothers had lived in since Mrs D'Arcy Billière had taken them in as refugees at the beginning of the war.

Perhaps realising that Katy was the wrong person to talk to about absent husbands, Louise drained her drink and stood up. She delved into her handbag for some money. 'By the way,' she said, 'what's going on at number forty-two? The house opposite Mrs Carter's?'

Katy turned round. 'I didn't know anything was going on,' she said. 'Why?'

'Well, there was a car parked outside just now,' Louise said. 'A military staff car with a driver and everything. It must be some kind of general moving in, I think.'

'A general?' Katy blinked. 'That can't be right. No self-respecting general would want to live in Mrs Butler's old house.'

Louise giggled as she wrapped her scarf round her hair.

'Well, he may not be self-respecting,' she said, 'but he's certainly got a nice car.' She waved an airy farewell. 'Oh, and Katy,' she called back from the door. 'Let me know when the mistletoe goes up. I want to be first in the queue.'

Some scare about an unexploded bomb had delayed the buses, and the evening session at the pub was already in progress by the time Ward arrived back. Malcolm, in a dirty nappy, and almost buried in foliage, was crying from hunger.

'Tough afternoon?' Katy asked sweetly as she lifted him out of the pram.

Ward smiled and ran his hands over his face. He was clearly exhausted from his first day out alone with his son. 'This child is a menace,' he said. 'Are you sure we can't switch him for an easier one?'

'He's not very keen on the pram,' Katy said. 'Now that he can walk a few steps, he prefers to toddle along on the ground. Or be carried.'

'So I gathered!'

'I know. It does make it all a bit slow,' Katy said, peering into the pram. 'But you got some lovely holly. Oh … and some mistletoe too.'

Ward glanced at her. 'That's what you wanted, isn't it?'

'Well, yes,' Katy said. 'We'll put it up tomorrow. But I don't want you kissing all the pretty girls under it!'

He laughed and pulled her to him. 'There's only one pretty girl I want to kiss,' he said.

But Malcolm wasn't having any of that. Redoubling his screams, he started to beat his fists against Katy's shoulder.

Reluctantly Katy broke away and took Malcolm upstairs to get him ready for bed, leaving Ward to man the bar.

I must try to get some more staff, she thought. Ward was happy enough to help, but he had hardly struggled all the way back from Germany just to be a barman. But staff were so hard to find nowadays. Since she had reopened the pub after her father's death, Katy had lost all her helpers one by one, as they joined up or were called up. Even Jacob Hoch, Aaref's younger brother, who helped out sometimes, was away on some schoolboy training manoeuvres this weekend.

Two hours later, the evening was in full swing, and even with Ward to help her, Katy was hard pressed to keep up with the orders. There were some Americans soldiers in and the bar was hot and noisy. Any minute now they would run out of glasses. The wireless was blaring out some military march. Katy could feel the beginning of a headache and longed for the evening to be over. She was sweating as she reached under the counter for some more bottles of the cold beer the Americans preferred to the draught everybody else drank.

Further along the counter Ward was serving Mr Lorenz with a small whisky. Despite his day in charge of Malcolm, he was looking relaxed, smiling at something Mr Lorenz was saying. Momentarily distracted, Katy's hand slipped on the bottle opener and a splash of lager caught her right in the face.

She was just trying to wipe it off with her sleeve when the door of the pub opened, and the most beautiful woman Katy had ever seen came into the bar.

Pausing on the threshold, she stood for a moment as though taking stock, or – the thought flashed across Katy's mind – to allow everyone to take stock of her.

Certainly the bar had fallen very silent. Even the band on the wireless had segued into a slow, sultry version of 'They Can't Black Out the Moon'.

The woman's face was a perfect pale oval, her nose was straight and her eyes were large and slightly slanting, with almost artificially thick lashes. Her lips formed a perfect red bow and her hair, under a pert little hat, bubbled in glossy dark curls to her shoulders. She was dressed in a figure-hugging lime-green coat, and when she finally stepped forward and approached the bar, it was with the telltale swish of real silk stockings, and a gliding swing of her hips like a model on a catwalk.

'Can I help you?' Katy asked faintly, aware of heads turning as every man in the bar followed her progress across the room.

The woman smiled, baring a set of perfect white teeth. 'I am Mrs James,' she said. 'I've just moved in up the road. Number forty-two. I was hoping you might let me buy a bottle of gin.'

'I'm afraid I don't sell bottles.' Katy waved a hand at the line of upended bottles with optics clamped to the shelf behind her. 'I only sell spirits by the measure.'

Mrs James looked taken aback. Her eyes fell on Ward, standing transfixed at Katy's side, and she gave him a little crestfallen pout.

Ward cleared his throat. 'Oh come on, Katy, surely we could make an exception?'

'We can't make an exception,' Katy said crossly. 'Gin is almost impossible to get hold of, and that bottle up there is the only one I've got. If I make an exception, I will be letting our regular customers down.'

'I hope I'll become a regular customer,' the woman purred. Her voice was slightly husky, with a slight hint of an accent; not foreign, more of a purring lilt of pressure on the wrong syllables.

On closer inspection, Katy realised she wasn't quite as young as she appeared on first impression. There was a slightly bruised look around her lips, and when she smiled you could see lines at the edges of her eyes, even though they were cleverly concealed with some kind of matt foundation or powder. Jen Carter would know, Katy thought. Jen was an expert with make-up. But despite the tiny flaws, there was no doubt Mrs James was remarkably attractive. More than attractive. Stunning was a better word. Ward wasn't the only one who looked stunned. Half the men in the bar did too.

Katy forced a smile on to her lips. 'Well of course I hope so too,' she said mendaciously. 'But I still can't sell you a bottle of gin.'

'How about four measures in a glass, then?' the woman said. 'To take away.'

'I can't let you take away a glass—' Katy began.

But Ward stepped in. 'Of course she can,' he said smoothly. He turned back to the woman with a conspiratorial smile. 'So long as you promise to bring it back tomorrow.'

Seething, Katy took a glass off the shelf and pressed to the optic four times, waiting in stony silence each time for the liquid to gurgle back into the measure.

By the time she turned back to the bar, the woman had taken a ten-shilling note out of her purse.

'Thank you,' she said, accepting the change. Slanting a grateful little glance at Ward through her lashes, she headed back to the door.

As soon as she had left, the pub erupted.

'Cor,' someone said, 'If four measures of gin is all it takes …!'

'It would take you four bottles,' another man responded.

'Four hundred, more like,' someone else called across, and everyone burst into laughter.

Ward turned to Katy. 'Shame we didn't put that mistletoe up yet,' he murmured.

He was joking. Teasing. He sounded as though he was teasing. But as Katy looked up into his laughing grey eyes, she felt something twist in her stomach.

'Don't worry,' she said crossly. 'There's still time. She's coming back again tomorrow with the glass.'

'You are late, Nurse Coogan!'

As Sister Parkes's stentorian voice rang out, Molly groaned inwardly. She had hoped there might have been some last-minute crisis to delay evening prayers and allow her to slip unobtrusively on to the ward without anyone noticing. But not much escaped Sister Parkes's notice. Even the patients lay at attention during her ward rounds. She was known as one of the hardest taskmasters at the Wilhelmina. And she had been the bane of Molly's life ever since she had joined Septic Ward Four.

'I'm sorry, Sister,' Molly muttered. 'But I—'

'I don't want excuses,' Sister Parkes's voice was like cannon fire. 'Sick patients won't wait for a nurse who's late, and nor will Matron. She was expecting you in her office five minutes ago.'

Molly was appalled. Being late on duty was one thing; being late for Matron was quite another. 'But I didn't know—' she began.

'If you had got here on time you would have known. Now tidy yourself up and go and report to Matron's office immediately. For once I will let you off ward prayers, but I expect you to make up your worship in your own time.'

'Yes, Sister,' Molly muttered. Tidy herself up indeed. How dare Sister Parkes treat her as if she was still a junior probationer? She could see the other nurses smirking, delighting in her discomfiture. Well they wouldn't be smirking when she came back and said she was moving to Croydon to start midwifery training. That would wipe the smiles off their smug little faces.

It was gone quarter to eight by the time Molly was called into Matron's office.

Matron was not a large woman. Her enormous desk had almost certainly been designed with a more substantial predecessor in mind. But her lack of bulk in no way diminished her aura of authority. She looked up from some papers as Molly came in.

'Ah yes,' she said. 'Nurse Coogan. You have applied for midwifery training in Croydon. I have your transfer papers here in front of me.' She took off her spectacles and laid them neatly on her desk. 'But I'm afraid I can't let you go.'

'What?' Molly couldn't believe her ears. She felt a sinking sensation in the pit of her stomach. For an awful moment she thought she was going to cry. 'But you've got to let me go,' she said. 'I've been accepted on the course.' She couldn't bear it. So much was hanging on this. Her voice rose in panic. 'I can't stay in London. I've got to get away. You've no right to stop me!'

Becoming aware of the sudden rigidity of Matron's thin face, she lapsed into silence. She knew she had gone too far. Far too far. Nobody spoke to Matron like that. Molly couldn't even imagine Matron's mother speaking to her like that a hundred years ago when Matron was a child. Even the doctors went quiet when Matron appeared. Everyone respected Matron. Because Matron had served in Siberia in the Great War.

Molly had once seen a hideous film about Siberia. There had been hordes of bloodthirsty Cossacks galloping about, and wild animals gnawing at the corpses of fallen soldiers. And she had wondered how a puritanical,

God-fearing woman like Matron had survived in such a wild, dangerous place. But then even a wolf would probably think twice before taking on Matron. If it had any sense.

Keeping her eyes fixed on a small mark on the lino under Matron's desk, Molly waited for a thunderbolt to fall.

'I have every right to stop you, Nurse Coogan.' Matron spoke calmly, but there was a hint of steel in her tone. 'Since this hospital is on a war footing, I am entitled to do whatever I need to ensure it is properly staffed. Normally I try to accommodate my nurses' specific requests, but in this case I cannot justify letting you go. We will soon be receiving an influx of injured servicemen from North Africa. I am quite sure that whatever your reasons for wanting to go to Croydon, they are less important than my desire to give these brave men the nursing care they deserve.'

Molly couldn't speak. She was conscious of her hopes crashing to the ground around her. She could feel herself shivering even though it wasn't cold. There was no way her pitiful wishes were going to be able to stand up against the irrefutable claims of heroic wounded soldiers just home from some godforsaken battlefield in Tunisia or Libya.

'Nurse Coogan?'

Molly looked up dully. 'Yes, Matron?'

'Do you understand what I have said?'

'Yes, Matron.'

Thinking the interview was over, Molly was waiting to be dismissed when Matron spoke again, slightly more gently this time.

'I can see you are disappointed. Would it help to tell me your reasons for requesting a transfer to midwifery when you haven't yet finished your training here?'

'No,' Molly said. 'I mean, no, Matron, I don't think it would help.' How could she tell Matron the real reason? She couldn't tell anyone. She could barely admit it to herself.

'Are you unhappy on Septic Ward Four?'

Yes, Molly wanted to scream. Of course I am unhappy. Sister Parkes is a bully and the other nurses think I am a joke. And all the patients die. But she shook her head again. If Sister Parkes found out she had complained about her, life wouldn't be worth living. 'No, Matron,' she said.

'Boyfriend trouble?'

Molly blinked. She was surprised Matron even knew what a boyfriend was. Nevertheless, for an awful moment she was tempted to unburden herself. If there had been an easy way to put her secret agony into words, she might even have done it.

'No, Matron. It's not that,' she said.

Matron continued to look at her for a moment, but when it became clear that Molly wasn't going to enlighten her any further, she picked up her glasses and put them on again.

'I see,' she said. 'Well, Nurse Coogan, as it is evident that you are clearly under some strain, I am prepared to overlook your reticence and your earlier outburst. But it proves my decision is the right one. You are still very young. I know you came to us in difficult circumstances. Another year with us will help you to grow up. To gain some maturity. If at that time you still want to transfer to another hospital, then I will be happy to reconsider your application.'

'But Matron—'

Matron held up her hand. 'In the meantime, I will tell Sister Parkes that I have released you from duty as of immediate effect. I am going to confine you to the nurses' quarters for a week. You are to rest and recuperate. You are not to go out, apart from to get some fresh air. I expressly forbid you to go to Lavender Road. Is that understood?'

'Yes,' Molly blinked. 'But how did you know …?'

'It is my job to know,' Matron said. 'I have been concerned for some while about the amount of time you have been spending at Katy Frazer's public house, but I didn't intervene as I realised she needed your support while her husband was missing. Now that he has returned, I will be expecting you to refocus your attention on your nursing.' She nodded a brisk dismissal. 'That will be all, Nurse Coogan.'

'Yes, Matron. Thank you, Matron,' Molly said automatically, turning back for the door.

But before she reached it, Matron spoke again. 'Oh, and Nurse Coogan. Running away is not always the answer. Sometimes we have to stand up and face our fears.'

Molly stopped with her hand on the handle and turned round.

'Is that what you did in Siberia?'

'In Siberia?' Matron looked startled. Then she lifted her chin a fraction and fixed Molly with a beady eye. 'No, not at all. In Siberia I just did my duty, the same way you are going to continue to do yours.'

I don't want to do my duty, Molly wanted to shout. I don't want to have to watch a lot of young soldiers die of septicaemia. I'm not cut out to be a nurse. I'm always being told off for saying the wrong thing, and the uniform makes me look like a demented pixie. But she didn't shout. She didn't say anything. She just nodded meekly and left the room.

So the blind man had been wrong after all. Nothing was going to change. She wasn't going anywhere.

I'm like that elephant at the potato fair, she thought as she walked back

28

to the nurses' quarters. I'm trapped in the wrong life.

Chapter Three

Jen Carter was feeling nervous. Much more nervous than she ever did on stage. Because she was about to have dinner with a highly respected and influential West End theatre producer called Henry Keller, and she knew that if she put on a good performance tonight, it might just be the making of her career.

She had originally been introduced to Henry Keller by Ward Frazer, who had met him through a mutual friend in the forces when he first came to England. At the time it had seemed like a lucky break. Henry Keller already had a number of sell-out theatrical productions to his name and Jen had had high hopes of the connection. But for some reason it had never quite worked out. Either she didn't quite have the experience or repertoire that he was looking for, or she had made a mess of the audition.

Then just when she thought she might finally have a chance of impressing him, she had developed a polyp on her vocal cords.

But now, thanks to her mother's admirer Mr Lorenz, who had paid for the operation, she had had the growth removed. Dr Goodacre, her surgeon at the Wilhelmina Hospital, had done a brilliant job and her voice was already almost back to normal.

And then, out of the blue, Henry Keller had invited her out to dinner, at a fancy West End restaurant called Maison Prunier.

Until she had said something about it to Katy in the pub one night, Jen hadn't realised that Maison Prunier was one of the smartest restaurants in London. But Louise, who was sitting nearby, had nearly fallen off her bar stool.

'Prunier's?' she had exclaimed. 'My word, Jen, you are going up in the world.'

Now as she teetered along war-torn Piccadilly towards St James's Street in a pair of painfully tight high heels she had seen in the window of Mr Lorenz's pawn shop, Jen realised she wasn't quite sure if she was ready to go up in the world. Even though she would rather have died than admit it, Louise's mocking incredulity had undermined her confidence.

Louise had been to finishing school. Jen had not.

Jen was only too aware that she didn't know the etiquette of these posh people, these posh places.

She squared her shoulders and lifted her chin. I am Jennifer Carter, she told herself. I have a solo part in a London show. Albeit a small show, in a lesser theatre. But a solo role was a solo role, and not to be sniffed at. She had certainly battled hard enough to get it. And amazingly, they had held it open for her for the last two weeks while she'd been recovering from the operation.

Not only that, but Henry Keller was interested in her. Admittedly she still wasn't quite sure if it was her voice or her body that most interested him, but either way, being connected to Henry Keller, in whatever capacity, was not going to do her career any harm. Unless she messed up tonight.

Prunier's was pretty much exactly as Louise had described it. Behind the heavily sandbagged windows, the restaurant was chic and modern. It had a huge circular pillar in the centre with protruding metal racks to hold glasses. Overhead, the whole ceiling was taken up in a great plaster halo containing magically recessed lights.

The waiters were foreign – French, Henry said – and thankfully not as stuck up as Jen had feared. And the food, smoked salmon, boiled chicken with rice and a chocolate mousse for pudding, was good. Although not quite as good, Jen thought privately, as the rabbit and vegetable pie her mother had cooked the previous night as a try-out for the café.

The clientele seemed to consist mainly of women in stylish outfits with tinkling laughs and genteel accents. The men were dressed, like Henry, in well-cut suits. Nobody was in uniform. Perhaps it wasn't à la mode to come to dinner at Prunier's dressed for war.

Henry had seemed gratifyingly pleased to see her. He stood up the moment he saw her enter the restaurant and came over to escort her to their table, handing her coat to an attentive waiter and settling her into her seat with such well-practised good manners that Jen felt nervous all over again. She wasn't used to this, to dates with men like Henry Keller, confident, suave and sophisticated. Men with important jobs, and the power to influence her career.

Her only previous boyfriend had been an itinerant young Irishman who had charmed her knickers off with his soft persuasive blarney and then disappeared back to Ireland without a backward glance.

But as the evening progressed, Jen began to relax. She had been worried about what they would talk about, but actually conversation proved to be easy. Henry knew Ward Frazer, of course, so they were able to discuss his miraculous homecoming, and Jen made Henry laugh out loud with her descriptions of Ward's attempts to help Katy in the pub.

She even found herself telling him that her little sister Angie was soon coming home from Devon. 'Reading between the lines, it sounds as though she has been fraternising with the enemy,' she said in mock disapproval. Then, belatedly remembering that she was trying to get into Henry's good books, she could have kicked herself. 'She's got a taste of her own,' she added quickly. 'I would run a mile before I fraternised with the enemy.'

But Henry just looked amused. 'Ah,' he said, leaning back in his chair slightly. 'So you don't go in for the jackboot look?'

'No!' Jen said. 'Not at all.'

He inclined his head. 'I'm glad to hear it.'

Jen eyed him doubtfully. Was he flirting, or was he laughing at her? She couldn't tell. The waiter came then, and by the time he had poured more wine, the moment had passed and Henry was asking her about how her voice was feeling after the operation.

'You need to build up gently,' he said when she told him she was rejoining her show the following week. 'It's a precious thing, that voice of yours. You don't want to overdo it at this stage of your career.'

Jen took a careful breath. The moment had come. The moment she had been waiting for all evening. 'Oh, it'll be fine,' she said. She gave a little regretful sigh. 'I've only got a tiny role. I'm always on the lookout for something a bit more challenging …'

Henry didn't respond at once, and when she looked up at him through her lashes, she saw that he was watching her. His earlier smile had faded and Jen felt colour surge into her face.

Oh no, she thought, he's seen straight through me. Why didn't I keep my stupid mouth shut? Now he's going to think I only came out to dinner with him to try to get a better job. And that wasn't the reason. Or at least not the only reason. There were probably a hundred aspiring actresses and singers in London who would give their lives, or if not their lives precisely, certainly their bodies, to curry favour with Henry Keller. And now he would think she was just like them.

Or maybe it was the other way around. For all she knew, he did this all the time. Invited pretty young actresses out for supper, and a bit more afterwards, on the promise of a leg-up with their career. There were plenty of people like that in the theatre. She'd been offered deals before. A leg-up for a leg-over.

But she didn't think so somehow. Henry didn't seem the type. He was a friend of Ward Frazer's, after all.

And sure enough, he just inclined his head, acknowledging her ambition. 'Of course you are,' he said easily. 'And I'll help you if I can. But first you need to get your voice back on top form.'

But it wasn't quite the same after that. He was still charming and courteous, apparently interested in what she said, responding politely to her attempts at humour. But some of the warmth had gone from his eyes, replaced by … by what? Jen couldn't quite decide. Disappointment? Distaste? All she knew was that the sparkle had gone out of the evening, and now she longed for it to be over.

Eventually it was. He offered to call her a taxi, but she insisted that she would get the tube. So he walked with her to Piccadilly Circus, where the famous Eros statue was still safely tucked away under its protective pyramid of sandbags. There he kissed her chastely on the cheek, brushed off her over-eager thanks for a lovely evening, said that he had enjoyed it too and that he hoped to see her again soon. And that was that.

It was already mid December. German attacks on British shipping had been especially brutal over the last couple of months, but even though Britain was suffering under the double strain of wartime privation and a cold, wet winter, at least some of the news was positive. The Russian were manfully holding their line at the Don. In North Africa, the Allied forces had pushed the Germans and Italians almost back to Tunis. And the RAF was busy bombing German industrial cities.

But regardless of, or perhaps just weary of, the bigger picture, what everyone actually seemed to be talking about was the new occupant of number forty-two Lavender Road.

'She's got a daughter,' Pam told Katy. 'Mr Dove told me she'd just been in to register them both for the meat ration.'

'What about her husband?' Katy asked. 'Louise says he's a general.'

'Really?' Pam frowned as she jiggled baby Helen in her arms. 'Mr Dove didn't mention a husband.'

'Mr Dove said she's very pretty,' George chipped in helpfully.

Pam chuckled. 'She must be absolutely gorgeous for old Mr Dove to notice.'

'She is,' Katy said. 'When she came into the bar on Saturday night, all you could hear was a clunking sound as the men's jaws dropped to the floor. And I'm still waiting for her to bring that glass back, which she promised to do yesterday.'

But Katy was out when Mrs James eventually brought the glass back, so it was Ward who first had the pleasure of properly making her acquaintance.

'Her name is Gillian,' he said, when Katy pressed him later for details. 'And her daughter is called Bella. She's about fourteen, I'd say.'

'Blimey,' Katy said. 'Mrs James must have started young.' She certainly hadn't looked old enough to have a fourteen-year-old daughter.'

33

'Maybe Bella is a bit younger than that,' Ward said non-committally. 'I didn't really look at her.'

I bet you didn't, Katy thought sourly, not with her mother in the room. 'So where has she suddenly appeared from?' she asked. 'What are they doing here?'

Ward looked vaguely surprised. 'I don't know. I didn't ask. I guess they just needed somewhere to live.'

'And she didn't mention a husband?'

'No, I kind of got the impression she might be a widow.'

'So who's the man in the staff car? Where does he fit in?'

Ward held up his hands. 'Hey, she just dropped off the glass. I didn't strap her to a chair and interrogate her.'

Katy glared at him. 'Well, what did you talk about?'

'I can't remember,' he said. He laughed at Katy's expression and pulled her into his arms. 'Yes, she is very beautiful,' he said. 'Very beautiful indeed. And so is the daughter actually. But surely you know I don't care about other women. It's you I love.'

To her surprise, Molly found that it was a relief that Matron had put Lavender Road out of bounds. It meant that she could put it, and its occupants, out of her mind and settle down to enjoying an unexpected week off.

At first it felt strange to have nothing to do, no obligations to fulfil, no ordeals to undergo, especially as the other nurses in her dorm were constantly rushing about, coming and going, changing uniforms or tarting themselves up for an evening out.

She was pleased when Aaref Hoch called to see how she was. She had always liked Aaref, ever since he had arrived in England as a refugee at the beginning of the war. She had really fancied him in the early days. He had never fancied her, of course, even though he had kindly pretended to sometimes. He had only really ever had eyes for posh, pretty Louise Rutherford. Or Louise Delmaine, as she was now. But it had been nice to have someone to go to the pictures with, someone to flaunt occasionally in front of those snarky nurses. And Aaref had needed someone to take his mind off Louise, and to prevent his unrequited love becoming a local joke. So the sham relationship had suited them both.

They went up to Mrs Carter's café for a cup of tea and a piece of cake. Aaref told her about the glamorous newcomer who had moved into Lavender Road, and the officer in the staff car who visited frequently but clearly wasn't living there.

'Perhaps he's her father,' Molly said, taking a sip of her tea.

'Perhaps so. He is surely old enough to be her father,' Aaref said. He glanced around to make sure nobody was listening. 'Or perhaps not. I don't think her father would stay until after midnight.'

Molly felt her eyes widen. 'You don't think …?'

He gave one of his little foreign gestures, a kind of shrug. 'She is a beautiful woman. It is wartime, people have to do what they can to survive, no?'

'No … well, yes, but …' Molly put the cup back in its saucer. She wasn't a prude. She knew that sort of thing went on, of course, in Soho and some of the seedier back streets of London. But not in Lavender Road. Not among people she knew.

But when Katy called in to see her later in the week with little Malcolm, she too seemed dubious about the widow.

'Apparently she's Welsh,' Katy said darkly, lifting Malcolm out of his pram and sitting down on Molly's bed with him on her lap.

Molly bit back a smile. 'Well, what's the problem with that?'

'It means that she has one of those soft, lilting accents that apparently drives men wild with desire,' Katy said.

'From what Aaref said, it isn't just her accent,' Molly remarked.

But Katy wasn't amused. 'Oh, for goodness' sake,' she said irritably. 'Not Aaref as well?'

Molly was startled by Katy's reaction. Katy was the most tolerant person she had ever known. Then she saw the expression on her face. 'Surely you don't mean Ward …?' She broke off as Katy plonked Malcolm down on the floor so hard his little legs buckled and he tipped over on to his hands and knees. Molly used the distraction to take a steadying breath. 'But … but Ward is mad about you.'

Katy was watching Malcolm crawling off around the room. 'That's what he says, but that doesn't stop him drooling every time he sees her in the street.'

'Ward would never drool,' Molly said indignantly. The thought was ridiculous. Ward Frazer was far too well-mannered to drool. He was far too cool to betray any untoward emotion like that, far too self-assured, far too perfect. She sighed, then, realising that Katy was looking at her oddly, flushed and tried to hide her confusion by rubbing her hands over her face with a weary yawn.

Katy's expression turned to one of dismay. 'I'm sorry you've got worn out, Molly,' she said. 'I shouldn't have asked you to help out so much. I know how hard nursing is, but you always seemed so strong, so resilient.'

Molly looked at her. How little she knew. 'You didn't ask me. I offered,' she said.

'I should have said no. It's just that I needed you so much.'

'Well,' Molly tried to speak lightly, 'you won't need me now Ward is back.'

Katy shook her head. 'It's not the same. He tries hard, but he's not a natural barman. He finds it boring. And he's nowhere near as good as you at pulling a pint.'

Molly could feel herself colouring again. She didn't like talking about Ward. 'Well, he's not as used to it as I am,' she said. 'He has different skills. I wouldn't be much use undercover in France.' She glanced at Katy. 'Talking of which, still no word from Helen, I suppose?'

Katy was watching Malcolm try to pull himself up on to his feet with the aid of Molly's bedside table. She pressed her lips together expressively. 'Ward went in to the SOE again yesterday,' she said. 'He says the new people there are a bunch of public school idiots, all so much in thrall to their own mystique that they can't admit they are out of control. Apparently there have been all sorts of problems: betrayals, agents going over to the Germans as soon as they arrive in France, that kind of thing.' She leaned forward to steady Malcolm as he lurched dangerously. 'That's what they thought André Cabillard had done, of course.'

Molly nodded. She remembered André Cabillard. The French secret agent who Helen de Burrel had fallen in love with only weeks before he was sent back to France. Molly had only met him once. But that was enough. It wasn't so much his rugged good looks and sexy accent that had upset her; it was the fact that he had the same hard, slightly remote look in his eyes as Ward Frazer had had in his just before he went to France that last time. It had made shivers run down her spine.

'They still think André might be a traitor,' Katy said. 'And Helen seems to have disappeared off the face of the earth.'

Just then Malcolm tipped over a chair, dislodging a pile of journals, which slid noisily to the floor. Shocked, he sat down and burst into tears.

'What on earth are these?' Katy asked, hastily gathering up the magazines and restacking them on the chair.

Molly pulled Malcolm on to her lap and tried to distract him with the threadbare stuffed donkey he had brought with him. 'They are copies of *The Lancet*, the doctors' magazine.'

'I can see that,' Katy said. 'But what are they doing here?'

'Sister Parkes sent them down to me with a note saying that she expected me to use this week to educate myself.'

'Goodness.' Katy eyed the turgid pile in dismay. 'Then I suppose I had better leave you to it.'

As she helped Katy get Malcolm back in his pram, Molly knew she should resist the impulse, but she couldn't stop herself. 'My week's curfew is up on Saturday,' she said. 'Shall I pop in on Sunday and see if you need a hand?'

Katy gave a guilty grimace. 'I ought to say no,' she said. 'Matron will probably kill me. But it would be such a help.'

Joyce enjoyed Jen's show, but more than that, she enjoyed the evening out. She and Mr Lorenz had travelled up to the West End in a taxi hired for the occasion by Dr Goodacre, the surgeon who had performed the operation on Jen's throat. Sister Morris, who had organised for Jen to see Mr Goodacre in the first place, had also been invited. Jen had given them all tickets as a thank-you.

Just that morning, Mr Lorenz had produced a smart winter coat for Joyce, which he claimed someone had left in hock in his shop and never redeemed. He thought it might be just the thing for her to wear to the theatre. But only if she fancied it, of course.

Joyce didn't really like feeling under obligation to Mr Lorenz. She didn't believe for a moment that anyone would voluntarily leave a lovely garment like that unredeemed, but she had been so worried about what to wear that she had accepted it gratefully. She hadn't always seen eye to eye with Jen, but she didn't want to let the side down among her benefactors.

And she hadn't let the side down. Dr Goodacre was one of the jolliest men she had ever met, and even Miss Morris, renowned for her abstemious ways, deigned to drink a small sherry in the interval. Joyce had already accepted their fulsome compliments about Jen's performance, which, fair's fair, had been good, even though it was only a small part. Now she made them laugh with her description of her and Jen hunting for the hibernating tortoise in the fog.

'Ah yes.' Dr Goodacre pricked up his ears. 'The tortoise. *Testudinidae*. A very interesting species. I believe the endoskeleton has the adaptation of an external shell actually fused to the ribcage.'

'I wish I had a shell fused to my ribcage,' Joyce remarked as a large, red-faced American officer barged past her to get to the bar. 'That bloke's got a bit too much testudinidae if you ask me.'

To her delight, Dr Goodacre let out a roar of mirth, while Sister Morris choked violently on her sherry and had to be slapped on the back by Mr Lorenz, who was chuckling so much his spectacles steamed up. After the show Jen had taken them backstage and introduced them to some of the cast, and that had been fun too, to see them without their stage make-up.

All in all it had been a good evening, Joyce thought in the taxi on the way home, as she tried to prise her right elbow out of Sister Morris's voluminous bosom. Jen, on her other side, seemed very bony and unyielding in comparison. It was dark in the taxi as it trundled through the blackout, so Joyce couldn't see her daughter's expression. When Mr Lorenz remarked that he thought Jen's voice was stronger than the leading lady's, she thought the least Jen could do was thank him. But she didn't.

'Yes indeed,' Dr Goodacre agreed enthusiastically. 'Not a hint of huskiness to be heard. So nice to know my handiwork is fully appreciated!'

Jen still didn't respond and Joyce nudged her irritably. Typical Jen, she thought. Just when she should be revelling in all the compliments, she was probably mulling over some imaginary mistake or missed note that nobody else had noticed.

Jen had indeed been mulling, but it wasn't over a mistake. Or not a musical one, anyway. She had been thinking about Henry Keller. A week had passed since the dinner at Prunier's, and she hadn't heard a squeak from him. She could have kicked herself. Why hadn't she just kept her mouth shut and let nature take its course?

'He's probably just busy,' Katy said consolingly the following morning. 'Ward told me he's got a new production in the pipeline, and I know he's involved with ENSA too.'

'But I want to be in his new production,' Jen groaned.

'Well why don't I ask Ward if—' Katy stopped as Ward came down the stairs carrying Malcolm.

'Ask me what?' Ward flashed Jen an enquiring smile, and not for the first time, she almost had to pinch herself to remind herself he was real. With his hair slightly damp, and with Malcolm clinging to his shoulder like a contented little monkey, he looked like every woman's dream.

But he was real, and it was mousy little Katy Parsons who had won him, and lost him, and now miraculously got him back again. Even now Jen could hardly believe it. It was like some happy-ever-after fairy tale. And any minute, the three of them would skip off into the sunset. Leaving her stuck at home with just her mother for company, a piddly role in a two-bit backstreet show, and no knight in shining armour anywhere to be seen.

'It's nothing,' she said, trying to glare Katy down. But Katy wasn't looking at her; she was looking at Ward.

'She thinks she put Henry off by hinting that she was hoping he might find her a better job,' she said.

'Pshaw!' Malcolm said.

Ward laughed and swung him to the ground. 'Absolutely right,' he said. 'I don't think you'd put Henry off as easily as that. He was probably hoping it was his body you were after, not his influence. But he's a bit of a one for

38

the ladies, so it won't do him any harm to be taken down a peg or two.'

'But I didn't mean to take him down any pegs,' Jen wailed. 'And I'm not averse to his body anyway! At least I don't think I am,' she added quickly.

Ward raised his eyebrows. 'Well, if I tell him that ...'

'No,' Jen screamed. 'No, don't you dare! Seriously, if you ever, ever mention my name to Henry Keller, I'll absolutely kill you.'

But as it turned out, she didn't need to kill him, because later that morning she received a note inviting her to audition for the part of Peep-Bo in a new production of *The Mikado*, a Gilbert and Sullivan comic opera.

Jen couldn't believe it. Peep-Bo was one of the famous 'three little maids from school'. It was a perfect role for her. Not the lead, but a good solo role nevertheless. A dream come true. There was no mention of Henry Keller in the letter. But she knew he was behind it. And if he had walked in just then, she would have shown him just how un-averse to him she really was.

When the moment came, Molly regretted her offer of going up to the pub on Sunday afternoon.

Even though she had slept nearly the whole week, she still felt tired. The thought of going back on the ward the following day filled her with horror. What was more, she had woken up with a headache, and a horrible spot on her face. There was one on her neck too. It was hardly the confidence boost she needed. Not for the hospital, nor for the pub.

To make things even worse, Jen Carter was in the pub, chatting with Katy, when Molly arrived.

Of course Jen noticed the spot at once. She recoiled in theatrical mock horror. 'Good God, what's that!'

'It's a spot,' Molly said crossly. How typical of blasted Jen to draw attention to it. Typical too that she should be in such high spirits. Crowing about an audition she had been invited to, for her *perfect* role, one that was going to launch her into the big time. As though her head wasn't swollen enough as it was. God only knew what she would be like if she really did become a West End star. Insufferable, that was what.

'Everyone gets spots when they are run-down,' Katy said placatingly. 'You shouldn't have come, Molly. You still look exhausted.'

Molly shook her head. 'I'll be fine,' she said. She glanced around apprehensively. Thank goodness Ward wasn't there. At least he wouldn't see her spot.

But only an hour or so later, he came in.

Something about his expression as he walked across to the bar made

Molly pause halfway through pulling a pint. Next to her Katy looked up, and she too froze with a glass in her hand.

'What is it?' Katy's voice was husky with fear. 'You've got news? Something about Helen?'

Ward nodded. 'Yes, I just called by the SOE and they'd received a signal earlier today.' He put his hands on the counter as though to support himself. 'Helen is alive. She's in a French field hospital in Oran in Algeria.'

'Algeria?' Katy said. 'What on earth is she doing there? She was meant to be in France.'

Ward shrugged. 'I don't know the details, but somehow she got there by submarine.'

'Submarine?' Katy was starting to laugh now, her relief bubbling over. 'So she's safe? Algeria is in Allied hands now, isn't it? So—'

But Ward leaned over the counter and put a hand on her arm. 'Hold up, Katy,' he said. 'It's not all good news. Helen's not well. She was unconscious for three weeks. That's why we didn't hear anything. Nobody knew who she was. She was shot in France. They did what they could on the submarine, but it seems now that the wound has gotten infected, and …'

Molly couldn't bear to hear any more. She didn't want to hear Katy's gasp of dismay. Or Ward's hasty step as he came round the bar to comfort her.

Poor Helen. And poor Katy. Katy had been a nurse. She would know the implications of an infected wound as well as Molly did. The doctors would do what they could with iodine and sulpha drugs, if indeed they even had such drugs in some unhygienic field hospital in Algeria, but if the infection had taken hold …

Wearily Molly leaned back against the wall for a moment and closed her eyes. This bloody war, she thought.

Wanting to give Ward and Katy some privacy, she was just pushing past Jen at the end of the bar when the door opened and Pam Nelson stuck her head through the blackout curtain.

'A terrible thing has happened,' she called across the room. 'I thought I ought to let you know. George has got chickenpox. I've just had the doctor. I don't know where he picked it up, but—' She stopped as she caught sight of Molly, and her eyes widened. 'Oh no …'

As everyone turned to look at her, Molly put her hand to her face. The spots. Her mind suddenly spun back to the unsavoury, pustulant child she had sat next to in the magician's tent at the potato fair. Oh no indeed.

And then Jen was backing away from her, knocking over a bar stool in her haste. 'No!' she screamed. 'Get away from me! If you've given me chickenpox, Molly Coogan, I'll bloody kill you.'

Chapter Four

Molly could hardly believe it. She didn't know what to do. Or where to go. She knew she wouldn't be welcome back in the nurses' home; they wouldn't want her infecting the other nurses, or the patients. Only a month ago, one of the staff nurses had been packed off home at a moment's notice when she had developed measles. But Molly didn't have a handy home to go to. And who else was going to take her in?

She certainly couldn't stay with Katy and Ward. Nobody would come to the pub if they thought there was a risk of contracting chickenpox. And the last thing she wanted to do was give it to little Malcolm, just as his first birthday was coming up. No, her best hope was to find somewhere where everyone had already had it, because she was pretty sure that you couldn't get it twice.

That didn't stop everyone backing away from her, though. Most people were less obvious than Jen, nobody else ran out of the pub screaming blue murder, but apart from Ward and Katy, there was a distinct sense of people moving out of range. And standing helplessly in the middle of the public bar, Molly was left feeling like a pariah, a leper, contagious and unwanted.

It was Pam Nelson who took pity on her. 'You had better come and stay with us,' she said. 'You can have Helen's room.'

'But what about you and Alan?' Molly asked. 'And the baby?'

'If we are going to get it, we'll get it from George anyway,' Pam said. 'So having you with us won't make any difference.'

So that was what happened. From one day to the next, Molly became the Nelsons' lodger.

Katy went down to the hospital to explain the situation to Matron and to collect some of Molly's things from the nurses' home, and George, delighted by the unexpected turn of events, carefully inspected Molly's spots and declared them nowhere near as numerous or impressive as his own.

Molly felt uncomfortable, oddly intrusive, walking into Helen de Burrel's bedroom. Some of Helen's things were still on the dressing table: a silver-framed photo of a handsome man smoking a cigar, a bottle of fancy Helena Rubinstein face cream, a tortoiseshell hair clip, a stick of Heavenly Pink lipstick, a burnt cork that she had probably been using as mascara, a jar of

42

Pond's cream and a nail file. A half-read French novel by Albert Camus lay on the bedside table. A lacy nightdress was folded neatly over the back of a chair; a dressing gown hung on the back of the door.

'She only took a few things with her.' Pam spoke from the doorway. 'I left everything as it was because I thought it might be bad luck to pack it away. But I'll make up the bed now and clear some space in the wardrobe so that when Katy brings your stuff you have somewhere to put it.'

'Thank you,' Molly said awkwardly. 'This is so kind of you. I hope Helen wouldn't mind.'

'I'm sure she wouldn't.' Pam turned away. But as she opened the wardrobe door, she suddenly let out a little sob and put her hand to her mouth. 'I'm sorry, Molly,' she said after a moment. 'Don't take any notice of me. It's just … the thought of her being all alone in a dirty French hospital in some godforsaken place in Algeria …'

Molly felt helpless in the face of Pam's distress. Someone more spontaneously outgoing might have given her a hug, but she didn't know Pam Nelson very well, and it didn't seem quite appropriate to hug her new landlady. Nor could she think of anything consoling to say. In the end, all she could do was agree. 'I know,' she said inadequately. 'I can hardly bear to think about it either.'

But Pam was already pulling herself together. 'I wish she had never been asked to go on that beastly mission,' she said angrily.

'I don't know how she had the guts,' Molly said. 'I would rather die than set one foot in enemy territory.'

'Me too,' Pam said. 'Imagine having to look over your shoulder all the time, knowing you could be shot at any moment. And if you were captured, God only knew what would happen to you.'

Molly shivered suddenly, as though someone had stepped on her grave. As she looked away, her eye fell on a photograph tucked into the corner of the mirror. Leaning closer, she saw Helen de Burrel standing under a tree, her beautiful face alight with happiness; close behind her, with his arms circling her shoulders, clasping her hands in his, right in front of her heart, was the French agent André Cabillard. Molly recognised his strong, rugged features, that lazy, heart-stopping smile. It must have been taken back in the summer, just before he returned to France and immediately disappeared off the SOE radar.

'You're right,' Molly said decisively. 'It might be bad luck to move her things. Let's leave everything exactly as it is for now. I'll just fit round it. I haven't got much anyway.'

Joyce was worried about Mrs Rutherford. When she had come in that morning, she had hung her coat on the wrong peg, and she had forgotten to bring the parsnips she had promised Joyce for today's soup. Joyce didn't want to pry, but when Mrs Rutherford mixed up two orders so that Mr Lorenz got a Camp coffee and Mrs Peacock got his national loaf toast and jam, she felt she had to ask if something was wrong.

And yes, there was. Mrs Rutherford had received a letter from her son, Douglas. It seemed he'd been due to do another two terms at his expensive public school in Oxfordshire, but now, through the father of a friend, he had been offered the opportunity of getting a commission with the Coldstream Guards.

'He says it's his duty to join up,' Mrs Rutherford went on. She tried to lift her chin. 'I know I should be proud, Mrs Carter, but after losing Bertie …'

Mrs Rutherford had lost her other son in action at El Alamein in Egypt, the same action, in fact, in which Joyce's son Bob had been taken prisoner. Joyce still didn't know where Bob was being held yet – she was waiting to hear from the Red Cross – but at least she knew he was safe, or as safe as possible. Unlike Bertie Rutherford, who was lying somewhere in the desert in an unmarked grave.

'But don't the Coldstream Guards just do guarding?' Joyce said. 'Of the King and that, at Buckingham Palace? Surely they are too smart to go into battle, with those fancy uniforms they wear?'

Celia gave a slight laugh. 'If only you were right,' she said. 'But I'm afraid they are just as likely to get sent to the front as any other regiment. I believe they have suffered considerable losses in North Africa, and that is why this opportunity has come up for Douglas.' She took a handkerchief out of her handbag and blew her nose. 'Who would be a young man in this day and age, Mrs Carter? It's so much easier for the girls.'

Joyce went back to chopping vegetables for the soup. Except for that poor Helen de Burrel, she thought. She wouldn't want to be in her shoes, stuck in some fuzzy-wuzzy hospital in Algeria.

Celia put her handkerchief away and braced her shoulders. 'Well, at least we'll have Douglas home for Christmas. And I've told him to bring a friend if he wants. It might be a bit tame for him to have Christmas lunch with just us and Louise.'

Tame? Horrific more like, Joyce thought. She'd rather sign up for the Coldstream Guards herself than have to sit down to lunch with sour-faced Greville Rutherford and hoity-toity Miss Louise.

'And I expect you are looking forward to Christmas with your Angie?'

Yes, Joyce thought. I am. She had never had any problem with Angie. Not like Jen. The fuss Jen had made about Molly Coogan having the chickenpox! She'd come flying into the house on Sunday night as though wolves were after her, gabbling about some audition and wanting to know if she'd had chickenpox as a child. And then was furious when Joyce couldn't remember. Well, with six children, how could she be expected to remember every childhood disease? And who cared anyway. Chickenpox was hardly life-threatening.

Yes, all in all it would be nice to have little Angie back. She'd try to make Christmas lunch a bit of a celebration. A welcome-home party for her long-lost daughter.

Pete would be there too, if he could get a couple of days' leave from his navy training college. God only knew what they'd all eat, though. There was no chance of a turkey. Mr Dove had even laughed in her face when she'd asked him to put a chicken by for her.

She would have to knock up some sort of pie with leftovers from the café. She liked inventing things, liked making something out of nothing, so long as it was tasty. Someone had said only yesterday that her food was better than the so-called British restaurants. Mrs Rutherford had been so worried that the new council-run restaurants would affect business at the café that she had been out to try the one in Wandsworth. But her report of being served a tough little rectangle of braised tongue followed by a minute portion of boiled pudding gave them confidence that people would still be prepared to pay a little more for better food.

'Oh, I nearly forgot,' Mrs Rutherford said, delving in her handbag and bringing out a newspaper cutting. 'I saw it in the *Wandsworth Borough News* this morning. It's a cookery competition.'

'*Calling all local cooks,*' she read out. '*This is your opportunity to create a tasty austerity menu for four for less than two shillings. Short-listed entrants will be invited to come and cook their menu in the town hall in front of a panel of judges and tasters.*' She looked up eagerly. 'What about it, Mrs Carter? Why don't you enter?'

Joyce recoiled in horror. 'I couldn't cook in front of a panel. And certainly not a panel of those posh WI women.'

'Nonsense,' Celia Rutherford said. 'You are a marvellous cook. And if you got through to the final, it would be tremendous publicity for the café. If you think up a menu, I'll get Greville's secretary to type it up for us neatly.'

'What's the incubation period for chickenpox?' Jen asked Katy.

Katy thought about it. 'Well, if Molly and George picked it up at that potato fair, then it must be about ten days. But I'm sure you won't get it, Jen. You probably had it as a child. Some children get it so mildly their parents don't even notice.'

'If I do get it, I'm going to murder that poxy little pixie Molly Coogan,' Jen said. 'Honestly, you'd think she'd have had the sense to stay away.'

'She didn't know she had it,' Katy objected. 'It wasn't her fault.'

'Of course it was her fault,' Jen said. 'Feeling ill and covered in spots, it's not that difficult. She's a nurse; you'd think she might have put two and two together.'

'She was hardly covered …' Katy began, and then gave up. When Jen got on her high horse, there was no point in arguing with her. It was easier just to change the subject.

'Any word from Henry?' she asked, and then regretted the question. Judging from Jen's frown, this was clearly not a good choice as a diversionary tactic.

'No,' Jen said. 'Not even a good-luck note for the audition.'

'Maybe it's nothing to do with him.' Katy said. 'Maybe he doesn't even know about it.'

'Of course he knows about it,' Jen said irritably. 'He pretty much *is* London theatre. He must have put me up for it. I'd never have got a sniff at it otherwise.'

'Well, there you are then,' Katy said. 'He's done exactly what you wanted.'

'I know,' Jen said gloomily, getting up to go. 'That's the problem.'

Left alone in the pub Katy began to sweep the floor. Some berries from the holly had fallen down and got squashed underfoot, staining the sawdust like spots of blood. As she swept the debris out of the door, she saw Mrs James emerge from her house further down the street. Katy was glad when she turned the other way and set off towards Lavender Hill. So far the glamorous widow hadn't been back to the pub. She had presumably found an alternative supply of gin.

Katy felt a bit guilty. Her natural instinct was to be friendly, but there was something about Gillian James that made her uneasy. It wasn't so much that she had come into the pub on her own. After all, Katy prided herself on running the kind of pub women could come into alone without being treated like tarts. And it wasn't just her looks, her evident sex appeal, although that was a worry, especially now, with the nice bunch of mistletoe hanging from the ceiling.

No, it was more that Katy sensed Mrs James was going to be trouble. She couldn't quite put it into words; it was something about her attitude, the way she wore her unpatriotically flashy clothes. And the daughter was so silent, so reserved, and yet so exceptionally pretty, with her glossy dark hair, perfect oval face and large almond-shaped eyes.

46

Pam Nelson had bumped into Bella James in the library while she was looking for a book on magic to keep George amused during his enforced incarceration. 'I see what you mean,' she said when she popped in to see Katy the following day. 'She's even more of a head-turner than her mother.'

But Katy didn't want to talk about Mrs James or her daughter. 'How are your patients?' she asked instead. 'Are they bored to death?' She felt guilty for avoiding Molly and George. But that morning she had received a letter from her mother confirming that she had had chickenpox as a baby, so now she *would* visit, despite her mother's insistence that she stay away from the sufferers in case she caught it again. Her mother had always been a worrier. That was why Katy had encouraged her to stay in the country with Ward's old aunts for the duration of the war.

Katy would have liked Ward to ask his parents the same question, but Ward was estranged from them. They hadn't approved of his decision to leave Canada before the war to pursue a journalistic career in Germany, and they had barely been in touch since.

Anyway, by the time a letter had travelled all the way to Canada and back, Molly and George's quarantine would be long over. Katy had managed to persuade him to stay away from the Nelsons' house instead, which was a shame because George hero-worshipped Ward and was always pestering him for information about spies and guns and how to make a catapult and the best way to string a conker. And Ward was always ready to respond. The catapult had been particularly successful, but had had to be confiscated by Pam when she caught George taking aim at one of Mrs Rutherford's hens over the back wall.

'Apart from the spots, you'd hardly know George was ill,' Pam replied. 'I think Molly is beginning to feel quite poorly. But she's been brilliant at keeping George amused. They have been learning conjuring tricks from the book I found in the library. They had me and Alan completely foxed last night with a disappearing handkerchief.'

Katy laughed. She couldn't imagine Molly performing magic. But when she went over the following day, she was completely flummoxed when Molly produced the ace of spades out of George's pocket, even though she had seen it in the pack with her own eyes only a moment before.

'You two ought to be on the stage,' she said. 'You'd make a fortune.'

George's spotty face lit up. 'We could have a tent like Mr Trickster,' he said.

Katy grinned at Molly. 'It could be a whole new career.'

Molly smiled rather wanly. 'If only,' she said.

Jen was appalled when Joyce told her that little Angie was going to have to sleep in her room.

'Pete's coming back for Christmas,' Joyce said. 'And I can't put her in with him.'

It was the last thing Jen wanted. For all she knew, Angie would snore or talk in her sleep. 'Why can't she go in with you?' she asked crossly. She saw Joyce flush and raised her eyebrows. 'Or are you hoping for a little bit of festive how's-your-father with Mr Lorenz?'

'Certainly not,' Joyce snapped. 'Don't be absurd. No, she's going in with you and that's that. And you be nice to her, poor little thing, she's been away for so long, she's bound to be a bit shy, and I want her to feel welcome.'

'All right, all right,' Jen said. 'I'll be sweetness and light.'

Jen had much more important things to worry about than her sister's arrival. Her audition for *The Mikado*. Already she could feel the tension in her stomach, the stab of nervous anticipation every time she remembered the ordeal in store.

She had chosen her pieces and practised them endlessly. She was word-perfect. She had even splashed out all her precious savings on a pianist to run through them with her. She wished she could have asked Henry Keller for advice too, but that was clearly out of the question. It would reinforce his impression that she was only after him for his influence.

On the morning of the audition, she was a bag of nerves. She had decided it would seem overconfident to sing the leading lady Yum-Yum's aria, 'The Sun Whose Rays Are All Ablaze', for the audition, so she had opted for two other Gilbert and Sullivan pieces instead, 'Poor Wand'ring One' from *The Pirates Of Penzance* and 'I Have a Song to Sing, O!' from *The Yeomen of the Guard*. Both were tricky numbers and she just hoped she could do them justice. As a backup she had 'Funiculi Funicula' ready too, which would prove beyond doubt that her voice was completely back to normal when she hit the top C in the finale.

Now, though, as she walked towards the Shaftesbury Theatre, where the auditions were to be held, she was worrying about her choices. Why on earth had she gone for such high, difficult pieces? Her technique would have to be spot on if she wasn't going to make a complete fool of herself.

'Douglas is coming back tomorrow,' Louise told Katy when she came in at lunchtime. 'He's joining up after Christmas. The Coldstream Guards, can you believe it?'

Katy could believe it. Typical of a cocky little public-school boy like Douglas Rutherford to find his way into a prestigious regiment, she thought. His older brother Bertie had once told her that Douglas was army mad. Poor Bertie. He'd been the complete opposite. But in the end he had done his duty, and like so many of the young men who had passed through the pub over the last year or so, he wouldn't be coming back, killed within weeks of arriving in North Africa.

'I expect your mother is worried sick,' she said, picking up a cloth to polish some glasses. It was quiet in the pub today. The only customers were a couple of old men smoking by the fire and three young soldiers from the anti-aircraft gun emplacement on Clapham Common.

'Yes, she is,' Louise said. 'But Daddy is awfully proud. He keeps making stupid comments about us all minding our Ps and Qs when there are Coldstreamers in the house. Christmas is going to be unbearable.' She gave a comical grimace, then sighed. 'I wish Helen was back so she could come for Christmas,' she said. 'That would take the wind out of their sails, knowing she had been working behind enemy lines and all that.'

Katy was about to put the glasses up on the shelf, but now she paused. Louise had been to finishing school with Helen de Burrel and still counted her as one of her best friends.

'Louise, you do realise Helen is very seriously ill?' she said. She felt something jolt in her heart as she spoke the words. 'She … she may not make it.'

Louise stared at her blankly. 'No,' she said. 'No. I can't believe it. I know you said her wound was infected, but … surely they can do something for her in this day and age?' She caught the look in Katy's eyes. 'I can't bear it,' she said. Her shoulders heaved convulsively as she began to cry. 'I hate this beastly war.'

It took Katy quite a while and two small whiskies to get Louise back on her feet, and all the time she was administering to her, and muttering reassuring words, she was thinking of Helen and wishing she could up sticks and go to Algeria to be with her. To nurse her if necessary. But of course it was impossible. You couldn't just go to Algeria. Not in the middle of a war. Even in peacetime, it was a million miles away.

'What about Helen's father?' Louise asked suddenly. 'Lord de Burrel? Surely he can help? He's awfully well connected. I thought he was some kind of ambassador or something.'

Katy sighed. 'The SOE are trying to contact him, but he's still in America and so far they haven't been able to track him down. There's some thought he might have gone skiing.'

'Skiing?' Louise looked astonished. 'While his daughter is lying half dead in Algeria?'

'Well he doesn't know that,' Katy said. 'I don't suppose he even knows she was in the SOE, come to that. She didn't volunteer for agent training

49

until well after he had gone off to America. It's hardly public knowledge. The only reason we know is because of Ward.'

Katy closed her eyes for a second. Ward was doing everything he could, but she knew he had lost confidence in the SOE. He was furious with them for sending Helen to France in the first place, for giving her so little backup, and now for dragging their feet in their efforts to get her home. It had been Ward who had recruited Helen into the SOE back in the early part of the war. But only as a research assistant, thinking her knowledge of France would come in handy. He had never in a million years intended for her to be sent overseas. Had he been here at the time, instead of in a German prisoner of war camp, he would have vigorously contested the decision to train her as an agent. And even though it had, in the end, been Helen's choice, Katy knew he felt responsible for what had happened.

Louise was still a bit tearful when Ward himself walked in, bringing a draught of icy December air with him.

'Look what I got,' he said, holding up a parcel. 'Malcolm's birthday present.'

Louise brightened at once, Helen apparently forgotten in her eagerness to put on a good face for Ward. 'Oh, what is it?' she asked.

'A push-along tank,' he said, unwrapping it proudly. 'It's a Crusader Mark Two. I saw it in Hamley's. It's kind of flimsy because it's only made of cardboard, but I think he'll like it. It's got this rotating gun turret, just like the real thing.'

'I'm sure he'll love it,' Louise said with a giggle. Then she glanced at the clock. 'Gosh, I'll be late for my shift if I don't get a move on.' She quickly shrugged on her coat. But halfway across the room she paused. 'Oh look,' she said, glancing back at Ward artlessly. 'I'm standing right under the mistletoe.'

Katy felt a stab of irritation, but Ward just laughed. 'Well, never let it be said that I am one to shirk my duty,' he said, and stepped across to give her a light kiss on the lips. Then, gently detaching her hands from his shoulders, he straightened up and threw Katy a comical glance. 'I know, I know, I'm a married man, but you wouldn't want me to leave a damsel in distress, now would you?'

Yes, Katy thought crossly as she washed up Louise's glass, I would. But she smiled obligingly and reminded herself that Ward could have married Louise if he had wanted to. But that he had chosen her instead.

'Thank you, Miss Carter.' The voice came out of the darkness in the auditorium, a male voice that sounded suitably impressed. Jen gave a polite smile in return, but inside she was gleeful. The *Pirates of Penzance* and *Yeomen of the Guard* songs had gone off well, almost faultlessly in fact. Her nerves had receded, making way for a thrill of adrenalin. For the first time in ages she was feeling confident of her voice, of her ability, and now she was hoping they would ask for 'Funiculi Funicula' so she could finish on a real high, in more ways than one.

She could hear the low voices out beyond the footlights, and for a moment she allowed herself to think how she would feel if they offered her the Peep-Bo part there and then, how unutterably brilliant that would be.

And then the voice spoke again. 'We'd like you to sing one more piece, Miss Carter.'

'Yes, of course,' she said brightly.

'Ideally we'd like to hear something from *The Mikado*. We were wondering about Yum-Yum's aria, 'The Sun Whose Rays Are All Ablaze', but you don't have it listed here. Do you know it by any chance?'

Jen felt sweat suddenly prickle in her armpits. What about 'Funiculi Funicula'? she wanted to shout at them. Why can't I just sing that? For a second she was tempted to deny knowing the Yum-Yum song; surely that was better than making a mess of it. But then, deciding honesty was the best course of action, she forced a rueful smile on to her lips. 'I do know it,' she said. 'But I haven't sung it for ages.'

There was another muffled consultation, and then the voice again. 'Well, how do you feel about having a go?'

I feel as though I might be sick, Jen wanted to respond. But of course she smiled again. She had to. She had to look professional. It was either that or run screaming from the stage. She took a steadying breath. 'If you could just give me a moment to look through the score?'

'Of course, take your time. Sing it from the piano if you wish.'

'Thank you,' she said.

Oh God, oh God, she thought as she walked over to the piano. It had all been going so well, and now she felt as though she was in the middle of a nightmare. 'Please help me,' she whispered to the pianist. 'I really don't know it that well.'

'You'll be fine,' he said. He ran his fingers over the keys, picking out the tune for her. 'They wouldn't have asked for it if they didn't like you.'

It was something. But it wasn't really enough. As she quickly flicked through the music with shaking fingers, Jen frantically tried to recall the tips her old mentor Mrs Frost had given her when they had worked on this piece two years ago. But her mind was a complete blank. She could barely remember the tune, let alone the finer points of technique needed to sing it successfully.

But the moment had come. She had to do it.

Get into role, get into role, she adjured herself as the pianist played the intro, and forcing herself to relax, she smiled wistfully and lifted her chin.

She got through it. That was the best you could say about it, she thought, as she stood waiting for a reaction from the audition panel. It was patchy and unexpressive, but she had at least got all the notes, and more or less in the right order.

'Thank you,' the voice said again. 'We will be in touch.'

And that was that.

Joyce was sitting at her kitchen table, working out a recipe, when someone knocked on the door. Frowning, she put her pencil down and stood up, but her eyes were still on the figures. It was hard to calculate how much all the small ingredients would cost. Did you have to include a cost for salt, for example, she wondered, or the flour she needed to roll the meat in to give the gravy a bit of thickness? She had no intention of entering the cookery competition, but it was interesting to work out exactly what sort of a meal for four you could knock up for less than two bob. Reluctantly she added another penny to cover the flour. Then she smoothed her apron and hurried down the dark passage to open the door.

Outside, the moonlight was bright. Somewhere in the distance, searchlights were patrolling the sky.

Standing on Joyce's doorstep with her hand raised for a second knock was a buxom young woman dressed in what looked like an RAF bomber jacket over a plaid skirt. Her hair was rolled back and held with a bright red and white polka-dot bow. In her arms she clutched a large, unwieldy parcel, badly wrapped in newspaper and tied with string. At her feet were two cardboard boxes and a bulging hessian sack.

Behind her in the road, wearing smart overcoats, tweed suits, V-necked jerseys and identical striped ties, stood two young men, one of whom Joyce dimly recognised as Douglas Rutherford.

Blankly Joyce turned a questioning gaze back on the girl, who was now smiling broadly, showing off a set of large white teeth under her bright red lipstick.

'You don't recognise me, do you?' The girl gave a scream of delighted laughter. 'It's me, Angie. Your daughter!'

Half deafened by the laugh, Joyce reeled back. Angie?

'Angie,' she said faintly. 'Is it really you?' Could this huge, blowsy girl really be her little Angie?

She peered at her more closely, but she could see very little sign of the shy, skinny child she had sent off to Devon for safety at the beginning of the war.

The girl laughed again, this time a kind of gurgling giggle. 'Of course it's me! Weren't you expecting me? I thought Mrs Baxter had written to you.'

'Well yes, well, no, not until tomorrow, actually, but …' Joyce tried to pull herself together, but found her glance drifting to the two smart young men waiting patiently by the gate.

'Oh don't mind them.' Angie waved her hand airily. 'We met on the train. I heard them mention Lavender Road, so we fell into conversation. And when we got to Clapham Junction, they offered to help carry my things.'

Thrusting the ungainly parcel into Joyce's arms, she turned back to the gate. 'Thanks, boys, I'm OK now. I'll see you later at the pub perhaps?'

The pub? But … Joyce tried to muster some objection, but the words failed her as she saw Angie give each of the young men a smacking kiss on the cheek and shoo them away. Obediently, with a rather shifty nod at Joyce, they sloped off down the road.

'So kind of them,' Angie said with breezy good humour, turning back to Joyce. 'I don't know how I'd have managed without them.'

Feeling the parcel slipping through her hands, Joyce fumbled to get a firmer grip on it. And on the situation. 'Angie, I really—' she began, but was interrupted by another raucous rattle of mirth.

'Watch out! You nearly dropped the turkey. Mrs Baxter sent it up for us for Christmas.'

Chapter Five

Jen was utterly exhausted by the time she got home from the theatre. The strain of the audition, followed by both a matinee and an evening show, had left her feeling as though she had been run over by a London bus. All day she been fretting about the audition, her hopes rising and plummeting alternately as she tried to work out how well she had performed. However much she told herself there was nothing she could do about it now, that her fate rested in the hands of the audition panel, she couldn't get it out of her mind. All she wanted now was to climb into bed, close her eyes and hope that blessed sleep would finally restore her equilibrium.

As she walked up Lavender Road, she noticed the staff car once again parked in the road outside number forty-two. The engine was idling, perhaps to keep the driver warm. Like everyone else, Jen had wondered about the so-called widow and her mysterious military visitor, but unlike everyone else, she didn't feel the need to pry into the poor woman's business.

But this time, just as she approached her own front door, the door of the house opposite opened and a tall man in an officer's greatcoat emerged. If she hadn't been standing exactly where she was, Jen wouldn't have seen anything more than that. But for a second, before the door closed again, she could see a woman wearing nothing but a lacy negligee silhouetted in the passageway behind him.

The driver of the staff car was already jumping out of his seat, dropping his cigarette and grinding it under his heel. He went smartly round the car to open the back door, and saluted, standing to attention as the officer climbed in. Within seconds he had closed the door, returned to his own seat, put the car into gear and driven away.

Jen stood for a moment rooted to the spot. It wasn't so much the fact of the officer leaving or the woman standing there half dressed that had stunned her. After all, the man could have been setting off for night duty at the War Office for all she knew. It was the fact that in that flash of light, Jen had quite clearly seen that the woman was not only looking completely dishevelled, with her lipstick smeared and her dark hair in disarray, but was holding what looked like a substantial wad of cash in her hand.

Good God, Jen thought. So that's the way the land lies. Then she giggled to herself. And in prudish old Lavender Road too. What was the world coming to?

She was still smiling when she opened the front door. But her amusement turned to astonishment as she heard an extraordinary noise coming from the kitchen. It was either mirth or a very high pitched sub-machine gun. What on earth …?

Her mother and an enormous rosy-cheeked girl were sitting at the kitchen table, sharing a wholesome picnic of bread, butter, cheese, apples and a big bottle of something that looked suspiciously like cider.

As soon as the girl noticed Jen, she jumped up, knocking over her chair and nearly overbalancing the cider bottle.

'Jen!' she screamed in delight. 'You must be Jen. Don't you recognise me? I'm your little sister Angie!'

And Jen found herself almost knocked off her feet as the girl launched forward and embraced her in a huge bear hug.

Good God, Jen thought. It can't be. The last time she had seen Angie, she had been a scrawny little thing, crying her eyes out at the thought of being evacuated. War had only just been declared. How on earth had she managed to change so much in just over three years?

Angie was standing back now, her eyes wide with awe. 'I don't remember you being so glamorous.'

'And I don't remember you being so huge!' Jen said, putting her hand to her chest, checking for cracked ribs.

She heard a slight gasp of objection from her mother at this, but Angie let out a good-natured guffaw.

'I know. I know. I'm enormous. It was all Mrs Baxter's lovely country food. We never went short on the farm. Look, I've brought a few bits and pieces with me. Do you want something? This is Mrs Baxter's home-made cheese. It's really good. Or there's a lovely ham pie in that box. Shall I cut you a slice?'

Jen glanced at her mother and bit back a smile. She had never seen Joyce looking so bemused. She wondered for a moment if she'd been at the cider, but then realised it was more likely the overpowering effect of her long-lost daughter.

'Well,' she demurred. 'I really need to go to bed. I've had a long day.'

'To bed?' Angie looked up from cutting a slice of pie. 'But it's only nine o clock. I was hoping you'd come over to the pub with me.'

'To the pub?' Jen repeated, and caught her mother's quick, urgent shake of the head.

'Yes, the Flag and Garter.' Angie nodded eagerly. 'I wanted to go earlier because I met some boys on the train who are going to be there, but Mum said she didn't think I should go on my own.'

'Boys?' Jen asked in amazement. 'What boys?'

'Douglas Rutherford and a friend,' Joyce said, meeting her eyes meaningfully. 'They carried her luggage up from Clapham Junction.'

Douglas Rutherford? Carrying her sister's luggage? Jen felt another surge of amusement. This was getting better and better.

Angie giggled as she thrust a plate towards Jen. 'It doesn't matter if I don't go tonight. They'll probably just think I'm playing hard to get.'

'Well I hope you *are* hard to get,' Jen said severely. She glanced at her sister's big rosy face. 'How old are you? Fifteen?'

Angie didn't reply because her mouth was full of pie, but she nodded enthusiastically.

'Angie's been telling me all about her fiancé in Devon,' Joyce remarked faintly.

'Fiancé?' Jen suddenly felt as though she had stumbled on to the set of a West End farce.

'Gino.' Angie clutched her chest and splayed her fingers over her heart. 'My lovely Gino.'

Reaching for the cider bottle, Jen carried it over to the sideboard and poured herself a glass. Then, righting the chair that Angie had knocked over, she sat down and took a good slug of the drink. She could see why her mother looked so frazzled. The combination of Angie and strong cider would be enough to finish anyone off. She was also beginning to see exactly why Mrs Baxter had sent her sister home.

'He's an Italian prisoner of war,' Joyce said.

'He's the love of my life,' Angie added, helping herself to another slice of pie.

'Good God,' Jen said. 'And how long is that going to last?'

'For ever.' Angie sighed dramatically. 'I miss him already. But we are going to write to each other. And when the war is over, we'll get married.' Then she let out another deafening salvo of her machine-gun laugh. 'But that's not going to stop me having a bit of fun first.'

Jen nearly choked on her drink. 'Well,' she said brightly, when she could make herself heard. She raised her glass to Joyce. 'Isn't it nice to have sweet little Angie back with us!'

For a while, despite the hideous spots, Molly hadn't felt too bad in herself, and had done her best to help Pam with the chores. She had discovered previously unknown talents in mangling the washing, wielding the new-fangled carpet sweeper and laying the fire. But the main way she had tried to help was by keeping George amused. If nothing else, it stopped him

56

scratching his spots and getting in Pam's way as she nursed baby Helen. It wasn't an easy task, because after the novelty of being kept home from school had worn off, George quickly became bored. He was a livewire with a short attention span, and Molly found him both endearing and exhausting.

The book of magic had proved to be a lifesaver. But now that they had perfected a number of tricks, the shortage of an audience was proving too much of a frustration, and George's interest had turned to the idea of making a go-cart. Being hopelessly untechnical, Molly felt ill-equipped to help with this project, but she was relieved at the change of focus, as the prospect of being required to perform a conjuring trick in front of Jen Carter or Ward Frazer made her feel quite faint. And in any case, by that time she had begun to feel really ill. So she was thankful that George was happy to tinker about on his own with the odd bits and pieces of wood, metal, spokes and bolts that Alan obligingly brought home from the brewery. It left her free to sit by the fire shivering under an eiderdown or, as her temperature rose to 102 degrees, to stay in bed.

For a couple of days she tossed and turned with aching limbs, a complete lack of appetite and a desire only to sleep. But thanks to Pam's care, and her nourishing offerings of Bovril, barley water and soup, she gradually began to recover.

As she began to feel better, she started to realise how much she would miss being here in this cosy, easy-going house. She would miss Pam's calm good sense, the homely warmth of the fire in the front room, listening to *The Brains Trust* with Alan, laughing at Lord Haw-Haw broadcasting from Germany with his idiotic claims about England being on the brink of collapse. She would miss baby Helen's little gurgles and her tiny clutching fingers. Most of all she would miss George's artless conversation and the family meals round the little table in the kitchen. She was beginning to dread going back to work.

In particular she was dreading the thought of being questioned on the medical journals Sister Parkes had given her to read. Molly couldn't imagine what she expected her to learn from them. Most of the articles were far too scientific even for someone with a Higher Certificate in Biology. Anyway, there seemed little point in educating herself when she had no chance to put any knowledge she gleaned into action.

But as her fever abated, so her fear of incurring Sister Parkes's wrath increased. Finally, on the Thursday before Christmas, while Pam took baby Helen and George out for some fresh air and to drop off the birthday card they had made for Malcolm, she forced herself to look at the journals again.

There were several articles about sepsis, of course, but they mostly focused on poor wound hygiene, contamination, and the ineffectiveness of sulphonamide drugs in fighting certain types of bacterium. She knew all that. But then as she flicked listlessly through a copy of *The Lancet*, her eye was caught by an article about a surprisingly effective type of mould, penicillin, which a London doctor, Professor Alexander Fleming, had discovered by chance thirteen years before, and which had apparently overcome many bacteria that the existing sulphonamide drugs did not affect. Having briefly outlined one specific case of a patient recovering unexpectedly from an extreme streptococcal infection, the article eventually reached it's conclusion, *in view of its potentialities it is recommended that methods for producing penicillin on a larger scale should be developed as quickly as possible.*

Yes indeed, Molly thought. So why on earth hadn't it been done? Surely thirteen years was long enough to test a new drug? Why wasn't it available to all the soldiers dying in their hundreds from infected wounds? If only this Fleming man had got a move on, so many lives might have been saved.

Then she found a piece in a more recent journal, this time quoting Professor Fleming himself: *Due to the toxicity of the penicillin chemical, the production of an effective therapeutic drug is very complicated and the difficulties are great.* She threw the magazine on the floor in disgust. So why raise everyone's hopes? Doctors, she thought crossly, men, they were all the same, so good at blowing their own trumpets, pretending they knew everything when they clearly didn't know much at all.

For a moment she leaned her head back in the chair, but then abruptly she stood up. She was fed up with being indoors. Surely if George was well enough to go and get some fresh air, then so was she. If she tied a scarf round her face, nobody would see her last remaining spots. She wouldn't infect anyone out in the open, and if she wrapped up nice and warm in Alan's overcoat, which was hanging on the peg by the door, nobody would recognise her anyway.

Joyce was struggling. Her limbs felt like lead and she had had a thumping headache all morning. Mrs Rutherford had looked rather surprised when she recounted the events of Angie's homecoming. 'That's odd,' she said. 'Douglas didn't mention meeting her on the train.'

'Oh.' Joyce wished she hadn't mentioned it either. It occurred to her that the Rutherfords wouldn't approve of their precious son hobnobbing with the likes of Angie Carter.

Mr Lorenz had looked concerned when he came in for his breakfast. 'Are you all right, Mrs Carter?' he asked. 'You don't look quite well.'

She had had to admit to having one too many glasses of Angie's cider the previous evening. 'Are you shocked, Mr Lorenz?'

'On the contrary,' he said courteously. 'I am looking forward to meeting your daughter. I remember her as a child, of course. But I expect she has grown up quite a bit since then.'

Joyce was surprised. She hadn't had much to do with Mr Lorenz in those days. Apart from taking the odd thing in to hock, of course. It was funny to think of him taking an interest in her family even then. 'She has certainly grown,' she agreed readily. 'I'm not sure about the *up*.'

He smiled slightly. 'Oh come now, Mrs Carter. You are always so hard on your children. Look at your Jennifer, she has turned into a delightful young woman. I expect she was pleased to see her sister.'

'Oh yes.' Joyce bit back a laugh. 'Absolutely delighted.' She had never seen anyone take the wind out of Jen's sails before. Joyce would have thought her older daughter was a match for anyone. But even Jen's acerbic tongue had proved powerless against Angie's relentless good humour. It was funny in a way, but later, as she began preparing the veg for lunch, Joyce was aware of a niggle of unease.

'I'll need to find something for Angie to do,' she remarked suddenly to Celia Rutherford. 'But she's not quite sixteen yet, and—'

'Perhaps we could use her here,' Celia suggested. 'We could do with some help with the washing-up and so on.'

Joyce had a sudden vision of letting Angie loose at the sink among their dainty cups and saucers, the precious plates and hard-to-come-by glasses, and quailed at the thought. On the other hand, it would mean she could keep an eye on her. Goodness only knew what Angie would get up to if she was left alone all day long. She had already expressed a desire to go up to town because she wanted to see with her own eyes all the different uniforms of the various nationalities of servicemen she had heard were at large in London.

'Well you'd better meet her first,' Joyce said doubtfully. 'See what you think.'

But when Angie appeared in the café later, Celia seemed delighted with her.

To Joyce's horror, Angie had brought with her the recipe Joyce had been working on the previous evening. 'I was just tidying up the kitchen and I found this under the bread board,' she said. 'I thought you might need it. Mmm.' She smacked her lips. 'Sausage and dumpling pie, it sounds delicious. And all for two shillings!'

Celia pricked up her ears. 'What recipe is that, Mrs Carter?'

'It's nothing,' Joyce muttered, scrunching up the piece of paper and throwing it into the rubbish bin. 'Just an idea I had for next week's lunch menu.'

59

To Joyce's relief, the bell clanged on the door just then. She was surprised to see Mr Lorenz again. He didn't usually come in twice in one day. Drawing her to one side and looking rather furtive, he pressed a small packet of Koray headache pills into her hand. 'I thought they might make you feel a bit more like it,' he murmured.

Joyce suppressed a smile as she thanked him, wondering what Jen would say about this latest love token.

Behind her Angie was gazing round the café. 'What a lovely place,' she said. 'You are clever to make it all so pretty. I bet your customers love coming here.'

'Oh we do,' Mr Lorenz said. 'It's the best café in town.'

'Ha.' Angie swung round with a wide smile. 'I remember you. You're Mr Lorenz. You mended my doll for me once when Mick pulled its head off and threw it over your wall.'

Mr Lorenz went a bit pink. 'No, no, I'm sure …'

'No, you did,' Angie insisted. 'And I thought it was very kind of you because Daddy was always so terribly rude to you. I don't know why. I always thought you were nice.'

'Well, I am delighted to have been of service,' Mr Lorenz said, avoiding Joyce's stricken glance. He offered his hand and winced as Angie shook it energetically. 'And it's a great pleasure to remake your acquaintance. Perhaps I could offer to buy you a cup of tea, or your mother makes a lovely cup of cocoa?'

'Cor!' Angie giggled delightedly. 'What a gent you are, Mr Lorenz. A nice cup of cocoa would go down a treat!'

'Well, she seems a very friendly girl,' Celia murmured to Joyce a few minutes later, as Angie and Mr Lorenz settled themselves at a table by the window and Angie began to regale him with a lively account of her former life in Devon. 'What do you think about offering her some work? She'd certainly jolly the place up a bit.'

It was cold outside, and Molly was already shivering by the time she got to the top of the road. Up on the common, without the protection of houses, the wind was strong. She could feel it buffeting against her, and she realised how weak and shaky she felt after being stuck indoors for days on end.

She would have liked to call at the pub to see if little Malcolm was enjoying his birthday, and whether there was any news of Helen. But it wasn't safe for her to go there yet. Thankfully, so far at least, no one else she knew had gone down with the disease, but until her spots completely disappeared, technically she was still infectious.

Skirting the gun emplacements behind their bristling barbed wire, and the allotments, now looking bleak and neglected, with only a few leeks and moth-eaten winter cabbages showing, she headed across the pockmarked grass towards the bandstand. The big chestnut trees on the Avenue were bare; like the grass, they had also suffered from their proximity to the anti-aircraft guns. Several bore shrapnel scars, two had broken limbs and one was burnt through. For weeks after the Blitz, despite the efforts of the fire brigade, that tree had smouldered on doggedly. Now only its trunk remained, eerie and blackened, pointing accusingly up at the sky.

There weren't many people about, and those who had braved the gale were moving briskly, hurrying along in heavy coats and shoes, muffled up in hand-knitted scarves and hats.

But then Molly saw someone running. A man. Purposefully, strongly, in khaki shorts and a thick navy sweater. Even from this distance she knew it was Ward Frazer, and though her first instinct was to hide, she couldn't resist stopping to watch him, the rhythm of his legs, of his whole body, moving in a steady, slightly lopsided stride. She couldn't imagine what he was doing. She'd never seen anyone running about on Clapham Common, certainly not in midwinter and not in shorts. But then she remembered that before the war Ward had been a sportsman. He'd rowed in the Canadian national team. And this kind of exercise was probably his way of trying to strengthen his knee.

He was nearer now, crossing her field of vision, and she could see his chest heaving, his breath misting on the cold air, the slight flinch of pain each time he landed on his damaged leg. Then suddenly, without warning, he turned down the path she was standing on, towards the bandstand. Towards her.

Hiding was already out of the question. Short of flattening herself against one of the chestnut trees or crouching behind the base of the bandstand, her only hope was to pull her scarf closer over her face and keep her head down. Reassuring herself that a man like Ward Frazer was hardly likely to give a second glance to a drab-looking woman dressed in a man's overcoat, she lowered her gaze and stepped casually to one side.

His stride didn't falter. She felt the drum of his boots on the path, felt the air vibrate as he passed, heard his laboured breathing and caught a slight, not unpleasant, suggestion of heat and sweat.

But then, behind her, she heard him drawing up. Quickly she began to walk away. And then she heard his voice, that lovely Canadian accent. 'Molly?' He was out of breath, but determined. 'Hey, is that you? Molly?'

Belatedly Molly realised that she had overlooked the fact that he was so observant. That was one of the many things that made her nervous of him. He saw what other people didn't notice. But then he was, or had been, a secret agent, and had presumably been trained always to be watchful, alert to danger. Not that she was likely to cause him any danger, of course. On the contrary ...

She suddenly felt rather breathless herself, but she could hardly ignore him, so she turned round. He was already walking back towards her. Behind him she could see two barrage balloons straining in the wind against their stays.

'Hi.' He smiled. 'I thought it was you. How's it going?'

Aware that she looked a complete fright, she took an involuntary step back. Then, feeling gauche, she mumbled something about still being infectious.

'You've had a rough time,' he said. 'Should you be out here in this cold wind?'

She shrugged and glanced pointedly at his bad leg. 'Should you?'

Now he was so close, she could see a livid scar running from the top of his sock up over his bare knee and disappearing under his shorts. The sight of his bare flesh made her feel quite peculiar. She wondered suddenly how Katy coped with having this man around all the time, let alone in her bed. Hastily averting her gaze, Molly found herself staring into his grey eyes instead. He looked amused.

'I'm trying to get fit again.' He was breathing more easily now, but she could tell from the tension around his mouth that he was in considerable pain. 'Build up my muscles.'

'But you might do more damage,' Molly said. 'Have you had it checked by a doctor? It could be your ligaments. Or you might have a haematoma.' Shut up, she told herself, just shut up. Ward Frazer's legs are nothing to do with you. Nothing.

He glanced down at his knee, flexing it experimentally. 'You want to take a look?'

'No,' she said. 'I'm not a doctor.' Hugging Alan's coat tighter around her, she made as if to walk on, but Ward put a hand on her arm.

'Hey, wait a moment. I want to ask you something.'

'About your knee?'

'No,' he said. 'About Katy.'

'Oh.' There was steam coming off him now, his body heat condensing in the cold air. She could see spangles of moisture like diamonds in his crisp dark hair.

'I want to get her something real nice for Christmas. Something to cheer her up. But what with rationing and nothing in the shops ...' He lifted his hands in appeal. 'Well, you're her best friend, so I thought you might have some ideas.'

Molly frowned. She guessed he was trying to flatter her with that best-friend malarkey, trying to win her over, but even so, she couldn't resist his seductive smile. Striving to ignore the sudden traitorous warmth that was curling round her heart, she tried to think of something Katy might want. Jewellery? A fancy pair of shoes? She didn't think so, but then she didn't know about those luxury things. Helen de Burrel would have been the person to ask. She really was Katy's best friend.

'The best gift you could give her would be to get Helen home,' she said.

That took the smile off his face. 'I've been trying to do just that. But the situation in Algeria is difficult. And she is so ill. It seems the drugs they've given her have helped a little, but …' He lifted his hands helplessly. 'You're a nurse, you know better than me that it's not sounding good.'

'Well if she's going to die, I'm sure she'd rather die here with her friends round her than alone in Algeria,' Molly said. 'Matron told me that there are hospital ships coming from North Africa all the time now, bringing wounded soldiers back to England. Why can't they put her on one of those?'

Ward made a slight gesture of frustration. He hesitated, glanced around quickly and lowered his voice. 'You know why she was sent to Toulon, right?'

Molly nodded. 'To blow up the French ships so the Germans couldn't use them.'

'Right,' he said. 'Well part of the problem is that she doesn't seem to trust the guy the Special Ops people have sent to debrief her. She won't tell him what happened in France. I guess I don't blame her after everything they've put her through, but—'

'Why don't they send someone she *does* trust?' Molly interrupted crossly. 'The truth is that they don't trust *her*. Probably because she's a girl. And because she fell in love with André Cabillard. Katy said they were beastly to her about all that …'

She stopped. Ward was suddenly gazing at her with a strange, arrested expression on his face. His eyes were fixed on her, but she could tell his thoughts were elsewhere. Or she certainly hoped they were. She didn't want him noticing the last scabby spot on the side of her nose, which itself was almost certainly unattractively red with cold by now, or her flat, lank hair, some of which had escaped from Pam's scarf and was even now whipping round her face.

But then he looked away, and for a second she was able to study his profile: the long black lashes, the strong nose, firm chin.

Then he was smiling. Smiling at her. And his grey eyes were sparkling. It was the same look she sometimes saw on George's face when he'd just

63

thought up a new prank.

'Thanks, Molly,' he said, reaching forward to grasp her hands. 'If you hadn't got chickenpox, I'd kiss you, right here, right now.'

And for the first time, Molly was grateful for the chickenpox, because if he had kissed her, she would have passed out cold right there at his feet.

She swallowed hard and withdrew her hands from his strong, warm grasp. 'Why?' she asked with a nervous shiver. 'What have I said?'

He just shook his head. 'You're cold. I shouldn't have kept you standing about in this wind.' He put a hand on her back and gently urged her forward. 'Go home and get warm.'

She was glad to get away, but she was surprised she could walk, her knees were trembling so much.

But then she heard his voice behind her again. 'Oh, and Molly?'

Gritting her teeth, she glanced back. He was standing in the middle of the path. Tall, strong, his dark hair lifting slightly in the wind, a conspiratorial look on his heart-wrenchingly handsome face.

He raised his eyebrows. 'Not a word to Katy, OK? It's our secret.'

'OK,' she mumbled, and quickly turned away again before he could see the tears filling her eyes. She didn't even know what his secret was, she realised, as she sniffed them back. But she knew what hers was all right. Yes. Now she finally had to admit it. The awful, agonising secret she had been trying to hide from everyone. Even from herself. She was in love with Ward Frazer. She had fallen hopelessly, and painfully, in love with her best friend's husband.

The following morning, Jen woke late to the sound of cats fighting downstairs. Or possibly dogs. Either way the sound was jarring, both unexpected and unwelcome. Blinking off sleep, she raised one shoulder to listen more closely and realised that it was actually her sister singing 'Chattanooga Choo Choo' at high volume and completely off key. It was more than Jen could bear. Sitting up only to yell at Angie to shut up, she slumped back down in the bed and closed her eyes. After last night, Angie was not in her good books anyway.

Jen groaned at the recollection. No wonder she had woken feeling so weary and headachy.

She had called in to see Katy at the pub on her way home the previous evening, only to discover Angie ensconced in the middle of some rowdy game which involved her dancing round in the middle of the room surrounded by a ring of young men. From time to time with a scream of laughter she would deliberately pass under the mistletoe, at which point, with a cheer of delight, her admirers would lunge forward, fighting each other off in an attempt to kiss her before she lolloped away again.

As she watched in mounting horror from the door, Jen couldn't help noticing that Douglas Rutherford was one of the more successful contenders. But since whoever kissed Angie, under the dubious rules of the game, had to take a big slug of beer, he was also extremely drunk, his self-satisfied, drawling public-school voice even more slurred than normal, and it was clear from the expressions of some of his less well-to-do rivals that the game was on the verge of turning nasty.

In response to Katy's agonised glance, Jen had been forced to intervene, grabbing Angie out of the circle and remonstrating with her while the young men booed and jeered behind her.

Give Angie her due, she hadn't taken it badly, but convinced that it would all start up again the minute she turned her back, Jen had felt obliged to stay on to supervise her until closing time, and was therefore now not only still cross but also exhausted.

So when she heard someone knock on the front door a few minutes later, she just groaned and buried her head in her pillow, leaving Angie to deal with the caller.

She heard an indistinguishable grumble of voices, then a peal of one of her sister's now familiar machine-gun giggles. This was followed by what sounded like a lively young elephant coming up the stairs. Then her door opened and Angie's face appeared in the opening. Even in blackout-curtain dimness, Jen could see that she was brimming with suppressed excitement.

'Jen? Are you awake? There's someone to see you,' she said. She adjusted her voice into a shrill, carrying whisper and added, 'He's ever so posh. And right handsome too. Is he your feller?'

Wishing she could throttle her, Jen sat up. 'Who is it?'

'I don't know. I didn't ask, but I think he might be the theatre man Mum told me about.'

Jen made a private note to kill her mother as well. 'Are you telling me it's Henry Keller? At our front door?'

Angie giggled and withdrew her head. 'All I'm telling you is there's a nice-looking gent asking for you,' she called back. 'But he's not at the front door, he's in the kitchen, and I'm happy to keep him company until you come down.'

Katy was having a bad morning too. The beer delivery was late, the dray horse had tried to bite her and the stupid drayman had dropped a crate of lemonade on the cellar steps. And she was pretty sure she'd still be charged for it. As she tried to clear it up, she caught her foot in the hem of her dress, one of her favourites, and ripped it, and moments after that, Malcolm broke the push-along tank Ward had chosen for his birthday and now he was screaming his head off in his playpen.

And on top of it all, lunchtime opening was coming up and there was no sign of Ward. He'd disappeared straight off into town after his run on the common yesterday and hadn't got back until after closing time, so he hadn't been there to help her quell the near riot caused by the rowdy drinking game that had developed after Angie Carter's unexpected arrival in the pub.

It had been a busy night. With only Aaref's young brother Jacob to help her, Katy had struggled to keep up with the orders and the empties. There were some new customers too, people she didn't know and two in particular that she hadn't liked the look of. And at one point Gillian James had made a brief appearance, once again on the hunt for gin. And once again Katy had witnessed the lascivious looks in the men's eyes as they followed her progress across the room. At that point, only that point, Katy had been glad Ward wasn't there.

He had helped her clear up, though, when he did finally come in. And in bed that night he had been extra affectionate, perhaps to make up for his absence earlier. But she had been cross and tired and then this morning he'd got dressed quickly and had gone off again before she'd even finished feeding Malcolm. And she hadn't seen him since.

Now she felt guilty. She loved him so much, so much it sometimes hurt, but what with the pub and Malcolm and the worry about Helen and the dreary winter and the endless depressing war it was sometimes hard to show it, hard to respond to him as she should. And that made her frightened, frightened of losing his affection, of losing him.

It was as she wiped a damp cloth over the counter that she suddenly felt something was missing. Running her eye along the bar, she saw the soda siphon, the beer mats, the ashtrays, the darts, the last-orders bell, the ice box, the glasses tray and the rather drooping pot plant she had retrieved from Ward's aunts' bombed-out house all those months ago. So what should be there that wasn't?

And then she knew. It was the Spitfire Fund Christmas collection tin. It was nowhere to be seen. She couldn't believe it. People had been putting their change in there for weeks. She wondered how much money had been inside. Not that it mattered now, she thought bitterly. It was all gone. Someone had clearly stolen it.

Jen had never got dressed so quickly in all her life. It was freezing in her bedroom and she came out in goose bumps the moment she leapt out of bed. Throwing on last night's clothes and scrabbling for her shoes, she could hear Angie's peals of laughter from downstairs. Dreading what they might be talking about, and what awful impression Angie was probably giving, she decided that she couldn't risk the time it would take to put on any make-up except a quick smear of lipstick. Henry would just have to see her au naturel for once. So fluffing up her hair and fixing a cool smile on her lips, hoping her nose wasn't blue with cold, she straightened her shoulders and went downstairs.

It was indeed Henry Keller. And, dressed in a pinstripe suit under a classy camel overcoat, he looked completely out of place in her mother's shabby kitchen.

'Aha,' he said, standing up as she came in. 'I'm sorry to call unannounced. I'm on my way to a fund-raising lunch in Wimbledon, and as I was more or less passing your door, I thought I'd pop in.'

Numbly Jen took the hand he offered, and was surprised when he drew her towards him and kissed her on the cheek. 'You look as ravishing as ever,' he murmured.

'Jen always looks ravishing,' Angie chipped in helpfully. 'Not like me. I look like I've been through a hedge backwards when I get out of bed.'

Henry glanced at Jen and smiled at her expression. 'Yes, I have met your delightful sister.'

Jen realised he was still holding her hand and withdrew it quickly. Was he being sarcastic, or had Angie been OK after all? Thank goodness he hadn't arrived while she was singing. But why had he come? She looked round rather wildly. 'Can I offer you a cup of tea or something?'

He raised his eyebrows slightly. 'I like the sound of *something*, but sadly I can't stay. I just wanted to bring you some good news.'

Jen's throat went completely dry. She suddenly felt rather faint. 'What sort of news?' she croaked.

'Well,' he said slowly. 'Not only are you going to be offered the part of Peep-Bo in the new *Mikado* production, but they also want you to be the understudy for Yum-Yum, the soprano lead. You should get a formal offer in the post tomorrow, but as I'd heard the news, I wanted to let you know as soon as possible. Rehearsals start next week, straight after Christmas.'

'No!' Jen couldn't believe it. After all the waiting and worrying, she could hardly take it in. Her dream come true. Having felt icy cold a moment before, now she felt suddenly feverish, as though beads of sweat were about to break out on her forehead. 'Oh Henry, I—'

Angie clapped her hands. 'Does that mean you are going to be a star?'

'Of course she is going to be a star,' Henry said.

Jen looked at him. Surely that was more than professional warmth in his voice. Quickly, before her courage deserted her, she stepped forward, reaching up to kiss him. 'Oh Henry, thank you so—'

But he put his hands on her shoulders and held her back. 'I should in fairness say that I am only the carrier of the news. I wasn't at the audition and I was in no way involved in the decision.'

Jen stared up into his smiling eyes. 'I don't care,' she said. 'I still want to kiss you.'

And to her surprise, he drew her close against him and kissed her back, coolly, competently and unnervingly sexily.

Behind her she heard Angie's irrepressible giggle. 'Cor, and to think you told me not to kiss people under the mistletoe.'

Jen felt Henry's choke of laughter against her lips. Opening her eyes, she turned her head and glared at her sister. 'This is completely different,' she snapped.

Henry was laughing openly now. 'Yes, it is,' he agreed. 'Wonderfully different.' He ran the back of his fingers over her lips, hesitated, then shook his head regretfully. 'Nevertheless, I really do have to go. My taxi is waiting.'

At the front door, he kissed her again, more chastely this time. 'I'm away over Christmas,' he said. 'But as soon as I get back, we'll celebrate properly.' He raised his eyebrows and his eyes held hers with a flicker of suggestive humour. 'Or perhaps not so properly.'

And then he was gone.

Closing the door behind him, Jen walked back down the passage to the kitchen. She took a glass off the shelf and poured herself a glass of water, then sat down at the table and put a hand to her head.

'What's the matter?' Angie asked from the doorway. 'Aren't you pleased?'

Jen looked up at her blankly. She should be pleased. She ought to be over the moon. She ought to be dancing with joy, savouring the news, relishing her triumph.

But she couldn't. Because suddenly she was feeling very peculiar. She was shivering violently and her head was thumping. And there was something itching round her waist. Irritably she scratched at it, then stopped and paled.

'Oh no,' she whispered. 'Oh God, please no.' Tugging her blouse out of the waistband of her skirt, she exposed a cluster of spots, very red against the white skin of her stomach. She stared at them in horror.

'Urrgh!' Angie craned forward with interest. 'What are those?'

Jen felt a surge of uncontrollable anger. Of furious despair. Of utter misery.

How could life be so unfair?

'Chickenpox,' she said, and picking up her glass, she threw it violently against the wall, where it smashed into smithereens.

Katy was down in the cellar tapping the beer when Ward came back in. She heard his quick step on the floor of the bar above her head, heard his voice urgently calling her name.

'I'm down here,' she called back, and looked up as he ran down the cellar steps.

There was something different about him, something purposeful and determined in his expression that suddenly filled her with fear.

'What's the matter? What's happened?' she asked.

'We've had a telegram from Lord de Burrel,' he said. He pulled a flimsy sheet of paper out of his pocket and unfolded it. '*Returning England Jan stop In meantime do what you see fit stop Keep me informed stop Can pull strings if necessary stop.*'

Katy stared at him nervously. His eyes were sparkling with suppressed excitement.

'And … what *do* you see fit?' she asked.

Ward went to speak, then hesitated for a moment and took her hands instead. 'Just tell me something, Katy,' he said, looking into her eyes, suddenly serious. 'Do you want Helen to come back to England?'

It was hard to think when he looked at her like that. All she wanted to do was melt. But she forced herself to concentrate. 'Yes, yes, of course. More than anything in the world. And I'm sure she would want to come, even if—'

'That's what I thought.' He smiled, kissed her and turned away up the stairs. 'Then I guess I'd better get moving.'

'Why?' Katy ran after him. 'Ward, wait! What do you mean?'

He stopped at the top of the stairs and turned back to face her. 'I'm going to get her.'

Katy felt her stomach turn over. 'Going where? You don't mean … not to Algeria?'

'There's a convoy leaving the Clyde naval base for North Africa tomorrow. I've managed to get a berth on one of the troopships. If I catch the train from King's Cross this afternoon, I should just about get up there in time.'

Chapter Six

Molly was appalled when she heard that Ward Frazer had upped sticks and gone off to Algeria. She felt so guilty she could hardly look Katy in the eye. Not only had she fallen in love with Katy's husband, but she also knew she had been instrumental in him heading off into renewed danger. 'Why don't they send someone she *does* trust?' she had said. And this was the outcome.

But it wasn't just the thought of him travelling on a slow, vulnerable convoy down into the Atlantic, round Spain and into the U-boat-infested Mediterranean that worried her; it was also the increasingly unstable situation in North Africa. The Germans and Italians had begun a new offensive in Tunisia, and the Allies had been forced to retreat almost back into Algeria. Molly had visions of Ward and Helen either being bombed to death in Oran or being captured by the advancing Nazis and sent off to a concentration camp, never to be seen again. And it would all be her fault.

When she heard on the wireless that a British convoy had been torpedoed in the Straits of Gibraltar and that a troopship, the SS *Strathallan*, had subsequently sunk just off Oran, she thought her worst fears had been realised. Then to top that off, on Christmas Eve it was announced that Admiral Darlan, the man the Allies had installed to run Algeria, had been shot dead and the country was once again in chaos.

And it wasn't just Ward Frazer that Molly felt guilty about. Jen Carter had succumbed to the chickenpox. And if that meant she lost the job she had been offered in a new West End production, Molly knew she would have made an enemy for life.

And yet despite her guilt and anxiety, Christmas 1942 was the happiest Christmas Molly had spent since her adopted family had died.

To her surprise, even though she was feeling considerably better, the Wilhelmina staff doctor had signed her off sick for another whole week. 'Technically you'll be out of quarantine on Christmas Day,' he had said. 'But you are still very weak and you need time to rebuild your strength before going back on the wards.'

So Molly was able to relax and enjoy Christmas at the Nelsons'. The tiny tree Alan had bought from a barrow in Tooting was now decorated with pre-war tinsel and baubles. On Christmas morning she found a sock on the end of her bed filled with two candles, an apple, a pack of funny wartime cards, a little bunch of lavender, a few precious nuts and a handkerchief Pam had secretly embroidered with her name. For lunch they ate chicken pie and a bright orange carrot sponge which, to George's delight, Alan set alight with a tot of brandy from the pub. They pulled crackers Pam had made from old newspaper and filled with barley sugar for Molly, liquorice sticks for Alan, humbugs for George and a piece of pink ribbon for the baby. After lunch they sat round the fire and listened to the King's speech and sang along to carols on the wireless.

Afterwards they played cards and Molly performed a new trick she had secretly perfected to surprise George and they all clapped, and it was all so homely and comfortable. So different from waking up on Christmas morning in a cold dormitory in the Wilhelmina nurses' home, watching while other girls opened their cards and gifts from home, the stiff ceremony of Sister supervising Christmas lunch on the ward, the excruciating afternoon service and the forced jollity of one of the doctors dressing up as Father Christmas and visiting the wards with pitiful, unsuitable gifts for the patients.

'Why don't you stay on with us?' Pam suddenly asked as she and Molly washed up. 'Instead of going back to the nurses' home. Do you think they'd let you?'

Molly blinked. 'I don't know,' she said. Truthfully there was nothing she would like more. And she was gratified that Pam and Alan would want her. But there were other considerations. Not least the close proximity to Ward Frazer, if he ever got home again. And financial ones too. 'But I earn so little,' she said. 'I don't think I could afford the rent.'

'Well, Alan and I were thinking we could offer you a low rent in return for helping me with George and the baby sometimes when you are off duty.'

Molly swallowed. It was so, so tempting. 'But what about Helen?' she asked suddenly. 'What if she recovers? What if she wants to come back?'

Pam looked at her in silence for a moment. They both knew that wasn't very likely, but neither of them wanted to admit it.

'Well then you and she can share until one of you finds somewhere else,' Pam said firmly. She wiped her hands on a tea towel and turned to face Molly with a warm smile. 'Have a think about it. You don't have to decide now.'

'I can't think of anything nicer,' Molly said. 'I'll write to Matron tomorrow to ask her permission.'

For Katy, Christmas passed in a complete blur. The bleak weather seemed to bring more people to the pub than ever. Some came for the conviviality, the lively banter, the jokes and the patriotic music; others came to listen to the news broadcasts on her wireless or drown their sorrows. And quite a few came just because Katy always had a good fire burning and it saved them the expense of trying to keep their own houses warm.

Keeping up with the busy trade and looking after Malcolm single-handed wasn't easy. With only Jacob to help her, she found it hard to keep her head above water. On Christmas Eve she ran out of glasses and had to start asking people to bring their own, and on Christmas Day she ran out of beer and everyone had to move on to her dwindling supply of spirits instead.

Thankfully Jen's brother Pete, back for a few days from his navy engineering course, took a few turns behind the bar, and Louise, grateful to have an excuse to escape from the Rutherford family Christmas, occasionally collected up the empties.

But Katy was glad to be busy. It kept her mind off her other worries, like who had stolen the Spitfire Fund collecting tin, and how she could be so mean as to constantly find herself wishing that someone else had gone to rescue Helen instead of Ward. Because Katy too had been in agonies about the sinking of the SS *Strathallan*. And relieved to learn from Douglas Rutherford – who, despite being a cocky little brat, seemed to know everything there was to know about the war – that it couldn't possibly be Ward's ship. Apparently not even a motor torpedo boat, the fastest vessel in the Royal Navy, could have got from the Clyde to Gibraltar in two days, let alone a ponderous convoy of mixed naval and merchant shipping.

In church on Christmas Day, she prayed for Ward and Helen's safe return. She hadn't heard a squeak from Ward since he had rushed away to catch the night train to Scotland. Not that she was expecting to. Nobody wanted news of movements or shipping to fall into enemy hands. The censor would intercept anything like that anyway. Please let them both be alive, she prayed. Please bring them come back safely. Oh, and while you are at it, I need help in the pub. I can't manage on my own. Not at this time of year.

And then at lunchtime on Boxing Day, Molly stepped tentatively through the blackout curtain. 'Alan said you were run off your feet. So as I'm no longer infectious, I thought you could use some help.'

Katy felt a surge of relief. At least one of her prayers had been answered. 'Oh yes please. I've been struggling to keep up ever since Ward left.' Molly had always been far and away her best helper. But noticing a sudden shadow cross her friend's face, she looked at her more closely. 'Are you sure you are feeling up to it?'

'Yes, yes, I'm fine,' Molly said quickly. 'Though I don't want Matron to find out. I'll have to hide in the cellar if anyone comes in from the hospital.'

Thankfully that eventuality was spared them, and with Molly's help for the next few evenings everything ran much more smoothly. There were no fights or thefts, the beer flowed freely and the customers were happy. And for the first time since Ward had left, Katy felt some of the pressure lift off her.

Perhaps it would all be OK after all, she thought as she counted her takings for the Christmas period and worked out the orders for New Year's Eve. Perhaps Ward would bring Helen home safely. Perhaps Helen would recover, and Ward would find some new and useful outlet for his skills and restless energy that didn't put him constantly in danger. And perhaps she would soon be able to afford to pay someone to help her full time so she could give him and Malcolm the love, time and attention they deserved.

Joyce was fed up with Jen. Not only had she spoiled the little lunch party Joyce had so carefully planned for Christmas Day by catching the chickenpox, but she was making an awful fuss about it too. Anyone would think she was dying, the way she was going on, complaining about feeling hot and cold, about having a splitting headache and spots on her face. What did she expect? She was ill, and she'd have to put up with it until she was better. And if she thought Joyce was going to keep a fire burning in the grate all day long just to keep the house warm for her, she had another think coming. Not unless Jen put her hand in her own pocket and paid for some fuel, which she wasn't likely to do, not if she wasn't working. No, if she was cold, she could stay in bed. And if she wanted the doctor to call every five minutes, she could damn well pay for him herself and all.

The problem was, of course, that Jen had never been ill before, not really ill with a temperature, a rash and aching limbs. Well, being ill wasn't meant to be fun. Yes, it would be a shame if she couldn't take up the new job she'd been offered, but it didn't mean that she had the right to take her temper out on everyone else in the house.

What it did mean, however, was that Angie had to share Joyce's room after all, which meant that Joyce got much less sleep than she was used to, because it turned out that as well as her constant daytime chatter and apparently unquenchable high spirits, the blasted girl even giggled in her sleep.

Oddly enough, Pete's presence helped a bit. Even though he had never been the brightest spark in the box, Joyce felt more comfortable letting Angie go out and about in the evenings when he was with her. And having suspected from an overheard remark of Jen's that Angie had been up to some high jinks in the pub, she was pleased to gather from Angie's artless bedtime conversations that Pete's solid, watchful presence at the Flag and Garter had apparently served to keep the attentions of Douglas Rutherford and his friends at bay.

When Pete went back to his unit, she felt obliged to have a word with Angie about the wisdom of allowing young men to take liberties with her. But it wasn't successful. Angie of course just thought it was a big joke.

'What, Philip Clarence-Webb and Dougie Rutherford, you mean? Oh, they don't mean anything by it. It's only a bit of fun.' She pressed her hand to her heart and made a comic soulful face. 'They know my heart belongs to another.'

It wasn't her heart that Joyce was worried about, it was her body. But as she knew only too well from her experiences with Jen at that age, too much disapproval might only serve to drive Angie into Douglas's arms. So she held her tongue and decided to pin her hopes on the fact that Douglas and his double-barrelled friend would surely be leaving soon to join their fancy regiment. And with any luck, that would be the last anyone would see of them for a while.

The one thing she knew for sure she couldn't do was mention her concerns to Celia Rutherford. She and Celia had always got on well; you could almost say they were friends. But that was partly because Joyce was careful not to overstep the mark.

Celia Rutherford came from a different social class, a smart, moneyed class, and Joyce knew only too well how quickly things could go wrong with those posh types. As long as you treated them nice and put up with their superior attitudes and swanky ideas, it was fine. It was all right for Mrs Rutherford to criticise Miss Fancy Pants Louise's flirtations or to bemoan Douglas's grandiose military ambitions, but for Joyce to imply that Douglas might be paying rather too much attention to her underage daughter would be just asking for trouble.

Mrs Rutherford owned the lease on the café. And the café was Joyce's salvation. She would rather cut off her own hand than put it in jeopardy. It was one of the reasons why she had so far resisted the idea of Angie coming to work there. The fear of what indiscretion Angie might let slip in front of Celia Rutherford far outweighed the potential benefit of an extra pair of hands or the desirability of being able to keep a close eye on how her younger daughter was spending her time.

So she was somewhat taken aback when Celia casually remarked one morning that she was very grateful to Angie and could Joyce pass on her thanks.

'What for?' Joyce asked, alarmed.

Celia smiled and drew a letter out of her handbag with a flourish.

'Because this arrived this morning and it's all down to her.'

'What is it?' Joyce asked.

'It's an invitation for you to cook in front of a panel of judges in the Wandsworth cooking competition in January. Only ten ladies have been chosen out of over a hundred entries.'

Joyce stared at her aghast. 'But I threw that recipe away.'

Celia looked smug. 'I took it out of the waste-paper basket and got Greville's secretary to type it up for me.'

Joyce didn't know what to think. On one level she was cross; on another she was thrilled. Her recipe had been picked out. But then the thought of cooking in front of an audience kicked in and she felt a sudden terror.

'But I can't,' she said. 'I told you. I'd be sick with nerves.'

'Nonsense. Of course you can,' Celia said briskly. 'Let's get Angie to come and help out in the new year, and that will give you more time to practise.'

Joyce was aware of sweat prickling in her armpits. She didn't know which made her feel more sick, the idea of having to cook in public, or the thought of letting Angie loose in her precious café.

After a couple of evenings back in the pub, Molly felt quite at home again. Immediately he saw her, little Malcolm had held up his arms to be picked up, and the regulars had seemed gratifyingly pleased to have her back too. Mr Lorenz had gone so far as to stand her a small port and lemonade. Yes, it was nice to be back in the fold, and so far the only fly in the ointment was Douglas Rutherford. It had only taken two nights for Molly to become fed up with him lording it about in the bar as though he owned the place. Well, OK, his father, as the local brewer, did in fact own it, but that was beside the point. Douglas was a jumped-up little git as far as Molly was concerned, even if he was about to join some fancy Guards regiment. And a chip off the Rutherford family block too, it seemed. It was bad enough that Louise had got her claws into Aaref; now it seemed that Douglas had got his eye on Jen Carter's younger sister, Angie.

Molly had been wary of Angie at first, especially when Angie inadvertently let slip that Jen now referred to Molly as the Poxy Pixie. But once she had got over that, Molly had quickly seen that, unlike Jen, there was no side to Angie. What you saw was what you got, a big, jolly, good-natured girl. Angie, with her gregarious nature and infectious giggle, was always the life and soul of the party. Molly would have liked to possess some of that unselfconscious conviviality herself. Angie was over-boisterous, but she was only fifteen after all, and it was understandable that she would get a bit carried away with all the attention she got from the boys. And yes, her laugh would soon drive you to distraction, but at least she wasn't going to stab you in the back like her sister.

The only problem was that Angie appeared to be completely indiscriminate about where she bestowed her affections. Whereas earlier in the week she had spent most of her time with the two public-school boys, now it was New Year's Eve and she was flirting with a group of local lads instead. And it was clear that Douglas Rutherford felt that her defection was a direct challenge to his manhood.

For Angie, the rivalry between these two groups was clearly all good fun, but Katy was concerned that it might turn ugly and had asked Molly to keep an eye on them. 'He's joining his new regiment tomorrow,' she had said, nodding towards the corner of the bar, where Douglas and his chinless friend, Philip Clarence-Webb, were bragging about how they would soon have to be measured up by some special Savile Row tailor for their new regimental dress uniforms. 'We don't want him turning up with a black eye.'

'Shame.' Molly had followed her gaze. 'I'd love to see someone wipe that smirk off his face.'

Katy giggled. 'So would I, but I don't want old man Rutherford closing me down because someone has tried to teach his son a few manners.'

So when a little bit later, as Molly came up from switching over the beer in the cellar, she noticed that both Douglas and Angie were missing from the bar, she asked Jacob if he had seen where they had gone.

'She went out to the lavatory,' Jacob said, tipping his head to the back door. 'Then Mr Douglas went also.'

'How long have they been gone?'

'I don't know, perhaps two minutes.'

'Did any of the others go?'

'I didn't notice.'

Molly looked over at the other boys. Philip Clarence-Webb was still there, but she couldn't remember how many local lads there had been. Even as she watched, one of them glanced towards the back door and made some comment. One of the others started rolling up his sleeves.

Oh no, Molly thought. Katy was upstairs seeing to Malcolm, so leaving Jacob at the bar, she went out to see what was going on.

Molly always pitied people caught short in the pub. Having to grope your way across the backyard to the Flag and Garter outside lavatory was not a pleasant experience at the best of times, and in the blackout it was even worse, although the pervading smell of urine did at least act as a guide. Katy tried to keep it clean, but the men who mainly used it either had a very poor aim or were too drunk to care. Molly avoided it like the plague, grateful that she had the privilege of using the new toilet Katy had had installed upstairs when the pub was renovated after the Blitz.

Now, as she stood waiting for her eyes to adjust to the darkness, she heard muffled voices and a sudden, quickly curtailed shriek of alarm.

'Hey,' she called. 'What's going on?' But she got no response.

Damn the blackout, she thought, and opened the passage door again, allowing light to spill out over the yard. It wasn't a salubrious sight, but the shaft of light made it look even worse, lighting up two old dustbins, a pile of crates, a broken beer barrel, a pool of oily water lying between a couple of concrete slabs. And in the far corner, as though caught in a silent movie spotlight, pressed hard up against the wall of the toilet by Douglas Rutherford, was Angie Carter, wriggling like a netted fish. It was clear that she was not wriggling in pleasure, even though Douglas was attempting to kiss her.

'Everyone deserves a kiss on New Year's Eve, and I'm off to war tomorrow.'

'Stop it.' Angie's voice was shrill. 'Douglas, stop it, it's not funny.'

It wasn't funny. Douglas had caught hold of her wrists now and had forced them against the wall above her head with one hand while he groped under her skirt with the other. This wasn't a successful seduction technique, Molly realised, as she watched in stunned horror, because it left the girl's legs free to kick, and Angie wasn't slow to avail herself of the opportunity.

Unfortunately her efforts only served to inflame Douglas further, but before his assault became even more violent, Molly ran across the yard, splashing through the puddle, shouting at him to let Angie go.

For a moment she thought he was going to carry on regardless. But then, abruptly, he released Angie and turned to face her. 'Oh look who it is,' he drawled in his smug upper-class voice as he smoothed back his hair. 'The Poxy Pixie. What's the matter, darling? Jealous?'

Gritting her teeth, Molly ignored him and looked at Angie, who was adjusting her clothes behind him. 'Are you all right?'

'Of course she's all right,' Douglas laughed and gave Angie a careless caress on the cheek. 'We were only having a quick kiss and a cuddle.' He turned back to Molly with a sneer. 'Not that you'd know anything about that. No self-respecting man would touch you with a bargepole.' He nodded towards the door. 'Haven't you seen them running a mile in there when you get anywhere near the mistletoe?'

It was cruel and entirely uncalled for. Even if it was true. Shocked into silence, to her horror Molly felt sudden tears sting her eyes. Luckily the light was behind her and, hoping neither of them would notice, she tried to think of an equally cutting retort.

But it was Angie who spoke first. 'Shut up, Douglas,' she said, rounding on her assailant. 'You were right out of order and you know it.'

Then Molly heard Katy's voice somewhere behind her. 'Why's this door open? What's going on out here?'

'Nothing,' Douglas said. 'But Miss Prudypants here had to come and poke her nose in.'

Silhouetted in the doorway, Katy drew herself up to her full height. 'How dare you speak like that?' she snapped. 'For goodness' sake, Douglas, try to act your age. Now go back indoors, and by the time I come in, I want you and your friend out of the bar. And I don't want to see you in my pub again.'

'But you can't—'

'Oh yes I can,' Katy said. 'I'm the landlady and I can do what I like. What's more, if I hear any more nonsense from you, I will be having a word with your father first thing tomorrow morning. I have to go to the brewery anyway to order some extra beer. I don't think Mr Rutherford will be at all happy to hear about your behaviour here tonight.'

To Molly's surprise, after a moment's pause, Douglas went.

But at the door, he turned. 'I'll soon be overseas fighting for King and Country. How does that make you feel?'

'Delighted,' Katy said. 'And shut the door behind you.'

He didn't shut it; he slammed it, and left them in total darkness. Molly felt the tension go out of her, to be replaced by a fit of shivering.

Angie was the first to utter a sound, and predictably it was a giggle. 'Cor,' she said. 'That put him in his place and all.'

'What *was* going on out here?' Katy asked.

'He got a bit fresh,' Angie said.

'Well let that be a lesson to you,' Katy said sternly. 'You need to learn where to draw the line.'

'I'd have kneed him in the privates if he'd gone much further,' Angie said. 'Gino taught me how to do that.'

Molly heard Katy give a slight choke as she reopened the door. But her voice sounded quite firm. 'That's as maybe,' she said, urging them back inside. 'But I want you to go straight home, Angie. And I would advise you to keep out of the way until Douglas leaves tomorrow.'

'Thank you for coming to the rescue,' Molly murmured when Angie had gone off obediently down the passage. 'You were marvellous. You sounded just like Sister Morris.'

Katy looked pleased. 'I model myself on Sister Morris in difficult situations,' she said.

'Would you really go and speak to his father?'

'You must be joking. Greville Rutherford would eat me for breakfast,'

Katy said. 'He hates the idea of me, a mere woman, running one of his precious pubs. But thankfully that jumped-up twit doesn't know that.' She paused, then glanced at Molly and lowered her voice. 'I heard what the little bastard said to you, Molly. I—'

'Oh, it's all right,' Molly said quickly, turning away. 'I didn't take any notice.'

But Katy knew her too well. She put a hand on her arm to stop her moving away. 'It's not true, you know,' she said quietly. 'Just because you don't tart yourself up like Louise, or Jen, it doesn't mean you aren't pretty. You've got really lovely eyes, you know. And a sweet smile. There are lots of men who find you very attractive.'

Molly sniffed. 'Are there?' she asked. 'Who?'

Katy paused again. 'Well, Ward for one,' she said. 'He said you looked beautiful at our wedding. Don't you remember?'

Molly felt her heart twist. 'He was just being kind. He said it to please you. We all know I looked a fright in that bridesmaid's dress.'

'Well, what about Aaref, then?' Katy persevered.

Molly only hesitated for a moment. 'Aaref and I have only ever been friends,' she said. 'We've never been a proper couple. The only person he wants is Louise.'

'Oh Molly, I'm so sorry. I'm sure you're wrong. But if that's true, then he's a fool.' Katy sounded quite cross. 'You're worth ten times more than Louise.' She squeezed Molly's arm. 'You will find someone nice. I know you will. Don't forget what the blind man said. Your moment will come. And I'm sure he's right.'

'He wasn't talking about boyfriends,' Molly said.

'Well, what about that fortune-teller at the potato fair? She said you'd meet a tall, dark, handsome stranger, didn't she?'

'They always say that,' Molly said. 'Anyway, it was a foreigner, she said, not a stranger. And I don't know any foreigners.'

'Yes you do,' Katy said. 'You know Aaref and … and those Americans who used to come to the bar, and Ward, of course. He's a foreigner.' She giggled suddenly. 'Oh dear, I do hope Ward isn't going to come home and suddenly sweep you off your feet. I wouldn't be too happy about that.'

Jen still couldn't believe her bad luck. How could it be that on the exact day when she had been offered a new, exciting and potentially life-changing opportunity – or two opportunities if you included the possibility of Henry's romantic intentions being serious – her whole life had crashed down around her?

Not only was she covered in horrible itchy spots, but now, as well as being convinced she would be disfigured for life, she also felt really ill. All she wanted to do was lie in bed and groan. Or cry. Or both. And as she lay there, she saw those exciting opportunities slipping through her fingers.

Mortifyingly, she had to warn Henry that she might have infected him, so she had sent him a stiff little note care of ENSA, which would probably be opened by his secretary. She had written to the production company too, explaining the situation and pleading for a week's grace. Which, to her amazement, they had given her. But then that week was up and she felt even iller than she had before. So she had had to write again, and this time there was no grace. Reluctantly, they said, they would have to withdraw their offer of employment.

Not only that, but she'd lost her current job too. Under the terms of her contract she was only paid for the shows she did, and they were entitled to replace her if she missed more than seven consecutive performances. As they had previously kept her job open while she had her throat operation, she was already well over her allotted quota of sick days. Too weak and dispirited to argue, she just had to come to terms with the fact that she was once again unemployed.

Henry's brief response to her note was sympathetic, if not effusive. *What bad luck*, he wrote. *But you'll be back on your feet soon and something else will crop up. Stay warm and rest. I'll come and visit you next week.*

No, Jen scribbled back. The thought of him seeing her covered in unsightly spots filled her with horror. *Please don't come. I don't want to see anyone.*

After that she didn't hear from him for a week and began to feel even more sorry for herself than she had before. But on New Year's Day a box of daffodils arrived. The post girl had left them on the step. Angie carried them upstairs with wide-eyed glee. Jen opened the brief note that accompanied them. *Get well soon. Happy New Year, Henry.*

Thankfully it seemed he had not contracted the disease.

'Cor,' Angie said. 'Mr Lorenz gave Mum flowers too. Roses. He brought them into the café and she went all pink. I wish my Gino would send me flowers.'

'I don't suppose they allow prisoners of war to send flowers,' Jen said. 'Or anything at all, come to that.'

'No,' Angie agreed. 'No, that's probably why he hasn't written to me yet. But I've worked out that if I send him an envelope with stamps on it, then he should be able to send it back.'

'I wouldn't hold your breath,' Jen muttered. She was fed up with listening to Angie going on about the legendary Gino. She was only fifteen, for goodness' sake. What did she know about love? She wouldn't be at all surprised to find that Gino was a figment of Angie's imagination.

But to her surprise, a week later, sure enough Angie's self-addressed envelope arrived home.

'Ha,' Angie said, flourishing it in front of Jen's nose. 'I told you so.'

'Well.' Jen levered herself up on an elbow. 'What does he say?'

'I'm not sure,' Angie admitted. 'I can't understand half of it.' She unfolded the flimsy piece of paper. 'He says it's difficile to scribe me, because limitations is very firm. It pleases him to record himself my beautiful face and he aspires that he is my faithful. The time makes very cold and—' She stopped as Jen gave a gasp of laughter.

'What?' Angie said. 'What's so funny?' Then she looked back at the letter and started to giggle. 'I forgot he can't speak English very well,' she said.

That made Jen laugh even more. But laughing exhausted her. Collapsing back on her pillows, she closed her eyes. 'Oh God,' she said. 'I'm weak as a kitten. Go away, Angie, I can't take any more of stupid Gino and his pidgin English. I don't know how you think you're in love with him if you can't understand a word he says.'

'He's not stupid,' Angie said. 'And I don't need language to know he loves me. He does,' she insisted as Jen gave a dismissive snort. 'You'll see when you meet him.'

'But I won't meet him, will I?' Jen said irritably. 'He's a prisoner of war. He's Italian. He's the bloody enemy, for goodness' sake. They're hardly likely to let him come waltzing up to London so he can tell you in person that *the time makes very cold*, are they?'

Angie looked momentarily crestfallen, then she shook her head. 'You're only cross because you're still poorly,' she said kindly. 'You'll soon feel better. That horrid spot on your forehead has nearly gone now. Look at Molly Coogan, she's completely fine again now and back at work and—'

'I don't want to look at Molly Coogan,' Jen snapped. 'I don't even want to hear her name. And I don't want to look at you. Just go away and leave me alone.'

Molly was indeed back at work. And it was just as bad as she had thought it would be. The other nurses were resentful that she had had so much time off, and several of her favourite patients had died in her absence. Sister Parkes, for her part, was as brisk and dismissive as usual.

'So did you read any of the medical journals I sent down to you?' she asked, drawing Molly to one side after morning prayers.

'Yes, Sister,' Molly said.

'And?'

'I found them very interesting, of course, but I didn't really know what you expected me to learn.'

'I expected you to use your initiative,' Sister Parkes snapped. 'You are not lacking in intelligence, but you lack self-discipline. I wouldn't go as far as to say you are slack, but I would like to see you demonstrate more determination and drive. You could still become a useful nurse if you would only pull your socks up and put your mind to it.'

'Well, there was one interesting article—' Molly stumbled into speech again, but Sister cut her off with an impatient wave of her hand.

'I've heard enough. It's clear to me that you wasted the opportunity.' She glanced at her fob watch. 'In any case, it's time for you to go back to work. Staff Nurse Roberts is waiting to brief you, and she will be expecting you to pull your weight. The other nurses have been working extra hard to cover your extended absence.'

'Yes, Sister,' Molly said meekly.

The only saving grace was that Matron, to everyone's surprise, gave her permission to move out of the nurses' home and in with the Nelsons on a more permanent basis, but only on the understanding that if her work suffered as a result, this privilege would immediately be withdrawn.

The best thing about it was that after an evening shift in the pub, instead of having to trek back through the freezing January darkness to the nurses' home, she merely had to pop across the road, which barely necessitated putting on a coat, to join Pam and Alan in their pre-bedtime cup of Horlicks in front of the fire.

She was looking forward to this little ceremony one evening as she helped Katy clear up after a busy evening when someone knocked on the door of the pub.

They both looked up surprised. It was late for anyone to call.

'Maybe someone has left something behind,' Katy said, and putting her mop back in the bucket, she tiptoed across the wet floor to unlock the door.

Molly straightened up and stood listening. There'd been two rather unpleasant men in the bar that evening, and it was common knowledge that Ward was away. Molly wouldn't have put it past one of them to come back and cause trouble, demanding more drink or with the aim of getting their hands on the contents of the till. Katy had told her that someone had stolen the Spitfire Fund collecting tin just before Christmas, and it seemed possible that one of these men might have been responsible.

But it was a woman's voice that spoke. 'This just came in, love, and I thought I should bring it up to you right away.'

And then she heard Katy's panicked voice. 'No, oh no, please no.'

Pushing through the blackout curtain, Molly found Katy white-faced and trembling. In front of her was a post girl with a telegram in her outstretched hand.

Everyone feared those yellow envelopes. Too many people had received bad news that way for anyone to accept them with equanimity.

'I'll take it,' Molly said. 'Come on, Katy. Come back indoors. We'll open it inside.'

But Katy wouldn't open it. 'I don't want to know,' she said. 'I just don't want to know.'

'But it might not be bad news,' Molly said, steering her into a chair by the dwindling fire. Still holding the dreaded telegram in her hand, she went over to the bar and poured a small brandy. Taking a quick sip herself first, she handed it to Katy and sat down next to her.

'You open it, Molly,' Katy whispered. 'I can't.'

Oh God, please don't let it be bad news, Molly prayed as she tore the envelope open with trembling fingers and drew out the flimsy paper.

Here safe stop Helen sends love stop Home soon stop Can you find hospital bed query Ward

Chapter Seven

Helen de Burrel was admitted to the Wilhelmina Hospital on the night of 20th January, the same day that a German bomb killed twenty-three schoolgirls as they waited in their school yard to see a production of *A Midsummer Night's Dream*.

Several bombs had fallen in south London over the last few days and nights. Three people had been killed in Thessaly Road, just a few streets from the Wilhelmina, and another man had been killed by a shell tube in Battersea. Even Buckingham Palace had been targeted. A report had been issued saying that although the royal family had not been affected, the Brussels sprouts in the royal vegetable garden had been completely ruined.

The air-raid warnings and the sudden resurgence of bombing had not made the final stages of Ward and Helen's already arduous journey any easier. The hospital train carrying them and a contingent of wounded servicemen from Southampton docks was delayed due to the bombing, only finally steaming into Clapham Junction at midnight to a waiting band of railway staff, orderlies, nurses and stretcher-bearers. In the car park was a fleet of camouflaged trucks and ambulances, ready to carry the sickest patients away to their assigned hospitals.

It was the first time that Molly had been present at such a homecoming, and as the train pulled in, shattering the silent, dark, ghostlike atmosphere of the station with a grating squeal of brakes, she was aware of a sense of nervous anticipation. No one knew what state the soldiers would be in, or even exactly how many there would be. Troop movements, even those concerning injured troops, were always shrouded in secrecy. Molly didn't know for sure that Ward and Helen would be on board, even though Katy said they were expected any day now, but when Sister Parkes had instructed her to report for collection duty, she braced herself just in case.

Over the last couple of weeks she had given herself a good talking-to. It was completely absurd to fall in love with a happily married man, let alone one who was barely aware of her existence. As Douglas Rutherford had so kindly pointed out, she was hardly the type of girl capable of luring a handsome man away from his wife, even if she wanted to. Which she didn't. Katy was her best friend. Her only real friend, come to that. So she had resolved to pull herself together, to get a grip and to put the blasted man out of her mind.

For a moment the great train stood still, steaming gently. With its windows all blacked out it emitted no light at all. It was only when the doors began to open, like the curtains in a theatre, that the dimly lit interior was revealed. The carriages had been refitted with lines of two-tier bunks. Each bunk contained a soldier or seaman, although some were so heavily swathed in bandages they were almost unidentifiable. Red Cross nurses were busying about, and the foul, all-too-familiar odour of sepsis and iodine began to permeate the night air.

And then there he was, Ward Frazer, dressed in RAF uniform, walking down the platform with his slightly uneven stride. Even in the dim, flickering light Molly recognised him immediately. She could tell it hadn't been an easy journey. Unshaven, with dark rings under his eyes, he looked like he'd come home from battle rather than from an errand of mercy. Raising her hand, she gave a nervous little wave and immediately he veered towards her. 'Molly? Is that you? I was hoping you'd be here.' And despite all her resolutions, all her private admonishments, it was as much as she could do to refrain from throwing herself into his arms.

But she didn't, of course. She just blurted out some question about Helen.

Ward's eyes flickered. 'She's not too good,' he said. 'She'll be pleased when this journey's over, that's for sure.'

'Katy's arranged a bed in Private Block,' Molly said. 'I'll find an orderly and we'll get her into an ambulance.'

It hadn't been easy to arrange a bed for Helen. Hospital beds in London were already in short supply, and the influx of wounded men from the North African battlefields was making it worse. But Katy had enlisted Sister Morris's support, and even Louise had helped, persuading her father, who was one of the trustees of the Wilhelmina, to have a word with Matron on Helen's behalf.

But now, as she followed Ward on to the train, Molly wondered if it would have been kinder to leave her in Algeria after all.

Lying still and silent under the grey army blanket, Helen was a shadow of her former self. They'd made her dye her blonde hair brown before she went into France, and now that it was growing out, it made her look even more ill and unkempt. It was impossible to believe this was the same fashionable, glowing girl as in the picture on the mirror in her room. She was so pinched-looking and thin, the bones showing clearly through the skin on her face. Molly had seen that translucent, hollow look before, all too many times, and she forced herself to hide her dismay as Helen's eyes opened at the sound of Ward's voice.

It took a while for Helen to focus, to understand where she was and what was happening. But even in this shocking state, her good manners didn't desert her. 'Hello, Molly,' she whispered through cracked, bloodless lips. 'Thank you so much.'

Katy was fast asleep when someone banged on the door. Because of the air raids, she and Malcolm had spent much of the previous night in the cellar, Katy on a camp bed and Malcolm tucked into an eiderdown in an old drawer. She didn't like being down there; it stank of beer, and despite all her best efforts to evict them, there was a family of mice living behind the beer barrels. The idea of a mouse running across her face was almost worse than the thought of a bomb crashing through the roof. Either way it made for a sleepless night. So it was a relief to be back in her own bed.

For a moment she lay there disoriented, heart hammering, still half in some strange dream about losing all the glasses in the pub and having to run up the street to borrow teacups to serve the drinks in. And the dream wasn't so far off the truth. Someone was stealing her glasses, and she had a fair idea who—

A shower of pebbles hit the boarded-up window of the bedroom like a salvo from a machine gun, and she suddenly realised that someone was trying to wake her up.

Dragging her dressing gown around her, she hastened downstairs. 'Who is it?' she called nervously.

'Who do you think?' a voice drawled in reply. 'Do men often bang on your door in the middle of the night?'

'Ward!' She dropped the key in her haste to unlock the door. 'Is it really you?'

And it was. He was standing there in the moonlight, his kitbag on his shoulder.

A moment later he had stepped inside and she was in his arms and he was hugging her tight against him.

'I'm sorry,' he murmured. 'I stink.'

'I don't mind. I like it.'

She felt the vibration of a chuckle in his chest. 'Now that's going too far,' he said.

'You're back, that's the main thing.' Katy looked up, but her smile faded when she saw his expression. 'You are both back, aren't you? Helen didn't …?'

His smile faded but he shook his head. 'No, she made it. It wasn't easy for her, but she's all tucked up in the Wilhelmina now, so let's hope I've done the right thing.'

'But how is she? How did she cope with the voyage? What did she tell you? How did she come to get shot? Is she going to be all right?'

He pushed her away, laughing. 'Hey, hold on. I promise to tell you everything, but first I want to know if you are OK? And Malcolm?'

No, Katy wanted to scream. No, I'm exhausted and I never want you to go away again. But all she said was, 'Yes, we're fine. We survived. What do you need? A drink? Shall I boil a kettle?"

'No, you're freezing. You go back to bed. All I need is a good wash.' Sweeping her into his arms, he carried her upstairs and lowered her gently on to the bed. Sliding gratefully back under the blankets, she watched him lean over Malcolm's cot and gently stroke his little pink cheek. Her heart filled. This kind, brave, strong, beautiful man. Her husband. She still could hardly believe it. I love him, she said to herself. I love him so much it frightens me.

Straightening up, he shrugged off his jacket and turned for the door. Then he glanced back at her. 'I'll only be a minute,' he said, and then grinned at her expression. 'And don't look at me like that. Not if you want any sleep tonight anyway!'

Joyce was also awake. She didn't sleep well with Angie in the bed. But Pete was home again and Jen had refused categorically to have Angie in her room while she was still feeling poorly. Joyce sniffed. Poorly? Malingering more like. As far as she could see, there didn't seem to be much wrong with Jen any more. Except she said she felt tired all the time. Well she wasn't the only one. As Angie snored away happily next to her, Joyce's thoughts turned to the ordeal that awaited her the following day. Because the day of the cooking competition was finally upon her. And more than anything she could have used a good night's sleep.

The bombing over the last few days had come as a very nasty shock. Joyce had got used to scurrying outside to the Anderson shelter night after night during the Blitz, but to find herself huddled in there all over again, this time with Jen and Angie, was no joke. Although in Angie's view that was exactly what it had been. She hadn't experienced an air raid before, but far from being scared, she had loved every minute of it, squealing with mock terror when they finally heard the planes, until Jen snapped at her to shut up. Thankfully the all-clear had sounded shortly after that and they'd gone back to bed, where Angie had insisted on speculating with gruesome fascination about where the bombs might have fallen and how much damage they might have caused.

Joyce prodded Angie with her foot, but it made no difference. Stanley had snored too. Joyce hadn't liked having him in her bed either, although for different reasons. She suddenly found herself wondering if Mr Lorenz snored, and decided that the pawnbroker was far too polite for that. And then she felt a hot flush creep over her. What on earth was she doing imagining Mr Lorenz in her bed? She turned over crossly and pressed her hot face to the cold pillow. It was out of the question. She didn't want anyone in her bed. She didn't want anything. Not Albert Lorenz, not the dubious privilege of being a finalist in a cooking competition, nothing. All she wanted was her bed to herself and for tomorrow to be over so she could go back to her nice, steady little life in the café.

When Ward came back into the bedroom, his hair was wet and he was naked apart from a towel round his waist. He hadn't shaved but he had clearly had a thorough wash. To Katy's surprise, he was also carrying his kitbag.

To her astonishment, he upended it and tipped the entire contents out on the bed. The first thing to fall out was a crushed RAF beret, followed by some dirty clothes, his shaving things, a towel, a flask, two rolled-up dusty puttees, a packet of foreign cigarettes, a notebook, a tatty French–Arabic dictionary, a box of matches, a dangerous-looking penknife in a sheath, two pencils, a compass and a dog-eared map of North Africa. This motley selection was followed by several small packets of highly pungent spices, a bunch of dried herbs, a bag of nuts, three lemons, a melon and half a dozen huge, waxy-skinned oranges.

'Oranges!' Katy exclaimed. 'I haven't seen an orange in three years. Let alone a melon!'

'Yeah, I thought Malcolm could do with some vitamin C,' Ward said. But his voice was distracted. It wasn't the fruit he was after. Then he gave a grunt of satisfaction. Out of a sandy shoe he drew a small package wrapped in newspaper covered in squiggly foreign writing and handed it to Katy with a slightly diffident smile. 'I bought this for you in Algiers on Christmas Day.'

Tearing the paper, Katy found a wad of cotton wool. Inside was an elegant gold bracelet, engraved all the way round with tiny hearts. It was the most beautiful thing she had ever seen.

'Oh Ward,' she said. She could feel tears pricking her eyes as she fingered the bracelet.

He sat down on the edge of the mattress and put an arm round her shoulders. 'Hey, why are you crying? Don't you like it?'

'Of course I like it,' Katy mumbled. 'I love it.' Desperately she sniffed back the tears. He wouldn't want to come back to a weeping wife. 'I ... I just ... I'm just so glad you're back safely. You didn't need to bring me a gift.'

Slipping the bracelet on to her wrist, she lifted her arm to show it off to him.

He took her hand and bent his head to kiss her fingertips. Then he looked up at her and smiled. That slow smile she knew so well. It was the one that curled round her heart and squeezed it so tight she could hardly breathe. 'Happy Christmas,' he said.

Katy gave a tearful laugh. 'But it wasn't happy,' she said. 'It was a nightmare.' She turned her head to look at him. 'Do you think we'll ever have a Christmas together?'

He touched her cheek with cool fingers. 'Next year,' he said. 'I promise.'

Katy pulled back slightly and glared at him. 'I'll hold you to that.'

His eyes glinted. 'I'd much rather you held me to your lovely body,' he said. He stood up, swept all the stuff on to the floor, shoved the kitbag under the bed, stripped off the towel and slid under the covers.

For a second the daunting prospect of tomorrow's tiredness crossed Katy's mind, but the next moment she forgot about everything. She forgot her anxiety that he might begin to find her too pedestrian and drab, she forgot about Gillian James, she forgot about her missing beer glasses, she even forgot about someone stealing the Spitfire Fund tin.

The feel of his skin against hers, the touch of his fingers, the strength of his limbs, the wicked sensuality of his lips was enough to drive all worries from her mind.

Later, much later, when she lay snuggled in his arms, as promised, he told her about his trip.

She listened in awe to his account of the cramped camaraderie on the troopship, the comically inadequate fire and lifeboat drills, the black-humoured defiance of the crew when the convoy was strafed by the Italian air force just off Gibraltar, his arrival in the shambolic port city of Algiers, the acrimonious discussions he had had with the SOE contingent there and the outlandish train journey through the desert to Oran.

The whole thing made Katy feel quite exhausted. Only Ward could suffer all that and then come home and laugh about it. It made her problems seem pitiful in comparison.

But he didn't laugh about the terrible state of the French field hospital. Nor the shock of finding Helen so very ill. Nor the arguments with the local officials and the difficulties of getting her on to a suitable ship for the return journey.

And then he recounted some of what Helen had told him about her last few days in France. The treachery of her SOE contact, who turned out to be working for the Germans. Her rescue by André Cabillard. Her two days of bliss at his family home. The deadly battle in Toulon harbour. And among it all, the awful processions of the homeless and destitute, mainly Jews, fleeing in front of the German occupation forces.

'We absolutely can't let that happen here,' Ward said suddenly. 'We've got to win this war. That bastard Hitler has got to be stopped.'

That was when Katy's heart sank. She had heard that tone in his voice before, that sense of conviction, that gritty determination. He was right, of course. The thought of people just like Aaref and Jacob or Mr Lorenz being herded up and sent to prison camps was unbearable. And there were new rumours now that things were even worse than that. That the so-called prison camps were actually death camps, and that Jews were being systematically murdered right across Europe.

But she didn't want Ward to be the one to stop Hitler and his beastly war machine. She didn't want him putting himself in danger. Not again. Not any more. She wanted him right here, at her side. In her life. In her bed.

It was generally agreed in the Wilhelmina Hospital that it was a miracle that Helen de Burrel had survived the journey. And indeed that she had survived this long at all. She was in a very bad way. The shoulder wound, where the traitorous SOE agent's bullet had entered, was badly infected. Staphylococcal bacteria were eating her from the inside like a worm in an apple, and the infection had entered her bloodstream. The skin on her arm was suppurating pus, and she was coughing up phlegm. Her temperature was high and she was in constant pain.

But despite her critical condition, it seemed that, in her view at least, Ward had made the right decision in bringing her home.

'You'll never know how glad I was to see him,' she whispered to Katy the following morning. It was clearly an effort for her to speak. She was heavily sedated. She could barely keep her eyes open and her breath was shallow and laboured.

'I'm so grateful to you for letting him come for me. I felt so ill.' Her lips moved into a faint smile. 'Well, to be honest, I don't feel brilliant now, but I thought I was about to die, and that beastly SOE man kept pestering me about what had happened in France. I didn't want to tell him anything. I didn't trust him. There've been too many betrayals and I didn't want to put André in any more danger than he is in already. But as soon as Ward walked into that horrid hospital tent in Oran, I knew everything would be all right.'

Katy felt her heart twist. Even during her brief career as a trainee nurse, she had never seen anyone look as ill as Helen. It was clear to her that everything was far from all right.

When Helen lapsed into a restless sleep, Katy went out into the corridor, where one of the Private Block SRN staff nurses was preparing a trolley.

The nurse glanced up and then quickly looked away again.

'She's not going to make it, is she?' Katy said.

The SRN shook her head. 'I don't think so.'

'How long has she got?'

The nurse looked uncomfortable. 'I don't know. Maybe a few days. A week at the most.'

Joyce was shaking like a leaf. Her heart was hammering and she was quite sure that if someone took her temperature, the thermometer would show a high fever. She had no idea that terror could make you feel physically ill.

Three long bench tables had been arranged in a semicircle in the large hall. There were two finalists to each bench. Joyce, dressed in a blouse and her workaday, rather faded floral wraparound café apron, was sharing hers with a tall, thin lady in a smart pale blue twinset and a large navy hat. A panel of judges sat facing them on upright chairs. They were well-heeled, tweedy WI types, just as she had feared, and they had neatly sharpened matching pencils and ominous-looking pads on their laps.

Behind the judges sat the audience. Each finalist had been allowed to invite guests. There weren't many there, perhaps thirty or so people, but among them, sitting together in an incongruous row, were Mrs Rutherford, Mr Lorenz, Pete and Angie. Joyce had expected Mrs Rutherford to stay behind to man the café, but earlier that morning she had hung a sign on the door: Due to the participation of Mrs Carter in the finals of the Wandsworth council cookery competition, the café will be closed for the afternoon. We apologise for any inconvenience caused.

Joyce had asked Jen if she wanted to come. Anything to stop her moping about all day long doing nothing. She'd thought it might do her good to get out of the house.

But Jen had refused. 'What? Come and watch a bunch of busybody WI ladies sniffing over your meat pie? I can't think of anything worse. Anyway, I don't feel well enough to traipse all the way up to Wandsworth.'

'It's a sausage and dumpling pie,' Joyce had retorted. 'And if you aren't well enough to drive up to Wandsworth in the taxi Mr Lorenz has ordered for us, then I think it's time you put your hand in your pocket and went to the doctor. You ought to be better by now. Molly Coogan has been back at work for weeks.'

'Bully for her,' Jen had said sourly. But she still hadn't come.

At least the others were there to support her, Joyce thought gratefully, even though it didn't help her concentration that every time she looked up from her preparation bench, Angie waved at her as though she was a child in a school play.

'So Mrs … Mrs Carter, isn't it? What are you making for us today?'

The sudden loud, posh voice interrupted Joyce's thoughts and she jumped, almost dropping her rolling pin. One of the judges had got up and was standing on the other side of the bench peering at the pastry she had just rolled out on the salvaged piece of roof slate she had brought with her for the purpose.

Joyce regarded her in some surprise. 'Well I'm making sausage and dumpling pie, like it said in my recipe,' she said. 'Isn't that what you wanted me to make?'

'Yes, yes, of course it is,' the woman said. She lifted one of her gloved hands and indicated the people sitting behind her. 'But I wanted you to tell the audience and to explain what methods you are using.'

Joyce felt the floor shake under her feet. She was here to cook, not to talk. Being here at all was bad enough. She felt as though she was about to have a heart attack as it was. But she certainly couldn't talk, not in front of an audience. Already, even at the thought of it, her hands had gone clammy, which wasn't going to do the pastry any good.

'I'm not using any methods,' she muttered.

'Speak up,' the woman said.

Joyce didn't want to speak up. What she wanted to do was to turn tail and run out of the hall, taking her dumplings with her. Either that or pick them up and sling them one by one into the smug, stuck-up faces of the judges. The thought made her feel more confident.

'I'm not using any methods,' she repeated a fraction louder. 'I don't know any methods. I'm just cooking the way I always do. Although I don't usually do it in front of an audience and a row of frosty-faced judges.'

Someone in the audience chuckled and her interrogator looked rather taken aback. 'Well you must have methods, Mrs Carter. Everyone has methods. For example, may I ask what is it you are using to roll your pastry on?'

'Well it's not a method, that's for sure,' Joyce said. 'It's a piece of roof slate I picked up from a bombed house in my road. It keeps the pastry nice and cool. Not that I need it in this great draughty place.'

'Hear, hear,' someone called from the audience, and more people started laughing.

'Ah yes, very resourceful,' the lady said patronisingly. 'We in the WI are great supporters of make-do and mend.'

'It's not so much make-do and mend,' Joyce said, dipping her fingers in a cup of water to dampen the edge of her dish. 'More like needs must when the devil drives. Not that I'm saying you judges are devils, mind, but I'm sure you'll complain if my pastry doesn't rise.' She glanced up then and caught sight of Mrs Rutherford clasping a hand to her mouth. Then Angie let out one of her irrepressible giggles, and a moment later the whole audience erupted in laughter.

That was too much for the interviewer. Hastily she moved along the bench to the twinset lady, who gave her much more satisfactory answers. As did the other contestants. And all in confident, plummy, well-to-do accents. They seemed to know everything there was to know about cooking, and they seemed delighted to have an opportunity to show off their methods. One was even using something called a bain-marie, whatever that was.

By the time Joyce's sausage and dumpling pie was ready to go in the communal oven, she knew she stood about as much chance of winning the competition as of flying to the moon. And she was right.

The judges did make some rather tight-lipped comments about the excellence of her pie, and deigned to commend her for the flavour and texture of her apple snow. But the prize went to the bain-marie lady for her baked trout and duchesse potatoes, although where you were expected to find a trout in south London for less than two shillings was anyone's guess. Joyce guessed that she had had it sent up to town from her country estate.

Not that Joyce cared. With her fancy methods and her cut-glass accent, the winner could go and jump in the lake on Clapham Common as far as she was concerned. Not that she'd find any trout in there, not any more; they'd all been fished out and eaten long ago, when rationing first came in.

'Well thank goodness that's over,' she said as Angie rushed up to congratulate her after the prizegiving.

'No, you were brilliant,' Angie said. 'We thought you should have won hands down, didn't we, Mr Lorenz?'

'Certainly we did,' Mr Lorenz agreed gravely as he approached. 'Your pie looked delicious, Mrs Carter. Very tasty indeed.'

'Wish we could have had it for supper,' Pete remarked gruffly with his shy laugh.

'Well I thought the whole thing was a right waste of time,' Joyce said.

'Not at all.' Mrs Rutherford was shaking her head. 'You did marvellously. And it was good publicity. Your name will be in the paper and I'm sure it will bring us in extra customers. And next time …'

Joyce was gathering up her things, but she stopped dead at that. 'There won't be a next time,' she said. 'I can assure you of that.'

*

Molly was helping one of the staff nurses dress a wound when she was summoned to Sister Parkes's office. She had already been there once that day, to be told off for helping Ward Frazer the night before.

'It has been reported to me that you neglected your post,' Sister Parkes had said.

'Well, yes, Sister,' Molly had admitted. 'But Helen de Burrel is a friend of a friend. And I wanted to help …'

'I don't care who she is. She should have taken her turn like everyone else. There's a system and we need to stick to it.'

'Yes, Sister,' Molly had said dutifully. She was only too aware that Ward had somehow managed to circumnavigate the system and had got Helen into an ambulance and away to the hospital almost before anyone else had disembarked from the train. She didn't quite know how he had done it, but the smile he had given her was worth any amount of telling off by Sister Parkes. She would do anything for that smile.

Now, as she washed her hands and headed up the ward a second time, she racked her brain for some other misdemeanour she might have inadvertently committed.

But this time it was a different matter completely. 'Ah, there you are, Nurse. What took you so long? Sister Donaldson requires your presence in Private Block.'

Molly suddenly felt a stab of anxiety. 'What for?'

'She didn't say. Now are you going to go or are you going to stand there asking unnecessary questions? And don't forget to change your apron.'

'I won't forget, Sister,' Molly said as she sped away. It was one of the rules of the Wilhelmina that nurses had to change their aprons if they went to another ward. It was a nuisance, but the rule had been introduced to help prevent the spread of infection. The only problem as Molly saw it was that the doctors quite happily moved from one ward to another without changing their white coats, and sometimes even without washing their hands. But then the doctors at the Wilhelmina were gods. Or they certainly thought they were. It was inconceivable that anyone might suggest they could be just as guilty of spreading infection as nurses.

Dr Mallet, the chief medical doctor, who was just coming through the swing doors to Private Block as Molly approached, was a case in point. Like his name, he was heavy-handed and authoritarian. For a moment Molly thought he was going to tell her off for running, another forbidden activity in the corridors of the Wilhelmina, but it was beneath him to address a junior nurse, and he swept past her in disapproving silence, with a waft of ammonia.

Sister Donaldson, looking rather pink, was standing just inside the swing

94

doors. With her was a middle-aged man wearing a camel overcoat over a well-cut suit and polished brogues. Healthy-looking and tanned, he wore his expensive clothes with a kind of careless panache unusual in these austere times. In his hand he held a grey fedora and a pair of leather gloves.

He looked as though he had just stepped out of an American film, Molly thought. And she wasn't far wrong. For this, as Sister Donaldson quickly pointed out, in a rather flustered manner, was Lord de Burrel, Helen's father, who had just arrived from America.

'And this is Nurse Coogan, sir,' she added grudgingly.

'Ah yes,' he said, holding out his hand to Molly with a smile. 'I gather you are a friend of my daughter's? I wanted to thank you for helping her last night.'

And to her astonishment, Molly found herself shaking hands with an earl. For a strange moment she thought she was going to curtsey. But she managed to restrain herself. His handshake was warm and firm. 'No, no, it was nothing,' she murmured. She could feel herself flushing. She had always liked Helen, but she would never have presumed to call herself one of her friends. Nor did she have any idea how she should address Helen's father. She decided, if necessary, to follow Sister Donaldson's lead and go for sir as the safest option.

He inclined his head and suddenly she could see the strain on his face. How awful it must be, she thought with compassion, to come all the way home from America to find your only daughter so terribly ill. She wondered if Dr Mallet had told him exactly how sick she was, and then she looked at him more closely and guessed he had. His natural courtesy and distinguished manners made him hide any private pain, but Molly could see it there in the rigidity of his features, the bleakness at the back of his eyes. What was more, she realised that Helen must have told him to ask for her, so he could put in a good word for her, maybe to prevent her being disciplined for her insubordination last night. What extraordinary people they were, she thought, to bother about her when things could hardly be worse for them.

But apparently Lord de Burrel wasn't going to leave it at that. He turned to Sister Donaldson with another of his charming smiles. 'After all my daughter has been through, I don't like to think of her being alone. Would Nurse Coogan be allowed to sit with her when her other duties permit?'

'Sir, I don't think …' Sister Donaldson lurched into a blustering objection, but she was no match for Lord de Burrel. Katy had once told Molly that he held some kind of high-powered liaison role with the American government. He now brought his diplomatic skills to bear.

'I'm sure you understand my concern, Sister,' he interrupted smoothly. 'I want my daughter to receive the best care possible.' He raised his eyebrows slightly. 'Perhaps if I had a word with Matron?'

'No, no, that won't be necessary, sir,' Sister Donaldson assured him hastily. 'I'm sure Nurse Coogan can be spared from time to time.'

'I hope that won't inconvenience you, Nurse Coogan?' he asked, turning back to Molly.

'No, no, not at all, er, sir. I'd be delighted to do anything I can,' Molly stammered. It was the first time anyone in the hospital had ever given a thought to her convenience.

'Good,' he said. He held out his hand to Sister Donaldson and clasped hers warmly. 'Thank you, Sister. I was sure I could rely on you. It is a comfort to know that my daughter is in such good hands.'

And so Molly began a strange backwards and forwards shuttling existence between Private Block and Septic Ward Four.

'Is this my father's doing?' Helen whispered when she woke later that day to find her sitting in her room.

Molly held a glass of water to Helen's dry lips. 'Yes, it is,' she said. 'He spoke to Sister Donaldson.'

'He said he would. But did he charm her or browbeat her?' Helen asked.

Molly smiled. 'A bit of both, I think.'

A minute or so elapsed before Helen spoke again, clearly worn out by even the effort of taking two tiny sips. 'He's not one to take no for an answer,' she said. 'Ward is the same. And André.' She closed her eyes, but Molly had caught the flash of despair that flickered across her thin face at the thought of André.

And so are you, Molly thought. Any normal person would have died by now.

But despite her tenacity, Helen's condition was clearly deteriorating. Dr Mallet had prescribed more sulpha drugs, but all they had done was bring her out in a rash.

She spent more and more time asleep, or at least not really asleep, more in a kind of semi coma. Molly ached for her. She wished there was something she could do. But there seemed to be very little anyone could do now, apart from dripping fluid into Helen's mouth and trying to persuade Sister to up the pain relief.

Molly didn't know Helen well, only as a friend of Katy and Louise's, someone who came into the pub from time to time. She'd always thought of her as a classy, well-brought-up girl with good manners and a polite smile. But her stoicism, and the way she coped with the awkward intimacy of their situation, made Molly wish she had known her better before. She hadn't met many patients capable of making light about the insertion of a catheter.

By the third day, Helen could no longer eat. So Molly just sat there, hour on hour, listening to her shallow laboured breathing. Pam lent her some knitting needles, and Molly joined the latest craze of knitting khaki balaclavas for RAF airmen.

Visiting time was an ordeal for everyone. It wasn't easy to know what to say to someone who was terminally ill.

Lord de Burrel was courteous and controlled. He had a natural air of authority which helped him get what he wanted. But it wasn't helping him get Helen any better, and the expression in his eyes as he left her room always made Molly's heart twist.

Katy put on a brave face and managed to make Helen smile with stories about Malcolm and events at the pub. Louise, on the other hand, ended up crying outside in the corridor, saying she couldn't come again as it was too distressing.

Pam and George's visit was particularly sad. George had pleaded to be allowed to see Helen, but when the moment came, he was uncharacteristically subdued. Forewarned by both Pam and Molly, he bravely tried not to let his dismay show and spoke in a hushed whisper. His little face was eager when he told Helen that they had named Pam's new baby after her, but it quickly became pinched with distress when Helen was unable to respond.

Ward Frazer came every afternoon. And every afternoon Molly found some excuse to be well out of the way. She simply couldn't bear to see the easy smile he put on his face as he entered Helen's room. Nor the way it faded the instant he left.

It was Ward who had introduced Helen to the secret world that had been her downfall, and Molly could tell he blamed himself for the condition she was in now. If only Ward hadn't discovered that she spoke fluent French, he never would have suggested that she joined the SOE and none of this would have happened.

'There must be something more they can do,' he said to Molly when he bumped into her in the corridor one afternoon as she waited for him to leave. And hearing that plea in his voice, she so wished there was. But even Lord de Burrel's influence and social standing couldn't magic up anything to alleviate Helen's suffering. She was bordering on pneumonia. Her racing pulse was uneven with arrhythmic fibrillation. Dr Mallet had prescribed morphine and digitalis. But nothing was helping her any more.

When Molly went back into the room after Ward's visit, there were beads of sweat on Helen's forehead, and she moved restlessly, unable to get comfortable.

'I'm dying, aren't I?' she whispered when she saw Molly. 'Everyone says I'll be fine, but I know you'll tell me the truth.'

Molly wiped her face with a flannel. 'Sometimes there are miracles,' she said.

Helen looked at her steadily. 'How long?'

Molly hesitated. 'Maybe a few days.'

Helen was silent for a long moment. Then she spoke again. 'Molly, I want you to do something for me.'

'Of course, yes, anything.'

'It's to do with André. You met him once, didn't you, in the pub?'

Molly nodded. 'Yes, yes I did. Briefly.'

'I left a picture of him, of us, at Pam's house. I don't know if it's still there. If you can find it, can you bring it in?'

'It's still tucked in the corner of the mirror in your room,' Molly said.

Helen nodded. 'I want to have it with me when I die,' she said. She took a difficult breath. Suddenly there were tears in her eyes, but she was unable to wipe them away. 'And after the war,' she went on, 'if you can, I'd like you to write to him. I don't know the exact address, but the Cabillard vineyards are at Domaine Saint-Jean, near Toulon. That would find him. If he's still alive. And tell him … tell him that I was holding him right at the end. Thinking about him. Because I will be.' There was another long pause, and then she spoke once more, very quietly. 'At least I hope I will be.'

That night before she went to bed, Molly sat at the dressing table for a long time looking at the photo of Helen and André. Dimly she could hear the wireless from downstairs. Alan and Pam were listening to the news. The newsreader was announcing that the British Eighth Army had taken Tripoli, the last remaining city in Mussolini's so-called African Empire. General Montgomery and his Desert Rats were even now crossing into Tunisia in pursuit of the retreating German and Italian forces. The Prime Minister, Winston Churchill, had received the news in Morocco, where he was meeting with President Roosevelt and the leader of the Free French forces, General de Gaulle.

According to Katy, that was where Lord de Burrel should have been too, at the summit in Casablanca, instead of attending his dying daughter's bedside.

The newsreader went on to report heavy fighting in Stalingrad. It was thought that the Germans were on the brink of collapse there too, with an estimated hundred thousand of their troops having been killed or having died of starvation or cold.

Molly knew she should feel pleased. She could tell from Alan's sudden shout of glee that he was pleased. The newsreader was clearly pleased too, or as pleased as he could show in his clipped, emotionless BBC accent. For once Hitler and Mussolini were on the run. But Molly just felt sick. Like everyone else, she hated the Germans, and the Italians, but she found it hard to celebrate so many deaths. In any case, a hundred thousand German deaths paled into insignificance against one imminent, local death.

With a sigh, she eased the photo out of the frame of the mirror and put it in the pocket of her cloak, ready for tomorrow.

Chapter Eight

Molly jerked awake just after midnight. For a second she thought it must be another air raid, and that the noise of a siren or the drone of bombers had woken her. But even though she strained her ears, she couldn't hear anything untoward. Certainly not anything that would have caused her heart to hammer in her chest.

But then she did hear a noise, a kind of whimper, as though from a trapped animal. Realising it had come from the direction of George and baby Helen's room, she waited a second to see if Pam or Alan would respond. When they didn't, she pushed back the covers, picked up her torch from the bedside table and crept out into the passage. Hearing the noise again, she quietly, carefully turned the door handle and stepped into the children's room. Silence.

She played the torch first over the cot, and was relieved to see that the baby was peacefully asleep.

There was no sound or movement from George's bed either. But nor was there any sign of George. On closer inspection, she saw that there was a mound under the covers half way down the bed.

Laying her hand on it, she felt a slight convulsion and realised that George was trying to conceal the fact that he was crying. She could sense him holding his breath.

Kneeling at the side of the bed, she peeled back the sheet and blankets a little way and whispered, 'Are you in there, George? It's me, Molly. What's the matter?'

There was a long pause, and then George's voice, muffled under the bedclothes, much smaller and more uncertain than usual. 'I don't want Helen to die.'

'Nobody wants her to die,' Molly whispered. 'Nobody wants anyone to die,' she added, and then thought what a ridiculous thing that was to say. In three separate tragic incidents earlier on in the war, George had lost both his parents and his younger brother. That was a high tally for someone so young, even in wartime. It was hardly surprising he was so upset about the prospect of losing Helen too.

'I thought hospitals were meant to make people better,' he mumbled.

Molly grimaced in the darkness. She had laboured under that delusion once too. But that was before she had learned about the relentless, indomitable effect of pathogenic bacteria.

'It's not fair. Why can't one of those stupid doctors do something to help her?'

Ward had said more or less the same thing, with almost equal despair, and Molly didn't know which one of them made her feel more tortured. Because she knew that Helen, like so many others suffering from serious septic infections, was doomed. Until someone discovered an effective treatment, there was nothing anyone—

She had reached under the blankets to stroke George's hair, but now she pulled away and sat back on her heels. Her mind flipped back to the medical journals that Sister Parkes had given her to read. Professor Alexander Fleming. Wasn't it a man with a streptococcal infection that his mould formula had unexpectedly cured? Or had she misremembered?

'What?' George was wriggling up the bed. 'What the matter?'

'I've just thought of something.'

'What?' He emerged from under the covers. 'What is it? Something to help Helen?'

'Shh!' Molly didn't want him to wake the baby. 'I'm not sure. I need to go and check something. Now listen,' she tucked him in again, 'you go back to sleep. Worrying won't help Helen. The best way we can help her is by being brave and strong.'

'Are you going to be brave and strong?' he whispered.

Molly shivered and pulled her dressing gown around her more tightly. She didn't feel very brave or very strong. She could already feel her blood running cold at the thought of approaching Sister Donaldson. It was unheard of for a junior nurse to query a patient's treatment. But now that she had remembered about Professor Fleming curing that man at St Mary's, she had to do something. She had to ask at the very least. Just in case. It was madness, but surely it was worth a try. 'Yes, I am.' She said. 'Or at least I am going to try to be.'

Joyce was just spooning out porridge for a customer when Mr Lorenz started choking at his table by the window. It was Angie who rushed over to him first, sending a chair flying as she went.

'Are you all right, Mr Lorenz?' she said. 'Do you want me to pat you on the back?'

As Mr Lorenz frantically shook his head, even while he gasped for air, Joyce suddenly had a vision of Angie whacking him so hard that she broke his ribs. 'No, no, I'll do it,' she called, hurrying across herself. 'A bit of toast must have gone down the wrong way.'

Mr Lorenz was trying desperately to catch his breath. He was bright red now and seemed to be stabbing a finger at the newspaper he'd been reading in the most peculiar way. For an awful moment, Joyce thought he was having some kind of a fit.

'Lift up your arms, that might help,' she suggested, slapping him on the back. It was the first time she had ever really touched him, and was surprised to find his torso rather more muscular than she had expected. He always wore a dark formal suit and stiff-collared shirt and tie, so that it was hard to tell what lay beneath.

She thumped him again, but already he was recovering, fumbling in his pocket for his handkerchief. He took off his spectacles and wiped his eyes. 'I'm so sorry to disturb you, ladies,' he wheezed, clearly mortified to have caused a scene. 'But I just noticed this in the Wandsworth Gazette ...'

Mrs Rutherford had joined them now, and it was she who picked up the newspaper.

'Oh, I say,' she said, with a gasp of delight. 'Listen to this. *The Wandsworth Council Austerity Cooking Competition took place this week. The first prize was taken by Mrs Delaney-Lawson for her poached trout and duchesse potatoes. But the real star of the event was Mrs Carter, who stole the show with her wit and repartee when questioned by the judges. Of all the contestants she had most entered into the spirit of the competition by rolling her pastry on a roof slate she had salvaged from a nearby bomb site. The resulting sausage and dumpling pie looked delicious and the good news is that you can taste it for yourself at her café on the corner of Lavender Road and Lavender Hill.'*

There was a moment's silence as she finished reading, then Angie clapped her hands in glee. 'Blimey, fancy that, Mum, to get your name in the paper. And the café too.'

'Yes indeed,' Mrs Rutherford said with considerable satisfaction, as a dozen or so customers joined in with Angie's applause. 'I think you had better make a few more of those pies, Mrs Carter.'

Mr Lorenz stood up and cleared his throat. He still looked rather pink and his voice sounded a little bit husky, although it was hard to tell if that was a result of the choking fit or some sort of emotion. 'I think this deserves a little celebration,' he said. He glanced round the café, encompassing the still clapping customers with a shy smile that widened slightly as it came to rest on Joyce's face. 'Perhaps I could treat everyone to a slice of your delicious apple cake, Mrs Carter.'

It was a very busy morning on Private Block. Some of the rooms had been commandeered by Matron to house an influx of patients injured when a building on Prince of Wales Drive had collapsed early that morning as a result of a so-called controlled detonation of an unexploded bomb that had fallen during the raids over the weekend.

So Sister Donaldson was not best pleased when Molly waylaid her in the lobby to ask whether she knew anything about Professor Fleming's work on a cure for septicaemia.

'It's called penicillin,' Molly rushed on when Sister just stared at her in blank amazement. 'He discovered it in some old mould years ago and he used it to treat a man with streptococcus infection last year. It was like a miracle cure and I wondered if we could find out if any was available for Helen de Burrel …'

At this point Sister Donaldson clearly couldn't control herself a moment longer. 'I don't know what you are talking about, Nurse Coogan. Have you taken complete leave of your senses? I have much more important things to do today than listen to some nonsense about a miracle cure.'

'But it's not nonsense,' Molly insisted. 'I read it in the—'

'I don't care where you read it. If such a cure was available, then Dr Mallet would have implemented it.'

'But he might not know—'

'Silence!' Sister Donaldson drew herself up to her full, considerable height. 'I will not listen to some pipsqueak of a junior nurse questioning the competence of one of this hospital's senior doctors.'

'No, Sister, but I just wanted to try and help …'

As Molly tailed off miserably, Sister Donaldson pursed her lips. When she spoke again, her voice was a little less strident. 'I'm sure you mean well, Nurse Coogan. I know you are a friend of Lady Helen's. And I do understand your concern. Her condition is critical. But our job as nurses is to carry out the doctors' instructions, calmly and efficiently. Not to come up with wild ideas of our own.' She fixed Molly with a penetrating gaze. 'So that's the last I want to hear about it. Is that understood?'

Molly sighed. 'Yes, Sister.'

Sister's eyes narrowed sharply. 'And I forbid you to mention anything about this to Lady Helen or her father. Or indeed to anyone else. Things are bad enough without you raising false hopes. For that's what they are. There is nothing on this earth that can fight the kind of infection that Lady Helen is suffering from.' She hesitated for a moment, and then added piously, 'If and when she is taken from us, then it will be God's will.'

'Do you really believe that, Sister?' Molly asked. 'About God's will, I mean?'

'Yes, of course I do,' Sister Donaldson replied. She glanced quickly at the fob watch pinned to her apron bib. 'And now, Nurse Coogan, I want you to return to Septic Ward Four. You can tell Sister Parkes I no longer need you here.'

'But ...' Molly suddenly felt very weary. Her night-time study was beginning to take its toll. She knew she had set herself a hard task, but she hadn't expected to fail so spectacularly. 'But Sister, I really need to see Helen. I promised to bring in a photograph she wanted.'

Sister Donaldson held out her hand. 'Well you can give it to me and I will pass it on to her.'

Reluctantly Molly delved in her pocket and brought out the picture of Helen and André. Sister Donaldson took it and glanced at it, but made no comment.

'You won't forget to give it to her, will you, Sister?' Molly asked anxiously.

'Of course I won't forget.' Sister's voice was even more clipped than usual. 'And in future, Nurse Coogan,' she added as Molly turned away, 'do try to behave in a more prudent and moderate manner, one befitting a nurse trained at this hospital.'

Jen stood waiting for the kettle to boil and wondered if she would ever feel well again. It was so cold in the kitchen that ice had formed on the window pane. If she'd been able to see through it, she wouldn't have been surprised to see a polar bear prowling about in the back yard. The only warm place in the house was in bed. She longed to crawl back under the covers right now, but was trying to resist. Spending so much time in bed hadn't made her feel any better, so now she was going to see if going out and taking some exercise might be a better policy. How come George and Molly Coogan had shaken off the dreaded chickenpox in a couple of weeks and she was still feeling lousy three weeks after the spots had gone? It wasn't fair. Nothing was fair.

Jen could hardly bear to think of *The Mikado*, the lost opportunity. What might have been: impressing the critics, impressing Henry Keller, maybe even the chance to step into the leading role, the notices she might have received. And instead of all the glitter, the parties, the acclaim, here she was in a freezing-cold kitchen, unemployed, broke and ill.

She had no strength in her at all. And no appetite either. It was even a strain to pour the boiling water over a teaspoon of Bovril in a cup. Why had everything gone so spectacularly wrong?

As she stirred the drink, she felt a stab of anger. It was all Molly Coogan's fault. Until Molly had given her the chickenpox, she had been doing so well: she had been fit and healthy, she had had a sophisticated and influential man interested in her, a decent job and every hope of a bright future.

Now all that had changed. She hadn't heard a squeak from Henry in the last week, and there was no work in the offing; even if there had been, she wasn't well enough to do it. And what was worse, nobody was sympathetic because they were all so concerned about Helen de Burrel, who was now apparently at death's door.

Things had gone from good to bad pretty quickly for her too, Jen realised. And it was a terrible thing, because despite her fancy name and privileged background, Helen de Burrel was all right. She didn't give herself airs and graces. She wasn't a jumped-up little snob like Louise. She wasn't really Jen's type. But she was nice enough and quite fun in a classy kind of way. Once, ages ago, when things had been going particularly badly for both of them, they had got drunk together and had both passed out on the floor of the pub.

No. Helen certainly didn't deserve to die. Especially after all that daredevil secret agent business. It made Jen shiver to think about it. She couldn't think of anything worse than running about all over Europe with the Nazis after you. But it would be nice, she thought, if someone would spare a tiny thought for her as well. Her situation wasn't quite as bad as Helen's, but it was bad enough.

Having Angie around didn't help either. Her sister's relentless high spirits made Jen feel even more depressed. Despite leaving her so-called fiancé in Devon, Angie was clearly delighted with her new life. She enjoyed her job at the café, even though it seemed her pay was docked almost every day for some breakage or another. And now she had decided to spend all her new-found wages on dancing lessons. She had gone to a dance hall up in Putney with a group of local lads earlier in the week and had come home full of chatter about some American servicemen showing off the latest craze of the Lindy Hop and the jitterbug.

'I've invited them to come over to the Flag and Garter next weekend,' she had said. 'One of them is good on the piano apparently, and if we clear some space maybe we can show off some moves.'

'I'm sure Katy will be delighted about that,' Jen had replied sarcastically.

'Oh, she is,' Angie agreed. 'She said she'd get some nice cold American beer in specially.'

And that made Jen feel even more irritated. She was meant to be the performer around here. Last year it had been she who had brought some American boys to the Flag and Garter. Stage-door Johnnies they had been, fans of her show. But they were nice boys and she had become quite fond of them. The aim then had been to boost Katy's trade during a lean patch, and they had certainly done that. Sadly they'd all been sent off to North Africa soon afterwards. Now it seemed Angie had taken over the role.

As she sipped her Bovril, Jen flicked through the local newspaper Joyce had left on the kitchen table. It was the one containing the review of the Wandsworth cooking competition. Jen glared at the article. Even her mother was getting good notices. What an irony was that.

Wondering if there might be a film she could go and see to cheer herself up, she turned to the entertainment section at the back, and immediately her eye fell on the word *Mikado*. She felt her blood run cold but she forced herself to read on.

New West End Mikado *production opens to rapturous applause. Slick and hilariously funny, the lively cast lost no opportunity to poke fun at our enemies Japan, Germany and Italy. The glittering first-night audience included Laurence Olivier and Vivien Leigh and the impresario Henry Keller (once again accompanied by the rising young actress Janette Pymm), who afterwards said it was one of the most entertaining evenings he had ever spent at the theatre.*

Jen closed her eyes. I bet he did, she thought bitterly. Janette Pymm was not only a starlet in the making, but also a considerable beauty, one of the forces' pin-up girls, in fact.

She made herself read the *Mikado* piece again. Talk about rubbing salt into the wound. It should have been her making the audience laugh, hobnobbing with the stars. But now, not only had she missed being part of a great show, it also sounded like she'd missed her chance with Henry too. If she had ever really had one. No wonder she hadn't heard from him if he was knocking around with the likes of Janette Pymm and Vivien Leigh. The unpalatable truth was that he was completely out of her league. He was hardly likely to be seriously interested in a two-bit wannabe from the back streets of Clapham.

Fighting the urge to scream or cry, Jen stood up, found some matches, tore out the article and burnt it in the sink. Then she picked up her cup of Bovril and went back upstairs to bed.

Molly arrived back on Septic Ward Four just as Dr Mallet was finishing his ward round. For once he looked as though he was in a good mood. The stethoscope round his neck swung jauntily as he nodded at something Sister Parkes was saying. Molly felt her heart accelerate. It somehow knew before she did that she was going to do something impulsive. Ward Frazer doesn't take no for an answer, she said to herself. And nor am I going to. But it took some nerve to step out in front of Dr Mallet as he turned to leave the ward.

Clasping her hands behind her back in the correct manner when addressing a superior at the Wilhelmina, she put on her most meek and polite voice. 'Dr Mallet, would it be possible to ask you a question about my friend Lady Helen de Burrel, who you are treating in Private Block?'

Dr Mallet looked at her in amazement. Even his moustache seemed to be bristling in displeasure at being waylaid. Then he turned to Sister Parkes, who was standing behind him with her eyes almost popping out of her head.

'Ah yes. Lady Helen de Burrel,' he said. 'A sad case. Terminal, I'm afraid, Sister. You probably heard they brought her back from North Africa.' He lifted his shoulders in a dismissive shrug. 'But I'm sorry to say her time on this earth is running out. Blood poisoning has taken hold. A severe *Streptococcus haemolyticus* infection. Nothing we can do now except keep her as comfortable as possible.'

'Yes, well that's what I wanted to ask you about,' Molly said. 'I wondered if you had heard of something called penicillin? Professor Fleming at St Mary's Hospital, Paddington, discovered it. He found it was effective against—'

'Nurse Coogan, I really must—' Sister Parkes lunged forward as though to physically push Molly out of the way, but Dr Mallet held up his hand, stopping her in her tracks.

'No, it's a fair question,' he said, still addressing Sister, as though Molly wasn't there. Sometimes she wondered if her junior nurse's uniform actually rendered her invisible. 'There have been one or two articles in the press about Professor Fleming's so-called miracle cure. But it's all pie in the sky, I'm afraid.'

At last he turned to Molly and put on a thin, patronising smile. 'Scientists, however eminent they are, sometimes do make extravagant claims for their discoveries. It's in their interest to do so; that's how they get funding for their research. But their assertions rarely amount to anything. If this penicillin had been proven as a feasible therapeutic cure, it would be available to the medical profession. And it's not.'

Molly felt a spark of hope. At least he had heard of it. 'Yes,' she said quickly as he went to turn away. 'But that's only because it's difficult to produce in sufficiently large quantities.'

Dr Mallet raised his hands, setting his stethoscope swinging again, but somehow less jauntily this time. 'Well there you are then. If in due course it turns out to be beneficial – which, to be frank, I and many other doctors doubt – then it will eventually be commercially produced and we will gain access to it. In the meantime, we use the skills and materials at our disposal. Our treatments have served us well up until now.'

'But they haven't,' Molly insisted. 'Not very well, at least. Far too many people die.'

Dr Mallet's eyes narrowed sharply. 'Nonsense,' he said. 'We have an excellent record in this hospital. We always do what we can, but ultimately we have to let nature take its course.'

'But that means giving up,' Molly said. Out of the corner of her eye she could see Sister Parkes twitching alarmingly, trying to attract her attention. She looked ready to explode. It was only the presence of Dr Mallet that was holding her back. Behind Sister Parkes, Molly could see two other ward nurses standing with their mouths open, clearly aghast at her temerity. But she wasn't going to stop now. Even if it did bring Sister Parkes's wrath down on her head. 'Surely we could contact Professor Fleming and at least ask him?'

'No, we certainly cannot,' Dr Mallet snapped. 'That is not how the medical profession works. Professor Fleming would be run off his feet if he had to deal with every Tom, Dick or Harry who felt he was entitled to a cure. There are procedures, licensing, trials. All processes that need to be—'

'But they are already doing trials,' Molly interrupted. She had spent virtually the whole night poring over the medical magazines, looking for anything she could find out about penicillin. She certainly knew a lot more about it now than she had known yesterday. But she could see from the steam coming out of Sister's ears that her own time on this earth was running out. 'It was in *The Lancet*. Why can't—'

'What were you doing reading *The Lancet*?'

The question stopped Molly in her tracks. She glanced at Sister Parkes and quailed. Sister's eyes were flashing fire.

But luckily Dr Mallet didn't wait for an answer. He was pretty angry himself now. 'You're a nurse, young lady, and you shouldn't start getting ideas above your station.' He swung round to address Sister Parkes again. His voice was frigid. 'Sister, this nurse needs to learn some respect and discipline.'

Sister Parkes was momentarily caught off guard, but she quickly recovered, kowtowing obsequiously and sweeping him away inexorably through the swing doors. 'I'm so sorry, Dr Mallet, I don't know what has come over her.'

A minute later she was back, with daggers in her eyes. 'I gave you those journals for your general edification, not so that you could embarrass me and yourself in front of one of our most eminent doctors.'

'Well if he's so eminent, why doesn't he try harder?' Molly said sulkily.

Sister's voice sounded like the crack of a whip. 'Nurse Coogan! You do not understand the complexities of the medical profession.'

'I do understand,' Molly said. 'And what I understand is that Helen de Burrel risked her life for the sake of this country and nobody here is willing to risk even a tiny bit of extra effort to try to save her.'

'That will do!' Sister Parkes's eyes had started to bulge ominously. 'I have never heard such cheek in all my life. As of this moment I am placing you on a disciplinary warning. You are to go straight back to your lodgings, where you should reflect seriously on your behaviour. Your pay will be docked. First thing tomorrow morning you will report to Matron. I hope between now and then you will have come to your senses and will be able to convince Matron that your appalling breach of conduct today has been a momentary aberration. Otherwise I am very much afraid your nursing career will be over.'

'I can't find my number one uniform belt,' Ward called down to Katy. 'The blue one. Have you seen it anywhere?'

Katy was counting glasses, but at this she ran upstairs, where she found him brushing his blue RAF jacket. She could see the dust motes circling in a shaft of thin winter sunlight coming through the half-boarded window. To her surprise he was dressed in his uniform trousers, pale blue shirt and neatly tied tie. 'Where are you going?' she asked.

'I could tell you, but then I'd have to kill you,' he said with a grin.

'No, seriously? Why are you so smart?'

He sat down on the dressing table chair and began to lace his shoes. 'It's a medical assessment,' he said. 'I need to prove I'm fit again. I can't sit behind a desk in London for ever. I want get back on active service. So I thought I should try to make a good impression, but now I can't find my damn belt.'

'Maybe it's still in your kitbag,' Katy said. Active service, she thought. Oh no. Oh no. She knew only too well what active service meant in Ward's secret world.

She reached under the bed and pulled out the canvas kitbag he had taken to North Africa. Delving into it, sure enough she found the belt; the buckle had snagged on the seam of the bag. But as she disentangled it, she found something else caught on the buckle too: a tiny package covered in the same flimsy foreign newspaper that her bracelet had been wrapped in. As she drew it out, the paper tore and she found herself holding a thin silver chain with a small oblong pendant hanging from it. She stared at it in silence. She was still kneeling at the bedside, with her back to Ward, and now suddenly her knees felt so weak she wondered if she would be able to get up again. Her whole body had frozen in sudden dread. This pretty thing had clearly been intended as a gift for someone. A woman. Obviously not her. But who?

Oh no, she thought. Oh no. This was worse than active duty. This was realisation of her worst fear.

'Any luck?' Ward's voice broke into her thoughts. Katy didn't know what to do. What to say. For a moment she even considered closing her fingers over the necklace in a vain attempt to deny its existence. Because she knew she wouldn't be able to bear it if he looked embarrassed. She didn't want to witness his guilt or a regretful explanation. She would rather not know at all than hear that there was another woman in his life.

'Katy?' She heard him laugh behind her. 'What are you doing? You look like you are saying your prayers.'

He wasn't far wrong, she thought, as she straightened up slowly. 'Yes, I found it,' she stammered, turning to face him. 'And I found this too.'

She hardly dared to look at him as she held out her hand with the necklace in it. But all he did was make a slight noise of surprise.

'Oh yeah,' he said, shrugging on his jacket. 'I'd forgotten about that. I bought it for Molly.'

'For Molly?' Katy couldn't believe her ears. Molly was probably the last person on earth to feature on her list of suspects for Ward's affection. 'What on earth for?'

'To thank her for suggesting I went to Oran to fetch Helen home.'

Katy stared at him incredulously. 'Molly told you to go to Oran?'

Ward was threading the belt through the loops. 'Well, not in so many words, but she certainly gave me the idea.' He nodded at the silver chain still lying on Katy's outstretched hand. 'I remembered you'd said she was doing some magic tricks with George, and that little dangly thing is meant to be a magic carpet. I thought she might kind of like it. But I've barely seen her since we got back, and with Helen so ill and everything, I completely forgot about it.'

Katy was conscious of a sense of relief so great it brought tears to her eyes. Turning away hastily, she rewrapped the chain with its tiny silver magic carpet in the piece of newspaper and put it on her dressing table. It seemed ironic somehow that of all the adoring women he could have bought a gift for, he had chosen Molly Coogan, the only one completely impervious to his charm.

Ward took his greatcoat out of the wardrobe, picked up his officer's cap and squared his shoulders. 'How do I look?'

He looked absolutely gorgeous. Like something off a recruitment poster for the RAF. Katy suddenly had an overwhelming desire to rip that smart uniform off him and push him back on the bed.

'Very smart,' she said. 'But you aren't fully fit. Your leg still—'

He pulled her to him and kissed her to stop the words. 'I know,' he murmured against her mouth. 'But I'm hoping to persuade them that I am.'

Katy didn't like the sound of that. Not at all. Nor did she like that purposeful, sparkly look in his eyes as he glanced back at her from the front door.

'Wish me luck,' he said, and was gone.

Katy turned to lift Malcolm out of his playpen. Hugging him to her, she tried to count her glasses again. But she kept losing track. Eventually she gave up and poured herself a tot of whisky instead. She wasn't normally a drinker, but suddenly she needed to feel that stinging warmth course down her gullet. She wondered why no one had ever warned her that loving someone could be so painful. And that loving someone in wartime was even worse.

Molly pushed out of the hospital doors and emerged on to St John's Road on shaking legs. Her decision to raise the topic of Professor Fleming's discovery had seemed quite reasonable in the middle of the night, but now, in the cold light of a January day, with a flea in her ear and her entire career hanging on the line, it seemed more like suicidal madness.

Sister Parkes had told her to go home and reflect on her behaviour. Well, she was already reflecting on her behaviour and had decided that she must have taken complete leave of her senses. Every aspect of her nursing training at the Wilhelmina had stressed the importance of adhering to long-practised procedures and maintaining total subservience to senior staff. There was no scope for some deranged junior nurse to suggest the use of an untested, controversial treatment, nor to question a senior doctor's professional competence. No wonder Sister Parkes had looked as though she was about to give birth to a canary. And as for Dr Mallet, it was probably the first time he'd ever realised that junior nurses had the power of speech.

Molly glanced helplessly up and down the street. The last thing she wanted to do was go back to the Nelsons' and sit agonising over her prospects all afternoon. Nor could she seek sympathy from Katy or Pam, because that would involve mentioning the existence of a potential miracle cure, which she had been expressly forbidden to do. Sister Parkes was right about that at least. It would be wrong to raise false hopes. That was the last thing Molly wanted. But what should she do? Where could she go?

Behind her she heard a whistle, a whoosh of steam and the dull, grinding vibration of a train pulling out of Clapham Junction station towards central London. Molly realised she was standing in the exact same spot where she had met the blind man all those weeks ago. 'Your moment will come,' he had said. Well, her moment certainly hadn't come yet. And it was unlikely to come in Matron's office first thing tomorrow morning either.

So much for not taking no for an answer, she reflected sourly. She wondered what Ward Frazer would do if he was in her shoes. And then she felt her heart do a double beat in her chest. It left her feeling faint and oddly light-headed.

No, she thought. No, I can't. Sister Parkes would kill me. She would crucify me. She would flay me alive.

Molly hadn't been into central London since she had taken George to the Potato Fair. On that occasion they had taken the train to Victoria and then the number 2 bus to Oxford Street. This time she stayed on the bus as far as Paddington station. Almost exactly one hour after leaving the Wilhelmina, she found herself standing in front of the red and white arched facade of St Mary's Hospital.

Huge and turreted, it was built to impress. A fine example of Victorian philanthropic vision. Daunted, but trying to remain resolute, Molly made her way through the heavily sandbagged front entrance.

Inside, she found herself in an imposing hallway. At the far side she could dimly perceive an elderly porter sitting behind a reception desk. Approaching him warily, her heels clicking loudly on the floor, she cleared her throat. 'I was wondering if it would be possible to see Professor Fleming,' she said.

'Are you a journalist?'

Molly wondered if the man was blind. It was rather dark, but all the same, she was clearly wearing a nurse's cloak and cap. 'No,' she said. 'I'm a nurse from the Wilhelmina Hospital at Clapham Junction.'

The old man shrugged. 'They are expecting a journalist up there, that's all. They asked me to get someone to show him up.'

'Well maybe you can get someone to show me up instead,' Molly suggested.

The man looked at her doubtfully, but then he spotted another porter crossing the hallway. 'Oi, Harry, can you show this young lady up to the inoculation department.'

All hospitals used older men as porters these days, because most men of fighting age had been called up, but Harry looked almost too old to work at all, and it was as much as he could do to get up the stairs. The ascent certainly didn't leave him enough breath to talk. But Molly was glad; she didn't want to have to answer any awkward questions. She was too busy working out her next step. It was too much to hope that this old fellow was simply going to usher her straight into Professor Fleming's office without any further checks or queries.

She was right. The inoculation department had its own reception desk, and it was manned by a sour-faced RGN staff nurse in a highly starched triangular cap.

'Can I help you?'

Molly quailed under her steely stare. 'I was hoping to have a quick word with Professor Fleming,' she said.

The nurse's brows rose. 'And you are?'

'Nurse Coogan.'

'Is he expecting you?'

'Well, no, but—'

'Then I'm sorry, Professor Fleming is very busy today.'

'But I really need to see him. I want to ask—'

A loud buzzer sounded on the nurse's desk. She stood up at once. Eyeing Molly coldly as she stepped round the desk towards a side door bearing a No Admittance notice, she said, 'I'm afraid the professor doesn't see unsolicited visitors. Will you find your own way out?'

'But …'

The nurse was gone and Molly was left staring at the closed door.

Before she could move, the entrance door opened and she heard the wheezing breath of Harry the porter once more. This time he was ushering in a thin man in a homburg, spectacles and a tweed suit.

This must be the journalist. He didn't notice Molly and was just about to ring the bell for attention when she stepped forward. 'Excuse me, sir, but are you here to talk to Professor Fleming?'

'Yes, indeed I am,' the man responded, swinging round in surprise. 'Are you his assistant?'

'No, not at all,' Molly said. 'I wanted to talk to him too, but they won't let me.'

'I am sorry to hear that,' the journalist said politely. 'What did you want to talk to him about?'

'I work at another hospital. I am nursing a patient there, a friend, who is dying of a septic infection. I was hoping Professor Fleming might let us try some of his new penicillin drug on her.'

The journalist's spectacles had steamed up, perhaps as a result of the arduous climb up the interminable stairs. Now he took them off and polished them on a cloth he took out of his pocket. 'But they won't let you see him?'

'No.' Molly stopped, realising that the No Admittance door was open and a man was standing in the opening.

He had swept-back blonde-grey hair and prominent, rather staring eyes, and was wearing a dark suit and a small, very neat bow tie. Ignoring Molly, he came forward and shook hands briskly with the journalist. 'Mr Wainwright? How do you do?' He spoke with a clipped upper-class accent

113

that rather belied his general air of geniality. 'I'm Professor Fleming. Perhaps you would like to come through to my laboratory?'

The journalist took a step back. 'I believe this young lady is before me. She wanted to ask if—'

'Yes, yes, I heard what she said,' Professor Fleming interrupted smoothly. He spread his hands in a clearly well-practised gesture of regret. 'But I'm afraid we don't keep any penicillin here at St Mary's.' He turned back to the journalist with a man-to-man smile. 'There is as yet, in actual fact, very little in existence at all. But if the extraction techniques can be refined, I believe we may well, in the future, be looking at a wonder drug.'

Molly was taken aback by his total indifference to Helen's plight. She felt herself flush. 'But ...'

But Professor Fleming was patting the journalist on the shoulder in a gesture of bonhomie. 'Now, Wainwright, if you'd like to follow me, I'll show you where I made my discovery.'

So that was that, Molly thought. Another failure. The end of the road. The end of Helen.

But instead of following Professor Fleming directly, the journalist put his hand in his pocket and handed Molly a card. 'I'll see what I can find out for you,' he murmured. 'Telephone me at my office at five o'clock.'

It was a long wait and it was very cold. And quickly getting dark too.

Molly would have liked to buy something to eat or drink, but she was down to her last few pennies and she needed to keep them for the telephone call. She didn't even dare spend them on a bus ticket. So she had walked all the way back to Victoria, via Bayswater and Hyde Park. She then spent the next hour loitering around the station, pacing back and forward past the telephone kiosks on Grosvenor Street, waiting for five o'clock.

When the moment eventually came, she dialled carefully. Despite the cold, her palms were clammy. She had never used a telephone kiosk before, but she knew you had to press button A when the person answered. She heard the first penny clunk into the metal box.

'*Daily Mirror*. Good afternoon. Can I help you?'

'Can I speak to Mr Wainwright, please?'

'Please hold the line.'

Molly heard a series of metallic pips and frantically thrust another penny into the slot. And another.

'I'm afraid he's not at his desk. Would you like to leave a message?'

Molly's heart sank. There was no point. He couldn't ring her back even if he wanted to. And she didn't have enough money to try again later. She was going to have to walk all the way back to Clapham in the dark as it was.

'My name is Molly Coogan,' she said helplessly as the pips went yet again. 'He asked me to telephone him at five o'clock.'

'Ah yes,' the voice said. 'I have a message for you. It reads: *Penicillin is being developed by Professor Florey at Sir William Dunn School of Pathology at Oxford University. Possibly worth a try for your friend. Good luck.*'

Chapter Nine

'Guess what?' Louise leaned over the bar. 'My friend Lucinda Veale is throwing a party in Henley. Everyone will be there and she wants you and Ward to come.'

'But I don't know Lucinda Veale,' Katy objected.

'Of course you do,' Louise said. 'She's a friend of Ward's. She came to your wedding.'

'Did she?' Katy said doubtfully. 'I don't remember her. But then of course my wedding passed in a complete blur. Adolf Hitler could have been there for all I knew.' She hesitated. 'So how well does Ward know her? He's never mentioned her since.'

'Ward used to be friendly with Lucinda's brother Ralph,' Louise said. 'Poor old Ralph was killed early on in the war, at Dunkirk I think. Anyway, when I told Lucinda that Ward had come home, she was desperate to see him again. Everyone is going to be there. All the old Lucie Clayton gang. You must come.'

'Mm.' Katy wiped a cloth over the bar. She didn't like the sound of being paraded in front of Louise's fancy finishing-school friends; already she could imagine their nicely plucked eyebrows rising when they discovered she ran a pub, smirking behind their well-manicured hands at the thought someone like Ward falling for a girl from the back streets of Clapham.

'I'm not in the mood for a party,' she said. 'Not with Helen being so bad.'

Louise made a face. 'I know. It's awful. I can't bear to see her any more. It's too upsetting. But the party's not until March.'

Katy didn't respond; she couldn't trust herself to speak. Louise had been friends with Helen much longer than she had. Helen had even stayed in the Rutherfords' house for a while. And now Louise couldn't even bring herself to visit her friend in her hour of need.

'I so wish Jack could come,' Louise went on, blithely unaware that Katy was fighting the urge to slap her across the face with the wet cloth. 'I hate going to things on my own. And I can hardly take Aaref. Lucinda would have a fit if I turned up with a Jewish black-marketeer. Maybe I'll ask Douglas to escort me. He'll be commissioned by then and Coldstream

116

officers have a really smart dress uniform.'

'Aaref isn't a black-marketeer,' Katy said. He was a fixer and a finder. But she didn't think he did anything downright illegal. She hoped he didn't anyway, because she'd just asked him to find her some new beer glasses, although how she was going to afford them was anyone's guess. Ward would offer to pay for them, of course, but it had become a matter of pride to her to keep the pub going without asking him for help. She knew he respected her for making a success of the business, and she didn't want to lose that respect. But she couldn't have done it without Aaref's help, and she didn't approve of Louise talking about him so dismissively. Aaref was worth a hundred times more than her nasty little brother Douglas.

Louise shrugged. 'Oh well, whatever he is, he's not suitable for Lucinda's party.'

'Then why do you spend so much time with him?' Katy said crossly. 'It's not fair on him to lead him up the garden path all the time.'

Louise tossed her head. 'I'm lonely, that's all. I don't see there's anything so wrong with going out to the cinema occasionally with a friend.'

'And how does Jack feel about that?' Katy asked sweetly.

'Jack doesn't know,' Louse said. 'But it's his fault for never coming home to see me.'

'For goodness' sake, Louise.' Katy could bear it no longer. 'You knew Jack was a naval officer when you married him.'

'Oh, don't be such a spoilsport, Katy.' Louise pouted. 'I can't help it if Aaref's sweet on me. He knows I love Jack. I'm not doing anything wrong. I'm only looking for a bit of fun. We all need a bit of fun. That's why I told you about Lucinda's party. But if you don't want to go, maybe Ward will take me instead.'

And he probably would too, Katy thought, if Louise gave him one of her little-girl-lost looks. That was the problem with Ward. He was too kind. But if Louise thought Katy would let him go to a fancy party full of glamorous, husbandless women on his own, she had another think coming.

'Goodness, is that the time?' she said. 'Sorry, Louise. I can't chat any more. I've got a million things to do before opening time.'

It was a long walk back to Clapham, and by the time she got to Lavender Road, Molly's feet felt like they'd been through Pam Nelson's mangle. And she was still no nearer to knowing what she should do next.

She had to report to Matron the following morning. If she missed that appointment, her nursing career would be over. On the other hand, if she didn't go to Oxford to follow up the journalist's lead, then Helen's life would be over.

To be honest, it would probably be over anyway, because the likelihood of getting any penicillin was one in a million. Or maybe ten million. Or a billion. And even then it might not work. It might even speed Helen's demise. Molly knew from her midnight reading that the toxicity of penicillin was one of the major problems hindering its development.

No, it was a ridiculous idea. It was an impossible task. She was crazy to even be thinking about it.

But the truth was that she had grown fond of Helen. Class didn't count for much when you were at death's door. And Helen had been so brave, so uncomplaining. Molly knew she herself would have made much more fuss. The chickenpox had been bad enough. She didn't have a tenth of Helen's resilience.

And she had grown fond of Helen's father too. Not that she had spoken to him much, hardly at all in fact, but she had seen the sparkle fading out of his eyes as he gradually came to terms with the fact that he was about to lose his only child. And yet he never lost his well-bred courtesy. He had always stood up to open the door for her as she left the room.

And then there was Ward. He had tried so hard. Molly couldn't bear the thought of all that effort being wasted. All his hopes being dashed.

She hesitated a moment outside the Flag and Garter, but then walked on. Much as she longed to ask Katy for help, for advice, it wasn't the right moment. Not with the pub full of people.

In the end, Molly didn't ask advice from anyone. She made her own decision. She woke up early, took the last few pound notes out of her savings box and let herself out of the house into the cold dawn.

As she once again boarded a train from Clapham Junction station, she tried not to think of Matron waiting expectantly for her in her office. She tried not to think of the wrath and retribution that would fall on her head. Defying a direct order from Sister Parkes was not going to have a pleasant outcome.

But there was enough to worry about without adding that into the mix. It wasn't just the prospect of arriving unannounced at the Sir William Dunn laboratory, it was the journey itself. Molly had spent her entire life in London. She had travelled the ten or so miles to Croydon for her interview at the maternity hospital a few months ago, but she had never been as far afield as Oxford. Once or twice as a child she had been taken on a charabanc coach trip to the seaside, but that was the extent of her travels.

So Oxford, when she finally got there three hours later, was a revelation. As she walked from the station into the centre of town, she felt she had somehow been transported into another time. All the magnificent college buildings were intact; there were no gaps or craters or boarded-up windows.

She had vaguely expected to see students with mortar boards and gowns, but there were none in evidence. Probably they had all joined up, like every other young man in the country. But despite the overcast skies and the icy wind, the ordinary people in the streets looked lively and well-to-do. Admittedly there were some military personnel about, and a few desultory sandbags banked up here and there, but apart from that, it seemed as though the war had somehow passed Oxford by.

She was standing by an ornate memorial statue trying to get her bearings when a policeman approached and asked her if she was all right. 'You look a bit woebegone standing there, love.'

Molly felt a bit woebegone. All this affluence and architectural grandeur made her feel small and insignificant. How could she possibly take on the might of Oxford University? The very thought was ridiculous. She ought to go back to London right now and plead with Matron not to dismiss her. She wasn't qualified to do anything other than nursing. She supposed she might find some kind of unskilled war work, but women's pay was pitifully small, probably not enough to enable her to afford even Pam Nelson's reduced rent. Suddenly she felt rather frightened.

She turned her head away from the policeman towards the statue, which she saw had been erected almost exactly one hundred years before in grateful commemoration of *Thomas Cranmer, Nicholas Ridley, Hugh Latimer, Prelates of the Church of England, who near this spot yielded their bodies to be burned, bearing witness to the sacred truths which they had affirmed and maintained against the errors of the Church of Rome.* What a mad world we live in, Molly thought. A world where people are prepared to die for their beliefs.

Realising that the policeman was still waiting for a response, she tried to pull herself together. 'I'm fine, thank you,' she lied. 'I was just wondering why there's no bomb damage here.'

The policeman laughed sourly. 'They reckon that blighter Hitler has his eye on Oxford for his headquarters when he invades,' he said. 'That's why he's left us alone. So far at least.' His face hardened. 'But if he thinks he's going to set up shop here, he'll soon have another think coming. It'll be over my dead body, that's for certain.'

With that, he touched his helmet politely and was about to move away when Molly heard herself asking one last question.

'Do you know where the Sir William Dunn School of Pathology is?'

He thought for a moment, then nodded. 'Yes, I know it. Modern building up by the University Parks. Go on up the Broad here. Left at the top opposite the Sheldonian, on past Wadham College, you get a nice view of the gardens over the fence, then right, up South Parks Road.' He glanced up at the glowering sky. 'But I should get a shift on if that's where you're headed, because it looks to me as though it's about to rain.'

Lunchtime opening was in full swing at the Flag and Garter when Katy looked up and saw the incongruous sight of her old mentor Sister Morris entering the bar.

Sister Morris did not approve of public houses; in fact when Katy had left the Wilhelmina to reopen the pub after her father's death, Sister Morris had presented her with a bible to keep her mind on the straight and narrow. Unfortunately, the same bible was currently propping up a small keg of cider that Aaref had procured for Katy from some undisclosed source. But Katy was far too worried about why Sister Morris had come at all to worry about that. As far as she was concerned, the only thing that would have brought Sister into her pub at this time of day – at any time of day, come to that – was a crisis. And the most likely crisis, as things stood at the moment, was one concerning Helen de Burrel.

Even as Sister approached the bar, Katy could feel the blood leaving her face. 'Oh no,' she said, clutching the counter for support. 'Please, Sister, don't tell me. Is it Helen?'

Sister Morris glanced around with some distaste, as though assessing the pub for hygiene and cleanliness and finding both wanting. She fixed two nearby drinkers with a steely glance, causing them to retreat a few paces further along the bar. Then she turned her attention to Katy.

'No,' she said. 'Not directly. Although you must be aware that Lady Helen isn't long for this world. You should be preparing yourself for that eventuality. I don't expect a nurse of mine to give in to any unnecessarily excessive emotion.'

Katy refrained from pointing out that she was no longer one of Sister Morris's nurses. It sometimes seemed that being trained by Sister Morris was like joining the Italian Mafia: once in, you could never leave.

'No, it's Nurse Coogan that I've come about,' Sister Morris went on imperturbably.

'Molly?' Katy stared at her. 'What about her? Has something happened to her?'

'That's what I'm hoping you can tell me. When did you last see her?'

'The day before yesterday, I think, but why …?'

'So she didn't tell you what happened yesterday?'

Katy shook her head. 'What did happen yesterday?'

Sister Morris pursed her lips. 'She was sent home in some disgrace for being rude to a doctor.'

'Goodness.' Katy bit back a sudden giggle. She had often felt like being rude to the doctors herself but had never dared. 'How brave of her,' she said. 'Which doctor was it?'

Sister Morris glared at her. 'It is no laughing matter,' she said. 'Nurse Coogan had been instructed to report to Matron this morning but she didn't appear. I have just called at her lodgings, but according to her landlady, Mrs Nelson, she left the house very early this morning.' She hesitated. 'It seems that Sister Parkes was somewhat harsh with her yesterday and—'

'And now you are worried she might have thrown herself in the river?' Katy said.

'I would be very disappointed if a nurse trained at the Wilhelmina did anything like that,' Sister Morris retorted. 'But yes, I can't deny that we are concerned.'

Katy thought about it. She was sure Molly hadn't jumped in the river. But why hadn't she called in yesterday when she was sent home? Surely the pub would have been her first port of call in a crisis?

But then Molly hadn't been herself recently. Since even before the chickenpox. She had been even more reticent than usual. Thinking about it now, Katy realised that a kind of constraint had sprung up between them. And there had been that awful scene with Douglas Rutherford. Suddenly she began to feel worried. And guilty. She was conscious that since Ward had come back from Germany, her attention had been focused on him, perhaps at the expense of her friends.

Katy had to serve a customer then, but when that was done she poured two small glasses of sherry and put one in front of Sister Morris.

'It's medicinal,' she said before Sister could object. 'So what did Molly say to the doctor that made Sister Parkes so angry?'

Sister Morris took a reluctant sip of the sherry as though it was indeed some unpleasant medicine.

'She queried Lady Helen's treatment,' she said. 'She'd got it into her head that not enough was being done.'

Katy frowned. 'But what else could be done?'

Sister hesitated. 'There are rumours that a new drug is being developed,' she said at last. 'There is some suggestion that it could be particularly effective in the treatment of septicaemia.'

'There's a cure for septicaemia?' Katy blinked at her. 'I never knew that. So why on earth—'

'No,' Sister interposed quickly. 'There isn't. This drug is in its infancy. It may be a flash in the pan for all we know. But somehow Nurse Coogan had found out about it and she asked Dr ... one of the doctors about it.'

'And he said it wasn't available?'

'It *isn't* available,' Sister Morris said. She took another sip of the sherry. Not quite so reluctantly this time. 'That's the whole point. If it was available, every doctor in the world would be prescribing it. Goodness, can you imagine the difference such a drug would make?'

Katy could imagine. She could also imagine that it not yet being available for Helen de Burrel might be the straw that broke the camel's back as far as Molly was concerned.

'Molly shouldn't have been allowed to nurse Helen,' she said. 'It's distressing enough nursing terminally ill patients, let alone someone you know.'

Sister nodded. 'I agree. I wouldn't have allowed it myself.' But she did allow herself another sip of sherry. 'Apparently Lord de Burrel was rather persuasive.'

Katy downed the last of her sherry and glanced at the clock behind the bar. 'It's last orders now. As soon as I've closed up, I'll ask around and see if anyone knows anything.'

As she escorted Sister to the door, she thought of something else. 'Oh, and Sister, I wonder if you could do me a favour and call on Jen Carter on your way back. She's not recovered at all well from the chickenpox. I'm worried about her too.'

The policeman had been right. It was about to pour with rain. And not just ordinary rain; this was a hideous mixture of stinging sleet and water that came down in torrents, as though someone had opened a sluice gate in the sky. By the time Molly reached the Sir William Dunn building, she was completely drenched. As she ran across an enormous forecourt and scurried up one of the two curving flanks of stone steps to the imposing first-floor entrance, she was berating herself for not bringing a mackintosh or an umbrella with her.

There were four people already in the large panelled hallway. Two men and two women. They had clearly been talking, but as Molly burst through the door, bringing a great noisy, billowing gust of wind and rain with her, they stopped abruptly and stepped back in alarm.

At first Molly could hardly see them, her face was running with so much water. She had decided to wear her nurses' uniform in the hopes that it might give her some credibility, but now her cap had collapsed into a sodden mess on top of her head.

She was trying to wipe her face with the corner of her cloak when one of the women spoke. 'Can we help you?'

Her voice was cut-glass English, matching her haughty upper-class face and smart clothes. The other woman, equally well dressed, seemed faintly amused, but the two men just looked irritated by the interruption. They both wore tweed three-piece suits. But there the resemblance ended. One was tall and slim, with smooth, slicked-back hair and wire-framed glasses; the other was heavier, distinctly foreign-looking, with a thick black cap of hair, a prominent nose and an impressive moustache. The four of them made an intimidating group, and Molly stared at them in considerable dismay. In comparison to their businesslike bearing and attire, she must look like some kind of demented gnome that had just scrambled out of a garden pond.

'I'm sorry to disturb you,' she stammered, aware that a puddle was forming round her feet. 'But I'm looking for Professor Florey.'

The taller of the two men spread his hands. 'Well, it seems you found me. I am Professor Florey.' He spoke with an accent Molly couldn't quite place. 'What can I do for you?'

Completely taken aback, Molly didn't know what to say. She had fully expected to be fobbed off, or passed from pillar to post. She certainly hadn't expected to stumble upon the person she needed the moment she stepped through the door. They were all looking at her expectantly now. She felt sudden heat rushing to her cheeks.

'I am trying to find some penicillin for a sick friend,' she said.

The two men exchanged glances. 'And so it starts,' Professor Florey said. He spoke with a kind of weary resignation. He nodded at the haughty-faced woman. 'I think you'd better deal with this, Margaret.' He pronounced the name as though it was missing the first r.

The woman nodded and moved forward, but before she could say anything, Molly rushed on. 'The thing is, I met Dr Fleming at St Mary's in London, and he—'

Professor Florey had been about to turn away, but at that he swung back with a frown. 'You've seen Fleming?'

'Yes.'

'And he sent you here?'

His voice was sharp, and Molly flinched. 'No, he told me he couldn't help me, but—'

Professor Florey made an impatient gesture. She thought she heard him say, 'Bloody man,' under his breath as he and the heavy black-haired man moved away.

The hard-faced woman stepped forward and tried to steer her back towards the door. 'Well I'm afraid we can't help you either. Penicillin is in very short supply. We can't even produce enough for our own research. It is certainly not available to the general public.'

Molly's heart sank. 'I know, but I've come all the way from London.'

'Then you have had a wasted journey. And I have to say that it was wrong of you to come barging in here without an appointment.'

'Nonsense!'

The fourth member of the group suddenly spoke for the first time, and Molly jumped in surprise, because her voice was surprisingly loud and off key. Oddly, she seemed to have the same twangy accent as Professor Florey. 'A nurse who shows initiative,' she said in the same strident tone. 'That's a rare thing.'

Staring at her in astonishment, Molly suddenly noticed that she was wearing a huge tortoiseshell ear trumpet. Apart from that encumbrance, she was a nice-looking woman, with wavy hair swept back off a high forehead.

'Show some heart, Margaret,' she bellowed. 'The poor girl is soaked to the skin. The least we can do is let her dry off.'

The stern-faced lady bristled. She too was speaking loudly now, and very clearly, as though to a gormless child. 'I can't be wasting time with everyone who wanders in off the street.'

'She hasn't wandered in off the street. She already explained that she has come from London specifically to see my husband.'

'But Ethel, your husband has decreed that all supplicants must be turned away. He doesn't want—'

'I don't care what he has decreed,' the deaf lady snapped. 'It's only common courtesy after all.'

Molly stared from one to the other. There was clearly no love lost here. And Ethel, the deaf lady, was Professor Florey's wife?

'No, no. Please don't worry,' she stammered, embarrassed to have these two terrifying women fighting over her. 'I'd just hoped—'

'You've already told us what you hoped,' the deaf lady bellowed. 'Hang up that wet cloak by the radiator there. While it dries I'll show you the laboratory, and then perhaps you will understand why we can't help you.'

'Good God,' Jen exclaimed when she opened the door to an imperious knock and found Sister Morris standing on the step. 'What are you doing here?'

'I had come to visit you,' Sister Morris said, drawing herself up to her full impressive height. 'But if you are going to blaspheme, I'll go away again.'

Jen groaned inwardly and stepped back. She was still in her dressing gown, and faced with Sister Morris in full nursing regalia, she felt at a distinct disadvantage. Jen had first encountered Sister Morris when Katy was a trainee nurse at the Wilhelmina at the beginning of the war. The old battleaxe had been poking her nose into their business ever since. Although give her her due, which at this moment Jen was reluctant to do, she had also been very helpful over various medical issues that had cropped up in the intervening years.

Leading the way along the passage into the kitchen, Jen moved a couple of dirty teacups off the table. There was nothing she could do about the dirty dishes on the sideboard or the crumbs on the floor, the result of a dripping sandwich Angie had made herself for breakfast before rushing off to work at the café, late as usual.

Sure enough, Sister Morris was looking around with distaste. 'Your mother works long hours in her café. I'd have thought the least you could do is keep the house clean and tidy for her.'

Gritting her teeth, Jen watched Sister Morris draw out a chair and sit down. Some of the kitchen chairs were a bit wobbly. In former times Jen might have relished the idea of Sister Morris collapsing on to the floor in disarray. She would have loved to catch a glimpse of Sister's underwear. She had always assumed it would consist of some kind of enormous chastity belt, or at the very least a pair of voluminous bloomers big enough to act as barrage balloons if necessary. But today she was glad that Sister Morris had chosen a strong chair. She didn't have the energy to find things like that amusing any more, let alone to haul Sister back on to her feet.

She sat down opposite her. 'I'm sure you didn't come here just to tell me to clear up my sister's crumbs, did you?'

'No.' Sister Morris glanced at the sticky table and folded her hands carefully in her lap. 'I came because I heard you were still feeling unwell and I wondered if I could help.'

'I doubt it,' Jen said ungraciously.

'What are your symptoms?'

Jen sighed impatiently. 'Oh, I don't know. I just feel tired all the time.'

'Do you have a temperature? Any aches and pains? A rash?'

Jen could feel Sister Morris's sharp eyes on her and she shook her head. 'No,' she said crossly. 'That's the problem. Nobody takes me seriously because I've got nothing to show for it any more except that I feel ill.'

Sister Morris took off her gloves and laid them on the table. Then she undid the top clasp on her cloak, lifted her fob watch and reached across to grasp Jen's wrist. After taking her pulse, she let go of Jen's arm and leaned over to pull down her lower eyelid instead.

'You look rather anaemic,' she observed, sitting back in her chair. 'Are you eating properly?'

'I've lost my appetite,' Jen said. 'Along with everything else.'

'But your mother is such a good cook. I saw an article about her in the paper.'

Jen groaned inwardly. Her mother had been cock-a-hoop since that blasted article had come out. According to Angie, they had been rushed off their feet in the café.

'Might you be pregnant?'

'What!' Jen almost fell off her chair at the unexpected question. 'No, of course I'm not pregnant.' She rolled her eyes. 'Chance would be a fine thing.'

Sister Morris eyed her closely. 'What do you mean by that?'

'I don't mean anything by it,' Jen said crossly. 'But I can assure you I'm not pregnant.'

'Your mother mentioned to me that you're stepping out with a theatre director.'

'Well she's wrong,' Jen said. 'I'm not seeing him any more.'

'And why is that?'

Jen glared at her. 'It's none of your business. Or my mother's. But if you must know, it's because while I had the chickenpox, he started seeing someone else.'

'Hm,' Sister Morris said.

'What do you mean, *hm*?'

Sister studied her thoughtfully. 'It is conceivable that you have picked up some kind of post-traumatic virus. But I suspect that what is actually happening is that you are allowing yourself to fall into a depression.'

'I'm not allowing myself to do anything. I'm just feeling ill.'

'If you think you are ill, you will feel ill. If you think you aren't hungry, you won't be hungry. Your thoughts affect your feelings.'

'It's nothing to do with how I think,' Jen said impatiently. 'It's reality. I've lost my job and my looks and my man. On top of that, I'm ill. It's a disaster.'

'Nonsense,' Sister said briskly. 'There will be other jobs. And other men.' She stood and picked up her gloves, grimacing as one of them stuck slightly to a smear of lard on the table. 'There are a lot of people in the world at the moment in very much worse predicaments than you. You should think about that.'

She did up the clasp on her hospital cloak. 'I won't tell you to pull yourself together, because that never helps anyone. But that's what I expect you to do. And the first thing you can do is get dressed, tidy up this house, then go to the chemist and buy yourself some cod liver oil.'

She saw Jen's expression. 'It's not pleasant, but it is very beneficial for lifting the spirits. Dr Goodacre swears by it. He takes a teaspoon every morning.'

Ignoring Jen's sudden choke of amusement, she turned abruptly and marched off down the passage. At the door, she stopped. 'I don't suppose you happen to have seen Nurse Coogan today?'

Jen shook her head. 'No. Why?'

Sister Morris pursed her lips. 'Because she seems to have disappeared.'

Jen stared at her for a moment, then burst out laughing. The first genuine laugh she had uttered for a long time. 'That's the best news I've heard in weeks,' she said. 'Maybe I don't need the cod liver oil after all!'

'Extracting penicillin is an enormously complicated procedure,' Ethel Florey said as she escorted Molly through a swing door and along a rather dark corridor. 'It is inherently unstable. My husband and his team have been working on it for years.'

'But what about Professor Fleming?' Molly began in surprise. 'I thought he …?'

Ethel Florey sniffed. 'Fleming discovered the antibacterial property of a certain culture of *Penicillium* many years ago,' she said. 'He named it penicillin, but he gave up on it when he was unable to isolate it in a way that retained its potency. All the subsequent work has been done here.'

She opened the door of a small laboratory. 'This is my husband's original counter-current extraction apparatus.' Following her into the room, Molly stopped and stared in amazement.

She hadn't known what to expect, but it certainly wasn't a dozen old milk churns, a six-foot bathtub and any number of bedpans, an old bookcase and a doorbell all joined together by metal pipes, wooden levers and dripping bottle contraptions. It looked like some kind of crazy jerry-built apparatus a mad amateur scientist might construct in his garage.

'Perhaps this explains why penicillin is not yet commercially available,' Ethel Florey said drily. 'Despite its appearance, this apparatus took years to perfect. Even now, we struggle to make enough penicillin to carry out clinical trials. And without satisfactory trial results, we cannot attract the funds or the commercial interest to develop the product further.' She shrugged her elegant shoulders. 'It doesn't help that this country's manufacturing capacity has been drastically reduced by the bombing. Plus, I am sure you are aware that the medical profession here is very conservative, somewhat hidebound by ethics and convention, and unwilling to take up new ideas.'

'Oh yes. I know that only too well,' Molly agreed. 'I'm already in trouble for mentioning to the doctor treating my friend that penicillin had been proved effective against staphylococcal infection. When they find out that I came here, I'll probably lose my job.'

127

Mrs Florey glanced at her. 'And yet you still came?'

Molly nodded. 'I had to do something. I had to try ...' She stopped and turned away as tears unexpectedly stung her eyes.

Ethel Florey closed the door of the lab and, after a moment's hesitation, led the way to a small, warm book-lined office. She sat down behind the desk and waved Molly to a chair on the other side.

'Tell me about your friend,' she said. 'What caused the original infection?'

Despite Mrs Florey's abrupt manner and extraordinary barking voice, Molly felt she could like this woman. She particularly liked the way she had put the snooty Margaret in her place earlier.

'It's all very hush-hush,' she said. 'But perhaps that doesn't matter so much now.' Reminding herself to speak up, she told Mrs Florey what she had gleaned about Helen's secret role in France. The sinking of the French fleet. The fatal gunfight at the harbour. Her escape on the submarine. The journey back from Oran on the hospital ship. And her subsequent deterioration.

'What is her current condition?'

Defeatedly, Molly listed Helen's symptoms: the high fever, the staphylococcal blood poisoning, the streptococcus bacterial infection of lungs and liver, the signs of meningitis, the constant suppuration of pus and phlegm from the shoulder wound.

'What about her family?' Ethel Florey asked. 'Next of kin? What do they feel about your visit here?'

'It's just her father,' Molly said. 'Lord de Burrel. I haven't said anything to him. I didn't want to raise any false hopes.'

'But you felt he would be receptive to an experimental treatment?'

'Oh yes,' Molly nodded. 'I think he'd agree to anything if there was the slightest chance of saving her.'

There was a pause. Ethel Florey looked at her thoughtfully. 'He is, of course, entitled to ask for a second opinion.'

'Yes, I suppose so,' Molly said doubtfully. 'But I don't know who he could ... ' She stopped and looked up. There was something in the woman's face, in her voice. 'Surely you don't mean ... your husband? But he didn't seem very ...'

Ethel Florey smiled. 'I actually meant myself,' she said. 'I am a doctor too.'

'I'm sorry,' Molly stammered, aghast. 'I didn't know. I've never met a lady doctor before. I didn't know such a thing existed.'

Ethel Florey lifted her shoulders. 'There aren't that many of us. I did my medical training in Australia. There is less prejudice against women there.'

She gave a sudden snort, as though at a private joke. 'In some ways.'

'And you mean … you'd be prepared …?' Molly stared at her blankly. Her brain was reeling. She couldn't quite take it in.

'I am in charge of the clinical trials for the penicillin project,' Ethel Florey said briskly. 'And as it happens, I am going to be in London tomorrow. I'd like to take a look at your friend. From what you have told me, it sounds like a rather interesting case.'

Molly tried to react. She suddenly felt light-headed. She tried to speak, but all that came out was a dry croak.

Before she could try again, Dr Florey held up her hand. 'But we have to go about this the right way. There are professional courtesies and procedures that need to be observed. We also have to be discreet. My husband is very concerned that if word gets out we will be inundated with requests that he can't satisfy.' She fixed Molly with a beady eye. 'And you must understand that even if your friend is presenting suitable symptoms, I'm still not promising anything. This drug is in its infancy. We have had successes, but we have also had tragic failures.'

'Yes, yes, I understand,' Molly said. But she wasn't really listening. Not any more. She couldn't believe it. She couldn't think. She couldn't concentrate. Somehow, miraculously, she had done it. She had succeeded in her quest.

If only Helen could just hang on for one more day.

Chapter Ten

As soon as she had got rid of her last customer, Katy lifted Malcolm out of his playpen, grabbed a blanket and went out into the back yard to get the pram out of the shed. She hadn't used the pram much recently, because Malcolm didn't like being in it now he could walk. But she didn't have time to dawdle along the street at his toddling pace today. When she opened the shed door, however, she recoiled in horror. The pram was there all right, or at least the carriage section was, but it no longer had any wheels.

'Oh no,' Katy groaned. First it had been the Spitfire Fund box, then her beer glasses, and now half of her pram had gone missing. She just hoped someone didn't pinch Malcolm as well. Or Ward, she thought sourly.

Hitching a protesting Malcolm up on to her hip, she ran back through the pub and let herself out of the front door, locking it carefully behind her.

A moment later, she was knocking on Pam Nelson's door. Pam answered holding baby Helen in her arms.

'I know it's a lot to ask, but could you watch Malcolm for me?' Katy asked. 'I'm going to go down to the hospital now to see if there's any news of Molly. And to see Helen.' She saw Pam's expression. 'I know. I don't think she's got long now. She didn't know me when I went yesterday.'

Tears sprang to Pam's eyes. She brushed them away crossly. 'What on earth is Molly doing running off now? It's not as though we haven't got enough to worry about.'

Fifteen minutes later, Katy was in the Wilhelmina Private Block. The first person she saw as she came through the swing door was Lord de Burrel. She had met him at the hospital several times before, but he had never looked as distraught as he did today. He was holding a silver cigarette case in his hand, revolving it backwards and forwards through his fingers. For an awful moment Katy thought the worst had already happened. But he looked up as he saw her.

'Ah, Mrs Frazer. How are you today?'

'Very well, thank you,' Katy responded. 'How are you?' How British we are, she thought. And now he'll say he's fine, when actually he's clearly close to despair.

But to her surprise, he didn't. Instead he hesitated for a moment, then drew her to one side. 'To be perfectly honest, I am in somewhat of a quandary,' he said. 'Apparently some kind of specialist in septic medicine research has telephoned from Oxford University asking if she can see Helen tomorrow.'

Katy gaped at him. 'Goodness,' she said. 'But surely that would be …?'

He lifted his shoulders impatiently. 'Yes. Yes. It sounds easy. The problem is that Dr Mallet doesn't feel that Helen will survive the night without another blood transfusion. And he is not prepared to …' his fingers clenched white on the silver cigarette case, 'to prolong her agony just so that some "damn fool" busybody, as he put it, can add a statistic to her academic thesis.'

Katy flinched. 'But is there a chance that this person could help Helen?'

'Not according to Mallet. He says her condition is too far advanced. Nothing short of a miracle will save her now.' Lord de Burrel's voice caught. 'He says it would be kinder to let her slip away.' He took a cigarette out of the case and looked at it thoughtfully. 'I wish I knew someone who could advise me, but the only decent physician I know is Lord Moran, and he's still out in Casablanca with Winston.'

Katy closed her eyes. Then opened them again. A miracle? According to Sister Morris, Molly had been talking about some kind of new miracle drug before she disappeared. That was exactly what her spat with Dr Mallet had been about.

'Has anyone mentioned Nurse Coogan?' she asked suddenly. 'Molly Coogan?'

Lord de Burrel looked startled at the abrupt change of subject. 'The little nurse Helen likes?' He shook his head. 'No, not to me. Why do you ask?'

'Because I think this might be something to do with her.' The more Katy thought about it, the more it made sense. It seemed incredible. But she was sure she was right. 'I think she may have tracked down something that might help. A new drug. I'm sure it's only a very small chance, and it may indeed be too late, but it might be a chance nevertheless.' She squared her shoulders. 'Lord de Burrel, I think you should insist on the transfusion. And if that beastly Dr Mallet won't do it, then we'll have to find a doctor who will.'

It was gone ten o'clock in the evening when Molly eventually arrived back in Lavender Road. The journey had been interminable: an air-raid warning had kept the train stationary and blacked out in Didcot station for an hour, and she had missed her connection at Reading. What was more, it was raining again, and her shoes squelched uncomfortably as she plodded along following the dim circle of light on the wet pavement thrown by her shaded torch.

Expecting Pam and Alan to be in bed, she let herself in quietly, but was surprised to find them still sitting up by the fire.

'Molly, thank goodness!' Pam jumped up. 'Are you all right? Is it really true you've been to Oxford about a new treatment for Helen?'

'Well, yes,' Molly stammered, blinking against the light. 'But how on earth did …?'

'Word travels fast in Lavender Road,' Alan said drily. He took Molly's coat.

'But how …?' Molly started again. Then she stopped and put her hand on the back of Pam's chair. She felt very odd. Shivery, and strangely empty. Belatedly she realised she hadn't eaten or drunk anything all day. A second later, her vision blurred and she collapsed in a dead faint on the floor at Alan's feet.

In the end it was Dr Goodacre who authorised the transfusion. And it was Sister Morris who had stepped in to resolve the situation when Dr Mallet predictably refused to co-operate.

'What is the meaning of this intrusion?' she had snapped when Katy burst on to the Ethel Barnet Ward in the middle of her afternoon round. Leaving a cluster of startled nurses by a patient's bedside, she had borne down on Katy like a battleship in full attack.

In former times, as a probationer nurse, Katy would have quailed under the lash of Sister Morris's tongue, but she knew her better now, and was aware that a warm heart lay carefully concealed behind that enormous, awe-inspiring bosom.

Drawing Sister Morris out into the corridor, she had explained the situation.

'This is most irregular,' Sister said. 'It flies in the face of all normal hospital procedures. And if Nurse Coogan really is behind it, I shall certainly have something to say to her.'

'I know, I know,' Katy said. 'But this is a life-and-death situation. What Lord de Burrel needs is a forward-looking doctor. Someone interested in new ideas, someone who might just be prepared to give Helen one last chance.' She crossed her fingers behind her back. 'Someone like you, Sister, who is prepared always to put the patient first.'

Sister eyed Katy suspiciously, then made her decision. 'Leave it to me,' she said. 'I'll have a word with Dr Goodacre.'

'Oh thank you,' Katy said. 'I was hoping you were going to say that.'

Jen couldn't sleep. It was ironic that she felt so tired all the time but couldn't sleep at night. She got out of bed, pulled on her dressing gown and crept downstairs. It was still warm in the front room. Joyce had had a fire in there earlier while she listened to the wireless and darned her stockings. Through the floorboards, Jen had heard the over-jolly voices of *ITMA*, followed by the restrainedly triumphant tone of a newsreader announcing that Berlin had been bombed in broad daylight just as Goering was about to deliver a broadcast celebrating ten years of Nazism. But when that idiot Lord Haw-Haw had come on afterwards with his fake upper-class 'Jarmany calling, Jarmany calling' voice, Joyce had abruptly turned the wireless off.

Angie had been out as usual; Jen didn't know where. Goodness only knew what she got up to at all hours of the night. Tonight Jen had heard her creep in at midnight. Creep, that was a joke. Angie didn't seem to grasp the meaning of the word. Her efforts to climb the stairs quietly reminded Jen of a stampede of buffalo she had once seen in a Western. That was probably what had woken her up. Either that or the car pulling up outside Gillian James's house.

During her self-imposed incarceration, Jen had become increasingly intrigued by the comings and goings over the road. It was perfectly clear that Gillian James was a kept woman. And the man keeping her was the officer with the fancy staff car. He obviously kept her pretty well. She was always having her hair done, and she seemed to have a good range of clothes and hats, although goodness knew where she got them, because there was nothing in the shops any more.

Hearing something in the street, Jen turned off the lamp and lifted the corner of the blackout. The car was indeed there. Silhouetted in the thin moonlight against the house behind. A big dark shape, like a great crouching frog. It was late for Gillian James's visitor to be calling. Normally he came at about ten and left around midnight. Two hours was apparently enough for him to get whatever he came for. And Jen was pretty sure it wasn't dinner.

As her eyes accustomed themselves to the darkness, Jen suddenly realised that the noise she could hear was voices. Gillian James's front door was open and she was out on the path arguing with the driver of the staff car. Jen couldn't hear the exact words, but she could get the drift of it. It wasn't hard to work out what was going on. It was like watching an overacted improvisation exercise in a drama class. The driver had obviously been sent round by his commanding officer to deliver some kind of message and, after having rather too many drinks, had decided to try his own luck with the racy widow.

Jen didn't really blame him. He must have spotted Gillian James in her lacy, revealing negligee often enough as she said goodbye to his boss. The sight of a beauty like her, half naked, wanton and dishevelled, was probably enough to drive any man wild. Especially one with too much booze inside him. Jen knew about drunks. Her own father had been a drinker. The whole family had suffered when he had come home with a skinful. Joyce had taken the brunt of it, of course. More than she'd ever let on, probably. Maybe that was why she was still holding poor old Lorenz at arm's length.

As the voices got louder, Jen wondered if she should go and intervene. But it wasn't any of her business. And then, after another brief altercation, Gillian retreated inside, the door closed and Jen saw the driver stagger back to the car. A minute later he had started it up, revved it violently and driven away rather jerkily up the road.

Glancing back at the house, Jen saw a flicker of movement in one of the windows as a curtain was redrawn, and realised she hadn't been the only person watching that little scene. Gillian's daughter had also been a silent observer.

Replacing the blackout, Jen sat back in her chair, hoping the girl hadn't seen her too. This is ridiculous, she said to herself. On top of everything else, I'm turning into some kind of awful old-spinsterish curtain-twitcher.

The next thing Molly knew, it was morning. Thin, low early February sunlight was slanting through the window. And Pam was standing by her bed holding a cup of tea.

'How are you feeling?'

Molly blinked at her in alarm. The only time Pam had ever brought her a cup of tea before was when she had the chickenpox. At the height of her fever. She felt oddly feverish now. Her brain was in turmoil. Images and thoughts jumbled in an incoherent panic. Trains. Foreign accents. Scientific apparatus. Milk churns. Bedpans. A telephone call.

'Oh no,' she said, sitting up. The bedroom looked just the same as always. Helen's things still stood neatly on the dressing table. Her dressing gown still hung on the back of the door. 'Please don't tell me it was all a dream.'

Pam put the cup and saucer down next to the alarm clock on the bedside table. 'No, it wasn't a dream. But you certainly overdid it. You were exhausted when you got back last night. And frozen to the bone. I think you should have a day in bed.'

Molly stared aghast at the clock and leaped out of bed. 'No, I can't possibly. I've got to go to the Wilhelmina.'

By the time she arrived at the hospital, it was already ten o'clock. She could hardly believe it was so late. Despite the porridge Pam had insisted she eat, she felt shaky and sick. She was going to be in such trouble. Pam had tried to calm her by recounting as much as she knew of the previous day's happenings at the hospital, but Molly wasn't convinced. She knew how the Wilhelmina worked. She knew only too well the rigid code of discipline.

And she realised at once that Pam's confidence had been misplaced. The first person she saw as she ran in, panting, was Nurse Spalding, one of the Private Block second-year nurses, who was pushing an empty trolley across the hall.

She stopped at once when she caught sight of Molly. 'Blimey, you've put the cat among the pigeons, that's for sure,' she said with poorly concealed glee. 'Sister Donaldson is hopping mad. I wouldn't want to be in your shoes.'

Trying to get her breath back, Molly caught sight of a new Winston Churchill poster on the wall by the porter's desk. *Your courage, Your cheerfulness, Your resolution will bring us Victory.* She glared at the pugnacious face behind the words. Helen de Burrel's courage and resolution had brought her to death's door.

Lifting her chin, she turned back to the nurse. 'There's a doctor from Oxford coming to see Helen de Burrel today. Dr Florey. Has she arrived yet?'

Nurse Spalding looked rather taken aback by Molly's sharp tone. 'Yes,' she said, rather more meekly. 'She's talking to Lord de Burrel and Dr Goodacre right now.'

'Has she seen Lady Helen yet?'

'I don't know.' She glanced up at the clock on the wall and smirked. 'All I know is that you've got to report to Matron. And sharpish. She was expecting you at eight thirty. I wish you luck!'

'Ah, Nurse Coogan,' Matron said coldly. 'How nice of you to rejoin us.'

Molly felt herself flush. 'I'm sorry. Matron. I know I'm in disgrace and I'm late and everything, but I can explain.'

'Unfortunately we don't have time for you to explain.' Matron's voice seemed to have come straight from the Arctic. 'Dr Florey has expressed a specific wish for you to assist her.' She paused and looked at Molly as though such a wish was beyond her comprehension. 'She is waiting for you in Private Block. So for the time being we will overlook the fact that you had absolutely no right to take matters into your own hands. That you disobeyed a direct order.'

Molly hung her head. 'I'm sorry, Matron,' she muttered.

'And so you should be. You have put us all in a very awkward situation.'

'I know,' Molly said. 'But if Dr Florey feels that penicillin could help Helen, then surely it will have been worthwhile?'

Matron's eyes narrowed sharply. 'That remains to be seen,' she said. Her voice was sceptical. 'I certainly hope so, for your sake.'

Molly looked up in surprise. '*I* hope so for Helen's sake.'

Matron regarded her in frigid silence for a moment. 'One thing I will say for you, Nurse Coogan, your heart is in the right place. However, you are not off the hook. I will decide what to do about you once this current situation is resolved.' Her lips tightened. 'One way or another. In the meantime, please remember that you are a Wilhelmina nurse, and from now on, try to behave accordingly.'

Molly was shocked by the sight of Helen. In the two days since she had last seen her, she seemed to have shrunk. The transfusion had only served to keep her alive, not to improve her condition. Already she was failing again. Molly could understand why Matron was dubious about Dr Florey's ability to treat her. You didn't have to be a nurse to know that Helen was at death's door. She was barely conscious and her breathing was laboured despite the oxygen mask over her face.

Dr Florey, dressed somewhat incongruously in a stylish navy-blue twinset, was in the process of examining her when Molly sidled into the room. Dr Goodacre was there too. As was Sister Donaldson.

'Ah, Nurse Coogan, there you are,' Dr Florey bellowed. Molly saw Sister Donaldson recoil in alarm. She clearly hadn't yet got used to Dr Florey's extraordinary style of speech. But it didn't stop her mouth tightening ominously as she caught sight of Molly.

'I must congratulate you, Nurse,' Dr Florey went on, oblivious. 'Your report of this patient's condition was exemplary.'

Leaving Molly flushing and Sister Donaldson looking as though someone had punched her in the stomach, Dr Florey blithely turned to Dr Goodacre. 'They call me a corpse-retriever in Oxford. I think we must agree that by any standard this is a very extreme case. However, I am prepared to proceed if you are, Dr Goodacre.'

Dr Goodacre looked delighted. 'Yes, yes, it would be an honour, Dr Florey. Penicillin indeed. Whoever would have thought we'd have a chance to trial it at the Wilhelmina?'

There was a moment's uneasy pause, but whatever anyone thought, nobody answered, because Dr Florey suddenly started barking out instructions about developing blood cultures, checking temperature and blood pressure.

'Accurate reports are essential for my research,' she said. 'We may in due course need to open the shoulder wound so that we can apply raw penicillin to the infected area. But she is far too weak at present. So we will

136

start with intravenous injections. The urine will have to be collected after every dose and brought back to Oxford every second day so that any undiluted penicillin can be extracted.'

Catching Sister Donaldson's astonished expression, she lifted her eyebrows in silent reprimand. 'Penicillin is in very short supply, Sister,' she shouted. 'I don't want to waste any.'

'No, no, I completely understand,' Sister stammered. 'But who …?'

Dr Florey smiled. 'I believe this is a task we can safely allocate to Nurse Coogan. She can convey your data to me at the same time. And bring back my recommendations.'

Ignoring Sister Donaldson's incoherent gurgle of protest, she took a small vial out of her bag. It looked extraordinarily insignificant. Molly stared at it in dismay. She had expected something much more dramatic. 'Goodness,' she said. 'Is that it?'

'Nurse!' Sister Donaldson expostulated in a vicious hiss.

Dr Florey didn't seem to hear Sister's intervention, or perhaps pretended not to. 'Yes, I'm afraid this is all we have available at the moment, Nurse Coogan. But it should be enough to start us off.' She regarded Helen's inert form thoughtfully. 'I am going to start with a relatively large initial dose of two hundred milligrams,' she said. 'If she survives that, we will follow up with a hundred milligrams every hour. Now if someone will bring me some sterilised water …'

Katy was sweeping the sawdust and debris from the night before out on to the pavement when she caught sight of Jen. 'Hey, Jen,' she called. 'Nice to see you out and about so early.'

For a moment Jen seemed to hesitate, then she crossed the road and came over. 'I thought a walk might do me good.'

'You're looking better.' Katy said encouragingly. She noticed that Jen was carrying something wrapped in brown paper that looked suspiciously like a small bottle. 'I hope you're not taking up secret drinking?'

She had spoken jokingly, but to her surprise, Jen flushed. 'What, this?' She glanced at the bag in her hand. 'No, no, this is …' She hesitated, then made a wry face. 'Well to be honest, it's cod liver oil.'

Katy regarded her with some amusement. 'Cod liver oil?'

'That old harridan Sister Morris recommended it,' Jen said. 'The mad old bat came to see me yesterday.' Her brow darkened as she caught Katy's guilty flinch. 'I thought at first Mum had set her on to me, but now I'm thinking it might have been you.'

Katy was tempted to deny it, but she didn't want Joyce to get it in the neck. Joyce and Jen's relationship was pretty fragile at the best of times. 'I was worried about you,' she said weakly. 'But I had no idea she was going to prescribe cod liver oil!'

For a moment it looked as though Jen was going to be angry, but then she relaxed. 'She says it's good for lifting the spirits. Apparently Dr Goodacre takes it every day.'

'Golly,' Katy said with a chuckle. 'Maybe I'd better start taking it too.'

'You don't need it,' Jen said. 'You've got lovely Ward to cheer you up.'

'Well, yes,' Katy agreed doubtfully. Catching Jen's quick, searching look, she hastened to explain. 'But what with worrying about Helen, and dealing with Malcolm, and not having enough bar staff to cope with all the Americans your sister is apparently bringing in on Saturday night, and these new air raids ...' She leaned on the broom wearily. 'I just wish this bloody war was over.'

Jen looked away up the bleak, war-battered street, then back again. 'Maybe I could help?' she said abruptly. 'Maybe I could work in the pub? Some evenings?'

'You?' Katy was taken by surprise. Jen had never lifted a finger to help in the pub. Even when she had stayed with Katy when Ward was away, the most she had ever done was a bit of singing on a busy evening, and even then only under sufferance.

'Jen,' Katy started nervously. 'I don't think ...'

'Please, Katy.' Jen raised her hands in theatrical supplication. 'I'm desperate. I've got no work and no money, and Mum won't let me off the rent.'

Katy was aware of a sense of foreboding. But she knew how much it must be costing Jen to plead. She also knew how upset she had been about losing the *Mikado* job. And about Henry's apparent defection. And she had been ill. Katy could feel herself weakening, and she knew it would be a mistake.

'But what about Molly?' she ventured, rather desperately. The thought of prima donna Jen and spiky Molly Coogan working together behind the bar made her feel quite ill herself. 'She often helps out in the evenings, and you and—'

'I thought she had disappeared,' Jen said. She laughed sourly. 'Sister Morris seemed to think she might have thrown herself in the river. Best place for her, if you ask me.'

'No.' Katy shook her head. 'It turned out she had gone off to Oxford to find some new medication for Helen. If it works, it will be a miracle.'

'Oh well,' Jen said, turning away huffily. 'If you'd rather have the wonderful St Molly working for you than me, your oldest friend, that's fine. I completely understand.'

And Katy heard herself saying that she would love to have Jen work for her. Molly wasn't there every night. They could maybe take it in turns.

Oh no, she thought when Jen had taken herself off. Oh no. What have I done?

Helen did survive the first dose. Everyone waited anxiously to see how she would react. Or indeed if she would react at all.

But nothing happened, and an hour later Dr Florey gave her another dose. Shortly after that, she departed, leaving instructions that Helen was to have a 100 mg intravenous injection every three hours.

Molly took her temperature and her pulse every hour. Dr Goodacre took blood for analysis every two hours.

As evening approached, there still seemed to be no change. Refusing to go home, Molly braced herself for the night.

It was a long vigil.

At ten o'clock, Helen suddenly seemed to settle into a more peaceful sleep. A sleep so deep and so still that Molly found herself checking her constantly for vital signs.

Her temperature had been 105.5 when she received her first injection. By midnight it had dropped to just over 102.

The next morning it was down to 100.

When she finally opened her eyes at lunchtime, she was very weak but fully conscious. And her temperature was normal for the first time since she had arrived at the Wilhelmina.

Nobody could believe it.

Sister Donaldson sent Nurse Spalding to fetch Matron from her office to witness the transformation.

Dr Goodacre was encouraging Helen to try and rest when Matron came in.

'I'm very happy to rest,' Helen was saying politely. 'But is there any chance I could have something to eat first? I'm awfully hungry.'

There was a moment's astonished pause. Then Dr Goodacre glanced at Sister Donaldson, who shook her head. 'I think it's too soon,' she said.

Molly frowned. Dr Florey hadn't said anything about withholding food. 'I don't see why she shouldn't eat if she feels like it,' she objected. She turned to Dr Goodacre. 'Why don't I fetch a bowl of porridge?'

But before Dr Goodacre could respond, Matron intervened. 'No,' she said in a voice that could have cut ice. She glanced at Sister Donaldson, who nodded grimly. 'Nurse Spalding can deal with that. It's time you went off duty, Nurse Coogan. You've been in here too long.'

'But I …' Molly started to object. She felt so involved. So protective. So responsible. She couldn't bear to let it go. What if something went wrong? What if Dr Mallet suddenly reappeared and started interfering? And she had so longed to see the look on Lord de Burrel's handsome face when he came in later and found Helen sitting up in bed eating a bowl of porridge.

'No but anything,' Matron said coldly.

She took Molly's arm in a vice-like grip and steered her out of the room. Closing the door firmly behind her, she stood Molly against the wall and regarded her with unnerving severity.

'Even if the result of your intervention turns out to be good,' she said, 'your behaviour has not been. I simply cannot let it go unpunished. I have discussed the matter with Sister Parkes and Sister Donaldson. We are all agreed that this has not been an isolated incident. Over the past two months your conduct and your attitude have both been unsatisfactory. Under normal circumstances I would be recommending your dismissal to the hospital board.' She folded her lips. 'But circumstances are not normal. And as one or two other members of staff have spoken quite strongly in your defence, I have decided merely to withdraw your privileges.'

Molly looked at her blankly. 'I didn't know I had any privileges,' she said.

Matron's eyes flashed dangerously. 'You have had the privilege of living in alternative accommodation,' she said quellingly. She inclined her head. 'So you will now go back to your lodgings. You can rest there for a couple of hours. Then you will pack your things and move back into the nurses' home.'

'Oh no! Matron, please.'

Matron held up her hand. 'It is perhaps partly my fault. I knew that you were not yet mature enough to be left to you own devices. But at least if you are in the nurses' home we can keep an eye on you. What's more,' she added, 'I don't want to hear any wild gossip emanating from you about Lady Helen's treatment. Dr Florey was most adamant that we keep it under our hats. In any case, it is very early days. I understand that penicillin is a very toxic substance. Lady Helen may yet suffer a serious reaction. And we have no idea yet whether it will be beneficial in the longer term.'

Molly looked at her in amazement. She sounded so unemotional, so matter-of-fact. She didn't seem to realise that something momentous had happened in that room during the night. A life had been saved. For now, at least, Helen was out of danger.

For a second, when Sister Donaldson had looked up in disbelief with the thermometer in her hand, Molly had thought this might have been the special moment the blind man had predicted for her all those weeks ago. She had overcome her fear and done something useful. Surely they would give her just a tiny bit of credit. But no, Matron had taken the wind right out of her sails.

Matron opened the door of Helen's room again. 'Nurse Coogan is going home to rest,' she said meaningfully to Sister Donaldson.

Following her into the room, Molly gritted her teeth, but she knew she couldn't argue.

But as she walked disconsolately over to the chair to pick up her night-duty cardigan and her knitting, Dr Goodacre caught her eye and gave her a conspiratorial wink.

'Matron's right,' he said. 'Get some sleep. I promise I won't let that old bugger Mallet loose on her while you are gone.' Then he went slightly pink, made a comical face and added, 'Excuse my French, ladies.'

Molly couldn't believe her ears. Nor, she could tell from the expression of shocked amazement on their faces, could Matron and Sister Donaldson believe theirs. Such irreverence in the hallowed halls of the Wilhelmina. And about Dr Mallet too. God himself.

Molly waited for the outburst. But none came. Sister Donaldson just looked away out of the window with a rather fixed smile on her face, and Matron bent over to pick something up from the floor. Molly stared at them in astonishment. If she had said something like that, they would have been down on her like a ton of bricks. I wish I was a man, she thought suddenly. Or a doctor.

She caught Helen's eye and saw that she was shaking with suppressed laughter.

For a second Molly almost felt like laughing herself. But she was too brought down by the thought of leaving the Nelsons' cosy, hospitable house and going back to the beastly old nurses' home.

So all she did was whisper, 'See you later,' to Helen and let herself out of the room.

By the time she left the hospital, Molly was seething. How dare they treat her so shabbily? She knew she had disobeyed orders. She had ignored their hallowed code of discipline. But if it wasn't for her, Helen de Burrel would now almost certainly be dead. And she had obeyed to the letter the instruction not to involve anyone else. It seemed cruelly unfair that in return for her discretion and the agonies of indecision she had suffered in the last few days, they would take from her the one thing she so relished. Her freedom.

She was so lost in thought that she was hardly looking where she was going, and as she rounded the corner opposite Mrs Carter's café, she bumped smack into Ward Frazer.

'Hey.' He steadied her as she recoiled in shock. 'You were going at a fair lick.'

Mumbling an apology, Molly tried to disengage her arm from his hand. But he was looking at her more closely now, the smile fading rapidly from his lips. 'It is Helen?' he asked, his voice at once rather husky. 'Is everything OK?'

Molly realised suddenly that everything she had done had been for this moment. She had so wanted to see his expression lighten when she told him the good news. She had wanted to see his relief. To hear the joy in his lovely voice. The joy he so much deserved. She had wanted to see him smile. To smile at her.

And now here she was, unable to speak, unable to do anything except stare at him in wonder at his sudden unexpected proximity.

'Molly?' He shook her gently, but his voice was urgent. 'Tell me what's happened.'

And then suddenly she was gabbling it all out. Like a waterfall. An idiotic, cascading, incoherent jumble of her trip to Oxford, Dr Florey's extraordinary decision to help, the tiny vial of penicillin, the awful vigil through the night, Helen's reduced temperature, the incredible fact of her suddenly wanting food.

And then, even as his puzzled frown began to lift, she blurted out about her own punishment, the small-minded meanness of it, the unfairness of it all.

'Let me get this straight,' Ward cut in after a moment. 'Are you telling me that Helen is on the road to recovery?'

Molly nodded. 'I think so,' she said. She looked away. On the other side of the road, through the window of the café, she could see Joyce Carter handing someone a plate of food.

'There may be setbacks,' she said. 'But if Dr Florey can find enough penicillin to keep treating her, then I think she could pull through.'

'My God.' He pronounced it 'Gard'. He put a hand to his head. 'I can't believe it. That is such good news.'

'So you see,' Molly gabbled on, 'I don't expect their gratitude, I know it wasn't just down to me, but surely they could at least admit that what I did was right. They shouldn't be punishing me for it.'

Ward shook his head slowly, as though to get his thoughts in order. 'You bucked the system,' he said. 'And that's a scary thing for any kind of institution. They need all those rules and regulations to keep the show on the road. But I bet they are impressed deep down. As am I.' He was smiling now all right, a bemused smile, almost of disbelief. He ran a hand through his hair. 'Seriously, I can't thank you enough, Molly. I don't know what to say.'

'It wasn't just me,' Molly said. 'If André Cabillard hadn't put her on that submarine, and you hadn't fetched her home, and—'

She stopped, because for a heart-trembling moment it looked as though he might kiss her. But then he blinked as though arrested by a thought, and delved his hand into his pocket. At once his smile widened.

'I have something for you.'

To her bewilderment, he brought out a small package wrapped in crumpled newspaper, a foreign newspaper covered in an indecipherable script.

'I got this for you in Algiers at Christmas,' he said. 'I've been meaning to give it to you for ages, but I never seemed to catch you alone. I guess now seems a good moment.'

Molly stared at the tiny package lying in the palm of her hand. Ward Frazer had been thinking of her in Algiers. At Christmas. He had bought her a gift.

'Thank you,' she whispered.

'Aren't you going to unwrap it?' he asked, and she could hear the smile in his voice.

Slowly, with trembling fingers, she unfolded the flimsy newspaper. Her heart was racing so hard she could hardly breathe. Wordlessly she gazed at the tiny charm on the thin silver chain.

'It's meant to be a magic carpet,' Ward said helpfully after a moment. 'Katy told me you'd been doing conjuring tricks with George.' He gave a diffident little laugh. 'The guy who sold it to me said it has the power to transport you to foreign lands.'

Molly felt herself starting to smile. She had never seen anything so beautiful in all her life. And to be given such a gift just now. By this wonderful man. Just when she had been so brought down by Matron's harsh words. That in itself was magic.

'I wish it *would* transport me to foreign lands,' she said. 'Well away from the Wilhelmina.'

Ward laughed. 'Be careful. I should have said he also told me that it had the power to make wishes come true.'

Molly looked at the little silver carpet again. Its tiny corner tassels seemed to be trembling, the whole thing vibrating in her palm, presumably because she was shaking so much.

'Then I'll wish that Helen makes a full recovery,' she said.

She looked up at him. He was watching her with his steady grey eyes, the curve of a smile on his lips. And suddenly that wasn't the only wish she wanted to make. She closed her hand over the magic carpet. Her fingers tingled. It was so, so tempting.

No, she thought. No, I mustn't. I mustn't even think it, let alone wish it.

And then to her horror, she felt tears stinging her eyes. Desperately she tried to blink them back. The last thing on earth she wanted was for him to see her all tearful and blotchy.

But already through her swimming eyes she could see his expression turning to one of concern.

'Hey, Molly, what's the matter? What is it?'

He put his hands on her shoulders and drew her to him, gently wiping the tears from her cheeks.

'Don't cry,' he said. 'You should be happy. You've done a wonderful thing. Don't worry about those old witches in the hospital. It's just sour grapes. They're jealous that you had the guts to go after what you believed in. They'll get over it.'

Molly was melting inside. The touch of his fingers on her skin was too much for her. She could see the warm, sympathetic smile in his eyes and feel the little silver ornament pressing into her palm. Maybe *this* was her moment, she thought. She had, after all, walked past this very spot with the blind man all those weeks ago.

'I wish—' she began, and then froze. Out of the corner of her eye she saw the café door swing open on the other side of the road and Jen Carter come marching out.

'I thought you'd have better taste, Ward Frazer,' Jen shouted across the road. 'But if you are going to snog that poxy little pixie, then I recommend you go and do it somewhere more private.'

Ward looked up, his eyes narrowing sharply. For a second he was still, then he dropped his hands from Molly's face and took a casual step to one side, chivalrously shielding Molly from Jen's gaze, and from any other prying eyes in the café. He gave a light, unconcerned laugh. 'I'm not snogging her,' he called back. 'I'm congratulating her. She may have just saved Helen's life.'

Jen glared at him. 'Well whatever you are doing, I wish you'd do it somewhere else,' she snapped. 'You're putting us off our food.'

As Jen flounced back into the café, Ward put his hands in his pockets and looked down at Molly. 'I'm sorry,' he said. 'Are you OK?'

She had to make a joke of it. Or try to. Anything else was too awful to contemplate. Swallowing hard and dragging her eyes away from Ward's all too perceptive gaze, she opened her palm and looked again at the magic carpet. She managed to produce a shaky laugh.

'I wish Jen Carter would be transported to foreign lands,' she said.

*

Later that evening, Jen was struggling to light the fire. Annoyed, she sat back on her heels and watched the tiny spark from the match die away yet again. Joyce always bought the cheapest, dirtiest coal, and the house was so cold, even the newspaper was damp. It was no wonder the blasted thing wouldn't light. And it was even less likely to when the front door suddenly opened and Joyce brought a gust of freezing-cold air in with her from the street.

Knowing that he mother had witnessed her angry outburst at lunchtime, Jen braced herself for a telling-off. But to her surprise, Joyce just looked at her in silence for a second, then dropped her gaze and pulled off her gloves. 'Do you know anything about a play called *The Mikado*?' she asked.

'It's not a play,' Jen said irritably, turning back to the fire. 'It's a comic opera. Gilbert and Sullivan.'

'Oh.' Joyce sounded slightly taken aback. 'Well whatever it is,' she went on, 'Mr Lorenz asked me if I'd like to see it. He saw a notice about it in the paper. It's on somewhere in the West End. Do you know anything about it?'

Jen swung round again to stare at her mother incredulously. 'Of course I do,' she snapped. 'I was going to be in it.'

Joyce was shrugging off her coat. 'Well how was I meant to know that?'

'You would if you ever took the slightest interest in what I do.'

Her mother's eyes snapped. 'Well you aren't *doing* it, are you. You are moping around here all day long and getting on everyone's nerves. What you need to do is earn some money.'

Jen threw the box of matches down on the grate and stood up. 'It's not my fault there are no acting jobs going,' she said. 'Anyway, I am going to be earning again. Katy's offered me a job at the pub.'

'The pub?' Joyce looked astonished. 'What, singing?'

'No,' Jen said. 'Serving, washing up and ... that sort of thing.'

Joyce stared at her for a moment in apparent disbelief, then gave a sudden chortle of amusement. 'Ha! I'll believe that when I see it.'

Pushing Jen out of the way, she kneeled down on the hearth and deftly reorganised the unruly pile of newspaper and coal into some new arrangement of her own. 'It would help if you bothered to clear out the grate first,' she muttered. Then she picked up the box of matches. 'You know your problem, don't you?' she asked over her shoulder.

'No,' Jen said dangerously. 'What is my problem, in your opinion?'

Joyce set a match to the corner of a piece of rolled-up newspaper and the fire took immediately with a confident whoosh. 'You shouldn't have let that nice Mr Keller slip through your fingers.'

Chapter Eleven

It wasn't all plain sailing for Helen de Burrel. Although her temperature had come down, it didn't stay down for long. And after a few days, Dr Florey decreed that the shoulder wound should be reopened and kept open so that powdered penicillin could be applied directly to the infected area inside. For a week or so it was once again touch and go. But then things really did start to improve. Helen's blood cultures showed that the number of bacterial colonies had dropped from a hundred and twenty-five per cubic centimetre to just one colony per cubic centimetre. And this time her temperature stayed down.

The wound was stitched up again and she gradually lost the emaciated, famine-victim look; helped along by the last two of Katy's precious oranges and the occasional dish from Joyce's café to supplement the tasteless hospital food, she finally began to put on some much-needed weight.

Molly's life had taken on a completely new routine. She barely noticed that she was back in the nurses' home, because she was now immersed in notes and statistics, blood cultures and pathology readings. And this was interspersed on alternate days with trips to Oxford carrying a glass jar containing Helen's urine. It had been a relief to everyone when Helen finally became strong enough to use a sterilised pan for herself and they could dispense with the uncomfortable and embarrassing catheter.

Molly relished the trips to Oxford. She felt free on that train. Important. She had a purpose, and she was interested in the process of reclaiming the penicillin from the urine. Indeed she found the whole penicillin production process fascinating, and her days in Oxford became increasingly enjoyable. The girls who worked in the penicillin lab were friendly, and Ethel Florey treated her not exactly as an equal but certainly as a junior colleague.

Professor Florey himself was an extraordinary man. He was blunt and outspoken, but he had a mind like a trap and he was kind to Molly in a brisk, unconcerned kind of way. Although she respected him, Molly couldn't help thinking that it wouldn't be much fun to be married to him.

The other key member of the penicillin team was the gruff, irascible Dr Chain, pronounced Khine, who was the moustachioed man Molly had seen on her first visit to the Sir William Dunn building. It turned out that Ernst Chain was a Jewish émigré. Disgusted with the new Nazi regime, he had left Germany in 1933 and arrived in England with only £10 to his name. His reputation had secured him a post at Cambridge University, where his innovative work on the biology of snake venom had caused Professor Florey to recruit him to Oxford. Ethel Florey once told Molly that Dr Chain was a brilliant musician and could equally well have become a concert pianist, which perhaps explained his volatile temperament.

'We haven't much money here, so we have to use our brains,' he said to Molly one day when she enquired why the penicillin project was not sponsored by the government. It seemed crazy to her that the development of such an incredibly useful drug was limping along, forced to use home-made equipment and such a meagre number of staff, when with a little financial backing it could make a huge impact on Britain's medical services, and indeed the war effort, by potentially saving thousands of soldiers' lives.

It had been Molly's reference to this surprising lack of funding that had caused Helen's father to donate money to the project as soon as it became clear that Helen was going to recover. Molly didn't know how much that gift had been, but it did perhaps explain why Dr Chain and Professor Florey treated her occasional presence in the department with a kind of benevolent tolerance.

But they were not very tolerant of each other. The funding of the penicillin project was only one of many contentious issues between them. Dr Chain believed that they should have patented the penicillin formula, but Professor Florey felt it was unethical to limit access to medicine. And now, as a result of Professor Florey sharing his expertise with colleagues in America, the USA was forging ahead with their own production.

'So it's too late now,' Chain said with an irritable shrug. 'It is slipping out beyond our control.'

'That's not fair,' Molly said hotly. 'I suppose I don't mind America having it. But I certainly hope the Nazis don't get hold of it.'

Dr Chain had given her one of his rare smiles then. 'You echo my feeling precisely,' he said.

Molly was not the only person for whom life had improved as a result of Helen de Burrel's recovery. Katy had been bracing herself for Helen's death. But now, visiting her at the Wilhelmina had become a complete pleasure, something to look forward to instead of being feared. Every day, as Helen's health continued to improve, it was like a weight lifting off her shoulders. There were still other weights, of course, other anxieties and problems, but at least for now she no longer had to worry about losing one of her best friends.

It wasn't all good news, however. On 16 February, Himmler announced that the 60,000 remaining occupants of the Jewish ghetto in Warsaw in Poland would be 'eliminated'.

Katy was listening to the story on the news when Aaref Hoch came into the pub carrying a small wooden crate. She quickly turned off the wireless. It was bad enough to hear about atrocities and inhumanities, but it was quite another thing to do so in the presence of someone who could so easily have been one of the victims. Someone, indeed, who could once again be in considerable danger if the Nazis ever did invade England. Katy hoped and believed that the British would never let such things happen here, but she knew from Ward that they were already happening in France and in Italy. Once the terrible fascist regimes took hold, they were so ruthless, so brutal, so powerful, there was little that ordinary people could do to resist.

In uneasy silence she watched Aaref settle the crate on to the counter. His long lashes were lowered over his dark eyes, concealing his thoughts. She knew she ought to say something about the radio report, but she couldn't for the life of her think of an appropriate comment.

Thankfully Aaref spoke first. 'I have brought you glasses,' he said, looking up and nodding to the box. 'Six beer glasses and six shorts.'

'Oh, Aaref!' Relieved, Katy stared at the crate and then at him. 'You are a complete star. Where did you get them?'

His lashes came down over his eyes again. 'It is better you do not ask me that,' he said. 'But I think you will like them, yes?'

'Yes indeed,' Katy said. She knew of old that it was better not to question the provenance of Aaref's lifesaving goods. So instead of pressing him, she opened the till and peered into it dubiously. 'Do you want me to pay you now?'

'There is no rush,' he said. Then he inclined his head politely and turned away towards the door.

'It won't happen here,' Katy said suddenly. 'I know it's happening in Europe. But we will never let it happen here.'

He paused at the door and glanced back at her quizzically. 'And if it does, you will hide us in your cellar, yes?'

'Yes.' Katy smiled. 'Yes, of course. As long as you promise not to drink all my beer!'

After he had gone, Katy glanced at the clock behind her. Jen should be here by now. She was late. Jen was always late. She simply didn't see the need to be prompt, that it might impact on the pub's smooth operation, or on Katy's peace of mind. When Katy had attempted to explain the importance of her well-practised routines and time-saving systems, Jen had airily brushed her off, saying she fussed too much.

Jen was also hopeless at practical tasks like lighting the fire, and was unwilling to get her hands wet or dirty, or to do anything that might run the risk of breaking her nails. 'An audition might just come up and I don't want to look like a skivvy,' she said, so Katy either had to hire Aaref's brother Jacob to be there on Jen's nights, or collect the empties, wash the glasses and do most of the preparation and clearing up herself.

Ward would always help, but he was often out in the evenings now. Katy didn't know precisely what he was doing, of course. As with so much of what he did, it was shrouded in secrecy, but she knew it was something to do with training Allied aircrew how to evade capture if they got shot down or had to bail out over Nazi-controlled Europe. The life expectancy of aircrew was very low, everyone knew that. There was a shortage of pilots, and getting them back to England so they could fly again was a high priority.

Katy smiled grimly to herself. That probably wasn't such good news for the pilots, but it was good news for her. It meant that Ward had this new, much safer role. And it all stemmed from a letter he had received from the medical assessment board, signing him off from active service for another two months.

'Two months,' Ward had said. 'Those damn doctors. I ask you. My leg is as good now as it's going to get. What difference is two months going to make?'

A lot to me, Katy had thought, turning away to hide her sigh of relief. She had felt another weight lifted off her shoulders. Two months of safety. Two months' less worry. What more could she ask for in the middle of a war?

Having got everything ready for evening opening, and battled through teatime with a recalcitrant Malcolm, who was now determined to feed himself rather than being spoon-fed, Katy was just about to unpack the new glasses when Jen finally breezed in.

'Sorry I'm a bit late,' she said. 'Mum's gone out with old Lorenz and I was helping Angie decipher one of Gino's letters.'

She shrugged off her coat and hung it on the peg behind the bar. 'I've never met an Italian, and I hope I never will, but if they're all like this idiot, Gino, I'm not surprised old Hitler is getting fed up with them.'

Katy couldn't help but laugh. 'Well, as long as Angie likes it, that's the main thing.'

'Oh, she laps it up,' Jen said scornfully. 'It doesn't seem to occur to her that he probably writes this pathetic hogwash to every girl he meets. Oh, and guess what,' she added, helping herself to a bottle of lemonade from the shelf under the counter. 'Mum's heard from the Red Cross. Bob's in a POW camp in Italy.'

Katy began unwrapping newspaper from round the new glasses 'Poor Bob,' she said. She'd always rather liked Jen's oldest brother, even if he was a bit of a ne'er-do-well. 'But thank goodness he's all right.'

'Oh, he'll be all right,' Jen said airily. 'If he's got any sense, he'll sit there safe and sound for the rest of the war. That's what I'd do in his shoes. But it's ironic, isn't it, that this damn Gino is here and Bob's there.'

But Katy was no longer listening. She was staring at the glasses she had taken out of Aaref's box.

'I don't believe it,' she said. She looked up at Jen. 'Aaref just brought these in for me, to replace the ones that have been stolen. But these *are* the ones that were stolen. These are my glasses.'

'How can you know that?' Jen said. She picked one up. 'Glasses all look the same.'

'No they don't,' Katy said. 'I recognise them. I've washed them up and polished the blasted things enough times. Look, this one has a tiny chip off the base. I always thought it was going to crack right across, but it never has.'

Jen took a sip of her lemonade. 'So whoever stole them is selling them on. And eventually they are getting back to Aaref. Unless it was Aaref who took them in the first place.'

'Of course it wasn't,' Katy said hotly. 'He would never do a thing like that. No, I think it's Gillian James.'

Jen almost choked on her drink. 'Good God, I shouldn't think so. From what I've seen, she gets paid quite well already.'

'What?' Katy stared at her, flabbergasted. 'You surely don't mean …?'

'Yeah,' Jen said. 'Her military visitor hands over a wad of cash every time he leaves.' She rolled her eyes suggestively. 'And by the look of her as she says goodbye, he certainly gets his money's worth. Although come to think of it, I haven't seen him or his car there recently. So maybe she is running a bit short.'

'Jen!' But appalled as she was at Jen's disclosure, Katy almost felt disappointed. She had been rather looking forward to catching the widow red-handed and thus having the excuse of banning her from the pub. 'I was sure she was the culprit. She was definitely in here the night the Spitfire Fund can was stolen. I don't know when the pram wheels disappeared, of course, but—'

Jen was fingering the errant glasses, but at that she looked up. 'Pram wheels?' she asked. 'Are you telling me someone stole your pram wheels?'

'Yes,' Katy groaned. 'That's why I'm having to walk Malcolm

everywhere. He loves it, of course, but he's so slow, it makes everything—' She stopped as Jen burst out laughing and headed for the door.

'What are you doing?' Katy screamed as Jen pushed through the blackout curtain. 'Jen, you can't go. It's nearly opening time. And it's only you and me here tonight.'

'Back in a sec,' Jen called back, and disappeared.

Katy stood rooted to the spot, aghast.

But before she could move, Jen was back, beckoning her to the door with a wicked grin on her face. 'If you're quick, you might be able to make a citizen's arrest.'

Bemused, Katy moved obediently over to the door. 'Jen, what on earth …?'

Jen held up her hand. 'Listen and learn.'

As Katy stepped out into the dusky street, she became aware of a strange kind of rattling rumble, and a moment later, out of the gloom, she saw George Nelson approaching on a lethal-looking home-made go-cart with a shrouded torch strapped to the steering mechanism, a rusty handlebar that had clearly once belonged to an old-fashioned bicycle. The chassis of the contraption had been constructed from two planks, and George himself was perched on a drinks crate attached to the frame with a length of fraying rope.

Skidding to a halt in front of them with an ungainly scuffle of feet and a rather violent bump on the kerb, he looked up at them with a half-guilty, half-defiant expression.

'This little blighter nearly mowed me down earlier,' Jen said.

'Did he?' Katy stared at her blankly. 'Yes, it does look rather dangerous, but I don't see …'

'*Katy!*' Jen leaned over and tapped one of the go-cart's wheels. 'Don't you recognise these?'

And then Katy suddenly did see. 'George!' she said. 'Are those my pram wheels?'

George began to shake his head, but honesty got the better of him. 'I didn't think you would need them any more now Malcolm can walk,' he said.

'He can't walk very far,' Katy muttered, trying not to laugh.

'I think we should call the police,' Jen said severely. 'You can't just steal things willy-nilly.'

George looked alarmed. 'It wasn't willy-nilly,' he said. 'I only borrowed them. Just to see if they would work.'

'But *how* did you borrow them?' Katy said in a choked voice. 'How come I didn't see you take them? You must have carried them through the pub right under our noses.'

He hesitated, fiddling with the handlebars for a moment. 'I learnt it in magic,' he finally admitted reluctantly. 'When Molly was staying. It's a technique. It's called distraction.'

'Ha, I might have known that poxy pixie was behind it,' Jen said.

Katy ignored her. 'What do you mean?' she said to George. 'How did you distract me?'

'*I* didn't distract you,' he said. 'It was the new lady from number forty-two. When she came into the pub, everyone started looking at her. So nobody saw me go past.'

'Good God,' Jen said. 'I wish I had that kind of charisma.'

'No you don't,' Katy said. 'It's character that's important, not looks.'

'Huh,' Jen sniffed. 'Tell that to Henry Keller.'

'Who is Henry Keller?' George asked, interested.

'Nobody,' Jen said quellingly.

'How can somebody be nobody?' George retorted with a cheeky grin.

'You're getting far too big for your boots,' Jen said.

George giggled and extended one foot. 'I'm not wearing boots.'

'You'll be wearing my boot round your ear if you don't get those wheels back on Malcolm's pram pretty sharpish,' Jen said.

Katy could see that George was about to take issue with this and intervened quickly. She wouldn't put it past Jen to put her threat into action. 'It's all right,' she said. 'You can keep them until the weekend. I won't need the pram before then.'

'You're too soft on him,' Jen said as they went back inside the pub.

'Poor little chap. It's nice to see him having fun after all he's been through.'

Jen looked at her incredulously. 'Poor little chap? He's a complete menace. Learnt it in magic indeed!' Then she laughed. 'My guess is he's not the only one who has been using Gillian James as a distraction. Next time she comes in, you'll have to completely ignore her and watch everyone else like a hawk to see who *is* pocketing your glasses.'

Joyce enjoyed *The Mikado*. It hadn't sounded much from the programme, what with all those Japanese names and such a complicated plot. But it had turned out to be quite fun, and funny, and even Mr Lorenz had had to dab his eyes with his handkerchief from too much laughing a couple of times. Despite the ridiculous fuss Jen had made about it, it was a shame she had missed the chance to be in it. Even Joyce could see that all that dancing and flirting, and the Lord High Executioner putting Hitler and Mussolini on his little list and all that, would have suited her down to the ground.

'Do you want to go straight home, Mrs Carter?' Mr Lorenz asked as they emerged on to the Strand. 'Or would you care for a small nightcap?'

As she hesitated, he added, 'I believe the Wellington is quite a nice place. It is where all the theatrical people go.'

Joyce wondered how he knew that. She couldn't imagine he came up to town very often. But perhaps he had come on his own to reconnoitre the area. In which case she didn't want to disappoint him. 'All right,' she said. 'Let's go there then. Just a quick one, mind.'

It was as Mr Lorenz settled her into a chair by a boarded-up window that Joyce glanced across the crowded room and spotted Henry Keller. She had only met him once, when Ward had brought him to a party at the café, but she recognised him immediately.

He was a nice-looking, well-built man, handsome you might even say, but posh of course. Even without hearing his voice you could tell he was well-spoken. It was the confident way he held his head, that lazy smile, and his slightly debonair clothes.

He was standing with a small group of people who clearly all knew each other. Two of them were arguing animatedly, gesticulating with their cigarettes. The others were watching, laughing, occasionally interrupting. Probably they too had just come out of a show.

Joyce was sure he wouldn't remember her. He'd only had eyes for Jen that night in the café.

But a few minutes later, perhaps aware of her gaze, he glanced in her direction. Caught unawares, Joyce gave him a kind of half-smile, then turned quickly to Mr Lorenz.

But before she could say anything, Henry Keller had detached himself from his group and was approaching their table.

'You are Jennifer's mother, aren't you?' he said. 'Mrs Carter? Forgive me. I didn't recognise you for a moment. How nice to see you. Have you been to a show?'

For an awful moment Joyce couldn't remember the name of the show they had seen, but Mr Lorenz supplied it as he and Henry shook hands.

'Ah yes,' Henry Keller said drily. 'The fateful *Mikado*.' He flicked an invisible piece of dust off the sleeve of his jacket. 'And how is Jennifer now? I hope she is fully recovered.'

He sounded casual, merely politely interested, but Joyce wasn't fooled. He wanted to know. And that confused her, because she thought he had given Jen the heave-ho. Or maybe his interest had only ever been professional, not personal. How was she meant to know how these fancy theatre people went on? Suddenly she had a terrible dread of saying the wrong thing and getting it in the neck from Jen. In the end she decided honesty was the only option.

'Yes, she's back on her feet now,' she said. 'But she was ever so disappointed when you disappeared off the scene.'

He looked surprised. 'I didn't disappear off the scene,' he said. 'She told me she didn't want to see me. Not while she was ill, at least. I assumed she would let me know when she was better.'

'Oh.' Joyce could feel herself getting flustered. Why on earth had she agreed to go for a drink? Why couldn't blasted Lorenz just have taken her home? The last thing she wanted was to be fighting Jen's battles. 'Well I don't know about that,' she said. 'All I know is that she's been like a bear with a sore paw since she lost that job you got her.'

'Yes, it was a shame she missed that opportunity,' he said. 'But I'd assumed, as I hadn't heard from her, that she must have found herself another job.'

'Yes, she has,' Joyce said. 'She's got a part-time barmaid job at the Flag and Garter in Lavender Road.' As a flicker of surprise passed over Henry's face, Joyce belatedly realised that that wasn't the kind of job he meant. She also realised it probably wasn't the kind of information Jen would want him to know.

'It's only to help out a friend,' she said quickly. 'Between you and me, she's not really suited to it, what with her fancy actressy ways. It's too messy for her. She doesn't like getting her hands dirty.'

He gave a short laugh. 'No, I don't suppose she does.' He glanced over his shoulder. One of the girls in the group had her eye on him rather possessively. He turned back to Joyce with an easy smile. 'I'm so glad I met you, Mrs Carter. And do let me know if there are any other shows you fancy seeing. I often get given tickets I can't use.' He nodded politely to Mr Lorenz as he moved away. 'Enjoy the rest of your evening.'

Joyce watched him rejoin his group. Watched the pretty girl put her hand on his arm. Free tickets indeed. She could imagine Jen's reaction if she let slip that Henry Keller had casually offered her and Lorenz free tickets. It didn't bear thinking about. None of it bore thinking about.

She sat in silence for a minute. Then she turned to Mr Lorenz. 'I don't think I'm going to say anything to Jen. About us bumping into him and that.'

Mr Lorenz inclined his head. 'No,' he agreed gravely. 'I think that's a wise decision.'

Catching his eye, Joyce found herself smiling. He understood. He knew Jen. He knew how touchy and proud she was. He knew how often Joyce had found herself on the wrong side of her. He knew what she was up against, even if he was too polite to say so. And she realised she was glad that he knew. It was nice, for once, to have someone on her side.

'About this party of Lucinda's next month,' Ward said, looking up as Katy came into the kitchen on Saturday afternoon. 'Louise is mad for us to go.'

He was cooking. Katy had forgotten that he liked to cook. He had cooked for her once on their honeymoon. And now suddenly, perhaps in celebration of Helen's improvement, here he was making some sort of North African dish, using the spices he had brought back from Algiers. It smelt strangely unpleasant to Katy's conservative nose. She had become aware of it wafting down the stairs as she cashed up the till after closing time. A powerful, rather heady aroma. She glanced into the pan nervously, hoping she was going to like it. So far it looked like a bowl of yellow sick.

'Louise is mad for *you* to go,' she corrected him. 'I don't think she's bothered about me.'

He laughed. 'Well I think we should both go, even if only to keep an eye on her. If she's not careful, she's going to mess up with Jack. And that would be a damn shame.' He picked up a knife and tested the blade on his finger. Clearly not satisfied, he rootled around in a drawer and found one of Katy's father's old sharpeners. 'It would be good for her to have something fun to look forward to.'

Katy watched him whisking the steel backwards and forwards over the knife blade. She was impressed. She had never got the hang of that. When she did it, the knives seemed to get blunter, not sharper.

Putting the steel back in the drawer, Ward glanced up with his eyebrows raised and a small smile playing on his lips. 'What do you think? We could make a weekend of it. Henley's a real nice place. The Veales always put on a good party. Helen might even be fit enough to come by then. And it would be kind of fun to see the old gang again.'

And Katy realised that *he* wanted to go. *He* wanted some fun.

Her heart sank. Lucinda Veale and her fancy friends were his gang, not hers. But worse than the thought of facing up to a whole bunch of people she didn't know, and probably wouldn't like, was the dread that if she said she wouldn't go, he might go on his own. Or with Louise.

'There'll be dancing,' he said.

It was getting worse and worse. 'I can't dance,' Katy said. 'I don't know how.'

'Sure you do,' he said. 'We don't have to do the Lindy Hop.' He gave a wry glance at his bad leg. 'I guess I might struggle with this damn knee. But hey, we can smooch, no problem.'

It was the thought of him smooching with someone else that made up Katy's mind. It wasn't Louise she needed to keep an eye on, it was him.

And it would give her a chance to show off the lovely bracelet Ward had brought her from Algiers.

'But what about Malcolm?' she said.

She saw his lips curve as he efficiently chopped a carrot into neat cubes; he knew she had capitulated. 'I'm sure Pam and Alan would have him for the night.'

'And what about the pub?' Katy said. 'I can't just close up.' The thought of her hard-won customers finding alternative, possibly preferable, drinking venues made her feel even more sick than the smell of Ward's North African stew.

'I'm sure Molly would hold the fort,' he said. He glanced over his shoulder, eyes sparkling. 'And, of course, we've got Jen now too.'

Katy's eyes widened in horror.

'They'll be fine,' he said. He waved his knife about. 'They are both grown women after all.'

Katy just looked at him. He grinned. 'OK, OK, I guess you're right. We'll hire Mrs Carter to come in as well. You can surely rely on her to keep the peace?'

And then on top of the party, Katy found she had something else to worry about. A letter arrived the following morning from Ward's aunts in Dorset. Katy knew their writing well and was just about to rip open the flimsy envelope when she realised it was addressed to Ward. Only to Ward. Normally the Miss Taylors' letters were addressed to both of them.

Ward's aunts were regular correspondents and Katy enjoyed their letters. They wrote with gentle humour about Katy's mother, who had gone to stay with them in the country months and months ago and never left, about Winston, their ancient, rather smelly, much-loved little dachshund, and rather less gently about what they'd like to do to Hitler and Mussolini if they ever had the privilege to get either of them alone in a room.

'You should have opened it,' Ward said when Katy handed him the letter later.

'I didn't like to,' she said, and he laughed.

'What's mine is yours,' he said, and slit open the envelope.

A moment later he swore softly under his breath. 'Good God!'

'What?' Katy asked, alarmed.

'My uncle is coming to visit.'

'Your uncle?' Katy didn't even know he had an uncle. 'From Canada?'

He looked at her blankly for a moment, then back at the letter in his hand. There was a strange, rather grim expression on his face that she had never seen before.

She watched him as he read the rest of the letter in silence. She knew so little about his family. Only that they had cut him off when he went to Germany before the war. He had met a Jewish girl and wanted to marry her. Tragically she had been killed during the awful Kristallnacht purge of the Jews in Berlin. Katy was sure that was partly why he was so determined to fight the Nazis in any way he could. In the early days, when she first met him, his aunts had thought he had a death wish. Probably the attitude of his family hadn't helped.

She crossed her fingers behind her back. Perhaps this uncle coming would be like an olive branch. The beginning of a reconciliation. She didn't like people being at odds with each other. And it would be nice for Malcolm to have a chance one day to meet his Canadian grandparents.

Ward folded the letter and put it in his pocket. 'He's coming over on some trade thing next month. And he wants to see me.'

Katy frowned. 'What about me? Doesn't he want to meet me?'

'Oh yes,' Ward said with an unhumorous laugh. 'I'm quite sure he wants to meet you too.'

'What do you mean?' Katy asked nervously. 'Why are you saying it like that?'

Ward looked at her, and at once his expression softened. 'Hey. It's OK,' he said. He came over to her and hugged her. Then he drew back and kissed her. 'It'll be fine,' he said lightly. 'Don't worry about it.'

Katy hadn't been particularly worried about it. But she was now. Very worried. And she didn't know why. 'What's your uncle like?'

'Uncle Maurice? I haven't seen him in years. He was pretty stiff when I was a teenager. Worse even than my father.' Ward smiled then, but it didn't quite reach his eyes. 'Let's hope he's mellowed in his old age.'

It was either because of Lord de Burrel's contribution to his research, or due to a general enthusiasm for his subject, that Dr Chain asked Molly if she would like to attend one of his lectures to preclinical medical students at the university. Whatever the reason, the invitation caught Molly completely by surprise.

'Me?' she said, almost looking behind her to see if there was someone else in the corridor. She realised Dr Chain was wearing his overcoat and hat. 'What, now?'

'Yes, yes,' he said. He checked the fob watch in his breast pocket. 'The lecture hall is five minutes away. I will speak only for forty minutes. The subject is the pathology of blood.'

She eyed him doubtfully. 'Do you think I'd understand it?'

'Ethel says you have a quick brain,' he said.

'Does she?' Molly was aware of a flush of pleasure. A quick brain? That was praise indeed from Ethel Florey. 'Then I'd love to come,' she said. But then she remembered the horror of being put on the spot by her teachers at school. The mocking hilarity of her classmates as she flushed beetroot red and stumbled out some incoherent response to a question in French or failed to decline a verb correctly. 'As long as you promise not to ask me any questions. In public, I mean.'

He gave a throaty laugh. 'I promise,' he said.

But oddly, when the lecture was over, delivered in his dictatorial, bombastic, heavily accented German accent, Dr Chain did fire a sharp final question at the assembled students, and Molly found that she knew the answer. Not that she volunteered it, of course. She was far too shy, and had already suffered some discomfiture at the curious glances the trainee medics had thrown her as she took a seat at one side of the small lecture theatre. They clearly were not used to having a lowly nurse sitting among them.

But as she travelled back to London on the train that evening, she felt absurdly pleased with herself. As they had walked back to the Sir William Dunn building, she had been able to answer Dr Chain's enquiry about her understanding of the lecture with some equanimity. And had even asked him one or two questions of her own, to which he had responded seriously and with evident pleasure. For once, she hadn't made a fool of herself.

But as she approached London and the Wilhelmina once again, she felt her spirits sinking. During her brief interludes at Oxford, despite her tenuous link to the penicillin project, she was treated with mild consideration, even perhaps a modicum of respect. But at the Wilhelmina, after a couple of days of inquisitive questions from the other nurses, which sadly had to go unanswered due to the secrecy shrouding Helen's treatment, she had resumed her normal status, constantly berated by Sisters Parkes and Donaldson, and quite often the butt of the other nurses' jokes.

There was also the faint but persistent sense of betrayal that she had experienced when she discovered that Katy had taken on Jen Carter to help in the pub, which meant that Molly's own visits to the Flag and Garter now had to be carefully scheduled so as not to coincide with any of Jen's shifts.

And as Helen's condition improved, it was no longer deemed necessary for Molly to spend time with her, and so, apart from brief visits to relay any recommendations on her ongoing treatment from Dr Florey, and to pick up Helen's urine and blood samples, even the small pleasure of making way for Ward at Helen's bedside was denied her.

But she did see some of Helen's other visitors. As Helen's strength returned, so other issues resurfaced. Issues about those last few days she had spent in France. Once again she was being questioned. Not by Ward, but by other SOE people, quiet, anonymous men who came and went with no introduction or farewell, leaving Helen stressed and unhappy.

Of course Molly wasn't party to any of these discussions, but she gleaned a certain amount nevertheless. And Helen soon filled her in on the rest. 'There's no point in worrying about secrecy now,' she said. 'It sounds to me as though the Germans know most of the SOE business already.'

The problem was that the French SOE resistance network had all but collapsed. The agent who had betrayed Helen had betrayed others too. The whole tenuous system had unravelled. All means of communication with their operatives in the southern section of France had been lost, and there seemed little chance of reactivating them.

Helen told Molly that André Cabillard had given her the grid reference of a landing site where a radio transmitter and supplies could be dropped so that he could carry on the struggle. He had requested that a coded message be broadcast on the BBC the night of the drop so that he could be ready and waiting. He had also asked that a similar message be broadcast to let him know if Helen had survived her injury.

Concerned that the wrong person might find André's note, Helen had memorised these instructions while she was on the submarine and destroyed the piece of paper they were written on. Now that she was finally out of danger, she wanted them put into operation. More than anything, she wanted André to know she was safe and well.

But so much time had elapsed since her escape, and in the absence of any proof that André was still alive and still on side, the bigwigs at the SOE were reluctant to comply.

The last thing anyone wanted was for supplies, especially a precious radio and the associated secret codes, to fall into enemy hands. But it quickly became clear that they were also concerned that in her trauma Helen might have misremembered the codes, or indeed that she might have misremembered whether André Cabillard really was playing for the right team. They suspected that her judgement might have been influenced by her attraction for him.

The fact that André had allowed the SS to commandeer part of his family's wine estate for their HQ made them nervous, even though Helen insisted that he believed it gave him valuable access and insight into their operations, and a certain immunity to their suspicions.

Eventually it was reluctantly agreed that, even though no equipment would be sent, no harm could be done by broadcasting the coded message saying that Helen was alive. So at the beginning of March, after what seemed like weeks of delay and pointless argument, finally the confirmation of Helen's survival – in the poignant words chosen by André, *The girl loves the fox* – was broadcast to France as one of the personal messages after the BBC overseas news.

Of course there was no way of knowing whether André had heard it. But at least it had been sent.

The following day, Helen was discharged from the Wilhelmina and went to stay with some friends near Oxford to convalesce. And Molly's strange double life came to an end.

Chapter Twelve

And then the Luftwaffe came back again. It wasn't like the Blitz, but it was bad enough, and rather too close for comfort. Incendiaries were dropped on Clapham Common. A house in Wakehurst Road had a great hole burnt through its roof. An anti-aircraft shell severed a gas main in Condray Street and the whole road had to be evacuated in case of an explosion. The worst tragedy was in Bethnal Green in north London, where an unexpected daylight siren caused nearly two hundred people to be killed as they trampled each other in their rush to get into the shelter.

'Poor buggers,' Joyce said. 'Bad enough to be killed by a bomb, but to be killed by just the thought of one really does take the biscuit, doesn't it?'

'They panicked, of course,' Mrs Rutherford said. 'I believe it is a Jewish area; perhaps they are more excitable.'

'I don't know about that,' Joyce said, looking up sharply from the cake mixture she was stirring. 'Mr Lorenz is a Jew and he's certainly not the panicking kind.'

'Oh no, not at all,' Mrs Rutherford agreed hastily.

'Anyway, it's not surprising they were frightened,' Joyce said. 'Angie told me that a friend of hers saw a German plane go past in broad daylight the other day. It was so low she could see the pilot grinning at her, and then a moment later he opened fire with a machine gun on some children in a playground.'

'No!' Mrs Rutherford looked appalled.

'Still, I don't suppose it's much fun in Berlin at the moment either,' Joyce said, putting a finger into her cake mix and tasting it with a nod of approval. The two real eggs that Mrs Rutherford had brought in from her chickens at home made all the difference. 'It said on the news last night that the RAF had dropped nine hundred tons of bombs on Berlin in half an hour.'

'Serves them right,' Mrs Rutherford said. 'They started it, after all. And the sooner we finish them all off, the better in my view.'

Joyce turned away to grease her cake tins. She knew Mrs Rutherford wanted the war to be over before her precious Douglas finished his officer training and got sent overseas. And she certainly wasn't alone in wanting the guts bombed out of Germany. The general mood in the café, and indeed in London, was one of belligerence and resolve. Since Italy had been pushed out of Tunisia, there was a feeling that the tide had turned in the Allies' favour. If Italian troops had been routed so comprehensively in North Africa, surely the Nazis could be too.

But of course it wasn't as easy as that. Because Winston Churchill and President Roosevelt refused to contemplate anything but total victory. And short of Germany capitulating – and nobody really believed that would happen; Italy possibly, but not Germany – that presumably meant invasion. But to get to Germany, an invasion force would first have to cross France, which was now under complete German occupation.

So much as she'd love the war to be over, and to get her own sons home safely, Joyce wasn't holding her breath. Because even she could see that while the Allied troops were still fighting the Nazis in North Africa, an invasion of France clearly wasn't going to happen any time soon. They were all going to have to suffer the bloody war for plenty of time yet. And that was a depressing thought.

On the other hand, the café was doing well. That piece about the cooking competition in the local paper had been good for trade. And having Angie there had brought quite a few younger people in as well. The weather had improved too. There were finally some signs of spring. It looked like the awful wet winter might finally be over.

'Guess what?' Joyce remarked suddenly as she slid her cake tins into the oven. 'Monty has woken up.'

Mrs Rutherford was clearly still thinking about the war. 'Monty?' She frowned. 'You mean General Montgomery in North Africa?'

'No.' Joyce straightened up with a chuckle. 'I mean the tortoise Lorenz gave me. Monty. When I looked in his box yesterday, his little face came poking out of his shell. He looked a bit peckish, though I wasn't sure what to give him. I offered him a drop of milk, but he turned his nose up at that.'

Mrs Rutherford smiled. 'I'll bring you in some cabbage leaves for him. He'll enjoy those.'

The warm spring weather encouraged Pam Nelson to invite Katy and Malcolm out for a walk on the common.

Pam had been apologetic when she learnt of George's theft of Katy's pram wheels. Ward, on the other hand, had been highly amused. And, having treated himself to a try-out on the infamous go-cart, he had told George that he could keep them a bit longer. 'It's a damn good machine he's made,' he told Katy when she had tried to remonstrate with him. 'It would be a shame to spoil his fun. I'll find some new wheels for the pram.'

As a result of this, Malcolm was now sitting on the go-cart being tugged along by George, while Pam pushed baby Helen – or Nellie, as she was now called – in her own, fully intact pram.

'Look at Malcolm,' Pam whispered. 'I think he's enjoying it.'

Katy glanced at Malcolm and saw with some alarm that he was wearing the same happy-go-lucky, daredevil smile his father had worn when he had tried out the go-cart a few days ago.

Closing her mind to the prospect of terrors ahead as Malcolm grew up, Katy reverted to her primary concern. 'This blasted party's next weekend and I've got nothing to wear. What am I going to do?'

For some reason, among so many other worries, the problem of what to wear to the party in Henley had only occurred to her the day before. She had immediately consulted Louise, hoping to be able to borrow something suitable. But Louise was taller and bustier than Katy and didn't seem very keen on the idea of lending her a dress, as anything she did lend would clearly have to be altered.

Jen, more generously, had offered Katy free rein in her wardrobe, but Katy secretly felt that Jen's clothes weren't quite the thing. They were a bit too flashy; not tarty, precisely, but definitely not classy. No, what she needed was a formal evening dress. Something chic and elegant that Ward could be proud of her in. He, of course, just said she should buy something new, and she did have enough coupons, but there was nowhere in Clapham that sold the kind of dress Katy wanted, and anyway, it seemed wrong to buy new clothes in these austere times when 'make do and mend' was the mantra.

The truth was that she had been hoping something would happen to prevent her from going to the party. That was why she hadn't organised anything to wear. It was ridiculous, she knew, but deep down she was frightened. And she knew why. It wasn't really to do with leaving her precious business in Molly and Jen's hands, although that was bad enough. No, her fear stemmed from her feelings for Ward and Malcolm.

The thought of losing either one of them made her feel physically sick. And over the party she was torn. She had said she would go to please Ward. More than anything she wanted to please Ward, but it meant leaving Malcolm behind in London. Little Malcolm, who was too young to put what he needed into words. *Mama* and *Dada* was the sum total of his vocabulary so far. She knew Pam would look after him, but Katy had never been separated from him before and she didn't know if she would be able to do it. He was so small, so vulnerable. She knew Ward loved him too, but it was different for Ward. He was a man. And he hadn't known Malcolm as a tiny baby. He hadn't nursed him, fed him, agonised over his health and revelled in every tiny development. How could he possibly understand the bond that existed between a mother and her child?

Katy glanced up ahead. The go-cart seemed to be going rather faster now. George was almost running as he pushed. She hoped Malcolm was still enjoying it. She was just about to call to George to slow down a bit when Pam spoke again.

'You ought to ask Gillian James where she shops,' she said. 'She's got some pretty fancy clothes.'

'I couldn't possibly,' Katy said, appalled. 'I wouldn't dream of it. For one thing, I hardly know her. And for another, I don't like her.'

She wondered about telling Pam what Jen had told her about Gillian. But then she decided against it. It wasn't her business if Gillian James was a kept woman. She didn't care what the blasted woman got up to, as long as it was under her own roof. In some ways she even felt mildly pleased about it. If the widow already had a satisfactory, paying lover, perhaps it made it less likely that she would be on the lookout for anyone else.

'It's a shame you didn't ask Helen before she left,' Pam remarked. 'She had lots of lovely clothes, but her father collected them before he drove her down to Oxford.'

'Oh, I never thought of that,' Katy said. 'How stupid of me.'

'You could write to her,' Pam said. 'Ask her to send you something. Or Molly's got to go to Oxford once more next week. Perhaps she could meet up with Helen and bring a dress back for you. It would save trusting it to the post.'

Katy frowned. Molly hadn't told her she was going to Oxford again. But Molly was still put out that Jen was working in the pub. And with due cause too. Jen seemed to delight in leaving all the nasty jobs for Molly. 'Oh, I'm hopeless at scrubbing,' she would say. 'Get St Molly to do it tomorrow.' If only Jen could find an acting job, Katy thought with a sigh, then everything could return to normal.

The thought had barely left her head when Pam gave a sudden shout of alarm. George had mistimed a corner, causing the go-cart to flip over on to its side, dragging George headfirst to the ground and spilling Malcolm off sideways on to the adjacent grass.

'Oh no!' Katy said, and began to run.

He'll have broken his leg, he'll have fractured his skull, she thought as she approached. He's only fourteen months old, after all. What on earth was I thinking, letting him ride on the go-cart? At the very least he would be utterly terrified and shocked.

But Malcolm was already up on his feet, toddling back to the lethal machine, trying to push it back on to its wheels. 'Again!' he screamed impatiently at George, who was still sitting on the path, looking rather

164

tearful, with a bloody nose and painfully grazed knees. 'Again!'

Katy put her hand to her heart. *Again*. It was the first real word Malcolm had ever uttered. She didn't know whether to laugh or cry.

Ethel Florey had indeed written to ask Molly to go to Oxford once more, and Molly was more than happy to comply.

The couple of weeks since Helen's departure had been even more difficult than usual. Molly was back on Septic Ward Four and Sister Parkes had been especially down on her, delighting in every small error. It was as though she was determined to put Molly back in her place.

Even Sister Morris had told her off for taking matters into her own hands, and Dr Mallet ignored her completely. The other nurses seemed to shun her even more than they had previously, as though she was somehow contaminating, dangerous to know, tainted with some mysterious, unspoken kind of disgrace.

Dr Goodacre was the only person who seemed to be on Molly's side, winking at her conspiratorially whenever he passed her in the passage.

Things up at the Flag and Garter weren't much easier. Katy seemed anxious and overly protective of Jen Carter, who by any standard was the laziest barmaid Molly had ever seen. Molly was always having to sort out problems caused by Jen's carelessness: bottles stacked in the wrong crates, the beer pump blocked because she hadn't cleaned it out properly, or dirty tea towels hidden under the counter because she was too proud to get her precious hands wet rinsing them out.

And either Ward Frazer wasn't there at all, which was bad enough, or he was there in all his glory, which was even worse. The last time she had seen him he had been stripped down to his shirt sleeves, fitting new wheels to Malcolm's pram.

Once again on the train, steaming away from London, Molly fingered the tiny magic carpet that now hung permanently, secretly, round her neck and was conscious of some of the tension easing out of her. For the moment at least she was safe from any unexpected encounters with Ward Frazer. Safe from vindictive nurses.

It felt good to be back on the train, liberated from the hospital, from her mundane little life. The sun was out, and through the small diamond cut out of the blackout on the carriage window she could see the countryside, green and fresh after the long, wet winter.

But at Reading station, a nasty surprise awaited her.

As usual, she had to change at Reading for the Oxford train, which was normally waiting on the opposite platform. But today there was no sign of it.

Instead there were a large number of soldiers standing about, which made her feel self-conscious dismounting from the train. When she stumbled on the bottom step, she heard laughter and a few token wolf whistles, and looked around rather desperately for someone to ask about the Oxford train. But the only railway official she could see was way up by the engine, talking to the driver, barely visible through a cloud of steam.

'Where you going to, darling?' one of the soldiers called out. 'Why don't you come with us?'

This produced another laugh, and Molly felt her cheeks turning pink.

'I've got a nasty wound on my inner thigh,' another lad chipped in. 'Would you like to take a look?'

More good-natured hilarity followed, until one of the men muttered a warning under his breath.

A group of four young officers with fresh, newly minted pips on their shoulders were approaching down the platform alongside the waiting train. Clearly relishing the novelty of their elevated status, they were deliberately strolling up and down so that the other ranks had to keep saluting them.

As the ribaldry faded away, Molly glanced gratefully at the officers. One of them raised his fingers carelessly to his cap, acknowledging the soldiers' salute, and, to her horror, Molly recognised the smug features of Douglas Rutherford.

He saw her at the same moment and did a kind of double-take. She quickly looked away and ducked her head. But he had seen her arriving at the Flag and Garter in her nurses' regalia too often not to recognise her.

'Well, well, if it isn't the Poxy Pixie,' he drawled, coming to a halt. He turned to the watching soldiers. 'Keep clear of this one, chaps, she's likely to give you a nasty disease.'

Several of the men laughed, although, to their credit, one or two looked uncomfortable. Not as uncomfortable as Molly felt, however.

'Probably not what you had in mind, though,' Douglas Rutherford continued with a smirk. 'I always thought nurses were meant to be pretty, until I saw this one.'

Molly wanted to kill him then, right there on the platform. She wished she had the courage to ask him if he had assaulted any teenage girls recently. But she didn't.

'I thought you'd be in North Africa by now,' she said instead.

'I will be soon. And that will be the last you see of Rommel and his Afrika Korps, I can assure you.'

'I'm sure he's quaking in his desert boots already,' Molly muttered, and was pleased when one of the servicemen chuckled. Douglas wasn't pleased, though. Molly saw his eyes narrow sharply and was relieved when whatever

166

he was about to say was interrupted by a bellowed order from a red-faced sergeant further up the platform. At once the soldiers broke ranks and surged forward to get into the train.

Stepping hastily to one side to avoid the crush, Molly watched the young officers stride away to a first-class carriage and found herself trembling. It was partly anger, partly embarrassment and partly something else. She knew she wasn't pretty. She only had to look in a mirror to know that. But somehow Douglas made her feel worse than just ugly. He was a bully and he sensed her weakness. But even so his derisive remarks had left her feeling pathetic and somehow ridiculous.

A minute later the last door clanged shut, there was a shrill whistle, a great gasping huff of steam and the train began to groan and wheeze its way out of the station.

'Those lads giving you a rough time, love?'

Molly jumped as the stationmaster suddenly loomed out of the smoke.

'No, no, I'm fine,' she said, but she could feel herself flushing again. 'But what's happened to the Oxford train?'

The man glanced up at the station clock. 'Running a bit late, delayed by an air raid.' Then, as the rail tracks began to vibrate again, he looked over her shoulder. 'Ah, here she comes now.' He gave her an encouraging nod as he moved away. 'Don't take it to heart. Boys will be boys, eh?'

'Douglas Rutherford deserves a smack,' Helen de Burrel said hotly when Molly recounted the incident to her later over a cup of tea at the Oxford Cadena in Cornmarket Street. Helen was wearing a stylish navy jacket over a Fair Isle jersey and a neat little skirt. She was looking much better. She was still very thin, but fresh air and exercise had put some colour back in her cheeks, and she had had her hair cut into a short, sleek bob. Molly could hardly believe the transformation. It made her feel even more plain in her unflattering Wilhelmina uniform and cap.

'He was so pleased with himself, with his officer's pips and his smart new uniform,' she said bitterly.

'I can't believe he's managed to get himself commissioned already,' Helen said, stirring her tea. 'But then of course the whole winter has kind of passed me by. It seems like one minute I was sweating myself to death in that horrid tent in Algeria, and the next time I look, it's spring.' She smiled at Molly. 'And it is all down to you. I just wish there was something I could do for you in return.'

'Find me a new life?' Molly suggested. She had meant it to sound funny, but it just sounded sad, and she flushed as Helen gave her a sympathetic glance.

'That bad?'

Molly shook her head. She didn't want Helen to feel sorry for her. 'No, I'm fine really. I just wish I could get away from the Wilhelmina ...' She stopped, because half of her wanted to get away from the Wilhelmina, away from Lavender Road, and half of her didn't.

Helen made a wry face. 'Be careful what you wish for,' she said. 'I wished I could see André just one more time, and look what happened. I was with him in France long enough to know I wanted to be with him for ever, and now I don't know if I will ever see him again. I don't even know if he is still alive.'

'I'm sure he's still alive,' Molly said stoutly. But of course she wasn't sure. How could she be? But after what Helen had been through, it would be a crying shame if she and André weren't able to be together one day. She also realised that in the face of Helen's lost love, her own problems seemed rather pitiful. Not that she would admit her idiotic infatuation with Ward Frazer to anyone. The very thought made her quail with mortification.

'Are you all right, Molly?' Helen was looking at her with some concern. 'Seriously, is there anything I can do to help?'

'No, I'm OK, I just ...' For a terrible moment Molly thought she was going to cry. Or worse, to blurt everything out. Helen was so nice. And before he had gone back to America, Lord de Burrel had written such a lovely letter to thank her, on beautiful heavy paper, embossed with the address of his club in St James's. *Please do not hesitate to contact me if you feel I can be of service to you in any way.* But there was nothing anyone could do to help. The problem was hers, and hers alone.

'Honestly, I'm fine,' she said again. 'Really.'

To her relief, Helen let the subject go then and poured them each another cup of tea. When she had dealt with the milk and spooned in the tiny ration of sugar they were allowed, she reached down under the table and brought out a parcel wrapped neatly in brown paper and tied with string.

'There are two evening dresses in there for Katy to try. Tell her she can have either of them altered if she wants. And tell her to give everyone my love.'

Molly looked up. 'Aren't you going to the party?'

Helen shook her head. 'I don't think I'm quite up to a party yet. And anyway, until I hear something about André, I don't really feel ...' She tailed off and gave a small shrug.

'Here.' Molly suddenly unclipped the chain from round her neck and offered the tiny silver carpet to Helen. 'Make a wish. Ward brought me this back from Algeria. The man who sold it to him said wishes you make on it come true.'

'Oh yes,' Helen said, fingering the little charm. 'I remember. He showed it to me. It's pretty, isn't it?' She held the charm in her slender fingers for a moment. Then she smiled and closed her eyes. 'I wish I could somehow help Molly Coogan to find herself a better life.'

'No!' Molly gaped at her in dismay. 'That's not what I meant at all. I wanted you to wish about André.'

Helen laughed as she handed the necklace back to Molly. 'I know.' She rubbed her thumb over the tips of her fingers as though they were tingling. 'But you've already given me my life back. It would be greedy for me to wish for more than that.'

Feeling choked, Molly clasped the necklace carefully back round her neck. 'Katy will be sorry you aren't going to the party,' she said. 'I think she was hoping for some moral support.'

'She'll be fine. Ward will look after her. He adores her.' Helen gave a wry smile. 'I think Katy sometimes forgets how lucky she is. He's such a great guy, isn't he? Don't you just love him to bits? I do.'

Molly tried to speak but felt her throat constrict. She couldn't talk about Ward Frazer. She couldn't. Already she could feel herself flushing. She pretended to catch sight of the café clock. 'Gosh. I must go,' she said, getting to her feet. 'I'm due at Dr Florey's at twelve.'

If Helen noticed anything untoward about her clumsy exit, she was too polite to show it. 'Say hello from me,' she said, picking up her handbag. 'When Daddy next comes back from Washington, he is going to take the Floreys out to dinner, and we want you to come too. No, no,' she waved away Molly's offer of money for the elevenses, 'this one is on me.'

'Oh, and Molly,' she added, as they said goodbye outside in the street. 'Don't worry about that spiteful little twit Douglas Rutherford. He'll get his comeuppance one day.'

Molly smiled gratefully and put her hand up to touch the little magic carpet at her throat. 'Then I wish that I can be there to witness it!' she said.

'I am looking for a book on what to feed tortoises,' Joyce said, and then felt herself colouring. Her request had come out rather more loudly than she had expected, especially in the hushed atmosphere of the library, but she had been waiting at the desk several minutes now and the thin-faced librarian had so far failed to acknowledge her presence. She seemed to be completely engrossed in making notations on some kind of lengthy list. But Joyce didn't have all day. She had only popped out of the café for a few minutes in the hope of finding out what to feed Monty. She was increasingly worried about him. He was looking a bit down in the mouth, to say the least. He had turned up his nose at the cabbage leaves Mrs Rutherford had given her. She had to find something that he would eat. And urgently too.

She gave a pointed cough. 'If you could just tell me which section tortoises would be in, I'll go and look myself if you are too busy to help me.'

At this the librarian did finally deign to lift her head and regarded Joyce over a pair of half-moon spectacles. 'Are you registered here?' she asked in a voice as hushed as the library.

'No.' Joyce had never previously set foot in the library. But when Mrs Rutherford had suggested that they might have a book on tortoise-keeping, she had decided to pay a call.

The librarian raised a thin pair of eyebrows. 'I can't let you take a book away if you are not registered.'

'Well how long does it take to register?' As Joyce spoke, trying to use the same low tone as the librarian, she became aware of a slight movement to her left and, to her surprise, saw Gillian James's daughter watching her from a nearby rack of books. As soon as she caught Joyce's sharp gaze, the girl looked away, her long lashes fluttering down over her blue eyes. She really was ridiculously pretty, Joyce thought. Prettier even than the mother.

The librarian pushed a form and a pen across the desk. 'It takes a few days, perhaps a week, for the paperwork to be completed.'

'A week?' Joyce stared at her, aghast. 'The tortoise will be dead by then.'

The librarian pursed her lips. 'If we do have a suitable book, you are perfectly at liberty to read it here.'

'Well *do* you have a suitable book?' Joyce asked irritably. This was a public library, for goodness' sake. Surely they were meant to help people gain knowledge. Even if it was only about tortoises. 'And if so, where is it?'

The woman stood up reluctantly. 'Follow me, please,' she said, leading the way through the shelves of books.

A minute later the librarian was handing her an enormous book entitled *Reptile Keeping*.

'Goodness.' Joyce stared at the tome in dismay. It would take her a year to wade through that. It weighed a ton and the pages were so closely written the words swam before her eyes.

She looked up in dismay. 'Would it be possible for you to find the information for me? All I need to know is what to feed him on now he's come out of hibernation.' As she offered the book hopefully back to the librarian, she caught sight of Bella James again. The blasted girl had clearly followed them through the library and was now lurking at the other end of the row, pretending to look for a book in the rack in the adjacent aisle.

'I'm afraid I don't have time for that,' the librarian said. 'But if you look in the index, you should be able to find what you need.'

'I doubt it.' Joyce muttered. She could feel the heat in her cheeks again. She had no idea where even to find an index, let alone how to use one if she did, but she was damned if she was going to display her ignorance to this snooty woman. Nor was she going to make a fool of herself in front of Bella James. She heaved the book back on to the shelf. 'I'll just have to try him again on the cabbage leaves,' she said, and turning on her heel, she marched out of the library.

'So that's that, then,' Ethel Florey said. 'A successful conclusion to a very interesting case.'

'I am so grateful to you, Dr Florey,' Molly said. 'Not just for what you and everyone here did for Helen, but also for your kindness to me. I—'

'Yes. It has been a good team effort,' Dr Florey interrupted brusquely. 'And you were part of that team.' She stood up and offered her hand. 'I have enjoyed working with you, Nurse Coogan. You have been efficient, sensible and reliable. I will be writing to your hospital matron to that effect.' She caught Molly's expression and smiled encouragingly. 'I know you aren't very happy at the Wilhelmina. But I'm sure you will go on to do great things.'

'I doubt it,' Molly said as she headed for the door. 'I'm more likely to end up as a boring old spinster staff nurse on Septic Ward Four.'

Ethel Florey gave a wry laugh. 'There are worse fates.'

If there were, Molly couldn't think of one, but she smiled dutifully as she said goodbye.

When she had left Dr Florey's office, Molly went to bid a final farewell to the masked girls in what was known as the mould room. They seemed genuinely sorry to see her go.

She wanted to say goodbye to Professor Florey and Dr Chain too, but Margaret Jennings told her that Dr Chain was giving a lecture and Professor Florey was in London trying to arrange a trip out to North Africa so that he could test penicillin on recently wounded servicemen.

On her way out of the building, however, she bumped into Dr Chain coming in through the swing doors.

He raised his hat politely. 'Ah, it's the little nurse. I think I haven't seen you recently.'

Molly smiled. 'That's because my patient is completely recovered.'

'The wonder of penicillin, yes?'

'Yes indeed,' Molly agreed. 'I'm so grateful to you all. And thank you for taking me to your lecture too. I really enjoyed it.'

He inclined his head. 'And have you thought any more about training to be a doctor?'

Molly stared at him blankly. 'It's not a question of thinking about it any more. I've never thought about it at all.'

He gave a jovial laugh. 'Well you should. We could do with some more intelligent young women in the medical profession.'

For a split second, as the implication of what he had said sank in, Molly felt a sudden thrill of gratified excitement, but reality quickly reasserted itself. Not only would you need a considerable amount of money to go to university medical school, you also presumably needed qualifications. 'But I don't know anything about physics or chemistry.'

Dr Chain peered at her in surprise from under his bristling eyebrows. 'Didn't you take sciences at school?'

'No.' Molly shook her head. 'Girls didn't do sciences at my school. Only biology.'

'Ach. Then that is a pity.' He glanced at his fob watch, gave her one of his formal foreign nods and strode away down the corridor.

As she walked back to the station, Molly had a brief vision of how wonderful it would be to be able to swan into the Wilhelmina in a doctor's coat with a stethoscope round her neck and start bossing the nursing staff around. It might almost be worth going to night school to study physics and chemistry just to see the look on Sister Parkes's face!

After her abortive visit to the library, Joyce had been in a bad mood all day. Now, as she walked home from the café, she was facing up to having to ask Jen if she'd go there to read up about tortoises for her. She could have asked Angie, of course, but she didn't think Angie was sufficiently well educated to know about indexes and all that academic mumbo-jumbo. All Angie seemed to know about was having a good time. But Jen had been clever at school. If it hadn't been for her mad idea of trying to become an actress, she might have done quite well for herself as a typist or even a secretary.

But as Joyce opened her front gate, she noticed there was something on the doorstep. It was a rusty baked bean can, half full of water, containing a bunch of dandelions. Under the tin was a folded piece of paper. The writing was neat and rounded. *For your tortoise.*

Swinging round, Joyce glanced over at the house on the other side of the road. There was no sign of anyone. No pretty face at the window. But it had to be her, she thought. It surely wasn't the po-faced librarian.

For a second she hesitated, then, unsure what else to do, she picked up the can, opened her front door and went inside.

Monty loved the dandelions. In fact he ate so many, Joyce thought he might be sick. So she held some back for the following day. Once again he fell on them with alacrity, his little eyes gleaming with excitement. The day after that, she left the empty can on her doorstep with a note under it. *Thank you.*

By the time she came home in the evening, it had been refilled. This time, as well as dandelions, there were some other unidentifiable weeds and two small stinging nettles.

Lucinda Veale's party was on 27 March. By ten o'clock that evening, Katy was wishing she had held to her original conviction and refused to come. She was hating it. She missed Malcolm more than she had imagined. Being away from him was like having a cord pulled out of her stomach.

But worse than that, she just didn't know how to behave. Talking to these smart, chic upper-class girls wasn't like standing behind the bar chatting to Mr Lorenz or Angie Carter. They were all so pretty and polite. Even in their not-quite-new dresses and last year's shoes, they exuded money. It was their bearing, their confidence, their assumption that everyone, especially the men present, would find them fascinating. And the men did seem to find them fascinating. Even Ward.

Not that Ward wasn't attentive to her as well, because he was. He was always coming to her side if she was alone, but she hated to hold him back. He was having fun; they loved him, they laughed at his jokes, teased him about his accent, and they loved pretending to pry into his secret work. They were impressed by him, and who wouldn't be. But they weren't impressed by her. Even dressed in Helen de Burrel's velvet evening dress, with the beautiful bracelet Ward had brought back from Algeria on her arm, in their eyes she was just a drab little wannabe, trying to move in circles quite above her station.

And then she met one who was even more pretty and not quite so polite. Her name was Felicity Rowe and she claimed to be an old friend of Ward's from way back when. She too had apparently been at Katy's wedding.

'Goodness, it was quite a turn-up for the books when we heard he was getting married. None of us could believe it. He had kept you very quiet. I wonder why? And Lucinda tells me you've already had a baby.'

While she talked, her eyes followed Ward round the dance floor as he waltzed with Lucinda. His bad leg didn't seem to be impeding his progress one iota.

'Malcolm?' Felicity Rowe tried to hide her giggle. 'What an unusual name. And how old is little Malcolm now?'

It took all Katy's self-control not to throw her glass of wine into the woman's smirking face. Instead she made some gauche, stumbling excuse and went to find Louise.

'Oh you don't want to worry about her. She's always had a bit of a pash for Ward.'

A pash? Katy was conscious of a flush of irritation. 'Well he's mine now,' she said. 'So she can keep her hands off.'

Louise laughed. 'Quite right,' she said. Then she jerked her head over to where two other girls were vying for Ward's attention now the waltz was over. 'But you'd better keep your eye on him, because Felicity isn't the only one who'd like to get her claws into him.'

And then it got worse. Two young men approached. One of them wore a confident smirk and a suave dinner jacket. The other wore a military uniform Katy didn't recognise. She guessed from his accent that he was American. The Americans were everywhere nowadays. There were always gangs of them in the Flag and Garter on a Saturday night, cavorting with Angie Carter to the sounds of Joe Loss on the wireless. Even as she had the thought, Katy experienced a stab of fear at what might be happening there tonight. There was so much potential for disaster: Jen might get distracted and inadvertently leave the till open, or a fight would break out, or a licensing official would call, or someone would steal the remaining glasses.

While Katy was lost in her thoughts, Louise monopolised the two newcomers, flirting coyly with the handsome civilian. Within minutes she had encouraged him on to the dance floor, leaving Katy to make stilted conversation with the other, who turned out to be a young pilot officer in the Royal Canadian Air Force.

'My husband is Canadian,' she said.

'Really?' He smiled politely. 'Where's he from?'

In Katy's experience, Canadians and Americans always wanted to know where their compatriots were from, but now, to her shame, she suddenly realised she couldn't provide the name of Ward's home town because she simply didn't know it.

'He's attached to the RAF,' she said, pretending she hadn't heard the question.

'Maybe I've met him,' the young officer said. He was looking around, clearly hoping to escape as soon as possible. Katy sympathised with him. Until someone came to rescue them, they were both hopelessly trapped in each other's company. 'What's his name?'

'Ward Frazer,' Katy said.

The pilot started in surprise. 'Ward Frazer?'

'Do you know him?' Katy asked.

He shook his head. 'I don't know him,' he said. 'But I know *of* him, of course. Everyone knows about Ward Frazer.' He looked at her with new interest. 'I didn't know he was married, though.'

'Well he is,' Katy said sourly. Then she looked at him more closely. 'What do you mean, everyone knows about Ward Frazer? Because of his lectures about escaping from a POW camp, you mean?'

'Did he? Wow! I didn't know about that.' The young man smiled at her ingratiatingly. She certainly had his attention now. There was no more glancing away in the hopes of salvation. 'No, I actually meant because of his background.'

It was Katy's turn to be surprised. She was conscious of a slight sinking sensation in the pit of her stomach. 'What do you mean?'

The pilot officer looked embarrassed. He shifted uneasily under her close scrutiny. 'Well. If he's the same guy I'm talking about, it was kind of big news when he went over to Germany for the Olympics and never came back.'

Katy's stomach sank another notch. They were obviously talking about the same guy. Ward Frazer. Her husband. She glared at her informant. 'Why was it such big news?'

The young man was squirming now. He was clearly labouring under the impression that he was being punished for speaking out of turn. It didn't seem to have occurred to him that she actually didn't know what he was talking about. 'I guess because of his father owning one of the country's largest aircraft manufacturers,' he muttered. 'Ewart Frazer is a pretty sizeable fish in Canada. It seemed a big deal when his son turned his back on all that.'

Suddenly Katy's brain was reeling. A big deal? He could say that again. Oh God, she thought. I am married to a man I don't know. The room spun for a moment. She put out a hand to clutch the back of a nearby chair.

'Are you OK, Mrs Frazer?' The young pilot sounded alarmed.

'I'm sorry,' Katy said. 'I feel a little faint. I just need to sit down for a moment.'

Chapter Thirteen

The Flag and Garter was indeed full of Americans. Mostly invited by Angie Carter. And because the Americans were there, so were the local girls, drawn as if by magic, or more likely by the whispered promise of nylons, lipstick and perfume.

All in all, by the middle of the evening the pub was as busy as Molly had ever seen it. The air was thick with the smoke of Lucky Strikes, Pashas and Wills. It was hot and getting hotter by the minute, and the smell of sweat and spilt beer mingled uneasily with the rather too liberally applied scents of the local girls. But the American GIs didn't care. They liked the Flag and Garter better than the West End pubs. A young marine called Randy had told Molly earlier that the guys could let their hair down here without feeling that everyone was on the snatch, like they were in central London.

And the GIs certainly knew how to let their hair down. Whether they had joined up from a factory in Detroit, or been drafted in from a farm in Iowa, they were all full of chat, banter and dance moves. Even now half a dozen of them were demonstrating their skill at the jitterbug over in the far corner to the music of Fats Waller on the wireless, while on the other side of the room, two lads from Chicago were noisily calling bets on half a dozen snails they had found in the back yard and which they were about to race across one of the tables.

None of them had ever been out of America before and they mostly had a very hazy idea of the geography of Europe, let alone that of North Africa. All they seemed to know was that there was a land mass called 'Yurp' that needed liberating. But that didn't appear to matter; they were all keen to do their bit, determined to get Hitler and Mussolini beat so they could return as soon as possible to their beloved US of A. And while they were waiting to be shipped off to the action, they were happy to spend their generous wages on pretty girls, cigarettes and beer.

And if they were happy to spend it in the Flag and Garter in Clapham, all the better, Molly thought, as she reached down into the ice bath under the counter for yet another bottle of Coors lager.

As she straightened up, she bumped into Jen, who was pulling a pint. 'Watch out, you idiot!' Jen screamed as a spray of froth splattered over her skirt.

'Why can't you look what you are doing,' Molly snapped back. 'Surely you could see I was down there. And for goodness' sake wipe up that mess before our shoes start sticking to it.' Jen never wiped up her spills. The surface of the bar was like glue from all the drink she slopped as she passed the glasses across to customers.

'I haven't got time. Do it yourself,' Jen said and waltzed off into the kitchen to mop herself up, leaving her disgruntled customer still waiting for his pint.

'Don't worry, Molly, I'll do it.' Joyce Carter suddenly appeared behind the bar with a tray of empties.

'I don't see why you have to clear up her mess,' Molly said crossly, opening the Coors with one hand while topping up the pint with the other.

'I'm used to it,' Joyce said grimly. 'I've been cleaning up after Jen for years.'

Before Molly could reply, some kind of a rumpus erupted at the other side of the room. It was followed by a peel of raucous laughter and a loud crash. Fats Waller gave a strangled squawk and died mid note.

'Good God, what's happened now?' Molly muttered.

'That sounded suspiciously like Angie,' Joyce said.

She was right. Her younger daughter's overenthusiastic jitterbug had resulted in her crashing into the wireless.

It was Aaref who brought the news over to Molly. Katy had asked him to spend the evening in the pub just in case of any trouble, and he had been talking to Alan Nelson over by the fire when the accident had happened. 'It is beyond repairing,' he said. 'Although one of the Yankees is trying.'

'Oh no,' Molly groaned. 'They're not going to stay long if there's no music.' She had a sudden vision of everyone leaving in disgust and going to one of the rival pubs in the area. Katy would be distraught if that happened. But there didn't seem to be much she could do about it, unless Jen would be prepared to play the piano and get a few songs going. There was little chance of that, though. Jen was always so concerned about straining her precious vocal cords.

She glanced back at Aaref and realised he was looking very down in the mouth. She knew why, of course. Louise hadn't asked him to the party in Henley. She'd preferred to go alone with Katy and Ward.

'You should learn your lesson,' Molly said. 'She's using you. She always has been. You're only of use to her if there's no one better around. You should try to find someone who will love you back.' She knew she was a fine one to talk, but she was fond of Aaref and felt impatient with him for wasting his efforts on a heartless, hoity-toity madam like Louise Delmaine.

Unfortunately Jen chose that precise moment to reappear out of the kitchen. 'Oh listen to the agony aunt,' she said sarcastically. 'What do you know about love?'

Heat surged into Molly's cheeks. She could feel Jen's mocking gaze on her.

Jen spread her hands dramatically. 'Careful!' she shouted suddenly. 'Don't move!' She laughed as everyone froze in alarm. 'Watch where you tread in case you step on one of the Poxy Pixie's pearls of wisdom.'

'I know more than you think,' Molly snapped.

'Well, what?' Jen challenged her. 'What could you possibly know?'

Molly had held back as best she could, but now she lost her temper. She was fed up with Jen and her snarky little remarks. 'Well one thing I do know is that love isn't about pretending you fancy some theatrical producer just so they can give you a leg-up with your career.'

Jen's face darkened ominously, and for an awful moment Molly thought she was going to hit her. But thankfully Joyce intervened. 'Leave her alone, Jen,' she said sharply. 'And do try to grow up. Why don't you go and do something useful for once, like playing the piano?'

A murmur of approval greeted this suggestion. But one voice stood out over the hubbub, an incongruously cool, cultured voice that belonged to a rather handsome man in an expensive-looking suit with a camel overcoat over his shoulders. Molly hadn't noticed him come in, but it was obvious from his expression that he had been there long enough to witness their angry exchange.

'Yes indeed,' he said evenly. 'Why don't you? I didn't know you could play the piano.'

Oh no, Molly thought. Oh no. She guessed at once who it must be. And the expression of mortified horror on Jen's face confirmed it. This sophisticated interloper was none other than Henry Keller himself.

In other, less calamitous circumstances Molly might have laughed. She had never seen Jen in such a state of shocked disarray. Her cheeks were scarlet, she had a beer stain all down the front of her shirt, and her copper curls, which had been teased into a fashionable neck roll when she arrived at the pub earlier, had become loose and had frizzed up in the heat, making her look like a demented poodle. When she finally managed to speak, her voice sounded as though someone had their hands round her throat. 'How did you know I was here?'

Molly saw Henry Keller's eyes flicker towards Joyce, who seemed to have become rooted to a particular spot behind the bar. Following his glance, Molly was surprised by the look of horror on Joyce's face. But Henry Keller was already turning back to Jen with a hint of ironic amusement in his eyes. 'Just a lucky guess,' he said blandly.

Uninterested in this exchange, a number of the regulars were still urging Jen to sit down at the piano.

'Come on, darling,' someone shouted. 'Give us a tune!' The refrain was taken up by one or two others. Even some of the Americans were joining in now.

'But …' Jen glanced uncertainly at Henry Keller, who had taken a packet of Gold Flake out of his pocket and was casually tapping out a cigarette.

He waved it unconcernedly in the direction of the piano. 'Your audience awaits,' he said. 'Don't mind me.' Then he turned to Molly. 'I'll have a small whisky, when you've got a moment.'

Molly stared at him aghast. He was cool, you had to give him that.

Taking a glass with a shaking hand, she held it up to the Famous Grouse optic on the shelf behind her. Reflected in the mirror, she could see Jen moving self-consciously over to the piano and taking up her position on the stool.

'I didn't really mean what I said before,' Molly muttered awkwardly as she put the whisky down on the counter. She didn't like Jen, but she didn't want to be the cause of her downfall. If nothing else, she knew Jen's capacity for revenge. 'She had annoyed me and I was trying to get back at her.'

Henry was lighting his cigarette with a gold lighter. 'I think you succeeded,' he said drily as behind him, on the other side of the room, Jen started thumping out the opening chords of 'I'll Never Smile Again'.

'I'm really sorry,' Molly said.

Henry looked at her thoughtfully through his exhaled smoke. 'Don't apologise,' he said. 'I think you may have done me a favour.' He waved his cigarette negligently. 'What is that expression they use in the military?'

Molly frowned. 'Don't shoot yourself in the foot?' she suggested.

He gave a sudden choke of laughter. 'No. I was thinking more in terms of "forewarned is forearmed"!' Giving her a quick conspiratorial wink, he pulled the glass towards him and swirled it around for a moment before raising it to his lips.

Then, leaning a casual elbow on the bar, he turned belatedly to watch Jen's performance.

'Why didn't you tell me?' Katy asked. She and Ward were sitting in a cool corner of the bar of the Leander Club. A series of rudders and long, engraved oars adorned the walls. In the adjacent room the party was still in full swing, the band leader segueing from a languorous smooch into a lively jive, and Katy could hear some laughing protestations as the swaying couples were forced to break up and show some action.

179

Ward had found her slumped, pale and feeling faint, on one of the sitting-out chairs at the side of the dance floor. Quickly he had escorted her out of the hot ballroom into the cooler bar. The Canadian air force officer had followed them, more, Katy suspected, with the intention of talking to Ward rather than out of any solicitude for her. But Ward had managed to get rid of him pretty swiftly, and having fetched Katy a glass of water had wasted no time in finding out what had caused her sudden collapse.

He had listened in silence as Katy blurted out the gist of the young man's comments. She had waited for him to deny it. But he didn't. He just looked rather grim and glanced through the doors to the other room as though wishing he could mete out some rough justice to the departed young officer for spilling the beans. Now, as she repeated her question, he sat back in his chair and ran a hand through his hair. 'What difference would it have made?'

Katy was feeling sick. She didn't know if it was the shock of finding out that Ward's family were rich and influential, or the wine. Or possibly the unexpectedly lavish food that Lucinda's parents had provided before the party. But at this she raised her eyes and gaped at her husband.

What difference? She didn't know where to begin.

'I guess I didn't want you to know,' he said. 'I didn't want you to be influenced by my background.'

Katy blinked. 'You thought I'd only want to marry you for your money?'

'No.' He shook his head. 'The complete opposite. I didn't want to scare you off. You were reluctant enough as it was.'

Katy remembered only too clearly how tongue-tied she had been with him in those early days. In some ridiculous way she still was. Even now, sometimes, when he looked at her in a certain way, she felt herself blushing and fumbling for words. But she was never reluctant. She was just shy.

He shrugged. 'I wanted you to marry me for who I am now, not for what I used to be. Anyway, I haven't got any money. Only what I earn.' He hesitated for a moment and his jaw hardened. 'That's why I am so angry with my parents. They should have helped you out while I was a POW.' He swore softly under his breath. 'Good God, it wasn't much to ask.'

Katy stared at him. 'Did you ask?'

'No, but my aunts did. And again when Malcolm was born.'

'They never said anything to me.'

'No.' He gave a slight smile. 'They are discreet old birds when they want to be.'

'But why didn't you tell me when we got married?' Katy persevered.

He had the grace to look slightly sheepish. 'I was going to. Of course I was, but somehow the moment was never quite right. And then when I eventually got back this time …' He paused for a moment. 'Everything had changed. You had Malcolm. You had the pub.' He gave a rueful grin that didn't quite reach his eyes. 'And suddenly you had me again. I knew it wasn't going to be easy for you. The last thing I wanted to do was to rock the boat.'

Katy flinched. It hadn't occurred to her to think of how much had changed while he had been away. When they had got married she had still been a wide-eyed, adoring little nurse. By the time he came back from Germany, not only had she become the landlady of a busy pub, but also a mother. He had been presented with a fait accompli. She had never thought to ask him if it was what he wanted.

'Anyway,' he went on steadily, 'it's *our* boat now. We're in it together. You, me and Malcolm. We'll live our life the way we want to. It's nothing to do with my parents.'

'But of course it is,' Katy said. She took a sip of her water. 'You are their only son. They're probably terrified you've married a guttersnipe.'

Ward's lips twitched. 'I'm not sure that my father'd know what that is.'

'He'll find out soon enough,' Katy said grimly. 'You uncle is probably coming to tell you they've disinherited you.'

'Let him. I don't want their money.'

Katy could understand that, to a certain extent. She had had the same feeling herself when her parents smothered her with caution as a teenager. But even though she'd resented their overprotective concern, even though she had longed to break away, she would never have abandoned them completely. It had never got that bad.

She looked at him, this man who she loved so much and suddenly seemed to know so little. 'So after the Olympics, you just didn't go back?'

'I did go back,' he said. 'But I left again pretty damn soon.' He saw her expression and shrugged. 'OK, maybe I was hot-headed. But once I'd seen what was happening in Germany … Good God. My girlfriend had just been killed by the Nazis. I couldn't let it go.'

Katy frowned. 'And your parents didn't understand that?'

'They didn't try to understand.'

Katy could hear the sulky resentment of the idealistic young man in his voice. There was no doubt his parents had handled the situation very badly. But she could understand their position. 'They didn't want you to put yourself in danger,' she said. 'They were frightened for you. That's what I feel about Malcolm. I'm frightened for him.'

Ward shook his head. 'The war will be well over by the time he's old enough to fight.'

'But there'll be another war,' Katy said. 'There'll always be wars while men are in charge of the world.'

He smiled at that, but didn't disagree. 'You wouldn't want to hold him back.'

'I'd try to protect him. Of course I would.' Katy thought of her anxiety when Malcolm had fallen off the go-cart. She knew that fear for him would never leave her.

'Maybe you're right,' Ward said. 'But if they think they can blackmail me, then they have another think coming. They tried that once before. There was a girl in Canada they wanted me to marry. They tried to bribe me into it.'

Oh no, Katy thought. This was getting worse and worse. She didn't dare ask who this other girl was. She didn't need to. Whoever she was, Katy knew that she would have been from a wealthy, classy family with a place in Canadian society. Exactly the sort of girl someone like Ward *should* have married. She realised she felt very sick again. She began to wonder if part of his motivation to marry her had been to punish his parents.

'We ought to go back to the party,' she said. 'They'll be wondering where we've got to.'

He reached across to take her hand. Lifting it to his lips, he kissed it gently. 'I think we should go back to the hotel.'

Katy felt a shiver run up her spine at the feel of his lips on her skin. 'But wouldn't it be rude just to leave?' she said. She was longing for her bed, but she didn't want to spoil his evening. Or to give his friends even more cause to sneer at her.

He stretched in his chair. 'I'll go make our apologies to Lucinda,' he said. He got to his feet slowly. 'I've done enough dancing for one night anyway.'

'But what about Louise?' Katy had no idea what had happened to Louise. She had last seen her swaying on the dance floor, wrapped much too closely in the arms of the smooth young man in the dinner jacket.

Ward looked impatient. 'Louise can look after herself.'

'But she can't,' Katy said. 'We are meant to be chaperoning her.'

'I don't care,' Ward said firmly. 'You need your bed.' He leaned over and touched her hot cheek with gentle fingers. Then he smiled his smile, the one that curled round Katy's heart. 'And I, rather urgently, need to convince you that I am exactly the same person as I was before tonight's revelations.'

In the Flag and Garter, still at the piano, Jen was seething. By any standard she was having the worst night of her life. Why, oh why, had blasted Katy decided to go to her fancy party? If only she had given in to her maternal instinct and stayed at home with Malcolm, none of this would have happened.

It was bad enough that Henry Keller had walked in when he had. But it was worse that he had stayed. How dare he watch her with that faintly amused smile curling his lips? How dare he chat so easily with her mother and with that treacherous little weasel Molly Coogan? Even Angie had given him a smacking kiss on the cheek. He seemed far more interested in all of them than in her. So what on earth was he doing here? Why wasn't he hobnobbing with Janette Pymm and Vivien Leigh in some fancy West End restaurant?

It had almost been a relief when the punters had clamoured for her to perform. Anything was better than having to face up to Henry after what Molly had said. If nothing else, she would show him. Even though she was no pianist, she would show him that she could work an audience.

And she had shown him. She had whipped them all up into a frenzy of singing, stamping and clapping. Much more of it and they'd blow the roof off. She was exhausted. But every time she'd tried to stop, they howled for more.

In the old days, Jen had refused to sing in the pub because of the smoke and the noise. But she didn't care about her voice any more. Her career was clearly over, so she might as well belt out tuppenny-ha'penny hits instead. She was in the middle of 'I've Got a Gal in Kalamazoo' now, and the Yankee soldiers were loving it.

And as she sang, so they bought her drinks, and she could feel herself getting increasingly tipsy. Not as tipsy as Angie, though. Jen could see her sister out of the corner of her eye, wrapped round a grinning young American soldier. If he hadn't been there to support her, Jen was pretty sure Angie would have slithered gracefully – or not so gracefully, given that it was Angie – to the ground. Not that anyone would notice; they were all well gone now, tipping back the ale as though there was no tomorrow.

So why didn't Henry just leave? Even he was on his third whisky now. The only consolation was that he must be hating it. This wasn't his normal milieu. He looked ridiculously out of place in his double-breasted suit and tie. Jen groaned inwardly as she launched into 'It's a Long Way To Tipperary'.

Who indeed, she thought grimly. Even an air raid would be preferable to this. As she thumped out her improvised version of the notes, she glanced hopefully over at Mr Broome. He was the local ARP warden after all. You'd have thought that on this night of all nights, that stupid bugger Hitler could have organised a few bombs to be dropped on Clapham. It was the least he could do. But no, Mr Broome was just sitting there next to Mr Lorenz by the fire, completely oblivious, clapping rather stiffly along with the rest. Surely if he had any sympathy for her plight he would be out at his ARP post at the end of the road, flashing his officious little warning cards and rattling his alarm, whether the Luftwaffe were approaching or not. Anything to bring this mortifying ordeal to an end.

Jen could feel the sweat damp under her arms. She could feel her hair working itself free from the chignon at the back of her neck. She could feel her voice getting husky. Once upon a time she had gone out of her way to try and convince Henry that she was a class act, a sophisticated, talented performer. An actress. It was too late for that now. Now he would know her for what she really was. A raucous pub entertainer, belting out raunchy numbers to a room full of drunkards.

And then finally it did come to an end. Molly rang the closing bell and the final notes of 'Crash! Bang! I Want to Go Home' were lost in a chorus of complaint. Everyone was so busy protesting that only Jen's most avid fans applauded her as she left the piano.

As she dragged herself over to the bar, she was conscious of Molly Coogan studiously avoiding her gaze. And so she damn well should.

Henry Keller was shrugging on his coat. 'Ah, Jennifer,' he said. 'Congratulations. That was a …' he paused, as though searching for the right word, 'an unforgettable performance.'

'It wasn't that bad,' Jen said crossly. 'I know I'm not much of a piano player, but—'

'Oh, I don't know,' he interrupted smoothly. 'You got one or two of the notes just about in the right places.'

Jen heard someone giggle behind her and guessed it was Molly. She felt her temper rise. She didn't like being mocked.

'You didn't have to stay if you didn't want to,' she snapped. 'You didn't have to come at all, come to that.'

He took a packet of Gold Flake out of his pocket and offered her a cigarette. When she shook her head, he lit one for himself and smiled thoughtfully. 'No, but I'm glad I did,' he said, his eyes narrowed slightly against the smoke. 'It's been a most enjoyable and … enlightening evening.'

Jen was just about to fire back a rude retort when she remembered that it wouldn't do to alienate Henry Keller. As Molly had oh-so-kindly pointed out earlier, he had it in his power to make her career. But he also had the power to break it completely. So instead of giving vent to her temper, she lowered her eyes. 'After what Molly said earlier, I thought you'd never talk to me again.'

'I clearly have a masochistic tendency.' He laughed, and she realised he was rather drunk too. He was about to say something else when a loud

American voice boomed across the room. One of the sergeants was standing by the blackout curtain trying to muster his men out into the street.

'Hey, Mr Keller, sir, just so you know. We'll be pulling out in five.'

Henry waved his cigarette. 'I'll be with you in two seconds,' he called back. He saw Jen's surprise and explained that the Americans had offered him a lift back to town in their truck.

The thought of Henry Keller, in his beautiful camel coat and pinstripe suit, trundling up to the West End in a canvas-sided wagon full of drunken GIs almost made Jen laugh. It served him right, she thought sourly, for ignoring her for weeks on end and then turning up out of the blue at the worst possible moment.

'So why *did* you come?' she asked. 'Was it to see me, or were you hoping to find Ward Frazer?'

'I came to see you.' He stubbed out his cigarette, and when he looked up, there was a slightly odd smile on his lips. 'I'm putting together a new ENSA show. I wanted to ask you if you would be interested in being part of it. There'll be some nice little solo roles.'

Jen stared at him. For a moment she wondered if she had heard him correctly. Or was she hallucinating? A new show? Solo roles? Did she want to be part of it? It was a job, wasn't it? Had he taken complete leave of his senses? Of course she was interested.

He glanced over towards the dwindling group of soldiers by the blackout curtain. 'I'd better go.'

'Henry …' She grabbed his arm as he went to move away. 'I … I don't know what to say. I'd love to be part of it. When are the auditions?'

He shook his head. 'You don't need to audition. I've got a pretty fair idea of your abilities.' He raised his eyebrows. 'Even if you are only pretending.'

Somehow they had crossed the room to the door. He was leaving and suddenly she couldn't bear for him to go. He was going to give her a job. A proper job. Without an audition. Such a thing had never happened to her before.

She could feel his eyes on her and she was aware of her pulse accelerating. 'What Molly said wasn't true,' she said suddenly. 'I wasn't pretending.'

He was smiling faintly, but she couldn't tell if he believed her or not.

'You are a terrible piano player, Jennifer Carter, but you are a good actress,' he said.

'I'm not acting,' Jen said. 'I mean it.'

He inclined his head politely. 'Either way, you shouldn't commit yourself until you know the details.'

'I don't care about the details,' Jen said crossly.

He ignored that. 'It's a touring show,' he said. 'Troop entertainment. In the UK at first, but then it will be going abroad. To North Africa. Egypt. Algeria. Possibly Tunisia, depending on the situation there. How do you feel about that?'

Jen stared at him in dismay. North Africa? Her previous ENSA tour had been bad enough, traipsing around England singing in hideous cold factories and smelly canteens. But North Africa? North Africa was a war zone. Her brother had been taken prisoner there. Helen de Burrel had nearly died there.

He saw her expression. 'You don't have to decide now. You'll want to think about it. I know it looks as though Rommel is finally on the run, but in wartime anything can happen.' He shrugged. 'There is obviously an element of danger. Don't feel you have to accept. There are plenty of people who don't want to go.'

Jen didn't blame them. It wasn't just Rommel and his beastly Afrika Corps that concerned her. What about the journey? Sailing over the top of who knew how many torpedo-laden U-boats, in full view of the Luftwaffe. All the way down round Portugal and Spain then through the Mediterranean. It didn't bear thinking about. *An element of danger* sounded like the biggest understatement of the year.

'Will you be going?' she asked as he held the blackout curtain open for her and stood back politely, allowing her to go through the door first.

There was much hilarity outside in the street. The soldiers already on the trucks were joshing and wolf-whistling those of their compatriots who were taking advantage of the relative darkness to bid passionate farewells to the local girls. Angie, in particular, seemed to be getting more than her fair share of attention. Jen gritted her teeth and hoped Henry wouldn't notice.

'I'll probably go out in advance to set things up,' he was saying. 'I couldn't expect my performers to go if I wasn't prepared to go myself. And it's not just the cast, of course. It's the stage hands and technicians as well. Obviously it's up to the individual. I can't force anyone.' He gave a short laugh. 'Although I do sometimes arm-twist the big names a bit.'

As she watched the sergeant trying to peel one of his men off her sister, Jen wondered idly what form Henry Keller's arm-twisting took. But as she wasn't a big name, she was hardly likely to find out.

But what she did know was that this was probably her last chance. Henry wasn't going to waste any more effort on her. If she turned him down, this would certainly be the last time she heard from him.

Having finally managed to get his men loaded up, the sergeant slammed the tailgate and turned to Henry. 'You can ride up front, sir, if you are ready.'

Henry offered his hand politely to Jen. 'Thank you for a delightful evening,' he said.

Jen squirmed inwardly at his pointed formality.

One of the GIs clearly also thought this was a bit meagre in the circumstances. 'Don't be so British, sir,' he shouted, leering out of the back of the wagon. 'Ain't you going to give her a kiss?'

Henry glanced at Jen for a moment. 'I prefer to do my kissing in private,' he said, and everyone laughed.

But when they moved towards the front of the vehicle, out of sight of the soldiers, Henry still didn't make any attempt to kiss her, and Jen could feel herself flushing in the darkness. She hoped he couldn't see. If he couldn't even bring himself to kiss her goodbye, then this really was her last chance. Maybe he had already changed his mind and was regretting the offer.

'I'm not scared of stupid old Rommel,' she said as he put his foot on the running board. 'If you are really sure you want me, then I'll do it.'

He paused and turned to her again. 'Oh yes,' he murmured. 'I want you all right.' He gave a half-laugh. 'Though God knows why after tonight.'

Then he swung easily into the cab and slammed the door. As the vehicle roared into life and pulled away, he rolled down the window and gave her a mocking salute. 'I'll send you a contract tomorrow.'

Jen was still standing in the street, watching the dimmed lights recede into the darkness, when she heard Angie's familiar giggle behind her.

'Cor, your Henry is a bit of all right, isn't he? I wish you'd marry him. Then we could all become really posh.'

'Nothing could ever make you posh,' Jen retorted. 'I've never seen anything like the way you carried on tonight. You ought to be ashamed of yourself.'

'I was only having a bit of fun.'

'You'll be having a bit of fun with an illegitimate baby if you're not careful.'

'No I won't,' Angie said. She gave a gurgle of laughter and lurched to one side, grabbing at Jen's arm to stop herself falling. 'I'm saving myself for Gino.'

'Lucky Gino,' Jen said with withering sarcasm. 'I wonder if he realises he has such a treat in store.' Shaking off her sister's clutching fingers, she began to walk away. She was fed up with Angie, and the mythical Gino. But for once she hadn't got the strength to argue.

She felt utterly drained. The whole evening had been a nightmare. What on earth had she let herself in for? The very thought of going to North Africa made her feel queasy. And after all that, she still had no idea where she stood with Henry Keller. Nor indeed how she really felt about him. How could she know when he always seemed to blow so hot and cold?

'Where are you going?' Angie called after her.

'Home,' Jen said.

'But what about the clearing-up?' Angie shouted.

'What about it?'

'It's your job to help, isn't it?'

'Not any more,' Jen said. 'I'm resigning as of now.'

'You can't just resign.'

'Just watch me,' Jen said. She turned round. 'Henry's offered me a job. I don't need to work in the pub any more.'

Unusually, Angie was silent a moment. Then she had one more try. 'But it's a right old mess in there tonight. It's going to take ages. You can't expect Mum to do it all.'

'You help her then,' Jen shouted back. 'Or better still, let Molly Coogan do it.'

Chapter Fourteen

Katy and Ward arrived back in Lavender Road late on Sunday afternoon. While Ward took their bags to the pub, Katy's first thought was to retrieve Malcolm from the Nelsons. To her relief, he had survived the separation with no ill effects at all. In fact he was so absorbed in watching George miraculously conjuring marbles out of baby Nellie's ears that he was reluctant to leave.

Her next priority was to see how the pub had fared. As she came in through the door with Malcolm squalling in her arms, she could hear Joyce Carter regaling Ward with the events of the night before. Molly, looking unusually flustered, was already pulling on her coat. As she thanked them for holding the fort, Katy's swift, assessing glance revealed two broken chairs, several ominous gaps on the glasses shelf, and, glinting in a shaft of sunlight, mysterious silver trails all up one wall.

'Snails,' Joyce said. 'They were racing them across the tables, and they must have escaped. I've looked all over for the damn things, but I can't find them anywhere.'

Illegal gambling, Katy thought, as Ward burst out laughing. That's all I need, to be closed down for illegal gambling on the premises.

But overall she preferred to hear about goings-on at the pub than talk about the party. She didn't want to tell anyone about Ward's revelation about his family. Not yet, at least.

And she didn't have to. Molly was already rushing off to get ready for two weeks' night duty. Joyce only stayed long enough to hand over the till money. And Jen, when she popped in later to resign from her pub duties, was far too full of her own sudden change of fortune to notice Katy's reticence.

Louise had been the most likely person to sniff it out, but she was also too preoccupied with her own affairs to notice anything amiss.

Affairs, or affair? Katy groaned inwardly. Goodness only knew what Louise had got up to in Henley. She had been back in her own bed in the hotel in the morning when Katy knocked tentatively on the door. But she had looked flushed and heavy-eyed, and although she denied it with a coy giggle, Katy had the nasty feeling that Louise's silver-tongued suitor of the previous evening had either only just left, or was even then hiding in the wardrobe. Over breakfast Louise had told them that his name was Charlie Hawkridge, and that he was something frightfully important in a City bank, and that was why he hadn't been called up.

'I never heard of banking being a reserved occupation,' Katy had whispered to Ward when Louise went back upstairs to fetch her ration book to prove to the rather fussy patron of the hotel that she was entitled to breakfast.

'No,' Ward had agreed, scraping his pitiful portion of margarine over a piece of dry toast with a look of distaste. 'He sounds like a right Charlie to me.' And Katy had got the giggles over her cornflakes.

It had been a relief to laugh. She had felt so fraught the previous evening. But of course Ward was exactly the same person he had been before. He hadn't really had to convince her of that, even though it had been a rather nice experience. So she had pushed the impending visit of his uncle and the pain of being separated from Malcolm to the back of her mind and tried instead to focus on enjoying the unexpected day off.

And she had enjoyed it. Ward had taken her rowing on the Thames, huddled up in his coat against the cold March breeze, then they had looked around the quaint little shops and he had bought her an advance birthday present of a beautiful off-ration hand-knitted cardigan from a lady in the hardware shop. And in accordance with her new policy of burying her head in the sand, Katy hadn't allowed herself to think about the ridiculously expensive price tag.

They had lunched at Lucinda's parents' enormous house with some other of the guests from last night's party, and even though she didn't precisely enjoy that, Katy hadn't found it quite as daunting as she had expected. Mainly because she spent most of the meal praying that Louise wasn't going to make a fool of herself over the oh-so-smooth Charles Hawkridge.

Now, back in the Flag and Garter, getting ready for the evening opening while Ward put Malcolm to bed, Katy felt as though the whole thing had been a dream. She very much hoped Charlie Hawkridge was a dream, because if not, she wouldn't be able to look Louise's lovely husband Jack in the face ever again.

It wasn't that easy to look Aaref Hoch in the face either when he came in later that evening to check that everything was all right on their return. The minute Katy saw his expression, she knew that Louise had deliberately let slip something about her new conquest.

'It was a good party, yes?' he asked stiffly. 'I hope you enjoy yourself as much as Louise?'

Katy looked into his hurt, earnest face and crossed her fingers behind her back. 'It was nothing,' she said. 'She only flirted with him. You know what she's like.'

'It is not my place to be concerned,' he said, lowering his long lashes over his expressive dark eyes. 'I am not her husband.'

The following day Louise pooh-poohed Katy's remonstration. 'Oh, Aaref will come round,' she said airily. 'He never sulks for very long.'

'And what about Jack?' Katy asked sweetly. 'How long will he sulk for?'

Louise gave a coy smile. 'Jack won't know anything about it. I'm hardly going to parade Charlie in front of him, am I?'

'I hope you aren't going to parade him in front of anyone,' Katy said.

'Oh don't be so square, Katy,' Louise retorted. 'Why shouldn't I see him? He's nice.' She rolled her eyes. 'Anyway, you're a fine one to talk, sloping off from the party so early. It's obvious what you and Ward were up to.'

Ridiculously, Katy felt herself flush. 'I wasn't feeling very well, that's all. Anyway,' she went on more strongly, 'Ward happens to be my husband, so we can get up to whatever we want.'

She felt cross with Louise, but even crosser with Jen for abandoning her job at the pub without a backward glance. Not only that, but Jen clearly expected Katy to enter fully into her mixed feelings about the new job.

'I must have been mad to say yes,' she wailed. 'North Africa! But it's such a good opportunity … If only it wasn't Henry Keller's show. Oh God. Henry! He makes me feel so self-conscious. I don't know what sort of person he wants me to be. It was bad enough before, but it's even worse now Molly Coogan's put her stupid foot in it.'

'Oh for goodness' sake,' Katy said eventually. 'Why not just be yourself and see what happens?'

She thought she'd managed to keep the irritation out of her voice, but Jen's eyes narrowed. 'It's all right for you,' she said, getting up and pointedly putting on her coat. 'It's so easy for you and Ward. Everything is perfect for you. You don't have anything to worry about. You don't know what it's like.'

Katy stared at her in amazement. Easy? Perfect? If only Jen knew. For a moment she was tempted to tell her what her life was really like. She could have done with a bit of sympathy herself. But Jen was already flouncing off out of the door.

There are times when I almost hate my friends, Katy thought.

In some ways Molly was quite relieved to be back on night duty. It meant she couldn't help Katy in the pub in the evenings and that meant she didn't have to worry about bumping into Ward. The last time she had seen him, when he and Katy came back from the party, she had been so overcome, all she had wanted to do was run away. Joyce Carter must have thought she was a complete idiot. Molly couldn't bear to think what Ward himself must have thought.

But she knew that at some point she would have to go up to Lavender Road. At the very least she needed to apologise to Katy for the missing glasses, and to explain that it had been impossible to keep an eye on them with everything else that had been going on that night. And she wanted to call on Pam too. She missed the Nelsons' cosy house.

So one afternoon, waking up at half past three, after six hours' sleep, she decided the moment had come.

It was nice to be out and about in the warm early April sunshine. The days were getting longer and there was a real feeling of warmth in the air. But as she began to walk the familiar route up Wandsworth Road and into Lavender Road, Molly felt her spirits drop.

Apart from the weather, nothing had changed. Despite all her efforts over the last few months, her life hadn't improved one iota. The blind man and that stupid fortune-teller had been completely wrong with their predictions. Her moment hadn't come. Or if it had come, it had gone again without her noticing it. And now once again she was stuck in the same old routine. With exactly the same problems as she had had before.

The only one of her wishes that had come true was that Jen Carter was going away. Now that *was* good news. Molly had to admit to feeling a certain gleeful relish at Jen's discomfort about having to going overseas. She didn't blame her for being anxious, but as far as Molly was concerned, it served her right for all her snide little 'poxy pixie' comments. And for shirking the dirty jobs in the pub. And although Molly didn't go as far as wishing disaster on Jen, she did hope she wouldn't come back too soon.

Jerked out of her reverie by some slight sound, Molly looked up blankly and realised that she had walked straight past the pub and was now standing by the bomb site that had once been the Miss Taylors' house.

She was about to turn back when something was thrust into her ribs and a voice behind her shouted, 'Bang! Put your hands up! You're dead!'

Swinging round, she saw George grinning at her with a toy gun in his hand. And behind him, emerging from the wreckage of his aunts' house, was Ward Frazer, guilty laughter sparkling in his grey eyes.

Molly gaped at him in dismay. Why wasn't he at work? And why wasn't George at school? And then she realised. It was Saturday. Why oh why hadn't she come up here yesterday, when it would have been safe? Being on night duty was messing with her mind. And suddenly being confronted with Ward Frazer was messing with her breathing.

'I'm so sorry, Molly,' he said as he stepped over the crumbled wall of what used to be the Miss Taylors' front garden. Then he turned to George. 'It's polite to allow someone time to put their hands up before shooting them dead, you know.'

'But she didn't put her hands up,' George complained.

'No,' Ward agreed gravely. He glanced at Molly with a smile. 'That was either very brave or very foolhardy.'

Molly was incapable of answering. But luckily George filled the gap. 'Ward was teaching me to be invisible like a spy. And it works. You didn't see us, did you?'

'No,' Molly said faintly. 'I didn't see you.' Her heart was still racing, but no longer from the shock.

'You have to keep really, really still,' George said, tucking the wooden pistol back in the waistband of his shorts. He stopped and looked at her more closely. 'Molly, are you listening?'

Molly nodded hastily, hoping the sudden heat in her cheeks wasn't manifesting itself in an unsightly flush. 'Yes, yes, I'm listening.'

'It's a bit like magic,' George explained. 'The person looking for you is expecting you to do one thing and you fox him by doing something else. If he's chasing you, he's expecting you to be moving.' He looked up at Ward for corroboration, and Ward nodded. 'He's looking for movement. You didn't see us because we were still.'

'But I wasn't looking for you,' Molly objected.

As Ward broke into sudden laughter, George looked taken aback. But he quickly rallied. 'Well, we'll try it again,' he said, glancing at her eagerly. 'Ward and I will go up the common. Then you come and see if you can find us. I bet you won't be able to.'

Molly told herself she couldn't resist George's wide-eyed, pleading look. But she knew exactly what it was she couldn't resist; it was the apologetic look in Ward Frazer's humorous eyes. She looked away quickly. It was either that or throw herself into his arms.

'Molly probably doesn't want to go traipsing all over the common,' Ward said. 'I'm sure she has better things to do.'

George looked astonished. 'What could be better than this?' He thought for a moment, then turned to Molly. 'If you get to the bandstand without seeing us, then we win; if you see us first, then you win.'

It was clearly too late to refuse. 'Oh go on then,' Molly said. She nodded up the road, carefully avoiding Ward's sharply perceptive eyes. 'When you're out of sight I'll count to a hundred, then I'm coming to find you.' If she had the strength. Her heart was beating so hard she might pass out before she got to the top of the road. I'm crazy, she thought as she watched them walk away, Ward with his slight limp, George scampering eagerly beside him. I'm completely crazy. It was one thing to humour George; it was quite another to find herself playing hide-and-seek with a man who gave her such heartache.

But despite her reservations, Molly was confident she would find them. The only place to hide between the end of Lavender Road and the bandstand was behind a tree. There were a couple of huts that people used to store things for their allotments, but they would be easy to check. The underground air-raid shelter would have been a possibility, but she knew it was kept locked until the sirens sounded. Further along, of course, there were the air-defence guns and the barrage balloon stands, but they were both surrounded by barbed wire.

So all she needed to do was walk a meandering route through the trees and she'd be bound to spot them, even if they did keep really, really still. How hard could it be?

But when, after diligently counting up to a hundred, she hurried up to the end of the road and crossed on to the common, there was no sign of a boy in a grey jersey or a man in a navy blue sports jacket anywhere. She studied the distant trees carefully. Some of them were certainly big enough for a man to hide behind, so she set off determinedly up the path.

There were a surprising number of people about. Some walking dogs, some working the allotments, and others just standing around in groups chatting in the bright sunshine. Feeling somewhat conspicuous, Molly forged off the path to check the trees, from time to time swinging right around in the hope of catching George's eager face poking out from behind a trunk. Twice she stopped and listened for rustling or giggling, but all she could hear was birdsong, a little traffic noise and the murmur of voices and laughter, none of it recognisable as belonging to Ward or George.

Conscious of the curious glances of a group of people nearby, Molly moved on quickly, tramping through the rough undergrowth. Wondering if they might have actually climbed a tree, she stared up into the branches. Most of the smaller trees were covered with blossom, pink and white like confetti against the blue sky, but there were no leaves on the big oaks yet. Clearly there was nobody up there.

Emerging from the trees by the bandstand, she circled it and stood helplessly looking around, wondering what to do. She felt stupid. Had they tricked her and gone off somewhere else completely? That was the sort of nasty prank her classmates had occasionally played on her at school; surely Ward wouldn't be so cruel.

It was as she swivelled round to glance rather desperately over towards the gun emplacements that she heard a slight scuffle behind her and a voice

194

said gleefully, 'Ha, ha! Bang! You're dead. We won!'

The two of them were standing there grinning. Ward's jacket was casually slung over his arm. He had rolled up his shirtsleeves, exposing lean, strong forearms and an efficient-looking watch. George had his jersey tied round his waist and the toy gun in his hand. They hadn't even been running. They were both breathing perfectly normally. Unlike Molly, who felt once again ridiculously breathless.

'How did you do that?' she gasped.

'We hid in the open,' George said, clearly thrilled with his victory. 'You were expecting us to be hiding. So you looked behind the trees.'

Molly nodded.

'You were looking for two of us. Dressed in grey and navy. So we changed our appearance and just stood with some other people. I borrowed a cap from that boy over there. We were watching you all the time. You didn't even look at us once.'

Molly glared at him. 'That's because I felt such an idiot marching about through the undergrowth. Everyone must have thought I was mad.'

Ward was smiling. 'Not mad,' he said. 'A little eccentric perhaps, when there is a perfectly good path leading right up to the bandstand.'

Molly groaned. 'I was hoping they might think I'd lost a cat or a parrot or something.'

That made him laugh, and she felt her heart twist again. For a second she allowed herself to revel in the warmth of his gaze, then she turned away and ruffled George's blonde hair. 'Well you win,' she conceded. 'But it wasn't really fair to pit me against a trained secret agent, was it?'

Ward looked amused. 'I thought you did very well,' he said. 'I was particularly impressed by your composure under fire.'

Molly knew then that she had to go. He wasn't going to be impressed by her composure if she stayed in his presence much longer. But she couldn't move. She couldn't speak. All she could think was how lovely it was to be standing in the sunshine with Ward Frazer looking at her with a teasing smile on his lips.

She was still trying to think of an excuse to escape when she caught sight of a man standing further up the path.

'Good God,' she exclaimed. 'That's Barry Fish. I thought he was still in jail.'

'Who?' Ward glanced at the man and then back at Molly, clearly concerned by her shocked tone.

'He used to be the pianist at the Flag and Garter,' she said. She glanced warily at George and saw he was busy putting on his jersey. She lowered her voice. 'He's a really nasty piece of work. He tried to lure Katy home

195

with him once. And he was always stealing from the till. He was in cahoots with Mrs Carter's husband. They both got arrested for looting in the end.'

She heard Ward swear softly under his breath. 'She never told me,' he said, and Molly realised she had spoken out of turn.

'It was while you were missing,' she said quickly. 'I'd forgotten all about him. Katy probably has too. Of course Stanley Carter died in jail,' she added.

'Shame Barry Fish didn't, by the sound of it,' Ward said grimly.

And then they saw what it was that had caught Barry Fish's attention. Gillian James was strolling along the path on the north side of the common. Her daughter, wearing a pale blue jersey and a skirt slightly too short for her, was crouched at the side of the path collecting daisies into a small basket. Even though she didn't like him, Molly didn't blame Barry Fish for staring. The two of them were certainly a sight for sore eyes. For a man recently out of prison, they must have looked like manna from heaven.

Gillian James was done up to the nines as usual, absurdly overdressed for a walk on the common. But under her stylish red hat, her hair was beginning to lose its perm, and Molly was pretty sure that the stocking seams up the back of her shapely legs had been drawn on with a crayon. None of that detracted from her breathtaking allure. Even the way she walked was somehow provocative.

She had certainly taken Barry Fish's breath away. For a moment he just stood there, looking. But then Molly noticed him lick his lips and look around furtively before cutting diagonally across the grass and turning to follow the two women along the pavement.

A muttered oath beside her told her that Ward had noticed too. Abruptly he looked down at George. 'What d'you say we go say hi to Mrs James and Bella?' he asked. 'Maybe walk them home?'

George didn't look too keen. Walking women home wasn't his kind of fun. But he clearly knew his hero's attention had been diverted. He kicked the ground despondently.

Molly felt sorry for him. And for herself – she was no match for a maiden in distress. Especially not a maiden who looked like Gillian James. 'I can stay here with George if you like,' she said.

'Thanks,' Ward said. He punched George lightly on the shoulder. 'You look after Molly now, OK?'

Molly tried not to watch him stride away across the grass in the direction of Gillian James. Tried not to see the sudden change in her demeanour, the alacrity with which she turned to greet him. Or the protective hand he put on Bella's shoulder as the three of them turned the corner into Lavender Road.

Instead she tried to feel pleased at the irritation on Barry Fish's face as he realised that he had been thwarted in whatever nasty little scheme he had planned.

'Do you want me to show you how to do tracking?' George asked disconsolately. Molly knew how he felt. He was trying to make the best of a bad job. But the sparkle had gone out of his day. And out of hers.

Unconsciously she lifted her hand to finger the little charm hanging at her throat. I've got to get away, she thought. I can't bear much more of this.

Joyce was packing up a box to send to Bob in Italy via the Red Cross when Jen came wafting into the kitchen wearing her dressing gown. It was Monday morning. Upstairs Joyce could hear Angie clumping about getting ready for another day's work in the café.

Ignoring Jen, Joyce surveyed the box. She had put in a couple of Bob's old shirts, and a pair of Pete's shoes. Nestled among them were two packets of biscuits and a tin each of jam, condensed milk, herrings, snoek and margarine. There were also two packets of cigarettes, a tin bowl, a pack of playing cards and two pieces of soap. Soap was on the ration now and was hard to come by. Joyce had hesitated over it, wondering if one bar would be enough, but she was sure his need was greater than hers. On the top lay a packet of American chewing gum and a Hershey chocolate bar, which Angie had donated from one of her GIs, and a new pair of socks that Mr Lorenz had dropped in the previous evening.

'Good God.' Jen was staring into the box. 'That must have used up most of our rations. I really don't see why he—'

'Read his letter,' Joyce interrupted sharply. 'That'll tell you.'

Bob had never been much of a letter-writer, she thought as she pushed the flimsy piece of paper across the table, but he had surpassed himself this time. He had written at the beginning of February. The letter had taken nearly two months to arrive. It was covered in postmarks, including an Italian military censor stamp, but oddly nothing had been crossed out.

Dear Mum,

I am writing from a POW camp in Italy. I'm still alive. Can you believe it?

When my unit was captured in North Africa an Eyetie officer told us, for you the war is over. And thank God for that, is what I thought. But that was before I knew what was in store. First we were kept in cages in the sun for three days without food or water. Guess who built those cages? Us Brits, that's who. We'd made them ready to house our POWs, but then we were driven back so the enemy were using them instead. The Eyeties thought that was very funny. Ha ha. Then we were moved to another place,

Derna it was called, and conditions there were worse. We were packed in like sardines. No proper latrines and we were plagued by flies. All they gave us to eat was one tin of Eyetie bully between two of us and a hard biscuit each. Nowhere near enough water. That's the only Eyetie word I know, acqua, that's what we were screaming at the guards all the time. I thought I was going to die there, I got such terrible runs.

But eventually we were moved out and shipped over to Italy and after endless transit places we got here to Camp 21 and now we can send letters via the Red Cross. Thank God the winter is over. When it was really cold we cut holes in our blankets and wore them over our heads, like Mexicans. There are decent latrines and that here. Being Italian the taps don't work very well, but at least we have some water. What we don't have is anything to eat out of, but I found an old food can on the rubbish dump and I'm using that as my mess tin for the portion of stew they give us each day. The stew has soft maggoty things in it they call macarooni.

It's pretty boring here of course. Roll calls and searches all the time. But the other lads are OK and I reckon I can sit it out here for the duration. It's not like Lavender Road, but it's better than being dead in the desert. Send whatever you can, food and clothes and that. Shoes if possible. Anything really. If I don't need it I can barter it with the other lads or the guards.

That's it for now, out of paper, your loving son, Bob

'Blimey!' Jen looked up laughing. 'Poor old Bob. He won't know what's hit him. He was always such a one for a cushy life.'

And he's not the only one, Joyce thought sourly. She'd like to see how Jen would cope with similar hardship. She'd be making a right old fuss and a half. Especially about the lack of sanitation. She had even made a scene the other night because Angie had left a soap ring round the bath.

'Send Bob my love,' Jen said as she turned to make herself a cup of tea. 'Tell him to spare a thought for his poor sister, kept on half-rations so he can have a nice blowout with his POW pals.'

Biting back a sharp retort, Joyce labelled the parcel with Bob's name and *Campo Concentramento 21 Italy c/o International Red Cross* as she had been instructed. She would take it to the café now and then nip out later when the post office opened to get it dispatched. 'I won't be in for supper tonight,' she said casually. 'I'm going up to the West End with Mr Lorenz to see a show.'

'Oh?' Jen's ears pricked up at that. 'What show?'

'It's that Ivor Novello one,' Joyce replied as she left the kitchen. '*The Dancing Years.*'

'Good God,' Jen called after her. 'How did old Lorenz get tickets for that? I thought it was sold out.'

'Henry Keller got them for us,' Joyce replied airily from the corridor.

'Henry? You've seen Henry?'

Joyce hefted the box on to her hip to open the front door. 'No, not since the other evening at the Flag and Garter. But we were chatting about it then and he said he'd leave tickets for us at the box office.'

She was already smiling smugly to herself as she shut the door on Jen's gasp of amazement and headed off down the street. It was rather satisfying to get one up on Jen for once. And it served her right for being so callous about Bob.

Joyce had been shocked by Bob's letter. He was her eldest and had always been her favourite. She hated to think of him suffering at the hands of those damn Italians. She couldn't help feeling resentful that the Italian POWs in England were having a much easier time of it. Certainly the ones in Devon were, from Angie's account at least. Hobnobbing with the local girls on the farms and that.

It didn't seem fair. There was often talk on the wireless about the Geneva Convention and how POWs should be well treated. But what use was that if the enemy didn't take any notice? It sounded as though Bob could have died in that camp in Africa with all that dysentery about. But then she'd always heard that foreigners weren't up to much on hygiene. Still, from what he'd said, things were a bit better now, thank goodness. And he'd be pleased when he got his parcel.

Jen's rehearsals started on 12 April, the day the Allies launched their so-called final push in Tunisia. Having not previously been much interested in the progress of the war, Jen now found herself listening to virtually every broadcast. Thankfully, on the whole, the news was good. Rommel was even now evacuating his troops from Tunis in the face of General Montgomery's advance. And the German industrial heartland was being bombed day and night. Only last week Winston Churchill had told the world that the RAF were 'carrying doom to tyrants'. In Russia, Stalin's Red Army was valiantly resisting a renewed Nazi offensive near Kursk.

Jen didn't care much about Europe or Russia, but she was definitely pinning her hopes on old Monty in North Africa. She certainly hoped he'd move on rather faster and more effectively than his namesake, her mother's precious tortoise, did in their back garden. She would feel a lot more sanguine about going to North Africa if she knew for sure that the last remaining Germans and Italians there had been well and truly ousted.

Not that that was her only concern, of course. She hadn't seen Henry Keller since that awful evening in the pub. All she had received was a short scribbled note accompanying the contract. *As promised, H. K.*

She still had no idea what role he was offering her. The contract had not been specific. But the wages were generous, more than she had ever earned before, with extra promised if the show was indeed taken overseas. So, with considerable trepidation, she had signed it and sent it back.

Not knowing what she might be required to do, and not daring to ask, Jen had spent the intervening time practising her scales and working on her breathing. And just in case dancing was required, she used the last of her savings to treat herself to some tap classes in the West End. Dancing had never been her forte, and the one thing she did know for absolute certain was that she didn't want to make a fool of herself in front of Henry Keller.

To her relief, Henry wasn't there when she arrived at the theatre on the first day, so she was able to check in and get her bearings without worrying about him.

ENSA had taken over the Theatre Royal in Drury Lane at the beginning of the war. Now, instead of posters advertising the latest musical productions, Jen was confronted by a brisk man with a clipboard who wouldn't let her pass until he had taken her name.

Having been duly issued with a white pass, she was told to report to the assistant producer in the auditorium. Most of the theatre's grand entrance hall had been divided up into offices, and through the thin walls Jen could hear the clack of typewriters and the buzzing of telephones. The pre-war days of society patrons parading in full evening dress were clearly long gone. Inside the theatre itself, things were even bleaker. The back of the circle and stalls had been hit by an HE bomb early on in the Blitz and were still cordoned off, and wobbly partitions reduced the famous stage to the size of an average military canteen.

Most ENSA shows consisted of groups of entertainers, magicians, contortionists or bands who had set routines and were already well used to touring around the country. Others were adaptations of existing theatre productions, slimmed down for the purpose of playing in mess halls or factories. But this new show was being created from scratch.

Gathering his new cast around him, the assistant producer explained that it was going to involve a series of skits and scenes from well-known films and musicals. Some were to be performed straight, some were to be comic parodies and some would probably end up nothing at all like the original. Members of the cast were expected to adapt and improvise, and play to their strengths.

Jen felt her heart sink. She had never worked like that before. Her previous producers had always told her exactly what they wanted. There had been no room for her suggestions or any change to the performance plan.

The following afternoon, Henry arrived. Jen felt even more out of her depth. And even more self-conscious. Henry was very much in charge, clever and decisive with his ideas. He seemed to know exactly what was going to work and what wasn't. The timetable was tight and he was keen to get everything organised as quickly as possible. It was obvious he wasn't going to put up with any nonsense. Jen could see the other girls nudging each other each time he addressed her. They knew he had hired her without an audition and they wanted to know why.

Singing in front of him at the pub that night had been bad enough, but this was a hundred times worse. Then, Jen hadn't realised she had anything to lose. Now, she had everything to prove.

But however hard she tried to impress him, nothing seemed to work. He always wanted more. Whenever she thought she had managed to come up with something, he said things like, 'OK, that's a start, I suppose,' or, 'Hmm, let's leave it there and move on,' or merely, dismissively, 'Oh well, that'll have to do for now.'

The whole thing was turning into a nightmare. As she left the theatre on Friday afternoon, Jen felt depressed. She had wanted this opportunity so much and now it was all going wrong. And it was Molly Coogan's fault.

Or maybe she just wasn't good enough. Maybe that was the real problem.

'Miss Carter?'

Jen stopped and turned round. One of the stagehands was hurrying down the steps behind her.

'I'm glad I caught you,' he panted. 'The other girls said you'd only just left.'

'What is it?' Jen asked.' What do you want?'

'Mr Keller wants to see you in his office.'

Chapter Fifteen

Joyce was busy clearing up the café kitchen. In the other room, Angie was laying out the cups and saucers ready for breakfast the following day. They were waiting for a batch of rock buns to finish cooking, and then they were going to drop off half a dozen up at the pub for a birthday gift for Katy on their way home.

Mr Lorenz said Joyce made the best cakes in London. Well, she didn't know about that, but they certainly seemed to go down well with her customers. And Katy deserved a little treat. She had been looking a bit peaky recently, and a couple of nice rock buns would be just the thing. Angie had told Joyce that Ward Frazer did most of their cooking now, often with some fancy herbs and spices he'd apparently brought back from North Africa. But he didn't do cakes. Of course, baking wasn't easy with wartime rationing and that. But Joyce had become quite a dab hand with the old powdered egg, and at bulking out the flour with some grated parsnip. Her latest trick was adding cream of tartar to dried milk to make an austerity cake mixture rise. Yes, she thought, as she opened the oven and sniffed the warm, sweet aroma appreciatively, she had discovered quite a few little tricks since she had been cooking in the café, and now—

'Mum!' Angie's sudden bellow made her nearly drop the tray of buns. 'There's a man here to see you.'

Joyce winced. Angie could have found a job as a train announcer down at Clapham Junction. She certainly wouldn't need a loudspeaker. Closing the oven door, Joyce carefully put the cakes on the sideboard.

But before she could turn round, Angie's face poked through the hatch. 'Did you hear me? There's a man—'

'Yes, yes, I heard you,' Joyce said. She lowered her voice. 'What sort of man is he?'

'He says he's from the council,' Angie said. Joyce felt her blood run cold.

Was it a hygiene inspector? Had someone complained? Or got sick? Or might he be something even worse, a Food Ministry man come to check they were abiding by the ration laws? Joyce quickly shoved the bag of sugar that Aaref Hoch had brought in that morning out of sight behind the mixer.

Wishing Mrs Rutherford hadn't gone off early, she straightened her

202

apron and emerged from the kitchen to find a stern middle-aged man with a briefcase standing by the counter.

'Are you Mrs Carter?'

'Yes,' Joyce said warily. Realising she was still holding the tea towel, she folded it nervously and put it down by the till. 'What is this about?' She glanced at the clock. 'It is rather late …'

'I told him we were closed,' Angie chipped in helpfully. 'But he would come in.'

The man frowned. 'I am sorry to disturb you,' he said stiffly, 'but I didn't think it was appropriate to come when you were busy with customers. My name is Mr Styles. I am head of the public liaison department.'

Joyce could feel her alarm rising. 'Go into the kitchen, Angie,' she said sharply. 'And make sure I turned off the oven.'

Mr Styles waited for Angie to go, then he smiled thinly. 'You have gained quite a reputation in the area, Mrs Carter,' he said.

Joyce stiffened. It sounded like a threat. And she didn't trust that smile. It looked fake. 'A reputation for what?' she asked.

She hated these officious, jobsworth council types. In her experience there was nothing they liked more than pulling the rug out from under your feet. It was all right for them, with their steady jobs and their lists of rules and regulations; it wasn't so easy for the likes of her trying to run a business in the middle of a war.

'For your cooking,' he said.

Joyce eyed him warily. Had he somehow got a sniff of the black-market goods young Aaref occasionally slipped in through the back door? Or had someone reported her for taking leftover veg home to Monty the tortoise? It was illegal nowadays to give human food to pets, but really, who cared about a few moth-eaten old lettuce leaves?

'We are aware that it is not easy cooking with limited ingredients,' Mr Styles went on.

Joyce ran her mind quickly through the contents of the cupboards in the kitchen and knew that she would be in the soup if Mr Styles asked to inspect them. As well as the extra sugar, there was a big pat of butter that would be difficult to explain away.

'But you seem very adept at turning out excellent food,' he said. 'Two of my colleagues were in here yesterday and they enjoyed an extremely nourishing meal.'

Joyce felt her temper rising. She didn't like the way he was pussyfooting around the subject. And she certainly didn't like the thought of entertaining council spies in her café.

'Why don't you just come out with it?' she snapped. 'Why are you here? What do you want?'

Mr Styles took a startled step back. 'We want you to do a cooking demonstration for us,' he said. 'At the council, for local ladies. Tips for making the ration go further. That kind of thing.'

As Joyce stared at him blankly, Angie's face appeared at the hatch. 'Oh, that would be brilliant,' she said, almost plunging through the opening in her excitement. 'It would be just like the cooking competition. Only better!'

Mr Styles blinked. 'Yes, I believe you made quite an impression at the competition,' he said. 'That's how we heard of you.'

Joyce had been so convinced he was after her blood in some way, she still couldn't quite believe she was off the hook. He had seemed so sinister, with his sly little comments and his fake smiles. Was he really serious? Or was it another trick?

'So what do you think, Mrs Carter?'

'Yes, yes, all right,' she said. 'I'll do it.' She just wanted to get rid of him. She somehow still couldn't quite believe he wasn't going to start poking his nose into her cupboards. Agreeing to show a few local ladies how to cook seemed a small price to pay.

Belatedly she realised that Mr Styles was speaking again. 'It will take a little while to organise,' he was saying. 'But we are proposing a date in late May or early June. How would that suit you?'

Joyce nodded dumbly. She didn't care when it was. One day was the same as the next as far as she was concerned.

'I will write to you with the details,' he said, picking up his briefcase. 'We aren't in a position to offer a fee; it's all part of the war effort after all. But we will of course cover the cost of the ingredients.' He turned to the door. 'And we will handle all the publicity. Posters and so on.'

Angie had emerged from the kitchen before he was even out of the door. Her eyes were wide with awe.

'Posters!' she breathed with uncharacteristically hushed wonder. 'Cor, you are going to be famous, Mum. Our Jen will be green with envy!'

Jen was indeed feeling rather green, but not with envy. Henry Keller's office was at the back of the theatre. In better times it had been a dressing room. By the time Jen had followed the stagehand in silence through the dimly lit warren of corridors, she was feeling distinctly sick.

She was certain Henry was going to sack her. Why else would he summon her to his office? She knew she was out of her depth in this show.

Last year, things had been good. She had had a nice, steady singing job and she had enjoyed staying with Katy in the pub while Ward was missing.

Even when Ward had come home and she had moved back in with her mother it had been all right. It was the chickenpox that had changed everything. Before the chickenpox she had been happy. Since the chickenpox every single thing in her life had gone wrong.

Crossing her fingers behind her back, she waited while the stagehand knocked on the door and announced her.

Henry was sitting behind a large desk. A score lay open in front of him, lit by a modern angled table lamp. A precarious looking pile of other papers had been pushed to one side next to a heavily laden in-tray. A cigarette smouldered in an ashtray beside his hand.

'Ah, Jennifer,' he said, pushing back his chair and standing up. 'Please. Take a seat.'

As she sat down on one of the upright visitor chairs, he resumed his own seat, picked up his cigarette, drew on it and studied her thoughtfully through his exhaled smoke.

'Tell me,' he said. 'Why are you holding out on me? Why aren't you giving me your best?'

Jen flinched. 'I am giving you my best,' she said. 'But I've never worked like this before. I've never been to drama school. I don't know what you want.'

He gave a dry laugh. 'I want a lot more than you're giving me,' he said.

Jen didn't like that laugh. It sounded mocking to her ears. Well she wasn't going to give him the pleasure of seeing her plead. 'I can't help it,' she said sulkily. 'You never should have hired me. It was a mistake. I'm clearly not good enough for you.'

He stubbed out his cigarette. 'You're right,' he said. 'It may well be a mistake. But not because you aren't good enough.'

He stood up then and walked to a small window that looked out over the narrow alley behind the theatre. Jen studied him covertly. This was the man who had taken her out to dinner, sent her flowers and spontaneously kissed her in the shabby passage of her mother's house. All that seemed a long time ago. She could hardly believe it had ever happened. He certainly seemed to have forgotten all about it.

'You have the ability but you aren't using it,' he said. 'You seem uneasy on the stage. Especially in the show skits. Hesitant. Nervous even. Why is that?'

He was right. She was nervous. 'I don't know,' she said.

Henry had turned round and was looking at her through slightly narrowed eyes. 'How well do you know the shows we are using?' he asked suddenly.

Jen could feel herself beginning to flush. A couple of times, when Henry or the assistant producer had asked the performers if they recalled a specific show or scene, she had nodded along with the rest. It was just too embarrassing to admit she didn't know what they were talking about. And now Henry, with his sharp eyes, had caught her out and she felt like a complete idiot.

'Not very well,' she muttered.

He frowned. 'How well? Which ones *do* you know?'

She bit her lip. 'I've never seen any of them,' she said.

'Good God,' he said.

'Going to West End shows isn't the sort of thing people in Clapham do,' Jen retorted defensively. 'Not people like my family anyway.'

He lifted his eyebrows. 'I suppose I assumed because your mother seemed interested in the theatre she would have taken you to—'

'Well, you assumed wrong,' Jen snapped. 'My mother isn't interested in the theatre. Or she never used to be. She didn't even bother to come and see me in my school plays.'

'How very remiss of her,' he said, and Jen glared up at him suspiciously. She didn't know if there was sympathy or mockery in his tone. Either way she felt annoyed with herself. She had put herself at a disadvantage. Opened herself to his derision. Why on earth had she mentioned her school plays?

Realising he was silent, she looked up and saw him checking his watch. He was obviously wondering how to terminate this embarrassing interview.

'Are you by any chance free this evening?' he asked.

Jen could hardly believe her ears. That was the last thing she had expected him to say. She was suddenly aware of a pulse beating against the hard chair under her knee. 'Well, yes, I suppose so,' she said. She wasn't, as it happened. She had promised to go and celebrate Katy's birthday. 'Why? Why do you ask?'

He spread his hands. 'I thought we could make a start on getting you up to speed.'

'What do you mean?'

He shrugged. 'I can't offer you the stage show, but the film of *Glamorous Night* is bound to be showing somewhere. If we are quick, we should be in time for the early-evening performance.'

'But ... but ...' But what? There were so many buts, Jen didn't know where to start. But ... I thought you didn't like me any more. But ... I am just an insignificant cog in the great Henry Keller wheel, a pitifully inadequate aspirant. But ... I'm completely terrified of going out with you, of doing or saying the wrong thing. Thankfully she didn't voice any of them; realising he was waiting for her proviso, she tried to muster a morsel of self-respect. 'I am perfectly happy to go on my own,' she said stiffly. 'You don't need to come with me.'

'It would be a pleasure,' he said with one of his dry, urbane smiles. 'It's my fault. I should have checked that you knew the shows. It's the least I can do.'

Katy wasn't having much of a birthday. The government had raised the duty on alcohol earlier in the week, and she had spent most of the lunchtime session explaining why she had had to put her prices up. One group of men in particular kept complaining about it, and she felt like telling them to drink elsewhere if they didn't like it. She certainly didn't like them, and she was pretty sure it was one of them who was pinching her glasses. But it was hard to keep an eye on them single-handed.

As the day wore on, she felt increasingly depressed. She had asked Pam to bring the children in for a birthday tea, but George had fallen over in the school playground and cut his face, so Pam had to take him to the doctor to get the wound dressed. Jen had promised to pop in after her rehearsal but had failed to turn up. Mrs Carter had dropped off some buns, but she hadn't stayed. Molly had sent a card apologising for not being able to come at all. Apparently they were short-staffed at the hospital and she had been working extra duty all week. There was no sign of Ward. And now it was nearly opening time and the only one of her friends who had come in to celebrate her birthday was Louise.

Katy hadn't seen Louise since the party. She guessed she had been off jaunting with Charlie Hawkridge, and her self-conscious smirk today confirmed it. At least she hadn't had the gall to bring him to the pub. It was probably only a matter of time before she felt the need to flaunt him in front of Aaref.

All in all, Louise wasn't Katy's favourite person at the moment, and that feeling intensified when Louise slanted her a sly glance and remarked that she hadn't realised Ward was so friendly with Gillian James. She had seen them walking down the road together the previous weekend and she had been dying to ask Katy what was going on.

As Ward hadn't mentioned the encounter, Katy was thrown into confusion. Louise raised her eyebrows. 'Oh dear, have I said the wrong thing?' She picked up one of Mrs Carter's rock cakes and inspected it carefully. 'Well you'd better keep your eye on him. Her military visitor has been conspicuously absent recently.' She nibbled the bun provocatively, clearly delighted to be getting back at Katy for criticising her liaison with Charlie Hawkridge. 'I hope Ward isn't about to take his place!'

Katy dearly hoped so too, but she wasn't able to respond because the door opened and Ward himself came in.

If he was aware of Katy's troubled expression or Louise's quizzical one, he gave no sign of it.

'Hi, Louise' he said easily. 'Have you had a good week?'

Then he turned to Katy. 'I've got a birthday surprise for you,' he said. 'Close your eyes and don't open them until I say.'

Katy was aware of feeling slightly sick. What on earth was this going to be? She didn't like surprises. She liked to be prepared for things, ready and steady. But she closed her eyes obediently and only opened them when she heard Louise's gasp of surprise and Ward's voice saying, 'OK, you can look now.'

And there, standing on the other side of the bar, dressed in a chic navy suit and a jaunty little hat, glowing with health and holding a bunch of beautiful yellow tulips, was Helen de Burrel.

On the way back from the pub, Joyce had found Bella James crouching by her front door with a bunch of dandelions in her hand.

Hearing Joyce's footstep behind her, the girl stood up abruptly, clearly disconcerted to be caught red-handed. She looked thin and unkempt. Her skirt was too short and her wrists were sticking out of the sleeves of her navy pullover. She seemed unnaturally pale too, and her eyes appeared even bigger and more wary than before.

Joyce was torn. She didn't approve of Gillian James and she didn't want to get involved with her daughter. But she was grateful for the offerings the girl had left for Monty. The least she could do now that she had caught her on the doorstep was volunteer to show her the tortoise.

'Thank you for the dandelions,' she said. 'Monty has enjoyed them. Would you like to see him?'

The girl looked tempted, but shy. She gnawed her bottom lip. Her mouth was slightly too wide for her face, which made her look older than her years and yet somehow vulnerable at the same time.

As she led the way down the passage to the kitchen, Joyce hoped Jen would have cleared up before she left for her rehearsals this morning. But no, she hadn't. What was more, she had obviously taken some of tonight's supper for her lunch. A cold leek and ham pie with a large slice out of it was sitting uncovered on the sideboard.

In the back yard, Monty was asleep in a patch of sunlight by the Anderson shelter.

Bella made a little noise of delight and crouched down beside him.

It took a moment for Monty to realise the girl was there. But then he obligingly poked his head out of his shell and blinked up at her. Joyce smiled to herself. They made an incongruous pair. The extraordinarily pretty girl, with her perfect skin and smooth, slender limbs, and the wrinkled old tortoise. Because even though she was obviously biased in his favour, Joyce couldn't by any stretch of the imagination say that Monty was good-looking.

'Am I allowed to pick him up?'

'Yes, of course,' Joyce said. 'As long as you are gentle.'

Bella was very gentle. As she stroked him under his chin, Monty closed his eyes in apparent bliss. And when she lifted him near to her face, he gave a little contented puff of breath. He had never done that to Joyce. Maybe he somehow knew it was Bella's supply of dandelions that had saved his life when he first came out of hibernation. Or maybe he just liked the look of her. What male wouldn't? She was a little beauty, with her delicate features, long, soft lashes and pretty mouth. She even had perfect teeth. Not like poor Angie, whose teeth wouldn't have looked amiss on a small Shetland pony. Either way Monty seemed to enjoy her touch. He waved his front legs and put one foot flirtatiously on her hand. He clearly had more guile than Joyce gave him credit for. He knew which side his bread was buttered.

Putting him back on the ground, Bella fed him a few dandelions and he ate them with evident relish. Then, seemingly feeling that she might be outstaying her welcome, she stood up and politely thanked Joyce for letting her see him.

As they went back into the kitchen, Joyce noticed Bella glance at the pie. She's hungry, she thought. That glamour-pants mother of hers isn't feeding her properly. No wonder the poor girl's so thin.

'Here.' She picked up a knife. 'Would you like a bit of pie?'

'No, no, thank you.' She had clearly been taught some manners. 'Mummy wouldn't like me to.' But she could hardly keep her eyes off it.

'Mummy needn't know,' Joyce said, sliding a slice of pie on to a plate and pushing it across the table.

'It's a fair exchange,' she added when Bella still hesitated. 'You've brought plenty of bits and pieces for Monty.'

Bella flushed slightly. 'How did you know it was me?'

'It was either you or that sour-faced librarian,' Joyce said. 'And it was hardly likely to be her.'

Bella didn't need any more persuading. She ate the pie with the same silent intent as Monty ate his dandelions. When she had finished, Joyce gave her another slice, and she ate that as quickly as the first. There was no doubt the poor child was starving.

'Thank you,' Bella said politely. 'It's very nice.'

I'll leave her something on the step tomorrow, Joyce thought, as she watched Bella cross the road a few minutes later. Another slice of pie, perhaps, or a sandwich. God knew how she was going to spare the food. And she dreaded to think what Jen would say if she knew her precious rations were going to feed Bella James. But Joyce felt sorry for the girl. It wasn't her fault that her mother was an improvident fancy piece.

And anyway, she felt they had forged a kind of bond over Monty.

Katy was delighted to see Helen looking so fit and well. 'I've been going to a marvellous physiotherapist in Oxford,' she said. 'Miss Smith. Dr Goodacre recommended her.' She smiled at Ward. 'You should ask him if he knows of anyone round here for your leg. It might make all the difference.'

Louise giggled. 'I should think there would be plenty of Miss Smiths happy to help with Ward's leg.'

As Katy looked away in exasperation, she caught Helen's eye and felt better. Helen knew what was what. She knew Louise of old. And she knew Ward. Katy realised she would be able to tell Helen about Ward's revelation at the party. Helen was from a rich, well-connected family herself. And she was discreet.

Katy was dreading someone finding out. Nothing stayed secret for long in Lavender Road, and the truth always got blurred. *Family money, you know.* People would nod meaningfully to each other. At best they would tease her about it and expect free drinks at the bar; at worst they might think they had deliberately been kept in the dark. And even if they believed she hadn't previously known about it herself, she felt it would say something about her and Ward's relationship, a lack of intimacy, a lack of honesty between them that she didn't want anyone to know.

But Helen knew Ward as well as anyone, probably better even than Katy did herself.

'I can sort of understand why he didn't tell you,' Helen said later, when she and Katy were chatting upstairs while Katy fed Malcolm and Ward manned the bar. 'It's to do with the kind of work he does.' She swirled her drink in her glass. 'Secrets become a habit. It's all part of the training. Your real life, your past, makes you vulnerable. And you can't afford to become vulnerable. It's much safer if everything is hidden away. Then things won't surface by mistake under … at the wrong time.'

'You mean if he got drunk or something?' Katy suggested. Not that Ward ever got drunk. It was one of the many things she admired about him. He liked a drink as much as the next man, he was convivial and hospitable, but he always knew when to stop. He never got mouthy and garrulous like so many men did.

210

'No,' Helen said. 'I actually meant under interrogation.'

Katy froze with the spoon halfway to Malcolm's mouth. 'You mean he …?'

Helen made a face. 'The Nazis certainly didn't make it easy for him. He was in the wrong place at the wrong time. I don't know how bad it got, but it wouldn't have been nice. But he didn't crack. Because he is good at it, Katy. Keeping secrets. And he's very brave. He couldn't have done what he did otherwise.'

Malcolm squealed and Katy handed him a spoonful of mashed potatoes, which he promptly smeared all over his face. She put her hand to her heart to steady its sudden erratic beat.

'He wouldn't want me to have told you that,' Helen said. 'But I think you need to know. To understand. It's not you he's keeping secrets from. It's everyone.'

The only thing Katy understood was that she felt very faint. 'But you aren't like that,' she said weakly.

'No,' Helen said wryly. 'But then I wasn't a very good agent. I wasn't able to detach myself in the same way that Ward can.'

Katy shivered. 'Are you going to go back to it?'

Helen shook her head. 'They don't want me. They say it's because I'm not fit, but I'm sure it's because of my liaison with André. They think my emotions influenced my judgement. And they are probably right.' She hesitated for a beat. 'In fact, I was wondering if you would like me to come and help you here instead.'

Katy stared at her. 'Here? In the pub? But you can't.'

Helen looked surprised. 'Why not? I'm getting bored in the country. It would do me good to do a bit of work.'

'But …' Katy paused in her effort to wipe a resisting Malcolm's face. She so badly needed help in the pub. Especially as Molly couldn't come so often with all these extra shifts she was doing at the hospital. She could hardly think of anything she would like more than having Helen working with her. Nor could she think of anything more unsuitable. 'But you're a lady. It's not fitting for you to work in a public house.'

Helen laughed. 'Come to that, from what you've told me, it's not fitting for the wife of Mr Highfalutin Ward Frazer either.'

Katy groaned. 'Don't,' she said. 'Don't rub it in. It was bad enough at the party. Everyone there thought I was a jumped-up little social climber.'

'Nonsense,' Helen said stoutly. 'I'm sure everyone thought you were lovely.'

Katy hesitated. Those people were Helen's set. They'd been to fancy boarding schools. 'Not everyone,' she said. 'There was a girl called Felicity

Rowe who certainly didn't. She as good as accused me of trapping Ward into marriage by getting pregnant with Malcolm.'

'No!' Helen put down her glass sharply. 'Damn. I should have warned you about Felicity. She's a menace. She set her cap at Ward from the start. He was footloose and fancy-free then, of course. And she is very pretty. He may have gone out with her a few times. But I don't think anything happened. At least, not much.' She looked up and caught Katy's expression. 'He didn't even know you then, Katy. Good God, you can't hold that against him.'

Katy was trying not to. And she was also trying not to think what might have happened, or might still happen, come to that, with other pretty women of his acquaintance. And exactly how much was *not much*?

Jen enjoyed the film. And she enjoyed sitting next to Henry Keller. In fact sitting next to Henry Keller made it quite hard to concentrate on the film. How could she worry about dangerous assassins, prototype televisions and gypsy weddings when her brain was busy mulling over the implications of this unexpected turn of events? It didn't help either that his right elbow and his right knee were in such close proximity to her, causing a tremor to run through her every time he moved. The dramatic shipwreck was the only scene that really caught her attention, making her feel quite queasy for a minute or two, but otherwise the whole thing passed in a blur.

'So do you think that will help?' he asked as they emerged from the Chelsea cinema.

It had been light when they had gone in, dropped by the taxi Henry had flagged down in Leicester Square, just in time to catch the opening credits. Now it was cold and dark and Jen couldn't see the expression on Henry's face.

'Yes,' she said. And it would, although probably not as much as the knowledge that Henry still had faith in her acting abilities. 'Although I do think all that television business is a bit far-fetched.'

She heard his low laugh. 'Not at all,' he said. 'If it wasn't for the war stopping development, people would even now be watching televisions in their own homes.'

'Rich people maybe,' Jen said.

'Well yes, at first,' he said. 'But it won't take long for it to become affordable. It's going to throw up all sorts of interesting opportunities for people like us.'

People like us. Jen felt a glow of pleasure at the words. Henry Keller was including her in his dream for the future. Only his professional dream, of course, but that was a lot better than the dismissal she had anticipated earlier that afternoon.

She shivered and pulled her jacket closed. She wasn't dressed for standing around on chilly street corners. The other patrons of the cinema had all disappeared off into the night. If this was a date, Henry would probably suggest going on somewhere for a drink, or maybe even something to eat.

But it wasn't a date, and all he suggested was finding her a taxi. Even as he spoke the words, Jen heard one come trundling up the King's Road towards them. And, just her luck, its dim For Hire sign was lit up.

'I can easily take the tube from Sloane Square,' she said, but Henry was already stepping forward to hail the cab.

'You're cold,' he said. 'You need to get home.'

'What about you?' Jen asked. Maybe he would come part of the way with her in the cab. Maybe she would get just a little bit more of his time. His attention. Perhaps, in the dark back seat of a cab, she might even get a good-night kiss.

'I live in Knightsbridge,' he said. 'I can walk from here.'

The elderly cab driver grumbled at having to go south of the river, but he stopped as soon as Henry handed him a couple of notes.

'I …' Jen knew she should object, but she also knew she hadn't the money to pay the driver herself. 'Thank you,' she mumbled, embarrassed, as Henry opened the door for her. 'You have been very kind.'

'It has been my pleasure,' he said politely.

Jen hesitated with one foot on the running board. 'I mean it,' she said. 'I really am grateful.'

'And I mean it too,' he said. 'It really has been a pleasure.'

The taxi pulled away with a sudden jerk and Jen was thrown back against the seat. As she struggled to straighten up on the slippery leather upholstery, she caught a glimpse of Henry turning away and walking purposefully off down the King's Road. In completely the opposite direction to Knightsbridge. A moment later he was lost in the darkness.

Jen hunkered down in her seat with a sigh and closed her eyes. She was none the wiser about how she stood with him. But at least he was giving her another chance. And that was a lot more than she had expected.

Despite Helen's reassurance, Katy had to ask Ward about Gillian James. She had to. It was going to eat her up otherwise. And she couldn't spoil her birthday now, because it was already over. She had opened all her presents. A set of hand-embroidered handkerchiefs from her mother, the latest Agatha Christie novel from Ward's aunts, the tulips from Helen, and a beautiful – and, she was certain, far too expensive – heart-shaped brooch from Ward. Aaref brought in a gift of four beer glasses that Molly had asked him to procure on her behalf, but disappeared again as soon as he caught sight of Louise. Jen hadn't materialised and Helen had now gone off to spend the night at the Nelsons'.

Mr Lorenz had stood Katy a celebratory small port and lemon just before closing time, and the resulting feeling of wooziness perhaps gave her the courage to broach the subject.

'Louise thinks Gillian James's general has stopped coming to see her,' she remarked as Ward came into the bedroom after checking on Malcolm.

Ward paused in unbuttoning his shirt. 'He's actually a brigadier,' he said. 'But she's right,' he said. 'He's been posted to Egypt.'

'How on earth do you know that?' Katy asked, averting her gaze from Ward's chest. Even now, the sight of his bare flesh had the power to make her go weak at the knees. And just now she needed all the strength she could muster.

'Mrs James told me herself,' he said, shrugging off the shirt and dropping it on the floor. 'I bumped into her and Bella on the common last weekend. She asked me if I could find out when he might be coming back.'

'But ...' She stared at him. He sounded so casual about it. So blasé. 'Why did she ask *you*?'

He yawned and a line of muscles rippled across his waist. 'I don't know. I guess someone must have told her I might be in a position to find out.'

'Really?' Katy was surprised. 'I can't imagine anyone telling her something like that.' Or talking to her at all, come to that. 'And *are* you in a position to find out?'

'Yes,' he said, as he unbuttoned his fly. 'I have found out. He's not coming back. He's been given a permanent staff appointment. In Cairo.' He flicked a brief glance at Katy from under his lashes. 'And his wife has gone with him.'

'Oh,' Katy said. 'Goodness.' She tried not to look as he sat down on the edge of the bed to pull off his trousers. 'Well it's a good thing he's gone then,' she said inadequately.

'Not for Mrs James,' Ward said. 'The bloody man had been paying her rent. Now he isn't. He's left her totally in the lurch.'

'You sound sorry for her.'

He had taken off his trousers and now stood for a moment in his undershorts, looking down at Katy. 'I am sorry for her. It's a bad position to be in. God knows what will happen to her, and to her daughter, if they get evicted from that house.'

Katy didn't know what she felt about it. Apart from her occasional foray to the pub for gin, Gillian James had kept herself to herself. People hadn't shunned her precisely, but they hadn't welcomed her into the community either. They were hardly likely to throw her an olive branch now.

Ward was naked and getting into the bed beside her. Katy was conscious of the cool strength of his limbs as he rolled over towards her. A moment later she was in his arms. She felt the steady beat of his heart against her breast. Her own heart accelerated. But she wasn't having any of that. Not yet at least.

'Why didn't you tell me you'd seen her?' she murmured, pulling back a little.

'I don't know.' He sounded surprised at the question. 'I guess it seemed kind of private. But if Louise knows, it won't stay private for long.'

'So what is Mrs James going to do about it?'

He adjusted his position slightly. 'I'm hoping she might look for a job.'

Katy sensed his hesitation and frowned. 'You weren't thinking of suggesting that I offer her one?

He stroked her cheek with cool fingers and an amused, tolerant smile. 'No. That wasn't what I was thinking.'

She looked at him suspiciously, trying to ignore the treacherous tingle of her skin under his touch. 'Anyway, I don't need anyone else. I've got Helen now.'

'Yes,' he said. His fingers paused for a moment. 'And you're pleased about that, aren't you?'

'I'm thrilled about it.'

'Good.'

She caught the faint hint of satisfaction in his voice and jerked back accusingly. 'You put her up to it, didn't you? It was you who suggested it.'

'Yes, I did,' he admitted, taking her hand and kissing it even as she tried to pull it away. 'Hey … don't be like that. I know it's your business and you want to run it your way. But I don't like you being here all on your own. Anything could happen. You never know who might come in. Most people are OK, but there are plenty of nasty guys around.'

'I've dealt with nasty guys before,' Katy said. She wanted to feel cross at his interference, but the warmth of his breath on her palm was sending tremors of desire through her body.

'I know,' he murmured against her skin. 'Guys like Mr Barry Fish.'

'Barry Fish is in prison.' Katy said. Thank God, she thought, shivering at the memory of the trouble that horrible man had caused her: his thieving, his slimy attempts at seduction, his nasty little threats of retribution. 'Anyway, how do you know about Barry Fish? That all happened ages ago.'

'Molly told me,' he said. 'But unfortunately Mr Fish is no longer in prison. And that's why I asked Helen to come and give you a hand.'

'I don't know why you think Helen could cope with Barry Fish any better than I would,' Katy said crossly.

Ward laughed. 'She's trained in unarmed combat, remember. Even with her bad shoulder, she'd have him in a cross-buttock in no time if he decided to cause trouble.' He drew her firmly back into his arms. 'And before you start complaining about something that I know you are basically happy about, I want to point out that it's nearly midnight and I still haven't given you a proper birthday kiss.'

Chapter Sixteen

Seeing *Glamorous Night* with Henry made a big difference to Jen's performance. A slight alteration here and there, a raised eyebrow or an overenthusiastic swoon, made the re-creation of the scenes in the new show much funnier. As a result her confidence improved. The following week Henry sent her off to see *The Wizard of Oz*, then accompanied her to a live production of *Show Boat* at the Stoll Theatre. This time he did suggest a quick drink afterwards.

During the show Jen had been enthralled, but in the bar she had begun to feel nervous again. Henry, however, had seemed unflatteringly relaxed. He was attentive in his courteous, well-mannered way. But he made no effort to woo her. He just talked about *Show Boat*, and his own show, explaining his vision, his ideas for enhancing her role. Jen was left feeling an urgent desire to please him. And she was hard pressed to hide her disappointment when he once again sent her home mid evening with an excuse about pressure of work. But at least this time he did give her a brief good-night kiss on the cheek.

'So what's happened to you?' one of the leading male actors remarked as she came off stage after a rehearsal the following day. He had been lounging in the wings watching her skit, waiting for his session. 'We all thought you were dead in the water, but you seem to have had a transformation.'

Jen glowed. This was praise indeed. Conrad Porter was a big name. He was one of the snooty Old Vic actors, not given to hobnobbing with the rest of the cast. Now he was looking at her with admiration in his eyes.

'Henry took me to see a couple of the musicals this show is based on,' Jen said. 'I think it really helped me.'

'Ha.' Conrad Porter made a smug, told-you-so face at another actor standing nearby. 'We guessed Henry had been working his magic on you.'

'What do you mean?'

The actor chuckled. 'They call it diva dienst in the operatic world. The way conductors deal with temperamental female stars. Henry has the same knack. It's a mixture of flattery, encouragement and advice. It does the trick every time.'

Jen blanched. That was exactly what Henry had done with her. She had hoped it was because he liked her for herself, but maybe it had only been for the good of the show.

But whatever it was, it had made her even more conscious of him. She didn't know if it was Henry himself or the aura of power that surrounded him, but she always knew if he was standing in the dark auditorium watching the rehearsals, even if she couldn't see him over the footlights. Or it could have been the way everyone hero-worshipped him. As rehearsals progressed, it became clear that his vision was true. He was inspired and inspiring. He confirmed over and over again his reputation of always getting the best out of his cast.

The dress rehearsal proved what the whole cast secretly knew. The show was going to be a success. But suddenly they were about to go off on tour, all the way to Scotland. And Henry wasn't coming.

Jen heard the news as she waited for her final costume fitting. They referred to the Drury Lane seamstresses as 'train-catchers' because they worked so fast. But despite the speed of their creation, Jen loved her costumes. They were pretty and flattering and she felt good in all of them. Like everyone else, she had to parade them individually for Henry's approval, and she was sure she caught an appreciative gleam in his eyes when she twirled self-consciously in front of him in her final somewhat skimpy outfit. 'Perfect,' was all he said, but that was enough to make her wish he was coming on tour with them.

But once they were on the road, there wasn't time to miss him. ENSA had set up a punishing schedule. They travelled by coach, with the scenery and costumes stacked up in the back. They arrived at hostels and bed and breakfasts in the dead of night, barely having time to sleep, let alone unpack, before they were called the following morning for the run-through. Then it was two full shows, the pack-up, and on to the next venue ready for the following day.

Henry did join them briefly at an army depot in Manchester, but only to sort out a problem with one of the cast who was sick and had to be replaced.

As soon as she heard he was there, Jen contrived to bump into him at the entrance to the NAAFI.

'Ah, Jennifer,' he said. 'How are you? How is it going?'

'I'm fine,' Jen said, feeling absurdly shy now the moment had come. 'I think it's going well.'

She had wanted to brag to him about the applause she was getting. The encores. The way the soldiers queued up for her autograph after the show. But she couldn't say anything because Henry was looking at her with a slight frown, and she felt a sudden stab of fear.

'You look tired,' he said. He put a finger under her chin to tip her face up. 'You've got shadows under your eyes. I hope you aren't burning the candle at both ends?'

'No,' Jen said, aggrieved. 'I'm not.'

The assistant producer approached then and Henry dropped his hand. 'Good,' he said. 'You need your beauty sleep. I don't want to hear that Conrad Porter and the Old Vic boys are making a nuisance of themselves.'

They weren't. Because Jen didn't attend the late-night drinking sessions. She was too exhausted. And anyway, she didn't like the flirting or the gossip. She didn't want to hear about Henry's past conquests, and she certainly didn't want to hear who he was seeing now. It was bad enough to overhear them talking about the Forces' Sweetheart, Janette Pymm, one night, and to discover that the pretty actress lived on the King's Road. Jen had a nasty feeling that that was where Henry had been heading so purposefully when he had put her in the taxi that night.

But she didn't have a chance to worry about it. And as the tour continued to Edinburgh and Glasgow and then back through the Midlands and Wales, it was as much as she could do to find time to eat, let alone sleep. She lost all track of the war.

Then, on the morning of 12 May, the soubrette she was sharing with ran into the room with the news that the war in North Africa was over. All German and Italian resistance in Tunisia had ceased. A quarter of a million enemy troops had been taken captive. And Mr Churchill had gone to America to discuss an invasion of mainland Europe.

A few days later, word buzzed round that the show would soon be heading back to London. There both cast and crew would get a week off. Then they would be leaving for North Africa.

Katy was enjoying having Helen around. Somehow she made everything seem more fun. She had even made a game of what she called the mystery of the missing glasses. She couldn't believe Katy had done so little about it and was determined to bring the culprits to account as soon as possible. Katy had in fact asked Aaref to try to trace the provenance of the glasses he had procured, but the underworld in which he operated was notoriously tight-lipped and he had soon been warned off. That route was clearly a dead end.

So one morning they carefully marked half a dozen of the pint glasses with a tiny distinctive scratch on the base and resolved to use those ones when they were serving the two men Katy suspected.

But when one evening two glasses disappeared, Katy and Helen had both been so busy they couldn't remember whether they had given the marked glasses to the right men or not. Helen's dismay was so comical that despite the loss of the glasses, Katy couldn't stop laughing.

Even Malcolm seemed happier. Helen had more time than Katy to dawdle around the common with him in tow during the afternoons. And Ward was happy because Helen being there meant he could go off on training trips with an easy heart.

And the war news was good too. Mostly. The victory in North Africa was wonderful. Some of the enemy prisoners had already been shipped back to England and there were pictures in the paper of people booing and jeering from bridges as the prison trains passed underneath.

But Katy's own jubilation faded abruptly one morning when she was shopping in Northcote Road and caught sight of Barry Fish talking to one of the men she thought was stealing her glasses.

She would have liked to avoid them, but unfortunately she had both Malcolm and George with her. As George had already run on ahead carrying Malcolm, screaming with delight, on his back, Katy had no choice but to follow in their wake, pushing the empty pram, which brought her face to face with her old tormentor.

Barry Fish recognised her at once. She saw him mutter something to the other man, who melted away, then he turned to face her with an ingratiating smile on his weaselly face. 'Well, well,' he said. 'If it isn't young Katy Parsons.'

'Hello, Mr Fish,' Katy said. 'Actually I'm Mrs Frazer now.' Looking down to avoid Barry Fish's leering grin, she realised that George was suddenly standing at her side, Malcolm still clinging to his back like a little monkey. Detaching Malcolm's fingers from George's shoulders, she lifted him into the pram.

'These are two nice little chaps,' Barry Fish said, glancing down at the children. He gave a knowing smirk. 'But they can't both be yours?'

'No,' Katy said crisply, moving a loaf of bread out of the reach of Malcolm's inquisitive fingers. 'Only this one.'

She cringed as Barry Fish leant over the pram and chucked Malcolm under the chin. Don't touch him, she wanted to scream. Get your filthy, dishonest hands off him. But she controlled herself and with a polite, dismissive nod steered the pram past him.

'You don't like him, do you?' George remarked as they walked away.

Katy blinked. She didn't think she had made it that obvious. Not to a child of George's age at least. 'No,' she said. 'Not very much.'

He glanced up at her. 'Would you call him a nasty piece of work?'

Katy looked at him in surprise. It seemed an odd phrase for him to use. 'Well, yes,' she admitted. 'I suppose I would.'

'I don't like him either,' he said blithely.

Katy began to feel slightly uneasy. She knew that innocent expression that George was wearing. It didn't bode well. 'You keep away from him, George,' she said sternly. 'He's not a nice person.'

George nodded. 'He's a bad man,' he agreed happily. 'Like Hitler.'

Delivering George back to Pam a bit later on, Katy felt drained. Dealing with one child was bad enough, she thought; two was completely exhausting. But Malcolm enjoyed the company. As she pushed him back across the road to the pub, she realised she didn't want him to be an only child. She had been an only child herself and she had often felt overwhelmed by being the sole focus of her parents' well-meant yet relentless concern. But the thought of having to cope with another child made her feel quite queasy.

Queasy? She stopped in the middle of the road. She had felt queasy rather a lot over the last month or so. Especially in the mornings. But she had put it down to all the spicy food Ward had been cooking. Now, suddenly feeling rather faint, she grasped the handle of the pram and lowered her head. Oh no, she thought. Oh no.

'Katy!' She heard footsteps and raised her head again. Molly was running up the road towards her. 'I saw you from down the street,' she gasped. 'What's the matter? Are you all right?'

'No,' Katy said. 'I'm not. I think I'm pregnant.'

Joyce stared in horror at the letter lying on the table in front of her. If there hadn't been a chair handy, she would probably have collapsed in a heap on the kitchen floor. 'Oh no,' she said. 'What have I done?'

'What *have* you done?' Mrs Rutherford asked, coming into the kitchen.

Angie was following her, carrying a tray of dirties. 'Are you feeling all right, Mum? You don't look very well.'

'I don't feel very well,' Joyce said. She turned to Mrs Rutherford. 'You know I told you about that man who came and asked me to do a cooking demonstration at the council?'

'Yes.' Mrs Rutherford nodded encouragingly. She had been all for it, of course, brushing all Joyce's concerns away in her enthusiasm for yet more promotion for the café.

'Yes, well,' Joyce said slowly. 'It turns out it's not just a demonstration. They want me to give a talk as well.' She swallowed. 'And they're expecting an audience of over a hundred people.'

'Good Lord,' Mrs Rutherford exclaimed. 'That's wonderful.'

Joyce looked up. Had the woman gone quite mad? 'It's not wonderful,' she said. 'It's awful. I can't talk to a hundred people.

'Over a hundred,' Angie corrected her. She had picked up the letter and was reading it excitedly. 'It says here there might be as many as a hundred and fifty.'

Joyce closed her eyes and then opened them again. 'I'll have to get out of it.'

'You can't let them down now,' Mrs Rutherford said. 'It would give a very bad impression.'

'It's all fixed for Saturday the nineteenth of June,' Angie added. 'They're getting posters printed and everything.'

'I don't care about the posters,' Joyce said irritably.

'I do,' Angie said eagerly. 'They might let me have one afterwards to put up in my bedroom.'

Joyce groaned. They didn't understand. A cooking demonstration was one thing, a speech quite another. Even now, she had butterflies in her stomach at the very thought of it. And not just small butterflies; these were great enormous things as big as birds, and they were flapping around as though they were trying to get out. She knew she would stumble over her words or clam up completely and not be able to speak. She would blush and sweat, and the mortification of it would be unbearable.

'Why don't you ask Jen to help you?' Angie suggested. 'She'll be home next week. And she must know about managing nerves and speaking out nice and loud and that.'

'That's a very good idea,' Mrs Rutherford said, smiling at Angie with approval.

'It's not,' Joyce said. 'Because Jen doesn't have any nerves. She's never been frightened of anything.'

So Katy was going to have another baby. Molly didn't know quite know how she felt about that.

She had only gone up to Lavender Road that day because she knew from Angie Carter that Ward was away. All it took was the purchase of a cup of tea in the café and a casual question and Angie would tell her all the news.

Until she had hit on this technique of finding out about Ward's whereabouts, Molly had been avoiding going to the pub at all. But she knew her fabricated excuses of having to work extra shifts were wearing thin.

'Ward is absolutely thrilled,' Angie told her as she poured out Molly's tea on Monday morning, slopping half of it into the saucer in her excitement. 'He's hoping it will be a girl this time, one that looks just like Katy.'

Katy, on the other hand, hadn't been happy about it at all. 'How am I going to cope?' she had wailed. 'Even with Helen helping out I'm going to struggle. It was hard enough managing the pub last time I was pregnant, and now I've got Malcolm and Ward to look after as well. What am I going to do?'

It was a good question. And predictably it was Ward who came up with a possible answer.

A few days later, Molly was sitting in the corner of the café, stirring a minuscule lump of sugar into her tea, when the door opened and Ward walked in. He saw her and at once approached her table.

'Hi, Molly, I hoped you would be here. Angie mentioned that you often came in at this time.' He glanced at the spare chair. 'Do you mind if I join you?'

Luckily he took the chair anyway, because Molly couldn't speak. She couldn't move. She had come straight off night duty. Not only was she conscious that she reeked of disinfectant, but she hadn't even bothered to glance in a mirror before she came out. She was also conscious of an overwhelming desire to wring Angie Carter's neck. Angie was meant to be *her* spy, not Ward Frazer's.

Even now the blasted girl was barging through the tables towards them, eager to take his order.

He asked for coffee, 'Easy on the chicory, though,' and Angie giggled delightedly in response.

'I'll see what I can do.' She glanced at Molly to share the joke, but didn't get the response she was expecting. 'Are you all right, Molly? You look awfully peaky this morning.'

'I'm fine,' Molly muttered. 'It was a long night, that's all.'

'You'll feel better when you've drunk your tea,' Angie said kindly. 'I made it nice and strong, the way you like it.'

Ward watched her go. 'She's cute, isn't she?' he said.

Molly nodded, although cute was hardly the word she would choose to describe Angie Carter. Traitorous was more like it.

He smiled. 'You British and your tea,' he remarked. 'I don't even like it, but for you it's the great cure-all.'

Molly glanced at her cup. If only it would cure her, she thought. But just now she couldn't even pick it up because her hand was trembling too much.

She knew she should say something about Katy's pregnancy, but it seemed somehow too intimate, too embarrassing, almost as though she was congratulating him for having sex.

But it seemed he had no such qualms.

'I want to talk to you about Katy,' he said, leaning forward. He smiled rather self-consciously. 'Or rather, I want to make you a proposition.'

Molly stared at him. A proposition? What sort of proposition? But even as a number of wildly improbable ideas began to run through her brain, he continued. 'Katy works too hard. She needs far more help than I can give her. At the moment she has Helen, but Helen won't be with us for ever.'

He stopped as Angie brought his drink. Molly noticed that he got much more sugar than the measly grain she had been given. She watched his strong, lean fingers as he stirred it into the coffee.

'You are way better than me or Helen in the bar,' he went on. He gave a grin. 'Let alone Jen. And I know how much you hate it at the Wilhelmina. So I was thinking. If you ever did decide to give up nursing, we'd kind of love for you to come and work at the pub full time. Maybe even take a share in the business?'

Molly was flabbergasted. She didn't know what to think. Certainly she didn't know what to say. She had heard the words, she understood their meaning, but she had no idea how to respond.

He picked up his cup and sipped his coffee. 'Obviously you don't have to say yes or no right now. There's no rush. Katy is OK for a few months yet. The baby's not due until December. I just wanted to give you time to think about the idea. But it would have to be what you want.'

Molly stared at him numbly. The only thing she really wanted was to touch his hand. It was hard to think about anything else when he was sitting so close, just there on the other side of the table, looking at her so intently with those beautiful grey eyes.

Desperately she tried to concentrate on what he was saying. The truth was, she was stunned by the offer. Ward and Katy wanted her, Molly Coogan, to share their business with them. In one way it was all her dreams come true, a way out of nursing, a chance to make a real life for herself, a means to earn some proper money. But in another way it was her worst nightmare.

He finished his coffee and glanced at his watch. 'I've got to go,' he said. 'Think about it, OK? Giving up nursing would be a real big decision. I wouldn't suggest this if you weren't so unhappy at the hospital.' He glanced at her questioningly, perhaps dismayed by her lack of response. 'But maybe you have something else in mind that you would rather do?'

Unconsciously Molly put a hand up to the little charm that hung at her throat. She did indeed have something else in mind that she would rather do, but she could hardly say it, because it involved being transported to a different world, a magical, beautiful, tropical haven of safety, and finding that Ward Frazer was already there and was half walking, half running towards her with his arms outstretched to greet her.

She was jerked out of her reverie by the scrape of his chair on the floor

224

as he stood up. 'I'm sorry,' he said. He looked down at her with a rueful smile. 'I can see you are dead on your feet. I should have chosen a better time. Go get some sleep. Put it out of your mind. We can talk again another day.'

Talk? That was a joke. Watching him banter with Angie as he paid for his coffee, Molly realised that she had barely uttered a word throughout their whole encounter.

When he'd left, she downed her cold cup of tea, stood up and went over to the till. But Angie waved her away. 'He paid for your tea,' she said. She wrinkled her nose. 'He's such a gentleman, isn't he? And so handsome. I don't know how you stay so calm. I go all a-flutter when I talk to him. If I wasn't waiting for my lovely Gino, I'd be head over heels in love with him by now.' She lowered her voice to a piercing whisper. 'Lucky Katy is all I say. I bet making that baby was fun!'

Jen arrived back in London at the beginning of June. In theory she was on leave; in fact there were a hundred things to attend to prior to her departure. The first thing she had to do was to report to the ENSA Overseas Section. She had to visit the Board of Trade at Euston to be allocated a special allowance of coupons. She had to queue up to be issued with malaria tablets and for painful TAB and tet-tox vaccinations, whatever they were, and just as she was thinking that ordeal was over, she was sent off to a ghastly doctor in the Euston Road to be jabbed with yellow fever and typhus, which left her with a throbbing arm and unable to sit down for several days

She found the required sun- and sand-glasses and a water bottle at Gamages in Holborn. Other items on the ENSA list included a sun hat, sandals, a swimming costume and hat, a mackintosh, a bar of soap and a packet of toilet paper, although how the person who drew up the list thought anyone could manage for four months on one bar of soap and one packet of toilet paper was anyone's guess.

The only thing she enjoyed buying were two brand-new, rather sexy summer dresses, which she found in Arding and Hobbs in Clapham Junction and looked forward to flaunting in front of Henry Keller on the voyage.

But then, shortly after that, the whole cast and crew were issued with uniforms. They were a hideous khaki, in a military style that made Jen feel like an absolute frump. It was only a precaution, they were told. In uniform they would be considered to be members of the armed forces and would therefore fall within the remit of the Geneva Convention if by any chance they were taken captive by the enemy. Most people thought it was really to stop Allied soldiers getting too frisky with the female cast members.

Security considerations meant that nobody knew the exact date they were leaving, nor indeed where they would be sailing from. All Jen knew was that she was safe until 19 June. After that she would be on twenty-four hours' notice to depart.

And then she discovered from one of the soubrettes that Henry Keller was leaving with a small advance party much earlier than that. The girl had rolled her eyes meaningfully as she relayed the news. 'There's a rumour that he's travelling with Janette Pymm. She's going out on one of her Forces' Sweetheart tours.'

For a moment Jen felt a jolt of jealous disappointment, which she had, of course, carefully concealed from the other girl. Because she knew she had to be realistic. Henry had flirted a little bit with her in the past, but he had made very little attempt recently to seek her out. With all her rushing about, her shopping and her inoculations, she had barely seen him since getting back to London, and certainly not in private. She just had to accept that he was in a different league to her. He moved in different circles. Glamorous circles of fame and fortune. He was hardly likely to be seriously interested in a girl from the back streets of Clapham. Or only in as much as she contributed to the success of his show.

But two days later, suddenly there he was, standing alone, in uniform, hat in hand, in the corridor as Jen emerged from an appointment with the wardrobe mistress.

'Well hello,' he said. 'Or rather, goodbye. I'm leaving later today.'

'Yes,' Jen said. 'I had heard.'

'It won't be long for you now either.' He glanced at the costume she was holding. 'Are you all sorted out?'

Jen nodded. 'Yes, pretty much,' she said. She wished he would just go. It was easy enough to write him off when he wasn't there; it was harder when he was standing right in front of her studying her with those observant eyes. He looked surprisingly good in his uniform too.

He smiled and raised his eyebrows slightly. 'How are you feeling?'

Jen fiddled with a button on the costume. 'Nervous,' she said. 'Terrified, in fact. I've never set foot on a boat in my entire life.' She hesitated, encouraged by that smile. 'I wish I was going with you.' It was true. She would feel a lot safer travelling in his company. Even if blasted Janette Pymm was on the same ship. There was something very calm and reassuring about Henry Keller.

'Really?' He looked surprised. 'That's funny, because I wish you were too.'

Jen looked at him uncertainly. She never knew whether he was teasing her or mocking her.

He snapped his fingers with a light smile. 'Damn. If only I'd known, I'd have put you on the advance party list. That would have lightened up my voyage no end.'

Jen was sure he was teasing her now. 'Well, you've got Janette Pymm to lighten it up for you instead, haven't you?' she said crossly.

He looked at her thoughtfully. 'I have indeed. But only for the voyage. She is going straight on to Egypt.' He put on a mournful face. 'So I'll be extra lonely by the time you arrive.'

Jen glared at him. The words were flirtatious, yet the way he had spoken them sounded as though he was mocking her. But the warmth in his eyes when he looked at her made her not so sure. She had absolutely no idea whether he meant what he said or not. Well, two could play at that game.

'I doubt that,' she murmured. 'Not when you look so gorgeous in your uniform.'

He laughed. 'Ah, that's more like it.' He took a step forward and put a hand on her shoulder, drawing her towards him. 'Goodbye, Jennifer Carter,' he said. He dropped a light kiss on her lips. 'I look forward to seeing you in Tripoli. Safe journey.' He moved on past her then. But at the end of the corridor he looked back. 'And don't fall in love with some damn sailor on the way over.'

Even though Katy was appalled about being pregnant again, she couldn't help being touched by Ward's solicitous concern for her welfare. He hadn't been there, of course, when she was carrying Malcolm. Nor at his awful, prolonged, life-threatening birth. Last time she had had to deal with everything on her own, or with her friends. But this time Ward was there and he couldn't stop working out ways to lighten her load. 'You are my wife,' he said when she tried to explain that she didn't need coddling every minute of the day. 'And I want to look after you.'

But even Katy thought that inviting Molly to work at the pub full time was a good idea. She trusted Molly implicitly. She really hoped she would decide to take them up on the offer. It would make everything so much easier.

But in the meantime, she and Helen were doing all right. When Katy totted up her takings for May, she found it had been her best month ever. Angie Carter's open-handed GIs and the victory in North Africa had helped enormously. So many people had friends and relatives in the army, it was a relief to know that for now, at least, they were safe. There had been plenty of rounds bought when Winston Churchill's celebratory speech to the American Congress had been broadcast on the wireless last week.

But the news wasn't good for everyone. Because although the ground forces were off the hook for the time being, there was no let-up for the boys in the navy or the air force. It hadn't been formally announced, for security reasons, but there was a rumour that a whole convoy had been lost in the Atlantic recently. Katy hardly dared to wonder how Louise's husband Jack and Joyce's son, young Mick Carter, were faring on their respective vessels.

But bad as it was for those at sea, the losses in the air were even worse. Bombers were constantly being shot down as they flew to Germany night after night, day after day, in their efforts to take the heart out of the Nazi war machine. Ward had told her that even in the recent, spectacularly audacious and daring dam-busting raid in the Ruhr valley, fifty-six of the hundred and thirty-three aircrew who had participated in the attack were now listed as killed or missing, including thirteen from the Royal Canadian Air Force. Katy couldn't help wondering if the fresh-faced young pilot she had met at Lucinda Veale's party might be among them.

So many young deaths. But the good news was that some of the downed aircrew were managing to get home again. The efforts of Ward and his colleagues were beginning to bear fruit. The lucky ones were being passed from town to town, village to village, smuggled down through Belgium and France and eventually over the border into Spain and then Portugal, where the British Embassy could arrange them a passage back to England. The dangers for their foreign helpers were great. The Nazis shot anyone found harbouring or assisting escaping airmen, or indeed escaping Jews. In some case reprisals were so harsh that whole families were killed, women and children included. The thought made Katy feel even sicker than she did already.

And then suddenly the Americans had gone, taking their business and their gifts of stockings, lipstick and cigarettes with them. From one weekend to the next they disappeared. And that Saturday night the Flag and Garter seemed very quiet and flat.

Katy had seen this happen before, last October. Then it had heralded the American landings in Morocco and Tunisia. Now it looked like another invasion was on the cards, but this time nobody knew where it would be.

But then news came in that the RAF had begun to bomb the island of Sicily from airfields in North Africa. It began to look increasingly likely that the next big push would be across the Mediterranean from North Africa into Italy. That wasn't the news that people wanted to hear. Most people had been hoping for an invasion across the English Channel, which seemed the shortest route to Germany. Helen de Burrel was disappointed too. For obvious reasons, she had been hoping for an invasion of the south of France.

Even as her till takings dropped alarmingly, Katy tried to look on the bright side. 'Everyone says Italy will surrender. So it won't take our forces long to get up to the border with France. And André is near there, isn't he?'

But Helen hadn't been so positive. 'People think the Italians are lily-livered and assume that they'd rather capitulate than fight,' she said. 'But I don't know. Mussolini is a vicious old bugger. I don't think he'd be likely to give in easily. Especially not with Hitler at his back.'

Molly couldn't stop thinking about Ward's offer. Far from putting it out of her mind, as he had suggested, she thought of almost nothing else. Even as she swilled out bedpans, administered bed baths, and tucked blankets into neat hospital corners, her feelings swung wildly between hope and despair. How could she possibly live and work so close to a man who inadvertently caused her such agony? But if she put her emotions aside, Ward's proposal was so, so tempting. Could she really just give up nursing, though? Just like that? And if she did give up nursing, was running a pub what she really wanted to do?

But Ward was right. Katy needed help. Helen obviously wasn't going to stay there for ever. She was definitely cut out for better things than being a barmaid. Even if she wasn't going to work for the SOE any more, she would soon be offered something else. And with her connections, better things wouldn't be hard to find. After all, her father was a friend of Winston Churchill. She had even been to his family home at Chartwell once as a child.

'All I remember was that he had lots of animals roaming around,' she said when Molly asked her what it was like. 'Not just dogs and cats, but pigs and goats too. While we were having tea, two chickens came into the drawing room and nobody batted an eyelid.'

'I wish I could meet him,' Molly said.

Helen looked surprised. 'Why? What would you say?'

'I'd tell him to stop smoking those cigars,' Molly said, and was surprised when Helen burst out laughing. 'No, I would,' she insisted. 'They can't be good for his chest. And we need him to stay healthy so we can win this blasted war as soon as possible.'

'You are wasted as a nurse,' Helen said. 'You ought to apply to be the Prime Minister's private physician. I'm sure you'd be better at it than stuffy old Lord Moran.'

If only, Molly thought now, as she painstakingly cleaned the pus out of a patient's wound prior to applying a lint gauze poultice. If only the world was a different place. Or if only she had a different position in it. Then amazing things like that could happen. As it was, her only real choice seemed to be between washing patients and washing glasses. And that was a decision she seemed entirely unable to make.

'Nurse Coogan!'

Molly looked up in alarm and saw that Sister Parkes was sailing down the ward towards her. 'What on earth are you doing? That should have been finished by now.'

'I'm sorry, Sister,' Molly muttered.

'It's no good being sorry. I don't know what's the matter with you. You have been half asleep for the last few days. But now you need to pull yourself together, because Matron wants you to report to her immediately.'

'Matron?' Molly's mind immediately began to run over all possible misdemeanours she might have unwittingly committed. 'But why?'

Sister Parkes pursed her lips in irritation. 'It would be nice if just once in your life, Nurse Coogan, you could obey a command without questioning it first.'

'Yes, Sister,' Molly responded, and thrusting the poultice into Sister's hands, she hurried away to change her apron.

As always, Matron was sitting behind her enormous desk. As Molly stood on the other side, with her hands correctly folded behind her back, she tried to imagine herself calmly telling Matron that she wanted to leave nursing in order to run a pub. The thought made her quail.

Perhaps aware of her sudden tremor of trepidation, Matron glanced at her oddly, then looked down at a letter on her desk.

'I received a letter from Dr Florey this morning,' she said.

She glanced up as though waiting for Molly to say something, but Molly just stared at her blankly.

'She seems to have a very high opinion of you,' Matron went on in a tone that implied that in her opinion Dr Florey needed her head examined.

'She's very kind,' Molly muttered.

Matron sniffed. 'I'm not sure if her current proposal is kind or not. It is very irregular, but in wartime we all have to make concessions.'

'Yes, Matron,' Molly said. She had no idea what Matron was talking about, but for some reason her heart had begun to beat faster and her hands felt clammy.

'I gather that her husband, Professor Florey, has recently arrived in Egypt, where he is intending to trial various forms of penicillin on recently wounded soldiers.'

'Yes, Matron,' Molly said again. She knew about Professor Florey's trip.

230

It had been mentioned last time she had been in Oxford.

'And it seems he needs someone to monitor treatment records and to train other nurses how to do the same.'

Molly nodded. She could see that he would find that helpful.

Matron glanced up at her again. 'I have consulted with Dr Goodacre and he felt I should at least mention it to you before responding. He sees it as quite an honour. But you are still very young. And very inexperienced. It clearly isn't at all suitable for you to go.'

Molly's pulse was accelerating harder now, making her feel quite faint. She felt a slow-welling excitement, but she wanted to be sure. Completely sure that she hadn't misunderstood. That she wasn't deluding herself. 'Go where?' she asked.

'To Egypt.' Matron spoke with some exasperation. 'For goodness' sake, Nurse Coogan, haven't you listened to a word I have been saying? Professor Florey has specifically asked for you to travel out and help him for a month or so. As you know their systems already, it would be quicker and easier than training up someone new. But as I said, nobody is going to put any pressure ...'

But Molly was hardly listening any more. This was her chance. Her chance to get away. If Jen Carter was brave enough to go to North Africa, so was she. And Matron herself had served in Siberia. Molly knew that if she didn't take this opportunity, she would regret it for ever. Katy and Ward could wait a month. Katy's bump was hardly even showing. They had Helen de Burrel for now.

'I'll go,' she said firmly. She would go, and while she was away she would decide what to do about her future. 'I'm happy to go. I want to go.'

Chapter Seventeen

If getting ready to travel to North Africa had been a rush for Jen, it was worse for Molly. She had even more to do. And everything was happening so quickly. It had been arranged that she would be temporarily attached to the Queen Alexandra Imperial Military Nursing Service and would be travelling to Egypt on the next available convoy with a small detachment of QA nurses who were being posted to the Number 70 General Hospital in Tunisia. It was impressed upon her by Matron that she would be under the command of a QA nursing sister on the voyage. 'I don't want you going off with the idea that you can behave in any way other than with the decorum, obedience and efficiency I would expect of a nurse trained at this hospital.'

Molly had nodded dutifully and had subsequently endured a ghastly day at Goodwood House, the QA headquarters, where she had been given numerous painful inoculations, completed countless forms and been generally treated as some kind of imposter by everyone she met, including the sister who would be in charge of the party, a formidable woman called Miss Summers, who spoke with such a cut-glass accent, Molly was surprised she didn't injure herself on it.

'I don't know why you have been foisted upon me,' Miss Summers snapped when they were introduced. 'I am certain any one of my nurses could have carried out the duties Professor Florey wishes you to perform. But it is not my role to question my orders, only to ensure that you are properly prepared.'

Once again Molly had nodded obediently. But in fact it was only a matter of days before she found herself disregarding several explicit QA directives.

The QA recommendation was that personnel travelling to North Africa should obtain their tropical supplies from Harrods. This, even with the extra coupons she was issued, Molly simply couldn't afford to do. If Jen had been prepared to co-operate, Molly could have saved a lot of time and money. But as Jen didn't seem to know the word, Molly had to scrabble around London trying to find the required items on her own.

In the end it was Helen de Burrel who saved the day by lending her a small trunk from out of her father's storage, a straw boater and a summer frock, which Molly would need to shorten when she had time, and generously equipping her with sunburn lotion, an umbrella and a Thermos vacuum flask, all of which were items on the QA North Africa essential requirements list. Aaref Hoch provided her with the padlock she needed to secure the lid of the trunk, but there were plenty of other items on the list, like witch hazel liquid, that Molly was simply unable to find.

'Goodness,' Katy remarked when she saw Molly's neat little trunk, packed in readiness and now waiting on standby to be summoned to Goodwood House for departure with the rest of the QA contingent. 'Is that all you are taking? You should see the size of Jen's trunk. And she's got a suitcase as well! I suppose she is going for longer, but even so …'

Molly eyed her luggage doubtfully. She had decided against taking the evening gowns, gloves, overcoat or wellington boots suggested by the QAs, as she was unable to imagine a scenario in a field hospital in the middle of a baking hot desert where she was likely to need them.

Nor was she taking the enormous bible that Sister Morris had given her, which, according to Sister Morris at least, was an essential item when travelling in heathen lands.

Dr Goodacre, who had appeared in Sister's office just at that moment, overheard the comment. 'Yes indeed.' He winked at Molly. 'You'll need to be very careful, Nurse Coogan. He's an unpredictable type of fellow, the Arab. I believe he's sent wild by the mere sight of a female ankle.'

Molly giggled nervously and wondered if that was why the wellington boots were on the QA packing list.

Dr Goodacre chuckled. 'I don't blame him, of course. A nicely turned talocrural joint is one of the most beautiful sights to behold. And if you don't mind me saying so,' he added gallantly, 'you two ladies both have very shapely specimens.'

'Really, Dr Goodacre,' Sister Morris expostulated. 'What will you say next!'

What indeed, Molly thought. As Sister Morris's ankles, clad as they were in thick black woollen stockings, wouldn't have seemed out of place on the brewery dray horse, Dr Goodacre clearly needed his eyes examined.

Katy burst out laughing when Molly relayed this story, and Molly suddenly realised how much she was going to miss her.

'Are you sure you don't mind me going?' she asked. 'I feel so guilty for leaving you short-handed.'

'You aren't leaving me short-handed,' Katy said. 'I've still got Helen. And Ward. And Jacob at the weekends. And it's only a month. You'll be back before you know it.'

As Professor Florey wanted her to bring more penicillin supplies out to Egypt with her, Molly had also had to fit in a trip to Oxford. There Ethel

Florey impressed upon her the importance of keeping the box of mould cultures safe. Until she left, it was to be stored in a refrigerated unit at the Wilhelmina, and on the ship, it was to be consigned to the care of the purser.

'Penicillin is about to become one of the Allies' secret weapons,' she barked. 'We don't want the enemy getting his hands on any.'

Molly felt a shiver of fear. 'I'll guard it with my life,' she said, and Ethel Florey had laughed.

'I hope it won't come to that,' she said. Then she looked at Molly more closely and her face softened. 'Are you all right, Molly? How do you really feel about this trip? When Howard suggested it, I just thought it might interest you. But you don't have to go, you know. I'm sure we can find someone else.'

'No, no, I want to go,' Molly assured her quickly. 'I do feel a little bit nervous, I suppose, but I promise to do my best.'

But on the train on the way back to London, she realised she hadn't told the truth. Fear was only a small part of what she felt. What she really felt was pride. The Floreys were trusting her with their precious invention. She was absolutely determined not to let them down.

And then as she sat there carefully nursing the box of penicillin on her lap, she realised that among all the rush of the preparations, her overriding emotion wasn't pride or fear. It was excitement.

This was her chance for a little bit of adventure. And she could hardly wait.

Joyce tried valiantly to get out of the cooking demonstration. But Angie had been right: the posters were already at the printer's, the invitations to all the WI and women's clubs in the area had been sent out, and Mr Styles had been very po-faced about any idea of cancelling. To such an extent that Joyce had eventually, reluctantly, agreed to go ahead with it.

And now the horror of it was looming larger every day. It wasn't the cooking that scared her. She knew she could cook as well as – probably better than – the next person. No, it was the performance side of things that terrified her, the thought of standing there looking out at a sea of expectant faces and feeling like a lemon because she had completely lost her nerve. Perhaps Angie was right. Perhaps she should ask Jen to give her some tips.

But predictably Jen wasn't helpful. 'Goodness, I don't know what you are worrying about,' she said. 'It's only a few old biddies from the WI; it's hardly an appearance at the Old Vic, is it?'

'It's all right for you,' Joyce said, trying to stay calm. 'You're used to it now, but you must have been nervous when you started out, in school plays and that. Weren't you?'

'I was, at it happens,' Jen retorted. 'But much you cared. You didn't even bother to come and see me perform.'

Joyce blinked, taken aback by the sudden accusation. It was true, but it wasn't her fault. They had all got so sick of Jen and her big talk. Her wild ideas of fame and glory. Even as a child she had behaved like a prima donna.

'Well, your dad never had any interest in theatricals,' Joyce said. 'We thought it was all a bit of a flash in the pan. How was I to know it was going to become your career?'

'I told you often enough,' Jen snapped. 'But you didn't care.' She threw Joyce a resentful glance. 'Just as you won't care if something happens to me in North Africa. I bet you won't send me food parcels like you send Bob. All I'll get is a letter telling me to pull myself together.'

Joyce flinched. 'I will care,' she said. 'I do care.' And she did, even though Jen made it so difficult. She tried to gentle her voice. Tried to be reassuring. 'Anyway, nothing is going to happen. And even if it does, you'll have that nice Henry Keller there to look after you.'

Jen's eyes flashed with irritation. 'I don't want him to look after me.' She pushed back her chair and stood up. 'Don't you understand? I want to be my own person.'

Joyce sniffed. She had tried to be nice, but she was losing her patience now. 'Well you are stupid then, because I wouldn't mind a man like that looking after me.'

'You've got Mr Lorenz,' Jen said, flouncing over to the door. 'Or you could have if you ever gave the poor man a chance.'

Wearily Joyce pulled round the chair Jen had vacated and sat down. Jen was right. She did have Mr Lorenz in a sort of way. But she had suffered too much at Stanley's hands to even think of making the same mistake again. The café had given her independence. It had given her money, her own money; not much, but enough to get by, money that was hers and that nobody was going to drink away or blow on the horses.

Men, she thought. Men and families. How much easier life would be without them.

On Friday 18 June, Goebbels triumphantly declared Warsaw free of Jews. Katy listened to the news in silence, head bowed, her hands flat on the bar. A whole city 'free of Jews'. A capital city. The largest in Poland. It would be like declaring London free of Jews. She could barely take it in. She certainly couldn't understand it, the hideous mindset that relegated one whole section of a population to the status of rabid dogs or rats. More than anything else they had done, it was the Nazis' utter inhumanity that made Katy feel the war was worth fighting.

All in all, she wasn't surprised when Mr Lorenz didn't come in that night. She didn't blame him. If the news was shocking to her, what must it be like for anyone who was Jewish. Nor did Aaref Hoch stay more than a minute when he called in to drop off some supplies. But that might have been for other reasons. Because Louise had chosen that night to bring Charlie Hawkridge into the pub.

'Don't look at me like that,' she muttered to Katy as Helen took Charlie's order at the bar.

'You didn't have to bring him down here,' Katy said crossly. 'It's like rubbing salt in the wound. What if Aaref tells Jack?'

Katy was fond of Jack Delmaine, Louise's husband. He hadn't had an easy time of it as a young officer in the navy. The last thing he needed was to find out that Louise was playing around behind his back with some self-regarding lothario.

She glanced over towards the bar. She could tell from Helen's over-polite smile, as she pulled a pint for Charlie, that she didn't approve of Louise's latest acquisition either.

Louise gave a smug little smile. 'Aaref would never betray me. He's far too sweet on me to do anything like that.'

Katy felt like slapping her. 'Well for goodness' sake don't get pregnant,' she said sourly. 'Because Jack will know exactly what's been going on then.'

'Katy! Really!' Louise's eyes widened in mocking incredulity. 'What do you think I am?'

'Blasted Louise,' Katy muttered to Helen a few minutes later, after she had endured a few minutes' conversation with Charlie Hawkridge. Give him his due, he tried hard, with his wide smiles and his smooth compliments, but Katy couldn't warm to him. 'Sometimes she almost makes my blood boil.'

'Talking of which,' Helen responded drily, 'look who has just come in.'

But Katy was already aware of a sudden hush. Glancing over to the door, she saw that Gillian James had made one of her entrances and was now standing just inside the blackout curtain, scanning the room as though she was expecting to see someone she knew.

'Look at Mr Hawkridge,' Helen whispered to Katy. 'His tongue is almost hanging out. I reckon Louise might have her work cut out to keep him in line!'

'Ha. Serves her right,' Katy muttered. She wished Charlie Hawkridge would abandon Louise for another woman, although she would prefer if it didn't happen in her pub.

Gillian James was at the bar now. She gave Katy a flicker of a smile and asked for a gin and tonic. After a moment's hesitation, Katy took a glass and turned to the optic to pour it. She had to. She couldn't embarrass the woman by refusing, even though that was what she longed to do. 'That'll be—' she began, but Gillian interrupted.

'I'm meeting a friend,' she murmured in her purring voice. 'He'll pay when he comes.' She looked at Katy through her long lashes. 'I hope that's all right?'

Katy hesitated. It wasn't all right. She never ran tabs. She had learnt from experience that they were more trouble than they were worth.

'OK,' she said reluctantly. 'But just this once, mind.'

She watched Gillian James walk self-consciously over to a small empty table, watched her sit down, take out a cigarette and then glance round hopefully for someone to give her a light.

'Keep an eye on the glasses,' Katy murmured to Helen, as Charlie Hawkridge leaned over obligingly with a silver cigarette lighter. Dragging her own gaze away from the widow, she cast a quick glance at the group of men in the corner. But they like everyone else seemed to be transfixed by the sight of Mrs James pouting her lips round the cigarette as she drew on Charlie's flame. The smile of gratitude she threw him afterwards would have melted the heart of a lesser man.

It took some time before the atmosphere in the pub returned to normal, and even then it was obvious from the subdued talk and forced laughter that everyone was very aware of the widow still sitting alone at her table for two.

'You know what she's up to, don't you?' Louise muttered to Katy when Charlie went out to the back to relieve himself. 'Charlie says he can spot women like that a mile off.'

Katy stared at her and then at Gillian James, who had crossed her shapely legs and was idly swinging her foot. Her dainty slingback shoe had slipped off her heel and was now hanging rather provocatively from her bare toes.

'How clever of him,' Katy said coldly. But she had a nasty feeling Louise was right.

At least half an hour elapsed and there was no sign of Mrs James's so-called friend. But if Gillian James really had come in with the intention of picking up a man prepared to pay for her services, then she wasn't so far having any luck. She had spun out her gin and tonic as long as she could and she was now sitting with an empty glass in front of her, perhaps waiting for someone to offer her another.

If Louise and Charlie had still been there, perhaps Charlie would have obliged. But they had gone, purportedly to the pictures, although judging from the way Louise deliberately brushed against Charlie as he held the blackout curtain for her, Katy privately doubted the truth of that.

When nobody else offered to refresh her glass, Gillian James approached the bar herself. And once again, Katy felt she couldn't refuse her. It was just too awkward with everyone in the bar hanging on the blasted woman's every move.

But when, after three gin and tonics, Gillian James eventually got up to go, Katy felt rather less tolerant.

'My friend must have got delayed,' Mrs James said. She gave a token little rummage in her handbag. 'Oh dear. I'm so sorry. I've forgotten to bring my purse. Can I settle up tomorrow?'

Katy wondered sourly what would happen if she insisted on payment now. Would one of the widow's reticent admirers leap forward with the cash? Or would she go home and return straight away with the money? Somehow Katy doubted it. 'OK,' she said grudgingly. She lowered her voice. 'But if I don't get it by tomorrow night, I won't serve you again.'

Katy wasn't the only one to notice Gillian flinch as she turned away.

'Goodness,' Helen remarked with a sideways glance at Katy. 'You certainly aren't pulling your punches tonight.'

As soon as Gillian James was out of the door, the noise in the pub increased dramatically. Katy grimaced as a rude, raunchy chuckle rang out from the men in the corner. It was obvious what they were talking about.

'I don't like her coming in here,' she said. 'Meeting a friend, my foot. If I'm not careful, she's going to give the place a bad name.'

Helen made a face. 'Well I felt rather sorry for her. You must admit she's got guts, coming in all alone like that.'

'Gall, I'd call it,' Katy said crossly. 'Not guts. And what's more, I've just realised that I won't be here tomorrow evening because Mrs Carter has invited us to her cooking demonstration. Molly has promised to come and help you here. Jacob will be here too, as it's a Saturday night.' She looked at Helen severely. 'So if Mrs James comes in without the money, you are not to serve her. Don't you dare let her off the hook.'

Helen was just about to respond when the door opened and Jen came in. Without a glance at anyone else, she came straight up to the bar. 'I need a drink,' she said. 'A whisky. Maybe even a double.'

Katy looked at her in alarm. Jen's pretty face was unnaturally pale. Her hand shook. 'What's the matter? What's happened?'

'We've been given the order,' Jen said. 'I'm leaving tomorrow.'

*

In an odd way, the news of Jen's imminent departure made Joyce feel calmer about her own upcoming ordeal. Jen had been told days ago to have her luggage packed and standing by, but needless to say, she still wasn't ready when the taxi came to pick her up. All the fluster and kerfuffle over Jen's last-minute items had taken Joyce's mind off the cookery demonstration. And what with rushing down to Northcote Road to get some salt, and squeezing into the outfit Angie had chosen for her, and loading up her own taxi, which Mr Lorenz had thoughtfully provided, she was at the town hall and setting up before she had time to feel properly scared.

In the end, she had thought of asking Ward Frazer for advice. Unlike Jen, he had been very helpful. He advised her not to worry about doing a separate talk, but just to chat about things as she went along. And sure enough, there he was, as promised, about halfway back, looking relaxed, smiling encouragingly, sitting between Katy and Angie. Mr Lorenz was the other side of Angie, and Mrs Rutherford was at the end of the row dressed in a tweedy suit and a large hat that must be completely obscuring the view of the person behind her. Not that Joyce cared if someone's view was obscured. The fewer people who saw her, the better. The outfit that Angie had picked out for her was a trim little suit that had once belonged to Jen. But the hall was hotter than she had expected and it wouldn't be long before she was sweating like a pig.

For a second or two, when she first walked out to face her audience, Joyce had almost turned tail and run. But she stood her ground. She was conscious of her knees trembling as Mr Styles introduced her, and hoped nobody could see. But once she had remembered to breathe slowly as Ward had told her, she began to feel better.

It all started off well. Ward had suggested telling them about her family. 'Get them on your side from the start,' he said. 'Make them realise we are all in it together.'

So she told the audience that she had recently been widowed, that her eldest son, Bob, was a POW in Italy, that Pete had just started at naval college, that Mick, always so naughty in his youth, was now in the merchant marine, had survived a torpedo attack and been decorated for his bravery, and that her elder daughter was just about to go to North Africa in ENSA. As she spoke, she could hear the murmurs of patriotic approval and she knew Ward had been right. They were lapping it up. As for her other daughter, she went on, pointing at Angie, who was scarlet with beaming pleasure, she helped her in the café, and her youngest son was still an evacuee in Devon.

'We are living through difficult times,' Joyce said, obedient to Ward's instructions. 'But if we want to get rid of that nasty, fidgety little man Adolf Hitler, we all have to do our bit. And for us women that means using whatever food we can get hold of in the most efficient way. So what I'm hoping to do today is to give you some ideas about how to make your rations go just that little bit further and your meals just a little bit tastier.'

So far so good. She had decided to cook a meat and veg pie, a rhubarb fool and a small cake on the side. It all sounded straightforward, but she hoped some of the ingredients would take people by surprise. For example, instead of meat, she was using a couple of tins of Canadian Spam. 'Once it's been fried crisp on the edges, you can hardly tell the difference,' she said.

She smeared a small scoop of lard into a frying pan and set it on the stove cooker the council had provided. While the pan heated up, she cut the Spam and a few potatoes into chunks and tossed them in a little salted flour. Then she chopped two carrots and carefully trimmed the leaves off a dozen radishes that Mrs Rutherford had grown.

It was as she began to reveal her other surprise ingredients that things started to go wrong.

'With so little in the shops,' she said, 'I started looking around for other nourishing things I could use. And when I discovered that my tortoise was partial to dandelions, daisies and stinging nettles, I thought, well, if they are good enough for Monty, they are probably good enough for me. So I tried them last week and I'm still here to tell the tale.'

Distracted by the audience's chuckle of amusement, she unthinkingly delved into a bag to draw out the edible weeds she had mentioned. But she had forgotten about the stinging nettles. As soon as her fingers closed on the vicious leaves, it felt as though her entire hand had caught fire. With a shriek of shock and pain, she jerked her arm out of the bag and rushed over to the sink, scattering stinging nettles, dandelions and daisy leaves in her wake.

But in her haste to get her throbbing hand under the cold tap, she bumped the corner of the table, and even as she felt the cooling balm of the water on her fingers, she saw her trimmed radishes start to roll off the chopping board. As she ran back, hand still smarting, to try to stop them falling on to the floor, she slipped on a dandelion and, clutching at the table to steady herself, inadvertently tipped over her bowl of dried egg powder.

Her eyes were already watering from the nettle stings and now, through a blurry haze of egg powder, she saw the audience staring at her open-mouthed. One lady in the front row looked as though her eyes were about to start out of her head. As the first two radishes dropped on to the floor, someone gave a muffled snort of mirth.

There was a hushed pause as the third radish teetered on the edge of the table, and then it too plopped on to the floor. This time there was a distinct rumble of amusement. At the same moment Joyce heard a distinct splash of water and realised the sink was overflowing. Several people were giggling openly now; someone towards the back of the hall seemed to be weeping with laughter.

And then, as she rushed to turn off the tap, Joyce heard a sharp collective intake of breath, and out of the corner of her eye she saw that her frying pan was on fire.

In the pub, Helen was rinsing out glasses while Molly helped Jacob Hoch with his maths homework. Jacob was a shy, studious boy. He had been helping Katy in the pub for over a year now. Molly had often found him poring over his books in the depths of the cellar. His ambition was to go to Oxford University to read law.

'No, for the circumference of a circle you multiply the diameter by pi,' Molly was saying now.

Jacob frowned down at the exercise book spread open on the bar. 'But I thought the formula was two pi r.'

'That's the same,' Molly said. 'R is the radius, two r is the diameter. Two pi r is the same as pi d.'

'Goodness, Molly, how do you know all that stuff?' Helen said, glancing over her shoulder.

'I liked maths at school,' Molly said. 'I always liked working out those formulas.'

Helen looked at her in wonder. 'I could never make head or tail of it. I was much more interested in languages.'

'I was hopeless at languages,' Molly said. 'Lucky old Jacob, however, is good at everything.'

The boy flushed and shook his head. 'No, no. I am very stupid at algebra. But I am pleased Miss Molly can help me.'

Helen moved away then to serve one of the regulars, and she had just handed over his pint and his change when the door of the pub opened and two strangers stepped into the bar.

Glancing up, Molly saw the elder of the two straighten his tie and look around with an expression of haughty distaste. Even though the younger man looked less severe, there was a certain resemblance between them. She guessed they were father and son. Clearly very much on their dignity, they were both dressed immaculately in well-cut dark suits and fedora hats. They looked clean, fit and expensive, completely out of place in the Flag and Garter. There was something oddly familiar about them, especially about the younger man, and Molly found herself studying him curiously as they approached the bar.

Beside her she heard Helen suddenly catch her breath. 'Oh my God,' she muttered. Molly turned her head in surprise. Helen wasn't normally one to blaspheme. But it was too late to ask her what the matter was, because the two men were already upon them.

'I am looking for Mr Ward Frazer,' the older one said. He sounded American, but his tone was so clipped it was hard to be sure. 'Are we in the right place?'

'Well, yes,' Molly said, bristling at the cold, assessing glance that accompanied his question. 'You are in the right place. But you've come at the wrong time. Because he's not here.'

The man's eyebrows rose. 'I would be obliged if you could tell me when he will be back.'

Molly didn't want to oblige such an objectionable man with anything. But before she could make an angry retort, to her bewilderment, Helen de Burrel suddenly leaned across the counter and extended her hand.

'Hello,' she said with a bright smile. 'My name is Helen de Burrel. I am a friend of Ward and Katy. I think you must be Ward's uncle? How lovely to meet you.'

Ward's uncle?

Molly did a double-take. Of course. That was why they looked familiar. The younger man in particular had a definite look of Ward Frazer about him. Or he might if he ever smiled. But how on earth had Helen known who they were? Molly glanced at her in bemusement and saw that she was biting her lip, trying not to laugh.

But even Helen's gushing welcome didn't appear to mollify Ward's uncle. He deigned to shake hands with her, but that was about it. He didn't bother to introduce his son, and noticing that the younger man was looking around with considerable interest, he cleared his throat to attract his attention and threw him an admonishing frown.

'And this is Molly Coogan and Jacob Hoch,' Helen went on blithely. 'We are helping out this evening while Ward and Katy are out.'

Molly nodded a cool greeting. She was damned if she was going to shake hands, even if he was Ward Frazer's uncle. Beside her she was conscious of Jacob nervously gathering up his books. A moment later he had disappeared down into the cellar.

Helen glanced over her shoulder at the big grandfather clock. 'I don't think Ward and Katy will be all that long,' she lied blithely. 'Perhaps you would like a drink while you wait.'

With some reluctance, the man accepted half a pint of beer for himself and a pint for his son, and they withdrew to a small table for two by the window.

They had barely sat down before Helen was dragging Molly into the little kitchen.

'Oh goodness,' Helen gasped. 'Your expression! I could hardly keep a straight face. I think he must have thought you were Katy.'

Molly glared at her. 'Well how was I to know who they were? Come to that, how on earth did *you* know who they were?'

Helen wiped her eyes. 'Katy mentioned a while ago that Ward's uncle might turn up. She thinks his family disapprove of their marriage, and judging from old sour-pants out there, she might be right.'

'But why would they disapprove of Katy?' Molly asked hotly. 'Nobody could be nicer than Katy. How dare they judge her without even knowing her? Katy will be really upset if he treats her like that.'

Helen grimaced. 'I know. We clearly have to soften the pompous old fool up before they get home.'

'But how?' Molly asked. 'He's hardly going to soften up much on half a pint, is he?'

'No,' Helen agreed. 'You're right. We'll have to get some more alcohol into him somehow.'

They heard the door go then, and to her dismay, Molly saw Gillian James standing just inside the blackout curtain, surveying the room. When she spotted the two distinguished-looking strangers sitting alone at their table, her eyes lit up and she gave them a coy little glance as she sashayed past them to the bar.

'Oh no,' Molly groaned. 'That's all we need.'

But Helen was smiling. 'No, she said. 'I think that's exactly what we need.'

With considerable astonishment, Molly watched Helen walk over to greet Mrs James with a friendly smile. She couldn't hear what she was saying, but the widow was clearly making some excuse about something. Pleading for more time.

Intrigued, Molly edged out of the kitchen and took up her previous position behind the bar.

'OK, I'll let you off the debt,' Helen was saying. 'I'll pay for yesterday's gin and tonics and I'll give you another now. But in return, I want you to do me a favour.'

Another customer came up then, so Molly missed the rest, but it soon became clear what Helen had been up to.

Taking the gin and tonic with her, Gillian James went and sat demurely down at the next table to Ward's relatives. Ward's uncle might be a disapproving old-school stickler, but even he apparently was not immune to Gillian James's startling beauty. She had positioned herself right in his line of sight, and it wasn't long before Molly saw him casting covert glances in her direction. When her handbag somehow slipped off her chair and fell right at his feet, he returned it to her with old-fashioned courtesy, and the smile he received in return caused him to run a finger round his collar as though it had suddenly become too tight. After that, it was easy work for her to inveigle her way on to their table, and within ten minutes he had offered her another drink.

It was when his son came up to the bar to order two double gin and tonics and another pint of beer for himself that Helen turned on her own charm, leaning across the bar with a flirty remark about it being a shame they hadn't been properly introduced, and why didn't he have something a little stronger to drink. Or a chaser perhaps?

When Ward and Katy arrived home an hour later, they found Ward's uncle full up to the ears with gin and tonic, virtually sitting in Gillian James's lap, and his son slumped on a bar stool, almost catatonic after imbibing four pints of beer and three large whisky chasers, trying unsuccessfully to explain to Molly how much he loved her.

Molly saw Ward and Helen exchange a meaningful glance. He took in the situation in a flash. 'Good God,' he said, biting back a laugh. 'What on earth's going on? Uncle Maurice? Is that really you? I hope you haven't been making a nuisance of yourself with our female customers. We run a very strict establishment here, you know. Katy, I'm ashamed to say this is my uncle, Maurice Frazer. And this drunken idiot here is my cousin Callum.'

As Uncle Maurice tried unsuccessfully to stand up, Katy rose magnificently to the occasion. Nodding politely, she said, 'I'm delighted to meet you. But I think we had better see if we can find a taxi to take you back to wherever you are staying.' Ignoring Maurice Frazer's attempt to bluster into speech, she turned abruptly to Jacob, who had appeared goggle-eyed at the top of the cellar steps. 'Run and see if you can find a taxi, Jacob. If you're quick, you might catch the one I saw just dropping off Mrs Carter.'

Five minutes later, Jacob and Ward were helping the two inebriated men across to the door.

'I do hope you will come and see us again when you are feeling better,' Katy called after them, and then turned and collapsed in uncontrollable hysterics.

When Ward came back in, he was laughing too. 'You wicked girls,' he said with a grin that made Molly's heart miss a beat.

'Well, they were awfully stuffy when they first came in,' Helen said, slightly shamefacedly. 'So we thought we should try and loosen them up a bit.'

'Loosen them up?' Ward started laughing again. 'You almost finished the poor man off.'

He turned to smile at Gillian James, who had stood up to leave. She too looked rather unsteady on her feet. 'Thank you,' he said. 'I really do hope my uncle wasn't a nuisance. I've never seen him behave like that in my life.'

Gillian James shook her head. 'Not at all,' she said, slightly regretfully. 'He was actually very charming.'

Choking back another laugh, Helen asked how Mrs Carter's demonstration had gone off.

Instead of answering, Ward glanced across at Katy, who started giggling again.

'Well,' she said. 'Mrs Carter did manage to make her dishes. In the end.' Her eyes were bright with guilty amusement. 'The funniest bit was when her frying pan caught fire.'

Ward shook his head. 'No, the funniest bit was when the button popped off her jacket and hit the organiser on the forehead.'

'Or when she said "Bugger, excuse my French",' Katy said, and they both dissolved into helpless laughter again.

Molly looked at them, disconcerted by their callous hilarity. 'Poor Mrs Carter,' she said reproachfully. 'It sounds awful.'

'It was awful in a way,' Ward admitted. 'But it was completely brilliant too. Like a comedy show. Although I'm not sure Mrs Carter saw it quite like that.'

'She must have realised from the applause that everyone loved it,' Katy said. Her eyes were dancing as she looked at Ward. 'We certainly enjoyed it.'

'Enjoyed it?' Ward pulled Katy into his arms and kissed her, then lifted his head to smile at Molly over her shoulder. Laughter was still sparkling in his eyes. 'All in all this has been one of the most entertaining evenings I've ever spent. And,' he murmured softly into Katy's hair, 'it's not over yet.'

It was as Molly turned away, partly in embarrassment and partly to hide the sudden pain that wrenched at her heart, that she saw Nurse Spalding stumbling through the blackout curtain in full nursing regalia.

'Thank goodness you're here,' Nurse Spalding panted. 'Matron sent me to fetch you. Your travel order just came through from the QAs. You've got to report to Goodwood House by nine o'clock tomorrow morning. So you'd better look snappy. Matron says you'll have to catch the milk train.'

*

245

An hour later, as they got into bed, Ward pulled Katy into his arms. 'Are you going to be OK without Molly and Jen?' he asked.

'Yes, I think so,' Katy said. 'I'll miss them, of course. But at least, in Molly's case, it's only for a month.' She snuggled closer against him. 'And what's more, I think I'll be able to face your uncle now he's had the wind taken out of his sails.'

Ward was silent a moment as his fingers trailed down her spine. When they reached the small of her back, they paused. 'I've just had a slightly worrying thought,' he said.

'What?' Katy asked in alarm, pulling away so she could look at him. 'What is it?'

'It sounds to me as though Molly and Jen might be travelling out to North Africa in the same convoy.'

'Oh Lord!' Katy stared at him in horror. Then she giggled, closed her eyes and sank back against him. 'Let's just hope they aren't on the same ship.'

Chapter Eighteen

Jen and Molly did find themselves on the same ship. Molly couldn't believe it. Her one chance for adventure and the whole thing was going to be soured by the presence of Jen Carter.

Molly had indeed taken the dead-of-night milk train. And having had to pay for a taxi from the station to get to Goodwood House in time, in a typically British triumph of organisation, two hours later she and the other QAs were taken back to the station by coach, where they boarded a train that travelled straight back through Clapham Junction. Had she joined the nurses' train there, she would have had time to say proper goodbyes to everyone. As it was, she had had to leave in such a scramble, she had hardly had a chance to say farewell to anyone except Helen, Katy and Ward Frazer. And the fond parting embrace she'd had from Ward had almost been her undoing.

'Be safe,' he had said, smiling as he held her face and kissed her lightly on both cheeks. 'Enjoy yourself. We'll miss you.'

She had had to pull away as her eyes filled suddenly with tears. Luckily everyone thought it was the emotion of leaving, but she knew it was the spine-tingling touch of his fingers on her skin, the warmth of his smile, the agony of not being able to bury her face in his chest and feel his arms close protectively around her.

As the train wound its laborious way north, with several long, unexplained delays and lots of shunting and coupling at indistinguishable stations along the way, she wondered if he would really miss her. As a helpmate for Katy, perhaps. And as a spare pair of hands to deal with Malcolm. Not as anything else. The way he had looked at Katy last night had shown Molly only too clearly how much he loved her.

But as the distance between the train and London increased, so gradually Molly began to look ahead rather than behind. The other five nurses in her carriage seemed very blasé about the forthcoming adventure. Unlike her, they were all fully qualified SRNs, and they all had posh, well-educated voices. After a few faintly patronising enquiries about the medicine box she was holding so carefully on her lap, they had left her alone. She clearly wasn't one of them, so they weren't going to bother with her. None of them had ever even heard of penicillin, and they clearly thought she was exaggerating its life-saving potential.

Molly didn't care if they thought she was beneath them. She didn't need their approval. They'd find out about the benefits of penicillin soon enough, and then they would have to eat their words.

As far as she was concerned, this trip was a chance for a bit of fun and freedom. She was determined to enjoy it, come what may.

So it came as a nasty shock when, late that evening, they finally arrived at Liverpool docks, and there on the quay, among an untidy group of yawning girls and lounging, eccentric-looking men dressed in an extraordinary mish-mash of uniform and civilian clothes, Molly spotted the unmistakable features of Jen Carter.

Jen was sitting on a suitcase, her chin resting on her rounded fists, looking tired and cross.

The ENSA contingent was almost completely surrounded by a plethora of suitcases and packing boxes, but if Molly had hoped to be able to slip past her old adversary without being noticed, that wish was quickly quashed. The arrival of the QAs had already caught the attention of the numerous ranks of soldiers who were also wearily awaiting embarkation. The sight of a squad of primly dressed nurses marching in brisk formation on to the already crowded landing stage was apparently more than enough to raise their flagging spirits.

Sister Summers tried to bustle her flock away from their suggestive comments and leering glances, but there was nowhere to go. On one side of them was a great pile of crates and military equipment waiting to be loaded; on the other was the ship, and in front of them was the formidable person of the loading officer, guarding the gangway from any unauthorised or untimely ingress. The noise was intense, the clamour of the loading machinery vying with shouted instructions and the clanking of chains. And pervading everything, the overriding smell of the sea, a pungent mixture of fish and oil.

Spurred on by the QAs' lack of reaction, the soldiers' banter increased in volume, and it wasn't long before Jen looked up to see what the rumpus was about. Out of the corner of her eye Molly saw her direct a glance in their direction. When Jen's bored expression changed to one of incredulity, Molly knew she'd been spotted. Jen stiffened, then got up and strolled over.

Accustomed as Molly was to Jen's normal flashy bravura, it seemed strange to see her looking so weary and dishevelled. The drab ENSA uniform didn't suit her. Even her unruly hair seemed to lack its usual bounce and lustre. But her caustic tongue was still the same.

'Good God,' she said. 'I suppose I might have guessed you'd turn up.' She slanted a quick mocking glance at the poker-faced QAs. 'Blimey. What a stiff-looking bunch.' She nodded at the medicine box Molly was still clutching. 'I don't suppose by any chance you've got something to eat in there, have you?'

Molly shook her head. She'd eaten the packed lunch she had been given before they'd even reached Crewe. She was pretty hungry herself.

'Damn,' Jen said. 'I'm bloody starving.' She glared at the loading officer. 'I had no idea it would all take so long.'

'How long have you been here?' Molly asked.

'Hours,' Jen said, turning away disgruntledly. She gave a dry laugh. 'And now it turns out we are priority Z, so we may not even get on.'

As Jen walked off back to her comrades, Molly felt a flicker of hope. Perhaps she was going to be spared after all. Miss Precious Fancy Pants Jen Carter categorised as priority Z! If she hadn't felt so on edge, she might have laughed out loud.

But the ENSA crew did get on. From the tiny porthole of the minuscule bunkroom she had been allocated in the bow of the ship with three other QA nurses, Molly saw the ramshackle group finally come aboard just after midnight. And her heart sank.

Joyce had spent the whole of Sunday in the house, hidden away from prying eyes. But on Monday she had to open up the café and face the world.

She was certain everyone would be twitching at their curtains to watch her go by, the madwoman who called herself a cook, the woman who'd nearly set fire to Wandsworth Town Hall, who had damaged the precious parquet floor and given Mr Styles a black eye when a button flew off her jacket and hit him right in the face. She wasn't sure how many people had noticed that particular incident, but for Joyce it was the final straw of her humiliation. If she had possessed a pair of sunglasses, a false moustache or some other disguise, she would have worn it that morning. Anything to prevent people seeing her as she scurried down to the café.

Once she got there, she shut herself in the kitchen, where nobody could get at her. She was determined to stay there all day if necessary.

Mrs Rutherford, when she came in, was typically bracing. 'No, no,' she said. 'I know a few little things went wrong, but your dishes came out perfectly in the end; the Spam and weed pie looked particularly delicious.'

'It was delicious,' Angie chipped in loyally. 'I ate it all when we got home.'

Joyce knew they were trying to be kind. But she wished they would go away and leave her to her misery. And when a journalist from the *Wandsworth Gazette* turned up wanting to interview her about the demonstration, she told Angie to tell him to bugger off. She knew what journalists were like, always wanting to rub people's faces in things, gloating about disasters, putting words into your mouth.

Expecting Mrs Rutherford to come marching into the kitchen to bully her into the interview like she'd bullied her into the demonstration, Joyce was surprised when Mr Lorenz tapped tentatively on the door instead.

'I'm sorry to intrude on your private area, Mrs Carter,' he said. 'But Angela told me you were feeling a little low after all the excitement of Saturday night.'

Low? That was an understatement if ever she had heard one. She actually felt like flinging herself into the river. Or perhaps putting her head in the gas oven would be better, because she might survive a fall into the river. She had been quite a good swimmer in her youth. Swimming was one of the few things in life she *had* been good at. But it was kind of Mr Lorenz to come in. Because she had nearly snapped his head off in the taxi on the way home.

'I'm sorry about Saturday,' she said gruffly. 'I never thanked you for getting the taxi and that.'

He brushed it off with a little dismissive gesture of his hand. 'Things hadn't gone quite the way you wanted. It is understandable that you were disappointed.' He flicked an invisible speck off the sleeve of his old-fashioned dark suit. 'But I wouldn't be surprised if some members of the audience thought the … er, comedy of the situation was intentional.'

Joyce stared at him incredulously. Nobody in their right mind would think that she had deliberately set her frying pan on fire or smeared dried egg powder everywhere. But she caught the cunning glint in his eyes and began to see what he was getting at. Or she thought she did. The shrewd old bugger. He was offering her a way to save face.

'You mean I should pretend I did it all on purpose?'

'Well,' he murmured solemnly. 'I believe humour is known to be an effective way of getting a serious message across.'

So in the end she did agree to see the journalist, and, with aplomb fuelled by outrage at the position she'd been put into, managed to tell him blithely that in her view, the evening had gone pretty much as planned. Yes, perhaps one or two of her little stunts had got a bit out of control, but her task had been to make people remember the key message: that it was possible to make nourishing meals even with very limited ingredients. And to that extent she had met her brief.

The journalist looked rather taken aback. But he diligently scribbled down what she had said. 'Oh yes, I see,' he muttered, looking up doubtfully. 'So overall you think the evening was a success?'

'Of course it was,' Angie chipped in helpfully. 'After all, she got a standing ovulation.'

A stunned silence greeted this contribution. Seeing the flabbergasted look on the journalist's face, Joyce felt a bubble of hysteria well up inside her. Biting her lip, she glanced helplessly at Mr Lorenz and caught a quick gleam of complicit amusement in his eyes before his dark lashes lowered.

'Absolutely,' he agreed firmly, courteously ushering the journalist towards the door. 'There is no doubt in my mind that the evening was a triumph. Mrs Carter is clearly destined to be a culinary star.'

When Molly woke, the ship was under way. She could feel the throbbing of the engines somewhere far below her, and a slight sway of motion. Her three cabin mates were still asleep, but by dint of twisting round on her bunk and folding herself up like some kind of contortionist magician's assistant, she found she could see out of the cabin porthole.

There was light in the early-morning sky. The sea below was moving in slow blue-grey swells. At the very edge of her vision she glimpsed another ship, a naval vessel, a corvette, she guessed, perhaps one of the escort ships for the convoy they were due to join somewhere out in the Atlantic.

There had been too much hustle and bustle last night to do anything about storing the penicillin. Thinking that this might be a good time to hand over her precious cargo to the purser, she climbed off her bunk, pulled on her uniform dress and shoes, tidied her hair as best she could and let herself out of the cabin.

The purser, when Molly eventually found him, after asking a passing midshipman for directions to his office, seemed surprised by her request. But he obligingly read the letter Dr Florey had given her and proceeded to escort her down numerous flights of metal stairs into the bowels of the ship. The noise down here was much greater, and Molly received several curious glances from the crew members they passed.

Eventually, after walking through what seemed like endless clanging corridors and pushing through numerous heavy bulkhead doors, they reached the galley. There the penicillin case was consigned to the care of the chief steward, an enormous man with a huge, rather unhygienic-looking beard, who shoved it to the back of one of his refrigerated units.

'Jerry won't get his dirty hands on it down here,' he said with a wink. 'So you can stop worrying your pretty head over it and relax and enjoy yourself until we get to Cairo.'

Feeling absurdly flattered by the compliment, Molly followed the purser back up to the main deck. There she found Sister Summers mustering her flock for breakfast.

The nurses had been allocated the early sitting for all meals on the mess deck, which meant they ate with the group of rather elderly army officers on board, and not, to Molly's relief, with the ENSA troupe.

After breakfast, and a short period for digestion, Sister Summers ushered her charges up on to the deck for what would prove to be a daily ritual: twenty brisk circuits of the deck followed by a series of stretching exercises. These latter caused considerable amusement among their fellow passengers, but in Molly's view the pleasure of being up on deck in the fresh air more than compensated for the embarrassment at being wolf-whistled by a few soldiers.

Having previously been convinced that she would rail against Miss Summers' rigid discipline, Molly actually found she was grateful for it. Sister Summers watched over her flock very carefully. Not only did she ensure that they had enough food, sleep and exercise, but her steely gaze and air of authority shielded them from unwelcome approaches from their male co-passengers, and from the general rough and tumble of shipboard life. The best thing, as far as Molly was concerned, was that it also, to a certain extent, shielded her against Jen Carter, and allowed her to enjoy the novelty of life on board ship in peace and quiet.

Jen, on the other hand, was not enjoying life on board at all. Prior to the war, the MS *Marigold* had been a heavy cargo vessel, and as far as Jen was concerned that was what it should have remained. But in 1939 it had been requisitioned as a troopship, and whoever had designed the conversion had clearly gone for quantity of passengers over quality of living conditions. If the tiny, windowless cabin Jen had been allocated with three other ENSA girls was anything to go by, he had also designed the accommodation with midgets in mind.

Thinking it would be less claustrophobic, Jen chose one of the top bunks, only to find that it was both hotter and shorter than the ones below. They weren't allowed to leave the cabin door open, and at night she felt the only thing she was breathing was the exhaled breath of the other girls. There was no space to store anything; they had one tiny shelf and room for three hangers each, and the four of them were constantly bumping bottoms as they struggled about, trying to get washed and dressed. At first they all apologised politely, but after a while they stopped being polite and just grunted irritably as they shoved past each other or trod on each other's toes. The basin in the cabin was minuscule, and there was only seawater in the tap, which left Jen feeling more sticky and unclean than she had before she started.

The endless clanking, thumping, throbbing and vibration of the ship got on her nerves. And that was only the noise the ship made as it steamed along. On top of that were the klaxons, the hideous wake-up bugle, and the constant clatter of hobnailed boots on metal companionways. Jen herself walked about as little as possible, because the way the floor shifted under her feet upset her balance, making her feel dizzy and nauseous. Having felt so hungry before boarding, since then she hadn't been able to eat a single thing. She didn't know if it was fear or seasickness, but the very thought of food turned her stomach.

Their vulnerability, and that of the whole convoy, had been well and truly drummed into them during the captain's safety lecture on the first morning. There was to be no smoking below deck, nor at night on the open deck in case of attracting unwelcome attention from the Luftwaffe. Alcohol was strictly forbidden, there must be no switching of cabins, all watertight bulkhead doors must be kept closed, and they had to carry their lifebelts at all times.

The threat of danger was reinforced further by the daily evacuation drill. At the sound of the klaxon, everyone had to instantly muster on deck and stand in total silence adjacent to their allocated lifeboat. Jen's boat looked far too small to accommodate all the people clustered around it. And as it would have to be lowered miles down the side of the ship before it even reached the water, the drill didn't exactly fill her with confidence.

The extraordinary thing was that everyone else appeared to be enjoying themselves. Especially the other actresses and singers. They seemed delighted to spend their time flirting with the army officers and the better looking of the soldiers and sailors. Or if no suitable man was around, they were equally happy to lean on the rail gazing out to sea, or to play endless noisy games of strip poker or charades in the lounge. It seemed incredible to Jen that they could be so relaxed when at any moment something unspeakably awful could so easily happen.

On their third day aboard, an enemy aircraft did fly overhead and an impromptu singalong broke up in disarray, some of the participants leaping to their feet to make rude signs at the pilot, and others falling over themselves in their haste to scurry for cover. Afterwards everyone thought it was a huge joke.

No, Jen felt completely out of it. Her only consolation was that Molly Coogan must be having almost as miserable a time as she was, stuck with those stuffy nurses. Things could be worse, Jen thought; at least she didn't have to do physical jerks every morning on deck under the direction of that po-faced QA sister.

Ward's uncle and cousin were staying at the Ritz, and that was where Ward had eventually visited them. It was there he told his uncle that, far from being the shoddy, gun-to-the head affair his father had assumed, his marriage to Katy had taken place in the local church; that Katy had been an innocent bride, not at all the drunken harlot his family apparently suspected; and that Malcolm was his legitimate heir.

'Not that it's any of his business,' he said when he got back to the pub. 'But I thought I should at least try to set the record straight.'

'And what did he say?' Katy asked.

Ward hesitated for a second. 'Well, to be honest, there wasn't much he could say,' he said wryly. 'He may be stiff, but he's not stupid. When he woke up with a sore head, reeking of Mrs James's perfume on Sunday morning, I think he knew he'd lost the right to criticise my behaviour.

'In any case,' he went on, 'Helen apparently laid it on pretty thick with Callum about you getting the pub going again when your father was killed.' He rolled his eyes. 'She also filled him up with a lot of guff about me, so much so that the stupid boy now seems to think I'm some of comic-book superhero.'

Katy smiled at that. 'I think you're a superhero too,' she said. 'But Callum's hardly a boy. He must be eighteen or nineteen.'

'Twenty,' Ward said.

Katy frowned. 'Then why isn't he in the forces?' she asked. 'I thought Canadians had been called up.'

'They have,' Ward said shortly. 'I gather Uncle Maurice made a case for keeping him at home. The aircraft industry being so important to the war effort and all that.' He gave a disapproving grunt. 'Callum's a nice kid, but he's always been very much under Uncle Maurice's thumb.'

'You don't think he'll break away like you did?'

'I doubt it. Maybe that's why Uncle Maurice brought him on this trip. To stop him kicking over the traces.'

Hearing the cynical note in his voice, Katy looked at him in concern. She had never seen him like this before. So edgy and disapproving. 'So what happens now?' she asked.

Ward shrugged irritably. 'Uncle Maurice wanted us to take Malcolm up to see them at the Ritz.'

Staring at him in consternation, Katy at once started to think of ways she could cover the bar. She couldn't leave Helen all on her own. If only Molly was still around.

'Oh no,' she said. 'When? What did you say?'

'I said if they wanted to meet you and Malcolm then they could damn well come here.' Ward raised his hands impatiently. 'I don't see why we should be running around all over the place just to suit them.'

254

'And are they coming?'

'Yes, but very reluctantly.'

'I'm not surprised he's reluctant,' Katy said. 'He's probably nervous of bumping into Gillian James. Or maybe he wants to keep Callum out of Helen's clutches.'

'I didn't think of that.' Ward laughed suddenly. 'It probably didn't help when I suggested it might be tactful if he brought you a bunch of flowers by way of apology for their behaviour on Saturday night, and to help alleviate the understandable dismay you were feeling about the nature of the family you had married into.'

'Oh Ward, you didn't!' Katy stared at him aghast.

It seemed to have taken days for the convoy to convene. But eventually the dozen or so ships sorted themselves into a straggling line and the whole shebang got under way, creeping slowly down towards Spain and the Mediterranean under the protective, shepherding attentions of the Royal Navy frigates. Or maybe they were corvettes. Jen didn't know. She didn't care. As long as they were there, in sight.

Even though she disliked the motion of the ship, she was glad to be properly on the move. She had hated tossing around in the Atlantic like a sitting duck, just waiting for a passing U-boat to take a potshot at them.

If only she could get some decent rest she might feel better, but trapped in the cabin with her snoring companions, heart hammering at every untoward bump or change of engine beat, sleep continued to elude her.

So she took to sleeping by day. As the convoy sailed south, the weather improved dramatically. While everyone else was sunning themselves on the deck, the ENSA girls flaunting themselves in racy little two-pieces under the disapproving gaze of the fully clad QA nurses, Jen crawled into her hot bunk and tried to relax.

On the tenth day of the voyage the convoy passed single file through the Straits of Gibraltar. The sudden echoing boom of the MS *Marigold*'s depth charges woke Jen and caused her to run, panicked, up to the main deck.

There she found everyone staring at the Rock of Gibraltar. When, through the heat haze, they spotted British soldiers on the shoreline watching them through binoculars, everyone started cheering. One of the ENSA soubrettes flung off the top of her two-piece and danced a little jig. Several of the others followed suit, and a roar of delight could be heard sweeping across the water from the shore at the sight of so many pert little bosoms.

Further along the rail, Jen heard a choke of shocked disapproval from the QA group. Sister Summers turned away in disgust. 'What a revolting exhibition,' she said. The nurses all looked very hot under the collar. Even in this heat they were still in their full uniform. Molly Coogan was there among them in her different but equally prudish uniform and sensible shoes.

'Little sluts,' one of the other nurses muttered. 'They ought to be ashamed of themselves.'

That was the best day of the whole voyage for Jen. The sea was completely calm. They could finally see the coast of North Africa, the occasional blur of distant white towns trapped between sky and sea, and there was a sense of relief and excitement that they were gradually approaching their various destinations. From Jen's point of view it was particularly amusing to see the increasing friction between the ENSA group and the nurses.

But during the night the weather deteriorated, the wind got up, the sea became rough and Jen no longer found anything amusing. Now she couldn't sleep at all, not even by day. But the minute she stood up, she felt sick.

There was a brief moment of respite from the heavy seas when they put into Algiers for refuelling. They weren't allowed ashore, but even through the driving rain they could see the damage the war had caused. The harbour was full of wrecked ships. Many of the great porticoed buildings on the front had either been damaged or had collapsed completely. Behind them the white city seemed almost to have been reduced to rubble. It was a sobering sight, but the relative calm of the harbour did at least allow Jen time to emerge from her cabin to get some fresh air.

But the following evening, back at sea, the storm got worse. Staggering out of the lavatory after a session of painful retching, Jen bumped into Conrad Porter.

'Well hello,' he said. 'I have to say, you aren't looking your best.'

'I'm not feeling my best,' Jen said acidly. 'I've never been so sick in all my life. And on top of everything else, we'll probably get struck by lightning and sink.'

'No, no,' he said reassuringly. 'We're much safer in a storm. At least the Luftwaffe can't get at us from Italy.'

Jen stared at him, appalled. That was one eventuality that hadn't so far occurred to her.

Conrad looked at her with amused concern. 'You ought to take a sedative.'

'I know, but nobody will give me anything. I even asked that awful QA sister,' Jen admitted. 'She just said I'd soon get my sea legs. Heartless old harridan.'

'I wasn't talking about medication,' Conrad chuckled. 'I was talking about a little tipple.'

'If only,' Jen said. 'But there's no alcohol on the ship.'

Conrad tapped the side of his nose and produced a hip flask from his pocket. 'If you don't tell, I won't,' he said.

She looked at him suspiciously. None of the Old Vic actors were known for their friendliness. 'Why are you being kind to me?'

As the ship heaved to one side, Conrad put out a hand to steady himself against the wall. 'Henry told me to keep an eye on you.'

'Did he?' Jen grabbed a nearby door handle. 'That's odd, because he told me to keep well clear of you.'

Conrad laughed. 'So the maestro has designs on you himself, does he? Well, well. Still,' he grinned disarmingly, waving the flask in front of her nose, 'you know what they say? When the cat's away …'

Jen made a half-hearted snatch for the flask. Unfortunately the boat lurched again at that moment and she was forced to clutch at Conrad's arm instead. Taking advantage of her loss of balance, he swung her round against him. 'Exactly,' he said, drawing her close and offering her the flask with the other hand. 'Now what could be nicer?'

Still clinging to his arm, Jen took a swig and felt the liquor burn down her throat. 'Blimey,' she spluttered. 'What's that?'

'Love potion,' he said. He raised his eyebrows. 'Is it working?'

Jen had to laugh. 'No.' Conrad Porter was a bit of an old roué, but he was nice-looking in a louche kind of way. And he was pretty famous. It was kind of reassuring to have a strong pair of arms round her when the boat was jerking about like an enormous bucking bronco. It didn't mean anything. Everyone else was flirting and joking. Why shouldn't she?

But then she caught a movement at the end of the long companionway and recognised the frumpy uniform and sharp, pointed features of Molly Coogan.

Jen groaned inwardly and, realising what it must look like, made an effort to disentangle herself from Conrad's embrace.

But when she looked round again, Molly had gone.

For a second, as she glared down the empty corridor, Jen wondered about running after her. Then she shook her head. She was feeling pleasantly tiddly now, and much less nauseous. The alcohol was definitely helping. Prudy little Pixie, she thought. Let her think the worst. Who cared?

Ward clearly had said something about flowers to his uncle, because sure enough, when Maurice and Callum Frazer presented themselves at the pub on the appointed evening, they were armed with a bunch of roses, which

Maurice presented to Katy with stiff formality.

'Mrs Frazer, please forgive my discourtesy last time we met,' he said. 'We had only arrived from Canada the day before. I guess we were both a little fatigued.'

'Yes,' Katy murmured, looking away hastily as she caught Helen's eye. 'I believe travelling can have that effect.'

To avoid any potentially embarrassing encounter with Gillian James, Katy and Ward had decided to entertain Maurice and Callum upstairs in the flat. There they met Malcolm, who was looking particularly endearing, freshly scrubbed and dressed in a pair of tiny pyjamas that Pam Nelson had made for him out of an old towel.

At first, awed by the two strangers occupying the armchairs, Malcolm behaved impeccably, peering at them through his long lashes from a position of safety on Katy's lap, while Ward went down to get the drinks. In fact his presence made their arrival much easier than Katy had anticipated. Even though she was very conscious of the wartime shabbiness of the sitting room, at least Malcolm looked clean and wholesome. And when he wriggled suddenly off her knee in order to toddle over to inspect the newcomers more closely, his expression of wary congeniality was so similar to Ward's that she knew any residual doubts that Maurice Frazer might be harbouring about his parentage would surely be dispelled.

Despite being very much on their dignity, Maurice and Callum Frazer seemed quite taken with Malcolm, and received the news that there was another baby on the way with apparent equanimity.

Maurice even unbent sufficiently to offer Malcolm a few coins to play with. 'He's a fine little fellow,' he said, watching approvingly as Malcolm solemnly stacked the coppers on top of each other on the table. 'He seems kind of advanced for eighteen months, I'd say.'

And when, a moment later, with a shout of glee, he sent the pile flying across the room with one swipe of his little fist, it made Callum laugh. 'I guess that shows what he thinks of only being given small change,' he said.

To Katy it seemed that the evening was going quite well. So she was surprised when, returning to the sitting room after putting Malcolm to bed, she saw that Ward was looking distinctly steely-eyed.

'Your father wants you to come home,' Maurice Frazer was saying.

He might have got away with it if he had left it at that, but he had clearly misjudged, or misinterpreted, Ward's guarded cordiality. 'He needs you in the business. The same way I need Callum. And it's a reserved occupation. You owe it to the family.'

'Katy and Malcolm are my family now,' Ward said.

'Yes, of course.' Maurice gave Katy a thin smile. 'But think of how much more comfortable you would all be in Canada. And how much safer. Not to mention your own personal financial advantage.'

'I am not interested in my personal financial advantage,' Ward said icily. 'I'm interested in winning this war.' He stood up, moved away slightly and took a long breath. When he turned back, there was anger in his eyes, but his voice was carefully under control.

'Haven't you seen the newsreels? Don't you know what happened to the Jews in Warsaw? Haven't you heard about the carnage that madman Hitler leaves in his wake?'

'Yes, yes, of course,' Maurice Frazer said placatingly. 'Sure, we get the news. But listen to me Ward, you've done your bit.' He looked pointedly around the shabby little room. 'And really—'

'And really nothing,' Ward snapped. 'Do you have any idea what people in London have gone through? The sacrifices they've made to rid the world of these ruthless tyrants?' He swung a hand in Katy's direction. 'Katy lost her father, for God's sake. I've lost countless colleagues both from the RAF and the SOE. And we're not alone. Everyone we know has lost friends and family. And all you can do is gloat about the business and how snug and safe you are in Canada.' He stopped, eyes narrowed dangerously. 'If you must know, I don't approve of you or my father making money out of the war. It makes me feel ashamed.'

Still standing frozen in horrified shock by Malcolm's bedroom door, Katy stared at Ward. She could see the angry tension in his lovely mouth, the pulse beating in his neck, and her heart swelled. I love him, she thought. I completely love him.

Callum was looking at Ward in awe, but his father was clearly outraged. He stood up angrily. 'Ward, really, I don't see what—'

'Don't you?' Ward was close to losing his temper now. 'Don't you realise that if Hitler marches in here, that will be the end of your lucrative British contracts? Surely you can understand that, at least, even if you can't understand anything else.' He stopped suddenly, clamped his mouth shut, then moved to the stairs. 'I'm sorry,' he said, abruptly. 'I'll go see if I can find a taxi to take you back to the hotel.'

As they listened to the sound of his footsteps on the stairs, an awkward silence fell.

After a moment Maurice Frazer exhaled and ran a hand over his face. He gave an irritable grunt. 'He always was headstrong.'

'He's not headstrong,' Katy said, jumping instantly to Ward's defence. 'He just has moral integrity. He's seen Nazism first hand. Both before the war, when his girlfriend was killed, and last year, when he was captured in France.' She glanced at Callum, who looked as though he had been electrocuted. 'I don't know if Helen told you the other night what Ward went through during that period. But I can assure you it wasn't nice.' She turned her attention back to Maurice Frazer. 'He would do anything in his power to defeat Hitler. He'll never give up on it. Never. So there's no point in pushing him. Maybe when the war is over ...' She tailed off. 'Perhaps then he'll want to come home.'

'That's assuming he's still alive,' Maurice remarked with callous brutality.

Katy recoiled. He was right, of course, but that didn't make his words easier to hear.

She lifted her chin. 'If he's not,' she said stiffly, 'at least he will have done his duty.' She hesitated, and tears sprang into her eyes. She sniffed them back. 'And I'll feel proud to have been his wife.'

Another silence greeted this declaration. Callum was staring at her with a stunned expression. Maurice Frazer was looking at her too. But before either of them could speak, Ward reappeared at the top of the stairs.

His eyes swept the room. He no longer looked angry, but neither did he apologise for his outburst. He just nodded at his uncle. 'Your taxi is here,' he said.

Maurice Frazer picked up his coat and hat, then eyed Katy grimly for a moment. 'Well if he wants to turn his back on his family,' he said as he turned for the stairs, 'I suppose that's his choice. And you will have to take the consequences.'

Katy felt her temper rise again. 'I think it's the other way round,' she called after him. 'It seems to me that his family has turned its back on him. And,' she added angrily, 'just so you know, we don't care about the consequences.'

Turning back into the room, she bumped into Callum, who was hovering at the top of the stairs. She brushed past him impatiently. 'Go on. Hurry up,' she said scornfully, ignoring his awkward attempt to say goodbye. 'Run after Daddy. Or you'll have to suffer the consequences too.'

On 8 July, the QA contingent disembarked at La Goulette in the Gulf of Tunis. The weather was foul. Hard, sheeting rain was whipping across the water, but Molly braved the deck of the MS *Marigold* to watch the nurses teetering down the gangway in the awkward shelter of umbrellas held by a gang of thin, dark-skinned men in sodden white tunics. Several more similarly bedraggled men scurried along behind, almost invisible under a mountain of luggage.

Molly hadn't liked the QAs very much, but she was oddly sad to see them go. Now she really was on her own.

She determined to avoid the ENSA contingent, and specifically Jen

Carter, until they disembarked at Tripoli in two days' time. Then, finally, she'd be able to relax. Until then, if necessary she could pretty much stay in her cabin, which she now, rather luxuriously, had all to herself.

It was later that night that she realised she wasn't the only person intending to benefit from the extra space afforded by the departure of the QAs.

Perhaps because of the terrible weather, the convoy had stayed longer at La Goulette than expected. They set sail during the evening, and as they rounded the Cap Bon peninsula and turned south through the Strait of Sicily into the eastern Mediterranean, they once again met the full force of the storm.

Almost immediately the ship began to buck and roll even worse than before. And over the noise of banging and rattling, and the clanking smack of the bow crashing repeatedly down into the water, Molly could hear voices in the corridor outside.

A moment later the door of her cabin was pushed open and a voice said, 'This one's empty. This will do.'

Recognising the well-modulated tones of Conrad Porter, Molly sat up, pulling the thin sheet up to her chin. 'It's not empty,' she said indignantly, glaring at him through the dim light. 'I'm in it.'

'Oh God,' another voice shrieked. 'It's the Poxy Pixie. I don't want to go in there.'

Molly would have known Jen's voice anywhere, but tonight she sounded as though she was ill, or possibly drunk. Molly saw that she was also clinging to the actor's arm.

'I'm so sorry to disturb you,' Conrad Porter drawled in mock apology. 'I'll try next door.'

'You aren't allowed to change cabins,' Molly snapped. 'Not unless you tell the purser.'

'Oh, don't be such a goody two-shoes.' Jen's voice was shrill and panicky. 'This is an emergency. If I don't lie down soon, I'm going to be sick.'

She did indeed look rather green. And very scared. 'What's the matter with your own cabin?' Molly asked.

'There are too many people in it.' And with that she was gone.

The door of Molly's cabin slammed shut, leaving her feeling angry and unsettled by Jen's palpable fear. As the boat once again crested a high swell and nosedived alarmingly into the trough, Molly suddenly felt rather frightened herself. Bracing herself against the wall of the bunk, she touched the tiny charm at her throat. 'Please don't let me drown,' she whispered.

*

261

Two hours later, there really was an emergency.

The convoy was attacked by two German U-boats, and the MS *Marigold* was hit amidships by a T3 torpedo.

Chapter Nineteen

At first Molly thought the ear-splitting explosion was another depth charge being dropped. That was bad enough because it meant that the captain feared a submarine was underneath them. But then, with a dying clang, the engine stopped and the dim cabin light went out.

The plunging ship went ominously quiet. So quiet that Molly could hear the waves slapping hard against the sides. She lay rigid, listening. And then she heard the rising wail of the klaxon. She struggled off her bunk in alarm, grabbing for her torch, her coat and her lifebelt, scrabbling around for the small 'panic' bag of essentials they had been told to have ready at all times.

As she opened the sealed door of the cabin, she could hear boots clattering on the deck above. But her own companionway was dark and deserted. It took her midnight brain a moment to remember that the QAs were no longer there. The cabins were empty.

Or were they? Clinging to the door jamb for support as the shipped rolled alarmingly, she flashed her torch at the closed door next to hers. She felt completely disoriented. Was it the same night? Were Jen and Conrad Porter still in there?

Suddenly the bell stopped and Molly froze again, the sound echoing in her ears. She was almost certain that had been the general alarm. But she didn't want to look like an idiot for overreacting. For a second, she even wondered if she was dreaming.

Then, from a different direction, she heard the ship's whistle start firing a volley of staccato honks. 'Oh my God,' she whispered as the final long blast echoed down the metal corridor. She knew that one all right. And she definitely wasn't dreaming. That was the signal for abandon ship.

And then the door next to her opened and she saw Conrad Porter's face squinting into the beam of her torch.

'Quick,' he shouted. 'I need help here.'

It had been drummed into them during muster drill that in an emergency they should immediately run for the lifeboats, leaving the crew to deal with any stragglers. But without thinking, Molly dropped her things on the floor and pushed past him into the adjacent cabin. Jen Carter was lying flat out on the bottom bunk, dead to the world.

'I can't wake her.' Conrad spoke behind her. His rich, theatrical voice now sounded harsh and anxious. And with due cause. Even when Molly shone her torch right into her face, Jen didn't react. Taking her wrist, Molly felt for her pulse and was relieved to feel a steady beat.

Clutching the edge of the bunk to steady herself against the erratic rocking motion of the ship, she looked round at Conrad accusingly. 'What's the matter with her?'

'She must have had too much to drink,' he said. 'She passed out as soon as she lay down. I didn't think I ought to leave her, so …'

'You shouldn't have got her drunk in the first place.' Molly snapped. She lifted Jen's shoulders and shook her hard. 'Now you know why alcohol wasn't allowed on board.'

'Good God, don't break her neck.' The actor gave a shocked laugh. He didn't sound a hundred per cent sober himself. 'And to think Jen told us you were a drippy little thing.'

'Did she?' Molly said grimly. 'I'll show her drippy.' And she slapped Jen hard on the face. 'I don't want to save your life,' she muttered. 'But I won't be able to face Katy if I don't try.'

'Katy?' Jen murmured. 'Is Katy here?'

Unsteadily, Molly reached down to pick up a towel lying on the floor and drenched it in water at the tiny sink. 'Jen, listen to me,' she hissed, squeezing it out over Jen's head. 'Just for once in your life, please try and co-operate. We've got to get you out of here.'

'Shtop it,' Jen mumbled, incensed. She struggled into a sitting position, trying ineffectually to push Molly away. 'Where's Katy? I want to see her.'

Holding the cabin door open with one hand, Conrad leaned forward and dragged Jen unceremoniously to her feet. 'I have no idea who Katy is,' he said grimly. 'But if we don't get a move on, neither of you will ever see her again.'

Thanks to the daily drills, Molly knew the way to the B deck muster station blindfolded. But by the time she and Conrad had battled their way up the ominously tilting stairway, dragging Jen between them, the lifeboat had gone.

The adjacent one was dangling from the hoist crane by its stern, twisting and jerking like an enormous fish on a line. Something had obviously gone badly wrong. One of the ropes must have snapped. Molly shivered convulsively, clinging to the cold, wet rail. Everyone on board would have been spilled out in the churning water below. She couldn't bring herself to look, but she could hear people shouting down there in the inky darkness. It was impossible against the wind and the driving rain to hear what they were saying, or indeed if anyone was doing anything to help them.

But she could hear voices further up the ship too and felt a surge of hope. If there were still some crew on board, there must be other lifeboats somewhere.

The MS *Marigold* was definitely listing now, but she wasn't showing any immediate signs of sinking.

'Try and find another lifeboat,' Molly shouted at Conrad. 'I'm going to fetch something from the galley. Don't wait for me.'

'Good God, girl, don't be ridiculous,' he yelled back. But she had already gone.

Molly didn't feel ridiculous. She felt almost numb with fear. But she also felt a blind determination to do her duty. And she knew her duty was to rescue the penicillin.

It seemed to take ages to reach the corridor that led down to the galley, but in reality it probably took only a few minutes, because for some reason, the bulkhead doors down there were open. But as she fumbled her way towards the next stairwell, she ran into a group of crew members coming the other way.

One of them grabbed her arm and they lurched together in a brief, ungainly dance. Regaining her balance, struggling to get free, Molly flashed her torch into his face and screamed. A second later she realised it was the bearded chief steward, bleeding hard from a cut on his face. For a mad moment she had thought she was grappling with an injured bear.

'What are you doing still on board?' he asked. 'Didn't you hear the abandon ship command?'

'I must get the penicillin,' Molly screamed at him. 'I promised to keep it safe.'

'No chance,' he said. He took her arm in an iron grip and steered her forcefully back the way she had come. 'The galley's flooding. Most of the bulkheads burst open in the blast. We've managed to jam a couple shut, but they won't hold for long.'

When they re-emerged on deck, lit up now by a fire burning at the other end of the ship, they found Jen, soaked to the skin, clinging to the rail, shouting abuse at Conrad, who had wedged himself in next to the lifeboat crane and was calmly smoking a cigarette.

The chief steward stared at them in astonishment. 'Good Lord,' he said. 'Why haven't you been evacuated?'

'There aren't any lifeboats,' Conrad said, waving his cigarette up the deck. 'They've all gone. We've resigned ourselves to our fate.'

'I haven't bloody resigned myself to my fate,' Jen yelled at him. Her voice was shrill. The howling gale had apparently worked wonders on her befuddled brain. Unfortunately it hadn't done anything to reduce her belligerence. Catching sight of Molly silhouetted against the crackling flames, she pointed her finger at her.

'You!' she screamed furiously. 'It's all your fault. If you hadn't made us wait while you ran off for your stupid medicine, we would be safely on a lifeboat by now.'

Molly couldn't believe her ears. 'Me?' She almost choked in outrage. 'My fault? If you had been in your own cabin instead of canoodling with Laurence Olivier here, we—'

'I wasn't canoodling,' Jen shrieked. 'I was just—'

'Not only that,' Molly interrupted bitingly. 'You were pissed as a newt, and—'

'Ladies, ladies.' The chief steward intervened with calm authority. 'You can continue this discussion later. May I suggest that we now proceed with some urgency to the bow, where we should find some reserve lifeboats.'

The chief steward was a man blessed with apparently imperturbable composure. Even as the fire raged at the other end of the ship and various crew members ran about shouting instructions to each other, he and his little team of cooks and galley boys opened a locker on the foredeck and produced a life raft kit, which they proceeded to fit together with efficient dexterity.

As soon as the makeshift craft, which he referred to as a Berthon boat, was assembled to the chief steward's satisfaction, it was slowly lowered over the side of the ship. 'There we go, nice and gently,' he murmured as it eventually landed in the water and immediately started bucking about on the waves below.

Instructing them to inflate their life jackets, he threw a rope ladder over the side and one of the crewmen climbed over the rail and began to shimmy down it. But just as he reached the life raft, the ship rolled heavily to one side and he swung way off target, clinging on to the ladder for dear life like an ape on a broken branch.

Entirely unfazed by the young sailor's predicament, the chief steward remained as cool as a cucumber. 'Take your time, lad,' he called down in his calm, impassive voice. 'Wait for her to come under you.'

Conrad Porter gave a grunt of amusement. 'Yes indeed,' he said. 'They always say that's the best way.'

Molly heard a couple of the other crewmen laugh at this, and she looked round at them in bewilderment. For the life of her she couldn't see what was so funny. Nor indeed how anyone could find anything funny at this precise moment, when the young seaman's life was quite literally hanging in the balance.

But then somehow the boy got a foot on to the raft and then next

266

minute he was down, pulling the little craft tight up on the rope. At once the next man began the treacherous descent.

As soon as the second sailor was in the boat and able to steady the ladder, the chief steward turned calmly to Molly. 'You next, my love,' he said.

Molly's fingers tightened on the rail. 'I can't,' she stammered. 'Let Conrad go first.'

'No, no.' Conrad waved his cigarette with lazy courtesy. 'Women and children first. I insist.'

'No, but …' Even in the fierce, sheeting rain, Molly could feel her palms sweating.

'Oh for God's sake,' Jen burst out impatiently. 'I'll go.' And pushing Molly out of the way, she clambered nimbly over the rail.

She was halfway down when her foot missed the next rung of the ladder.

'Take it steady,' the steward murmured reassuringly, as she screamed in alarm. 'There's plenty of time.'

But it was clear to Molly that there wasn't plenty of time. 'Oh come on, Jen, hurry up,' she shouted.

The ship was groaning and creaking as it plunged up and down on the swell. It was listing so badly now that it was impossible to stand upright without holding on to something. Molly could hear flames crackling behind them. Her eyes were stinging from the acrid smoke billowing on the wind.

At last Jen reached the bottom of the ladder and dropped into the life raft. Then firm hands were helping Molly up and over the rail.

And now Molly could see why Jen had had problems. The metal rungs were cold and slick and the side ropes were rough and abrasive and kept trapping her fingers against the rungs as the ladder whipped wildly from side to side.

She had no idea how she did it, but shamed by Jen's gritty example, somehow, in utter terror, and by dint of scraping most of the skin off the palms of her hands, she made her way down into the flimsy little lifeboat.

Conrad was next. But shimmying down rope ladders clearly wasn't part of a Shakespearean actor's repertoire. He had no idea about using alternate hands and feet, and his unbalanced descent caused the ladder to twist and turn alarmingly. The young rating tasked to hold it steady was almost torn in two in his efforts to keep it in place. When a sudden wave crashed up against the lifeboat, he lost his footing completely and was flung head first into the bottom of the boat, leaving the actor dangling helplessly over the churning sea, legs flailing as the ladder lashed wildly beneath him like a demented snake.

'Steady does it.' The chief steward's unruffled voice drifted down from the MS *Marigold*'s deck. 'Give him a hand, someone, if you can. Easy does it. Take your time. There's no rush.'

The young sailor seemed to have been knocked out cold by his fall, the other deckhand was already having trouble holding the boat steady, and Jen clearly wasn't going to do anything, so Molly struggled to the edge of the life raft and, clinging to a rowlock with one hand, eventually managed to grab hold of the writhing ladder with the other.

But just as Conrad struggled down the last few feet, another buffeting swell lifted the raft, and she caught the metal heel of his shoe hard in her face. With a strangled cry, she let go of the rope and she too fell back into the bottom of the boat, with Conrad Porter on top of her.

As she lay there, winded, she saw the cook and the two galley boys shimmying efficiently down the ladder. The galley boys immediately took up position at the oars.

Last, but not least, was the chief steward. He came down the ladder hand over hand, not even bothering to use his feet. Molly was glad he was so quick. The MS *Marigold* was leaning so far over them now, it almost looked as though his weight on the ladder would bring the ship down on top of them.

'Man the oars,' the chief steward grunted, as he dropped heavily into the small craft. 'Ready all. Row.'

When nothing happened, he turned his head, cupping his hands to his mouth. 'Row, you lazy cunts!' he bellowed. 'Row! There's not a moment to lose. If she goes down now, she'll take us all with her.'

'Well you've certainly changed your tune,' Conrad Porter remarked sardonically as he levered himself off Molly. 'I thought you said we had all the time in the world.'

The chief steward gave an apologetic laugh. 'Excuse my French, ladies. But better safe than sorry.'

Even as he spoke, one of the young sailors missed his stroke and the tiny boat rocked alarmingly. Somewhere behind her, Molly heard Jen's piercing voice. 'Safe?' she screamed incredulously. 'You call this safe?'

I hate her, Molly thought, as a sudden wave of fear washed over her. I really hate her. But as she lifted her head to tell her to shut up, one of the oars caught her on the back of the head. A sharp pain shot through her temple, and she lost consciousness.

Joyce was fretting. She had woken up just after midnight, bathed in sweat. She lay tense, listening, then got out of bed. Pulling on her old pink candlewick dressing gown and a pair of bedroom slippers, she shuffled out on to the landing and listened again. Nothing. But hearing nothing was ominous in its own right. Normally there would be snoring coming from Angie's bedroom.

Sure enough, when Joyce opened the door, the bed was empty.

Joyce had known this would happen the moment Jen went away. Angie was wary of her sister. Understandably so: nobody in their right mind would want to get on the wrong side of Jen. Joyce suddenly wondered how that nice Mr Keller would cope with her when she got to Libya. She smiled wryly to herself. Poor man. He didn't know what he was in for.

Padding down the stairs, she stood indecisively in the dark hallway, wondering what to do. Something was wrong. She knew it in her bones. Angie was often late, but not as late as this. She was so young. And so innocent. It was far too late for her to be out. Who knew what might be lurking out there in the darkness? Men like that predatory weasel Barry Fish.

She knew it was ridiculous to look outside. But she couldn't go back to bed wondering if Angie was slumped unconscious in the front garden. Taking a breath, she opened the front door.

As she looked out, she realised she could hear voices. Indistinct voices. A woman and a man. A low circle of shrouded torchlight preceding them. And the click of high heels on the pavement. It wasn't Angie; Angie's voice could never be described as indistinct.

Terrified of being spotted in her old dressing gown and rollers, Joyce flattened herself against the front wall of the house. And then, as the couple approached, she heard the slight Welsh lilt in the woman's voice. 'Not too noisy now, mind. I don't want to wake my daughter.'

It was Mrs James. Joyce couldn't see who the man was, but she heard the drunken leer in his voice as he said, 'You didn't say you had a daughter. I bet she's a pretty little thing if she takes after you.'

There was a slight hesitation as Mrs James fumbled to find the keyhole in the darkness. 'No, no, she's not at all pretty,' she said. 'Sadly, she takes after her father.'

And that's a right porky, Joyce thought as they went indoors. Gillian James either needed her eyes examined or she was lying deliberately. Either way it was clear she was up to no good. Joyce wondered how much the lucky man had agreed to pay for his night of fun. She also wondered what everyone in the street would say if they found out what was going on. One regular gentleman caller was bad enough, but nobody was going to take too kindly to the thought of a little private brothel in Lavender Road.

She was just about to go back into the house when Angie loomed up out of the darkness. Catching sight of Joyce, she recoiled with a shriek.

'Crumbs, Mum! You made me jump out of my skin. I thought you were a ghost.' She nodded across the road. 'Did you see who that was?' Her eyes were round as saucers. 'They were on the train from Victoria. I followed them all the way home. What do you think she's up to?'

'I don't know. And it's none of our business,' Joyce said firmly. If Angie didn't understand about ladies of the night, so much the better. 'Anyway,' she added sternly as she closed the door, 'where have you been? I was worried to death.'

'I was up at Rainbow Corner,' Angie said. 'The Americans' club at Piccadilly. There was a dancing competition. I got into the final and lost track of the time, that's all.'

'Well it's very naughty of you to be so late,' Joyce said.

Angie giggled. 'I know, but at least I'm not bringing strange men home and selling sex for money.'

It took the sailors a terrifying few minutes to manoeuvre the life raft clear of the sinking ship. Behind them they could hear shouting as another Berthon boat was lowered into the water. But as their distance from the burning vessel increased, the sound of voices faded. For a while, each time they rose on the swell, Jen could see the ship burning behind them. Then, suddenly, it was gone.

Through the darkness she heard the chief steward's voice. 'There she goes,' he announced.

'I'm sorry, Chief,' another voice said. 'What a shame. She was a useful little ship.'

'She can't have been that useful,' Jen snapped, 'or she wouldn't have sunk.'

'It wasn't her fault,' the second voice responded defensively. 'A ship that size can't do much against a bloody torpedo. It's a miracle she stayed afloat as long as she did.'

Jen felt her heart jolt. She hadn't realised they'd been hit by a torpedo. That put a whole new complexion on their predicament. 'You mean there's a submarine underneath us right now?'

'Possibly,' the chief steward said calmly. 'More likely he's gone off hunting the rest of the convoy.'

'Oh my God,' Jen groaned. But even the jeopardy they were in paled in comparison with how awful she was suddenly feeling. Her stomach was cramping again and she was conscious of an ominous tightness in her gullet.

But at least Molly Coogan had finally shut up. That was one blessing. Jen was fed up to the back teeth with her disapproving looks and her pious little reprimands. Jen's recall of the events preceding their descent into the lifeboat was somewhat hazy, but she was damned if she was going to let that righteous little goody-goody lecture her about what she should or shouldn't do or say.

'OK, folks.' The chief steward's steady voice came out of the darkness again. 'Let's take stock. Are we all present and correct?'

Present, maybe, Jen thought sourly, as someone switched on a torch, but hardly correct. Jammed in like sardines, there were clearly far too many of them for such a small boat. If you could call the flimsy thing they were sitting in a boat. The canvas bottom was already awash; Jen could feel the water swilling round her feet.

'Chief?' one of the galley boys called out suddenly.

'Be careful!' Jen screamed as the boat rocked alarmingly. 'You're going to tip us up.'

'What is it, Joe?' the chief steward's calm voice responded.

'It's Robbie Jones,' the boy said shakily. 'He's not breathing. I think he's dead. I think he's broke his neck.'

As the beam of his torch flashed wildly, Jen screamed in horror. The water lapping at her feet was red with blood. And lying in it like a broken doll was Molly Coogan.

Jen felt her gorge rise, and leaning forward, she was copiously sick into the bottom of the boat.

Katy felt guilty about Ward's uncle's disastrous visit. It had left a bad taste in her mouth. She hated conflict. Arguments always upset her. Ward, on the other hand, seemed to have put the whole thing out of his mind.

'Certainly not,' he said, when Katy asked if he was intending to see Maurice again. 'We made our position clear, and if he doesn't want to accept it,' a flicker of amusement crossed his handsome face, 'well then, he'll have to take the consequences.'

Katy grimaced at the memory of her angry words. 'But I feel I should apologise for being so rude.'

'You weren't rude,' Ward said. 'You were loyal. You stood up for me and I really appreciate that.' He gave a wry laugh. 'Poor old Uncle Maurice, I don't think he'll forget this trip to England in a hurry. One minute he's getting seduced by Gillian James, the next he's set upon by you. It's probably the most excitement he's had in his whole life.'

And that had made Katy feel even worse. But as a week had now elapsed with no word from them, she began to wonder if they had gone home to Canada.

So it was with considerable dismay that she opened the door on the morning of 9 July and found Callum Frazer standing on the step outside, dishevelled and distinctly ill at ease.

It was the last thing she'd expected, or indeed wanted. She felt tired and dirty herself. She had had a wakeful night, compounded by Ward having to leave early to catch a train. Normally Katy would have been able to go back to sleep for an hour or so after he had left, but this morning she had felt uneasy, edgy and restless, so she had got up and scrubbed out the cellar instead. She had only opened the door to throw out the dirty water, and to bring in the milk before someone pinched it.

'Goodness,' she said. She cast a nervous glance over Callum's shoulder, but thankfully he seemed to be alone. 'What are you doing here? I thought you'd be long gone by now.'

'We've been in Scotland,' he said. 'My father wanted me to see Edinburgh.'

'How nice for you,' Katy said politely, sloshing the dirty water out into the street. 'So where is your father now? I thought you were joined at the hip.'

When he didn't reply, she looked at him more closely and realised he was glaring at her resentfully.

'You don't understand,' he said.

Katy suddenly remembered her own overprotective parents, and how feeble she had been at resisting their smothering care. How much more difficult it would be with a stiff, autocratic old tartar like Maurice Frazer. 'Oh, I think I do,' she said. She bent down to pick up the small bottle of milk that was standing on the step. 'You'd better come in. You look as though you need a cup of tea.'

When Molly next opened her eyes, it was light. For a second as she stared up at the forbidding grey sky, she couldn't remember where she was. Then it all came back to her and a weird sense of exhilaration washed over her. She was alive. Then she remembered that she hadn't managed to rescue the penicillin, and the elation was replaced by disappointment. But as she began to take in what was going on in the small boat, the frustration of her failure was superseded by a creeping sense of fear.

She had been dragged up into the prow and was propped up, half lying, half sitting, between the legs of two men. She could feel their knees, surprisingly warm and bony, pressing into her arms. It had stopped raining, but the sea was still very rough. The canvas bottom of the boat was awash with water. From time to time, on a particularly violent swell, it splashed right up into her face.

Two of the crewmen were scooping the water up in buckets and throwing it over the side, but as soon as one lot had been bailed out, another wave would buffet the small craft and more would pour in. To make things even worse, someone had been sick and the vomit was swilling about in the water. Molly's sodden cloak stank of it.

Molly knew she must look a fright. But the others didn't look up to much either. They were certainly a motley crew. The two young ratings at the oars had given up rowing and were now just trying, not altogether successfully, to steer the tiny craft's bow into the oncoming waves. Another sailor was curled up awkwardly in the stern, apparently fast asleep, his life jacket over his face.

Opposite her, Conrad Porter was leaning forward, elbows on his knees, hunched over a cigarette. Always somewhat eccentrically dressed, the actor was now an extraordinary sight. He was wearing his yellow life vest over a purple velvet smoking jacket; his shirt, splattered with blood, possibly hers, was open at the neck. A paisley cravat was tied round his head, giving him a rather jaunty, piratical look.

Next to him, Jen was almost unrecognisable. Clutching the edge of the boat with one hand, she had the other round her knees, either for warmth or perhaps to keep her bare feet out of the fetid water. Her hair hung in rat's tails, and she was shivering convulsively. Under her life preserver, her little black evening dress was clinging to her like a second skin. Her toes were blue with cold, and her tarty red nail polish was chipped and scratched. But pitiful as she looked, there was nothing wrong with her sharp little eyes.

'Good God,' she said, through chattering teeth. 'Watch out, everyone. The goblin has woken up.'

Molly ignored her, turning her head instead to peer up at the chief steward. He wasn't looking his best either, his beard encrusted with blood from a great gash on his forehead that had virtually closed his left eye.

'What happened to the *Marigold*?' she asked.

'She sank,' he said shortly. Then he patted her in a fatherly way on the shoulder. 'How are you feeling, love? You've been out a long while.'

Tentatively Molly flexed her limbs. Her head felt as though someone was driving nails into it, her nose was blocked, her mouth was dry, she had lost a piece off one of her front teeth and her legs were numb with cold. But the worst thing was the pain that shot up her arm when she tried to move her hand.

'I think I've broken my finger,' she said.

Jen started laughing. 'Lucky you.' She nodded at the motionless sailor in the stern. 'That poor bugger broke his neck.'

Molly flinched, shocked at her callous insensitivity.

'We'd thought you'd gone the same way and all,' one of the sailors remarked.

'No, no, I'm fine,' Molly said.

'Well I'm not,' Jen said. 'I'm bloody freezing.'

'At least you're alive,' Molly snapped. 'Thanks to me and Mr Porter.'

'Conrad, please,' the actor murmured. 'I think in the circumstances we can drop the formality.'

Molly glanced at him coldly, then turned back to Jen. 'If it wasn't for us, you'd be dead by now.'

'I wish I *was* dead,' Jen said. 'You should have left me on board. I'd rather have gone down with the ship than bloody freeze to death.'

'Now, now, girls,' the chief steward intervened. 'I'm sure we'll all be right as rain. You'll see.'

A sceptical silence followed this optimistic pronouncement.

'What happened to the rest of the convoy?' Molly asked after a moment. 'Surely the rescue boat will search for us now that it's light?'

'Of course they will,' the chief steward said.

'Of course they won't,' Jen snapped. 'They're probably in Tripoli by now. Thanking their lucky stars it wasn't them that got torpedoed.'

'I think we're being swept south,' one of the sailors remarked.

'Let's hope so,' another said grimly. 'We don't want to tip up in France or Italy.'

'North, south, who cares?' Jen said. 'Nobody will find us in the middle of this damn great ocean. We're obviously going to die. Soon we will have to start eating each other.'

I wish someone would eat Jen Carter, Molly thought. Then, in sudden dread, she lifted her good hand and felt for the little magic carpet necklace that Ward Frazer had given her. It was still there. She sighed with relief and fingered the tiny charm. Please let us be rescued, she whispered to herself. Please send someone to save us.

'We was going to have roast chicken in the mess hall tonight,' the cook said suddenly. 'Shame that's all gone to waste.'

Conrad Porter choked on his cigarette. 'What about dessert?' he asked.

'Jam roly poly,' the man replied mournfully.

The actor threw the cigarette butt into the water and watched it fizzle out. 'Now that really is a shame,' he drawled. He caught Molly's eyes on him and winked. 'I'm rather partial to a bit of roly poly.'

Despite herself, Molly couldn't help giving a shocked little giggle.

'Oh shut up, Conrad,' Jen said irritably. 'And stop talking about food. You're making me feel sick.'

After a while the chief steward glanced at the body in the stern of the

274

boat. 'I think we should let Robbie go,' he said.

There was a moment's silence, then the two nearest crewmen turned and began to manoeuvre their former shipmate on to the edge of the boat.

'This is going to sound awful,' Jen said. 'But do you think I could have his jumper before he goes?'

The sailors hesitated and glanced at the chief steward. He nodded. 'And check his pockets in case there's something we can send his family.'

A minute or two later, just as the grim-faced sailors were about to release the body, he held up his hand. 'Hold on, lads,' he said.

He lowered his head. 'Unto Almighty God we commend the soul of our brother departed,' he intoned in his deep voice. 'And we commit his body to the deep.' There he paused.

As everyone waited, heads bowed, for him to go on, he added, 'You'd better let him go, lads, because I can't remember the rest.'

As they pushed the body over the stern, one of the young sailors gave an audible sniff. 'Good luck, Robbie,' he muttered.

With swimming eyes, Molly watched the corpse bobbing face down in the rough sea behind them. At first it looked like it was going to follow them. But then it was bowled roughly away by a sudden wave. For a minute or so she could still see it when they rose on a swell.

And then it was gone.

It didn't take Katy long to ascertain that the Frazers' father-and-son trip to Scotland had not been a success. It took a little longer to work out why.

Having rushed down to Clapham with the aim of seeing Ward, Callum was put out to find only Katy at home.

'Dammit,' he said, picking up a beer mat and fiddling with it nervously. 'Why did he have to go out so early?'

Katy, with Malcolm perched on her lap, was stirring the tea in the teapot. 'Because what he does is important,' she said coldly. 'It's often a matter of life and death.' She looked up at him. 'There is a war on, you know.'

Then she felt guilty, because Callum blanched.

'That's why I fell out with my father,' he said. Dropping the beer mat, he took a jerky breath and stood up abruptly with an expression of sheepish defiance. 'I told him I wanted to join up.'

Katy nearly dropped the teaspoon. 'Oh Lord,' she said with a choke of laughter. 'I bet that put the cat among the pigeons.'

Setting Malcolm down on the floor, she stood up and fetched a bottle of whisky. 'Here,' she said, pouring him a small tot. 'You look as though you need something a bit stronger than tea.'

It seemed that Callum had spent most of the trip to Scotland agonising about how best to impart this change of heart to this father. It was only on their return to London late the previous evening that he had summoned up the courage. His announcement had provoked a blazing row and he had stormed out, vowing never to speak to his father again.

'He said it was your fault,' he said now, sipping the whisky gratefully.

'Mine?' Katy choked on her tea.

Callum shrugged. 'Well, yours and Ward's. He said you'd influenced me.'

Katy looked at him in surprise. 'And had we?' Until today, she had barely exchanged two words with Callum. She certainly hadn't intended to influence him. In fact, despite his athletic figure, she had written him off as a bit of a sissy.

'No ... well, yes.' He sat down again and sighed. 'I don't know. I guess I just feel guilty. The war was very far removed in Canada. But seeing the damage and hearing what you all have been through ...' He hesitated, then made a self-conscious gesture. 'And finding out some of what Ward has done. I guess it's kind of made me think ...'

Katy never heard exactly what it *had* made him think, because at that moment the door opened and Helen came in, followed by George, dressed in school uniform with his satchel on his back.

Helen's eyes widened as she saw Katy's visitor. They widened even more when she spotted the whisky bottle on the table. 'Well hello,' she said. 'How nice to see you again. But isn't it a little early for alcohol?'

Jumping to his feet in some confusion, Callum began to stammer out an explanation, but he was drowned out by Malcolm's squeals of delight as he tried to climb up Helen's leg. Feeling sorry for the young Canadian, Katy introduced him to George, explaining that Callum was Ward's cousin.

As Helen grappled with Malcolm, George eyed Callum with interest. 'Are you a secret agent too?' he asked.

Catching Helen's eye and trying to keep the amusement out of her voice, Katy explained that Callum had just that morning decided to join up.

Helen abandoned her mock battle with Malcolm and hoisted him into her arms. 'Good for you,' she said at once. 'Congratulations. That's a brave decision.'

'Yeah, I guess ...' Callum flushed and glanced awkwardly at Katy. 'But the thing is, now I've told my dad I never want to see him again, I don't know what to do next. I thought Ward would help me, but ...'

George was regarding him with considerable surprise. 'I'd know what to do if *I* was old enough to join up,' he said. 'I'd go straight to Germany and kill Mr Hitler.'

Callum looked somewhat startled at this unexpected intervention. Biting

276

back a laugh, Katy nudged George with her toe. 'And how exactly would you do that?' she asked.

'I'd pretend I wanted his autograph,' George said at once. 'Then when he was busy writing his name, I'd whack him on the back of the head. Or if I couldn't get close enough to do that, I'd get him in the eye with my catapult. Or I'd run him over with my go-cart. Or I'd take a knife and stab him in the heart. Or else I'd do a card trick on him and make sure he chose the poisoned card.'

'Wouldn't it be easier to bomb him?' Callum asked suddenly, breaking in on this bloodthirsty agenda. 'We could fly over Berlin and drop a neat little blockbuster bomb right on his headquarters.'

'Well, yes,' George admitted reluctantly. 'But I don't know how to fly.'

'No, I guess not,' Callum said. 'But I do.'

'Do you?' George looked at him with new respect.

'Sure I do. I've been flying all my life.'

'Then you should join the Royal Air Force,' Helen said.

'Or the Canadian Air Force,' Katy murmured thoughtfully.

Helen gave her a quick look, then turned to George. 'Hey, you're going to be late for school,' she said, and whisked him away.

Leaving Callum to keep an eye on Malcolm, Katy went upstairs to tidy herself up. Callum had looked nervous about being left alone with the toddler. He clearly wasn't used to children. But being the well-mannered boy he was, he had accepted the responsibility without expressing the dismay he obviously felt.

He was nice-looking too, Katy thought as she quickly washed and dressed. He seemed young for his age, but he already had the same easy grace in his movement as Ward had, the same attentive look in his eyes.

Katy could see a bit of Ward in him, and also perhaps what Malcolm might become. Her heart twisted. What would she feel like in the future if Malcolm suddenly decided to join up, to put himself in danger, without even discussing it with her? What if something happened to him and she hadn't had the chance to say goodbye? She wondered what Callum's mother would think of his plans.

She had barely had the thought when she heard a piercing scream from the bar. Racing down the stairs, the first thing she saw was Malcolm flying up towards the ceiling, his limbs spread wide like a little starfish. As he began to plummet down again, her heart stopped and she watched in frozen terror.

There was no time to think, no time to move. Then she saw Callum step forward to catch him easily in outstretched arms.

Realising that he was just about to toss Malcolm skywards again, she stumbled down the last couple of stairs. 'What on earth are you doing?'

Callum started nervously and hastily lowered Malcolm to the floor. 'Teaching him how to fly,' he said. He glanced down at Malcolm, who was holding his arms up for another go, and gave her a sheepish grin. 'He seems to kind of like it.'

'Of course he likes it,' Katy said crossly. 'He likes anything dangerous.'

What was it with these Frazer men? she wondered. You only had to look away for a moment for them to start risking life and limb in some mad exploit.

'You should go back to Canada and join up there,' she said, picking Malcolm up and hugging him to her. 'Do it properly. I'm sure the Canadian Air force will snap you up.'

Callum looked horrified. 'But I'm already here,' he said. 'It's such a waste to go back.'

'You'll have to be trained up wherever you are. So it might as well be in Canada.' Katy put Malcolm down in his playpen. 'It's not fair on your parents to jump ship now. Especially your mother.'

'But Ward did it.'

'I know,' Katy said grimly. 'And look what trouble it caused.'

'But—'

Katy held up her hand. 'No buts,' she said. She crossed her fingers behind her back. 'I know Ward will agree with me. You should go back to your hotel right now and talk to your father. Tell him you've thought it through, but that you've made up your mind. You want to enlist. And that you'd like his help to facilitate that decision.'

'I can't,' Callum said. 'I can't face him.'

Katy poured another tot of whisky into his glass. She handed it to him and chinked her teacup against it.

'Of course you can,' she said. 'You have to. You have to show him that you have the maturity to make your own decisions. The maturity to serve your country.'

Chapter Twenty

Molly heard the seagulls before she saw them. For a mad moment she thought the sound was babies crying on a maternity ward. But then reality reasserted itself and she caught sight of the birds circling in the distance. She had seen seagulls before, of course, earlier on the voyage. Huge great things, much bigger than the ones in London, flapping and screeching as they searched the wake of the convoy ships for fish, or titbits of waste from the galleys. But she hadn't noticed any during the sixteen hours they had been tossing about in the lifeboat. Wondering if their presence might, by some miraculous chance, mean that land was nearby, she mustered what little strength she had left and sat up to peer in their direction. That was when she saw the boat.

Her first attempt to alert the others was soundless. Licking the salt off her parched lips, she coughed and tried again. 'There's a boat,' she gasped. 'I'm sure I just saw a boat.'

At first nobody believed her, but sure enough, a minute later, as they crested a particularly high swell, they all saw it. And heard it too. A small fishing trawler with a stubby mast and a throbbing engine.

'Who do you think they are?' one of the sailors asked as they all started to shout and wave.

'Who cares,' Jen said. Despite the dead sailor's jumper she was now wearing under her lifebelt, her lips were blue with cold. 'Surely they'll rescue us, whoever they are.'

'Let's hope they're from North Africa,' the chief steward said. 'In which case they'll be on our side.'

'In theory,' Conrad Porter said drily.

But although they were deeply tanned, the crew of the fishing boat didn't look at all like the white-robed Arabs Molly had seen on the dock in Tunis. These men wore dark peaked caps, and despite the weather, the sleeves of their workaday shirts were rolled up to their elbows. Their heavily lined faces looked reasonably benign, but judging from the edgy silence with which they cautiously approached the floundering life raft, they weren't going to take any chances.

'What do we do now?' one of the sailors whispered nervously.

'We could overpower them,' the chief steward murmured. 'There's only four of them.'

Conrad gave a choke of laughter. 'Good God, man, have you seen the condition we are in? I don't know about you, but I'm pretty much numb from the waist down.'

As the trawler circled around them, the men on board caught sight of the two bedraggled girls and stared in wonder. One of them suddenly yelled a rapid volley of questions.

The sailors glanced at each other blankly. 'What language is that?' one of them asked nervously.

'I think it's Italian,' Jen said.

Conrad turned his head in surprise. 'Do you speak Italian?'

'No,' Jen said. 'But my sister has been trying to learn it and I recognise some of the words.'

'Well answer him then,' the chief steward urged her. 'Explain who we are and that we need their help.'

'I've no idea how to say that,' Jen said crossly.

'Say something else then,' Molly said.

Jen glared at her. 'I can't,' she said. 'It's Angie who was learning it, not me.' She thought for a moment, then shook her head. 'The only thing I can remember how to say is, I want to be your wife and have your babies.'

Conrad raised his eyebrows. 'You could try that,' he said drily. 'It would probably do the trick.'

One of the sailors gave a muffled gasp of amusement. A moment later the chief steward started chuckling. Conrad joined in, and the next minute everyone on the lifeboat was rocking with laughter. Even Molly found herself giggling. It was partly the ridiculousness of it, but mostly it was the relief of no longer being alone on the ocean without food or drink.

The funniest thing was the bemused expressions on the faces of their potential rescuers. But soon even they were laughing, their teeth shining white in their weather-beaten faces as they leaned over the rising and falling rail of their boat to inspect the raft more closely.

'*Italiani?*' Jen shouted up at them tentatively.

'*Siete Italiani? Bene, bene, ci siamo Siciliani,*' the fishermen responded delightedly, and followed this exchange with another burst of incomprehensible questions.

'Oh, this is hopeless,' Jen said, turning away in disgust. 'I have no idea what they're saying. Why can't the idiots speak English?'

Molly saw one of the fishermen recoil in horror. 'Inglesh?' he said. He turned to his cohorts. '*Non sono Italiani. Sono Inglesi.*'

Molly couldn't bear it. Kneeling up on her seat, she clasped her swollen hands together in a pleading gesture. 'Yes, we are English,' she called up pitifully, trying to keep her balance as the little craft bucked and plunged beneath her in the swell. 'I know we are your enemy, but we are going to die if you leave us here. So please, won't you let us get into your boat? Or at the very least, give us something to drink?'

They clearly had no idea what she was saying, but they got the gist of what she wanted. After a brief discussion among themselves, they produced a long wooden pole with a fearsome kind of hook on the end. Brandishing this nerve-racking weapon with practised skill, they quickly caught up the prow rope of the raft.

A minute later they were reaching down to haul them unceremoniously, one by one, like sacks of fish, up off the lifeboat and into the trawler.

Hearing the pub door open, Katy looked up nervously. She was terrified that Maurice Frazer might appear, and didn't want to have to face him without Ward there to protect her. She was certain Ward's uncle would be mad as fire when he discovered Callum had come running to the pub for moral support. That would surely rub salt in the wound that had been inflicted by his son's determination to join up. She wondered if Callum's resolve would hold in the face of his father's inevitable fury. It wasn't going to be easy for him. For either of them, come to that. Maurice Frazer wasn't going to suffer defeat readily. But in the circumstances, she felt she had done the best she could. Although she was pretty sure Ward's uncle wouldn't see it like that.

But it wasn't Maurice Frazer who came brushing arrogantly through the blackout curtain; it was Douglas Rutherford, which in Katy's view was almost as bad.

'Oh God,' she muttered to Helen, who was standing next to her behind the bar. 'That's all we need. All I can say is thank goodness Molly isn't here.'

'Yes indeed,' Helen agreed. 'Lucky Molly. At least she'll be spared this.'

Douglas was wearing a well-tailored khaki officer's uniform with the distinctive red flash of the Coldstream Guards across the top of his sleeve. A highly polished leather Sam Browne belt circled his waist, with a smaller strap leading up over one shoulder. As he entered the room, he took off his peaked forage cap with an ostentatious flourish that made its silver badge catch the light.

Beside him, clinging to his arm, was Louise, looking very proud of her fine younger brother. And he did indeed look very smart. The picture of a young Guards officer, in fact. But that didn't stop Katy feeling irritated at the sight of him. She hadn't forgotten his appalling behaviour last time he'd been in.

'Long time no see,' she said brightly, as Douglas swaggered up to the bar and ordered two gin and tonics. 'So you're still in England, then?'

'As you see,' he said with a patronising sneer.

'He's responsible for guarding Windsor Castle,' Louise said.

'Goodness, how brave,' Helen murmured.

Katy bit back a giggle. 'Well I am surprised,' she went on artlessly as she pressed the shorts glasses up to the optic. 'I thought from what you said last time you were in here that you'd have been on active service in North Africa by now.' She smiled as she reached under the counter for the tonics. 'I was disappointed, actually, that I didn't hear your name in the news as single-handedly responsible for the rout of Rommel.'

A slight flush tinged Douglas's cheeks, but his voice was as smug as ever. 'No. As it happened, I didn't get the chance.' He lifted his shoulders in a negligent shrug. 'But I don't mind. It's obvious they are keeping my squadron back for some special assignment.'

'Funny you should say that,' Helen chipped in cheerfully. 'Molly Coogan has just gone off on a special assignment. Do you remember her? The nurse that worked here sometimes.'

Douglas's eyes flickered uneasily to Helen's face, but he was apparently reassured by her innocent smile. 'I think so.' He gave a short chuckle. 'You mean the one people called the Poxy Pixie?'

'Well, yes,' Helen said doubtfully. 'But obviously only stupid people who have no manners or finesse.' Studiously ignoring Katy's sudden choking fit next to her, she went on blithely. 'Anyway, she's just gone to North Africa. She should be there by now, actually. She volunteered to go. Don't you think that was brave of her?'

Douglas laughed contemptuously. 'Hardly,' he said. He took out a leather wallet and tossed a note carelessly on to the bar. 'North Africa is old news. There's no danger there any more. Italy is where the action will be next. We've already taken a couple of the southern islands. I reckon it will be Sicily next.' Katy handed him his change, and he tossed the coins up and caught them again with a snap of his hand. Dropping them in his pocket, he picked up the drinks with a self-satisfied smile. 'Yes. Italy will be the place to be. You'll see. Mussolini won't last long once I get there.'

As he turned away, Katy wanted to scream. Either that or swear. But she couldn't, because Louise was still standing at the bar.

'I've had a letter from Jack,' she said gloomily.

'Oh, Louise.' Katy brightened at once. 'That's great news. Is he OK? Does he say where he is?'

'No, he can never say where he is.' Louise grimaced. 'But he does say he will be home soon for a week's leave.'

'That's great. You lucky thing. How wonderful.'

'But what am I going to do about Charlie?'

Katy saw Louise's expression and rolled her eyes. 'Oh for goodness' sake, Louise. Jack is your husband. He loves you. You love him. Or you did. Don't let this idiotic business with Charlie get between you.'

'It's not idiotic,' Louise said. 'You have no idea. Charlie is wonderful. I'm completely mad about him.'

'You were completely mad about Jack a few months ago,' Katy said sourly. She glanced over at Helen. It was ironic that on the one hand there was Louise, getting good news from her husband and not wanting it. And on the other there was Helen, desperate for news of André and never hearing anything. The world suddenly seemed very unfair.

'Come on, Louise,' Douglas shouted across. 'It was you that wanted to come for a drink. I haven't got all night.'

'Oh, look at Mr Officer, suddenly so authoritative,' Louise giggled. 'To think he's my baby brother.'

'Yes,' Helen murmured, as Louise hurried over. 'And if he was *my* baby brother, I'd give him a good smack.'

'They both need a smack,' Katy said.

If anything, the trawler was an even less salubrious vessel than the life raft had been. Mainly because it involved travelling in the company of a huge number of dead and dying fish. No wonder the seagulls had been circling the boat, Molly thought, eyeing the squirming silver mound at her feet. The smell was disgusting. She wasn't surprised to see Jen retching over the side. Even the chief steward and the other young merchant seamen looked somewhat green about the gills, and Conrad Porter had taken the precaution of wrapping his paisley cravat over his nose.

Used to the hideous aroma of septicaemia, Molly could just about bear the smell, but she found the sight of the fish's desperate eyes and gasping mouths hard to take. It wasn't quite the salvation she'd wished for, but at least they were no longer tossing about aimlessly in the flimsy little lifeboat. Whatever the future held, surely nothing could be as bad as that.

Molly knew from her nursing training that it was the dehydration that would have killed them. The body could cope without food for several days, but they were all desperately weak from lack of fluids.

The fishermen had already used up most of their provisions, but they at least produced warm jackets, along with a few pieces of dry bread, a couple of slices of thin, salty sausage, a bottle of rather brackish water and a metal flask of a colourless but fiery liquid, which burnt its way down to Molly's stomach.

And then some other boats appeared. They were clearly all part of the same small fleet, returning to harbour. With a lot of shouting and gesticulating, their rescuers steered close alongside to show off their unexpected haul. One or two of the new arrivals tossed over bits and pieces of food and then watched eagerly to see what the castaways would do with it, for all the world as though they were feeding some exotic species in a zoo.

The captain of one of the other trawlers spoke a bit of broken English, and when the two boats came within yelling distance, he engaged in an intermittent shouted conversation with the chief steward.

Molly couldn't really hear what they were saying. She was past caring anyway. The alcohol in the metal flask had gone straight to her head. She felt woozy and exhausted. Her broken front tooth was painfully sensitive and her hand was throbbing again as a result of her being hauled aboard. But even those discomforts had been dulled by the fiery liquid. Curling up against an enormous bundle of damp, stinking fishing nets, she closed her eyes.

Katy woke up when Ward got home. He came upstairs very quietly. She heard him tiptoe in to check on Malcolm in his cot, then listened to him moving about in the kitchen: the clunk of the breadbin, the chink of a plate in the basin, the creak of a chair, then a long pause, which surprised her. He wasn't one for sitting around late at night. But then normally he didn't go to such lengths not to wake her either.

'Are you OK?' she asked when he eventually eased himself into bed beside her.

'Yeah, I'm fine,' he said. He stroked her hair gently. 'Go back to sleep. It's very late.'

But Katy was wide awake now. 'A terrible thing happened today,' she murmured.

She felt him flinch and went on hastily, 'Well, quite terrible anyway.' Turning over, she told him about Callum's visit.

Ward listened in silence. She could hear his steady breathing. But he wasn't reacting to her story quite as she'd expected. She had thought he'd sympathise about the predicament Callum had put her in, even perhaps find it amusing. Certainly speculate how his uncle would take the news.

'Do you think I did the wrong thing?' she asked nervously when he didn't respond.

'No, you did fine,' he said.

It seemed a rather meagre response, and Katy felt slightly aggrieved. After all it was his blasted cousin she had had to deal with. And it hadn't been easy.

And then it occurred to her that he wasn't touching her either. Even if he wasn't intending to make love, which he obviously wasn't tonight, he would normally at least caress her, smoothing her skin, stroking her gently off to sleep.

'Where've you been?' she asked suddenly. 'Why are you so late?'

There was a long pause in the darkness. Then he gave a slight groan. 'Why aren't you asleep?'

She felt a flash of fear. 'I don't know, but I'm not. What is it?' she added. 'Why are you being so peculiar?'

He sighed. 'Something has happened,' he said. 'I didn't want to tell you until tomorrow.'

Oh no, Katy thought, he's been with another woman and now he's feeling guilty. All her previous fears of his infidelity came rushing back. She sat up and peered at him through the darkness. Please don't let it be Gillian James, she thought. For some reason she felt she could bear anything except that.

'Tell me. Please. I want to know now.'

The bed moved as he sat up too. He reached over to turn on the bedside lamp. 'I called at the office on the way back and there was news coming in about a convoy being attacked in the Mediterranean. It seems quite a few ships went down. That's why I'm so late home. I wanted to try and get more details.'

Katy couldn't take it in. It was so different from what she'd expected to hear. No wonder Ward hadn't been interested in her burbling on about Callum. Her concern about Maurice Frazer turning up in the pub had already paled into insignificance.

'It's not definite,' Ward said. 'And even if their ship was hit, they may still be OK. Plenty of survivors have been picked up. But it's very unclear at the moment. The rest of the convoy scattered into different ports, so things are pretty confused. We'll hear more in a day or two, once they sort out which vessels are where.'

'But they've been gone so long. Surely they should have arrived by now,' Katy said.

Ward hesitated, a frown creasing his brow. 'There seems to be some thought that the convoy was deliberately delayed.'

Katy blinked. 'Why? What do you mean?'

'The invasion of Sicily is kicking off tomorrow. They may have been using the convoy to lure the subs out of the way.'

Katy put her hand to her mouth. 'Oh my God,' she said. For a second she sat there, staring at him. Her vision blurred as tears welled in her eyes;

she didn't even try to stop them falling. She could feel a constriction in her throat, a bubble of emotion, of dread, of fear, of anger. And suddenly she was sobbing. Great heaving cries, rocking her whole frame. After the tension of the day, it was all too much. Jen and Molly. The very thought of their names caused another sob to rack her body.

'Hey, sweetheart.' Ward pulled her into his arms and tried to wipe her eyes. 'It may not be so bad. They may be fine, for all we know.'

But she couldn't stop crying.

'Katy, come on,' Ward murmured into her hair. 'Take it easy. You'll wake Malcolm.' He put a hand on her stomach. 'And think of the baby.'

Katy pushed his hand away. 'I don't want to bring another baby into such a horrid world,' she said.

A group of armed men in black shirts and tight knitted hats were waiting for them on the dock. It seemed that one of the fishing boats had gone in ahead to alert the port authorities about the unusual haul that was about to arrive. These nasty-looking militia formed the welcome committee. The fishermen stood by uneasily as their captives were ordered off the boat at gunpoint and herded roughly along the quay.

'Welcome to Sicily,' Conrad murmured, smiling benignly at the groups of dark, silent people standing at the entrance to the harbour.

Molly had always understood that Sicily was some kind of impoverished outpost of Italy, so she was taken aback by the elegant cobbled streets, tree-lined squares and ornate, imposing buildings of the town that rose up the hillside behind the small port. She felt she had been misled. If this proud, grim grandeur was anything to go by, Italy wasn't going to be quite as easy to dismiss as the British propaganda was leading people to believe. Nor did the ominously leaden sky and brisk wind do anything to lift her spirits.

'What's going to happen to us?' she whispered nervously to the chief steward as she stumbled along beside him, clutching her wet cloak tightly round her against the incomprehensible but clearly hostile taunts of their captors. She felt cold and dirty, and her swollen finger throbbed painfully even though she had made a rudimentary splint for it from a small sliver of wood she had found on the fishing boat, strapped on with a strip torn off her handkerchief.

'Goodness knows,' the chief steward replied. 'There's been a lot of bombing in the last week. That's why they're so jumpy. They think the Allies might be working up to an invasion.'

'So we may get rescued pretty soon?' Molly said hopefully.

'I certainly hope so,' the chief steward said. 'Because the Merchant Navy stops our pay from the moment the ship sinks, and my wife's going to suffer if I'm stuck here for long.'

'Oh dear,' Molly said inadequately. She couldn't believe he was thinking about something as trivial as pay. Her own mind seemed suddenly to have become completely numb with fear. She felt like some kind of automaton, able to move, and follow orders, but unable to comprehend what was going on, let alone do anything about it.

Jen's spirits, on the other hand, seemed to have improved considerably now that she was back on dry land. She was still wearing the dead sailor's navy jumper, but the damp, skimpy dress below it, clinging to her bare legs, was causing quite a lot of interest among the bystanders in the street. Taking her lead from Conrad Porter, she stared defiantly back with a gritty smile, even though the uneven surface of the road must have been painful on her bare feet.

They arrived at some kind of police barracks in the centre of town, and mercifully that seemed to be where they were going to stop. But as they turned through a high stone archway into a courtyard filled with military vehicles, the most officious member of their escort indicated with a wave of his pistol that it was only the two girls who were to be housed there.

'Oh, please don't split us up,' Molly pleaded. They had been a surprisingly comradely little group. The ordeal on the life raft had bonded them together, and the thought of being suddenly separated was unbearable. It also meant she would be alone with Jen Carter.

But their captors didn't care. With a lot of angry, incomprehensible commands, Molly and Jen were pushed past the vehicles into a small room. The door was locked behind them. Through a barred window they could see the rest of their little party being marched off elsewhere.

Molly had to swallow hard and turn away to prevent Jen from seeing the tears that sprang to her eyes.

The cell was perhaps eight feet square. All it contained was three wooden chairs, a small table and an unsavoury bucket.

Molly could feel the fear, and fought against it. 'We've got to do something,' she whispered suddenly.

'Oh really?' Jen raised her eyebrows. 'And what do you suggest?'

'We've got to escape.'

'Escape?' Jen said incredulously. 'Have you looked out of the window? The whole place is teeming with armed men. We can't possibly escape.'

Molly frowned. How typical of Jen to be so defeatist. 'The best time to escape is in the first twenty-four hours after capture,' she said doggedly. 'When they expect you to be tired and disorientated.'

Jen looked at her pityingly. 'I think you must be disorientated already,' she said. 'Who told you that anyway?'

'George Nelson.'

'George Nelson?' Jen's eyes widened. 'George Nelson is eight years old. What does he know about it?'

'I think Ward told him.' To her dismay, Molly felt a sudden flush creep into her cheeks as she said the name, but luckily Jen didn't seem to notice.

'Oh, great. So we are secret agents now?' Jen scoffed. 'What on earth would we do if we did escape? Neither of us can speak a word of the language.'

'No, but if the invasion is imminent, surely we could hide somewhere until the Allies find us.'

'Oh for goodness' sake,' Jen said. 'You're a piddly little nurse and I'm a piddly little two-bit actress. We'd be caught within five minutes.' She yawned. 'Look, nobody is going to harm us. We can just stay here until the Allies find us.' And with that she sat down on the hard floor, leaned her head back against the wall and closed her eyes.

Molly glared at her. Of all the people she could be stranded in Sicily with, it would be Jen Carter. Any normal person would surely want to talk through their situation. To discuss their, admittedly limited, options.

But all Jen did was snooze gently until someone slid open the little wooden panel on the door, at which point she shouted that she wanted something to eat.

'I'm bloody starving here,' she yelled at whoever was peering in. 'For God's sake. Surely you have some food in this godforsaken place?'

'They don't understand,' Molly said. 'I don't think anyone speaks English.'

'They don't want to understand,' Jen snapped. She made a knife and fork eating gesture. 'It's not very difficult, is it?'

Eventually someone did come in.

He was a well-built man with a florid complexion, short curly yellow hair and unattractively thick lips. His dark uniform was very neat and crisp, with a badge of what looked like two flashes of lightning on his collar. He wore high, very shiny black leather boots. Under his arm he carried a stiff peaked cap.

Scrambling to her feet from the uncomfortable chair she had been sitting on for hours, Molly eyed him with considerable alarm. He seemed pleased by her reaction, less so by Jen's lazy regard from her position on the floor.

'Ah, the two English girls. How charming,' he said, clicking his heels in a kind of mock salute. 'I have been looking forward to meeting you.'

He was clearly German. Molly didn't recognise the sinister uniform, but she knew that guttural accent from war films she had seen, and it caused her armpits to prickle and goose bumps to spring up on her arms.

But Jen seemed oblivious to his nationality. 'Oh, thank goodness,' she said, standing up lazily. 'Finally, someone who can speak English.' She gave him an encouraging smile. 'We've been trying for hours to get something to eat and drink, but nobody seems to understand.'

He did not return the smile. 'You will be given food and clothing when you answer a few simple questions. Do you understand?'

Molly nodded obediently and sat down. Jen didn't move.

'Please,' he said. 'Sit.' His tone was studiously polite, but there was an underlying hardness that even Jen seemed to recognise. In any case, to Molly's relief, after another moment's hesitation, she sat down.

'So.' He pulled up the third chair and sat astride it as though riding a horse. Then he took a notebook out of his breast pocket and uncapped a fountain pen. 'Tell me your names.'

When they both obliged, he nodded. 'Good.'

Having checked the spelling, he put down his pen and tapped his fingertips together. 'Now tell me what are you doing here.'

'We aren't doing anything,' Jen said. 'You may not have noticed, but we have been locked in this filthy little cell ever since we arrived.'

His pale blue eyes narrowed. 'We were on our way to North Africa,' Molly stammered hastily. 'We were torpedoed and our ship sank.'

Very slowly he transferred his cold gaze from Jen to her. 'You came to Sicily by boat?'

'Well, yes,' Molly said. 'But—'

'You are not part of the British armed forces, I think?'

'Of course we aren't,' Jen said irritably. 'Do we look like soldiers?'

'No.' He sat back in his chair and inspected his nails for a moment.

Then, with no warning at all, he jerked his head forward and snarled at them, 'You are spies. Infiltrators. Sent in advance of the invasion, yes?'

Molly was suddenly too frightened to open her mouth. Notwithstanding his menacing tone, the word *spies* sent a shiver of terror down her spine. She knew only too well from her association with Helen and Ward the fate that awaited spies in Nazi Europe.

She knew she should deny his accusation, but she was frozen into immobility. Long years of nursing training had taught her to respect authority. Standing up to one of the nursing sisters at the Wilhelmina was bad enough. Contradicting this man seemed utterly unthinkable.

But it seemed Jen had no such inhibitions. 'Don't be absurd,' she said. 'Of course we aren't spies. I am a performer with ENSA, a singer and actress, and Molly here is a nurse.'

The officer didn't even glance in Molly's direction. But he ran his eyes over Jen in a way that made Molly squirm.

'A singer?' He smiled, but it wasn't a kindly smile. More like that of a crocodile before the kill. He stood up and turned his chair round.

Settling himself back down, he crossed his legs comfortably. 'So. I am fond of music. Perhaps you would give me a song?'

A pregnant pause followed this request. Molly could feel her heart hammering in her chest. Her hands were clammy in her lap. She wanted to turn to look at Jen, but her neck muscles seemed to have seized up.

Then, quite calmly, Jen pushed back her chair and got up. Moving towards the window, she inhaled a long breath. Then she turned, clasped her hands in front of her chest, and, to Molly's utter horror, launched into a vibrant rendering of 'Land of Hope and Glory'.

Her voice was audaciously strong and, in the confined space of the cell, almost ear-piercingly loud.

It took a moment or two for the German officer to realise what she was singing, and by then, through the window, Molly could hear the sudden grumble of male voices joining in, and realised that their shipmates were obviously still within earshot and were taking the opportunity to show their defiant solidarity. She thought she could make out Conrad's well-enunciated baritone and the deep bass of the chief steward, and her eyes suddenly swam with emotion.

As their distant voices swelled to a roar and merged with Jen's, the German jumped to his feet. 'Stop!' he shouted. 'Stop this now.'

'Jen, for goodness' sake ...' Molly whispered, as Jen took a breath before launching into the second verse.

'If we are going to be killed, we might as well go down singing,' Jen muttered, dodging round the small table as the German advanced menacingly towards her. Depleted as she was, dehydrated and exhausted from the constant vomiting, she was agile on her feet. Molly looked at her with new respect. Much as she disliked her, she had to admire her spirit. She knew that she herself would never in a million years be able to do what Jen was doing. Even performing a card trick for the Nelsons had made her quake at the knees.

But then Jen did stop, because the door opened and another man strode in. He was also wearing a uniform Molly didn't recognise, with three stars and a crown on his epaulettes. In complete contrast to the German, this was a tall, dark-haired, aristocratic-looking man with a Roman nose and humour lines round his eyes. But he wasn't laughing now. On the contrary, he was white-lipped with anger.

'*Cosa sta succedendo? Si supera la vostra autorità.*'

This was addressed to the German officer, who had stopped in his tracks and was now visibly discomfited. The two men glared at each other like rival lions scrapping over a carcass.

The German clicked his heels in a kind of grudging salute. 'My apology, Colonel, but you were not here …'

'Hermann Goering here asked me to sing,' Jen murmured. 'To prove I wasn't a spy.'

Something flickered in the Italian's eyes, but he didn't even glance at her. He merely held the door with exaggerated courtesy for the German, who, after a moment, turned stiffly on his heel.

As he left, he fixed his eyes on Jen for a moment. 'You think you are clever, no? But I believe it is also possible for a spy to sing.' His tongue ran briefly over his thick lips. 'We will meet again.'

'Not if I can help it,' Jen retorted.

They listened to his heels clicking down the passage. Then the Italian colonel relaxed slightly, looked them over briefly and issued a brisk command to someone outside the door.

'You will receive food and water and some wardrobe.'

Molly glanced at Jen, willing her not to laugh. 'Thank you,' she said shakily. She nodded at the door. 'For coming when you did.'

He inclined his head. 'Hauptsturmführer Wessel exceeds his authority. The Tedeschi, the Germans, do not rule our country. Not yet.' His eyes narrowed slightly. 'I think it is better that you do not fall again into their hands.'

'We would rather fall into British hands,' Molly said hopefully.

'Regrettably this is also not possible.'

'We aren't spies.'

The colonel spread his hands. 'Maybe so, but unfortunately you are still our enemy.' He turned to the door. 'Now you eat and perhaps sleep. I try to arrange for beds. Tomorrow we take you to a better place.' He lifted his shoulders in a weary, ironic shrug. 'That is, if we survive the bombings from your RAF this night.'

Chapter Twenty-One

Four hours later, Jen was feeling aggrieved. It wasn't because the Italian colonel hadn't kept his word, because he had, more or less. The promised 'wardrobe', when it had eventually materialised, had consisted of two rough grey shirts and two pairs of cotton khaki trousers. None of it was new, but it was at least clean and dry. Jen had also got a pair of canvas boots that looked as though they had been made out of an old rucksack. They had also been given some bread and two pieces of very hard cheese, and a jug of what, bizarrely, seemed to be red wine. But the colonel's idea of beds fell very short of Jen's expectations. Two thick blankets did not, in her view, comprise a bed. And a bucket of cold water was hardly what she had meant when she demanded that they be allowed to wash.

His prediction about the bombing hadn't been far wrong either. They hadn't been killed yet, but the booming of the anti-aircraft fire seemed to be unnervingly close, and that, combined with her inability to get even remotely comfortable, meant she couldn't sleep.

It would be a cruel irony, she thought, as she turned over for probably the fiftieth time, if, after all they had been through in the last couple of days, they were killed by an overzealous British pilot.

In the light of a sudden flare, she glared over at her companion curled up on her blanket on the other side of the cell. That was what made her feel aggrieved. Because despite the noise outside, Molly was fast asleep. The blasted girl seemed to be able to sleep at the drop of a hat. Jen wondered if it was years of night duty at the hospital that had helped her develop the skill, or whether she simply had no sensitivity. She certainly didn't seem to have much pluck. Despite her idiotic talk of escape, Molly had been meek as a mouse with that ghastly German officer. Not that Jen entirely blamed her. She had been pretty frightened herself. But she wasn't going to admit that to Molly Coogan.

Giving up on sleep, Jen sat up and hugged her knees. No, her bravado with the German officer had been one big act. But it had been worth it to see the look on Molly's stupid face. And on the German officer's. She smiled grimly to herself. She had met bullies like that before, back-street theatre producers mostly, who put on seedy second-rate shows. Who thought they had power over you and wanted you to know it. She knew from experience that the only way to deal with people like that was to stand up to them. Even if they did have a pistol tucked ostentatiously into a holster on their belt.

But she had been reasonably confident that, however much the horrible man had blustered, he wouldn't really harm them. They were civilian women, for goodness' sake. There were international conventions and things about that.

She stood up and went over to the window. It was still dark and she could hear the wind whistling around the buildings. She tried to breathe calmly, to settle her racing pulse.

But it wasn't easy. It was so unfair that this should happen just when she had once again got a lucky break. It seemed as though she was being thwarted at every turn. But surely their incarceration wouldn't be for too long. There must be some system for handing back civilians.

Reassured by this thought, she settled down on her blanket again.

She felt she had only just closed her eyes when she heard the rattle of boots on concrete.

A soldier flung open their door. '*Venite per favore!*'

When they sat up and stared at him blankly, he beckoned urgently. '*Sbrigatevi!*' They had no idea what he was saying, but it was obvious what he meant.

Molly was already on her feet. Jen had just pulled on her new boots and was about to follow her out when she had a thought. Crouching down again, she gathered her discarded clothes and her blanket. She hesitated, then grabbed Molly's too. Whatever lay ahead, they might as well keep what little comfort they already had.

Outside in the courtyard, lights were suddenly blazing everywhere. Some of the trucks, loaded with soldiers, were already manoeuvring out through the archway. Others were firing up, belching smoke. Men were shouting and running about all over the place.

A sudden burst of gunfire nearby made Jen scream. A second later a plane roared overhead, gun blazing. The aircraft was so low that had it been daylight, Jen would have been able to see the pilot's face. Even so, she caught a glimpse of goggles in the cockpit. Then she realised Molly was shouting at her.

'This is our chance,' she was screaming. 'Look, if we are quick, we can get through the gate.'

Following her pointing arm, Jen saw that the arrival of the British plane had spooked the guards at the arched entrance to the courtyard. Two of them were trying to help a fallen comrade, two more were aiming their guns skywards; others were running into the building, whether to fetch weapons or to get under cover for the pilot's next pass it wasn't clear, but either way the archway was temporarily unattended.

'Quick,' Molly shouted. 'Run!' And she began to sprint across the courtyard.

But she wasn't quick enough. The young soldier who had fetched them was hot on her heels. Within seconds he had caught her, throwing her to the ground just as the plane roared over again. Jen saw his leg jerk as the plane's gun rattled once more. Then strong arms grabbed her, and she was half lifted, half thrown into the back of some kind of jeep, blankets and all. A second later, Molly was bundled in beside her. Two other men climbed in, the driver started the engine, and the vehicle roared out of the courtyard, almost tipping over as it cornered sharply on to the wet road.

With some difficulty, Jen disentangled herself from the blankets and eased herself up on to the metal seat. Molly was still lying on the floor. The makeshift bandage had come off her hand and intense pain showed on her face at every jolt and swerve of the truck.

'Are you all right?' Jen asked.

Molly tried to struggle up and winced. 'My finger hurts,' she said. 'I must have fallen on it again.'

As far as Jen was concerned, it served her right. But biting back her irritation, she helped Molly up on to the spare seat and wedged the blankets around her as best she could.

'What on earth were you playing at?' she said. 'You nearly got killed.'

Molly glared at her. 'If you hadn't just stood there like a great goop, we might have got away,' she snapped.

Jen stared at her incredulously. If she hadn't been clinging for dear life on to the side of the speeding vehicle, she would have hit her. What a bloody cheek, she seethed silently, turning her face away. As though it was her fault that Molly had been felled to the ground by an Italian soldier.

They were climbing steeply and had soon left the town. Mercifully the driver slowed a fraction, and a few minutes later, at a command from the man in the passenger seat, he stopped. Getting out, he produced a length of rope and grabbed Jen's right wrist. At the same time, the other soldier reached for Molly's bad hand.

'Please don't do this,' Molly whimpered, white-faced. 'Please just leave us here. We are no danger to anyone.'

'You bloody sadist,' Jen shouted at him, trying to jerk away.

But the soldier was too strong for her, and within seconds she and Molly were tied together.

The man in the front turned round. 'You are danger to me,' he said. 'I lose you, I get shot.'

Jen stared at him angrily. He looked back steadily. He had a thin, sallow face with premature frown lines on his forehead. 'Who are you?' she asked. 'Where are you taking us?'

'I am Capitano Guzzoni,' he said. 'I am to be your escort. I apologise for your discomfort. But I must hold you safe.' He nodded to the grim-faced soldier in the back. 'Caporale Rocca assists me. We go now to Messina. It will take some hours.'

Jen wanted to ask more, but the driver was back in his seat now and the engine was roaring.

'Are you all right?' she muttered awkwardly to Molly as they moved off again.

Molly nodded, but Jen could see she was close to tears. She wasn't surprised. The rope was tight and abrasive. God knew what it must feel like jerking against Molly's swollen hand.

They travelled on in jolting silence for an hour or so, swerving wildly from time to avoid occasional vehicles coming the other way. At last they rounded a high, steep bend in the road with a heart-numbing drop to one side. A second later, Captain Guzzoni shouted something and the driver screeched to a halt. The three men leaned forward to see out of the fly-splattered windscreen, and one by one they went rigid. Corporal Rocca swore under his breath.

Jen craned over to see what had caught their attention. Beyond the precipice they were perched on, the land swept down ahead of them towards the coast. It was still dark, windy and overcast and at first she couldn't see what they were looking at. Then she gasped. There, out on the wave-flecked sea, spread across the cloudy horizon, were masses and masses of ships.

She couldn't believe her eyes. They must be Allied ships, she realised. This must be the invasion.

But the scene was curiously static. Nothing seemed to be happening either out at sea or on shore. The only movement she could see was some animals – sheep, or maybe goats – ambling slowly across a distant hillside. The whole tableau was just poised there as though waiting for a signal to start.

And then, way below them, there was a booming roar as a coastal defence battery went into action. Flashes of flame began scudding across the rough sea towards the armada. And through the drifting plumes of smoke she noticed something else, almost invisible against the grey sea: a swarm of strange snub-nosed aircraft, swooping in towards the land.

'What are those?' she asked.

'*Alianti*.' Captain Guzzoni was looking through binoculars now.

'Gliders.' His voice was husky with shock. 'They bring your soldiers behind our positions.' He pointed to a large town on a promontory at the far edge of the island. 'I believe they try to cut off Siracusa.'

'Blimey,' Jen said. 'They don't look very safe.' It was clear even to her unpractised eye that the flimsy aircraft were being blown way off course by the strong wind. They seemed to be coming in too high, and too fast. She looked down at the patchwork of tiny fields and roads. 'Where on earth are they going to land?'

The officer just shrugged.

'But—'

Before she could speak, she saw one of the gliders crash into the side of the hill where the sheep were grazing. Even as she watched in dawning horror, she saw two more overshoot the town completely and nose-dive into the sea beyond.

Beside her, Molly put a hand to her mouth. 'Oh my God,' she whispered.

The driver gave a grunt of satisfaction and started up the vehicle again. And then a curve in the road put the dreadful scene out of sight.

As they turned away from the coast through the mountains, they began to encounter convoys of Italian tanks and trucks coming in the opposite direction. They were full of tense-looking young soldiers. The jeep was constantly having to pull over on the narrow road to let them trundle by.

Then they were away from the turmoil, driving along quieter roads in a bleak, treeless landscape, passing straggly villages where men were sitting, smoking calmly, on benches in front of shabby little bars, and old women dressed all in black were already working in tiny, steep fields. Later again they came upon a small gaggle of children in school uniform with tiny leather satchels on their backs, who waved and ran after them, shrieking delightedly.

Their high-pitched voices seemed to bring Molly to life again. Leaning forward, she tapped Captain Guzzoni imperiously on the shoulder. 'Where are our friends?' she shouted. 'The men we came with. What's happened to them?'

He looked round, clearly surprised by her temerity. 'They go to special camp,' he said. 'For seamen.'

'Oh dear.' Jen gave an exaggerated grimace. 'Poor old Conrad. That doesn't sound much fun.'

Molly's head snapped round. 'Don't you care what happens to him?'

'Not particularly,' Jen retorted irritably. 'Anyway, there's nothing I can do about it, is there?'

But in fact she had ended up quite liking Conrad Porter, and she would miss his dry humour. Yes, he had tried it on with her a bit at first, but it hadn't been serious. She knew she should tell Molly that nothing had happened between them, other than a bit of late-night drinking, but she just couldn't be bothered. She didn't care what Molly thought.

Soon after that, they hit wider roads, and now they began to encounter hastily erected military checkpoints. Nervous soldiers flagged them down and stared with open-mouthed amazement at Jen and Molly, roped together, wrapped in their blankets, clinging on like white-faced limpets with their free hands.

And then they were dropping down towards another substantial town, beyond which was a huge harbour half filled with ships.

Captain Guzzoni swung round in his seat. 'Here is Messina,' he said. 'From here we go to the mainland.'

It took a moment for Jen to realise the immediate import of what this meant. 'Oh no,' she wailed as her stomach heaved in anticipation. 'Not another sea voyage.'

Joyce couldn't believe it. No one would dare torpedo Jen. It was impossible. Not Jen.

She had heard the news from Ward Frazer earlier that morning. Katy had thought she would want to know, he had said. But Joyce didn't want to know. Especially as there were no details. No certainty. That made it worse. Because she didn't know how to feel. She couldn't mourn, not when there was still hope. But nor could she be normal when she knew something awful had happened. So she was stuck in an awful kind of limbo, and that made her feel low and cross.

Even Angie was subdued. After a brief burst of tears, she had mopped herself up and was now putting on a brave face. But it wasn't her usual sunny face, and that made Joyce even more irritable, because it meant people would soon start asking what was wrong, and she didn't want to talk about it. Not yet. Not until she knew more.

So when she bumped into Gillian James on her way to order next week's meat from Mr Dove in Northcote Road market later that day, she was not in the mood to be forgiving.

'Watch out,' she snapped as they collided on the corner of Wakehurst Road. Realising who it was, she stepped abruptly to one side. 'Oh, it's you,' she sniffed. 'I'm surprised you are up and about so early.'

Mrs James stiffened. 'What do you mean?'

'What do you think I mean? This is a nice neighbourhood and we don't need types like you giving it a bad name.'

The glamorous widow lifted her chin. 'I don't know what you are talking about.'

'Oh don't you?' Joyce sneered. 'Well it's not very difficult. Once word gets out what you are up to, there will be all types of unsavoury men prowling around Lavender Road. And that's not good. You aren't the only one with a teenage daughter, you know. Not that you seem to care about yours.'

'What do you mean by that?' Gillian James's neatly plucked brows drew together dangerously.

'Entertaining men while your daughter is in the house. That's disgusting. What a way to bring her up.'

'You mind your own business.'

'How can I, when the poor little thing is half starving?' Joyce retorted.

Gillian James's beautiful eyes flashed. 'So you are the busybody who's been giving her food. I don't know who you think you are to interfere in my life, but we don't need your charity or your opinion.'

Joyce had an urge to slap her pretty face, but managed to suppress it. 'What you need is a proper job. There is a war on, you know. There are people dying for the good of this country.' Her eyes filled unexpectedly with angry tears. 'My daughter, Jen, may be one of them,' she said. And then she walked away.

For ten days, one of the greatest tank battles ever had been raging around Kursk, just south of Moscow. It ended on 13 July with an overwhelming defeat for the German army. Hitler's prediction of a German victory that would 'shine like a beacon around the world' now looked like empty rhetoric.

It was good news, and Katy's takings increased that night as the Russkies were once again toasted for their valiant resistance to the Nazi war machine.

On the other hand, news that the French Resistance leader Jean Moulin had died after being captured and tortured by the Gestapo sent a shiver through her.

It also caused Helen to start worrying anew about the fate of André Cabillard. 'If he is still alive, he's not going to take that lying down,' she said. 'I just wish that I could get news of him before he does anything rash.'

It turned out that Ward had actually known Moulin. 'God, if only I could get my hands on whoever did that,' he said. And he and Helen had exchanged a glance that left Katy feeling sick.

There was also terrible news of an American air mission to bomb the guts out of the German aircraft industry at Regensburg. Sixty US bombers had been shot down in one night.

But overriding everything else, good news and bad, was Katy's desperation to hear word of Jen and Molly.

They knew now that four ships in the convoy had been sunk. A few lifeboats had been picked up. Many others were feared lost in the rough seas. Ward had been in touch with Henry Keller in Tripoli. It seemed that most of the ENSA group on the MS *Marigold* had been rescued and, having regrouped in Tripoli, were now intending going on as best they could with the scheduled shows. But six people were still unaccounted for, including Jen and Conrad Porter. In the absence of any other information, Henry was having to work on the assumption that they had all perished in the torpedo attack.

The bad weather had also affected the invasion of Sicily. But by 14 July, despite the shocking loss of the majority of glider crews during the advance landings, the Allies had taken Syracuse, Ragusa and Augusta, and it was rumoured that Hitler had summoned Mussolini to a meeting in northern Italy to discuss the worsening military situation.

Even though she was pleased about the Allied success, Katy wasn't particularly interested in the invasion of Sicily. Like so many others, she would have preferred them to try to take back France. Sicily seemed such a long way away. But at least the plethora of news about it, and her sorrow about Molly and Jen, had taken her mind off Ward's uncle.

So when, one morning in the middle of July, Maurice Frazer came into the pub, he took Katy completely by surprise.

She was even more surprised when he diverted on his way to the bar to lean over Malcolm's playpen. 'Well, young man,' he said with hearty bonhomie. 'It looks like you've grown even since I last saw you.'

Malcolm seemed pleased by this tribute and stood up to give his great-uncle a beaming smile. He offered him the toy he had been playing with. 'Air polane,' he said. 'My air polane.'

Maurice Frazer took the rather haphazard wooden aeroplane Ward had made out of an old drinks crate and inspected it critically. 'Hm,' he said, glancing at Katy. 'Did Ward make that?'

Katy nodded nervously and waited for some new tirade about Ward's disrespect for the family business. But it didn't come. Maurice Frazer merely handed the toy back to Malcolm. 'Let's hope my young fool of a son ends up flying something rather more airworthy than this contraption,' he said.

Katy could hardly believe her ears. 'You mean …?'

Maurice patted Malcolm on the head and straightened up. 'I've come to apologise,' he said gruffly. 'And to thank you.'

Katy blinked. 'To … thank me?'

He let out a slow breath. 'I know,' he said. 'You're surprised. And you have every reason to be. I'm sure you can imagine my reaction when Callum announced he wanted to enlist.' He gave her a beady look. 'Although I daresay you don't need to imagine it, because I know he told you. I wasn't pleased when I found he had come running over here.'

Avoiding his eye, Katy swallowed and turned silently to pour two small glasses of whisky. It was rather early for whisky, but he looked as though he needed it. It wouldn't be long, she thought to herself, somewhat hysterically, before Ward's relatives had drunk her out of house and home.

Maurice Frazer picked up the glass, swirled it absent-mindedly, then took a good swig.

'I was frightened,' he said. 'I didn't want to lose him.' He looked up at Katy with an almost pleading expression in his eyes. Pleading for understanding. 'He's my only son.'

Katy nodded. She did understand.

He looked at her but didn't speak. 'You are a good girl,' he said at last. 'I know what you said to Callum. You sent him back to me. You gave me a chance to reconcile myself. That's why I wanted to thank you.'

'You don't have to thank me,' Katy said. 'I just didn't want the same rift to come between you and Callum as has come between Ward and his father. Life is too short.' She thought suddenly of Molly and Jen. 'Especially at the moment.'

Maurice Frazer downed his whisky and, putting the glass down on the counter, held out his hand. 'We leave tomorrow,' he said. 'But I hope one day we will meet again. And then we will see what we can do to heal that rift.'

Katy blinked back sudden tears. 'Say goodbye to Callum for me,' she said, as they solemnly shook hands. 'He's a fine young man. Wish him luck. I'm sure he will make you very proud.'

By 23 July, US forces had taken Palermo, the capital of Sicily, trapping an estimated 50,000 Axis troops up in the north-west of the island. The remaining German and Italian troops were busy evacuating by ship via the north-east channel to the mainland.

General Eisenhower, the Allied commander-in-chief, described the capture of Palermo as 'the first page in the story of the liberation of the European continent'.

Katy was just absorbing this when a post girl came to the door with a telegram.

Telegrams were not normally good news, but as Katy couldn't imagine who would be sending one to her, she opened it quite calmly.

With regret I inform you, as Miss Molly Coogan's NOK, that it is feared Miss Coogan lost her life when MS Marigold *was sunk during torpedo attack 8 July.*

Katy couldn't take it in. She had no idea that Molly had put her down as next of kin. She was still staring at the page when Ward burst in through the door.

'I've just heard,' he said.

'So have I.' Katy could hardly breathe. She held up the telegram. 'They died when the ship went down.'

'No, no, they didn't,' Ward said. 'At least I'm pretty sure they didn't. We just got some intel back from the invasion forces. A lot of Italian prisoners were taken. They've been questioned and several of them have been talking about a group of people arriving in Sicily from a shipwreck. They were merchant seamen, but there was also a flamboyant character in a velvet smoking jacket.' He put his hands on Katy's shoulders. 'And two girls. The descriptions fit. And listen. It seems one of the girls started singing "Land of Hope and Glory" when she was being interrogated by a German SS officer. It apparently caused quite a stir. That just has to be Jen, doesn't it? And wait, there's more. The other girl tried to escape, but she was quickly caught.' He shook his head. 'That's Molly, for sure.'

Katy looked at him blankly. It didn't sound remotely like Molly to her, but she was willing to hope. 'So where are they now?'

Ward's eyes flickered. 'It's not clear. The invasion put everything in turmoil. The Italians were caught completely off guard. They hadn't expected it so soon, or on such a bad night. All we know is that the girls were taken off somewhere in a jeep. To an internment camp probably.'

An internment camp? Katy's mind was reeling. How could he sound so casual when it all sounded so awful. 'What about the SS officer?' she asked. 'What was he doing in Italy?'

'Italy is full of Germans,' Ward said. 'Hitler's trying to bolster their defences.' He caught Katy's expression. 'Sweetheart, it is good news. They are alive. They survived the torpedo attack.'

Katy's eyes were swimming. 'You must go and tell Joyce. She may have had the same telegram.'

Ward drew her into his arms. 'I already told her. I called at the café on the way back. And I sent a telegram to Henry in Tripoli too.'

Katy was glad to have Ward's arms round her. She felt strangely light-headed. Jen and Molly were alive. But her relief was mixed with a whole new anxiety. How on earth were they going to cope stuck in an internment camp together?

'What did Joyce say?' she murmured against Ward's chest.

Ward smiled. 'Not much. She seemed a bit overcome, but Angie was over the moon, and Mr Lorenz offered to stand everyone a cup of tea.'

Two days later, Benito Mussolini, the fascist dictator of Italy, was deposed.

Molly and Jen were in a train when they heard the news. They had spent a lot of time in trains since leaving Sicily. On their arrival on the mainland, they had sat in the first one, just outside Foggia station, for nearly three days.

Locked in a hot, stuffy compartment, with very limited access to any sanitation, in considerable danger from repeated Allied aerial attacks on the railway, they had spent their time watching other trains shunting around them, glaring at the numerous railway officials and soldiers who peered in as they pushed up and down the crowded corridor, and eating the flat dry bread and tomatoes that Corporal Rocca or Captain Guzzoni occasionally brought them. The rest of the time they had slept, or tried to sleep, hanging Molly's cloak over the door to give themselves a modicum of privacy as they lay along the wooden seats with the blankets folded under them to provide at least a tiny bit of comfort.

They had already suffered considerable discomfort in a dirty police cell at the port while they waited for room on a ship. The additional delay at Foggia had nearly driven Jen mad. 'I thought the only good thing about blessed Mussolini was that he made the trains run on time,' she grumbled.

'I don't know why you're so bothered,' Molly muttered. 'It's not as though we are going anywhere nice.'

'It's bound to be nicer than this,' Jen retorted.

Molly wasn't so sure, but eventually that train had moved off. It soon stopped again. They lost track of time. The bad weather had long gone, and during the daytime, the carriage was baking hot. Now they used Molly's cloak to swathe the window, trying to stop the sun blazing in, and no longer cared when men peered in through the corridor door, startled at the sight of Jen stretched out in her little black evening dress and Molly in a man's military shirt and not much else.

The first they knew of Mussolini's departure was when the train pulled into a dark station late one evening. As it sat there, puffing and wheezing, they heard screaming and shouting on the platform outside, and saw a group of people running through the station shouting, '*Benito finiti! Fascisti finiti!*'

One of the railway officials hurled a framed portrait of Mussolini out of the stationmaster's window, and several people jumped off the train and ran over to stamp on it, crunching the glass in a wild stomping dance. Others began tearing down a fascist eagle emblem from the wall.

Molly and Jen looked on in astonishment. For a wonderful moment they thought the rumpus meant that Italy had capitulated and that the war was over. But Captain Guzzoni quickly disabused them of that idea. Opening their door a few minutes later, he explained that Mussolini had been deposed, but that King Victor Emmanuel had appointed Marshal Badoglio in his place. Martial law had been declared. Italy would keep her pledge to Germany and the war would go on.

That evening they stopped again, this time in a siding in the middle of the countryside. Beside the tracks was an enormous field of sunflowers, their faces turned towards the setting sun. Moving slowly among them, tending them in some way, were half a dozen wizened old women, once again dressed all in black. Beyond were two lines of tall, very thin dark green trees. Distant hills were dotted with clusters of tiny red-roofed houses shimmering in the sunset.

The train sat there the whole night. In the early morning, a flock of thin goats, followed by an old man and a rangy dog, began making its way along the track, grazing the longer foliage, apparently unworried about the prospect of being mowed down by a passing locomotive.

'This is absolutely ridiculous,' Jen said for perhaps the hundredth time. 'Why doesn't that bloody man at least tell us what's going on?'

'Oh shut up,' Molly snapped. Jen was constantly trying to pick a fight with Captain Guzzoni. But in Molly's opinion, the captain was doing his best, in clearly difficult circumstances, to keep them fed and watered and protected from the other inhabitants of the various trains they had been on. He wasn't enjoying the journey any more than they were. They occasionally saw him or his surly sidekick Corporal Rocca on the verge outside, smoking, chatting, in the company of other soldiers. They looked tired and weary too. Their occasional laughter sounded bitter.

Molly had it in her heart to feel sorry for them. Not only was their country under Allied attack from the south, but it seemed they were also being browbeaten to stand up for themselves by the Germans to the north. In the middle was Captain Guzzoni, stuck in a siding, unable to do anything about any of it. It wasn't surprising he looked so morose.

The next day, taking pity on their boredom, Captain Guzzoni produced a pack of cards. It was an odd pack; there were only ten cards in each suit, and instead of diamonds, hearts, clubs and spades, there were cups, coins, swords and batons. The number cards only ran up to seven; the court cards were knave, knight and king. There was no queen at all. It was very strange and foreign.

It quickly became clear that Jen was no card player, so Molly amused herself with endless rounds of patience. With her injured finger, it was painful handling the cards, but she persevered, reckoning it was good physiotherapy. But even that palled after a while. Then, remembering the techniques she had learnt with George Nelson, she began to practise shuffling and riffling, until the snap and rustle of the cards began to get on Jen's nerves.

But just as Molly was about to put the cards away, Jen changed her mind. 'Go on then,' she said suddenly. 'Do a trick on me.'

Molly cringed. With her scathing remarks and sharp little eyes, Jen had to be the worst audience she could possibly imagine. But she knew she would mock her if she refused.

Before she even began the trick, Molly could feel her hands shaking. But Jen was gratifyingly impressed when the four aces appeared on top of the pack. And even more so when the seven of swords, which she had memorised and carefully slid back into the middle of the pack, turned up lying on the seat next to her.

The heat and her nerves were making Molly's hands sweat. The cards were already slick in her palms. So she decided to finish off her routine with a French drop, using the silver magic carpet from the necklace that Ward had given her as her prop. Under cover of a nod towards the door and a comment about Captain Guzzoni passing down the corridor, even eagle-eyed Jen didn't notice her palm the tiny ornament.

'How on earth did you do that?' Jen exclaimed, when Molly had successfully magicked it out of one of her discarded boots. 'If we ever get out of this godforsaken country, you ought to jump ship and join ENSA.'

Molly felt unduly gratified by this compliment, but just as she was preparing to slip the charm back on to the chain, Jen reached over and took it from her hand. 'What is this anyway?'

'It's a magic carpet,' Molly said, fighting an urge to snatch it back. She didn't want Jen handling her precious gift.

Jen studied the tiny silver charm. 'It's nice,' she said. 'Where did you get it?'

'Ward Frazer gave it to me,' Molly said. She could feel herself beginning to blush. 'To thank me for helping with Helen de Burrel.' She sensed Jen's eyes on her and rushed on. 'He told me it has the power to make your wishes come true.'

Jen rolled her eyes mockingly as she handed the charm back to Molly. 'Then I wish that this damn train would start moving again,' she said.

The words were barely out of her mouth when, with a sudden jolt and a wheezing vibration, the train came to life. The timing of it made them both laugh.

It felt strange. As Molly put the necklace on again, she realised it was probably the first time she had laughed since leaving England. It was certainly the first time she had ever laughed with Jen Carter.

But the unexpected rapport didn't last.

They pulled into Rome late that evening. It was immediately clear from the battered state of the station and the lines of damaged trains that their previous delays had been as a result of extensive Allied bombing of the railway system.

When Captain Guzzoni came in with the familiar length of rope, he looked more glum than usual. Taking advantage of his evident shock at the state of his capital city, Jen pleaded with him not to rope them together.

Guzzoni hesitated. 'OK,' he said. 'But one of you run, we shoot both, yes?'

Assuming that Jen had made the request with an ulterior motive, Molly at once began to wonder if there might indeed be a chance to escape. Surely in such a big city they would be able to hide out until the Allies arrived. Captain Guzzoni was hardly going to shoot them in a crowded street. But when Jen saw her glancing around, she nudged her sharply in the ribs.

'Don't you dare,' she hissed as the two men led them out of the enormous station concourse into a long, unbelievably hot street.

'We've got to try,' Molly whispered.

'We haven't got to try anything,' Jen snapped. 'I'm damned if I'm going to get shot just because you got some mad ideas from bloody Ward Frazer.'

'I'm worried about what they are going to do to us,' Molly muttered.

'They aren't going to do anything,' Jen said. 'They are probably going to register us or something before arranging to hand us back.'

Jen was wrong. They were registered. But they weren't handed back.

Instead, after two days of being locked in a hot, airless room on the third floor of the building, they were handcuffed and taken by truck to a prison camp for female enemy aliens.

There they were forcibly stripped naked, hosed down with cold water, and inspected for lice by two large, grim-faced female warders. They were then issued with loose-fitting grey trousers and tunics embroidered with big red diamond-shaped POW identification patches, and pushed into a stifling bunkroom, where they were allocated two hard slatted beds, one on top of the other.

So that's it, Molly thought, as the door of the hut banged shut behind them. We've failed. We've missed our chance of escape. There's no way we are going to get out of here.

It was very hot in London too. The pub was crowded, people spilling out into the street to get cool.

Katy was just wondering how to keep track of the glasses when she saw

Aaref pushing through the jam. 'Please, Katy,' he called urgently, white-faced and clearly harried. 'You must come!'

'What is it?' Katy asked, alarmed. 'What's happened?'

'It's Louise,' Aaref said. 'She is screaming and screaming. I don't know what to do. I thought of her parents, but ...' He tailed off and lifted his shoulders in one of his foreign shrugs. They both knew that Louise didn't have a good relationship with her parents. They, more than anyone, had disapproved of her messing around with Aaref, and now they disapproved of her messing around with Charlie Hawkridge.

Katy looked around in dismay. The bar was busy and she didn't like to leave Helen on her own, especially not with Malcolm asleep upstairs. But there didn't seem to be any choice. So she told Helen what had happened and that she'd be back as soon as possible, and followed Aaref out into the street.

Louise was still wailing as Katy and Aaref climbed the fire escape that led to the little attic apartment she rented from Mrs D'Arcy Billière. She was lying curled up in a tight ball on a mattress on the floor. Her eyes were screwed shut and she was howling like an injured animal.

'Louise?' Katy shook her shoulder gently. 'It's me. What's the matter?'

But Louise didn't respond. She was completely hysterical. Glancing rather helplessly round the room to see what on earth might have caused her distress, Katy noticed a crumpled piece of flimsy yellow paper in the corner.

A telegram.

Oh no, she thought, picking it up and smoothing it out.

It was cruelly brief and to the point.

Important. From Admiralty London. Deeply regret to inform you that your husband C00820791 Lt Jack Delmaine has been killed on active service. Sincere sympathy.

Katy sat down on the bed and put her hand to her head.

Jack Delmaine. Young, eager, fresh-faced Jack Delmaine.

She thought suddenly of Louise and Jack's wedding. Louise's gleeful delight. Jack's pride in his beautiful, glowing bride. He had been so eager to please her. So excited. So in love.

Katy closed her eyes. It was too cruel. She couldn't bear it. But nor could she bear the awful noise Louise was making.

Looking up, she realised that Aaref was still standing by the door, watching her.

She stood up and handed him the crumpled telegram. 'It's Jack,' she said. 'He's dead. I'm going to fetch Mrs Rutherford.'

By the time Katy eventually got back to the pub, it was nearly closing time.

Her hand was on the door when she saw Ward jogging up the street towards her.

'Katy, what are you doing out here? Is everything OK?'

'No, not really,' Katy said. She told him what had happened and he swore under his breath and hugged her close.

'Oh no. Poor Louise. Poor you. I know you were fond of him. He was a real nice guy.'

But then he hesitated, and she sensed he had news of his own.

She leaned back from his embrace to look up at him. 'What is it? Have you heard something more about Molly or Jen?'

He shook his head. 'No. It's not that.'

'Then what?' Katy insisted, pulling back further. 'What is it?'

He let her go, grimaced, and ran a hand through his hair. 'I guess it's a bad time to tell you,' he said. 'But I may have to go away.'

'When?'

'Soon.'

Katy swallowed. There was something in his eyes that told her it wasn't going to be a quick overnight trip to some RAF base in Norfolk. 'Where?'

'I shouldn't tell you.'

She glared at him. 'Tell me.'

He drew her into the doorway and lowered his voice. 'Corsica. But that's only between you and me. No one else must know.'

Katy stared at him blankly. Corsica? For a second she couldn't even think where Corsica was. An island in the Mediterranean somewhere. Underneath France. Next to Italy.

He saw her confusion. 'It's currently occupied by the Germans, but technically it's part of France and there's a strong resistance movement there. They want someone to go in and help.'

'But you aren't fit.'

He shrugged. 'I was passed fit this morning.'

He was trying to sound regretful, but he couldn't keep the excitement out of his voice. Katy suddenly realised that he wanted to go. He'd wanted to go all this time.

'But the pub? Malcolm? The baby?' She could hear the desperation in her voice.

So apparently could he. He drew her into his arms again and hugged her close. 'I know, sweetheart,' he murmured. 'I know. But this is important. This is a chance to do some real damage to the Nazis. It won't be for long.'

Important? Not for long? Katy had heard those words before. Before his last dreadful trip to France. And now he was going to abandon her again.

For a second she was still, rigid. Then she jerked out of his embrace.

'Then go,' she shouted at him, taking a step back. 'Go and get killed like Jack Delmaine. See if I care.'

Chapter Twenty-Two

Ward did go. He left at the end of August, the day after a war conference between Winston Churchill and President Roosevelt ended in Quebec with a buoyant 'forward now to Victory' communiqué to the press.

Katy had made up with him long before then. The morning after her outburst in fact. After a silent, awkward night, one of the most horrid nights she had ever known, she had apologised for snapping at him. Ward said there was nothing to forgive. He understood. He sympathised with her anxiety. But it was wartime and he had to do his duty, just like everyone else. He'd hugged her and kissed her. And afterwards, on the surface at least, everything went back to normal. He didn't mention the incident again. He was the same loving husband, kind, attentive, helpful in the bar in the evenings, sweet with Malcolm, happy to cook and clean up, everything a perfect husband should be.

He had even taken steps to provide some extra help for her in his absence. He had recently met a Jewish family who, like some of the downed aircrew, had escaped France by dint of an arduous trek over the Pyrenees into Spain. By using the last of their salvaged jewellery to bribe the captain of a merchant vessel, they had eventually managed to get themselves to England, but had then been interned as enemy aliens.

It was as he interviewed them about their journey through France that Ward gleaned that before the German invasion, the daughter had worked in a bar in Paris. He had suggested that when her release was arranged, she should come and see Katy with a view to possibly doing some work in the pub.

On his last morning Ward told Katy that he loved her and would be back as soon as he could. She tried to believe him.

But after he had gone she not only felt bereft, she also felt she hadn't apologised enough. She desperately wished she could take those bitter words back. It was too late now. He was gone. There was still so much she wanted to say to him, so much more she wanted to explain. She had wanted to plead with him to be careful, not to do anything rash. But the faint flicker of dismay in his eyes when she tried to broach the subject stopped her. There was a new constraint between them. It was barely noticeable, but it was there nevertheless.

All in all, the day after his departure, Katy wasn't feeling her best. It didn't help that the pregnancy was still making her feel nauseous and weary. Thinking of Ward made her want to weep. Superstitiously, she wished there was something of his that she could keep with her at all times, like a talisman, or a good luck charm. And then she remembered the jewellery he had given her. She couldn't wear the brooch, not on her work pinafore, but she could wear the bracelet he had brought her back from North Africa. She had been keeping them both for best, but with Ward gone away there wouldn't be much best.

Pleased with the idea, she ran upstairs and went over to her dressing table. But when she opened the little trinket box her parents had given her as a child, she stared in dismay.

It was empty. Completely empty.

She was still standing there in shock when Helen arrived for work. 'Katy, are you all right? What's happened?'

What had happened was that someone had clearly come upstairs into her and Ward's private space and stolen her jewellery. Katy felt as though she had been kicked in the stomach.

'But how?' Helen asked. 'Who could get up here without being seen?'

Who indeed? It was impossible to know. Katy hadn't looked in the jewellery box for several weeks. After some thought, they decided that the most likely opportunity for a burglary had been the night when Louise had received the telegram about Jack.

'Distraction,' Helen said. 'We were distracted and someone took advantage of it.'

'Well, we can't blame Gillian James this time,' Katy said. The widow hadn't been in the bar that night, and, anyway, it was increasingly clear she had other fish to fry. She had been seen on more than one occasion letting men into her house.

'You've got to go to the police,' Helen said.

Katy sighed. 'They didn't take any notice of me when I told them the glasses were going missing.'

'Well you'll have to make them take notice this time. This isn't petty pilfering, this is downright theft.'

Having been so frightened by the German officer in Sicily, Molly was relieved when the Italian authorities accepted their story of the torpedo attack and registered them merely as enemy aliens.

The ruthlessness of their reception at the prison camp had been a shock, but once Molly had got over that, and learnt the ropes, she settled into the new routine. Her broken finger was improving and her broken tooth had become less sensitive, though she still had a black eye from when she had been knocked out on the lifeboat. Jen had kindly told her that she looked as though she had been run over by a double-decker bus.

There weren't actually many ropes to learn. Molly was used to communal living, and in an odd way this wasn't so very different from the Wilhelmina nurses' home.

There were about thirty women incarcerated in the camp. Many of them were Italian Jews. Few of them spoke English. There were also two rather posh Englishwomen whose Italian husbands had apparently been too outspoken about their dislike of the fascist regime. The two women had known each other prior to their internment and spent all their time together, muttering darkly about the 'situation' and lurking around the warder's office trying to catch the news broadcasts on their jailors' wireless.

As Molly couldn't understand a word of it, there was no point in her listening to the news, but the two English ladies, Nancy and Betty, passed on snippets of information. Despite the incessant jingoistic rhetoric, they were convinced that Italy would soon surrender.

But until that happened, all Molly could do was queue for meals, practise the exercises the QA sister on the boat had taught her, and play endless rounds of patience with the pack of cards she had failed to return to Captain Guzzoni. Mostly she lay or sat on the ground, enjoying the beautiful weather, thinking nostalgically about London and the life she'd left behind.

Her secret passion for Ward Frazer had subsided into a dull ache, almost a distant dream. Dr Florey, Katy, Helen de Burrel, George and the Nelsons seemed to belong to a different world. She even thought quite fondly of the Wilhelmina. How safe and untroubled her little life there now seemed. And yet how she'd longed to get away. Maybe she should have been more careful about what she wished for.

Automatically she lifted her fingers to her throat. She had been allowed to keep the charm necklace. The female warders were strict and hard-nosed, but they weren't inhuman. Even the army blankets Jen had stolen from the police station in Sicily had been restored to them, and their ragged clothes, such as they were, had been washed and embroidered with a big red square that denoted the status of POW, presumably in case they made an escape attempt.

Not that there was much chance of that. The soldiers who patrolled the double perimeter fence of the camp were diligent and alert. The fence was high, and the only exit, the main gate, was controlled by the warders. And even if they did get out, where on earth would they go? Maybe Jen had been right all along, Molly thought, leaning back against the wall and turning her bruised face to the sun. Maybe it was better to sit it out and wait for the Allies to arrive.

Jen, on the other hand, hated the camp from the word go. The mortifying indignity of their arrival had appalled her, and the communal living didn't suit her at all. She railed at everything: the hard bunks, the drab uniforms, the dour warders, the other women, the lack of privacy, the smelly huts, the unspeakable lavatories – basically a stinking hole in the ground – the excruciating heat, the mosquitoes. And the food.

When she'd moaned to Molly about the food, Molly had said it was better than what they got at the Wilhelmina. Well as far as Jen was concerned, that just went to show how mad anyone was who wanted to become a nurse. Nobody in their right mind could enjoy a meal that looked (and tasted) like white slugs basking in a pool of oily blood-red gravy.

And as for the communal washroom. Well, in there, modesty went straight out of the window. Jen couldn't believe how casually some of the other women stripped off, brazenly exposing bottoms and bosoms with no apparent embarrassment.

Jen hated stripping off in public. Once, at the beginning of her acting career, desperate for money, she had reluctantly agreed to pose nude in a tableau in a back-street variety show. It had been the worst experience of her life. Worse even than the torpedo attack. Humiliated by the catcalls from the leering drunken audience, she had felt degraded by the whole experience, and had sworn never, ever to put herself through something like that again.

There had only ever been one person Jen had been comfortable being naked in front of, and that was Sean Byrne, the young Irishman to whom she had lost her virginity back at the beginning of the war. She wondered now how she could have been so bold, but there had been something about his humorous Irish charm that had made it seem easy and natural.

It would have been different with Henry Keller. Henry was so polished, so well groomed, so assured, so observant and so critical. The thought of him thinking she was too thin, or too freckly, or that she wasn't doing it right, gave her the shivers. No, as far as she was concerned, sex was a minefield, best avoided.

But she would rather have sex with Adolf Hitler himself than stay much longer in this beastly camp. She couldn't understand how Molly seemed so relaxed, chatting with those two stuck-up Englishwomen and endlessly playing clock patience with her stupid playing cards.

Jen knew nobody in the camp liked her, but she didn't care. She knew her attitude was making it worse for herself, but she couldn't help it. She was bored and angry. She remembered the letter her mother had received via the International Red Cross from Bob, also a prisoner of war somewhere in Italy. She felt a bit more sympathetic than when she had read his stupid letter. His griping no longer seemed quite so unjustified. She wished the Red Cross would visit this camp so that she too might receive food parcels and be able to send letters home, but as yet no one had materialised. And the old harridans in charge of the camp just shrugged their shoulders irritably and pretended not to understand what she was talking about when she tried to ask if her family would have been told where she was.

The only thing that gave Jen any pleasure was the admiring glances she got from the guards when she occasionally ambled round the perimeter fence whenever it wasn't too hot, trying to muster some amusement at the sight of Molly doing her idiotic exercises. Some of the other women had joined Molly now, and the sight of them all bending and stretching in unison was enough to make a cat laugh.

The soldiers on sentry duty thought it was hilarious too. If their superior officer wasn't present, they would try to talk to Jen, egging each other on, trying to outdo each other with their flattery and gesticulating enthusiastically when she tried out some Italian words. They weren't much more than boys, farmhands and factory boys, feeling important because they had been given a uniform. She guessed they wouldn't be far different from Angie's so-called fiancé Gino. She would certainly give Angie what-for about that when she got home. If she ever got home.

The young soldiers were clearly idiots, but at least it was a relief to know they didn't think she looked a complete fright, not like Molly Coogan with her bruised face, broken tooth and lank hair. Jen's own hair had gone dry and frizzy in the heat and she had taken to tying it back with a strip ripped off her old dress.

That was another annoying thing about Molly: she didn't seem to mind the heat, whereas Jen could hardly bear to stay in the sun more than a few minutes. Even that caused her skin to burn and her lips to blister. Mostly she lay despondently on her bunk, scratching her bites, half listening to the desultory conversations of the dreary Jewish women, who also generally huddled indoors, and wishing that she hadn't been quite so dismissive of Molly's earlier attempts to escape.

Katy was on the way back from the police station when she bumped into Pam, George and baby Nellie heading up to the common so George could have a dip in the pond. On hot days, the Long Pond on Clapham Common had become a magnet for local boys, some of whom seemed to spend their entire time trawling the bottom, trying to find pieces of shell casing and shrapnel from the nearby ack-ack guns. It wasn't the most salubrious place to swim but Pam had found it a reasonably satisfactory way of keeping George amused and out of mischief during the summer holidays.

She had been shocked to hear about the theft of the jewellery. 'What did the police say?' she asked now.

'Not much,' Katy said.

'But do they have any suspects?'

Katy grimaced. 'I think they've got their eye on a couple of men who drink in the pub. The Garrow brothers. They're pals of that awful Barry Fish. I've seen them together. But they've got no evidence against them. Or him.'

Pam frowned. 'So what are they going to do?'

'There seems to be nothing they can do,' Katy said with a sigh. 'Not unless they catch one of them red-handed.' She felt so cross, so bitterly upset. 'It was bad enough when the glasses went missing, but Ward gave me that jewellery, and now he's gone away and ...' she stopped, aware of George's eyes on her, and tried to pull herself together.

'In some countries people who steal things get their hands cut off,' George said. 'Does that happen here?'

Katy gave a choked laugh. 'No, I don't think so.'

'Well it should,' he said. 'If I found someone stealing my things, I'd run him over with my go-cart.'

When Katy got back to the pub, Helen was reading a letter from her father.

'He's just arrived back in Washington from Canada,' she said. 'He was at the summit in Quebec. He says they had some sumptuous dinners and the PM was looking quite fat.'

'Winston Churchill always looks fat,' Katy said. 'I'm sure all that food and drink can't be good for him.'

Helen laughed. 'That's probably why he always takes his doctor with him when he travels.' She folded the letter and put it away. 'By the way,' she added, 'you just missed Louise.'

'Oh dear.' Katy still felt guilty for her irritation with Louise that evening when the telegram had come. Louise had taken Jack's death very hard and it didn't look as though she was going to bounce back easily. Jack's parents had been up to see her. Katy remembered them from the wedding and felt so sorry for their loss. They were such nice people, so proud of Jack. So concerned for Louise. They had offered to have her to stay for a while if she wanted, but Louise declined. She was too unhappy to go anywhere. She just wanted to stay in the flat where Jack had made her so happy.

Helen had raised an eyebrow when she heard that. 'Oh really?' she had remarked. 'I thought it was Charlie Hawkridge who had made her so happy in that flat?'

'Don't,' Katy said. 'I suppose we should be thankful she hasn't turned to him for comfort.'

'I don't see him as the comforting type,' Helen said drily.

In fact over the first weeks of her bereavement, it was Aaref Hoch who had borne the brunt of Louise's grief. He listened to her agony, brought her flowers to cheer her, walked with her on the common to make her take some fresh air, and took her to the café to encourage her to eat.

'She was in a bit of a state,' Helen said now. 'She's been told that if she doesn't go back to work soon, she'll lose her job.'

'Oh, poor Louise,' Katy said. 'I do feel sorry for her.'

'So do I,' Helen said. 'But it is wartime, after all, and there are plenty of people who have lost loved ones and been back at work the next day.'

Katy glanced at her. It wasn't like Helen to be so hard. But she was suffering too, of course. Nine months had elapsed since she had left France in that submarine the previous November. And in all that time, through her illness, her recovery, and her subsequent hard graft at the pub, she hadn't heard one word from or about André Cabillard. Not one single thing to give her even a flicker of hope. Katy knew only too well what that sort of silence was like. It was enough to bring anyone down. Even someone as resilient as Helen de Burrel.

Joyce was skinning beetroot when Angie's face loomed through the hatch.

'That feller of Jen's has just come in,' Angie said. 'That Henry Keller. He's back from North Africa and wants to know if he can have a word.'

'Oh Lord,' Joyce responded. She looked at her bright red hands. 'You'd better tell him to sit down. And give him a cup of tea. I'll be there in a minute.'

Joyce had always been a bit shy of Henry Keller; he seemed so grand, somehow, with his elegant good manners, his big shows and hobnobbing with the stars and all that. But today he looked less calm and collected than normal. He was just as handsome as usual, perhaps even more so with a healthy tan from the North African sun. But there was tension in his courteous smile.

'I am so sorry to intrude,' he said. 'But I had to come and see if you had any more news of Jennifer. Ward Frazer sent me a telegram to say that she'd been seen in Sicily, but I've heard nothing since.'

'Nor have we,' Joyce said. 'Apart from about her singing "Land of Hope and Glory" to some SS officer.'

'Good God,' he said.

He looked momentarily impressed when she told him what she knew, but he didn't seem very amused. He actually looked rather pale under his tan. 'Mrs Carter, I'm so sorry. This is all my fault. If I hadn't asked her to go …'

Joyce shook her head. 'It wasn't your fault. She needed the work.'

'Well, yes, perhaps, but even so …'

He stopped, and Joyce looked at him more closely. She could see the strain in his eyes and wondered fleetingly if he felt equally responsible for his other missing cast members. Or if he had his own reasons for being so especially concerned about Jen. If he had been a lesser man, she might have patted him reassuringly on the arm. But it didn't quite seem appropriate with Henry Keller.

'I'm sure Jen will be all right,' she said instead. 'She always falls on her feet.'

He seemed doubtful. 'Does she? I'm not sure how easy it would be to fall on your feet in occupied Europe.'

'Well, no,' Joyce agreed. The blasted man was making her feel all anxious again now. And she needed to get back to her beetroot. 'But I'm sure I'll hear something from the Red Cross soon. I've given them her name and description and all.'

Henry took out a smart leather wallet and extracted a business card. 'Let me give you my address,' he said as he stood up. 'If you hear anything, anything at all, perhaps you could let me know?'

'Of course,' Joyce said.

He wanted to pay for his tea, but Joyce wouldn't let him. 'Good gracious, no,' she said. 'It's the least I can do after you got me and Mr Lorenz those theatre tickets.'

He smiled then, that well-mannered smile. 'That was my pleasure. But thank you, I appreciate it.'

Angie scurried over to the window to watch him walk off down the street. Then she turned to Joyce. 'I know he's all cool and sophisticated and that. But I think deep down he's sweet on Jen, don't you?'

Joyce was just wondering how to respond when she was distracted by the sight of Bella James walking up the other side of the road. After her spat with Gillian James, she had left a note in the jam jar saying she didn't need the weeds any more as there was enough food in the garden for Monty.

It was true, but Joyce felt bad about it. The girl was so thin, so pretty, so silent. The last time she had seen her was up on the common, sitting on a bench all on her own, with her nose in a book. It wasn't her fault she had such a slut of a mother.

Picking up a bun, she pressed a slice of Spam into it and called Angie over. 'Here, run out and give this to Bella James,' she said.

She glanced at Mrs Rutherford, who was clearing a nearby table. 'You don't mind, do you? That poor child's not getting enough to eat.'

As Mrs Rutherford nodded her approval, Joyce watched Angie running across the road. She saw the girl's start of surprise as Angie thrust the bun into her hand.

Next to Angie, Bella James really did look like a waif. They were roughly the same height, but Angie probably weighed twice as much as the younger girl. Angie certainly wasn't short of food, Joyce thought drily. Working in the café hadn't been good for her daughter's figure, mainly because she ate everyone else's leftovers. Not that there were many leftovers. Nevertheless, Angie was about the only person in London who looked rosy-cheeked and well nourished. If it wasn't for the hops she went to in the evenings, she would probably be the size of a barrage balloon by now.

Angie crossed back over the road. But before she got to the door of the café, she was waylaid by Barry Fish.

Barry Fish was the last person Joyce wanted Angie talking to. She rapped on the glass to attract her attention. But it was too late. Angie was smiling at him and shaking her head.

And then she was back in the café. 'She said to say thank you,' she said.

'What were you doing talking to Mr Fish?' Joyce asked crossly.

'Who?' Angie looked puzzled. She followed Joyce's glance out of the window. Barry Fish was still standing on the kerb outside, staring up the street in the direction Bella James had taken. 'Oh, that bloke. He's always hanging around. He's harmless enough. He's lonely, I think. He's always offering me sweets and bits of make-up and that.'

Joyce stared at her, appalled. 'I hope you never take it?'

'Oh no,' Angie said airily. 'It's all rubbishy stuff. Anyway, I told him my fiancé wouldn't approve.'

Joyce felt mildly relieved at this. But she was increasingly concerned about Angie's constant references to the absent Gino. Sometimes she wondered if he even existed.

'Have you heard from Gino recently?' she asked later as they cleared up together after closing time.

Angie shook her head. 'No, he's not very good at letters,' she said.

Joyce hesitated. 'But you are sure he knows he is your fiancé?'

'Oh yes,' Angie said. She put some dishes in the sink and turned on the tap. 'He asked me to marry me when I was on the farm.'

'A lot of young men say that sort of thing,' Joyce suggested tentatively.

'But they don't always really mean it.'

Angie looked up, surprised. 'Oh, Gino meant it,' she said. 'I know he meant it.'

After what had happened to Molly and Jen's ship, Katy was relieved to receive a telegram from Ward saying that he had arrived safely in Tunis. She wasn't so pleased with the second part of the message. *Will be out of touch for a while now stop Don't worry stop Back asap stop All love W*

'It's war,' Helen said. 'It's what happens. It's hideous, but it has to be done.'

Katy sighed. 'I'd feel better if I trusted the SOE to let me know if anything happens to him.'

Helen hesitated. 'I still know people there,' she said. 'I can ask them to keep an ear out.'

'Would you?' Katy asked eagerly. 'And about Molly and Jen too?'

Glancing up suddenly, she caught a pensive look on Helen's face and frowned. 'But I don't want you going back there if it upsets you.'

'No.' Helen shook her head. 'I was just thinking about—' She stopped abruptly and flushed slightly before starting again. 'They promised to let me know if they had any news of André and they never have. I don't want to give up hope. But ...'

'No,' Katy said fiercely. 'You must never give up hope. Never. I of all people know that.'

On 3 September, Allied forces landed on mainland Italy.

The news broadcasts on the prison warders' wireless now took on a different tone. Even to Molly's untutored ears, the Italian voices sounded both nervous and angry. The two English ladies, Nancy and Betty, told her that Winston Churchill was insisting on unconditional surrender, but the Italian government were refusing to capitulate. They had rid themselves of fascism and they felt they deserved some credit for that. Italy had her pride. She would fight on to the death rather than surrender on those terms.

It didn't sound promising.

But then suddenly, unexpectedly, on the evening of 8 September, Italy did surrender. Marshal Badoglio announced that hostilities between Italian and Anglo-American forces would cease forthwith.

Molly was walking back to her hut carrying a dish of rice and meatballs when she heard one of the warders shouting through the gate to the soldiers outside. At first the sentries looked bemused, then they gave a desultory cheer. One of them laid his rifle on the ground and started dancing round it. '*Armistizio! La guerra è finita!*'

318

Nancy and Betty were delighted. They too danced a little jig of joy.

'So what happens now?' Molly asked.

But nobody seemed to know. The Allied forces were still absolutely miles away, right down in the south of Italy. There was no chance of them arriving any time soon. And what about all the German troops who had evacuated to the mainland from Sicily? It seemed unlikely that they would just pack up and go home.

'So are the Italians now fighting the Germans?' Molly asked.

'It's not clear,' Nancy said. 'Badoglio wasn't specific. He certainly hasn't declared war on Germany.'

'Well what has he done?' Jen asked.

'He's gone off to Brindisi with the King,' she said.

'It sounds like a complete shambles,' Jen said irritably.

It was a shambles. But by the following morning, the sentries had taken matters into their own hands by melting away into the countryside. A couple of hours later, the female warders decided that their role had also come to an end and they too disappeared, taking their wireless and all the food from the kitchen with them.

'What on earth do we do now?' Jen asked.

'Betty and I are going to wait for our friends to come and collect us,' Nancy said stolidly. 'They know where we are.'

'Well that's all right for you,' Jen said. 'But Molly and I haven't got any friends.'

Or any money, Molly thought. Or indeed any idea of where to go, or what to do. If only Ward Frazer was here, she thought. He would know exactly what to do.

'Let's give it one more day,' she suggested. 'Surely some government official will come and help us.'

But the following morning it wasn't Nancy or Betty's friends, nor an Italian official, who appeared at the camp, but a troop of grim-faced German soldiers in round metal helmets.

They arrived in a small truck, an open field car and two sinister-looking motorbikes with sidecars, which they parked across the gates.

Hearing the roar of engines, Molly ran with several of the other women to the entrance to see who it was. Oh no, she thought. Why didn't we leave when we had the chance? How could we be so stupid?

Half a dozen of the men had already taken up positions either side of the gates. The rest, at a barked command from an officer in the car, spread out around the perimeter.

Once the camp was secure, the officer got out of the car. Straightening up, he glanced at the group of inmates clustered at the entrance. 'My name is Hauptmann Kleber,' he said pleasantly, in almost perfect English. 'I need you to assemble in silence on the parade ground immediately. This camp is now under my command.'

Just as he began to repeat this statement in Italian, to Molly's dismay one of the English women, Betty, stepped forward. 'Under what authority?' she asked.

Hauptmann Kleber looked at her for a long moment as she stood there trembling angrily in front of him. Then he slowly peeled off one of his gloves.

'Under the authority of the Third Reich,' he said, and lifting the glove, he slapped it hard across her face. He watched with indifference as she reeled back in shock, tears springing to her eyes. 'And the Third Reich does not permit insubordination. Is that understood?'

Chapter Twenty-Three

Hauptmann Kleber had a thing for roll calls. That first day he kept them standing on the parade ground in the broiling sun for an hour and a half while one of his men took down their names and nationalities. Four others searched the huts for weapons or anything else that might help them escape.

'This is your fault,' Jen hissed at Molly. 'I said we should leave when we had the chance.'

Molly glanced nervously around to make sure none of their new guards were in earshot. Talking was forbidden. She didn't know what the penalty would be, and certainly didn't want to find out.

'Well you didn't say it loud enough,' she muttered. 'Yes, we should have gone, but we didn't. But surely we'll be rescued soon. The Allies are on their way. We have to look on the bright side.'

'The bright side?' Jen's voice rose. 'There's not going to be any bright side of this. Not with these Nazi thugs in charge.'

'Shh,' Molly said. 'I'm sure it won't be as bad as all that. Not if we keep our heads down and do what they say.'

But after a few days she had to admit that Jen had been right. They were still fed, just about. They were still allowed to wash twice a day, even if it was now only in cold water. Molly and her fellow fitness addicts were still allowed to do their exercises. But that was about it.

The atmosphere in the camp had changed, and not for the better.

Since Hauptmann Kleber had slapped Betty on the face, there had been no more physical assaults. But the new regime practised a different kind of cruelty, a kind of casual indifference. At first Molly had braced herself for an interrogation. But it quickly became apparent that Hauptmann Kleber and his men didn't really care who their prisoners were. They evinced no interest in their history, how they had come to be there, let alone in their personalities.

Whether a deliberate ploy or not, this utter disinterest had the effect of sapping everyone's spirits. They began to feel more like animals on a cattle farm than human beings.

But their new guards hardly seemed human either. It was as though all normal feelings had been expunged from them. As if they had seen and

321

done things no human being should. Nevertheless, their loyalty to the Nazi cause was apparent. Every time they caught even a glimpse of an officer, they stiffened to rigid attention and gave the Nazi salute with utter conviction.

Not that any of them were blonde or Aryan. An uglier bunch would have been hard to imagine. But then Adolf Hitler had never exactly been a pin-up boy either. Kleber was the blondest of the bunch, which was perhaps why he was in charge. That and his predilection for order and obedience.

Intimidating as their new captors were, Molly was also intrigued by them. But it was impossible to get to know them, because fraternisation was forbidden. Not that these men wanted to fraternise. On the contrary, they made it clear that the women in the camp were unworthy of their attention, unworthy of even basic good manners. That didn't stop them looking, of course, but unlike the Italian soldiers, there was no charm in their leering stares. They clearly felt they were a superior species, members of a precious Nazi elite, future rulers of the world.

And even Molly, used to being treated as the lowest of the low by the doctors at the Wilhelmina, found it hard to keep her spirits up in the face of such contemptuous belittlement. It didn't help that she was still angry with herself for not taking the opportunity to leave the camp when they'd had the chance.

Looking back, she realised that even then, a kind of imprisonment malaise had affected her. She could see it affecting the others too, even more so now they were under German command.

It manifested itself in a sense of despondency and despair. When all decisions and sense of identity were taken away, it was hard to remember that such things as free will or hope even existed.

Even Nancy and Betty seemed to have given up. They no longer plotted and grumbled. They, more than anyone, must be kicking themselves for not getting away during the armistice. They had homes in Italy to go to, lives to resume, friends and relations to protect them. With no access to any news to motivate them, they, like everyone else, just sat about listlessly, waiting for the next roll call, or the next meal.

Jen was the most lethargic of them all. She was always last on parade, often ambling over so slowly to take up her allotted position that in Molly's opinion she was asking for trouble.

'You should watch out,' Molly said to her. 'You're drawing attention to yourself. We just need to keep our heads down and wait for a chance to escape.'

'There was a chance and we didn't take it,' Jen said.

Molly gritted her teeth. 'I know, but another may come. We just have to bide our time.'

Jen made a sceptical face. 'They'd love you to try. They've been itching to shoot someone ever since they got here.'

Molly frowned, but Jen was right. The chance of escaping seemed remote indeed. They were clearly going to be stuck here for some time. It was bearable, just. What she didn't want was for it to get any worse.

And then it did get worse.

One night the weather broke with a massive thunderstorm. Within hours the previously parched earth of the camp had turned into mud. Now, instead of suffering the intense heat, the problem became how to keep dry.

A couple of days later, they were locked in their huts while a new fence was erected across the middle of the camp. The women in the huts in the newly partitioned zone were told to move into the huts on Jen and Molly's side of the fence.

But there weren't enough bunks. It looked as though some of the women were going to have to double up.

'We ought to offer,' Molly said to Jen. 'At least we know each other.'

'I'm not offering,' Jen said. 'I hardly sleep a wink as it is. I don't want your smelly feet in my face.'

In the end it was the Jewish women who were told to double up. That was bad enough, but the increased numbers put extra pressure on the washroom, which quickly got dirty and unhygienic. There wasn't enough water, and the mud and slime from their feet kept blocking the drains.

It became clear why this new arrangement had been instigated when men began to be brought in to the huts on the other side of the fence. Many of them were young Italians.

All Italian soldiers had apparently been ordered to report to their nearest German command, but few had obeyed this instruction and the German military police, the Feldgendarmerie, were now busy rounding up every young man they could find. They could be heard every morning setting off in a great roar of vehicles.

It was made clear that there was to be no communication with these new arrivals. Hauptmann Kleber announced that anyone going within six feet of the fence would be shot. But even so, a certain amount of information was surreptitiously exchanged.

Via Nancy and Betty, Molly learned that Italy was now almost entirely under Nazi occupation. The instant the armistice had been declared, the Germans had brought several armoured divisions down into Italy through the Brenner Pass. Rome was already in their hands. Mussolini had been liberated and had been reinstated as leader of a German-controlled puppet government.

And so far, the Allies only had a tiny foothold in the far south of the country.

The Clapham police were hopeless. They didn't do anything. The Garrow brothers carried on drinking in the pub, Barry Fish still roamed the streets. And Katy continued to mourn the loss of her jewellery.

'Maybe we should offer a reward,' Helen suggested one evening when they were clearing up after the last drinkers had left. 'We could put an advertisement in the paper.'

'I can't afford a reward,' Katy said.

'I can,' Helen said. She held up her hand as Katy went to demur. 'No, seriously, it's the least I can do after what you have done for me.'

'I suppose Ward would pay you back when he gets home. If he gets home,' Katy said, crossing her fingers. It was like a superstition. Not to talk about his return as if it was an inevitability. After four weeks of silence, it no longer seemed inevitable that he would return.

She had heard on the wireless that there was fierce fighting going on in Corsica between the Germans and the French Resistance. But of Ward there had been no word. As promised, Helen had tried to get news from the SOE. But apart from discovering that the submarine that had secretly delivered Ward into Corsica had been one of the ones she had helped liberate from Toulon harbour all those months ago, she had been unable to glean any information about what had happened since.

'No news is good news,' she had said, and Katy had managed to prevent herself pointing out that she had been told that before, when no news had certainly not been good news. There was no news from the Red Cross either, and Katy couldn't bear to think about what might have happened, or be happening, to Jen and Molly.

At roll call one morning, the Jewish women were told to step forward. They were then herded together by the entrance and loaded on to trucks at gunpoint. More Jewish women soon arrived to take their place.

'Where do you think they're going?' Molly asked Nancy when the second lot were dispatched.

'Germany, I suppose,' she responded. 'Poor blighters.'

On the other side of the fence, the first batch of young Italian deserters were being shipped out too. Molly could tell from the tone of the boys' voices that they were frightened. They had been told that as they had given up their uniforms, they were classed as civilians, and therefore weren't protected under the Geneva Convention. Molly quailed when she heard that. It didn't bode well for her and Jen either.

Whatever the rights and wrongs of the German's categorisation, it was clear the camp had become a kind of transit unit. Both men and women were now brought in on a regular basis, and not just Italian Jews. There were Yugoslavs and Poles too. Even a young Dutch woman and her mother who had been caught sheltering some Jews in Rome. Many were moved out again soon after their arrival.

Rumours of what happened to these departing prisoners were rife, and the awful command '*Un passo avanti!*' – 'You, one step forward!' – quickly became dreaded by all.

It all made the atmosphere very tense. Nobody wanted to be shipped out. The relative security of the camp was much more appealing than unknown dangers in Germany. More and more Molly longed for a visit from the Red Cross, but it never materialised. She hated to think that nobody in England knew where they were. They probably thought they had died in the torpedo attack. Molly hadn't quite begun to wish they had, but occasionally she had come close, and had had to force herself to think positive, to exercise, and to try to keep healthy.

Because the more crowded the camp became, the more people began to get sick. Several women developed boils. Flea and mosquito bites got infected. Without access to scissors or nail files, ingrowing nails also became a problem.

Finding out that she was a nurse, people began to ask her for help. But there was very little she could do without medical equipment. She had summoned up the courage to ask one of the guards if she could have some disinfectant, but even though he agreed to pass on the request, she never heard any more about it.

Then, one day at roll call, Hauptmann Kleber ordered anyone with medical training to step forward.

Molly's heart jolted in alarm. Was she going to be sent away? Without Jen?

She didn't like Jen, but she suddenly realised that she didn't want to be separated from her. She had got used to her. Jen was her only link with home. For a split second, as terror washed through her, Molly hesitated, but then she realised that Hauptmann Kleber must know perfectly well that she was a nurse. It might be fatal to defy his command.

Molly was the only person who stepped forward, but she wasn't taken away. She was taken instead to wait outside Hauptmann Kleber's office.

He made her stand there for ten nervous minutes before calling her in.

He looked her over as she stood in front of his desk. 'You are English, yes?'

Molly nodded. She clasped her hands behind her back to stop them trembling.

'A nurse?'

Molly nodded again. 'Yes.'

'Next week the camp is to be inspected,' he said. 'It is important that the women are healthy. I wish for you to make sure this is the case.'

Molly stared at him aghast. Next week? What was she meant to do? Wave a magic wand?

'But that's impossible,' she stammered. 'Some of them are very sick. I've got no medicine, no equipment …' She stopped abruptly, heart hammering, as his hand cracked down on the desk.

She thought he was angry, but a second later his glance was indifferent. He picked up a pen and uncapped it. 'What do you need?'

Molly suddenly felt short of breath. She knew this was an opportunity, but for a terrible second her mind had gone blank. What *did* she need? There might be things she could ask for that might be useful in other ways, not just for treating the women. She tried to remember what had been on the ward trolleys in the Wilhelmina, but it all seemed so long ago, like a distant dream. Think, she shouted at herself silently. Think.

'Disinfectant,' she stammered. 'Carbolic soap. Dressings. Swabs. A thermometer. Distilled water. Iodine. Sodium bicarbonate.' She took a breath. 'Scissors. Bandages. Tweezers. A suture needle. Thread. And plenty of boiling water.'

He looked up as she finished her list and capped the pen. 'I will see what I can do,' he said.

Molly felt something was expected of her. 'Thank you,' she said.

He barked out a command and one of his men stepped into the room and gave the Heil Hitler salute. 'My corporal, Gefreiter Henniker, will let you know when you can begin.'

Molly looked at the man who had come in. He didn't even glance at her. 'Thank you,' she said again.

But as she turned to leave, Hauptmann Kleber stopped her. 'Not the Jewish women, you understand. This is not necessary.'

Molly gaped at him incredulously. 'But some of them are even worse than—'

'It is not important.'

'It *is* important,' she said hotly. 'They are human beings too.'

His eyes narrowed dangerously. 'Be careful, Nurse,' he said. 'It would not be sensible for you to overstep the mark, yes?'

Molly swallowed but remained silent. There was no point in trying to appeal to Hauptmann Kleber's better nature, because he clearly didn't have one. As she walked out, her knees were trembling.

She couldn't believe what she had just heard. She knew the Germans hated the Jews. But to witness such callous injustice first-hand was almost unbearable.

But at least there was going to be an inspection. Thank God. At last. This must finally be the Red Cross, or something similar. And if so, surely they would insist on some kind of medical treatment for the Jewish women too.

On 4 October, Corsica fell to the French Resistance. The following morning everyone in London was talking about it. It was the first department of France to be liberated from the Germans.

Helen de Burrel was delighted, and even more so when she found out from the SOE a few days later that Ward had been instrumental in that success. She came straight back to the pub to tell Katy that he was alive and well. 'He still won't be able to contact us directly,' she said, taking off her coat. 'It's all in a muddle over there. But I promise he's OK.'

The relief was enormous. 'Thank God,' Katy whispered. 'And thank you for finding out.'

She put her hand on her enlarged stomach and closed her eyes. She took a deep breath and tried to steady her pulse. Opening her eyes again, she saw Helen watching her in concern.

'Katy, are you all right? You've gone awfully pale.'

'Yes, I'm fine,' Katy said. 'I just suddenly felt a bit faint. It happens sometimes when the baby kicks.' She took another breath and let the air out slowly. 'And what about André?' she asked tentatively. 'Any news?'

Helen shook her head. 'No. Nothing.' For a second she looked as though she was going to say something else, but then she seemed to change her mind.

'By the way,' she said in a different tone as she began to rinse out some glasses. 'I bumped into Louise earlier. She's looking much better. She's back at work. But I'm afraid she's going out with Charlie tonight.'

'Oh no,' Katy groaned.

'Oh yes,' Helen said. 'They are going to the pictures to see *The Night Invader*.'

'How appropriate,' Katy said drily.

Helen laughed. 'Oh, and look.' She dried her hands quickly and drew a copy of the *Wandsworth Gazette* out of her handbag. 'Our advertisement is in the paper.' She flicked to the right page. '*£20 reward offered. For information* *leading to the recovery of some personal jewellery stolen from the Flag and Garter public house, Lavender Road, Clapham.'*

She looked up. 'Now all we have to do is hope that's enough to tempt one of those light-fingered bastards to rat on his friends.'

The imminent inspection was clearly of some considerable importance to Hauptmann Kleber, because over the next couple of days efforts were made to pull the camp into better order. The prisoners' clothing and bedding, such as it was, was washed. The showers were scrubbed and the drains cleared. Even the food ration was slightly increased. Inevitably it was the Jewish women who were tasked with doing the laundry and cleaning, but nevertheless, conditions for everyone, on the women's side of the fence, at least, improved considerably.

For an hour a day Molly was installed in a room in the administrative block. Not everything she had asked for had been provided, but the basics were there. And there was a table and a sink and even occasionally some hot water.

'I've got bandages, scissors and tweezers,' she whispered to Jen that evening in the bunk room. 'If I can smuggle them out of the treatment room, will you help me hide them?'

'I'm happy to try,' Jen said. 'But I can't think where, when they search the huts every single day.' She gave a sour laugh. 'And frankly I can't imagine how a few bandages are going to help us escape.'

Molly sighed. The truth was that she had no idea either.

She had had some vague thought of using the bandages to tie up their guards, or picking the lock of the hut with the scissors. It was the sort of thing that would happen in a film. It was not, however, the sort of thing likely to have any chance of success in reality. Not when she was constantly under the eagle eye of Hauptmann Kleber's sycophantic sidekick, the impassive but observant Gefreiter Henniker.

With true German efficiency, all the items in the treatment room had been listed and had to be checked off against an inventory each time she finished a session. Everything she used had to be noted down, and the master list adjusted accordingly. It all took ages and Molly couldn't see how she would ever be able to purloin anything useful, especially as her prison tunic had no pockets. On the other hand, it was good to be able to give some relief to some of the ailing women, and she found she relished the time she spent in her makeshift clinic. She was able to lance boils, dress wounds, trim toenails, and soothe infected bites. She even managed to stitch a nasty cut that the pretty young Dutch girl had suffered when she slipped in the mud and caught her shin on the corner of one of the huts.

'Thank you,' the girl, Olga, whispered bravely, when Molly had finished and neatly cut off the thread.

'I'm sorry it was so painful,' Molly said. 'But they didn't give me anything I could use to numb the skin.'

'Are you going to bandage it?' the girl asked.

'No, I think it is better for it to have the air ...' Molly began. Then stopped. She cast a cautious glance at Gefreiter Henniker. 'Let me look at it again. No, on second thoughts,' she went on blithely, 'I think it does need bandaging.'

If the burly corporal noticed her change of mind, he gave no sign of it. It wasn't his job to question her treatment. Only to make sure she didn't steal the equipment.

Molly felt she ought to try to get to know her silent observer, but he was so unresponsive, it was hard to find a way in. But then one day, as they checked the list for perhaps the hundredth time, she noticed him wince slightly as he moved his arm.

'Do you have an injury?' she asked.

'No,' he said.

She frowned. 'But you have something wrong with your arm?'

She saw a slight flush stain his cheek and was surprised. Maybe he was partly human after all.

'It is only, how do you say, a splint?'

'A splinter?' Somehow she managed to keep a straight face. It seemed suddenly hilarious that this thickset, poker-faced member of the brutal Nazi machine would be troubled by something as trivial as a splinter.

'Do you want me to look at it?'

'It is not allowed.'

Molly glanced at the closed door. 'No one would know.'

She waited, and after a moment he undid the buttons at his cuff and pushed up his sleeve to expose a muscular white forearm.

Just above his wrist there was a deep wound surrounded by blue-grey bruising.

'It is nothing,' he said.

'It's not nothing,' Molly replied, looking up. 'It's a nasty gash. How did you get it?'

He didn't answer, and Molly realised his colour had risen again.

'Oh,' she said, and dropped her eyes back to the wound, feeling stupid. From the bruising and abrasion, it looked as though he had been attacked with something hard and rough. A plank of wood perhaps. Probably he had been trying to disarm someone resisting arrest. One of the deserters? Or a Jewish husband trying to prevent his wife being dragged away? She

329

wondered grimly what had happened to the person wielding the weapon.

She looked at Gefreiter Henniker. She didn't want to help him. She didn't want to touch him. But it occurred to her that it wouldn't do any harm for him to feel that he was in her debt.

'It's becoming infected,' she said briskly. 'At the very least I should try to take the splinter out. It will only get worse if you leave it.'

Without waiting for a response, she began to prepare a needle and a pair of tweezers, rinsing them in the remainder of the hot water she'd used earlier.

It was a tricky thing to do, made more difficult by the wound not being fresh. She knew she must be hurting him. But he didn't make a sound throughout the whole probing operation. As his blood dripped on to the table, she suddenly thought of Ward Frazer suffering the operation on his leg at the hands of some brutal German butcher, and was tempted to let the needle go in much deeper than it needed to. But she restrained herself.

And she was glad she had, because when eventually it was over and she dropped a long splinter of dirty wood on the table, he gave her a tentative smile. She had never seen him smile before and it lightened his whole face. 'I think you are a good doctor,' he said.

She swabbed the blood and pus from the open wound. 'I don't like to see people suffer,' she said. 'Whoever they are.' She pressed a gauze pad over the lesion. 'That is why I want to treat the Jewish ladies.'

Gefreiter Henniker's smile faded at once. 'This is not possible,' he said.

She gritted her teeth and in silence wrapped a short length of bandage round his forearm to hold the dressing in place, tucking in the end neatly.

He pulled down the sleeve of his uniform and rebuttoned his cuff. His eyes flickered uneasily to the door. 'I also do not like to see women suffer,' he said. 'But I have my orders and I cannot disobey.'

The rain had only lasted a few days and the camp was once again sweltering under a blazing-hot sun. The ground had dried out rough and pitted. Two women twisted their ankles, another bruised her knee. On Molly's instruction, Jen hurt her wrist. All these injuries ostensibly needed extensive bandaging. Olga, the pretty Dutch girl, lost the bandage from her shin and had to be issued with a fresh one.

It wasn't much, but it was a start, and it gave Molly a tiny sense of satisfaction that she was pulling the wool over her captors' eyes. Nobody remarked on the surprising number of bandages on display at roll calls. Nor did Gefreiter Henniker seem to notice that none of the bandages ever returned to the treatment room. Encouraged, Molly began to rack her brains about how she might be able to extract something that would be more use in an escape attempt.

Gefreiter Henniker's own injury was healing well. Molly hadn't raised the subject of the Jewish women again. He seemed appreciative of her aid and she didn't want to alienate him. In any case she was convinced that the Red Cross would take issue with Hauptmann Kleber about the discrepancies in the care of his prisoners. But so far there had been no sign of the upcoming inspection.

On 20 October, however, it became clear that something was about to happen. Hauptmann Kleber seemed unusually ill-tempered when he took the early-morning roll call.

'Today we will have visitors,' he announced. 'It is important that you tidy yourselves in preparation. I wish to have your best behaviour. Is this understood?'

Even the guards seemed on edge, and that made Molly feel increasingly optimistic. It looked as though they were expecting to be reprimanded in some way. And surely that was going to be good news for the prisoners.

They hadn't been told exactly who the visitors were going to be, but they were hoping for someone with the authority to check sanitation, sleeping conditions and the standard of food and medical provision. They were also anticipating boxes of extra supplies and long-awaited letters from loved ones. So when, later that morning, vehicles were heard approaching, a sense of excitement ran through the camp.

At once the whistle for roll call sounded.

But it wasn't a group of well-meaning Red Cross officials who came in, but three men in grey uniforms with black collar tabs and cuff bands, and a civilian in a mackintosh carrying a small black case. The four men had barely stepped through the entrance before the gate guards came to attention and lifted their arms in the Nazi salute.

From her position in the second row, Molly couldn't see the visitors' faces, but next to her she heard Jen take a sharp intake of breath.

'What is it?' Molly whispered as the men disappeared into Hauptmann Kleber's office.

Jen turned her head. 'Didn't you see?'

'No, what was it?'

'It's that man,' Jen said. 'The awful one from Sicily. The SS officer. I'm sure it was.'

Molly stared at her aghast. But there was nothing they could do, even if Jen was right.

They were kept waiting in the hot sunshine for fifteen minutes. During that time Molly's brain was racing. Where was the Red Cross? Why were these men here instead? And who were they? Surely Jen had been mistaken.

German uniforms all looked much the same. Blonde-haired Germans all looked much the same.

But Jen had not been mistaken.

As the new arrivals emerged on to the parade ground with Hauptmann Kleber, Molly immediately recognised the fat lips and pink complexion of Hauptsturmführer Wessel, last seen in the cell in Sicily, and for whom Jen had so valiantly sung 'Land of Hope and Glory'.

'Keep your eyes down,' Molly whispered. 'He won't recognise us after all this time. Not at this distance.'

'*Sei still! Silenzio!*' Hauptmann Kleber shouted. There was something edgy in his voice. Almost as though he wasn't pleased to see the visitors either. But it was also clear from his attentive, subservient demeanour that whatever they were up to, he wasn't going to stand in their way.

'We are honoured to have important visitors,' he said. 'You will now be inspected. If you are required to step forward, do so quickly and without question.'

It was an odd thing to say, because there was never any question. But it was too late to speculate about it, because two of the newcomers were already moving forward. And one of them was Hauptsturmführer Wessel.

The two men walked slowly along the front row. They took their time, murmuring to each other in German as they inspected each woman in turn. It was almost as though they were at a market, deliberating over the best produce. Three of the women, including Olga, the young Dutch girl, were instructed to step forward.

And then they were turning to the second row.

They stopped in front of Jen.

Molly held her breath, heart hammering, staring at the ground, her nails digging into her palms.

There was a long pause.

Then she heard Hauptsturmführer Wessel's silky voice. 'So,' he said. 'My two little spies. We meet again.'

In London, it was a lovely sunny autumn day. Katy was playing ball with Malcolm on the common when she noticed Barry Fish talking to half a dozen schoolgirls by the bandstand.

When the girls came giggling past a few minutes later, she stopped them.

'Was that man bothering you?' she asked.

The girls seemed surprised. 'Oh no, he's often there,' one of them said. 'Sometimes he gives us sweets.'

'You shouldn't take sweets from strangers,' Katy said. But they just giggled and walked on.

A minute later Barry Fish himself approached.

'Well, well,' he said, as Malcolm picked up the ball and eyed him with interest. 'He's growing up fast.'

'Yes,' Katy said coldly. 'He is.'

'A shame your husband is not here to play with him too. Little chap like that needs a man around the place.'

Katy suppressed a shiver. 'He'll be back very soon,' she said firmly.

Barry Fish smiled, baring a set of unpleasantly stained teeth. 'Well I hope so, obviously. For your sake.'

He put out his hand for the ball, and after a moment's reluctance, Malcolm handed it to him. Barry Fish dropped it to the ground and pretended to kick it, laughing as Malcolm began to run.

'And I hear you lost some jewellery.'

Katy felt her heart jump. 'Yes. It was stolen.'

Barry Fish jiggled his toe on the ball, apparently unaware of Malcolm's baleful expression. He hadn't appreciated being tricked. 'I'm sorry to hear that. I hope it wasn't anything too valuable?'

'No, not valuable,' Katy said. 'But precious to me.' She hesitated and tried to keep her voice pleasant, casual. 'I don't suppose you or any of your friends know anything about it? We are offering a reward for information.'

'Yes,' he said. 'I heard that as well.'

Katy waited, but he just stood there for a moment. Then he drew back his foot and suddenly booted the ball hard away across the common.

As Malcolm let out a cry of fury and trundled off after it, Barry Fish gave her a mocking wink. 'Be careful,' he said. 'You think you're clever, don't you? But when all's said and done, you are just a silly little girl. And if I was you, I'd keep my nose out of other people's business.'

Jen stared defiantly into Hauptsturmführer Wessel's pale blue eyes.

'I am not a spy,' she said.

He ignored her and glanced at his companion. 'This one is pretty, yes?' He turned back to Jen. 'Step forward.'

Jen stood her ground and lifted her chin. She was damned if she was going to move at his command. 'Why should I?'

With the speed of a snake, he grabbed her bandaged wrist and twisted it deliberately. Jen gritted her teeth. He wasn't to know that there was nothing wrong with it. But even so, it was painful, and she felt her eyes water.

He brought his mouth close to her ear and spoke very quietly. 'I think you were told not to question my order. Now.' He dropped her wrist. 'Step forward.'

There was no choice. She had to step forward, and she stood there seething while he glanced indifferently at Molly. 'This one is not pretty,' he said. And moved on.

In total eleven women had been asked to step forward. As soon as the inspection was over, they were taken to a room in the admin block. There they were each given a small glass beaker by some kind of orderly and escorted to the toilet block to produce a sample of urine.

'What's going on?' Jen asked angrily. 'I'm not producing anything until you tell me what all this is about.'

The orderly shrugged. 'It is a medical check. We wish to make sure you are healthy.'

'And what if I can't produce a sample?' Jen said.

'Then you will wait here until you do.'

Once again Jen had to capitulate. The toilet block was not somewhere anyone wanted to hang around for long, and Jen hated it more than most. The smell almost made her retch.

Back in the room, the eleven women were kept waiting again. Then, one at a time, they were called out.

Olga was first. She had only been gone a few minutes when the remaining women heard her scream.

They looked at each other. 'What the hell?' Jen muttered. She suddenly felt very frightened. She barely knew these other women. They were mostly recent arrivals. The only one she had ever actually spoken to was Nancy, the better-looking of the two English women.

Jen had always kept herself to herself in the camp, and now, even though they were all crammed into this tiny room, she felt very much alone. Ridiculously she found herself wishing Molly was there.

A few minutes later another woman was taken out. This time there was no scream.

And then it was Jen's turn.

Carrying the beaker, she was taken along the corridor and ushered into the room Molly used for her consultations. An upright chair had been placed near the door. Sitting on the other side of the central table was Hauptsturmführer Wessel and his grey-uniformed colleague from the earlier inspection.

The civilian, who now wore a white doctor's coat and steel-rimmed glasses, was waiting inside the door with a clipboard. He told her to put her urine sample on the table next to the others and then to sit down.

'English?'

Jen swallowed nervously. 'Yes.'

'Name?'

'Jennifer Carter.'

'Age?'

'Twenty-two.'

'You have proof of this. Papers? Passport? Identity document?'

Jen shook her head. 'No.' She was about to explain once again that she had lost them on the boat when he looked up from his notes.

'You are suffering from any diseases?'

'No.'

'Any other problems?'

Jen blinked. In other circumstances she might have made some quip about exactly how many problems she did have. But not now, not with Hauptsturmführer Wessel sitting there, clearly itching for a chance to humiliate her.

'No.'

The man glanced at the bandage on her arm. 'What is wrong with your arm?'

'I twisted my wrist,' Jen said.

He pushed up her sleeve and quickly undid the bandage. Oh God, Jen thought, now Molly's going to get into trouble. As he rotated her wrist, she tried to wince convincingly. He seemed satisfied and made a note on his pad. 'Some recent bruising,' he said. 'No lasting damage.' Realising that the bruising was the result of the pressure of Hauptsturmführer Wessel's painful grip on the parade ground, Jen almost sighed in relief.

But her relief was short-lived.

Taking a leather strap from his case, the doctor wrapped it round her upper arm and pulled it uncomfortably tight. He then flicked the skin inside her elbow a couple of times, grunted in satisfaction and picked up a vicious-looking syringe.

'No, please …' Jen gasped in horror.

But it was too late. He was already inserting the needle painfully into her vein. The shock made Jen cry out, but she knew if she pulled away it would be even worse. Tears inadvertently filled her eyes. As he slowly drew her blood into the syringe, she had to blink and bite her lip to stop them falling.

And then it was over. He untied the strap, pulled out the needle and told her to press her other thumb over the wound, while he transferred the blood to a glass vial waiting on the table.

Then he turned round.

'So,' he said briskly. 'Now please take off your clothes.'

Jen stared up at him. Her heart was thumping so hard she thought she must have misheard. 'What?'

'Take off your clothes. I need to check your body.'

Jen thought she was going to pass out. She suddenly felt hot and cold.

335

She couldn't breathe. She sat helplessly, numbly.

'No,' she whispered. 'No, I won't.'

'I'm afraid there is no option to refuse.' The doctor glanced at Hauptsturmführer Wessel, who nodded. The man sitting next to him began to roll up his sleeves.

Jen knew she had no choice. She remembered the Dutch girl's scream. Three men against one girl was no contest.

Trying not to think about what she was doing, she began to undress.

It didn't take long; she wasn't wearing much, only the cotton smock and trousers they had been given when they first arrived at the camp. Her bra and panties had disintegrated long ago.

And then she was standing there naked.

She didn't look at them. She couldn't. She wanted to scream. To cry. To die. She had never felt so mortified in all her life, but she was damned if she was going to show it. Her whole body burnt with fury. I hate them, she thought. I hate them. What she really wanted to do was to kill them. But she couldn't. She couldn't do anything. She just had to stand there and submit to their casual, indifferent regard.

'Turn round, please,' the doctor commanded. He made a few notes, then nodded to the two men on the other side of the table. 'No blemishes. Some ugly freckling. But otherwise fair skin. Straight spine. Rather thin, but this is to be expected.'

He turned back to Jen and indicated the chair. 'Sit, please. I need to listen to your chest and your heart.'

Jen flinched as he placed the cold stethoscope on the overheated skin of her back.

'Breathe. In. Out. In. Out.'

She gritted her teeth as he repeated the process on her front, shrinking away from his hand so close to her breast.

Taking the stethoscope out of his ears, he nodded. 'The lungs are strong. The heart too.'

He took a dental mirror from his bag. He put a hand under her chin and tilted her head back. 'Open your mouth, I wish to check the teeth.'

Jen felt his fingers pushing back her lips, then he was probing around her tongue. The invasion and the metallic taste of the mirror made her gag. She could feel bile rising in her throat. She longed for the courage to bite.

Withdrawing the mirror, he went to the sink and rinsed his hand. Jen wanted to spit, but she didn't dare. She felt too vulnerable, too naked, too humbled.

The doctor glanced down at his list. 'Have you ever given birth to children?'

Jen shook her head. 'No.'

'Are you virgin?' He pronounced it 'wirgin'.

Jen froze. Her mouth was dry now, so dry she could hardly speak. 'That's none of your business,' she muttered.

He looked at her steadily and asked again. 'Are you a virgin?'

Jen met his gaze and saw his eyes flicker with impatience behind the wire-rimmed glasses. He raised his thin eyebrows and glanced towards the table. 'You wish me to check?'

'No,' Jen muttered. 'I'm not a virgin.'

The doctor made a note on his list, turned to the other men and nodded.

Hauptsturmführer Wessel stood up and came round the table. He stopped in front of Jen and let his eyes run over her slowly. His fat lips opened in a satisfied smile as she trembled and dropped her eyes. 'So, my little spy,' he said. 'You are not quite so bold now, I think.'

'I am not a spy,' Jen muttered.

'No.' He put his hand under her chin and jerked her head up so she was forced to look straight into his cold blue eyes. 'You are right. You are nothing. Nobody. You understand? You no longer exist. It is only from the goodness of my heart that I keep you alive.'

He waited for a long moment, then patted her on the cheek. 'That is all. For now. You can go. No, take your clothes. You can get dressed outside.'

Chapter Twenty-Four

Having assumed she would never see Jen again, Molly could hardly believe how relieved she felt when she saw her walking across the parade ground towards the accommodation block and realised she hadn't been taken away for good.

But Jen looked as though she had seen a ghost. Her pretty face was ashen and she was visibly trembling.

'Jen, are you OK? What on earth happened?'

Jen flinched away. 'I don't want to talk about it. Leave me alone.'

Molly looked at her in concern. 'But—'

Jen's eyes flashed. 'I told you. I don't want to talk about it.' She swung away and disappeared into their dormitory hut.

Molly didn't know what to do. Jen was always spiky and difficult, but this was something completely different. She had seemed to be on the verge of tears. And despite all they had been through, Molly had never seen her cry. Certainly she had never seen her look so shaken. She decided to leave her in peace for an hour, and then go and see if there was anything she could do.

But before the hour was up, Molly herself was summoned to the medical room.

Gefreiter Henniker was already there. He nodded towards the sink. 'You are required to wash up.'

Looking round in surprise, Molly saw a dozen or so glass beakers on the table, containing what looked and smelt like urine. A stethoscope also lay on the table, an open black medical bag beside it. Inside she could see an untidy selection of probes, spatulas and syringes, and tucked in on one side, a small pair of nail scissors.

Dragging her eyes away, she noticed a patch of blood on the floor and gave an involuntary shiver. There was a strange smell in the hot, muggy room. Not just urine. But another smell. Sweat. Fear.

She glanced back at Gefreiter Henniker, who was still standing by the door. 'What have they been doing in here?'

'They check the women's health.'

Molly frowned. Judging by Jen's reaction, it hadn't been a pleasant process. 'But why did they only choose the good-looking women? Why not everyone?'

'I don't know.' He spoke quickly, too quickly, and Molly looked at him more closely.

'Are you sure you don't know?'

He looked uncomfortable.

'I did you a favour,' Molly said steadily. 'I took out your splinter. I think it only fair now that you tell me what is going on.'

He glanced nervously at the door and lowered his voice. 'There is talk,' he said reluctantly.

Molly nodded encouragingly. 'What talk?'

'Talk of places for the officers to go.'

'What do you mean?' Molly asked. 'What sort of places?'

He flushed slightly. 'Places to amuse themselves.'

Molly looked at him blankly.

'With women,' he added, avoiding her eyes.

'Oh my God,' she said. She put her hand to her mouth in horror as the implication of his words finally sank in. 'You mean brothels?'

'Maybe also to breed good children for the party.'

He saw her horrified expression and went on quickly, 'But it is only talk. I do not know if it is true …'

Molly shuddered. 'But surely the authorities … the Red Cross … Jen and I were both registered by the Italians in Rome.'

He shrugged uneasily and glanced once more at the door. 'It is not so difficult for the Waffen-SS to disappear people. They call it *Nacht und Nebel*. Night and fog. There is no record. You understand?'

Molly didn't understand. Not really. It was hard to understand the unthinkable. But she understood enough. And the thought of Jen …

It was beyond comprehension. For the first time in her life, she suddenly felt glad not to be pretty.

'*Komm.*' Gefreiter Henniker clearly felt he had already said too much. 'You must wash the glasses. It must be done before they finish lunch, yes?'

But the word *disappear* had triggered something in Molly's brain. Even as she moved obediently towards the table, her eyes flickered back to the doctor's bag and her heart accelerated sharply. Perhaps the Waffen-SS weren't the only ones who could disappear things.

She was shaky with shock. But she knew she had to take the risk.

She glanced at Gefreiter Henniker. He had moved forward to stand near the sink.

It would only take a moment. She had disappeared cards often enough while doing tricks with George. She had palmed the little charm from her necklace when she had done the magic trick on Jen in the train all those weeks ago. This would be much harder. But not impossible.

But she would have to make sure Gefreiter Henniker was looking away. She needed a distraction. Or Miss Direction, as George Nelson used to call it.

She could see how to create one. But it had to be right. Exactly right. And already her palms were going clammy at the very thought of it. What if it went wrong? What if she was caught?

Picking up two of the glass beakers, she carried them over to the sink. Having emptied them and rinsed them, she set them casually upside down on the draining board. Having repeated the process with the second two, she was just about to lift the third pair off the table when she glanced back towards the sink.

'Oh no,' she said urgently. 'Look! That one's slipping. It's going to break!'

As she had intended, Gefreiter Henniker swivelled towards the sink. Seeing one of the glass beakers lodged precariously right on the edge of the draining board, he instinctively took a step towards it, his right hand outstretched to steady it. In that moment, Molly's left hand flicked into the doctor's bag.

She found the nail scissors instantly. Then she was lifting them out of the bag. Carefully. Silently. Slowly. The magic book had been explicit on that point; quick movement invariably drew attention. But palming a pair of scissors slowly was easier said than done when there was an eagle-eyed Nazi already turning back towards her.

'Oh phew,' Molly said. She lifted her hand dramatically to her mouth, allowing the scissors to slither along her sleeve to the elbow. 'Thank you. I thought it was going to fall.'

Heart racing, she raised her hand even further to smooth her hair. Then, clamping her upper arm tight against her ribcage, she casually picked up two more beakers.

Five minutes later the task was finished. The beakers were stacked neatly, clean and dry, back on the table. It hadn't been easy to conceal the fact that she had a pair of nail scissors hidden in her armpit, but if Gefreiter Henniker thought she was moving unusually stiffly, she hoped he would put it down to her understandable fear of the SS.

'So what's going to happen now?' she asked. 'Will they take the women away today?'

'No,' he replied. 'I believe they will be carried by train in one or two days.'

Molly hesitated. 'You know one of them is my friend?' And she realised as she spoke the words that it was the first time in her entire life that she had thought of, let alone referred to, Jen Carter as a friend.

She looked up at him as he opened the door to let her out. 'We don't want to be separated. If there is anything you can do …'

He shook his head. 'There is nothing I can do. There is nothing anybody can do. These men. They make their own rules.'

Joyce couldn't understand why she had heard nothing about Jen. Surely people couldn't just disappear. Not even in wartime. Not civilians. Even in the middle of the Blitz there had been wardens making lists of the injured and missing. You could hardly blink nowadays without filling out some kind of official form. You had to register for everything, for ration books, for medical attention, for work, even for a damned library card. And she couldn't believe it was much different in other countries.

She had had news of Bob from the Red Cross almost as soon as he had arrived in Italy. She had assumed that when Italy surrendered, both Bob and Jen would be rescued by British troops and sent home. But that hadn't happened. The Nazis had invaded Italy instead. And poor old Bob had been shipped off to another prisoner of war camp, this time in Germany.

Italy had, at last, declared war on the Germans. But there was still no news of Jen.

At first Joyce had been sure she would turn up safe and sound, like she always had in the past, like a bad penny. But it was a long time now and she was beginning to get seriously worried.

She wasn't the only one. Everyone was worried. Not least Henry Keller. He had called at the café several times since that first visit, even though Joyce had promised to send word if she heard anything, to save him struggling all the way down to Clapham. A posh, busy man like that, you'd think he had better things to do with his time.

Katy, of course, was also hoping for news of both Ward and Molly Coogan. That poor Helen de Burrel still hadn't heard a squeak from that young man of hers in France. And in a different way, Mrs Rutherford was worried about Louise.

'She's carrying on with this frightful fellow in the City,' she had confided only that morning. 'It's most unseemly. It's not three months yet since Jack died.'

'Well at least she hasn't turned her flat into a brothel like that other widow up the road,' Joyce said.

Mrs Rutherford recoiled so sharply she almost dropped the pile of dirty plates she was carrying. 'Good Lord,' she said. 'What an appalling thought. Even Louise wouldn't go that far.'

Joyce gave a slight chuckle at the look on her face. 'Well then. You should be grateful for small mercies. And while you're at it, I'll have those veg scraps for Monty. I'm trying to fatten him up ready for hibernation.'

It seemed a trivial thing compared to losing Jen, but she was worried about Monty too. He hadn't grown much over the year. And she didn't know if she should be feeding him up or not.

On the way home that afternoon, she stopped outside the library and glanced dubiously at the formidable wooden doors. She wondered if she would ever be able to find that book on tortoises again. She glanced around hoping nobody was watching her dithering on the steps, but the only person she could see was young George Nelson, fiddling with his shoelaces on the other side of the road.

Joyce was just bracing herself to face the librarian again when the library doors opened and Barry Fish came out.

'Well, well,' he said. 'If it isn't Mrs Carter. How nice to see you. I must come and try the wares in your café one day. Some of them look very tasty.'

Joyce met his smarmy gaze head on. 'I hope it's my cakes you are talking about, Mr Fish,' she said. 'Not my daughter.'

He laughed. 'Oh, you always were quick on the uptake weren't you? Even in Stanley's day.'

Joyce shuddered. She didn't want to be reminded of Stanley.

Barry Fish gave a knowing chuckle. 'I hear you are up to no good with that Jewish pawnbroker,' he said. 'Stanley wouldn't have approved of that, you know.'

To her dismay, Joyce felt herself flush. She wasn't up to anything with Mr Lorenz. But she had become fond of him. Mr Lorenz was a good, kind man, even if he was a pawnbroker.

Lorenz was worried about Jen and all. Only the other day he'd asked if there was anyone he could write to on Joyce's behalf. He had seemed quite brought down about it when Joyce told him the only person he could write to was that bastard Adolf Hitler. But whatever Lorenz did or didn't do, it was none of Barry Fish's business. 'I don't know what you're talking about,' she said.

He winked and tapped the side of his nose. 'Oh I think you do,' he said.

As he touched his hat in a mock-courteous farewell, Joyce nodded at the library doors. 'Funny place to find you,' she said. 'I wouldn't have pegged you for a reader, Mr Fish.'

He drew his lips back in one of his nasty little smirks. 'It's surprising what you can find in a library,' he said. 'If you know where to look.'

Joyce watched him walk away with a sense of unease. She hadn't liked that smile. She wondered what he had been looking up. How to crack open a safe most likely, or how to tell a genuine diamond from a fake one. He certainly wouldn't have been looking for a book on tortoise-keeping.

She frowned. Maybe she could ask George Nelson to help her. But when she glanced across the road, the damn child had completely disappeared.

Joyce suddenly wished she hadn't snubbed Bella James all those weeks ago. Otherwise she could have asked her. She would have been able to look up about hibernation on a flash. She was in and out of the library all the time.

Turning away with a sigh, Joyce began to walk home. The thought that Barry Fish had been in the library put her off. Anyway, she wanted to make sure Monty was all right. It was cold and getting dark and she didn't want him suddenly to go into hiding in the garden. That was what had happened last year, she suddenly remembered. And Jen had helped her find him. She felt another sudden shiver of apprehension as she turned the corner into Lavender Road and crossed her fingers superstitiously. I hope Jen's all right, she thought, squeezing them tight. Please God let her be all right.

As she walked back across the parade ground, Molly couldn't believe she'd got away with it. She was certain there would be a shout behind her and she would be stopped and searched and caught red-handed with the scissors. Her first thought was to put them in a safe place. She chose the patch of ground where she often sat playing patience. She sat down and carefully let the scissors slip back down her sleeve into her hand. Then she buried them discreetly in the ground, pressing the earth over them to hide the shape. Nobody would ever find them there.

Standing up again, she let out a long breath and went to find Jen.

Jen was lying curled up on her bed in the bunk room. But her eyes were open.

'Are you all right?' Molly asked tentatively. 'I would have come sooner, but Gefreiter Henniker made me clear up the room.'

Jen was shivering. 'Did he tell you what it was all about?'

Molly shook her head. 'Some kind of medical, he said.'

'But did he tell you why?'

Now it was Molly's turn to be reticent. 'No. He didn't say much.'

Jen sat up and eyed her beadily. 'What did he say?'

Molly shook her head. 'Honestly, Jen, you don't want to know.'

'I do want to know. Tell me.'

'Jen, I can't. '

'What did he say?'

Molly felt herself squirming. She couldn't bring herself to say the words. It was all too awful.

343

'It's not certain,' she stammered. 'He may be wrong. For all I know he was joking. Just to scare us.'

Jen looked at her grittily. 'Tell me.'

Molly sighed. 'He said he thought it might be some kind of sexual thing. Providing women for the SS officers.'

The colour left Jen's face. Her eyes widened in horror. 'They can't do that,' she whispered. 'Surely even beastly old Hauptmann Kleber wouldn't allow that?'

But it seemed he would.

Two days later, ten of the women who had had the so-called medicals were called forward at the early-morning roll call and told to pack their things. Molly just had time to catch Jen's bleak, agonised look when her own name was called out. She was told to report to Hauptmann Kleber.

Oh no, she thought in horror. They've discovered about the missing scissors.

But it wasn't scissors that Hauptmann Kleber wanted to talk about.

'Ten women have been selected for special duties,' he said. 'In the service of the Third Reich.'

Molly looked at him, wondering if he was going to explain what those special duties entailed. But he didn't. Instead he said that it was important that they arrived at their destination in good health. 'I have therefore decided,' he continued, 'to send you with them to ensure that this is the case. Do you understand?'

Molly nodded shakily. She understood all right. Hauptmann Kleber didn't want any repercussions from the SS if anything happened to the women on the way. He wanted a scapegoat.

But it seemed she had maligned him.

'It is Gefreiter Henniker who suggested this,' he added. 'He has been impressed by your nursing skill. He believes you will be a calming influence.'

Even though they were told they could take their blankets and their spare clothes with them, Molly was sure they would be searched before they left the camp. She decided to wind her stolen bandages round her bust and waist in the hope that they wouldn't be asked to strip.

She wanted Jen to do the same, but Jen refused.

'Have you gone completely mad?' she said as she bundled up her few possessions. 'Things are bad enough as they are without getting punished for trying to smuggle out some stupid bandages.'

For once Molly hadn't argued, because she knew Jen was in a bad way.

Since the so-called medical, she had been even more irritable than usual. It wasn't surprising. The prospect of working under duress in a Nazi brothel was enough to knock the stuffing out of anyone. Molly was still struggling to believe that even the Nazis could be capable of such evil.

The previous night she had conjured up a vision of Ward Frazer and tried to imagine what he would do if he was in her shoes. Then, clutching the little magic carpet charm in her hand, she had made a wish. 'Please, please don't let this happen,' she'd whispered. 'Please help us. Please show us a way out.'

There wasn't time to ask any of the other women to help her smuggle out the bandages. In any case, she didn't trust them not to give the game away. The rumours about what lay ahead had spread and they were all in varying states of agitation. So she wound yet one more bandage round her bosoms and hoped that none of the guards would notice that she had developed a voluptuous bust overnight.

In other circumstances it might have been funny, Molly thought, as she stood in line waiting to be patted down. But nothing was very funny any more. In any case, she was still holding her breath in case the scissors were discovered.

But the camp guards were so used to her carrying a pack of cards around that none of them bothered to check inside the card box when she casually laid it on the table with her few other things: her blanket, her Wilhelmina cloak and the shirt and trousers she had been given in Sicily. If they had, they would have found that she had carefully cut the middles out of just enough playing cards to conceal the scissors.

She had no idea what she was going to do with them, or indeed the bandages, but it was the best she could think of. At the very least, she'd be able to keep her toenails trimmed.

And, she thought grimly, as clutching their pitiful bundles they were loaded at gunpoint on to a canvas-sided truck, if the worst came to the very worst, then maybe she and Jen could use the bandages to hang themselves.

Katy was washing the windows when she saw the brewery wagon approaching up the street. Reluctantly she put down her cloth and went over to greet the drayman. The dray horse tossed his head as she drew close, and she jumped hastily out of the way.

The drayman roared with laughter as he tied the animal to the lamp post. 'He nearly got you that time.'

Katy smiled mirthlessly. The dray horse was an enormous animal with a face the size and colour of a suitcase and teeth as big as dominoes. She didn't like how he looked at her, nor the way he twitched every time a fly landed on him. Not only that, but he made her sneeze.

Normally she avoided him like the plague, but unfortunately Helen had taken Malcolm out to pat him a few weeks ago, and Malcolm had taken a liking to the brute. Now, every time he heard the clatter of hooves or the creak of harness, he started squealing to be allowed out of his playpen to greet his new-found friend.

Already Katy could hear him starting up indoors. But she hadn't the energy to go in and fetch him. He would just have to wait until she'd counted the barrels.

It was as she was unlocking the pavement hatch that she saw a man in uniform approaching up the street.

For a second, she froze, thinking it was Ward.

It wasn't, of course. But even as she turned away in disappointment, the young officer lifted a hand in greeting. Who on earth …?

But then she noticed the Canadian shoulder flash. And now she recognised him. 'Callum? Is that really you?'

'It sure is,' he said. He was carrying a parcel, which he now tucked under his arm so that he could give her a self-conscious salute. 'Pilot Officer Callum Frazer of the Royal Canadian Air Force reporting for a glass of beer,' he said. Then he opened his arms, showing off his uniform. 'What do you think?'

Katy laughed. 'You look amazing.'

It was true. He had always been nice-looking, but now there was a new confidence in his step. A sharper look in his eye. It was surprising what a couple of months' military training could do, Katy thought wryly.

'And you are commissioned already? That was quick.'

'You were right,' he said. 'They snapped me up.' He lifted his shoulders slightly. 'I'm on my way to a unit in North Africa. I had to stop over in London for a few hours, so I thought I'd call by.' He glanced at the drayman, who was waiting to roll the first barrel down the ramp into the cellar. 'But it looks like I've come at a bad time.'

'No,' Katy said. 'You have come at an excellent time. Could you go and fetch Malcolm out so he can stroke the horse?'

Callum glanced at the dray horse, which was now relieving itself copiously in the street. 'Sure,' he said. 'I kind of like horses.'

Katy watched him go into the pub, then tentatively eased herself through the hatch and down the rickety steps into the cellar so she could tell the drayman where to put the fresh barrels.

It didn't take the man long to unload, nor to take out the empties. 'That's it then,' he called down to her. 'See you next week.'

'Could you close the hatch,' she called up. 'I'll come up the other way.'

Katy wasn't concerned to find neither Callum nor Malcolm in the bar when she emerged from the cellar a minute later. Malcolm had probably insisted on staying with the horse until the last possible moment.

But when she went over to look out of the door, she nearly had a heart attack.

The dray was moving off briskly down the street, the horse already breaking into a trot. And perched on its enormous back, wobbling alarmingly from side to side, was Malcolm.

'Stop!' Katy yelled. 'Stop!'

The drayman glanced round in surprise but obediently pulled up the horse, which stopped with a great rattle of hooves. It was only then that Katy realised that Callum had been running along on the other side of the horse, holding Malcolm in position. Now, hearing Katy's panic-ridden voice, he lifted Malcolm down.

'I'm sorry,' he said, as soon as he saw Katy's expression. 'I thought he might kind of like it.'

Malcolm was making it quite clear that he had kind of liked it. 'Again,' he was shouting, wriggling like a fish in Callum's arms. 'Horsey. Again.'

Katy suddenly felt rather faint. She knew she had overreacted, but that didn't stop her heart racing.

'Are you OK?' Callum asked, looking at her in concern, even as he grappled to cling on to Malcolm.

Katy didn't know whether to laugh or cry. She put her hand on her stomach. The baby was complaining. Maybe it wanted a ride on a horse too. 'I think I need to sit down,' she gasped. 'You Frazer men. You're going to be the death of me.'

The canvas back panel of the truck was rolled down so the women couldn't see out, and they were driven for about an hour under armed guard to a railway station. There, after a long delay in the hot lorry, they were herded on to a train, bundled down the narrow corridor and shoved into a compartment designed for six. A moment later the door was slammed and locked behind them.

It was a similar train to the ones Jen and Molly had travelled on before. Then, they'd had a whole compartment to themselves. Now, the first thing they had to do was work out a way for everyone to get the chance to sit down. As there were eleven of them, it wasn't easy. There was a language problem too. The English woman, Nancy, had been shocked into silence. None of the Italians nor the two Polish women spoke any English. And the young Dutch girl, whom the guards had earlier had to drag screaming from her mother's arms, was still crying.

In the end they arranged it that four women would cram in on each side. The most agile two, Jen and the Dutch girl, would climb up and lie on blankets on the luggage rack. Molly volunteered to sit on the floor under the window.

It was very uncomfortable and it didn't take long for Molly to regret her magnanimity. She had become so thin that her bottom bones quickly got sore pressing on the hard, jolting floor. The other women, wedged together on the wooden benches, at least had each other to lean against. And up on the luggage rack, Jen looked as though she was comfortably asleep.

As Molly bunched her spare clothes together to make a kind of makeshift cushion, she wondered if Gefreiter Henniker had intended to do her a favour by recommending that she went with the other women. Or perhaps he really had thought she would be a calming influence.

Well if that was the case, she thought sourly, he was wrong. She didn't want to calm the other women, she wanted to motivate them. Since the missed opportunity of the armistice, there had been no possibility of escape. But on a long journey there might just be a chance. After all, Ward Frazer had escaped from a train in Germany.

Gefreiter Henniker wasn't one of the escort guards. Instead Hauptmann Kleber had allocated three of his most surly men. But maybe, just maybe, Molly thought, their callous inattention might play into her hands.

'We're going to have to try to escape,' she said suddenly.

Nancy laughed sourly. 'And how do you suggest we go about that?'

'I don't know. But we have to keep our eyes open,' Molly said doggedly. 'An opportunity might come up and we must be ready.'

Nancy's translation of this was greeted by a nervous outcry of objections.

'They think we will get shot,' she said.

'Maybe,' Molly said brutally. 'But surely it's better to risk getting shot than end up working in an SS brothel.'

Apart from the horse incident, Katy was enjoying Callum's visit. He was full of his new adventure and keen to catch up on all the news. He was impressed that Ward had been involved in the liberation of Corsica. 'Wow, that's pretty cool,' he said.

He enquired politely after Helen and seemed mildly disappointed that she had gone up to town for the morning. But he nearly fell off his chair when he asked about Molly, and Katy told him what had happened to her.

'My God,' he said. 'And you've heard nothing since August?' He looked at her, aghast. 'How can you be so calm about it?'

'I'm not at all calm,' Katy said. 'But it's the war. We've all had to get used to waiting and hoping.'

'I guess,' he said. It looked as though he was going to say something else, but he stopped himself and flushed slightly. He took a glug of his drink. 'Well I sure hope she's OK,' he said gruffly.

It was only as he stood up to go that he remembered the parcel he had brought with him.

'Oh yeah,' he said. 'Ward's mom gave me this to bring over for Malcolm. It's some old thing Ward had when he was a kid.' He made a doubtful face. 'It's pretty tatty, but she thought Malcolm might like it.'

Unwrapping the parcel, Katy found a threadbare teddy bear inside. He was dressed in faded striped pyjamas. One of his ears was slightly torn. But he had a kind face and very soft paws. Suddenly she had an image of Ward hugging him as a young child, and tears filled her eyes.

She didn't know if Malcolm would like it or not. It didn't matter. Because it wasn't just a tatty old bear. It was an olive branch.

Now she had an excuse to write to Mrs Frazer. And that was something she had wanted to do for a long time.

'Thank you, Callum,' she said, as she hugged him tearfully goodbye out on the street. 'Thank you for coming. Good luck in North Africa. And be safe.'

'I'll do my best,' Callum said with a brave smile. 'And good luck to you with the baby.'

With that he turned quickly away. But after a few paces he stopped. 'Oh, and hey, Katy,' he called back. 'If I let you know where I am, will you write me?' He hesitated. 'And if you do hear anything about Molly, good or bad, I'd kind of like to know …'

It was Jen who noticed the crack in the window.

'Good God,' she remarked suddenly. 'Molly, look. The glass is chipped.'

Molly stood up to see. The train's jolting was causing the ragged blackout curtain to swing to one side, and sure enough, behind it there was indeed a hairline crack running up the top right-hand side of the dirty window pane.

Molly thought back to the damaged trains they had seen at the station in Rome. 'It probably happened during a bombing raid,' she said. 'And nobody noticed because of the curtain.' If Jen hadn't been perched right up there on the luggage rack, none of them would have noticed it either.

'The glass is really thick,' Jen said, levering herself up on to her elbows to have a better look. She ran her finger over the crack. 'We still wouldn't be able to break it. Not unless we had something really sharp to poke into it.'

'I've got a pair of scissors,' Molly whispered, and Jen turned her head to look down at her in amazement.

'How on earth …?'

'Shh,' Molly said. She hadn't much faith in the discretion of their fellow captives. But it was too late. One of the Italian women had already swivelled round to see what they were looking at. Spotting the crack, she started chattering excitedly. One of the Polish women leapt to her feet and started banging her fist on the glass.

'No.' Molly grabbed her arm, desperately hoping the clunking rattle of the train would have drowned out the noise. 'Wait. We must think about this carefully.'

But the women were all animated now, taking it in turns to scramble over each other to inspect the window.

Molly glanced up at Jen in despair.

Jen leaned out from her eyrie. 'Sit down!' she hissed. The women looked up at her in alarm, but even though they didn't understand the words, they understood her angry glare and her mime as she pointed expressively at the door. 'We don't want the guards getting suspicious. For goodness' sake, just sit down and shut up, and give us a chance to think.'

As the women subsided, she rolled her eyes at Molly. 'Any ideas?'

Molly's mind was racing. She knew they would only get one chance. And they had to get it right.

The train was travelling at considerable speed, so they clearly couldn't jump out as it went along. Nor would they be able to escape at a station. Stations were invariably full of German soldiers.

Their best chance was to wait for an unscheduled stop, preferably in a siding.

'But what happens if it doesn't stop?' Nancy asked.

'It will,' Molly said confidently. She thought back to their earlier train journeys and looked up at Jen for corroboration. 'Italian trains stop all the time.'

'But what if we reach our destination before then?'

'We must be going some distance or they would have taken us by truck,' Jen pointed out grimly. 'For all we know, we're on our way to Germany.'

Nancy flinched. 'So when we stop,' she said. '*If* we stop. We simply break the window and jump out?' She gave a sceptical sniff. 'Don't you think someone would notice?'

Molly grimaced. 'Yes,' she said. 'They would notice. That's why we have to time it just right. If we stop for any length of time, some of the men are bound to get out to stretch their legs.'

'And to pee,' Jen said. The Dutch girl giggled. Molly looked up at her and realised she looked better already. They all did. The cracked window had given them hope.

But their excitement made her nervous. It will never work, she thought. How could it possibly work?

'So we wait until they get on again,' she said, 'and then we break the window. If we can. Then we climb out quickly before the train moves away.'

Jen glanced out of the window. 'It's an awfully long drop if there's no platform,' she said doubtfully. 'And there are eleven of us. It's not going to be easy.'

Molly picked up her spare shirt. 'The first thing we have to do is drape something over the glass in the corridor door, like we did before. Get the guards used to not being able to see in.'

Then she lifted her tunic and began to unwind the bandages. 'If we plait these, maybe we can use them as a rope.'

Jen's dry laugh held a hint of her old sarcasm. 'You're not just a pretty face, are you?' she said.

Molly glanced up at her. 'Thankfully not,' she said. And that wiped the smirk off Jen's lips.

'OK,' Jen turned grimly to Nancy. 'It's up to you to make sure these idiot women do exactly what they are told. If anyone messes up and gives the game away, I'll kill them with my own hands.'

The words were barely out of her mouth when the train began to slow. It creaked and groaned, and a few minutes later came to a grinding halt. Peering out of the window, Molly saw that they were indeed in a siding.

Despite it being late October, the sun was still blazing down. The grass at the side of the track was dry, the bare earth in the adjacent fields cracked and pitted. The parched landscape was only interrupted by a few thin trees clustering round a distant red-roofed farmhouse.

Nervous chatter broke out as the women began to look excitedly towards the window.

Molly shook her head. 'No,' she said. 'Not here. It's too soon. We aren't ready.'

'But—' Nancy began, but she was interrupted by the sound of voices outside the door.

While Jen made sure the curtain was covering the crack, Molly hastily sat down again with the bandages bundled up behind her back. She was just in time. A second later, one of their guards opened the door.

The nearest women flinched back guiltily. Molly gritted her teeth, but the soldier was used to his prisoners looking nervous. If anything, he seemed pleased by their scared faces.

But he wasn't pleased about the shirt covering the glass panel in the door. 'No,' he said, reaching round the door to pull it down. 'This is not permitted.'

'Oh, please leave it,' Molly said. 'It's so hot in here and the girls want to take off some clothes, but people keep staring in at them.'

The man hesitated. He turned to consult someone in the corridor, then nodded grudgingly. '*Ja.* OK.'

'So next time you want to come in, please will you knock first?' Jen asked sweetly. 'We wouldn't want to shock you. Oh, and if there's any chance of a drink ...?'

He glared at her and slammed the door.

A minute later, they saw him outside the window, smoking with his cronies at the side of the track. After a while, as Jen had predicted, they started to fumble with their flies. But then, perhaps aware of the women's eyes on them, they moved out of sight along the verge.

Ten minutes later they heard the doors slam, then the whistle blew and the train jerked and grumbled back into action.

'OK,' Molly said, turning back from the window. 'Let's get these bandages plaited so we're ready for the next time.'

Two hours elapsed before the next suitable stop. A couple of times their hopes had been raised when the train slowed, but either it had picked up speed again, or it had pulled into yet another station with an unpronounceable name.

'We should have had a go in that last siding,' Nancy kept saying in her posh voice. 'For all we know, we might be getting off at the next station.'

'Oh do shut up,' Jen said irritably. 'There's nothing we can do about it now.'

'There'll be another chance,' Molly said placatingly as Nancy bridled. 'We just have to hold our nerve.'

But even she had begun to get nervous. She would feel such a fool if they really had missed their chance. But it would have been hopeless to do anything until they were ready. Now, with Nancy laboriously translating, they had finally worked out a plan. They all knew what to do. They just needed a chance to put it into action.

And it came sooner than they had expected. The train had only been travelling about ten minutes out of a station called Viareggio when it once again ground to a halt. Molly glanced up at Jen and felt her pulse accelerate.

The terrain was different here. The railway seemed to be running through a wide plain. There were a few straggly bushes growing between the track and the adjacent fields. The landscape beyond was flat, patterned in long, narrow lines of low trellised vines, and bisected by a road that ran parallel to the railway line. In the distance, some way ahead of them, Molly could see two wooded hills, topped with small red-roofed towns. 'I don't know,' she said doubtfully. 'There's not much cover.'

Hearing the clunk of a door opening further up the train, Jen leaned down to peer out of the window. 'Our guards have got out,' she murmured to Molly. 'I think it's now or never. I don't think we'll be able to contain these madwomen much longer. Not now they've got the prospect of freedom.'

She was right. The women were already fidgeting impatiently.

'All right,' Molly said. And even as she spoke, she felt her heart accelerate. 'Let's get ready.'

Twenty minutes later they saw the soldiers outside stubbing out their cigarettes.

'OK. This is it,' Molly whispered.

When the train's whistle blew, they were ready and in position. Jen and Olga were lying on their backs on the luggage racks ready to start putting pressure on the window. One of the Polish women had tied one bandage rope to the overhead rack and another to the door handle, to delay anyone coming in for as long as possible.

Molly was poised with her shoe in her hand, ready to hammer the scissors into the crack.

As the doors began to slam shut, she gave the shoe a first tentative knock on the scissors.

Nothing happened.

She tried again. At the same time Jen and Olga started pushing their feet against the glass.

Molly's heart sank. It wasn't going to work. Despite the crack, the glass was still too tough. She heard the train's engine give a low, throbbing cough as it came to life.

'For goodness' sake give me the shoe,' Nancy said. Snatching it out of Molly's hand, she began frantically hammering the heel on the scissors.

And suddenly, miraculously, the fissure deepened.

'Come on, you bastard,' Jen muttered.

A moment later, with a sharp, splintering crack, the glass shattered and smashed out on to the ground outside.

As one, the women fell silent, terrified that there might still have been someone outside to hear the crash. But there were no shouts. No alarms. In fact the train was already beginning to creak and groan, its normal procedure prior to moving off.

'Quick,' Molly whispered to Nancy. 'Go.' She dropped the blankets out of the window. 'Try to cover yourselves with those. And don't forget to lie completely still, as close as you can to the track. And make sure the others do too.'

It had sounded easy, but it seemed to take an age for Nancy to clamber from the seat to the glass-encrusted sill. She balanced precariously for a moment, then levered herself over, grabbing the knotted rope and sliding down the other side to the ground.

They all waited tensely for a shout or a shot. None came. Olga was much quicker, and the other women followed obediently.

Molly and Jen had agreed to go last. The train was already moving by then, juddering as the engine rolled slowly over the points.

'Good luck,' Molly whispered as Jen grabbed the rope and shimmied efficiently over the sill.

Then it was her turn. As on the MS *Marigold* all those weeks ago, it was harder than it looked. And once again it was made more difficult by the fact that she was shaking all over and her palms were slick with sweat.

But she managed it. The jagged glass on the sill caught briefly on her tunic, and then she was out, bumping hard against the side of the moving train, scraping her knuckles painfully against the grey paintwork.

Reluctantly she let go of the rope and crashed to the ground, keeping her head down as she had instructed the others to do. She could feel the turbulence in the air as the metal wheels hissed and thumped over the track only inches from her head, but she didn't move. She remembered George and Ward hiding in the ruins of the Miss Taylors' old house. 'It's movement that attracts attention,' Ward had said. 'If you keep still, nobody will notice you.'

Molly kept still. She kept still for so long that when someone tapped her on the shoulder, the train was completely out of earshot.

She lifted her head in alarm, expecting to see a German officer training a rifle on her. But it was only Jen, crouching beside her. Behind Jen, further back down the track, Molly could see the other women already on their feet, brushing themselves down, gathering up their bundles.

Jen's trousers were torn. Her knees were grazed and beginning to bleed, but there was a big grin on her face. 'We did it,' she said. Her voice was unusually husky. 'It looks like we did it.'

She glanced around at the empty countryside and gave a shaky laugh. 'But now what do we do?'

Chapter Twenty-Five

It didn't take long for the euphoria of their escape to wear off. Five minutes later, dazed and disoriented, the eleven of them were still standing at the edge of the railway line, nervously clutching their bundles of clothes and blankets.

The siding seemed to be in the middle of nowhere. An expanse of gnarled vines stretched away in all directions, the bare branches trained on to low parallel lines of rope or wire. Apart from a couple of dusty bushes, there was nowhere to hide. The only route away from the railway was a narrow track that Molly assumed would lead to the road she had seen from the higher vantage point of the carriage window earlier.

'What will they do when they realise we've escaped?' the Dutch girl asked anxiously, glancing up the track.

'God knows,' Jen said. 'They'll probably stop at the next station and radio for a search party to come and find us.'

'We should split up,' Molly said. 'Go different ways in pairs and threes. There's no hope for us if we stay as a gang.'

But nobody wanted to be the ones to break away. When Jen and Molly started to walk down the track towards the road, they soon found everyone else trailing behind them like lemmings.

'Safety in numbers,' Nancy said, when Jen complained. 'We have to get to the road. Then we'll decide what to do.'

The road did seem the obvious choice. They clearly wouldn't get far tramping through the lines of vines. But when they reached the road, another argument broke out. Nobody wanted to go in the direction of the villages they could see on the nearby hills for fear of meeting Germans, or some Italian sympathiser who might turn them in.

'Look,' Jen pointed out. 'There's a crossroad up the other way. Let's go in that direction and then we can divide.'

But well before they reached the junction, they were overtaken by a young boy on a bicycle.

And the incomprehensible, high-pitched announcement he delivered as he whizzed past galvanised the women into instant action.

'What's happening?' Molly asked in alarm as they all started running off up the road.

'The Germans are coming,' Nancy said. She nodded back towards the villages. 'They are only a mile away, the other side of the hill. The local mayor saw us escape from the train and sent the boy to tell us that we should hurry.' And she set off in hot pursuit of the other women.

Molly held on to Jen's sleeve as she went to follow them.

'We don't stand a chance that way, she said.

'We don't stand a chance any way,' Jen snapped.

Molly looked around. 'We can hide in the field.'

'But there's no cover. They'll see us from miles away.'

'No they won't.'

'What on earth are you talking about?' Jen said. But she followed Molly off the road.

As they ran up through a line of vines, Molly could hear Jen panting behind her. 'For goodness' sake,' Jen gasped. 'What are you doing? Have you gone mad?'

Molly stopped and looked around. The other women were straggled out along the distant road now, the fitter ones still running, the rest dropping behind. She looked the other way. The road stretching back towards the villages was empty. She couldn't see any vehicles, but as she squinted against the glare of the sun, she thought she heard the distant grumble of an engine. At once she dropped her bundle. She would have liked to go further, but this would have to do. She turned to Jen, who was standing behind her, head bowed, clutching her sides. 'Do you still have that black dress?'

Jen looked up in astonishment.

'We need to look like old women working the fields,' Molly said. 'Like we saw in Sicily and from the trains.'

It took a moment for Jen to cotton on, but then she swung into action, dragging the black dress out of her bundle and ripping it into scarf-sized pieces.

Working quickly, they draped the dark army blankets over their shoulders and belted them at the waist with more strips from the dress.

'Now what?' Jen said when they stood there looking like two shabby nuns.

'Ninety per cent of recognition depends on body posture and gestures,' Molly muttered. 'How do we make ourselves look old?'

'I don't know.' Jen shrugged. 'I've always been hopeless at improvisation.'

'Oh for goodness' sake,' Molly said impatiently. 'I thought you were meant to be an actress.' She tensed. 'Listen,' she said. 'It's too late. They're coming.'

Jen swore under her breath. 'Bend over,' she said. 'Look hunched. Move slowly. Pretend to be checking the leaves or something.'

Out of the corner of her eye Molly saw two vehicles, an open car and a canvas-sided truck, coming quite fast along the road from the direction of the village. The car was flying a swastika flag from the aerial.

'Oh God,' Molly whispered. 'Oh God. Let's pray they don't stop.'

They did stop.

A man in field-grey uniform and officer's cap got out of the lead car.

'Now we're for it,' Jen muttered.

'Ignore them,' Molly whispered.

The man shouted something in Italian.

They ignored him.

'OK, clever clogs,' Jen said when the man shouted again. 'What do we do now?'

Molly swallowed. Her heart was jumping all over the place. 'I don't know,' she said. 'Act?'

And to her surprise, Jen did act. She turned round slowly, shading her eyes and face with a bent arm as though she had poor vision. Her other hand was on her back as though she had lumbago.

Seeing he had her attention, the man called out again, pointing towards the railway line.

Jen continued to stare in dumb silence. Then, to Molly's utter amazement, in a voice that sounded exactly like that of an old crone, she shouted, '*Non ho visto niente.*'

The man immediately responded with another question.

'What's he saying?' Molly whispered out of the corner of her mouth. 'What did you say?'

'I said I hadn't seen anything,' Jen said. 'But I have no idea what he is saying now.'

The German shouted over again.

'I'm fed up with this idiot,' Jen muttered.

Still shielding her face, she suddenly waved her other fist at the vehicles and yelled out another phrase in her screechy old woman's voice. '*Va fanculo, tedeschi sporchi.*' Then she spat on the ground and turned back to the vine.

Molly almost passed out with shock. She could feel her head swimming. Her palms felt clammy.

'What did that mean?' she asked after a moment.

'I'm not sure,' Jen said. 'But I know it's rather rude. The Italian boys in the camp said it all the time. I hope I got it right.'

Despite her terror, Molly had to bite her lip to stop herself laughing.

'What is he doing?' Jen asked.

Molly took a surreptitious peek from under her makeshift scarf. 'He's talking to the driver of the car. No, wait. He's getting back in. It looks like they're going.'

'Thank God for that,' Jen said as the vehicle roared away up the road. 'I'm sweating like a pig under this damn blanket. What shall we do? Go back to the road? Or run the other way?'

Molly shook her head. 'No, we must stay where we are. In case they come back the same way. They might get suspicious if we aren't still here.'

Five minutes later the vehicles did come back the same way. And huddled together in the back of the truck, under armed guard, were their former camp mates, looking most forlorn.

'I hope they don't recognise us,' Jen said, bending over the vine again as the vehicles swept past.

'They won't,' Molly said confidently. 'We're part of the landscape. Hidden in plain sight.'

When the truck had disappeared, Molly stood up and exhaled. Her knees were trembling.

'Phew,' she said. She glanced across at Jen. 'You were brilliant. You had them completely fooled.'

Jen shrugged. 'You weren't so shabby yourself,' she said. 'Who taught you how to do that? No.' She held up her hand. 'Let me guess. George Nelson?'

'Well, yes,' Molly admitted. She crouched down to pick up her things. 'And Ward Frazer.'

When she straightened up again, Jen was looking amused, and for a terrible moment Molly thought she had guessed her guilty secret. But then Jen gave a light laugh. 'It's a good trick,' she said. 'It certainly worked this time. But we can't stand here for ever. We'd better find somewhere to hide. It won't take them long to realise they haven't caught everyone.'

But finding somewhere to hide was easier said than done. Both born and bred in London, they had no idea about landscape, vegetation or where they might conceivably find shelter and water. Molly had only identified the foliage twisted on to the wire trellis as vines because she had noticed that some of them still had little bunches of shrivelled grapes hanging from them. Hoping that they might help relieve her thirst, Jen had picked some to try, but spat them out at once. 'Yuck,' she said. 'That is disgusting.'

Soon after that, she thought she saw a snake and thereafter refused to wade through the dry grass that grew along the centre of the gaps between the trellises. Instead she insisted on teetering along as close to the vines as possible. 'There's no point evading the Germans if we get bitten by a snake instead,' she pointed out.

Molly had no idea if there were poisonous snakes in Italy – she thought what Jen had seen was probably a lizard – but even she had to admit that they were completely out of their depth. They seemed to have been walking for ever and they were no nearer to finding a hiding place.

'This is ridiculous,' Jen said when they reached the end of yet another row. 'I can't go on much further. I'm absolutely exhausted. My legs feel like jelly.'

'Well you should have done some exercises at the camp,' Molly snapped. 'Instead of just laughing at me.'

But she was finding it hard going too. The land was rough and dry, parched from months of sunshine. Dead leaves crackled underfoot. Clouds of dust and insects swarmed up around them at every step.

Eventually they stumbled across a track that seemed to be leading towards one of the hill towns they had seen earlier, but then immediately fell out about whether to follow it or not.

'It's too dangerous,' Molly said. 'What's to stop them turning us in?'

'The mayor sent that boy to warn us about the Germans coming,' Jen pointed out. 'They must be on our side.'

'Yes, but it may not have been the mayor of this village,' Molly said. 'For all we know, every village might have a mayor.'

'I don't care how many blasted mayors there are,' Jen said irritably. 'We are going to have to trust somebody sooner or later. Or else we're going to die of thirst.'

It was as they stood arguing that Molly noticed something shimmering like a mirage at the end of the track. It was impossible at this distance to tell what it was. At first she thought it was a goat or a horse, but then, as the little dust cloud gradually approached, they realised it was once again the boy on the bicycle.

Drawing up in front of them, he immediately launched into one of his excited speeches. Molly stared at him in dismay. She had absolutely no idea what he was saying. But Jen, with the aid of some calming hand gestures and some stumbling Italian questions of her own, seemed to be able to get the gist of what he was trying to communicate.

'He wants us to follow him somewhere,' she said. 'I've no idea where. And then we must wait until dark. Someone will come and help us.'

Molly was impressed. 'How on earth can you understand him?' she asked as the boy zoomed off and they began to walk along in his dusty wake. 'When did you suddenly learn Italian?'

'I don't know,' Jen said negligently. 'I suppose I picked up some words from the Italian soldiers, and from listening to the women in the camp. Mind you,' she added, 'It would help if the stupid brat didn't insist on talking so fast. He doesn't seem to grasp that we can't speak Italian. He's clearly missing a few cogs in the brain department.'

'I think he's rather sweet,' Molly said. 'He reminds me of George Nelson.'

'Oh God,' Jen groaned. 'That's all we need.'

But whether the boy was missing mental cogs or not, he managed to lead them to a small forest on the edge of a hill. Leaving his bike lying on the ground, he guided them along a tiny indistinguishable path to a clearing in which stood a derelict hut. It had probably once belonged to some kind of woodsman. It had long since been abandoned. Half the roof had caved in, and there were weeds and even a small tree growing inside. But at least it was shady. And pretty much invisible.

Patting the air with his hand in the kind of stay gesture you would make to an attentive dog, the boy fired off a final salvo of Italian and disappeared back the way they had come.

Jen looked around dubiously. 'So now we wait until dark,' she said.

Katy glanced at the clock. It was unusual for Helen to be late. And having been delayed by Callum's visit, she was struggling to get ready for the lunchtime opening on her own. She was relying on Helen more and more now that her pregnancy was getting advanced.

Helen had gone up to town to the SOE. She had been several times recently. But as the organisation had no effective underground networks yet in Italy, there was little chance of picking up word on Molly or Jen.

In France, however, even though the British efforts had faltered, the resistance movement was strengthening. News had come in that members of the French Resistance had attacked a prison in Lyons and released fourteen of their imprisoned comrades. Helen hadn't said, but Katy knew that she had wondered if André was involved, either as one of the attackers, or as one of the released prisoners.

Hearing the door open, Katy looked up in relief. But instead of Helen breezing in past the blackout curtain in her smart little Eisenhower jacket and pencil skirt, Katy saw a thin, black-haired young woman in the shabbiest coat she had ever seen.

'Can I help you?' Katy asked coolly as the girl approached the bar. There had been rumours recently of foreign beggars importuning local landlords for money or food, and if anyone looked like a beggar, this girl did.

But the girl seemed more nervous than aggressive. 'My name is Elsa Distel,' she said, looking at Katy expectantly. Her eyes were very dark, with unusually long curling lashes. 'I hope I come to the right place?'

Katy stared at her blankly. 'The right place for what?' she asked.

'You are Katy, yes?'

'Yes, I am.' Katy frowned and glanced at the clock. The first customers would be arriving in a minute and she hadn't even given Malcolm his lunch yet. He had been grizzling disconsolately in the playpen ever since Callum had left.

The girl lowered her eyes and took a step back. 'Perhaps I mistake. I thought you would expect me. I met a man. I think your husband. He mention to me that you might need a barmaid?'

Suddenly the penny dropped. Katy stared at the girl in dismay. This pitiful creature was the Jewish refugee that Ward had thought might work in the pub? She didn't look strong enough to lift a flea, let alone manoeuvre barrels of beer or carry crates up from the cellar. Nor did she look capable of dealing with irascible customers. But she clearly couldn't turn the poor girl away out of hand.

'I'm sorry,' she said. 'Ward didn't give me your name. So I—' She stopped abruptly as the door swung open and Helen came rushing in.

'Katy, I'm sorry,' she said. 'But something has come up and I need to talk to you urgently.'

'What about?' Katy asked, hurrying out from behind the bar in alarm.

'I've been offered a job,' Helen said. She gave Katy an agonised look. 'I should have mentioned it before, but I didn't want to leave you in the lurch. I was hoping Ward would come home. But now they're pressing me and—'

'What sort of job?' Katy asked, even as her heart sank. She knew it was going to be with the SOE.

Helen threw a quick glance at Elsa Distel and lowered her voice. 'In Tunisia.' She grimaced. 'At first I said no. But it's not undercover or anything like that. They need someone to co-ordinate things between the various agencies.' She hesitated. 'I might have a chance to find out what's happened to André. And maybe even Jen and Molly.' She stopped again and touched Katy's arm. 'Katy, listen. If you don't want me to go, I won't.' She grimaced. 'But they want me to make a decision today.'

Katy realised she felt faint. She put a hand on the bar to steady herself and tried to breathe normally. It suddenly seemed as though all her friends were deserting her. She still had Louise, of course. But if Louise had anything to do with it, Katy would soon be losing her to Charlie Hawkridge.

'I think I'm falling in love with him,' she had whispered to Katy a couple of nights previously. 'He seems to be awfully well off, and without Jack's salary I can't really afford the rent on the flat. So I'm going to hint that we ought to get married.'

But however much she wanted to thwart Louise's plans, Katy knew she couldn't thwart Helen's. Not if there was even the remotest chance of her finding out what had happened to Molly and Jen.

'When would you have to go?' she asked faintly.

Helen shook her head. 'I don't know. Quite soon, I think. But there's a lot to do here in London first. ' She screwed up her face apologetically. 'And they want me to start straight away.'

Katy stared at her in silence for a second. Then she turned to Elsa Distel, who was still standing patiently at the bar. 'It looks as though you've got yourself a job,' she said.

The hut wasn't exactly cool, but at least it allowed Molly and Jen to get out of the sun. And having laid the blankets out on the bare earth floor, they both flopped down in considerable relief. They were tired, hungry and very thirsty. But at least, for the moment, they were free.

Molly had wanted to doze, but she couldn't relax. She kept reliving the events of the last few hours. The image of those women scrambling out of the train window would be embedded in her brain for ever.

'What do you think will happen to the others?' she asked after a while. She could tell from the way Jen twitched every time an insect landed on her that she wasn't asleep either.

'I don't know,' Jen replied drowsily. 'Let's hope the guys who picked them up have more guts than Hauptmann Kleber. If so, they might make some effort to protect them from that bastard Wessel.' She give a visible shudder as she spoke, and Molly knew she was imagining what might have awaited her at the end of the journey.

Molly felt her own flesh creep. 'It's the first time in my life I've been glad I wasn't pretty,' she said.

Jen sat up and stretched. 'You know, you actually aren't that bad-looking,' she said. 'Since we've been over here, you've got tanned and it suits you.'

Molly shook her head. 'I look like a pixie,' she said. 'You've said it often enough yourself.' She touched her chipped tooth with her tongue. 'And now I've got a broken tooth as well.'

Jen had the grace to look guilty. 'I was only being mean. I was furious about the chickenpox business and I wanted to get back at you. I reckon you should change your hair, though. You'd look better with layers and a fringe.'

Molly glanced at her suspiciously. 'You're just being nice to me because

362

of the train.'

'I'm not,' Jen said. She laughed. 'Well, maybe a bit. If you hadn't smuggled out those bandages and the scissors, God knows what would have happened.'

Reaching over, Molly slipped the scissors out of the card packet and looked at them thoughtfully. 'Would you do it for me now?' she asked.

'What?'

'Cut my hair?'

For a second she thought Jen was going to refuse. But then she laughed. 'Why not? It's not as though we've got anything else to do.'

It felt odd having Jen crouching so close to her. Feeling her fingers in her hair. Hearing the crunch of the scissors. Flinching at her occasional muttered oath or command to keep still. It seemed to take ages, and Molly couldn't help feeling nervous as the little piles of hair on the blanket grew.

When Jen eventually laid down the scissors, Molly fingered her remaining hair experimentally. 'How does it look?' she asked.

Jen tilted her head on one side. 'It looks a bit like a rat's gnawed at it,' she said. 'But apart from that, it's OK. Better than it was, anyway.' She ran a negligent hand through her own hair. Her perm had long grown out and her reddish hair was lank and full of split ends. 'One of the things I miss most is going to the hairdresser.'

Molly picked up the scissors. 'Do you want me to have a go at yours?'

'You must be joking.' Jen recoiled in horror. 'I'm not letting you loose on my hair with a pair of nail scissors. No, I'm going to wait until we get home, and then I'll treat myself to a nice cut, wash and set in a posh West End salon.'

Molly bit back a sharp retort. That was so typical of Jen. To be quite nice one minute and uppity the next.

Turning away, she touched her hair again. It felt good. Light and cool. She wondered what people would think of it when they got back. She wondered whether Ward—

'What do you miss most about England?' Jen asked suddenly.

Molly nearly said his name without thinking. But she stopped herself just in time, and seeing Jen's eyes on her, she felt herself flush.

'I don't know,' she said quickly. 'Everything, I think. My life seemed so ordinary, so routine, but I miss it now. What about you? What do you miss most? Apart from the hairdresser.'

'My mum's cooking,' Jen said. She lay back and rested her head on her hands. 'I keep wondering how she got on with that demonstration in Wandsworth.'

Molly looked at her in surprise. 'Didn't you hear? No, I suppose you'd

363

already left.' She thought back to that evening. To Ward and Katy's guilty amusement. 'I think it was a bit of a disaster. Katy said your mum got into a terrible fluster. And because she was so nervous, everything went wrong.'

There was a long pause. 'I should have given her more help,' Jen said eventually, and lapsed into silence.

'What about Henry Keller?' Molly asked after a while. 'Do you miss him?' She hesitated. 'Or Conrad Porter?'

Jen looked up at her sharply. 'I didn't go to bed with Conrad on the boat.'

'I wasn't asking that,' Molly said.

'Weren't you?' Jen said. 'Well I've been wanting to tell you anyway. Conrad was fun and he gave me brandy to stop me feeling sick. Too much brandy as it turned out. But I didn't go to bed with him.'

She took a long breath and exhaled heavily. 'I don't know if I miss Henry or not. He made me so nervous. It's like I was in his thrall. It seems weird looking back on it.'

'Well he is pretty important, isn't he?' Molly said. 'And rather gorgeous.'

'Do you think so?' Jen gave a slight laugh and slanted Molly a sly glance. 'I'm surprised you noticed,' she said. 'I thought you only had eyes for Ward Frazer.'

It was entirely unexpected, out of the blue. Molly wasn't ready. And it felt like a blow to the heart. She suddenly found it hard to breathe.

Mortification, horror, embarrassment ran through her. On top of everything, it seemed a cruel irony that of all people, it was Jen Carter who had guessed her guilty secret. And now, she thought bitterly, Jen would never let her hear the last of it.

At that moment Molly hoped they never would get back to England. The thought of Jen teasing her in front of him, or laughing up her sleeve, was completely unbearable.

Jen was already grinning now. 'Katy always thought you didn't like him, but I ...' She caught Molly's agonised expression and stopped in surprise, her smile fading.

'Hey. Don't take it so hard. You're not alone. We've all been in love with Ward Frazer at one point or another. Louise, Helen, me ...'

'You?' It came out as a strangled gasp.

'Sure.' Jen shrugged. 'In the early days. I probably still am a bit. He's just one of those perfect men. Handsome, nice, kind, funny, bags of sex appeal.' She made a wry face. 'And unfortunately, having someone like him around makes it hard for any of us to fall for anyone else.'

Molly stared at her incredulously. She could hardly believe her ears. Jen wasn't mocking her. She wasn't laughing at her. On the contrary, she understood. She even sympathised.

Molly couldn't speak or think. She felt completely dazed. For a moment she even forgot where she was. The predicament they were in. She was so overwhelmed by relief, it was like a heavy burden falling off her shoulders. A deliverance. She wasn't mad. She wasn't alone.

Jen lay down again. 'Bloody men,' she said. 'They're a menace. When I get back to England, I'm not going to have anything to do with any of them.'

Chapter Twenty-Six

It turned out that Elsa Distel had walked all the way from Ealing in west London to see Katy. She had set out at six o'clock and had had nothing to eat or drink all day.

Thanks to Ward's intervention before he went away, the whole Distel family had finally been released from the internment camp at Lingfield Park racecourse in Surrey. But as 'enemy aliens' they had no access to work permits and therefore no means of supporting themselves. They had been allocated one small room in a tenement building by the Central Office for Refugees. They had to share a kitchen and a bathroom with ten other families. Elsa wasn't complaining. She was appreciative of the help they had been given. But it clearly was a desperate situation.

While Helen manned the bar, Katy took Elsa upstairs and gave her and Malcolm some bread and cheese and a small glass of milk each. The girl was pathetically grateful for the food. And even more so for the offer of paid work.

'You do not mind that I am a Jew?' she asked, clearly anxious to make sure there was no misunderstanding.

'Of course not,' Katy said. 'I already have a young Jewish boy, Jacob, helping me at the weekends. He and his brothers are also refugees; they came here from Austria right at the beginning of the war.'

Elsa seemed pleased about that. She gave Katy a shy smile. 'I look forward to meeting him,' she said.

'If you work as hard as him, then I will be pleased,' Katy said.

She nodded eagerly. 'I will. I am good worker.'

And she was.

Katy had intended just to show her the ropes that day, explain how things were done. But Elsa was so eager to help that it wasn't long before she was busy washing glasses and wiping tables.

She didn't talk much, although she was pleased to discover that Helen spoke French, but she was quick, clean and efficient and she did exactly what she was told. It was clear that she had indeed worked in a bar, a much smarter one probably than the Flag and Garter. She didn't know much about beer, but she knew about shorts and measures. And despite her fragile appearance, she was strong.

366

The only problem was that she lived such a long way away.

'She can't come traipsing over from Ealing every day,' Katy said as Elsa exchanged a few shy words in English with Aaref Hoch, who had brought in two new beer glasses to replace a couple that had disappeared only the previous week, despite her and Helen's continued vigilance.

Katy frowned as she rinsed the new glasses and put them up on the shelf. These petty thefts really were getting beyond a joke.

'She could have my room when I go,' Helen said. 'I'm sure Pam Nelson wouldn't mind.'

'But what about the parents and sister?' Katy asked, lowering her voice. 'I don't think she's going to want to leave them in some hideous slum in Ealing.'

Helen hesitated. 'What about Mrs Carter?' she said. 'She's only got Angie there now. Do you think she'd have them?' She caught Katy's shocked glance and added quickly, 'Just for a while, until Jen gets back, I mean.'

To her horror, Katy felt sudden tears sting her eyes. 'You don't think she and Molly are coming back, do you?'

'I do, I do,' Helen said quickly. 'But there are no escape networks in Italy yet. So unless they can somehow make contact with our invasion forces, I really can't see …' she tailed off and bit her lip. 'I'm sorry, Katy. I didn't mean to upset you. Are you really sure you don't mind me going away?'

'I do mind,' Katy said. 'But I know you have to go.' She glanced across the bar. Aaref had gone and Elsa was humming happily to herself as she methodically swept the floor. 'At least I've got Elsa now,' she said with a watery smile. 'I'll be fine.'

The man crept up on them so quietly that even though she had been listening for someone, Molly nearly jumped out of her skin when she heard his low murmured greeting.

His arrival had been drowned out by the incessant high-pitched hum of frogs and crickets. They had heard the same pulsating sound every evening in the camp. It had been Nancy who had eventually told Molly what it was. From time to time, when an individual chirrup seemed really close Molly had tried to find the culprit. She had never seen a cricket in her life. But as soon as she got close, the sound invariably stopped, only to start up again somewhere else a moment later. So far she hadn't seen either a frog or a cricket, but there were plenty of mosquitoes. She was just swatting one on her arm when she heard the man's voice.

Jen was dozing on one of the blankets, but she sat up when Molly prodded her foot.

'Blimey,' she muttered, blinking at the figure silhouetted against the opening of the hut. 'Where did he come from?'

In the dusky light, it was hard to make out their visitor's features, but Molly could see that he was a stocky man wearing a baggy old patched corduroy suit and a felt hat that he now took off politely.

'*Permesso?*'

He seemed rather bizarrely to be asking permission to enter, and Jen choked back a giggle. 'Do come in,' she said grandly, waving her arm round the dilapidated hut. 'We are delighted to see you. I'm Jen and this is Molly.'

'I am Gianni Bandini,' he said, shaking hands. 'You are Inglese, yes?'

'Yes,' Jen said. 'Unfortunately we are.'

These formalities over, Gianni Bandini produced a small paraffin lantern from the sack he carried over his shoulder. Crouching down, he lit it efficiently. In the new, hazy light, Molly saw that he was younger than she had previously thought. A large moustache obscured his mouth, but his eyes were bright and watchful. As well as the lamp, he had also brought a flat loaf of bread, a piece of cheese wrapped in newspaper, and a bottle of what proved to be a rather pleasant, sweet fizzy drink that tasted vaguely of apples. Laying these provisions out carefully on a large white handkerchief, he gestured politely.

'*Prego*. Please. It is for you.'

'You're a star, Gianni,' Jen said, and took a long swig from the bottle.

'Thank you, Mr Bandini,' Molly said with a reproving glance at Jen. 'You are very kind.'

'You are welcome,' he said. He seemed to have a reasonable grasp of English, and while they gratefully ate and even more gratefully drank, he asked how they came to be there.

He was shocked by their story, but not altogether surprised.

'These Tedeschi,' he said as they came to the end. 'They take everything they want. They are like pigs.' He frowned. 'Is this the right word?'

'Exactly right,' Jen mumbled, her mouth full of bread and cheese.

'So can you help us?' Molly leaned forward eagerly. 'Can you find us somewhere to hide?'

'*Uffa.*' he lifted his chin and clicked his tongue on his teeth in an expression of doubt. 'It is not easy. Many people have fear. The Germans they make reward for escape prisoners. You understand?'

'I think so,' Molly said dubiously. 'But nobody knows we are here.'

Gianni Bandini's teeth flashed briefly in the glow of the lantern. 'Everyone knows you are here. Many people in the village see you among the vines. This is why I send my nephew to bring you here.'

It hadn't occurred to Molly that if they could see the distant village on the hill, then people in the village could see them.

'But how did they know we weren't just local women working there?'

He lifted his shoulders and nodded towards the now almost empty bottle in Jen's hand. 'The *vendemmia*, the harvest of grapes, is finished. Nobody works among the vines now.'

'I'm glad the Germans didn't know that,' Jen said drily. Her voice suddenly sounded oddly slurred, and Molly looked at her in concern.

But Gianni Bandini was smiling again. 'Yes,' he agreed. 'This is fortunate.'

'It wouldn't be for long,' Molly said pleadingly. 'Only until the British get here.'

His smile faded. 'This is not soon, I think. The Tedeschi are very strong. It will not be easy for your Allies to come here.'

'We don't even know where we are,' Molly said.

Obligingly Gianni Bandini drew a rough outline of Italy in the earth with his finger.

He pointed to a spot towards the top left of the country. 'We are here,' he said. 'In Toscano. Between Pisa and Genoa.' He tapped the map right at the bottom on the boot of Italy. 'Your forces remain only here.'

Molly peered at the map, wondering why the lines had suddenly gone so fuzzy. 'Where were the Germans taking us?'

Gianni ran his finger up the side of his map, curling round to the left at Genoa. 'This train, he travels from Rome to Marseilles in France.' He shrugged and moved his finger the other way. 'From Genoa it is not so far to Milan, Bolzano and then Austria and Germany.'

'Ha,' Jen remarked. 'So it's lucky we got off when we did.'

Got off? Molly almost choked on the piece of cheese she was eating. Jen somehow made it sound as though they had casually disembarked at a convenient station with a helpful porter to hand them down on to the platform and help with their luggage. It was all suddenly too much for her. She caught Jen's eye and they both began to giggle.

Gianni Bandini looked at them in surprise and shook his head. 'You English,' he said. 'You like to laugh in the face of danger, yes?'

Molly shook her head helplessly. 'No,' she said. 'I think it must be the wine. We've drunk too much wine.'

Joyce Carter was not prepared to let Elsa Distel have Jen's room.

'Goodness,' she said when Katy went down to the café to broach the subject later that afternoon. 'I daren't. My life wouldn't be worth living if Jen came home and found some refugee family living in her room.'

Noticing a tempting Victoria sponge on the counter, Katy hitched Malcolm up more firmly on her hip to keep him out of reach.

369

'Anyway,' Joyce went on, 'Pete's coming home for Christmas. And maybe Mick too. His last letter said he might be back in Liverpool around Christmas time and he'd try to get a bit of leave.'

'And I've invited Gino,' Angie chipped in.

'Is he going to come?' Katy asked, when Joyce failed to respond to this interpolation. 'I suppose he's allowed to travel around now that Italy's no longer our enemy.'

Angie wrinkled her nose. 'He hasn't replied yet,' she said.

Katy glanced at Joyce and saw a strange expression on her face. 'What is it?' she asked as Angie went off to serve a customer. 'Don't you want him here?'

'I don't mind him coming,' Joyce said. 'But she hasn't heard from him in months.'

'Oh dear,' Katy said, watching Angie flirting with a couple of young men at a table by the window. 'Poor Angie. Is she upset about that?'

'Upset?' Joyce's eyes widened. 'Not her. No, she just says he's not very good at writing letters.' She shook her head wearily. 'Between you and me, Katy, sometimes I wonder if the damn fellow even exists.'

'Well Ward isn't very good at writing letters either,' Katy said. 'And he certainly exists. Or at least I hope he still does.'

Joyce's jaw clenched. 'He'll be back soon,' she said stolidly. 'They all will. You mark my words.'

'I hope so,' Katy said with a sigh, moving aside to make room for Mrs Rutherford, who was coming out of the kitchen bearing a tray of cups and saucers. 'But in the meantime, I must find somewhere for this Jewish family to live. I need this girl. I can't manage the pub on my own.' She heaved Malcolm over on to her other hip and patted her stomach with her free hand. 'Not with these two to cope with.'

'What about Louise's flat?' Mrs Rutherford suggested as she squeezed past. 'She'll be giving that up at the weekend. I'm sure Mrs D'Arcy Billière would be happy to take in some more refugees.'

'Louise? Giving up her flat?' Katy nearly dropped Malcolm in her surprise. Taking advantage of her inattention, Malcolm leaned forward and plunged his finger into the Victoria sponge. Katy took a hasty step back, hoping Mrs Rutherford hadn't noticed. 'Why? Surely she can't be marrying Charlie Hawkridge already?'

It was Celia Rutherford's turn to be surprised. 'Marry that dreadful fellow?' she gasped. 'Certainly not. No, the truth is, she can't afford the rent, not on her own. Not now poor Jack is no longer with us. And as Greville has refused to bail her out, she's going to have to come back and live at home.' She pursed her lips. 'I think it's for the best. We certainly don't want her going the same way as that awful Mrs James.'

In the end, Gianni Bandini decided to take them to his uncle.
'It will not be easy,' he said. 'But is not safe to stay here. Tomorrow I think the Germans will be coming to hunt more for you.'

'It will not be easy' was one of Gianni Bandini's favourite English expressions. But despite Molly and Jen's state of inebriation, and the night-time curfew imposed by the Germans, he managed to escort them about ten miles up into the hills, where his uncle had a farm.

It was a gruelling trek. How he found his way with only the shallow moonlight to guide him, Molly had no idea. But as they stumbled behind, he led them unerringly along murky woodland tracks, through olive groves and up several steep shale inclines, until at last, to their considerable relief, they emerged from a dense, dark pine forest and saw in front of them a ramshackle homestead flanked on each side by tumbledown outhouses.

He made them wait outside while he went to consult with his uncle.

'Good God,' Jen muttered, slumping against a rickety fence, on the other side of which stood two large cows, chewing the cud and staring at them with mournful interest. 'It looks like we've arrived at Cold Comfort Farm.'

But there was nothing cold about Gianni Bandini's uncle. He was a swarthy man with an even larger moustache than his nephew's. But unlike his nephew's, Enrico Bandini's was accompanied by a thick beard, a bulbous nose and a pair of twinkling eyes.

'Welcome, welcome,' he said, when Gianni eventually ushered them into the kitchen. He peered at them eagerly and clapped his hands in delight. 'My nephew says he has two English beauties with him, but I do not believe it until I see with my own eyes.'

Molly warmed to him at once. Perhaps her new hairstyle really had made a difference, she thought.

His wife seemed rather less keen on the idea of housing two refugees on the run from the dreaded Tedeschi. But on Enrico's command, she obediently went off upstairs to make up beds for them.

'It is agreed you can stay,' Gianni told them. 'But you must remain very quiet and keep out of sight. If the Germans come, you must take your things and run straight away into the trees.'

To Molly, who had never in her life set foot on a farm, let alone an Italian one, Enrico Bandini's farm was a fascinating place. The back of the house was built into a steep hillside. The stove in the kitchen was situated in a crevice that had been chiselled out of the actual rock face. Candles dripped off a mantelpiece apparently hewn from an enormous log, and a huge copper pot hung over the fire on a heavy chain. There was a well-worn stone sink and an ancient low chest with a removable top, which Signora Bandini referred to as the *madia*, and in which she stored the flour for making her bread and pasta.

Despite there being no clocks in the house, Signora Bandini ran the household on a very regular timetable, which mostly revolved around food.

Breakfast, consisting of a cup of revolting coffee made from acorns, and leftover stale bread, took place just after sunrise.

At the mid-morning *merenda* they were given a slice of hot flat bread, freshly baked by Signora Bandini, a small piece of cheese and a glass of wine.

Lunch, *pranzo*, was a portion of maize pudding with sliced sausage, or a soup made with dried beans.

At sunset they settled down to a small dish of pasta with oil, or a slice of thick omelette with mushrooms that Signora Bandini had gathered from the woods.

Although the meals were frequent, they weren't plentiful, and it didn't take long for Molly to realise that their presence was a strain on the household. Nevertheless, her repeated offers to help with the chores were always rejected. The kitchen was Signora Bandini's domain and nobody else was welcome there except at mealtimes.

Molly was, however, allowed to assist with the weekly wash. This was an extraordinary event. The threadbare linen off the beds and various well-patched items of clothing were all carried in a basket up to a kind of trough in a stream at the top of Enrico Bandini's land, where they were vigorously scrubbed on a huge flat stone before being rinsed and hung out to dry over the adjacent bushes and olive trees.

It was all very primitive, and Molly couldn't help wondering what Sister Parkes would make of it. It was a far cry from the relentless bleaching, starching and airing that went on at the Wilhelmina.

Jen, entirely uninterested in the domestic side of things, amused herself by trying to learn Italian from their host.

Enrico Bandini found her attempts to speak Italian hilarious, and he was quite happy to spend his entire day chatting to her while he busied himself with his endless tasks around the remote little farm. One of the many reasons he hated the Germans was that only the previous month they had confiscated five of his cows. He lived in fear of losing the rest of his animals and had prepared a secret pen in the woods to hide them if necessary.

'We cannot survive without them,' he said simply. 'We starve.'

The two remaining cows, both blessed with enormous udders, needed milking twice a day. Enrico also tended about twenty tall, long-legged sheep. Some of these wore bells, and Molly got used to the clinking and clanking sound they made as they meandered about the adjacent hillsides.

Enrico Bandini loved his livestock. But his pride and joy were two bad-tempered geese, with extraordinary sensitive hearing, which flew cackling and hissing and flapping at any stranger who dared to come within a hundred yards of the farm while they were on the loose during daylight hours. It wasn't clear if he had somehow trained the fearsome birds to do this, or whether it was a natural instinct, but either way it enabled Molly and Jen to scurry into hiding in the house before any passer-by had a chance to catch sight of them.

As yet there had been no unwelcome visitors. But as soon as Enrico discovered that Molly could do magic tricks, he threw caution to the wind and invited all his friends to come and witness this extraordinary phenomenon, clapping his hands proudly when she obligingly conjured up cards they had memorised, or discovered them up on the mantelpiece or hidden underneath Signora Bandini's *madia*.

Enrico also had a home-made wireless, and occasionally, in the evening, when he was sure there was nobody in earshot, he was able to pick up the BBC overseas news. But reassuring though it was to hear the familiar, well-modulated accents of the BBC newsreaders echoing round the Bandinis' kitchen, telling them that Winston Churchill had arrived in the Middle East for talks with President Roosevelt and Marshal Stalin in Tehran, or that Christmas turkeys in England were very scarce, Molly and Jen soon realised that their hopes of an early rescue were unrealistic to say the least.

Despite a successful landing at Naples, the Allied troops were making very slow progress. At first, each night, the BBC reported an advance of one mile or perhaps two. But then, just as the weather broke at the end of November, it was reported that the Allies had met unexpectedly stiff resistance by German snipers entrenched in a monastery on a hill at a place called Monte Cassino, which Enrico told them was more than a hundred miles south of Rome.

'At this rate it will take them months,' Jen said in disgust. 'Why don't they get a move on?'

'These Germans,' Enrico said grimly. 'They fight to the death. Because if not they get sent to Russia, where they die anyway.'

It annoyed him that the BBC kept exhorting the people of Italy to rid themselves of the Germans. 'How do they expect us to do it?' he asked, waving his hands around in frustration. 'It is like asking a field of sheep to rid themselves of a pack of wolves.'

Not only that, but the round-up – or rake-up, as Enrico called it, the *rastrellamento* – of Italian young men and deserters was continuing. The Germans were also hunting escaped Allied POWs, and, of course, Jews. A friend who called to see Enrico one evening told him of the hideous cruelty meted out to Jews in Pisa.

The only sign of the Allies came one morning when they saw about thirty shiny Liberators fly over in formation. Later they heard on the BBC that Genoa and Perugia had both been heavily bombed.

As she came downstairs the following evening, Jen overheard, and understood, an announcement on the German-controlled Italian wireless channel. From now on, anyone found harbouring an escaped prisoner, a deserter or a Jew would be summarily sentenced to death. Large payments were offered for information that led to such a discovery.

'I hope the Bandinis don't turn us in,' she whispered to Molly when she relayed this information in the privacy of their bedroom later.

Molly was sure they wouldn't. But she also knew the time had come to leave. It had become obvious that Signora Bandini was living in terror of the dreaded *denunciato*. The Bandinis had housed them long enough. Too many of their friends and relations already knew they were there. It wasn't fair to make them risk their lives any longer.

'We'll have to go,' she said. 'We'll have to find someone else to help us.'

Jen raised her eyebrows. 'Yes, that's easy enough to say,' she said. 'But who?'

Molly took a breath. This was the moment she had been dreading.

'I think we should go and find André Cabillard,' she said.

Jen looked at her as though she had taken leave of her senses. For once she was literally speechless, then she gave a low, incredulous laugh. 'You want us to go to France?'

Molly nodded. 'A fortune-teller once told me that if I found a certain man, a foreigner, but not a stranger, he would be my salvation. I think it's André Cabillard. I've been thinking about it, and he is the only person I know in the whole of Europe. Not that I really know him. But I have at least met him once.'

'Yeah,' Jen said with a scoffing laugh. 'And that blind man told you that your moment would come. That hasn't exactly come true, has it?'

Molly frowned. She was surprised that Jen remembered about the blind man, but it was typical of her to throw cold water on her suggestion.

She fingered her necklace nervously. The little magic carpet hadn't let her down so far. Everything she had wished for had come true. Admittedly not in the way she had expected, but nevertheless …

'There's no way we can go south,' Jen said suddenly. 'We'd never manage to cross the German lines. So we might as well go north.'

'West,' Molly said. 'France is west of here.'

'OK, whatever,' Jen said. 'But even if we did go to France, how would we find André Cabillard?'

'I know where he lives,' Molly said eagerly. 'It's near Toulon. Helen gave me the address of his family's vineyard ages ago, when she thought she was dying. She wanted me to contact him after the war to tell him that she died holding a photograph of him on her heart.'

Jen was silent.

'So let's get this straight,' she said after a moment. 'You are suggesting we travel hundreds of miles with no money or identity papers, cross a heavily guarded border into another country teeming with Germans to find a man neither of us will probably recognise, and who in any case might not even still be alive?'

'Yes,' Molly said. 'People escape from France all the time. André did himself. And all those pilots that Ward Frazer deals with. There are networks to get people out.'

'But how on earth would we get to France?' Jen asked.

'I've thought about that,' Molly said. 'I think we should go by train. It won't be easy, but—'

Jen gave a sudden chuckle. 'You sound like Gianni Bandini,' she said. 'But what the hell, let's go for it. After all, what have we got to lose?'

Chapter Twenty-Seven

In November, his Russian campaign deteriorating, Hitler once again turned his attention on London. Having had a modicum of peace over the summer, it was a nasty shock to be having to carry gas masks and running to shelters again when the sirens sounded. But in south London people knew the threat was real: without any warning a bomb fell on a dance hall above a milk bar in Putney and killed nearly a hundred people.

It was only a matter of luck that Angie Carter had not been there that night; the Cinderella Dance Club had been one of her favourite haunts. She had been intending to go, but that morning had slipped on a piece of cabbage in the café kitchen and twisted her ankle quite badly.

Two weeks later, a high-explosive bomb destroyed a food shop in Beaufoy Road, demolishing the adjacent houses and killing seven people. When officials from the Food Executive arrived to try to prevent the premises being looted, there was an ugly scene. Katy began to worry about what would happen if a bomb fell in Lavender Road. The Flag and Garter had been looted before, but the business wouldn't survive if she lost everything again. And with the likes of Barry Fish, the Garrow brothers and the other unsavoury characters now hanging around Lavender Road thanks to the proclivities of Gillian James, she had a nasty feeling that, alone and heavily pregnant, there wouldn't be much she could do to protect it.

If only the police were more effective, she thought. Or if someone would at least come forward to claim Helen's reward. Then she might feel less anxious.

No. As far as Katy was concerned, apart from the arrival of Elsa Distel, November had not been a good month. And the icing on the rather bitter cake came with a casual telegram from Ward.

Just a bit more to do here stop Missing you and Malcolm stop All my love Ward

But if things were bad for Katy, they were even worse for Louise.

Over a period of just a week, she had lost her flat, her independence and, it seemed, her lover.

She had put up a fierce fight against her father's edict that she had to move back into Cedars House. But despite her protestations, and a number of delaying tactics, in the end she had been forced to capitulate, because she simply couldn't afford to maintain the flat on her own. Not on her meagre women's war-work pay.

Her best chance of avoiding a humiliating return to her parents' home would have been on the arm of Charlie Hawkridge, but when she appealed to her lover for a longer-term commitment, it had not been forthcoming. Nor had he been in touch since. It seemed he was happy enough to see her when she had a nice little flat in which she could entertain him at his leisure. One sniff of Mr and Mrs Rutherford and he had run a mile.

'I don't know why she's surprised,' Helen had remarked when she and Katy were chatting one evening. 'We only had to take one look at him to know he was a cad and a bounder.'

Katy had smiled at that, but in a way she would have preferred Charlie Hawkridge to have kept Louise sweet for just a little bit longer.

It hadn't escaped Katy's notice that Aaref had been around more than usual since Elsa Distel had started working at the pub. Nor that Elsa was more animated when he was present. But now, as usual, Louise was turning to Aaref for comfort in her disappointment. 'Charlie treated me very shabbily when I think about it,' she confided to Katy. 'He used me. I don't want a man like that. I want someone who really cares for me and who likes me for myself.'

Someone like Jack, Katy thought rather sourly, but managed to hold her tongue.

Louise had sighed. 'Of course Aaref has been in love with me for ever. I suppose I always knew I'd end up with him in the end. I've decided to ask him to come to Christmas lunch. Douglas has finally got his movement order. And I can't spend Christmas just with Mummy and Daddy all on my own.'

It didn't bode well for Elsa, but Katy knew there was nothing she could do about it. 'So Douglas is finally off overseas,' she said. 'Where's he going?'

'Somewhere in North Africa,' Louise said. 'He doesn't know exactly where, but he's frightfully excited. He told Mummy that from there he'll be sent to Italy. He's convinced he's going to liberate Rome single-handed.'

'I wish he'd liberate Molly and Jen,' Katy said crossly to Helen later.

'Molly would rather die than be liberated by Douglas Rutherford,' Helen said. 'And I don't blame her. He's the nastiest little git I've ever had the pleasure to meet.'

Katy chuckled. 'It will be funny if you bump into him in North Africa.'

Helen rolled her eyes. 'Don't worry,' she said. 'If I see him, I'll avoid him like the plague. But I tell you who I might see, and that's Daddy. I had a letter this morning. He's travelling round the Middle East and North Africa with the Prime Minister and President Roosevelt at the moment. He's due back in America for Christmas, but it sounds as though we might just overlap in Tunisia.'

Katy smiled and said the right things, but all this talk of Christmas was beginning to make her panic. The baby was due at Christmas. And she only had Elsa Distel to help her.

She had briefly considered asking her mother to come up for her confinement, but the thought of entrusting Malcolm to her mother or to Wards' lovely but somewhat ancient aunts made her feel quite anxious. He would run rings round them. No, it would be better to close the pub, even though that would mean losing custom, and ask Pam to have Malcolm. Anyway, maybe, just maybe, by then Ward would be home and everything would be all right. In the meantime, she was going to ask Aaref to take a couple of photographs of Malcolm so she could send one to her mother, and one to Ward's mother as a gesture of Christmas goodwill.

Enrico Bandini was reluctant to let Molly and Jen go, but in the end he accepted their decision. However, he persuaded them to wait until they could consult with Gianni.

The following night, summoned by some mysterious local bush telegraph, Gianni appeared at the farm.

'France?' he gasped, his serious dark eyes nearly popping out of his head. 'By train?' He sat back and eyed them uncertainly. 'I think you have again drunk too much wine, yes?'

'I don't mean we should go to the station and buy a ticket,' Molly explained. 'But, after all, we managed to get off a train in a siding, so maybe we could get on one too. And you said yourself that the line runs round into France.'

'*Uffa.*' Gianni clicked his tongue. 'But the border. How will you cross it? This is controlled by the Germans. It will not be easy.'

Jen caught Molly's eye and giggled. 'Don't worry,' she said airily. 'I'm sure Molly will find a way to magic us over.'

Molly wasn't sure of that, but she didn't want to linger at the farm any longer than they had to, so she nodded confidently. She had a feeling their time there was running out, and she couldn't bear the thought that they were putting these kind people's lives at risk.

They left at dusk the following evening, guided by the boy, Enzo, who Gianni had sent up to the farm that afternoon. Enzo had brought with him two dark jerseys, two schoolgirl hats and two navy-blue knee-length skirts; outfits that Gianni apparently felt two young Italian women might be likely to wear on a journey to France.

Leaving was hard. Even Signora Bandini shed a few tears, although Jen said afterwards they were probably tears of relief. She had already prepared a *merenda* picnic for them to take with them: bread, cheese, sausage, a wine bottle full of fresh milk and a jar of pickled beetroot. Now she also presented them each with a curious vest-like undergarment she had knitted specially from wool spun from the fleeces of Enrico's sheep.

'The time is becoming cold,' she said, the first words of English she had spoken during their entire visit. 'This hold you warm, yes?'

'Yes indeed,' Molly responded gravely, as Jen took one look at the garments and collapsed in hysterics. 'Thank you so much.'

She would have liked to give the Bandinis something in return. Some small token of her gratitude. But she had nothing to give. It was only as they said their final goodbyes that she thought of the playing cards and offered them to Enrico.

'It's not a full pack, of course, but I'd love you to have what's left of them. There are still enough to play patience,' she smiled. 'Or to do tricks.'

To her surprise, he took the depleted pack in a trembling hand, tears of delight filling his eyes. He fondled the dog-eared cards reverentially, then held them to his heart. 'You are to me like the daughters we never have,' he said in a choked voice. 'I hope you don't forget us.'

'Never,' Molly said, tears welling in her own eyes. 'I'll never forget your kindness to us.'

He patted her on the arm. 'If you learn more tricks, you come and show me after the war, yes?'

Molly could only gulp and nod. Tears were running down her face. She could no longer speak.

'*Arrivederci,*' he called after them mournfully as they followed Enzo and Gianni down the track into the wood. '*Fortuna. In bocca al lupo!*'

'He's saying something about a wolf,' Jen said, looking round in some alarm. She questioned Enzo tensely, then sighed in relief. 'Apparently it means good luck.'

Taking a deep breath, she turned round and cupped her hands round her mouth.

'Eh, Enrico,' she yelled. 'Don't worry. If we meet a wolf, I'll make him eat Molly first.'

The sound of his laughter followed them all the way down the valley.

On 5 December, a few days before she was due to leave for Tunisia, Helen finally heard some news at the SOE offices.

'Someone in Corsica intercepted some German radio traffic from Italy,' she told Katy that evening. 'It seems the SS have been hunting for two young English female spies.' She opened her hands as Katy looked at her blankly. 'There aren't any SOE female agents in Italy. I checked with the Secret Service and Military Intelligence as well. I think it must be Molly and Jen.'

'Spies?' Katy said faintly. 'Molly and Jen aren't spies.'

Helen made a slight face. 'I know,' she said. 'Goodness knows what they've been up to, but at least it sounds as though they are still alive and haven't been spirited away to Germany.'

'When was this?' Katy asked.

'A few weeks ago. Nothing has been heard since. The radio buffs at Bletchley Park are on to it now. They think they would have heard if they had been recaptured.'

'Does Ward know about this?'

'Yes.'

'Why didn't he tell me in his telegram?'

Helen looked surprised. 'He couldn't. It was too risky. We can't let the Germans know we have the codes to monitor their radio traffic.' She leaned forward eagerly. 'But I think that's why he is staying on in Corsica. If the Germans mention them again, he'll be able to work out where they are and then he'll try to go in and get them.'

Katy felt the blood leaving her face. She pulled up a chair and sat down abruptly.

'Katy, are you all right?' Helen asked in concern. 'Perhaps I shouldn't have told you, but I thought you'd be pleased.'

Pleased? Katy looked up at her incredulously. She loved Molly and Jen. But she loved Ward too. And she had suddenly realised she didn't want him to risk his life in an effort to save theirs. But then she felt a sickening wave of guilt. How could she even think that? The thought of Molly and Jen all alone, probably terrified, in Italy was more than she could bear either.

She put her head in her hands.

'This bloody war,' she mumbled. 'I don't think I can take it much longer.'

She heard the clink of a bottle on a glass, then Helen thrust a small whisky into her hand.

Katy shook her head. 'It's not good for the baby,' she said.

'It's not for the baby,' Helen said. 'It's for you.'

Katy was still sipping the whisky when George Nelson sidled into the bar.

George was also unhappy about Helen going away. He had nearly lost her once before. The fact that she had recovered and come back to live with them had slightly compensated for that. But now she was leaving them again.

'I've been thinking,' he said to her earnestly. 'I think it would be best if I came with you. I know all about spying. Ward taught me lots of things and I've been practising, and I've got really good at it.'

Katy saw Helen's lips twitch, but when she spoke, her voice was serious. 'It's true, you would be really useful,' she said. 'But unfortunately I'm not allowed to take anyone with me.'

'Oh.' He looked crestfallen. 'But I thought we could go and find Molly. I'm sure Mummy and Daddy wouldn't mind. It's nearly the Christmas holidays, so I wouldn't miss much school.'

Helen threw a quick glance at Katy and then drew George slightly to one side. 'Well,' she said. 'I'd obviously like to take you with me. But,' she lowered her voice, 'the thing is, I'm relying on you to keep an eye on Katy. She's going to have a new baby soon, and without Ward here she's going to need someone to look out for her and protect her. I can't think of anyone better to do that than you. A trained spy.' She paused and looked at him gravely. 'What do you think?'

It was clear from George's expression that keeping an eye on Katy didn't compare at all well with an exciting adventure in North Africa. But then, after disgruntledly kicking the table leg a few times, he looked up.

'The thing is,' he said. 'If I'm going to protect Katy, I'll need a weapon.' He slid a speculative glance at Helen. 'And you did say you'd get me a catapult for Christmas.'

Katy saw Helen give a slight grimace. 'I know I did. But Pam told me that you nearly killed one of Mrs Rutherford's chickens with the last one you had, so ...'

'Oh, I wouldn't do that again,' George said. 'I'm not interested in chickens any more. They're too easy.'

Helen hesitated, but she clearly couldn't resist the expression in his limpid blue eyes. 'Well if you absolutely promise not to aim at any animals or birds,' she said.

He nodded eagerly. 'I absolutely promise,' he said. 'Cross my heart and hope to die.'

'OK,' Helen said warily. 'But I'm going to check with Pam. If she says it's all right, I'll pop into Hamleys on my way home tomorrow and see if they've got one.'

George looked surprised. 'Oh, you don't need to go to Hamleys,' he said. 'Mr Lorenz has got a really nice one in the window of his shop on Northcote Road.'

To start with, at least, everything went to plan.

Enzo guided Molly and Jen efficiently back to the hut. It was already getting light when they arrived, and he took them out to the edge of the wood, from where they could just make out the distant railway line running through the wide valley below them. Diligently he pointed out the path they would need to take at nightfall. The path through the vines to the lonely siding where their previous train had stopped.

Then he solemnly shook hands and disappeared into the trees.

Molly and Jen looked at each other. Now they were on their own.

The sky was overcast and a light wind rustled the tops of the trees above them. It was chilly in the hut and they were glad of Signora Bandini's hand-knitted vests. Tired from the trek, Jen spent most of the day asleep, curled up in her blanket.

Molly was too nervous to sleep. She felt bereft without her playing cards. They had kept her going through so many long, boring days. And this one seemed even longer than most. But eventually it began to grow dark and they drank some milk and ate a little bit of their picnic. They had no idea how long Signora Bandini's *merenda* would need to sustain them, so they carefully bundled up the rest in their blankets and set off down the path.

In the cold darkness it seemed much further than they remembered. Molly wondered how they had ever managed it in the full heat of the day, and decided that adrenalin must have played a large part.

Having eventually found the railway siding, they took up position a few yards back, tucked in among a line of vines. It was unlikely that any dismounting passengers would wander very far at night.

But the track was totally silent. Some distant rumbling and lights in the sky to the north-west made them guess that Genoa was once again being bombed, and they began to wonder if that was why there were no trains passing in either direction.

They had been there several hours when they finally heard a slight buzzing vibration run along the rails. A moment later there was the distant grumble of a train coming from the south. But was it going to stop?

Suddenly, with a thumping bang, the huge engine powered out of the gloom. They flinched back in disappointment as it thundered past them with a swirl of dust.

But then they heard the brakes, the familiar clunk and squeal of the buffers, the hissing and grinding as the train gradually lost speed. It seemed immensely long. The swishing noise of the passing carriages seemed to go on for ever. But eventually it came to a wheezing stop.

It seemed to be comprised of both passenger carriages and freight cars, some of which, towards the back, were the open sort with no roof. It was exactly what Molly and Jen had been hoping for. Now they just had to choose a suitable wagon, make sure no one was looking, and climb aboard.

They were about to make their move when they saw the blink of a light approaching and heard the crunch of feet on gravel. They froze just in time to see a man walking along the side of the train, flashing a torch at the freight wagons.

It was too late to hide, too late to do anything except hold their breath and pray he wouldn't shine the torch in their direction. But thankfully he seemed more interested in checking the locks than in the adjacent countryside. In the darkness it was impossible to make out what sort of uniform he was wearing, but as he passed between them and the train, they could see the glint of a weapon. He was obviously some kind of security guard, and that made Molly nervous.

'What do you think?' she whispered when he had gone well past.

'I think we should risk it,' Jen said. 'Mainly because I can't face walking all the way back to that bloody hut. And we may not get a better chance.'

It was surprisingly easy to half climb, half haul themselves up over the side into one of the open-topped freight cars. It was more difficult, in the dark, to work out what the wagon was carrying.

There seemed to be half a dozen long, lumpy packages lying along the floor. Several other large, oddly shaped items filled the rest of the space. Everything was wrapped in swathes of rough sacking tied with twine.

'I can't make out what it is,' Molly whispered, poking her fingers gently into one of the bundles. 'It feels really hard and cold and all curved shapes.'

'Who cares what it is?' Jen said. 'It's perfect. Nobody will notice us among all this lot.'

Whatever it was, it did indeed seem ideal for their purpose. And nestling themselves carefully in among the enormous packages, they settled down to wait for the train to move on.

Joyce was thinking about Christmas. Or, more specifically, Christmas lunch. She had already invited Mr Lorenz of course, but it wasn't going to be much fun for him to spend it just with her and Angie. She had been secretly hoping that Jen would somehow magically reappear in time. But according to Helen de Burrel, that didn't sound very likely now.

Henry Keller had looked appalled when she had told him what Helen had said. 'What?' he had exclaimed. 'On the run from the SS? I can't believe it.' His handsome face had gone quite white. He groaned. 'Oh my God. How can this have happened? If only I hadn't put her in that damn show …'

Joyce had made him a nice strong cup of tea and tried to reassure him. But it wasn't easy. She felt rather shaky about it all herself.

She had very little expectation of the elusive Gino materialising either. And if he didn't, then Angie would be down in the dumps, which was the last thing anyone wanted at Christmas lunch.

Christmas Day had been bad enough last year, what with Jen making all that fuss about having the chickenpox. No, what she needed this year, Joyce decided, was someone to make them laugh. And the perfect person to do that was Dr Goodacre.

But she could hardly invite Dr Goodacre without also inviting Sister Morris, and that was a somewhat more daunting prospect. Nevertheless, the previous evening, after closing up the café, she had bravely written out two invitations and dropped them off at the hospital.

Now all she had to do was wait and see what would happen.

What happened was that at crack of dawn the following morning, Dr Goodacre came bustling into the café.

Pausing only to wipe his steamed-up glasses, he advanced purposefully on Joyce, who was already busy at the counter even though it was still dark outside. 'Christmas lunch,' he boomed. 'What a delightful treat that would be. There's nothing I like more than a nice slice of turkey.'

Joyce stared at him with dismay. She had thought a small chicken would do the trick. She hadn't a hope in hell of getting her hands on a turkey. 'What about Sister Morris?' she asked. 'Do you think she'll come?'

He pulled a mock-serious face. 'Sister Morris feels it is her duty to spend Christmas on the ward.'

'Oh dear,' Joyce said with some relief. 'What a shame.'

'Aha.' He winked and went on quickly, with the air of someone pulling a rabbit out of a hat. 'But when I got your charming invitation, I took the liberty of having a quiet word with Matron, and she decreed that this year Sister Morris will be excused her Christmas duty.'

'Oh,' Joyce said faintly. Four more customers came in then, and she called into the kitchen for Angie to come and take their order. 'Well that's wonderful news.'

'It is, it is,' Dr Goodacre agreed, rubbing his hands. 'And now I think, Mrs Carter, if you would be so good, I'll have a nice cup of tea and one of your delicious—' He stopped abruptly as he caught sight of Angie hobbling out of the kitchen. 'Good Lord,' he said. 'What's happened to her?'

'She slipped on a cabbage leaf and twisted her ankle a couple of weeks ago,' Joyce said. 'But I don't think it's anything very serious.'

'Not serious? Good gracious me. You should have brought her straight to me. It might be a hyperdorsiflexion fracture for all we know.' He

384

beckoned Angie over. 'If you don't mind, my dear, I'll have a look at it now. I am very interested in the workings of the talocrural joint.'

'Perhaps not right in the middle of the café ...' Joyce began. But it was too late. And actually, maybe it was for the best. Dr Goodacre was a specialist after all. And it would save her having to shell out on a visit to the GP.

'Cor,' Angie said, sitting down and stripping off her sock eagerly. 'I've never been looked at by a proper doctor. '

Dawn was just coming into the sky when Molly woke up. Beside her, Jen was still fast asleep, curled up in her blanket. They hadn't intended to sleep, but the rhythmical motion of the train had obviously lulled them off. Molly wondered where they were.

She yawned and rubbed her eyes. She was cold and stiff. Her hair was thick with dust and she could taste salt on her dry lips. Stretching awkwardly, she turned her head and found herself nose to nose with an unnervingly lifelike white face. Aghast, she lurched back, only just managing to suppress a scream.

It took a moment for her to regain her composure. She realised that the oddly shaped parcels that had puzzled them the night before were actually a collection of statues and sculptures. Some of the sacking had come away from the one lying next to her, exposing the blank, sightless face of a life-size Roman figure. Behind him a heavily carved handle protruded from what was clearly an enormous stone urn.

Cautiously Molly lifted her head to peer cautiously over the side of the wagon. To her surprise, she saw blue sea glistening some way below them. Tiny white houses clung in higgledy-piggledy tiers to the steep cliffs. On the other side of the train the ground rose steeply. A light mist hazed everything with a pink glow.

It was extraordinarily beautiful. But even as Molly drank in the view, enjoying the feel of the fresh, salty breeze on her face, the train started to slow. Squinting ahead through the haze of smoke, she saw barricades and reams of glittering barbed wire running at right angles to the track. She had barely withdrawn her head when the train drew to a shuddering halt and at once she heard voices. German voices.

She shook Jen urgently. 'For goodness' sake wake up,' she muttered. 'I think we must be at the border.'

Jen sat up. 'But we haven't been through Genoa.'

'We must have slept through it,' Molly said. 'Or maybe they diverted because of the bombing.'

Jen looked round sleepily. Catching sight of the statue's face, she recoiled. 'Good God, who's that? Julius Caesar?'

Molly's sudden giggle died on her lips. Tucked under the sides of the car, they were invisible from the platform, but now, as well as voices, they suddenly heard the clunk of metal as someone climbed into the adjoining carriage.

Molly glanced at Jen in alarm. Anyone looking over into their wagon would be bound to see them. Quickly she took out her scissors and began cutting through the ropes on one of the prostrate statues.

'Lie back down,' she whispered to Jen. 'I'll cover you in some of this sacking.'

It didn't take a moment to tuck Jen in neatly, but it was much harder to wrap herself.

There was a long pause. Not daring to move a muscle, Molly strained her ears to hear what might be happening.

The voices gradually receded, but then once again she heard footsteps, a low grunt and the scrape of a bolt being opened. She felt the car creak and tilt slightly as someone came aboard. Then a long, agonising silence. Molly was certain that whoever it was would be able to hear her heart thudding against the floor of the truck.

Then the wagon creaked again, and through the rough weave of the hessian, Molly saw a pair of black leather jackboots and, tucked in above them, the all-too-familiar field-grey trousers. The man was so close, she could smell the polish on his boots.

She screwed up her eyes and tried not to breathe, tried not to think of her own feet poking out of the end of the sacking, surely in full sight. But it was hard. Her skin was prickling, twitching. Her mouth was dry. Despite the cold, she felt a bead of sweat trickle down her armpit. After all they had been through, surely it wasn't going to end like this …

She tensed as the soldier moved again. She could hear the slight clink of keys or coins in his pocket. Again there was silence. Perhaps he hadn't noticed her and was moving away.

But no, he was just getting into a better position. A moment later something cold touched her temple. Gradually the sack was peeled back over her hair.

She could feel the cool morning breeze on her face.

And opening her eyes, she found herself looking straight up the barrel of a gun.

As Molly struggled into a sitting position with her arms in the air, the German soldier aimed the gun on the sacking that contained Jen.

'Raus!' he said, giving her supine body a sharp kick. 'Hände hoch!'

386

He was obviously expecting it to be a man, and looked surprised when Jen emerged.

He was small and wiry, somewhat older than the soldiers at the camp had been. As he gestured with the rifle for Jen to sit up and raise her hands, Molly saw that he had a thin mouth and foxy, calculating eyes.

He glanced from one to the other and then focused on Molly. '*Wer sind Sie?*' he snapped. '*Was machen Sie hier?*'

Molly could feel her hands trembling above her head. She knew that if she spoke, she would give the game away. Turning her head very slowly, she caught Jen's eye.

Jen nodded slightly and lowered her hands slowly into the prayer gesture. She gave the man a shy, pitiful smile. 'Please,' she said in Italian. 'We had papers and a permit but they were lost in the bombing in Genoa.'

Molly didn't understand every word, but she got the gist of it. So did the German. He clearly didn't believe her, but he relaxed slightly and lowered the gun.

He walked to the edge of the wagon and leaned out to flick a glance up and down the train. Apparently satisfied, he turned back to his captives. '*Haben Sie Geld?*' When they looked blank, he rubbed his fingertips together in the traditional money gesture. '*Soldi?*'

Jen shook her head regretfully. 'Those British pigs,' she said in Italian. 'They have left us with nothing.'

The soldier's eyes narrowed. Turning to Molly, he indicated with a jerk of his gun that he wanted her to open the small sack that contained their picnic. He looked disgusted when all she drew out was the remainder of the bread and the jar of pickled beetroot.

Belatedly it dawned on Molly what he was up to. He wanted them to bribe him with money. Or valuables. He wanted them to buy his silence. Otherwise he would turn them in.

And then she saw him looking at Jen in a certain way, and she suddenly realised that, if money wasn't available, he had something else in mind. Something much more sinister.

Jen was by no means looking her best. The schoolgirl clothes Gianni Bandini had given her were covered in dust. Her hair was a tangled mess, and she had a smear of beetroot across her cheek. But even the dirt and disarray couldn't disguise her pretty face and slender figure.

As Molly watched, the soldier licked his lips, and she saw the pleading expression on Jen's face change to one of horrified alarm.

Instinctively she lowered one hand to the little magic carpet at her throat. Please help us, she whispered silently. Please help us. But the soldier had caught the movement. As he turned towards her again, his greedy little

387

eyes lit up. Oh no, Molly thought. Oh please, no. But she knew it was their only hope.

With shaking fingers, she undid the necklace and offered it to him.

He took it, fingered it briefly, gave a grunt of satisfaction, then slid it into his pocket. As it disappeared from sight, Molly was aware of a physical pain in her heart.

But then he turned back to Jen. Raising the gun, he took a step towards her, his lips curled into an unpleasant smile.

Before he could take a second step, someone further up the platform shouted something in German. It sounded like a command or a warning. At the same moment, the train jolted slightly. The engine began to vibrate.

The man swore under his breath. He turned away and jumped down off the truck. They heard the other voice shouting again, and his response. '*Ja. Ja. Alles in Ordnung.*'

With an angry grunt, he heaved the metal gate back into place. The bolt slid across.

Doors slammed, a whistle blew, and gradually the train began to move.

Keeping her head well down, Molly held her breath, waiting for a shout, a police whistle, a screech of brakes. But nothing happened. After a minute, the train plunged into a long, noisy tunnel, and when it emerged, it was still picking up speed.

Jen let out a long breath. 'That was a nasty moment,' she said. She still looked very pale 'You know what he wanted, don't you?'

Molly nodded. 'Would you have done it?' she asked after a moment.

'God, I don't know.' Jen thought about it and shuddered. 'Yes, I probably would have done it. Rather that than get handed back to that bastard Hauptsturmführer Wessel.' She attempted a smile. 'But I'm very glad I didn't have to.'

Molly suddenly felt choked. The blasé, gung-ho attitude Jen had adopted since their escape had obviously been covering up an intense fear.

Jen could be so annoying, with her proud, dismissive prima donna ways, but she was quick on the uptake, and you couldn't question her courage. Molly was suddenly conscious that in a tight spot, she would rather have Jen Carter at her side than almost anyone else in the world.

'I'm sorry,' Jen added when Molly didn't immediately respond. 'I know you loved that necklace.'

Molly swallowed and shook her head. 'It's only because Ward gave it to me,' she said.

Only a month ago, she could never have brought herself to say such a thing. Especially not to Jen Carter. But since her confession on the day of their escape from the train, everything had changed. It was almost as though her terrible secret had been cut off with her hair. At last she could talk about Ward without blushing. Her infatuation no longer seemed so awful, so shocking, so wrong. Thanks to Jen, it now seemed bearable. Almost normal.

It didn't make it any easier to lose the necklace, though. She sighed, feeling as though she had somehow let him down. 'The man who sold it to him told him it had the power to take you to foreign lands.'

'Well he was obviously right,' Jen said, settling back against the huge urn. 'Because it's taken us into France.' She gave a small, shaky laugh. 'Now all we have to do is find André Cabillard.'

Chapter Twenty-Eight

Helen left on the morning of 7 December. It was a tumultuous farewell. Katy and Pam Nelson cried. Malcolm shouted, 'Want to go in car, want to go in car!' at the top of his voice. Baby Nellie wailed and threw her rag doll out of the pram. And George had to be forcibly restrained from using his new catapult to fire a conker at the back window of Helen's taxi.

'Do you think she'll be all right?' Pam asked as the cab turned on to Lavender Hill and disappeared out of sight.

Katy blew her nose and nodded. 'I think so. She's hoping to meet her father out there. He's been travelling all round the Middle East with the Prime Minister and the President.'

'Yes,' Pam said, picking up the still wailing baby. 'I heard on the news last night that Mr Churchill had been trying to persuade the Turks to come into the war.' She grimaced as she jiggled Nellie in an attempt to soothe her. 'Poor old Winnie. I expect he'll be glad to get home. Dealing with all those ghastly foreigners must be exhausting. And he never looks very healthy at the best of times.'

Katy gave a slightly tearful smile. 'Molly always used to say he smoked too many cigars.'

Pam chuckled. 'Molly should have been a doctor,' she said. She watched Katy crouch awkwardly to pick up the discarded doll. 'You look as though you're about to pop,' she said. 'I'll do what I can, but I think you are going to need a lot more help than I can give you.'

Molly and Jen's plan, such as it was, had been to travel as close as they dared to Toulon and then somehow get off the train and find their way to André's village. But now that the German soldier knew they were on board, it seemed imperative that they disembark as soon as possible.

But getting off was more difficult than getting on had been. Because now that it was in France, the blasted train never stopped.

'We don't want to go too far,' Molly said nervously as yet another small village flashed past.

They had already passed through Monte Carlo and Nice, so they knew they were going in the right direction, but they didn't want to overshoot. Finding their way to the Cabillard vineyard was going to be hard enough.

390

They didn't want to have to struggle any further than necessary.

They were just finishing off the meagre remains of their picnic when they finally felt the familiar jolt and sway as the brakes engaged.

'OK,' Molly said, glancing round at Jen. 'Are you ready?'

But Jen wasn't ready. She was busy doing something to one of the prostrate statues. As Molly stared in amazement, she dipped the tip of her little finger into the jar of pickled beetroot juice and then pressed it on to the exposed stone face.

'Jen!' Molly said. 'What on earth are you doing?'

'Getting my revenge,' Jen said. 'I'm giving Julius Caesar here a nice dose of chickenpox.'

Molly glanced at the statue. She couldn't believe her eyes. Or Jen's gall. Dots of purple beetroot juice already covered the emperor's head and shoulders; some had sunk in straight away, others were bleeding slightly at the edges.

'It looks more like a variola rash to me,' Molly said. 'Smallpox, not chickenpox.'

Jen gave a choke of laughter. 'You should be a doctor,' she said. 'You're wasted as a nurse.' She applied a final dab of the beetroot to the statue's left eyeball and sat back and looked at her work with satisfaction. Then she quickly pulled the sacking back over the statue and tied it up again with the rope. 'Whatever it is, I hope someone will get a nasty shock.'

Molly chuckled. 'I don't think there's any doubt about that.' As she spoke, she heard the hiss and squeal of the train decelerating sharply and caught a whiff of the burnt orange smell of the brakes. Picking up Jen's blanket, she bundled it up and thrust it into her arms. Then she made sure her own cloak was securely buckled across her chest. 'Are you ready? If necessary, we'll have to jump for it.'

But it was too late.

The train was already passing through a built-up area. A moment later it pulled into Toulon station.

And lining the platform was a group of purposeful-looking German soldiers.

Jen swore. 'That's all we need.'

There was no choice but to climb out of the other side of the wagon and jump down on to the tracks. They clearly didn't stand a chance on the platform. Even if they avoided the soldiers, they would never get through a ticket barrier. Their only hope was to sneak back down the line alongside the now stationary train and pray that another one didn't come the other way and mow them down.

They made it about a hundred yards. But then they heard a shout, and throwing caution to the wind, they dropped their bundles and ran.

They ran until Jen got cramp. 'Leave me,' she gasped, hopping to a halt. 'You go on.'

Molly could still hear voices in pursuit, but she and Jen were beyond the platforms and station buildings now, and over to the side she noticed a gap in the perimeter fence.

In front of them a train was approaching fast. 'Quick,' Molly said, grabbing Jen's arm. 'This way.'

Half running, half jumping over the hissing tracks, they darted across in front of the oncoming train. Molly felt the rush of turbulence lift the back of her hair as it thundered past. Then they were through the gap and stumbling across a patch of rough ground towards an alley between two industrial buildings.

Ahead Molly could see more buildings, a road and some traffic. If only they could get in among other people, they might stand a chance of evading their pursuers. But Jen was clearly in considerable pain.

'Come on,' Molly urged her. 'Not far now.'

But then something zinged over her shoulder, and a second later she heard the crack of a gun. A piece of masonry fell off the wall beside her.

Dragging Jen with her, Molly veered off blindly down another alley, and then another, and then suddenly, unexpectedly, they erupted like corks from a bottle on to a proper street lined with tall yellow stone buildings with ornate ironwork balconies.

Two people on the pavement swerved abruptly to avoid them. Another paused, but then, hearing the sound of German voices echoing behind them in the alley, hurried quickly away.

There was nowhere to hide. All the shops were closed. To their left, at the end of the street, there seemed to be some kind of square with a fountain and a few bare trees. On the corner in front of it a smartly dressed man with a black apron round his waist and a napkin over his arm was standing outside a discreet, expensive-looking restaurant watching them with mild interest.

But as they hobbled towards him, his interest quickly turned to dismay. He took a hasty step back, and was about to retreat into the restaurant when Molly called out in English, 'No! Please! Help us!'

She stumbled to a stop in front of him. 'Please let us come in,' she gasped. 'We are being chased by German soldiers.'

The man looked absolutely astonished. As well he might. It probably wasn't every day of the week that two wild-haired overgrown schoolgirls came running up the street screaming at him in English to let them into his select little restaurant.

Already he was taking another step back, shaking his head and raising his hands as though to fend them off, and Molly felt her heart sinking. Beside her Jen was wheezing in pain. The Germans were surely not far behind them. They hadn't a second to lose. Automatically Molly lifted her hand to touch the charm at her throat.

But of course it was no longer there.

Thoughts jumbled frantically through her head. A smart restaurant. Expensive food. Expensive wine. Toulon. Vineyards. Surely it was possible? Surely it was worth a try? She crossed her fingers and prayed he spoke English.

'Do you by any chance know someone called André Cabillard?' she said to the man. 'I'm sure you know his wine. He's a friend of ours and we need to send him an urgent message.'

It was as though she had waved a magic wand, or spoken a secret password. Whether he understood English or not, as soon as he heard the name, the man's demeanour changed.

But he didn't look any more friendly or eager to help. On the contrary, he looked as though she had punched him in the stomach. All the colour drained from his face. Beads of sweat appeared on his brow.

For a second he stood there as though frozen to the spot. Molly could hear the rapid clatter of boots on concrete as the soldiers searched the alley. They were much closer now. Any minute now they would be on the street, and that would be that.

But just in time, the man jerked his head towards a small flight of steps leading down to some kind of cellar under the restaurant. '*Allez là-bas*. Go down there,' he muttered. 'Through the door. But no further. And remain silent.'

It was pitch dark inside the door. The wall was cold and slightly damp.

They had only been there a second when they again heard the sound of running feet and urgent German voices. A barked demand. The impassive reply. A question. A denial. A suggestion.

Molly and Jen stood rigid, hardly daring to breathe.

And then the scrape of hobnails on tarmac as their pursuers ran on, across the road on to the square.

'Crumbs,' Jen whispered when it was silent again. 'That was a close shave.'

They heard someone tiptoeing down the steps. They tensed. But it was only the maître d'. Holding his finger to his lips, he turned on a light and ushered them swiftly along a corridor to a small office at the back. 'Wait here,' he said very quietly. He looked behind him nervously. 'But please. No noise.'

It had taken Aaref several days to lay hands on a camera, but he finally appeared with one only a couple of hours after Helen had left. He had tracked it down at Woolworth's for the bargain price of three shillings, which included a film of six prints. Katy knew it was already too late to get the film developed and a picture sent off to Canada in time for Christmas. But it was the thought that counted after all, and she would still be in time to send one to her mother and Ward's aunts in the country.

But as she stood in the street outside the pub, trying to stop Malcolm wriggling long enough for Aaref to take the photo, she felt the familiar hand of panic close round her throat. What would happen if she died in childbirth? What would happen to Malcolm then? She couldn't expect Pam to look after him for ever. But if Ward wasn't back …

Sometimes, recently, despite his occasional reassuring telegrams, she had begun to wonder if Ward actually wanted to come back.

'Smile, Katy,' Aaref called, looking down into the camera. 'You do not look very happy.'

'It's Malcolm you're meant to be taking, not me,' Katy said, alarmed. 'I'm not dressed for a photo.'

'I take you both, mother and child. It is nice. But you should smile, I think. This would be better.'

Jen and Molly waited a long time in the restaurant basement. The pervasive smell of food made their stomachs rumble. On the floor above they could hear the scraping of chairs, the popping of corks, the rattle of plates, the grumble of conversation, the occasional burst of raucous laughter. The diners in the restaurant were clearly having a jolly time.

Occasionally they heard footsteps on a staircase, the sound of water and the flush of a lavatory. Once they heard a cavernous fart, and despite, or perhaps because of, their nervous tension, they both nearly got the giggles.

And then gradually, eventually, the noises died down. The lunch service was obviously drawing to a close.

But still nobody came.

'I'm bloody starving,' Jen whispered. 'Do you think there might be some leftovers?'

'Shh.' Molly glanced nervously at the door. She had caught the sound of a slight rustle in the corridor. A low, murmured remark. Perhaps a warning. Or an apology.

And then they heard a firm tread.

The door handle turned.

The door opened.

And there, just as tall and strikingly attractive as Molly had remembered, was André Cabillard.

He was wearing a stylish jacket over a high-necked grey jumper and navy trousers. His dark hair was clean and crisp, his eyes hard and alert.

Even though he had a pistol in his hand, she recognised him at once. The strong, aristocratic features, the sense of leashed energy, the hint of danger.

He was a fraction slower to recognise her. But, amazingly, recognise her he did.

'It's Molly, isn't it?' he said, his eyebrows rising with surprise. It was the same voice. The same sexy French accent. He made a slight, rueful gesture and discreetly slid the gun into his pocket. '*Je m'excuse.* I'm sorry, but these days one can't be too careful.' He smiled and turned to Jen, his eyes narrowing slightly in concentration. 'And you are Jen, I think. I saw you once perform at the theatre.'

Molly couldn't believe it. Here he was. As large as life. Gorgeous as ever. André Cabillard. Helen de Burrel's fiancé. And even though he hadn't seen them for well over a year, though she and Jen looked as though they had been pulled through a bush backwards and they were standing in a damp, dimly lit room underneath a restaurant in the south of France, he was acting as though it was some pleasant, mildly unexpected encounter with a couple of old acquaintances.

But he wasn't a hundred per cent relaxed. There was a watchful look about him. His smile hadn't quite reached his eyes.

Molly was aware of a sudden frisson of fear. Behind his charm and easy manner, he looked distinctly dangerous. Almost angry. No wonder the maître d' had been so nervous when she mentioned his name. And she began to wonder if they had made a terrible mistake.

He waved them back to their chairs with an authoritative gesture. 'I don't wish to sound discourteous,' he said, 'but can I ask what you are doing here? Jean-Marie told me you had a message for me.'

'I just wanted him to help us,' Molly stammered. 'I thought if I mentioned your name ...'

She stopped helplessly as a strange look flashed across his face. His hand clenched into a fist and she saw him make a deliberate effort to relax.

'Tell me,' he said slowly. He looked suddenly pale. His voice was husky, his accent slightly more pronounced. 'Before we talk of anything else. There's something I need to know.' He stopped abruptly, as though he couldn't bear to frame the question.

It was Jen who cottoned on first. She suddenly gave a little gasp of comprehension and leaned forward in her chair.

'She's alive,' she said. She gave a sudden nervous laugh. 'Helen de Burrel. She is alive and well. Or at least she was when we left England.'

If either of them had ever doubted the strength of André Cabillard's feelings for Helen, in that second those doubts were dispelled. His whole body seemed to shudder in relief. He closed his eyes and held his palms to his forehead. He stood like that for a long moment. Then he dropped his hands, shook himself and attempted to speak.

'I'm sorry,' he said. 'I ...' He stopped again and clenched his teeth together.

Molly stared at him through watering eyes, unbearably moved by his emotion. She wondered if any man would ever feel like that about her. It seemed unlikely.

Then he took a long breath, looked up and gave a self-conscious smile. 'I have waited a very long time to hear this news,' he said. He raised his hands in a little Gallic gesture of deprecation. 'Of course I had feared the worst.'

'But they sent a coded message on the BBC,' Molly said.

He frowned. 'I waited for this message, but I never heard it.'

'It was a long time later, because for a while she was very ill, but—'

A look of pain crossed his face. 'The bullet wound?'

'Yes.' Molly nodded. 'It got infected, and Katy's husband, Ward Frazer, went to fetch her back from North Africa—'

'Molly saved her life,' Jen chipped in suddenly. 'It was all thanks to her. She found some special new drug that cured her.'

Molly felt a rush of heat flood her cheeks. Glaring at Jen, she opened her mouth to demur, but before she could think of what to say, André stepped forward and held his hands out to her.

Unthinkingly, she took them and he pulled her to her feet. For a shocking moment she found herself staring up into his midnight-blue eyes. And then he leaned down and kissed her full on the lips. '*Merci*,' he murmured, hugging her to his hard chest. 'Thank you from the bottom of my heart.'

Stunned, cheeks flaming, when he released her, Molly almost fell back into her chair.

Jen's eyes were brimming with laughter. 'Who cares about Ward Frazer now?' she murmured.

'But Helen is healthy now?' André asked sharply. His eyes flickered. 'And happy?'

Molly nodded dumbly. She was suddenly finding it hard to think of anything except the feel of André Cabillard's lips on hers. 'Healthy certainly,' she stammered breathlessly. 'She's been really brave. But she misses you terribly.'

There was a moment's silence, then he relaxed. '*Mon Dieu,*' he said. 'I am so pleased you came here. Later, if it is safe, we will go home. But first …' He glanced at them questioningly, acknowledging their dishevelled appearance with a wry smile. 'You look as though you perhaps need something to eat.' He raised his hands with a smile. 'As you have chosen to come to one of the best restaurants in Toulon, I suggest we eat here.'

He had barely uttered these wonderful words when someone tapped on the door and the maître d' came into the room bearing a silver tray with a bottle of wine and three glasses.

He seemed delighted at André's suggestion that the chef might like to prepare them lunch, and entered into a brisk discussion in French of what delicacies might be most acceptable.

Once that was decided to André's satisfaction, the man bowed obsequiously and backed away.

'He's changed his tune,' Jen murmured wryly, as the door closed behind him.

André looked surprised.

'He didn't seem very pleased to see us when we first got here,' Molly explained. She was still feeling shaky and disorientated from that unexpected kiss, but she didn't approve of Jen mocking the maître d'. After all, he had probably saved their lives.

André stared at them for a moment, then threw back his head and laughed. 'Poor Jean-Marie. I'm not surprised. Didn't he tell you? The restaurant was full of German officers.'

Jen started laughing too. 'Oh my God, she said. 'We had no idea.'

Molly stared at them aghast. So it wasn't fear of André Cabillard that had sent the poor maître d' into a cold sweat. It was fear of what he was going to have to do *for* André. The risk he was going to have to take in bringing her and Jen in and keeping them right under the noses of his Nazi clientele.

André was already casually pouring the wine. 'Now,' he said, raising his glass and smiling at them over the rim. 'Tell me everything.'

They ate a meal of tender fried cutlets in a mushroom sauce, fresh vegetables and delicate creamed potatoes sculpted into clever little whirls, following it up with chocolate mousse for Jen and something called an île flottante for André and Molly. It was the most delicious meal Molly or Jen had ever eaten. Jen remarked wryly that it had been worth five months of hell to get a chance to taste food like that. André translated her comment

397

for the maître d', and he summoned an elderly chef in a high white hat, who eyed them somewhat askance but seemed pleased with the compliment.

And they did indeed tell André everything. At first it was hard to know where to begin. But André was so gratifyingly furious at their treatment at the hands of the Germans, and so amused by the story of Jen painting spots on to the stolen statue, that they soon lost their inhibitions. The relief of unburdening themselves was tremendous.

Falling over each other in their efforts to give him all the gory details, they forgot that they were still in enemy-held territory, that this was only a temporary reprieve, that they were penniless fugitives from German martial law.

But André Cabillard didn't forget. Despite his relaxed, easy-going manner, his attentive interest in their garbled story, he was always listening, alert, his hand never too far from his pocket.

And when the moment came to leave the restaurant, he installed them in the back of a wine van, hidden among some empty crates.

'We will have to pass roadblocks,' he said. 'But they know me. With luck they won't search in the back.'

Even when they reached the vineyard, he had to leave them in the van, because there were some German officers standing in the driveway right outside the house.

He had already explained over lunch that part of his family estate, the Domaine Saint- Jean, had been requisitioned for use as an SS officers' headquarters. He had lifted his shoulders in a dismissive shrug. 'This is why the SOE mistrusted me. But it is safer this way. I can watch them. And listen to them. And they are so stupid, so confident in their Nazi superiority, that they have no idea that we are running refugees and resistance fighters in and out under their fat noses.' He laughed with mocking derision. 'Nor do they know that they are drinking the dregs of our wine. From bottles with the best labels, of course.'

He had glanced at Jen with glittering eyes. 'I will keep my ears open, and if your Hauptsturmführer Wessel ever sets one foot in this area, you can be sure that he will meet with a very nasty end.'

It was much later, when they had finally been smuggled into the magnificent house, been introduced to André's charming, aristocratic father, taken it in turn to bathe in a huge bath of hot water, and were tucked up in two clean, comfortable beds in a spacious room with tall windows discreetly closed off by heavy wooden shutters, that Molly found herself thinking it was no wonder at all that Helen de Burrel had been so distraught at having to leave this magnificent man. No wonder that she had been pining for him ever since. Molly wasn't far off pining for him herself.

'Oh dear,' she whispered into the darkness. 'I think I've fallen in love with André Cabillard now.'

She heard Jen's chuckle. 'So have I,' she said.

Joyce was watching Mr Lorenz talking to Katy's new barmaid, Elsa. She was a nice little thing, pretty in a dark, foreign way, and Mr Lorenz seemed quite taken with her. She was Jewish, of course; that probably helped. But Joyce wished he'd stop chatting and come and sit down. She felt awkward waiting for him all alone with no drink.

Mr Lorenz had invited her to the Flag and Garter for the occasional drink before. Normally they sat in the public bar. But tonight he had escorted her into the saloon. 'There's something I wanted to ask you,' he had murmured as he settled her courteously at one of the corner tables.

When she had looked up at him questioningly, he had just smiled faintly and gone for the drinks.

'So what was it you wanted to ask me?' Joyce asked when he eventually came back with a pint of beer and a half of Guinness for her. She had wondered if it might be about Angie's foot. She knew he was worried about that. Thanks to blasted Dr Goodacre, Angie was off work for a week. And now the lazy madam was lying around at home all day long, listening to the wireless, pleased as Punch, with a damn great bandage wrapped round her leg. Or he might want to ask her something about the lease on the café, which was coming up for renewal.

She eyed him nervously. She hoped he wasn't going to ask her to pay back the money he had put into the business. That would be a disaster. Things were worryingly tight as it was.

But it wasn't either of those things.

'I wanted to ask if there was anything you would particularly like for Christmas,' he said. 'I was thinking of making it a surprise. But in these difficult times I wanted to make sure it would be something you really wanted.' He adjusted his spectacles. 'I was wondering about a piece of jewellery or a new outfit? Or perhaps tickets to a show? Or even,' he coughed and lowered his voice, 'I thought you might like to take a little holiday. Perhaps to a nice hotel somewhere?'

It was not at all what she had been expecting. A hotel? Joyce had never set foot in a hotel. Nor had she ever had a holiday. Not a proper one. Although she had once been to Devon to visit the farm that Angie and Paul had been evacuated to. Ward Frazer had given her a lift in a car he had borrowed. People could still get petrol in those days. That seemed a long while ago now. Well before he and Katy were married.

Of course there had been a lot of heartache since. And now Ward was absent again and the new baby was due any moment now, judging by the look of Katy. She'd had a very bad time with the last birth. But at least last time she had her friends there to give her support. How the poor girl was going to cope on her own she couldn't imagine.

Joyce sighed. If only people didn't fall in love. Things were so good at the beginning. In the heat of the moment. But they so often seemed to go wrong in the end.

She realised that Mr Lorenz was watching her anxiously. He coloured when he heard her sigh, perhaps feeling he had overstepped the mark. 'We would have separate rooms, of course,' he murmured. 'I wasn't suggesting ...' He tailed off in some confusion. 'Not that I wouldn't want to,' he added. 'I mean ... only if you wanted to.'

Joyce couldn't believe her ears. Was he really suggesting ...?

She gaped at him and saw the mortification in his kind eyes. It was unlike Lorenz to lose his composure. Usually he was so calm, courteous and correct. For a moment then he had sounded like a schoolboy propositioning his first love. She suddenly had a terrible urge to laugh. She forced it back. She didn't want to hurt or embarrass him. But what she really didn't want to do, she suddenly realised with a jolt of alarm, was lose him.

Feeling rather flustered herself, she dropped her gaze and saw how tightly he was holding his glass. His long, clean fingers. The neatly trimmed nails. So very different to Stanley's rough, clumsy hands. She had noticed Lorenz's hands before. And the slender, wiry strength of his arms.

To her surprise, she felt a sudden slight heat somewhere in the region of her groin. It was a sensation she hadn't felt for such a long time, she didn't immediately recognise it. She didn't want to recognise it. Not yet. Not here in the pub.

She took a quick breath and tried to drag her mind off the idea of sharing a hotel room with Mr Lorenz.

'I'm not sure about a holiday,' she said. She saw his long eyelashes flicker down to hide his disappointment, and hurried on nervously. 'I don't think I'd feel right enjoying myself with Jen still missing.' She stopped abruptly. What was she saying? What was she implying?

She took a grip on herself, and before he could speak, she went on quickly. 'But there is something I'd like for Christmas.'

He looked up then, eagerly, gratefully. 'Yes? What is it?'

'A turkey,' Joyce said.

'A turkey?'

Joyce nodded. 'Yes. I've asked Sister Morris and Dr Goodacre to join us for Christmas lunch, and what with Angie and the boys, I don't think a chicken will be enough.'

Something flickered in his eyes. She saw him bite back a smile.

'I don't know why you're laughing,' she said indignantly. 'You can't get a turkey for love nor money these days, but I thought you—'

'Not for money,' he murmured. 'But perhaps for love.'

She gulped.

He took her hand and held it in a surprisingly firm grip. 'I have loved you for a very long time, Mrs Carter. Joyce. I know you don't feel the same. And I would never ask you to do anything you didn't want to do. I know you are worried about Jen and your boys. I know it's not the right moment. And I don't expect a reply. But if you ever felt you might like to marry me, I would promise to protect you and look after you until the day I die.'

Chapter Twenty-Nine

Joyce was thinking about Mr Lorenz's offer of marriage as she unlocked the café the following morning. She hadn't said yes, but she hadn't said no either. As a matter of fact, she hadn't said anything much at all. She couldn't. Not there in the pub. It had all been too awkward. So she had stammered out something about being very grateful, and then to her relief there'd been a bit of a rumpus in the bar. Louise Delmaine had came in and caught Aaref Hoch chatting to the new barmaid.

As Louise had apparently been waiting for nearly an hour at her parents' house for Aaref to come and take her to the pictures, this had not gone down well. Miss Fancy-Pants Louise had been in a right old stew, accusing Aaref of both standing her up and letting her down, and all sorts of other hysterical nonsense.

Things had settled down eventually. Aaref had taken Louise away. Elsa had carried on with her work in her usual silent way. Mr Lorenz had bought another round of drinks and enquired politely about Angie's ankle. He hadn't referred to the proposal.

Nor had Joyce told anyone, even though Angie had been agog when she got home.

'You've been out so long,' she said. 'I thought something exciting must have happened.'

Joyce was conscious of heat in her cheeks. To cover her confusion, she told Angie about Louise and Aaref.

'Ha,' Angie had said. 'Serves her right. That Aaref is a nice bloke. But she's made him wait too long. You can't keep men hanging on a string for ever. They're bound to look elsewhere.'

It was a busy morning in the café. Mrs Rutherford wasn't in yet. And with Angie still out of action, Joyce was run off her feet. It was as she hurried out of the kitchen with some water to top up the almost empty tea urn that she found Mr Lorenz at the counter.

'Ah, good morning, Mrs Carter,' he said in his usual courteous way.

Joyce put the jug down rather unsteadily. Glancing at his unperturbed face, she suddenly found herself wondering if she had imagined the events of the previous evening. Perhaps it had been a dream, or a hallucination. Maybe he hadn't proposed to her at all. Or perhaps he had forgotten all about it. But then she felt a sinking feeling. Of course he couldn't have forgotten. Nor about her idiotic request for a turkey as a Christmas present. In preference to a weekend away with him.

'I'm sorry about last night,' she mumbled. 'I—'

He held up his hand. 'No, no,' he said. 'There is no apology needed. If there is any blame, it is mine for speaking out of turn.'

'No, not at all,' Joyce said quickly, looking up in dismay as the bell jangled and yet another customer came in. There was steam hissing out of the urn now. It would explode if she wasn't careful. She knew how it felt. It was bad enough managing the breakfasts single-handed without having to deal with her own emotional turmoil as well. 'I mean, it wasn't out of turn. Not that we were taking turns, but it changes things, and I—'

Mr Lorenz bent forward slightly and lowered his voice. 'Nothing has changed,' he said. 'I suggest we go on exactly as before.'

Joyce felt a sense of relief. Of affection for this kind, patient man. Dragging her eyes away from his, she took a cloth, lifted the lid of the urn and poured in the cold water. The steam subsided at once.

She relaxed and turned back to Mr Lorenz. There were two people queuing up behind him now. He was watching her with a fond smile on his lips. She smiled back. 'Tea and toast, then? Same as usual?'

She saw a flicker of amusement in his dark eyes. 'Yes indeed, Mrs Carter,' he said gravely. 'When you have a moment. Tea and toast. Exactly as usual.'

And suddenly she felt better. He could wait a bit longer. She didn't think he was likely to look elsewhere. Not yet.

As the morning progressed, Joyce gradually realised that the ball of dread that had been lodged in her stomach overnight had somehow transformed itself into something nice. A little nugget of pleasure that she could visit from time to time. Someone loved her. Mr Lorenz loved her. But otherwise everything was the same.

Except that without Angie, she was struggling to keep on top of the chores. The piece in the paper about the fateful cooking demonstration had indeed been good for the business, a bit too good.

It was already getting dark outside when she glanced through the hatch into the kitchen and saw the mounting pile of washing-up. She was just wondering how long she and Mrs Rutherford could manage on their own when she noticed Bella James standing outside in the street talking to Barry Fish. Or at least Barry Fish was talking. Bella was looking shy and embarrassed, and very cold.

But even as Joyce watched, she saw the girl raise her eyes and smile shyly at him.

Without thinking, she rushed to the door.

'Bella,' she called out sharply. 'Come in for a moment, there's something I want to ask you.'

The girl jumped in surprise, as well she might, because Joyce hadn't spoken to her in weeks. Murmuring some kind of apology to Barry Fish, she dutifully came in.

'You should keep clear of men like that,' Joyce said, nodding towards the window. Barry Fish was still outside, staring disgruntledly at the café door. As Joyce glared at him, he was forced to take a hasty step to one side as George Nelson suddenly zoomed past, dangerously close, on his go-cart.

Bella quickly smothered a giggle and Joyce eyed her suspiciously. Despite her nose being blue with cold, the girl really was ridiculously pretty. It was no wonder men wanted to talk to her. Even George, young as he was, seemed to be smitten with her. Joyce was quite sure that near-miss had not been an accident.

'What are you doing out and about in the dark?' she said. 'Why aren't you at home?'

Bella's lashes came down swiftly. 'Mummy doesn't like me being in the house when she has visitors,' she said.

As she looked into the girl's shy, innocent face, Joyce felt a bubble of fury well up inside her. If Gillian James had come in then, she would have happily whacked her round the head with a frying pan. She knew she should say something. At the very least she should issue a stronger warning about the danger of talking to strangers. But before she could open her mouth, Mrs Rutherford came bustling out of the kitchen drying her hands on a tea towel.

'Mrs Carter, I've just realised that I have to be at the WI by five o clock. I'm sorry to leave you with all the washing-up, but …' Apparently only just then noticing Bella's presence, she stopped and looked her up and down, taking in the second-hand school uniform coat, far too thin for December weather, the bare legs and tawdry, down-at-heel shoes. For a second, Joyce was worried she might be going to shoo the girl out.

But Celia Rutherford merely raised her eyebrows. 'You are Miss James, aren't you?' she said.

Bella nodded.

'Do you know how to wash up?'

Bella looked startled at the question, but she nodded again.

'Well then, how would you like to earn a little pocket money after school for a few days?'

The girl blinked. 'Really?' She turned eagerly to Joyce. 'You wouldn't mind?'

But Joyce was staring at Mrs Rutherford.

'Of course she wouldn't mind,' Mrs Rutherford said in her brisk, no-nonsense way, ushering Bella into the kitchen.

'Well why not?' she added under her breath to Joyce. 'We need some help. And it will at least keep her out of harm's way for a couple of hours while her mother is otherwise engaged.'

Despite the luxuriousness of their new accommodation, Jen and Molly were even more restricted at the Domaine Saint-Jean than they had been at Enrico Bandini's farm. They certainly couldn't go outside, not even to get some fresh air. The risk of them being seen by one of the resident SS officers was too great. André said he could explain away occasional political refugees, passing them off as wine experts or itinerant workers, but accounting for two English girls would tax even his powers of invention.

'And it is not just the SS we must be careful of,' he warned them. 'But also the local population. Not everyone is a sympathiser or a collaborator, but the Germans are ruthless and people are frightened. Some will do anything, or say anything, to save their skins.'

Molly and Jen weren't the first women to be sheltered at the Domaine. André was reticent about his own activities, but they learned from his father that in the absence of support from the SOE, André had used his own contacts, friends and relations to build a network of opponents to the pro-German Vichy regime. These he drew on for specific tasks, intelligence and acts of deliberate sabotage. He had also helped smuggle Jewish and other political refugees out of France. Sometimes hiding them from the SS, and the equally vicious Milice Française, in a crypt under the family chapel, alongside his hoard of gelignite and other weapons stolen from the Germans, until reliable local guides could be found to help them make the hazardous trek through the Alps to Switzerland. Or the equally arduous trek over the Pyrenees to Spain. Now, though, due to the harsh winter weather, both these routes were impassable.

While André put his mind to how to get them away by some other means, Molly and Jen of necessity spent most of their time in their room. Due to the proximity of the SS contingent, they could only talk in whispers, but in fact for the first two days they barely spoke at all. Because they suddenly found they were completely exhausted. The strain of the last few months had finally caught up on them. All they wanted to do was sleep, and eat.

It was no hardship to laze in their comfortable room, or indeed the adjoining bathroom with its huge claw-footed bath and ceramic toilet, the height of luxury after months of battling with hideous holes in the ground.

They also spent a lot of time stroking and cuddling André's two kind-faced mongrels, who, rather dangerously, took to visiting their room, scratching imperiously on their door for admittance.

When the coast was clear, one of André's henchmen, a man called Raoul, would bring them food, or André would pop in for a quiet chat over a bottle of wine. He was keen to talk about London. About the war. And, of course, about Helen.

In the evenings, dressed in Helen's abandoned clothes, they would creep downstairs, and after supper Molly sometimes played cards with André's father, who, like Enrico Bandini, quickly became a fan of her tricks.

But it clearly wasn't an arrangement that was going to last for long. It was fraught with danger. One night, when André was out on some undisclosed business, Molly took the opportunity to thank his father for risking so much for them.

'My dear girl,' Monsieur Cabillard said, looking up from his cards. 'It is our pleasure. Our world here has been very dark this last year. Since you arrived, André is a changed man. You have brought him hope. This is good for me too. André has taken many risks in his efforts to undermine the occupation forces.' He smiled. 'Now, perhaps, with the knowledge that Hélène is alive and waiting for him, he will take a little more care.'

'Do you think he will find a way to get us out?'

'*Mais bien sûr*. Of course.' He looked surprised. 'André will move heaven and earth to get you to safety.'

Bella James proved to be a big asset in the café. She was clean, tidy and willing. And unlike Angie, she never broke anything. Nevertheless, Joyce and Mrs Rutherford kept her well concealed in the kitchen. For one thing, they didn't have a work permit for her. For another, having all their male customers flirting with Angie was bad enough; they couldn't imagine what would happen if they let Bella James loose on them.

The only person unhappy with the new arrangement was Angie. 'You aren't going to want me to come back,' she said disconsolately one evening. 'Now you think Bella is so good.'

It was unlike Angie to be morose. Joyce wondered if she had secretly begun to doubt the mythical Gino's devotion. It had been reported on the news that Italian prisoners of war were now entitled to fight on behalf of the Allies. Or they could become 'co-operators', continuing to work on the land in return for wages and more freedom than they had previously enjoyed. If Gino had availed himself of either of these opportunities, then presumably he would have been able to come to London to reacquaint himself with his so-called fiancée.

But when Joyce assured Angie that Bella's employment was only a temporary measure, she brightened at once. 'Oh, I don't mind her working there,' she said airily. 'I just don't want to lose my job. Because I'm saving up for my bottom drawer. Me and Gino will be setting up home soon, and I'll need sheets and towels and what not.'

But the café couldn't afford to employ both girls, so when Dr Goodacre eventually declared that Angie was once again fit to work, Joyce decided to ask Katy if she fancied taking Bella on. After all, Katy needed extra help even more than they did.

'I don't know how the poor girl manages in that pub,' Celia Rutherford said. 'Especially with the baby coming.'

Katy was understandably dubious about the idea of employing Gillian James's daughter. But, encouraged by Joyce's fulsome recommendation, she agreed to give her a try-out. So the following day Bella stopped washing up cups and saucers in the café, and began washing up glasses in the pub instead.

André did not have to move heaven and earth, but he did have to pull in a favour with the Free French government-in-exile's intelligence service, the Bureau Central de Renseignements et d'Action.

'I have given them some assistance over the last few months,' he said. 'Now I hope they will be able to help me.'

'So when will we go?' Jen asked. 'And where will we end up?'

But André was evasive about the details. 'It is best perhaps if you do not know too much.' He lifted his shoulders in an apologetic shrug. 'There is some slight danger that we may get intercepted before we reach the people who will help you. I do not wish to put any more lives at risk than necessary.'

Molly shivered. She knew what he meant. If they were intercepted, as he so politely put it, they would almost certainly be made to talk, to reveal the escape plan and who was helping them.

She caught Jen's eye and grimaced. Once she might have protested that they would never reveal anything. But Molly knew only too well that, faced with someone like Hauptsturmführer Wessel, it would be impossible to hold out for very long.

'I'm sorry,' she murmured. 'I'm sorry for putting you and your father in danger.'

'Nonsense,' André said. 'You and Jen have shown much courage and resilience.' He opened his hands with one of his charming smiles. 'It is an honour to assist you.'

*

Since the day that Louise had thrown a tantrum about Aaref chatting to Elsa, Katy had been dreading a confrontation between the two girls. But so far there had been no uncomfortable scenes. And although Katy often noticed Elsa sliding a glance at Aaref when he was in the bar, the two of them made no attempt to converse, and Katy began to wonder if she had imagined their former rapport.

But now she was faced with the problem of having not just one but two pretty young women working in the pub, one of whom was not only distinctly underage, but also the daughter of the local prostitute.

In an effort to keep Bella out of the public gaze, and remembering that Joyce had once remarked that the girl was a big reader, Katy had suggested that she read Malcolm a bedtime story. This had proved a big success. Bella and Malcolm immediately hit it off. So for the next few evenings Katy let her play with him, give him his supper and get him ready for bed while she and Elsa manned the bar.

The first night Bella had clearly been somewhat reluctant to go home, and Katy asked if her mother would worry about her being out so late.

Bella lowered her eyes as she shook her head. 'She doesn't mind. She doesn't like me being there when she has visitors. And the money you give me will help with the housekeeping.'

Early in the evening of 14 December, a telegram arrived from Helen de Burrel.

Arrived Tunis stop Daddy here too More news soon stop love H

So Helen had managed to meet up with her father after all. Katy was pleased for her. She had thought she might have missed him, because she had heard on the wireless that President Roosevelt was already back in America. There had been no mention of Winston Churchill arriving back in London, however, even though he was long overdue, so perhaps Lord de Burrel had stayed on with him.

But at least Helen was safe, that was the main thing.

Katy was just folding the flimsy paper when she heard the sharp crack of something smashing against her front window.

Everyone stopped talking and Katy swung round in alarm just in time to see the glass explode into the bar.

There was a moment's silence, then instant panic. Elsa screamed. Men started shouting. One of them thought it must be machine-gun fire. Thinking it was a bomb, someone else started barging towards the cellar.

Frozen in the middle of the bar with the telegram in her hand, Katy's first thought was Malcolm, but before she could call up to Bella to bring him down to safety, the pub door opened and George Nelson came in carrying his catapult.

'It wasn't a bomb,' he said, looking rather taken aback at the panic he had caused. 'It was a stone. I'm really sorry. But it was a good shot.'

It took a second for this news to sink in.

'A good shot?' Katy said incredulously. 'Please don't tell me you were aiming at my window?'

George looked incensed at this accusation. 'Of course I wasn't,' he said. 'I was aiming at the lamp post. I hit it, too. But the stone ricocheted off and hit your window.'

And now, indeed, Katy could see a large pebble lying on the floor.

'What on earth were you doing firing your catapult so close to the window anyway?'

'Helen told me to protect you,' he said sulkily. 'So that's what I was doing.'

'I can't see how breaking my window is protecting me,' Katy said.

He flushed slightly. 'I was practising for something else.'

'What?' Katy asked suspiciously. 'What were you practising for?'

But he wouldn't answer. He clearly felt he had already said too much. And if she wasn't grateful for his protection, then he wasn't going to divulge any more.

Katy took one look at his mulish face and gave up. In any case, the deed was done. There was no point in being cross. All she could do now was try to find someone to board the window up. She could hardly leave it wide open for some light-fingered passer-by to help himself from the bar during the night. Nor indeed could she leave it open to the elements. Already there was a chill wind blowing in, buffeting the blackout curtains. Some of her customers were shrugging on their coats, drinking up, putting down their empties and preparing to leave. Nobody wanted to stand in a howling gale with glass crunching underfoot.

'Elsa,' Katy called. 'You'd better turn off some of the lights. We don't want to attract the attention of any German bombers. Or the blackout warden.'

George blanched, perhaps belatedly realising the extent and severity of his crime. 'You won't tell Mum and Dad, will you?'

Katy glanced down at him. He suddenly looked very young, all his former bravado gone, probably at the thought of having his precious catapult confiscated.

'No,' she said. 'You're going to tell them. They're bound to hear what's happened anyway. But I promise to make sure they realise it was an accident, as long as you promise not to do any more damage.'

He hung his head. 'I promise,' he said.

'So go home and tell them. And ask Alan to come over and help me board up the window. I've got some old planks in the shed. Oh, and tell Pam that Helen arrived safely in Tunisia too.'

'Tunisia?' George's eyes widened in awe. 'Blimey,' he said. 'I wish I'd gone with her.'

Katy glanced at her rapidly departing customers. I wish you had too, she thought grimly.

It took Katy and Elsa half an hour to sweep up the glass. It was another hour before the window was boarded up to Alan Nelson's satisfaction.

'I'm so sorry, Katy,' he said. 'We've confiscated his catapult for a few days. But between you and me, I think he's already learned his lesson.'

Katy nodded, but she privately doubted that. 'He said he was practising for something,' she said. 'I dread to think what it was?'

Alan was about to reply when they heard a gasp and turned to see Elsa blinking at the draining board. 'We are missing six beer glasses,' she said. 'I count them twice and look everywhere, but they are not here.'

Katy stared at her, but before she could gather her wits, she heard a thump upstairs, followed by a shriek and the sound of running footsteps. A second later, Malcolm came tumbling head over heels down the stairs.

Reaching the bottom, he lay sprawled on the floor for a moment. Then, laughing, he scrambled to his feet and set off across the room shouting, 'I scape, I scape!'

Bella appeared at the top of the stairs. 'Mrs Frazer,' she said in her soft, shy voice. 'I'm really sorry, but Malcolm has just learnt how to climb out of his cot.'

Katy put a hand on her stomach and closed her eyes. Oh God, she thought.

'Katy? Are you all right?' She heard Alan's concerned voice. 'You'd better sit down. Do you need a doctor?'

Katy shook her head. She opened her eyes and forced a watery smile. It was all too much. 'No,' she said. 'I need my husband.' And then she burst into tears.

When the moment came, it was determined by the weather. Cocooned in their shuttered bedroom, Jen and Molly hadn't paid much attention to what was happening outside. They had arrived in France in bright sunshine. But now, a week later, the temperature had dropped sharply, and a thick fog descended over the Domaine Saint-Jean.

As they finished dinner that evening, the telephone rang in André's office. It was a very short call. When he came back into the room, he glanced at his father and nodded.

'*Alors*,' he said as he sat down again. 'Tonight we leave. Wear your warmest and darkest clothes. Be ready when I tap on the door.'

He sounded so casual, so matter-of-fact, that for a second Molly thought she had misunderstood.

But he wasn't casual when, later that night, he ushered them out of the house and into the back of the wine van. He was quick, careful and efficient.

On a low command, three of his men loomed out of the shrouded darkness to push the van silently out of the yard. The engine only fired when they were well clear of the house. Even then they proceeded very slowly, coasting up to every junction so one of the men could get out and creep forward through the fog to check for roadblocks. Once, even Molly and Jen had to get out to help push the heavy van backwards for some considerable distance to avoid a Milice Française patrol.

But André clearly knew the roads well. He took a different turning and they were on their way once more.

The rendezvous was in an old barn. Again André was very careful. He stopped the van well away. While Molly and Jen waited with Raoul, he and the other two men moved cautiously forward into the gloom. But it seemed everything was in order, because a minute later, André was back. 'Come,' he murmured. 'But be very quiet. We are close to a German coastal battery.'

And indeed, as they groped their way through the foggy darkness to the barn, Molly could hear the sea grumbling in the distance. She could smell it too, that same salty tang she'd noticed on the train from Italy.

Three men were waiting for them in the barn. In the dim light from a small lamp, Molly could see that they too were dressed in dark clothes, all with hats or berets pulled well over their faces. They shook hands with Raoul and the other men, but despite them eyeing her and Jen with obvious interest, there were no introductions. No chit-chat.

André settled Molly and Jen on a pile of sacks in a corner. 'You could try to get a little sleep,' he murmured. 'We may be here some time.'

But the atmosphere was far too tense for sleep. It was obvious that the men were listening for something.

It was a long wait. When eventually a slight noise outside broke the silence, they all produced guns and flattened themselves against the walls.

But when they heard a low whistle, they relaxed. Two of the men left the barn and the rest moved towards the door.

'What do you think is going to happen now?' Jen whispered nervously to Molly.

'I have no idea,' Molly whispered back.

'I have a nasty feeling it's going to involve a boat,' Jen said.

But before Molly could reply, André was beckoning them over. 'Be careful how you tread,' he said. 'Stay close to me. It will be steep and very slippery.'

In total silence, the little group filed out of the barn. Keeping very close together, they crept through some kind of plantation. Molly could smell the scent of pine. There was no light to guide them. Whoever was at the front of the line clearly knew the terrain like the back of his hand. Soon the pines gave way to spiky scrub, which tore at their shins and made the going even more difficult.

The sound of the surf became louder. It was an odd, disorientating experience walking in the yellow darkness, unable even to see their own feet.

At one point, as they came on to harder, more uneven ground, they heard muffled German voices drifting out of the fog, and the line stopped abruptly. As the voices receded, André urged Molly to take his hand. 'Now we climb down,' he murmured. Telling Jen to wait, he led Molly down a slippery, almost sheer rock face. If she hadn't had his hand strongly gripping her own, she would surely have slipped.

Leaving her clinging to a ledge, he went back to get Jen, and then they were scrambling down a steep fissure in the rock, so narrow they could use the cliff wall on either side to steady them.

At the bottom, they finally dropped down on to a beach. Molly could feel the soft crunch of sand under her feet.

Over the sound of the breaking waves, she heard André's voice. '*Voilà*,' he said. 'So far, so good. But now we may not have much time. We are meeting a boat.'

'I knew it,' Jen groaned.

'It is an Italian MAS torpedo boat, now under the control of the Free French,' André continued. 'If all goes well, they will take you to Corsica. There, I think, you should find some British forces. They will be able to get you back to England.'

'And if all doesn't go well?' Jen asked. 'Apart from me getting seasick, I mean?'

They heard André's low chuckle. 'I am sorry,' he said. 'I didn't know. This is the best I could do.' He hesitated. 'If there is any problem, the captain will make for Spain.' He pressed a soft packet into Molly's hand. 'Here,' he said. 'This is some money. You may need it. And a letter for you to take to Hélène in London. But if you do meet problems, please destroy it at once. And tell no one that I have helped you. The Germans have spies everywhere, and it is important they do not find out who I am. You understand?'

'I understand,' Molly whispered. 'But we can't take your money. You've done more than enough for us already.'

'It is nothing compared with what you have done for me,' he said. Then he stopped abruptly and listened. 'They are here,' he said. '*Eh bien.* There will not be time to say goodbye. So I'll say it now. I look forward to meeting you both again after this war is over.'

Even as he kissed Jen, there was a low call. '*Venez, vite!*'

He quickly drew Molly close and she felt the touch of his lips on her cheek. Then he swung her effortlessly up into his arms and waded into the water.

They passed three other people wading out. They were carrying a large crate, taking care to keep it clear of the water.

Molly heard the slap of water on metal, a splash on her face, and a second later André hefted her up on to a slippery deck. Cold hands pulled her aboard. And then Jen was scrambling up next to her.

Already André was lost in the fog, but they heard his low voice across the water. '*Au revoir, Molly et Jen. Bon voyage. Bonne chance.* And take all my love to Hélène.'

Within half an hour, Jen was sick. It wasn't surprising; it was the bumpiest ride Molly had ever been on. At first the small crew had rowed strongly and silently. But then at some unspecified point, presumably deemed safe, they had fired the engines. The noise was deafening, and as the power surged through the small vessel, the bow rose out of the water and it had felt for all the world as though they were going to flip over backwards.

They didn't flip over. Instead they started thumping and bouncing over the invisible water like there was no tomorrow. And indeed, at one point, when they heard another engine closing on them, there nearly was no tomorrow.

A sharp German command had been bellowed through a megaphone. Molly thought she heard the crack of weapons being fired. But the MAS boat just swerved and increased its speed, the bow lifting up even further.

Molly felt sorry for Jen as the Cabillard's lovely dinner splattered over the side of the boat, but she herself couldn't help but feel exhilarated by the blind, reckless headlong speed of the boat into the swirling fog. As the salt spray splashed in her face and the wind whipped through her hair, she found herself thinking back to her encounter with the blind man in the fog in Clapham. It seemed a long time ago. He had predicted change for her. She wondered if she would ever get a chance to tell him how right he had been.

The journey seemed to go on for ever. Gradually, very gradually, the sky began to lighten, but the fog still hung on the water. And now, for the first time, Molly allowed herself to think about the future. About getting back to London. About helping Katy with the baby, which must be almost due. About the pub. About whether she would give up nursing. And even whether she might, perhaps, look into the possibility of—

Then suddenly, as though they had passed through a magic wall, from one moment to the next they were out of the fog.

It was extraordinary.

The sky was clear blue. The water was flat calm, shimmering faintly pink in the early-morning light. And ahead of them, a distinct navy-blue outline on the horizon.

'Jen,' she shouted. 'Look! We're nearly there!'

One of the boatmen gave a gleeful laugh, and even Jen raised a thin smile. 'It can't be soon enough for me,' she said.

As they approached the island, the blue blur of mountains gradually crystallised into hillsides and headlands, inlets and rocky coves. Now Molly could make out individual villages, patches of cultivated land, and a colourful town sprawling up the hill.

As the boat rounded a groyne, the captain cut the engine, the bow dropped, the vibration settled and they cruised gently into a small port.

The harbour was fringed by tall bomb-damaged buildings, all tinged pink in the morning light. In the centre, a huge yellow church with two cupolas dominated the little town.

It was still early, but there were plenty of people about. Many of them were staring in their direction, startled, but not particularly alarmed, by the arrival of an Italian torpedo boat.

The captain threw out a couple of fenders and pulled in neatly against the pier. At once the smell of fresh coffee drifted across from the café tables set out on the harbour wall.

'Bastia,' the captain said gesturing with evident satisfaction as he turned off the engine. 'La Corse.'

It was as she climbed up on to the pier and stood swaying on shaking legs that Molly saw Ward Frazer.

It was like a mirage. A miracle. As though she had somehow conjured him up. He was standing with two men in British Army uniform, but even as she stared at him in wonder, recognition dawned and he took a sudden step forward.

And then he was half walking, half running towards them. It was like a slow-motion scene from a film. Almost the exact same scene, in fact, that

414

Molly had once imagined in Mrs Carter's café.

Ward was wearing shorts and a T-shirt that clung to his chest. His hair was wet, as though he had just been swimming. His eyes were wide with incredulity

'Tell me I'm dreaming.' Molly murmured to Jen.

Jen laughed. 'You're not dreaming.'

But Ward Frazer looked as though he was dreaming. In all the time she had known him, Molly had never seen him look so bemused. So dumbfounded.

And as he approached them, hands outstretched, a smile of amazed delight just beginning to curve on to his lovely mouth, Molly found she was laughing too.

Laughing and crying.

But it was all right. She felt all right. She was amazed and delighted to see him. She was glad to see that his limp was less pronounced than it had been. But that was all. Her infatuation had mysteriously vanished. The spell had been broken.

She felt a sudden surge of relief. Of pride. Of confidence. She remembered all the times she had thought about Ward Frazer over the last few dangerous months. All the times she had thought how much they needed him. All the times she had longed for his help. His expertise. His support. And in the end they hadn't needed any of it.

She and Jen had done it all on their own.

Chapter Thirty

Despite the devastation the Germans had left behind, Bastia was enjoying its liberation. And within minutes of arriving on the island, Molly and Jen were enjoying theirs too. It seemed incredible that from one day to the next they no longer had to talk in whispers, no longer had to look over their shoulders, and more than anything, they no longer had to be scared.

There were a million things they wanted to ask Ward Frazer, but it was impossible to talk as they were suddenly swamped by well-wishers who, discovering where they had come from, and some of that they had been through, wanted to shake their hands.

Jen, her seasickness forgotten, was in her element. But Molly was glad when Ward extracted them from the melee and walked them to a small hotel to freshen up while he went to arrange for messages to be sent to the Wilhelmina, to Katy and to Mrs Carter.

'How is Katy?' Molly asked him. 'When did you last see her?'

'August,' he said. 'I got sent out here to help with the liberation and I've been here ever since. But I've been offered a berth on a ship leaving Ajaccio direct for England tomorrow. If I can get you girls on it too, we might just about make it home for Christmas.'

'Hurrah,' Jen said. 'I fancy a bit of roast turkey.'

But Molly was looking at him aghast. 'You've been here since August? But how's Katy coping? Is she OK? The baby must be almost due.'

'It's due any day now.' Ward ran a hand through his hair and Molly realised she had touched a nerve. Under the tan she could see now that his handsome face looked strained. 'She says she's OK. But only a couple of her letters have got through, so I don't know much detail. She's been worried to death about you two, for sure. She has found some new staff, but I guess she's missing Helen ...'

As he tailed off with a sigh, Molly felt the blood drain from her face. Visions of a sudden fatal relapse flashed through her mind. Penicillin was, after all, only an experimental drug. 'What's happened to Helen?' she asked, alarmed. 'Surely you don't mean she's ... died?'

Amusement sparkled suddenly in Ward's eyes. 'No. Far from it,' he said. 'She's rejoined the SOE and has been posted to Tunis.'

He clearly expected Molly to be delighted by this evidence of Helen's total recovery. But Molly just stared at him in dismay. 'Helen's in Tunisia?'

She turned slowly to Jen. But Jen held up her hands. 'Oh no,' she said. 'I know what you're thinking. But you can count me out. The only place I'm going is back to England.'

Molly frowned. 'But we've got to see her,' she insisted. 'We promised André that—' Aware of Jen's warning cough, she stopped abruptly and tried to change the subject.

But Ward wasn't a spy for nothing. His dark brows rose at once. 'André? Helen's André? Good God, was it André Cabillard who got you on that boat?'

As Molly nodded, Jen gave a slight chuckle. 'Ha,' she said. 'Now you've let the cat out of the bag.'

Molly glanced at Ward apologetically. 'He told us not to tell anyone. But yes, it was him who arranged it all. We'd made our way from Italy to Toulon specially to find him. He was the only person we could think of that might be able to help us.'

Ward gave a low, incredulous laugh. 'There have been rumours of someone operating pretty effectively in the Toulon area. I guess now we know who it is. I'd sure like to make contact with him.' He saw Molly's expression and held up his hands. 'But don't worry. His secret is safe with me.'

Molly fidgeted uneasily. 'The thing is, he gave us a letter for Helen.'

'He gave *you* a letter for Helen,' Jen muttered.

Molly glared at her. 'And I promised to deliver it personally.'

Ward looked at her thoughtfully for a long moment. 'In that case,' he said, 'I'll just book Jen on my ship to England. And I'll have to see if I can figure out a way of getting you to Tunisia.' He hesitated for a fraction of a second. 'Unless you want me to come with you?'

In the past, the idea of spending time on a ship with Ward Frazer would have been Molly's dearest wish. Even now it was tempting. If nothing else, the thought of setting off all alone to yet another country was daunting to say the least.

But studiously ignoring Jen's sudden choke of laughter, Molly shook her head. 'No,' she said adamantly. 'You must go back to Katy. She needs you far more than I do.'

'Your blood pressure is rather high,' the health visitor said. 'You should be taking more rest. Now, if you stand up, I'll just have a quick feel of your uterus to see where the baby has positioned himself.'

'I can't rest,' Katy said crossly. 'I haven't got time.' But she obediently unbuttoned her blouse, exposing her huge, bloated stomach.

'Well you must make time,' the health visitor said reprovingly. 'All my other ladies are putting their feet up for at least three hours a day.'

Bully for them, Katy thought. I don't suppose they have a pub to run, a toddler to supervise and a husband who shows no sign of ever coming home. But she bit it back. They had had this argument before. 'How do you know it's a him?' she asked instead.

'I can tell from the bump,' the health visitor said. 'A big, low bump like yours always indicates a boy.'

'My husband wanted a girl,' Katy said.

'Well I'm afraid he'll have to wait until number three,' the woman said complacently.

Number three? Katy almost recoiled in horror. 'I'm not having any more,' she said. 'I can't go through this again.'

'Nonsense,' the health visitor said briskly, as she rubbed the stethoscope with her hand. 'It's our duty as women to create big, happy families. Now lean back as far as you can. I'm afraid it's a little bit cold.'

Cold was an understatement. The metal plate was icy on Katy's hot flesh.

As she flinched back in an ungainly half-naked sprawl against the bar, wishing she had locked the door, Aaref Hoch appeared through the blackout curtain.

He looked appalled to catch her in such disarray. 'I brought your photographs,' he stammered, brandishing a small sealed package. 'But I can come back later when it's more convenient.'

'No,' Katy cried in alarm. She pushed the health visitor out of the way and hastily adjusted her blouse. 'Leave them here. I want to post them off as soon as I can.'

Averting his gaze, Aaref reluctantly stepped forward and dropped the packet on the bar.

'I'm sorry they have taken so long,' he muttered, retreating hastily. 'But everything is so damn slow these days.'

'Now, now,' the health visitor tut-tutted. 'No complaining. There is a war on, you know. Everyone is trying to do their bit.' She eyed Aaref's civilian clothes with disapproval. 'And if you don't mind my saying so, you two should both be doing your bit too. Not lowering morale with unpatriotic sentiment.'

Katy did mind her saying so. Doing her bit? She could hardly believe her ears. She had been doing her bit for years. More than her bit. And surely Aaref had done his bit by escaping from Jewish purges in Austria and bringing his younger brothers to safety in England. And now he was working his socks off to pay for their education.

418

As Aaref flushed and beat a hasty retreat, Katy suddenly longed for the courage to summon up some unpatriotic sentiment and stuff the stethoscope into the health visitor's prim little mouth. That would certainly lower her morale and no mistake.

When Ward came back to the hotel two hours later, he had not only dispatched the messages and secured an extra berth for Jen on the ship, but he had also persuaded a pilot he knew in the American Air Force to take Molly on a supply flight to Tunisia the following morning.

He had also armed himself with a picnic of freshly baked French bread, smoked sausage, tomatoes, oranges, a bag of small chestnut doughnuts filled with soft cheese and a couple of bottles of wine.

He had been asked to debrief the girls about their adventure. He said their recollections and observations would be useful for intelligence purposes. And what better place, he suggested, than a nearby beach. It was only about half an hour's drive in a jeep. They could relax on the sand, paddle or swim in the sea if they wanted to, and talk without fear of being interrupted.

But then he looked them over meditatively. 'Although I guess I really ought to get a doctor to give you a check-over first.'

'No.' Jen recoiled in sudden panic. 'I don't want to see a doctor.'

'No. No,' Molly added hastily. 'We're fine. I know we are a bit thin, but otherwise we are perfectly healthy.'

Jen nodded. 'If Molly she says we are fine, then we are fine. I trust her judgement much more than some stupid doctor.'

Ward had looked at her in some surprise, but he didn't push it. 'OK,' he said easily. 'Then let's go to the beach.'

It was a magical place, and a magical afternoon. Even though it was mid December, the sun was shining, the air was scented with wild herbs, the sand was warm under their bare feet, the sea clear and blue. High cliffs each side of the cove sheltered them from any unwanted breezes, and the picnic was delicious.

Ward Frazer was the perfect interrogator. He was a good listener and his questions were relaxed and unhurried. But it was an odd thing. Having divulged all the gory details to André, this time, perhaps because they were already trying to forget the worst aspects of their ordeal, they found themselves giving a lighter, funnier version.

At one point, clearly aware that they were glossing over the details, Ward cut in. 'You don't have to tell me if you don't want to,' he said quietly. 'But we kind of need to know if you were ever actually … mistreated.' He hesitated. 'Physically, I mean.'

Molly and Jen looked at each other. They knew what he meant. Then Molly shook her head. 'No, although once it was pretty close.'

'Molly had to use that necklace you gave her to bribe a German guard to keep his hands off us,' Jen said.

Molly gave him an apologetic look. 'It was the only thing we had left,' she said. 'I was sad to lose it, because all the wishes I'd made on it up until then had come true.'

Ward stared at them for a moment, as though transfixed. Then slowly he leaned forward and poured some more wine. 'You girls,' he said, lifting his glass. 'You never cease to amaze me.'

'No, but really, it was all down to Jen,' Molly insisted. 'If she hadn't picked up so much Italian, we'd have been sunk.'

'No,' Jen said. 'It was all down to Molly.' She nodded wisely. 'But then of course she had been very well trained in escape and evasion.'

Ward looked startled. 'By who? Helen?'

'No,' Jen said. 'By George Nelson.'

And Ward could only watch in astonishment as they both collapsed back on the sand laughing.

Somewhat to their surprise, they had been joined on the expedition by a large dog with a long nose, a huge lolling tongue and a set of very large teeth.

'I call him Lucky,' Ward had said. 'He got caught up in some nasty crossfire in an ambush when the Germans were retreating and he was lucky to survive. Since then he's kind of adopted me.' He had grinned and encouraged the animal to jump in next to Molly on the back seat of the jeep. 'Or maybe I have adopted him.' He glanced affectionately at the dog. 'I'm thinking of taking him back to London as a Christmas present for Malcolm. What do you think?'

Molly had a fair idea of what Katy would think at being lumbered with an enormous boisterous animal like Lucky. On the other hand, he would make a good guard dog. He would certainly keep the likes of Barry Fish at bay. And she had little doubt Malcolm would adore him. As long as Lucky didn't eat him first.

Now, lying back on the sand, shading her eyes, Molly surreptitiously watched Ward strip down to a pair of swimming trunks and run down the beach with the huge dog gambolling at his heels, barking its head off as they both plunged into the water

Ward Frazer. Intelligent. Intrepid. Patriotic. Gorgeous. He was exactly the same. But she, mercifully, was different. She still liked him. Fancied him. Even perhaps adored him. But she was no longer in his thrall.

Jen was grinning at her. 'That's a sight for sore eyes. Do you need a cold compress?'

Molly giggled. 'No,' she said. 'I'm fine. I really am. I'm over it. I still think he's wonderful. But that's all.' She glanced at Jen. 'What about you? Are you really OK? You seemed a bit edgy about the idea of seeing a doctor.'

Jen grimaced. 'I was. Thanks for getting us out of that. I never liked doctors at the best of times, but now I may have a lifetime phobia.'

'That's a shame,' Molly said mildly. 'Because I'm beginning to wonder if I might try to become one.'

'A doctor?' Jen looked dumbfounded. 'Women don't become doctors.'

'They do. Some do. Dr Florey is a woman. And I'm fed up with being bossed around by those stuffy, dim-witted sisters at the Wilhelmina.'

Jen laughed. 'I can't wait to see Sister Morris's face when I tell her!'

Molly sat up, appalled. 'Don't you dare tell her,' she said. 'Or anyone. Not yet. I want to look into it first. See what qualifications I need. It may not be possible.'

'Good God,' Jen said. 'If we can escape from Nazi Europe, anything is possible.'

Molly gazed at her for a moment, then lay back again and shut her eyes. *Anything is possible.* She wondered if that was true. Lying on the beach, in the warm glow of Ward Frazer's flattering admiration, it felt true, but it might not feel quite the same back in the strict confines of the Wilhelmina.

But she didn't have long to think about it, because Jen's voice interrupted her reverie.

'Watch out,' she warned. 'Here comes Mr Wonderful and the Hound of the Baskervilles. And they are both soaking wet.'

As Lucky bounded up, Jen screamed and ran away, leaving Molly to get showered with seawater as the dog shook vigorously right in front of her.

Laughing apologetically, Ward shooed him away and handed Molly his towel. 'I'm sorry,' he said. 'He has no manners.'

Molly tried not to look at him as she wiped her face. She tried very hard. But he was standing right in front of her. And Jen was right. Ward Frazer was a sight for sore eyes. Fresh from his swim, he looked like an advertisement for health and vitality. His legs were long and strong. His swimming trunks were clinging to him. His tanned chest was gleaming wet. And droplets of water were sparkling on his long dark lashes like diamonds.

In some desperation, Molly buried her face in the towel.

'I like your new hairstyle,' he said. 'It suits you.'

Molly cautiously lowered the towel. He was smiling down at her, and she felt a stab of alarm. His smile had always been her undoing. But now she found herself able to smile back, almost normally. 'Jen did it,' she said.

Jen was still some distance away, keeping a wary eye on the dog, but she heard the comment. 'It's good, isn't it?' she called. 'It makes her look quite pretty, don't you think?'

'Jen!' Molly swung round indignantly.

Ward laughed. 'I've always thought Molly was pretty,' he said. 'But now she's more than pretty. Enchanting might be a better word. Entrancing perhaps. But definitely much more than just pretty.'

The photographs were disappointing. Malcolm at least was smiling, but even so, Katy felt they didn't quite do him justice. And she looked plain and ridiculously fat.

Louise was there when she opened them up. 'Good God,' she said, looking over Katy's shoulder.

'I know,' Katy said mournfully. 'I can't possibly send any of these to Ward's mother. She'll think he's married a whale. '

Laughing, Louise took the pictures and flicked through them.

And then suddenly she wasn't laughing. She was staring at the last one with a look of shock on her face.

'What is it?' Katy asked in alarm. She pulled the photo out of Louise's rigid fingers.

It was a picture of Elsa, her new barmaid. It only took Katy a second to realise what had happened. Having taken the photos of Malcolm, Aaref must have realised that there was one exposure left on the reel and had used it to take one last shot.

But this wasn't just a photograph. It was more than that. It was a declaration of love. It was clearly carefully posed. Elsa was turning her head up to catch the light. A small, shy smile was playing on her lips and her eyes shone with emotion. To make things even worse, the picture had been taken at the top of the fire escape that led up to the flat at the top of Mrs D'Arcy Billière's house. The flat Louise had been so reluctant to give up.

Louise took a shuddering breath. 'So that's why he's been avoiding me,' she said. Her shoulders slumped. 'I've lost him. I always thought he loved me. But now I've lost him as well. Why? What is about me that turns them away? Why can't I ever keep hold of them?'

Katy looked at her uneasily. Because you only think about yourself, she wanted to say. Because you only seem to want men as trophies to show off, not as people to love for who they are, what they are. But that wasn't the kind of thing you could say, not even to a friend. Certainly not to one as volatile as Louise.

'You didn't turn Jack away,' Katy said. 'He loved you. He married you. And I'm sure one day you'll find another Jack.'

'I won't,' Louise said. She started to cry. 'And even if I do, they'll run off with someone else. Some little flibbertigibbet barmaid.'

Katy glanced at the clock. Elsa would be arriving any minute; the last thing she wanted was a scene.

'Oh for goodness' sake, Louise,' she said. 'You must admit you've treated Aaref very badly over the last couple of years. It's not really surprising he's found somebody else. Elsa isn't a flibbertigibbet. She's a nice, intelligent girl. I think they're very well suited.'

Expecting sympathy, Louise seemed taken aback by Katy's blunt assessment. Or perhaps she heard the exasperation in her voice. Either way, instead of succumbing to a bout of self-indulgent misery, she sniffed back her tears and wiped her eyes on her sleeve.

'What you mean is she's nicer than me,' she said. She lifted her chin. 'Well then, if that's all it takes, I'm going to turn over a new leaf. I'm going to be a nicer person.'

'Excellent,' Katy said briskly. 'In that case, if I quickly write a Christmas note to my mother to go with the photograph, perhaps you can take it down to the post office for me.'

Molly had never been to an airfield before. She had certainly never stood right beside an aeroplane. She looked up at the huge machine in considerable alarm. It seemed awfully unlikely that this hulking great thing would ever be able to get into the air, let alone fly.

But Ward, of course, took the whole thing in his stride.

'I've sent a signal to Helen telling her you are on your way,' he said to Molly after introducing her to the pilot and crew. 'She'll try to fix up a passage home for you from there.' He reached forward and put his hands on her shoulders, looking at her steadily. 'Are you sure you'll be OK?'

'I think so,' Molly said. She glanced dubiously at the aeroplane. 'But I wish I still had that magic carpet.'

He smiled, that slow, warm smile that had so often been her undoing. 'You'll be fine,' he said, patting the side of the aircraft. 'The C-47 is a reliable old bus, and you'll have a fighter escort. And don't forget, you're tougher than you think. The kind of thing you've just been through would have broken most people. It hasn't broken you. Quite the opposite. I reckon you can face anything now.'

He lowered his head and kissed her on the cheek. 'Goodbye, Molly. And remember, when you get home, our offer of a share in the pub still stands.'

After a second's hesitation, Molly reached up and kissed him back.

'Thank you,' she said. 'Give Katy my love. And tell her I'll be back as soon as I can.'

And then the moment came to say goodbye to Jen.

Jen had been watching her farewell to Ward with gleeful interest. But now, as Ward went off to talk to the pilot, and Molly turned to face her, the laughter faded from her eyes.

'So this is it,' she said. 'I can't believe you are abandoning me after all we've been through.'

Molly looked at her indignantly. 'It's you that's abandoning me. How am I going to cope in Tunisia without you?'

'You'll be fine. You're much better at this travelling lark than me. I never want to meet another foreigner as long as I live.'

'They weren't all bad,' Molly said. 'What about Enrico and Gianni and little Enzo? And André, he's foreign. And so is Ward, come to that. What's wrong with him?'

'He's a man,' Jen said sourly. 'They're all men. I'm fed up with men and their stupid war. No, I'm looking forward to a nice quiet Christmas with Mum and Angie. And then I'm going into a nunnery.'

Molly laughed. 'I'll believe that when I see it. By the time I get back, you'll probably be married to Henry Keller and starring in some West End show.'

'Molly?' Ward called across. 'It's time to go.'

'Say hello to Helen,' Jen said. 'And good luck.' She hesitated. 'You're all right, Molly Coogan. I'll miss you.' She gave a self-conscious laugh. 'And I never thought I'd say that.'

Then suddenly, to Molly's surprise, Jen stepped forward and hugged her.

It was the first time they had ever embraced. Compared to Ward Frazer, Jen's thin body felt bony and fragile, and the ferocity of her embrace brought unexpected tears to Molly's eyes.

'I'll miss you too,' she said gruffly. 'And I certainly never thought I'd say that either. Not in a million years.'

It was quarter to three in the afternoon and Katy had just rung last orders when Pam called at the pub. She had promised to take Malcolm out for a walk on the common with George and Nellie.

Some of the Flag and Garter customers were already beginning to drink up and shrug on their coats, but the stalwarts were moving to the bar for the chance to get one more pint in before closing.

Leaving Elsa to deal with them, Katy came round the counter to get Malcolm ready for his outing.

'Bit worrying about Winston Churchill, isn't it?' Pam remarked as

Malcolm stood up expectantly and began to rattle the side of his playpen. She saw Katy's blank look. 'Haven't you heard? It's just been on the wireless. He's ill. In the Middle East somewhere. It didn't say exactly where, I suppose for security. But that's why he hasn't come home.'

Katy had been just about to lift Malcolm out of the playpen, but now she left him where he was and swung round in concern. 'Not seriously ill, surely?'

'Yes.' Pam nodded. 'Well, serious enough for that Lord Moran, his private physician, to feel it should be announced. Apparently Mrs Churchill flew out there yesterday to be with him.'

'Blimey,' Katy said. 'That doesn't sound good.'

'No,' Pam agreed. 'I expect bloody old Hitler will be rubbing his hands in glee.'

She was right, Katy thought. Winston Churchill was the person they were all relying on to bring them out of this mess. They needed him. The whole country would panic now. And it must be serious if his wife had been flown out. God only knew what would happen if …

She didn't have time to complete the thought, because at that moment the post girl came in with a telegram.

'Oh no,' Katy said at once. 'I don't want to open it.' As she spoke, she was aware of a hush falling over the room. The only person who didn't hush was Malcolm, who was getting increasingly impatient to go out for his walk.

Ignoring his cries of frustration, Katy opened the telegram with shaking fingers.

Girls safe stop Molly going to Helen stop Jen and me home for Xmas bracket as promised bracket W

As the meaning sank in, the words blurred in front of her eyes. Katy handed the flimsy paper to Pam. 'They're safe,' she said. 'Molly and Jen. They're alive. They're safe.'

Suddenly everyone was cheering and clapping. And that made Katy feel even more tearful.

'But what's this about Helen?' Pam said when the noise subsided. 'Helen's in Tunisia. Why would Molly be going there? Why isn't she coming home with Ward and Jen?'

It was indeed a mystery. And it was as Katy reached over to take another look at the telegram that out of the corner of her eye she saw one of the Garrow brothers slip a pint glass inside his coat.

It was so quick, so practised; like a magician spiriting away a playing card. If she hadn't glanced up at that precise moment, she would have missed it. He had clearly decided to use the distraction of the telegram as cover for his move.

Already he was edging casually over towards the door. Katy didn't know what to do. Glancing around wildly for someone to help her, she called out his name.

'Mr Garrow. Please. Wait a moment.'

But he didn't wait.

And nor did Malcolm.

Infuriated by the delay, Malcolm had already been grappling angrily with the side of his playpen. Now, like an agile little monkey, he suddenly pulled himself up the bars, wriggled a foot up on to the wooden rim and a moment later was rolling over the top and tumbling down on to the floor. Undeterred by the fall, he scrambled to his feet and set off at high speed towards the door, and freedom.

Mr Garrow had his sights on the same thing. He was already through the blackout curtain, and was just in the process of opening the door when Malcolm cannoned into the back of his legs.

Mr Garrow let out a grunt of surprise. Glancing down to see what had hit him, he caught his foot on the sill, lost his balance and plunged head first on to the pavement outside, with Malcolm sprawled on top of him.

As the blackout curtain swung shut behind them, there was a moment's stunned silence. Then, with a strangled cry, Katy lurched towards the door.

Outside in the street, she found Malcolm sitting on the pavement, looking rather stunned by his escapade. George, whom Pam had left outside to guard Nellie in her pram, was studying the prostrate figure of Mr Garrow with considerable interest.

'He's bleeding,' he said. 'And groaning.'

Hauling Malcolm into her arms, Katy eyed her erstwhile customer with dismay. He was indeed groaning. And a small pool of blood was forming in the gutter under his stomach. She turned her head to Pam, who had hurried out behind her. 'Would you send someone to go and fetch the police,' she said. 'He'd stolen one of my glasses. I saw him take it. I think it must have broken underneath him as he fell.'

As Pam turned to find a volunteer among the onlookers, George prodded Mr Garrow with his foot.

'Will he get his hand cut off?' he asked hopefully.

'No,' Katy said with a choked laugh. 'I told you. That sort of thing doesn't happen in this country. But he might just get sent to prison.' And at the very least I'll be able to justify banning him and his brother from the pub, she thought with satisfaction.

She hugged Malcolm to her. 'You clever boy,' she said. 'You've caught my thief.'

But George was eyeing Malcolm with some disfavour. 'I suppose the police'll give Malcolm the reward now,' he said. 'But it's not fair. He didn't mean to catch him. He wasn't even trying.'

For a second Katy didn't know what he was talking about. She had all but forgotten about Helen's reward. 'No,' she said. 'The reward was for finding my jewellery. And sadly we are no closer to finding that, not unless Mr Garrow spills the beans, which doesn't seem very likely. But I have got good news for you, George,' she added consolingly. 'I just heard that Molly and Jen are safe. And Ward is coming home for Christmas.'

It hadn't occurred to Molly that she would be able to see out. But the American pilot of the C-47 had installed her in a bucket seat right next to a small oval window in the side of the cavernous aeroplane.

As the huge plane revved up and rumbled down the bomb-damaged runway at Poretta airfield, Molly suddenly caught sight of Ward and Jen waving by the makeshift huts. She waved back but she didn't think they could see her.

Suddenly she felt very alone. And very frightened. What am I doing? she thought. I must be mad. Instinctively she put her fingers to her throat. But of course the lucky charm was no longer there to help her.

Pressing her nails into her palms to try to stop the sense of impending doom overwhelming her, she was thrust back in her seat as the plane accelerated. Outside she saw piles of recently unloaded construction material flash past. There was some earth-moving machinery too, and lines of khaki tents, presumably belonging to the troops tasked with rebuilding and extending the airfield almost destroyed by the retreating Germans. Ward had told her that due to its strategic position in the northern Mediterranean, Corsica was soon going to become one enormous airbase. USAF fighters and bombers from Corsica were already giving support to the Allied troops still pinned down at Monte Cassino in Italy.

And then they were in the air and Molly's stomach lurched sickeningly as the airstrip peeled away below her. She saw the jagged coastline, some tiny white towns and the distant snow-covered peaks of a mountain range. Momentarily she caught sight of the two small escort planes, but before she had a chance to feel reassured, the engine noise of the C-47 changed and the wing on her side dropped so low she was certain they would slide sideways out of the air and crash.

But gradually, after a long, slow turn, the plane steadied out, and her heartbeat returned to normal. Releasing her grip on the safety strap, she opened her eyes again. She could see the island, green and hazy, drifting underneath, and then they were out over the sea, heading for North Africa.

427

Chapter Thirty-One

Joyce was queuing up in the butcher's when the door burst open and Angie came hobbling in brandishing a telegram. 'Look,' she panted, pink from her exertions. 'The post girl brought this to the café and I knew you'd want me to open it. Then Mrs Rutherford said I should come and find you.' She took a gasp of air and her voice rose with excitement. 'Jen's safe! And Molly Coogan! They're with Ward Frazer in Corsica. Wherever that it. And he thinks they'll be home in time for Christmas.'

As Joyce stared at her incredulously, Angie raised her voice even further and glanced hopefully at Mr Dove, who was busy chopping up a bit of scrawny-looking meat for Mrs Trewgarth, the verger's wife. 'What a shame we haven't got a turkey to celebrate,' she remarked pointedly. 'Do you remember last year I brought that nice one up from Mrs Baxter in Devon?'

Joyce did remember. It seemed inconceivable that Angie had already been back for a whole year. And now Jen was coming home and all. Joyce could hardly believe that either.

But already, thanks to Angie's raucous announcement, people in the queue, people she didn't even know, were offering her congratulations, trying to shake her hand. And she was getting all tangled up with her shopping basket, her umbrella and her gas mask box. Angie was still dancing about like a mad thing. The only person who seemed oblivious to the news was pernickety old Mr Dove, who carried on chopping Mrs Trewgarth's brisket as though nothing untoward had happened.

But when, having sent Angie back to the café, Joyce finally reached the front of the queue, Mr Dove drew her to one side and murmured that she should pop round the back when she'd finished her order.

And to her surprise, when she met him outside the storeroom a few minutes later, he thrust a heavy package into her arms. 'It's a turkey,' he said. 'A nice ten-pounder from Norfolk. You've been a good customer to me this year, Mrs Carter, and I thought you deserved a little something special for Christmas. Especially now your daughter's coming home. But keep it under your hat.'

She would need a very large hat to hide a ten-pound turkey under, Joyce thought, as she took the ungainly parcel and tucked it beneath her arm.

Mrs Rutherford was busy spreading sandwiches, but she put down her knife as soon as Joyce came in.

'Oh Mrs Carter! Angie told me the news. Isn't it wonderful? You must be so relieved.'

Joyce nodded. She certainly felt rather faint, although whether from relief or from lugging the turkey up the hill she wasn't sure. 'I can hardly believe it,' she said. 'And you'll never guess what. That tight old bastard Mr Dove has given me a turkey to celebrate.'

Celia Rutherford looked surprised. 'But I thought you said Mr Lorenz was getting you one.'

Joyce flushed as she heaved the turkey into the larder. 'He did say he might, but he hasn't mentioned it since. And I didn't want to look a gift horse in the mouth.'

'Well, no,' Celia agreed. 'But you ought to let Mr Lorenz know you've already got one. Turkeys are very hard to come by this year.'

But her warning came too late.

As Joyce walked home with Angie that evening, they saw Mr Lorenz crossing the road towards her house. He was carrying a large box, which made it difficult for him to lift his hat as they approached.

'Hello, Mr Lorenz,' Joyce said brightly to cover the gurgling noise of Angie giggling at his awkward contortions. 'What on earth have you got there?'

'A turkey,' he said. 'From Norfolk.' Catching her blink of dismay, he frowned. 'That was what you wanted, wasn't it? I wasn't sure what size to get, but I thought this would be about right.'

'But we've—'Angie began, but Joyce interrupted her firmly.

'A turkey! Yes indeed.' Lifting the lid of the box, she blanched at the size of the enormous pink bird inside. It must be at least fifteen pounds, she thought. It would feed an army. 'It's a beauty,' she said. 'It's exactly what I wanted.'

'But—' Angie started up again.

'Run ahead, Angie, and open the door,' Joyce said sharply. 'Poor Mr Lorenz's arms will fall off if he has to hold this bird up for much longer.'

As Angie lumbered off obediently, Joyce smiled at Lorenz. 'I wasn't expecting it,' she said. Not after ...' She stopped and hastily started again. 'Oh, I must tell you, Mr Lorenz. I got a telegram earlier. Jen's safe. She's on her way home with Ward Frazer.'

As Mr Lorenz gaped at her in silence through his wire-rimmed spectacles, she thought he really was going to drop the turkey. He seemed to sway slightly and his eyes watered. For a second she thought he was going to cry. Taking pity on him, Joyce put down her basket and lifted the box out of his arms.

But then he got a visible grip on himself. 'I ... Oh, Mrs Carter, my dear Joyce,' he said. 'I'm so pleased. I don't know what to say.' He took out a pristine white handkerchief, blew his nose and coughed self-consciously. 'Good news is so rare these days. It's hard to cope with it.'

Unexpectedly Joyce felt tears stinging her own eyes at the sight of his emotion. She sniffed and nodded down at the box. 'You are too kind. I don't deserve this.'

He shook his head. 'You deserve much more than I can give,' he said. And raising his hat again, he walked away.

The flight to North Africa took five hours. It was noisy and cold, and once again Molly was glad of the Wilhelmina hospital cloak that had travelled with her ever since she had left the UK. It had to be admitted that it no longer looked its best. Sister Parkes would have a canary if she ever clapped eyes on it; if indeed she was able to recognise it for what it was under all the grime it had acquired on its journey. But it was the only one of Molly's garments that had survived the rigours of the last few months, and having hated it in London, she had now developed an affection for its practicality and enveloping warmth.

At one point the co-pilot brewed up some American coffee on a small gas cylinder, which seemed to Molly to be an extraordinarily dangerous thing to do in mid air. But there was no explosion, and even though she wasn't a fan of coffee, she was grateful when he handed her a tin mug of the warm, sweet liquid.

It was late afternoon when eventually Molly glimpsed land out of her window. At once she heard the engine noise change. Her ears popped and she took a firm grasp of the safety strap.

As they came down, it seemed that they were about to land in the middle of the desert. Sand stretched in all directions, interspersed only by occasional vehicle tracks. There was no sign of any houses, or, indeed, of any people.

The plane dropped sharply, touched down, lifted and then bumped down again. Clinging on for dear life, Molly saw huts and tents flash by, a wire fence, a huge hangar, some military vehicles, a fire engine, three lines of small stationary camouflaged planes and a group of young blue-uniformed air force men sitting on chairs, perhaps taking in the last rays of the rapidly setting sun. And then the C-47 was slowing and turning and taxiing back the way it had come.

'Welcome to El Aouiana,' the pilot called back to Molly, as he flicked off some switches. 'Wasn't so bad, was it? At least for once Jerry left us alone.'

The whole sky was turning pink as Molly climbed stiffly down the steps on to the sandy concrete. The atmosphere was warm and dusty, completely different to the fresh, herb-scented air of Corsica. Even with her eyes shut she would have know she was in a different country. On a different continent even. And her heart accelerated. Another adventure lay ahead. But this time instead of scrabbling around helplessly with Jen Carter, she would have the cool, sophisticated, well-travelled Helen de Burrel to ease her way.

As she walked with the pilot over to the admin hut, she scanned around for a glimpse of Helen, but there was no sign of her. Nor indeed, she soon discovered, of a car to transport her to Tunis.

What there was, on the other hand, was a number of keen-eyed young pilots and aircrew, all eager to catch a glimpse of this rare phenomenon, a young British woman alone in this godforsaken place.

Having been told to wait outside while the somewhat harassed duty officer made enquiries, she was pulling her cloak closer around her, trying to avoid the curious glances of a group of young officers sitting in a small circle of deckchairs, playing cards, when she heard someone say her name.

'Molly?'

It was a male voice. A voice she vaguely recognised. An American accent. Doubtful, almost disbelieving. But with the enormous red setting sun behind them, she couldn't see who had spoken.

And then one of the pilots stood up. Easing himself out of the circle, to the humorous jeers of his fellow card players, he came towards her. Under his peaked cap, he looked vaguely familiar, but she still couldn't place him. Was it one of the boys who had been to the Flag and Garter? But none of them had been in the American Air Force as far as she remembered.

'Molly?' he said again. A tentative smile broke out on his face. 'It is you, isn't it?'

And then she realised. It wasn't the US Air Force insignia he was wearing, it was Canadian. 'Oh my goodness,' she said incredulously. 'You're Ward's cousin. Callum.'

He seemed pleased that she had remembered his name. She was utterly astonished that he had remembered hers. Last time she had seen him, he had been drunk out of his mind, ogling Helen de Burrel, while his father leered over Gillian James. She had written him off then as a soft, smug little daddy's boy, too posh and rich for his own good, with his cushy civilian job in his father's business. So what on earth was he doing here dressed in the uniform of a Royal Canadian Air Force pilot, looking tough and honed and, frankly, rather gorgeous?

But even though she knew nothing about him, he seemed to know quite a lot about her. 'Last I heard, you'd been taken prisoner in Italy,' he said.

'So what happened?'

Molly smiled. 'I escaped,' she said. 'But what about you? Last time I saw you, you were a civilian. What happened?'

'I joined up,' he said.

And they both laughed.

But before they could say more, the office door opened and the duty officer called out to Molly that her transport had just come through the main gate and would be there in a moment.

Molly glanced ruefully at Callum. 'It's been nice to see you,' she said. 'Good luck with the flying.'

He seemed reluctant to let her go. 'But what are you doing here?' he asked. 'Where are you staying?'

Molly could hear the car now. 'I'm going to be staying with Helen de Burrel,' she said. 'You remember her? She was in the pub that night. She's working here in Tunisia now.'

She thought he'd be interested in Helen's whereabouts, because he had seemed so keen on her that night. But all he did was groan. 'Yeah,' he said. 'Don't remind me. That awful night. I behaved like a complete idiot.'

'You weren't as bad as your father,' Molly said, and he laughed again.

She went to turn away, but he touched her arm. 'Hey, listen, Molly, maybe we can meet up sometime? I'd kind of like to hear what you have been up to, how you escaped and all. I bet it's a good story.'

He was trying to sound casual, but there was a hesitant eagerness in his voice. Molly glanced at him in surprise and realised he was flushing. He was shy about asking her out. He didn't want to make a fool of himself. It was a revelation. The new haircut really must have made a difference, she thought. No man had ever been shy of her before.

'I'll probably only be here a few days,' she said. 'I really need to get back to England.' And suddenly she felt regretful too. It might have been be fun to go out with Callum Frazer.

He looked disappointed. 'I'm on duty this week. But I'm free after Christmas. Do you have a number where I can reach you in case you are still here?'

The duty officer was calling her impatiently now. Ignoring him, Molly groped in her pocket and drew out the piece of paper Ward had given her with Helen's details. Callum took out a pen and wrote the number on his hand.

And then there was a cry of delight, and Helen was running towards her.

She was wearing a stylish yellow frock with strappy sandals, and a brightly patterned scarf draped round her elegant shoulders. Against the soft, rosy glow of the sky she looked like a film star, a picture of beauty, health and vitality. Molly felt completely eclipsed.

'Molly!' Helen kissed her in the continental fashion on both cheeks. 'I'm *so* glad you're safe. I can't believe it!'

'Nor can I,' Molly said. She had been looking forward to this moment. There was so much she wanted to say, but now she couldn't say anything, not with Callum still standing there. 'Do you remember Callum Frazer?' she asked awkwardly. 'Ward's cousin?'

'Yes, of course,' Helen said at once, shaking hands. 'How lovely to see you, Callum. Katy told me you had joined up.' She grimaced apologetically. 'But Molly, I'm afraid we really do have to go. We are already running late.'

While Molly wondered what they could possibly be running late for, Helen gave Callum one of her charming smiles. But he wasn't looking at her. He was still looking at Molly. 'I'll call you,' he said. 'We'll make a date.'

The car was enormous. Molly was amazed. And even more amazed when the military chauffeur opened the door for her. She'd always known Helen was posh, but she hadn't expected such luxury in North Africa. It was very warm inside the car and Molly slipped the cloak off her shoulders.

'Coo,' Helen said as she slid in beside her. 'A date with Callum Frazer. That was quick work!' But as soon as she turned to face Molly, her teasing smile froze on her lips.

She put a hand to her mouth. 'You've seen him,' she breathed through her fingers. 'You've seen André?'

Molly stared at her. Against the red aftermath of the sunset, Helen's face was very pale.

'Yes.' She nodded as the big car pulled away smoothly. 'But how on earth did you guess?' She knew Ward wouldn't have mentioned it in his signal.

Helen gave an unsteady laugh. 'You're wearing my skirt,' she said. Her voice was shaky with emotion. 'It's one of the ones I left at his house.' She swallowed and clutched Molly's arm in a vice-like grip. 'Oh Molly, tell me. Is he all right?'

Molly nodded, tears welling in her eyes. 'He's fine. He sends all his love.' She pulled André's letter out of her pocket and thrust it into Helen's trembling fingers. 'He gave me this to give you. That's why I came.'

Jen stared at the SS *Nancy* in dismay. She already felt rather queasy after the mad dash in a military Land Rover across the island to reach the harbour in time. Whatever other delights Corsica might offer, its roads were not something to write home about. Jen had never been more jolted and rattled in all her life. She hadn't been feeling her best when they had set off. After

433

everything they had been through together, it had been oddly distressing to see Molly zoom off in an aeroplane. And now she was faced with a long journey home on a rusty-looking tramp ship.

But at least she had Ward Frazer to keep her company. Surely that would make the time go by easier. And this time she was going to take a bit more notice of the safety drills.

An hour later, she and Ward were standing together on the stern deck of the SS *Nancy* watching the land recede. Ajaccio was already looking like an idyllic toy town in the distance, nestled under the green hills behind, the war-damaged yellow buildings shrinking and blurring in the dusky evening light.

'She's a neat little ship, isn't she?' Ward said. 'She feels pretty fast too. Let's hope the other ships in the convoy are as well. If so, we should definitely be back in England for Christmas.'

'Providing there are no torpedo attacks,' Jen said.

He gave her a reassuring smile. 'We should be OK. The Royal Navy has pretty much cleared the U-boats out of the Mediterranean. I guess the only time we might get into difficulties is round the Bay of Biscay.'

'Oh great,' Jen said. 'Thanks for telling me that.'

He laughed. 'You aren't really scared, are you? After what you've been through, I would have thought this would be a doddle.'

Jen thought about it. A doddle? Maybe he was right. Maybe this time it would be different. Maybe this time she would take it in her stride. It was true, she had certainly faced much worse things over the last few months. But then she had had Molly at her side. She felt a stab of regret. Perhaps she should have gone with Molly to Tunisia after all. It would have prolonged the adventure. Even among a load of hideous Arabs surely they would have found something to giggle about.

But no, she thought, as she leaned on the rail and watched the wake of the ship froth and foam on the gently rolling sea behind them. She had made the right choice. She wanted to go home. She wanted to see her family. She wanted to see Katy. She wanted to be back in London, back in Lavender Road. She had had no idea how much all that meant to her until she had thought she would never see any of it again.

As the SS *Nancy* began a slow, juddering turn straight into the path of the setting sun, Ward glanced at his watch. 'Do you want to take a few minutes to freshen up? Then how about we meet on the mess deck for a sundowner before supper?'

It was the word *supper* that did it. The thought of food.

At once Jen's stomach started cramping. Her throat tightened alarmingly. A moment later she clamped a hand to her mouth and ran for the lavatory.

Helen read the letter in silence. For a minute she was silent. Then she blew her nose and started asking questions. She wanted to know everything, all about André, about his father. About Molly and Jen's escape. About Ward Frazer. And more about André. She couldn't stop saying his name. Over and over, as though it was a miracle. A miracle of Molly's making.

As first, as they talked, Molly was oblivious to the terrain they were passing through. It was getting dark now and she couldn't see anything much except endless bleak-looking desert. But when they passed a couple of military encampments, she began to pay more notice.

Soon they were speeding through the outskirts of a city, Tunis presumably. In certain areas here all the buildings and trees had been completely flattened. There was ruin and rubble everywhere. The fighting had clearly been catastrophic. It was like a wasteland. Molly dreaded to think what had happened to the inhabitants. Certainly no one seemed to have yet made any effort to clear up.

Further on they saw some bedraggled Arabs dressed in dark cloaks and strange little round hats. Some were straggling along the roadside; others huddled watchfully on broken walls as the car swept past. Once a group of dark-skinned children ran after them screaming and laughing and the driver opened his window and threw a few coins out into the road.

The car slowed up slightly as they approached an area of more substantial, less damaged houses. They were waved past several American military checkpoints and cordons. Wherever they were headed, the security was very tight.

'Where are we going?' Molly asked suddenly. 'Why are we in such a hurry?'

Helen hesitated. 'We are going to see my father,' she said.

'Your father?' Molly had had no idea that Helen's father was in Tunisia. 'What's he doing here?'

Helen threw her a guilty look. 'I'm not allowed to tell you, not until we get there.'

Molly blinked. 'Why not?'

'Because it's top secret.'

A minute later the driver pulled up at another guard post. This one was manned by British soldiers.

'I'm afraid you'll have to get out, ladies,' the driver said. 'This is the final checkpoint. You'll need to sign in.'

As he was speaking, Helen was peering anxiously out of the window. Suddenly a wicked smile formed on her lips.

'Brace yourself,' she said to Molly. 'I think you are going to enjoy this. But let me do the talking.'

Molly stared at her in amazement. For a second, as she climbed out of the big car, she had no idea what Helen was talking about. But then she saw Helen jerk her head meaningfully towards the guard post. Following her gaze, Molly saw a young officer standing by the gate. But it wasn't just any young officer. It was Douglas Rutherford. Molly would have known that self-satisfied smirk anywhere. Even under the shiny peak of his Coldstream Guards forage cap.

She was startled enough. But at the sight of her, his supercilious little eyes nearly popped out of his head. 'Good God,' he gasped. 'What on earth are you doing here?'

'I'm afraid we haven't got time to chat,' Helen said briskly. She drew out a document and handed it to him in silence. 'You will see that Molly has been summoned to see the Prime Minister.'

Douglas Rutherford looked as though he was about to pass out. Involuntarily he ran a finger round his shirt collar. 'But—'

'Please hurry up, Douglas,' Helen said. 'I know you take your guard duties very seriously. But really there is no time to lose.'

She turned to Molly, who was gaping at her in total bemusement. 'As you can see, Douglas hasn't yet had the opportunity to go into action. But I'm sure his time will come one day.' She smiled sweetly at him. 'Molly has just escaped from a Nazi prisoner of war camp in Italy. Perhaps if you ask her nicely she will give you some tips about dealing with the enemy.'

As a livid flush stained Douglas Rutherford's cheeks, Molly heard one of the other guards give a snort of laughter. She almost laughed herself.

And then they were signing their names on a list, climbing back into the car, the barrier was rising, and they were driving through, leaving Douglas Rutherford staring after them as though he had seen a ghost.

Helen sat back in her seat with a gleeful giggle. 'Well? That was worth coming for, wasn't it? I told you he'd get his comeuppance one day.'

Molly was aware of feeling rather peculiar. She gave a nervous laugh. 'His face was certainly a picture,' she said. She took a breath and looked at Helen carefully. 'But you were joking, weren't you? About the Prime Minister ...?'

Helen gave a slight grimace. 'Not entirely,' she said. 'It's Daddy's fault. When I told him you were flying in today, he told me to bring you straight here.' She waved her hand at a beautiful, stately white house just coming into view ahead of them. 'This is General Eisenhower's villa, La Maison Blanche. Mr Churchill arrived here a week ago from Egypt. It's all been kept terribly secret. Nobody is meant to know he's here. But he collapsed as soon as he got here and he's been ill ever since. And Daddy thought you might be able to advise about whether penicillin might help him.'

'What!' Molly couldn't believe her ears. 'But …' There were so many objections she didn't know where to begin. And in the end she didn't express any of them, because as soon as the car pulled up, Lord de Burrel was running down the steps to greet them. He was wearing a lightweight cream linen suit that made him look like someone out of the film *Casablanca*.

'My dear Nurse Coogan,' he said. 'How very kind of you to come. I do hope you had a good journey?'

Taking her arm, he steered her inexorably up the steps past yet another uniformed guard and into a cool, ornate hallway. A man in a turban took her cloak, and then they were climbing a wide, curving marble staircase. Molly glanced back in desperation to Helen. But Helen was clearly intending to wait in the hall.

'I hope Helen has briefed you?' Lord de Burrel asked as they rounded a corner and entered a kind of antechamber.

'No,' Molly said. 'Not really. Please. Lord de Burrel, sir, I'm not qualified to do this. I really must—'

But she was too late. He was already tapping on a door, and when it opened, he ushered her inside,

'This is the girl I was telling you about, Winston,' he said, following her in. 'The girl who saved my daughter's life.'

Chapter Thirty-Two

On first glance, the room seemed full, but actually there were only four people in it. Two men dressed in formal dark suits, a nurse, and the Prime Minister, reclining under a pile of blankets in a large, comfortable-looking bed.

Molly found herself gazing in disbelief at the familiar pugnacious features she'd seen on so many posters and newsreels. She had never seen Winston Churchill in the flesh before, but it was obvious he wasn't at all well. He looked flushed and feverish. His eyes were bloodshot. He barely seemed able to turn his head in her direction. But even so, even in the rather odd enormous vest-like garment he was wearing, she could feel his presence, sense the aura of power that hung about him.

I can't believe it, she thought. I am in Winston Churchill's bedroom. She suddenly realised she couldn't wait to tell Jen. She would probably die laughing at the thought.

Even as she choked back a slightly hysterical giggle of her own, Molly was dimly aware of Helen's father introducing the two other men, Dr Pulvertaft and Sir Charles Wilson, Lord Moran.

Trying to get a grip on herself, Molly dragged her gaze away from the rotund figure in the bed and tried to work out which of the two very upright men was Lord Moran. She had no idea who Dr Pulvertaft was, but even she had heard of Lord Moran. Apart from being Winston Churchill's private physician, he was one of the most eminent doctors in the world. She had heard him on the wireless once. He had been one of the panel of experts on *The Brains Trust*, a programme Alan Nelson had always listened to on a Wednesday night.

Lord de Burrel didn't bother to introduce the nurse by name, but Molly nodded to her anyway and then belatedly realised that she recognised her. It was one of the QAs from the boat, one of the toffee-nosed girls she had shared a railway carriage with from London to Liverpool all those months ago. If she hadn't felt so bemused by the whole situation, she might have laughed out loud at the nurse's dumbfounded expression as recognition dawned on her too.

And oddly, it was the presence of the QA that made Molly finally pull herself together. Whatever the doctors might think of her, she didn't want to let herself down in front of the snooty nurse.

Silence fell. Looking around uncertainly, Molly noticed a portable X-ray machine, and a number of blue-grey exposed plates lying on a table by the door next to an open leather medical bag.

It was Lord Moran who spoke first. Molly recognised his voice.

'So you know something about penicillin, do you?'

His manner was dismissive, and before Molly could answer, he had turned to the Prime Minister and raised his voice slightly. 'You will remember, sir, the so-called miracle drug that Fleming discovered. At St Mary's, Paddington.'

Molly frowned. She knew that disparaging tone. It was the one that doctors invariably seemed to use when addressing nurses. And she didn't like it. Already she could feel her hackles rising.

'Well it may have been Dr Fleming who discovered it,' she said. 'But my understanding is that he gave up on it when he failed to stabilise it. It's Professor Florey and Dr Chain at the Sir William Dunn School of Pathology in Oxford who have developed it into a therapeutic drug.'

Lord Moran looked somewhat put out by this, but Winston Churchill seemed to find it amusing. Rousing himself from his lethargy, he gave a crack of laughter. 'Ha,' he said. 'That's put you in your place, Charles.' But his distinctive gravelly voice was husky and his breathing was laboured.

Leaning forward slightly on his pillows, he peered at Molly with interest. 'So tell me, young lady,' he growled. 'Do you think your penicillin might help me? Lord Moran is against it. But Pulvertaft here thinks it might be worth a try.'

Molly stared at him in dismay. Talk about being put on the spot. If she could have killed Helen de Burrel at that moment, she would have. She heard Lord Moran take a sharp breath and saw him exchange a glance with the other man. She suddenly felt the ground swaying beneath her feet. If she wasn't careful, she was going to make a complete fool of herself. Not only that, but a black mark against her name would be certain to put the kibosh on any chance she might have of ever going to medical school.

But then she realised suddenly that this wasn't about her. Or her secret ambitions. Or about doctors. This was about something much more important. This was about Winston Churchill.

The world was relying on this man. She remembered the poster of him in the lobby of the Wilhelmina. *We will go forward together.* Without the drive and dogged determination of Winston Churchill, the world might not go forward at all. It could so easily sink backwards, and succumb to the vicious tyranny of Adolf Hitler.

And she, for one, didn't want that to happen. It was time to put her

439

pride and her chagrin to one side. Honesty was the only option.

'I don't know, sir,' she said. 'It would depend entirely on the nature of your illness.'

Winston Churchill nodded impatiently to Lord Moran. 'Well go on, Charles. Give her your diagnosis.'

'The Prime Minister is suffering from a severe case of pneumonia.' Lord Moran's lips tightened. 'But he is already responding well to the sulphonamide treatment sulphapyridine.' He gave her a thin, patronising smile. 'His temperature is down to a hundred.'

'Have you been able to check his blood count?' Molly asked. It felt terribly presumptuous to be interrogating a doctor of Lord Moran's standing. Any doctor, come to that. She couldn't imagine what Sister Parkes would say if she could hear her. But she had no idea what pathology might be available in this godforsaken, battle-scarred country. And if she was going to give anything like an informed opinion, she needed to know the full picture.

Certainly Lord Moran looked taken aback by the question, even though he must have known as well as she did that the blood count was the acid test. 'Yes,' he said. 'The blood count is improving day by day.' He saw her glance at the X-ray machine and went on swiftly before she could ask the question. 'The radiographs show a considerable reduction of the congestion in the lungs.'

Molly nodded. 'Has there been any fibrillation?'

'Yes,' Lord Moran said grudgingly. 'But I have prescribed digitalis and there is some improvement there as well. The attacks are less frequent and less prolonged.'

Molly thought back to Helen de Burrel lying white-faced and shivering in the Wilhelmina. Helen had never shown any sign of improvement. Not until the penicillin had been administered, at least. Her deterioration prior to that had been swift and continuous. That was exactly why Molly had gone in search of the miracle drug. She wouldn't have made all that effort if Helen had shown any sign of recovery.

Molly glanced quickly at Dr Pulvertaft, then at Lord de Burrel, who was still standing by the door, watching her, with his hands in his pockets. He nodded encouragingly. She gave him a nervous smile and turned back to the Prime Minister.

'It sounds to me as though Lord Moran already has you on the mend, sir,' she said. 'And in that case, unless you suffer a relapse, I don't think there would be any particular benefit in introducing penicillin. Even though it does appear to have miraculous properties, it is a very new drug, still in development, and it's probably best not to experiment on someone as important as you. Except perhaps in an emergency.'

Winston Churchill thought that was hilarious. He threw back his head and roared with laughter, which brought on a fit of coughing. 'This girl is wasted as a nurse,' he gasped as he lay back weakly on his pillows and closed his eyes. 'But take her away before she kills me.'

Molly couldn't resist a quick glance at the QA. The woman's prim little eyes were almost popping out of her head.

But Lord Moran looked mollified. It had clearly galled him to have to justify his diagnosis and treatment to some pipsqueak nurse. His shoulders relaxed and his demeanour towards her became more civil. Not quite approving, but certainly more tolerant. In any event he clearly felt that good manners obliged him to make some mild conversation as he ushered her to the door. 'I understand you have recently arrived here from Italy,' he said.

His tone was complacent, unemotional, and Molly suddenly felt another unwanted giggle bubbling up inside her. The blasted man made it sound so easy. So simple. As though she had been holidaying there.

'Yes,' she said, trying to emulate his blasé, impassive tone. 'My friend and I were taken prisoner by the Italians when our ship was torpedoed. Then after the armistice our camp was taken over by the Germans.'

He paused at the door. 'That sounds rather uncomfortable,' he said. 'I expect you were glad to be rescued.'

Molly had been about to step past him out of the room, but at that she paused too, provoked by his bland assumption. 'Actually, we weren't rescued,' she said. 'We escaped.'

'Really?' His brows rose slightly. 'How did you manage that?'

Molly felt a stab of irritation. How did you manage that, indeed? She didn't want to brag, but really, his air of patronising scepticism was hard to take.

She hesitated for a moment, then pointed at the leather doctor's bag on the table. 'The last time I saw a bag like that, it belonged to a very unpleasant medical officer in the Gestapo. I managed to steal a pair of scissors and we used them to crack open a train window.' She gave him a bland smile. 'That's how we escaped. Some Italian peasants hid us until it became too dangerous. Then we made our way to France and made contact with someone in the French Resistance. He helped us get to Corsica.'

Lord Moran looked as though she had slapped him round the face with a wet fish. 'Good God,' he said.

Pleased to see that she had finally succeeded in wiping the condescending look off his face, Molly nodded politely and stepped out on to the landing, where Helen's father was now waiting to escort her down the stairs.

441

But to her surprise, Lord Moran followed her out and pulled the door to behind him. He gave a slight cough and cleared his throat. 'I imagine that you will be keen to get back to England,' he said. 'But ...' He put up a hand to adjust his tie. 'But if you were able to stay on for a few days ... just in case there is a relapse. It might be useful to have you at hand if we do have to consider getting hold of some penicillin.'

Molly turned to glance at Lord de Burrel. She saw the laughter in his eyes. 'Of course,' she said at once. 'I'll stay as long as necessary.'

On 19 December, Malcolm's birthday, Katy went down to the courtroom to watch Mr Garrow being brought up in front of the magistrate. To her relief, bail was refused. He was remanded in custody, charged with larceny. It was a serious charge in wartime, but despite an offer of leniency if he implicated his accomplices, he obstinately refused to open his mouth.

'Honour among thieves,' the arresting sergeant said sourly to Katy afterwards. 'But it's my guess there's worse things than thieving going on, and he knows his nasty little pals aren't going to make life easy for him if he spills the beans. He'd rather do his time than have his house burnt down.'

Katy shuddered. She hoped none of Mr Garrow's unsavoury friends and relations would think to burn the pub down in revenge for his capture. It was a worrying thought, but more worrying at the moment was the idea of going into labour during the night with nobody there to help her. Malcolm might have a knack of catching thieves, but he wasn't going to be much help if her waters broke at two o'clock in the morning.

As she walked heavily back up the hill to Lavender Road, she racked her brains to think of someone who might be prepared to sleep in the pub with her, just in case. But with all her best friends away, it wasn't easy to think of who to ask. Bella James was clearly out of the question. Angie Carter was far too excitable. Joyce would have been the best, but she wouldn't want to leave Angie on her own. Pam and Alan had their hands full with George and baby Nellie. In the end, the only person she could think of was Elsa.

Elsa, of course, was only too pleased to help out. But it seemed an imposition on the poor girl when she was working all hours of the day and night for her already. Katy explained that she wasn't expecting her to deliver the baby or anything. But at least she could fetch help if the worst happened.

When Louise heard of the arrangement, when she brought Malcolm one of her brother's old footballs as a birthday present, she was incensed that Katy hadn't thought of her.

'I am much more your friend than Elsa,' she said huffily. 'Why didn't you ask me? Especially when I'm trying to be so nice.'

The truth was that it hadn't occurred to Katy to ask Louise. Nice or not, Louise always made such a fuss about everything. And the last thing Katy was going to need in the middle of her labour was some hysterical outburst. But now she felt guilty. 'I'd love you to come and sleep here,' she said weakly. 'Maybe you and Elsa could take it in turns?'

'I don't want to take it in turns,' Louise said. 'I'll sleep here until Ward gets back and you can tell that stupid Elsa you don't need her after all.'

Katy hadn't the energy to argue. If only Molly was here, she thought. She would feel so much more confident about the baby, and the bar. 'Well OK,' she said reluctantly. 'But only if you promise not to snap Elsa's nose off every time you see her.' The repercussions of the fateful photograph had rumbled on, with Louise cold-shouldering Aaref and bad-mouthing Elsa whenever she got the opportunity. Neither of which made for a peaceful atmosphere in the pub.

Louise brightened at once. 'OK, I promise,' she said. 'I'll go and get my things right now.' She giggled guiltily. 'I've been looking for an excuse to get out of Mummy and Daddy's house. It's so boring there in the evenings, and Daddy keeps banging on about me getting a more ladylike job, somewhere I might meet more respectable men. I ask you. Anyone would think I was about to hang out a sign offering sex like Mrs James.'

Katy couldn't help laughing at that. She knew it was exactly what Louise's parents feared. But it wasn't really funny. Mrs James hadn't precisely hung out a sign, but it was well known locally by now that she was willing to exchange her favours for anyone prepared to pay.

It made it awkward for Katy having Bella working in the pub, but she felt sorry for the girl. And Bella had turned out to be invaluable for keeping an eye on Malcolm, especially now that he had learned how to escape from both his cot and his playpen.

Katy put a hand to her stomach as the baby kicked painfully. Oh God, she thought. The combination of Louise, Elsa and Bella was not one she would ever have chosen for her hour of need.

The only good news was that Winston Churchill was apparently getting better. It had been in the paper that evening: *The Prime Minister's temperature is subsiding and the pneumonia resolving. There has been some irregularity of the pulse, but he is expected to make a full recovery.*

The following evening, Henry Keller knocked at Joyce's door in Lavender Road. He had come to thank her for letting him know about Jen, and had brought with him a twenty-pound turkey. 'I have a friend with a farm in Norfolk,' he said over his shoulder as he lifted it out of the taxi. 'I thought you might like it to celebrate Jen's return.'

'Goodness me, Mr Keller,' Joyce stammered. 'That's very kind of you.'

Looking up into his smooth, handsome face as he handed over the neatly plucked and trussed bird, she suddenly felt flustered. She knew she ought to ask him in. But she couldn't. Not with Mr Lorenz's turkey already sitting in a bowl of salt on the sideboard. So instead she heard herself inviting him to come for Christmas lunch. It was the only thing she could think of, and the minute she had said it, she regretted it. She didn't want Mr Lorenz to find out that she had more than one turkey. And it would be bound to come out.

Jen might not get home in time anyway. Even if she did, Joyce had no idea what sort of a state she would be in after her ordeal in Italy.

And what about the others? Mr Lorenz would be all right, he had met Henry Keller before. And Sister Morris and Dr Goodacre were perfectly civilised. And Angie was always raving on about what a gentleman he was. But what on earth were Pete and Mick going to say when they found a complete stranger, and such a posh, sophisticated one at that, sitting at the lunch table with them? And what on earth would he think of them? On top of that, where were they all going to sit? She hadn't thought of that. The kitchen table was only big enough for four, or five at a pinch.

I must be mad, she thought, I must have gone stark raving bonkers. But she could hardly rescind the invitation now she had offered it.

Realising that Henry hadn't responded, she glanced at him nervously. 'You've probably made other arrangements already,' she suggested hopefully.

'As a matter of fact, I have,' he said. 'But I will be passing quite close, so I could pop in for a drink beforehand?'

A drink? What sort of drink? Joyce was assailed by a new panic. She had no idea what a man like Henry Keller would expect to drink on Christmas morning. And now she would have to ask Dr Goodacre and Sister Morris to come a bit earlier and all.

But it was impossible to refuse Henry Keller. There was something about him that made you agree with everything he said. No wonder he was so successful, she thought, as he got back in the taxi. She was beginning to understand why Jen had got her knickers in such a twist over him.

'It's completely ridiculous,' Joyce said to Mrs Rutherford the following morning. 'I didn't think I'd get sight or sound of a turkey this year, and now I've got the damn things coming out of my ears.'

Suddenly she realised that this was an opportunity to repay some of Celia Rutherford's kindness.

She felt herself colouring slightly. 'I'd rather like to keep the one Mr Lorenz's gave me,' she said. 'But you should have the one from Mr Dove.

And we'll serve the other one up in the café.'

Tunisia was in a state of flux. The fighting had been over for several months, but the signs of war were evident everywhere. The pitiful groups of homeless displaced persons. The lines of broken, abandoned vehicles. The rusting carcasses of tanks and trucks. The lethal, often unmarked minefields still hidden in the desert sand that meant you couldn't walk more than six inches off the side of the track. The debris of abandoned camps. The endless reams of tangled wire. And the huge numbers of Allied soldiers, who, having just completed one campaign, were now waiting to be dispatched to the next one in Italy.

Having only recently arrived in Tunisia herself, Helen was keen to explore. She casually borrowed both a jeep and a driver from the secret special operations camp where she was based, and she and Molly amused themselves by searching out sights of interest. They visited the fort at Kelibia, the arch of Bab El Bhar and the Roman ruins at Carthage, which to Molly's uncultured eye were not much different now from the rest of ruined Carthage, except there were slightly more goats.

They took a camel ride on a beach, recently declared free of mines, and browsed in the medina, which had already sprung up again in the tiny lanes and alleys in the heart of the city. Compared with the endless expanses of drab desert surrounding the city, the souk was an astonishing place of colour and scent, with hundreds of little stalls selling spices, cloth and fruit. It seemed incredible to Molly how quickly normal life – or at least what apparently passed for normal life in this bizarre world – had resumed. At least for the lucky ones who had survived two years of hell as Allied and Axis troops battled it out back and forth across their country.

Using a little bit of the money André had given her, Molly bought a selection of spices for Ward, a pair of leather slippers with orange tassels for Katy, a brightly painted camel on wheels for Malcolm, an ingenious double yo-yo for George, a crocheted doll in traditional dress for baby Nellie, and a box of sugared almonds for Pam and Alan.

She also splashed out on some of the beautiful materials on offer, and Helen took her to a wizened old tailor, who made her up four skirts, five blouses and two neat little suits in twenty-four hours. Another Arab in a dark hovel under a bombed-out building in Carthage measured her feet and made her three pairs of shoes. But nowhere, even though they trawled through nearly every silversmith and jewellery stall in Tunis, could she find a replacement for the little silver magic carpet.

The weather was warm and balmy. At the end of each hot, dusty day, they would inevitably end up back at the villa in Carthage where Helen's

445

father was staying while he was in town, only a few hundred yards from General Eisenhower's Maison Blanche, and where Molly had been allocated a small room on the top floor. There they were able to sit on one of the balconied terraces, sipping mint tea and gazing at the view across the Bay of Tunis to Cape Bon, before eating dinner served by silent men in white robes and ornate turbans.

It was all awfully grand and exotic. Molly had never experienced anything like it in her life before. But she knew it wasn't going to last for long.

Dr Pulvertaft, the nurses and two other doctors had all been staying at the villa too. It turned out that they had been brought over from Egypt at the request of Lord Moran. Now, as Winston Churchill's health slowly but surely continued to improve, they were sent away again. No summons had come for Molly, and she began to feel she was overstaying her welcome.

But Helen had no such qualms. 'I think you should stay until the New Year,' she said that evening when she arrived for supper. 'Daddy will fix it.' She raised her eyebrows. 'And that way you'll definitely get a chance to go out on your date with Callum. I had a message from him earlier today. He wants to know if you are free for dinner on Boxing Day.'

Dear Katy,

Thank you for the Christmas note and the photograph, which arrived today. What a handsome little man Malcolm has become. But we are all terribly worried about you. You looked so peaky and wan in the picture. So we have decided to spend Christmas in London. We don't want to be a nuisance, but we feel you could do with some help before (and after) the birth. Certainly until dear Ward gets home. And it will put your mother's mind at rest. We can stay with the Rutherfords at Cedars House. Celia Rutherford wrote to invite us a few days ago. She said that someone has given her a nice turkey, and with Douglas away in North Africa they would be delighted to have some company to eat it. I know poor Louise has moved back in, but perhaps it will do her good to have a few cheerful faces around. And I'm sure it will do you good too. We will arrive on Christmas Eve on the afternoon train. Fingers crossed for no delays or disruptions.

With love until then,

Your friends, Thelma and Esme Taylor

To Thelma and Esme Taylor. Thank you for kind offer stop Ward on his way home stop No need to come stop Better in New Year perhaps after baby born stop Happy Christmas stop Katy

To Katy Frazer. All arranged now stop Tickets booked stop Looking forward to seeing you tomorrow stop Thelma Taylor

Christmas Eve in the Flag and Garter was always one of the busiest days of the year. But even with the crush of bodies in the bar, it was cold. If only she could have got the window mended, Katy thought, as she poked irritably at the ineffectually smouldering coals in the fireplace. But apparently, as well as shortages of everything else, there was now a shortage of glass.

What was more, Bella hadn't turned up, and Katy was getting cross. Needless to say, there was no sign of Louise either. And Katy needed them desperately. There was a queue of customers at the bar, her mother and Ward's aunts were due any minute, and Malcolm was whining for his supper. There was no way she and Elsa were going to be able to cope on their own.

'I'm going to have to take Malcolm over to Pam,' Katy said to Elsa. 'He'll have to spend the evening there.'

But as she bent over the playpen to lift him out, a stab of pain gripped her abdomen. For a second she couldn't breathe. Oh no, she thought, surely not. Not tonight. Please not tonight. But then the moment passed, and she sighed with relief.

'I'm so sorry,' she said to Pam a few minutes later. 'But I'm short-staffed again and I just haven't time to feed him. It'll only be for a couple of hours. Do you mind?'

'No, of course not,' Pam responded automatically. But she was looking distracted, worried. 'We can't find George,' she said. 'Alan's gone out looking for him.'

'Oh no,' Katy said. But she couldn't worry about George just now. She had enough on her plate already. 'He's probably off on some prank,' she said.

'That's what I'm worried about,' Pam said grimly. Then she looked at Katy more closely. 'Are you all right? You look very pale.'

'I'm fine,' Katy said, backing away hastily. 'I'm just cold. I forgot to bring a coat.'

Waddling back across the dark street, she glanced hesitantly at Gillian James's house. The last thing she wanted was a confrontation with Mrs James, but if Bella had just got her nose in a book and forgotten the time, then …

Blasted girl, she thought. For putting me in this situation.

It took Gillian James a long time to open the door. And when she did, she was dressed up to the nines. She had obviously been expecting a customer for a Christmas Eve special, Katy thought sourly.

'I thought she was with you,' Mrs James said when Katy enquired if Bella was there.

'Well she's not,' Katy said shortly. She was cold and cross and out of breath, and the sight of Gillian James looking like a million dollars when she herself was standing there on the doorstep fat and ugly like a great panting whale made her want to cry. She knew it was unreasonable, but she suddenly blamed the glamorous widow for everything that had gone wrong over the year. The thefts, the unpleasant clientele in the pub, even for making things difficult between her and Ward. The damned woman was just too beautiful. Too sexy.

Katy wasn't jealous exactly, but Gillian James's presence in Lavender Road had definitely changed the atmosphere of the street. And the pub.

'It's most inconvenient,' she said irritably. 'Because I particularly needed her tonight.'

'It's not my fault,' Gillian James said. 'I don't know where she is.'

'Well you ought to know,' Katy snapped. 'She's far too young to be out on her own at night. If it wasn't for your—'

Hearing running footsteps, Katy turned back to the gate. In the light from Gillian James's doorway, she saw George Nelson pelting up the street as through wolves were after him.

She stepped out on to the pavement to intercept him. 'George? What are you doing?'

He gave a cry of alarm and swerved into the road. Then, realising who it was, he screeched to a halt.

'Oh, I'm glad it's you, Aunty Katy,' he said cheerfully. 'Because I think I've just killed Mr Fish.'

'What!' Katy stared at him aghast.

'I didn't mean to. But the stone must have hit him harder than I thought.'

Katy leaned weakly on Gillian James's gate as another stab of pain cramped her stomach. 'George, what are you talking about?'

'I'd got it all planned. I told Bella to go with him.'

As the pain receded, Katy found she was shivering uncontrollably. She could see her breath freezing on the icy air. She looked at George incredulously. 'You told Bella to go with Mr Fish?'

He nodded enthusiastically. 'Yes, she'd agreed to help me. But—'

'Help you to do what?'

He looked surprised. 'To get your jewellery back. He's got this lock-up, you see. But he's got so much stuff in there, I didn't know which was yours.'

Katy suddenly felt as though her blood was popping in her veins. It was making her feel very strange. She wasn't even sure if she had heard correctly. She turned her head and saw that Gillian James was still standing in her doorway, looking equally dumbfounded.

'Where is Bella now?' Gillian asked sharply.

'She's still with Mr Fish.'

'Oh my goodness, George,' Katy cried in horror. 'What have you done?'

A sulky look came over George's face. 'It was Malcolm who gave me the idea.'

'Malcolm?' Katy wondered if she was going mad.

'But you'd better come, because if he's not dead, he might wake up and kill her.'

Knowing Barry Fish, being killed was going to be the least of Bella's problems, Katy thought, but before she could muster a suitable retort, Gillian James was reaching for her coat and a torch.

And then the three of them were hurrying down the street.

'Where are we going, George?' Katy gasped as they turned on to Lavender Hill. 'I've left Elsa alone in the pub, and—'

'It's not far,' George said. 'It's an alley opposite the library. I've followed him there lots of times. He's always telling Bella he's got something nice to show her, and she doesn't like him, so she always says no, but this time I told her to say yes. And I knew that's where he'd take her, so I lay in wait. Like an ambush. And—'

Gillian James gave a gasp of dismay, as well she might.

'The stupid girl,' Katy said angrily. 'She really ought—'

'Don't call my daughter stupid,' Gillian said hotly.

'Well she is stupid. Surely she—' Katy stopped abruptly as another stabbing cramp forced her to double over.

Through a blur of pain, she felt the torch beam on her face and heard Gillian James's voice. 'Are you all right?'

'I've got a stitch,' Katy muttered. 'You go on. I'll catch you up.'

As they ran off, Katy tried to breathe. It's a stitch, she said to herself as she stumbled after them down the dark pavement. That's all it is. Just a stitch.

When she reached the alleyway a minute later, she found it all just as George had described.

In the light from the half-open door of the lock-up she could see Barry Fish sprawled face down on the ground with George's catapult lying incriminatingly beside him. The man was completely motionless. And when Katy crouched awkwardly by his side, she couldn't feel a pulse, either in his

449

wrist or his neck. Bella James, in her school coat, blue-nosed and shivering, was standing a few yards away.

'Oh no,' Katy whispered. She picked up the catapult. But apart from that, she had no idea what to do. She felt paralysed with shock.

'He dead, isn't he?' George asked.

Straightening up painfully, Katy nodded. 'I'm afraid he is.' She hadn't liked Barry Fish, but she hadn't wanted him dead. Nor had she wanted George to be the one to kill him. She looked at the boy's anxious face and felt a need to spare him the responsibility. 'I think he must have bumped his head when he fell.'

'Oh dear,' George said, somewhat crestfallen. 'Does that mean I won't get the reward?'

Katy barely heard him. She felt totally disorientated. All she wanted to do was run away. But she couldn't run away, not least because another crippling pain was cramping her stomach.

When it passed, she turned to Bella. 'What on earth were you thinking?'

Bella looked close to tears. 'I wanted to help you,' she whispered. 'You've been so kind to me, and George said—'

But she was interrupted by her mother. 'Mrs Frazer?' Gillian James's husky voice was low and shaky. 'I think you had better come and take a look in here.'

She was standing in the doorway of the lock-up. The door was wide open now, and Katy noticed that the keys were still dangling from the open padlock. Barry Fish had clearly been on the point of ushering Bella inside when George had taken aim.

Seeing the expression on the widow's face, Katy stumbled forward.

She had no idea what she was going to find, but what she saw made her blood run cold.

A jumble of jewellery littered the top of a grey Formica table. And there were glasses too, lots of them, all neatly lined up in size order on a grubby sideboard. Presumably ready to sell on.

But there was more than jewellery and glasses. A lot more.

Katy could only hope that George and Bella had not understood the significance of the metal bed with the stained candlewick counterpane, the half-empty bottle of whisky, the table mirror, the array of cheap, tacky make-up in front of it, the saucer of boiled sweets, the pile of dirty magazines, the ashtrays full of cigarette stubs, the camera, the factory lights, the four chairs, the thin ropes hanging from the bedstead.

She wasn't sure if she fully understood it herself, but nevertheless, she suddenly felt very sick. Once, a long time ago, Barry Fish had tried to befriend her, tried to persuade her to go home with him.

'What are we going to do?' Gillian James whispered. 'I don't want anyone to know that Bella was involved in any of this.'

'We must send George and Bella home,' Katy said. 'Then we'll get the police. We'll tell them we found Mr Fish in the alley by chance.' She felt fraught with tension, as though a terrible pressure was pushing down on her. She clenched her hand convulsively on the catapult. 'But you'll have to do it. Because I don't think I—'

And then the pain came again. This time it was accompanied by a distinct popping noise and a gush of fluid poured down between her legs.

'Oh my God.' Gillian gaped at the pool of bloody water. She glanced uncertainly at the bed. 'You'd better lie down.'

'No!' Katy screamed through her pain. 'No! I'm damned if I'm going to have my baby in Barry Fish's sordid little love nest.'

Gillian gave a choke of shocked laughter. 'Then at least sit on a chair,' she said. 'And stick that damn catapult up your jumper so the police don't see it. I'll be back in a minute.'

Chapter Thirty-Three

Gillian James was surprisingly efficient. Within minutes, George and Bella had been dispatched back to Lavender Road with strict instructions to say nothing about what had happened. The police had been summoned, and Gillian had told them that she and Katy had been on their way to the hospital when they had heard Barry Fish cry out. When they had rushed up the alley to help him, they found him dead on the ground.

'We think he must have tripped and hit his head on a stone,' she said, casting her eyes down demurely.

Whether the police believed her was another matter, but her beautiful, tragic smile was enough to take their minds off the implausibility of the story. And once they had taken a look inside the lock-up they didn't care anyway. A quick flick through some photographs they found in a drawer turned any qualms they may have had into an overriding desire to get the two women out of the way so they could set up a trap for the rest of Barry Fish's gang.

It therefore didn't take too much fluttering of Gillian James's eyelashes for them to agree to take Katy to the Wilhelmina in one of their vehicles.

'But what about the pub?' Katy wailed. 'I can't just leave it. There's only Elsa there. She'll never cope on her own. And, oh, my goodness, I'd completely forgotten, my mother and Ward's aunts are arriving any minute, and—'

'And you are going to hospital,' Gillian interrupted firmly. 'I can explain to your mother what has happened. As for the pub ...' She hesitated, and her eyes flickered. 'I know you don't like me going in there. But if you want, I can help out tonight. I'm sure Elsa will tell me what to do.'

Katy had never imagined that she would be grateful to this woman for anything. But now she wanted to kiss her. She waited for another contraction to pass, then gasped out her thanks. 'And I'm sorry,' she added. 'I know I've been mean to you, but I don't like all the men that ...' She tailed off, aware of a policeman approaching.

Gillian patted her on the shoulder. 'It's all right. I understand,' she said. 'I don't like them much either. But beggars can't be choosers. Especially not these days.' With a swish of her hips, she turned to the policeman and put her hand on his arm. She pulled him close and looked at him conspiratorially through her lashes. 'Now you take care of her, do you hear me? And don't leave her side until she is tucked up nice and snug in a hospital bed.'

The young constable looked completely overcome. If Katy hadn't been once again doubled over in pain, she would have laughed out loud. As it was, it was all she could do to totter to the police car.

The SS *Nancy* docked at Southampton late on Christmas Eve.

'Thank God,' Jen said, as she staggered on shaking legs down the gangplank with Ward Frazer and the dog, Lucky. 'I hereby announce that I will never, ever travel by ship again.'

Brisk easterly winds had speeded up the voyage but had also contributed to the swell, and Jen had had to suffer a week of constant seasickness.

Ward had tried to help her as much as he could by bringing her ginger ale, tasty morsels from the mess deck and reassuring chit-chat. But none of it had helped. Jen was feeling as weak as a kitten. Even now on terra firma she was shivering. The same wind that had caused her so much discomfort the whole way home was now biting through her thin Mediterranean clothes. Even the heavy jacket André had lent her wasn't thick enough to keep it out.

Lucky, on the other hand, had relished his time at sea. According to Ward, he had spent most of his time in the galley. Unused to any kind of restriction, he was now struggling about like an enormous fish on the length of rope Ward had attached him to.

'So what shall we do?' Ward asked, swinging his kitbag on to his shoulder. 'Are you feeling up to a train journey up to London? Or do you want to stay here for the night?'

'I want to stay here for the night,' Jen said at once. But then she saw a flicker of dismay cross Ward's face. She groaned. 'You want to get home, don't you?'

His mouth curved in a rueful grin. 'I promised Katy I'd be home for Christmas,' he said. 'And if the trains are running, I might still make it. Here, you hold Lucky and I'll go and check it out.'

The last thing Jen wanted to do was to sit on a bleak railway station waiting for some non-existent milk train to transport them to London. But nor could she refuse Ward Frazer. She hadn't gleaned much on the voyage, but she had come to understand that Ward was suffering from some misconception about Katy. Reading between the lines, they had had a falling-out before he left, and he was worrying about how to make amends.

Jen thought that was funny. It wasn't exactly going to be hard for someone like Ward Frazer to make amends, she thought. She knew how

Katy felt about him. One kiss from those lovely lips, one stroke of his hand and Katy would forgive him anything. She had toyed with telling him that, but had decided to refrain. She reckoned it was good for him to suffer.

She rather liked the thought of men suffering, she realised, as she grappled with Lucky, who seemed determined to break free so he could follow Ward. They had made her suffer enough over the years. She thought of Sean Byrne, leaving her without a backward glance. She thought of the various men in the theatre who had tried to take advantage of her. And of Hauptsturmführer Wessel.

She shuddered. She wasn't a bloodthirsty person, but she very much hoped some evil magic would lead that SS bastard to the Domaine Saint-Jean. She had every faith that André Cabillard would keep his word. And Wessel would deserve everything he got.

And then she thought about Henry Keller. According to Ward, Katy had mentioned in one of her letters that Henry had been tearing his hair out with worry about her. It sounded unlikely – she couldn't imagine Henry Keller doing anything as undignified as tearing out his own hair – but if it was true, it served him right. He should have made his feelings clear. Then she would have known where she stood. Or would she?

It occurred to her that it wasn't Henry's feelings that mattered, it was hers. And even now, even after all she had been through, she didn't know how she felt about Henry. What she did know was that she was no longer prepared to kow-tow to him. Or to anyone else come to that. If Henry decided he didn't want to help her with her career, and she couldn't make it on her own, then so be it. She would do something else. If Molly could make up her mind to give up nursing, then she could make up her mind to give up acting.

'Apparently there are no trains,' Ward said, reappearing in the company of a dock official. 'And all the hotels are shut.'

The dock official shook his head. 'Everything has closed down for Christmas,' he said. 'The trains are all up the creek.'

'So what happens if Hitler invades tonight?' Jen asked, hauling on the rope in an effort to prevent Lucky licking the dock official to death.

The man took a step back. 'Hitler won't invade now, darling,' he said complacently. 'The Jerries are well on the run.'

'They weren't when I last saw them,' Jen said sourly. 'Come to think of it, it's a shame Hitler didn't invade while he had the chance. I've just come from occupied Europe. The trains work perfectly well there.'

Laughing, Ward pulled her away. He swung his kitbag back on to his shoulder and took a firm grip on Lucky's rope. 'We'll have to try and get a taxi,' he said. And Jen resigned herself to a long night.

Sure enough, the one taxi they found only had enough petrol to go thirty miles. They decided that was better than nothing. But when the driver saw Lucky, he refused altogether.

At that point Jen lost patience. 'Oh for goodness' sake,' she said. 'What do you think he's going to do? Eat you?'

Ward intervened hastily. 'My friend here has recently escaped from a prison camp in Italy,' he said. 'She has travelled halfway across Europe to get back to England. All she wants is to go home to her family for Christmas.'

'That sounds a right cock-and-bull story,' the taxi driver said, but he nodded grudgingly. 'All right then, get in. But if that animal misbehaves, I'll charge you extra.'

Joyce stared in dismay at Mr Lorenz's turkey. She had been up at five o'clock in order to get it into the oven. It was going to take forever to cook. The damn thing only just fitted in the oven at all. She had had to bring a baking tray back from the café to roast it in because she didn't have a big enough one herself. She had hoped to get an early night on Christmas Eve. But the boys had arrived back, and what with Mick's wildly improbable stories of life at sea, and Pete's shy account of his naval engineering course, and Angie's delight at seeing her brothers again, the evening had stretched into the night.

What was more, at some point Mick had gone over to the pub and come back with some far-fetched story about Katy Frazer murdering Barry Fish and being carted off in a police car. When Joyce went over there herself, she was told that Katy had in fact gone into labour and had been taken to hospital in a police car organised by Gillian James. That seemed almost as unlikely as the previous story, but when she saw Gillian James and Katy's mother beavering away at the sink, and Ward's ancient aunts stumbling around collecting glasses under the direction of Louise Delmaine, she gleaned that things at the pub were at least vaguely under control, and she could return to her own Christmas preparations with a clear conscience. Nobody she talked to seemed to know anything about Barry Fish, but if he had been murdered, then as far as Joyce was concerned, it was good riddance.

But now it was eleven o'clock on Christmas Day. And she was ratty and flustered from lack of sleep. And notwithstanding the undercooked turkey, she still had a million things to do before her guests arrived.

Earlier she had sent the boys down to the café to fetch extra chairs while Angie helped her lay the makeshift table in the front room. They had combined the kitchen table with two dressing tables from upstairs. Joyce eyed the final result critically. The levels weren't quite right, but covered in a white sheet like a restaurant tablecloth, decked out with glasses, plates and cutlery from the café, and decorated with the holly she had snipped off the bush in Mrs Rutherford's garden and the crackers Angie had laboriously made out of the pages of one of Jen's acting magazines, it looked quite festive.

Mr Lorenz certainly seemed to think so when he arrived at eleven thirty. 'My word, Mrs Carter,' he said. 'You are doing us all proud.'

'You won't feel proud when you taste the pudding,' she said. 'I had to make it out of potato and carrot because I couldn't get enough suet.'

His eyes twinkled. 'I'm always proud of you, Mrs Carter. Whatever you do. Surely you know that by now.'

It had been a long night. By midnight Katy had been convinced she was going to die of exhaustion. Over the next four hours, the contractions became increasingly rapid and intense but the baby still showed no sign of emerging. And there was still no sign of Ward. She had been aware of her mother coming, and rather quickly going again. Katy had pleaded with her to stay, but she said it was too stressful. 'I can't bear to see you like this,' she said. 'It upsets me too much.' And after she had gone, Katy wept copiously.

'Good Lord,' Sister Morris said when she sailed into the room a few minutes later. 'What a fuss you are making. Anyone would think you hadn't given birth before.'

'I nearly died last time,' Katy gasped. 'And I'm definitely going to die this time if it doesn't come soon.'

'Nonsense,' Sister Morris said briskly. 'The midwife says it's all going very smoothly.'

'Smoothly!' Katy couldn't believe her ears.

'I am going off now for Christmas lunch at Mrs Carter's,' Sister said. 'But I will call later to see how you are going on. And if necessary, I will ask Dr Goodacre to take a look at you then.'

And through her blur of agony, Katy realised that it was the first time she had ever seen Sister dressed in mufti, a vast lilac twinset that somehow emphasised her enormous bosom even more than her uniform did. She wondered briefly what Dr Goodacre would think of it, but then another stab of pain took all thoughts out of her brain. By the time it was over, Sister Morris had gone.

It hadn't occurred to Joyce how crowded her front room would seem when her guests arrived. What with the improvised table and her three hulking children, there was hardly room to swing a flea in there, let alone a cat. And how was she meant to entertain them to a drink when she was running into the kitchen every few minutes to check on the turkey?

She had looked at the damn thing so often, she felt as though she had almost been living in the oven. And now, flushed and sweating, with her new Christmas perm already collapsing, she found herself forcibly thrusting Dr Goodacre into the front room, where he stood with his nose almost pressing against Sister Morris's voluminous violet bosom. Not that he seemed to mind. On the contrary, he was rubbing his hands with glee.

'Well, well,' he said, turning with some difficulty to address Mr Lorenz. 'How charming this is. We are going to have a delightful party, aren't we?'

'We are indeed,' Mr Lorenz agreed, trying to retain his balance as Angie squeezed between them carefully nursing a small glass of sherry for Henry Keller. 'All we need now is for Jennifer to arrive home. That would certainly make my day complete.' As he spoke, he caught Joyce's eye. She felt a stab of panic. She knew what that quizzical look meant. He was still waiting. Still hoping.

'Hear, hear,' Henry said and everyone laughed.

Flustered, Joyce muttered something about the turkey, and stepped hastily back into the passage.

Feeling a draught, she turned, and saw that the front door was still open.

And there, standing on the doorstep, dressed in an extraordinary selection of clothes, thin as a rake, with dark shadows under her eyes, was Jen.

In the end, the hospital midwife relented and gave Katy some gas and air.

After that, Katy didn't know what was happening. It didn't seem to make any difference to the pain, but it did make her feel light-headed and dizzy. Several times she dropped the mouthpiece in her delirium. Someone kept screaming nearby and it annoyed her. It took her several minutes to realise the screams were emanating from her.

Through a hazy blur, she could hear the midwife chatting unconcernedly with another nurse. They were bemoaning the fact that they were on duty at Christmas. A doctor glanced in briefly, but even he seemed to be concerned only with getting the baby born in time for Katy to tuck into a nice hospital Christmas lunch. She didn't have the energy to tell him what she would like to do with his Christmas lunch. But it certainly wasn't eat it.

At one stage, flat on her back and racked with pain, she even thought she heard Ward's voice. He seemed to be remonstrating with someone outside her room.

'She may be your patient,' he was saying. 'But she's my wife. And I want

457

to see her. Right now.'

And then, slightly louder, 'Get out of the way, you stupid woman. You have no right to stop me. In that case ...'

Then the door burst open and there, wild-eyed, panting and dishevelled, as though he had run all the way from Corsica, was Ward.

He took one look at Katy spread-eagled on the bed, writhing in agony, with her feet up in stirrups, and rounded angrily on the midwife who was standing at the end of the bed.

'What on earth's going on?' he shouted. 'I could hear her screaming from the other end of the corridor. Why aren't you doing anything to help her?'

The midwife recoiled in alarm. 'It's perfectly normal, sir,' she stammered. 'A certain amount of pain is natural during childbirth. But I must protest. This is most irregular. Husbands are not allowed in the delivery room. If you don't leave now, I will have to call the doctor.'

'You can call whoever you damn please,' Ward said grimly. 'I'm not going to stand out there listening to her screams.'

'But your wife won't want you to see her like this.'

He strode over to the bed. 'I guess that's a question we need to ask my wife,' he said. He stood looking at Katy for a long moment. Then he lifted her clenched fist and folded her fingers round his own hand. 'Do you want me to go away?' he murmured softly, raising it to his lips. 'I don't want to, but I will if you want me to.'

Katy looked hazily up into his grey eyes. She saw the tenderness there, the emotion, and the anxiety. She felt the hard strength of his hand on hers. And even in her weakened state, even drugged with gas and air, panting and exhausted, with the next hammering contraction already taking hold, she felt that fatal frisson, the one that curled round her heart and squeezed it tight.

She knew he was asking more than an immediate question. He was asking if she had forgiven him. Forgiven him for abandoning her for so long. For doing what he did. Perhaps even for being who he was.

She wanted to answer, she really did. She wanted to tell him to stay. To stay for ever at her side. She wanted to tell him never to leave her again. But she couldn't say anything.

Perhaps it was the rush of emotion, the relief at seeing his face again. Or perhaps it was just the right time. Whatever it was, an excruciating burning pressure suddenly bore down inside her. She could barely breathe, let alone speak. Clamping her teeth together, digging her nails into Ward's hand, she felt her whole body tense up into an involuntary, paroxysmal push.

'Good God,' Ward muttered. 'I had no idea it was like this. Surely there must be an easier way?'

'This is the easy way,' the midwife said irritably.

And Katy's gasp of hysterical laughter turned into a convulsive, strangled scream.

Five agonising minutes later, the baby was born.

Jen couldn't believe it. She had struggled halfway round Europe in order to get home for a nice quiet Christmas. She had been looking forward to having time to clean up, to sleep, to relax and regroup. And instead she was faced with a house full of people.

She had seen them through the window as she pushed open the gate. Not just any old people, but her two idiot brothers, her old bugbear Sister Morris, Dr Isn't-Everything-Fascinating Goodacre. And worst of all, by a long chalk, Henry Keller.

She had heard his voice as she walked up the path. And her heart had started to race uncomfortably. Oh no, she thought. Oh no.

And now her mother was standing in the doorway, dressed in a greasy apron, her face bright red, gaping at her as though she had forgotten who she was.

Jen knew that she must look a bit of a fright herself. She hadn't had a bath for well over a week. Her clothes stank of vomit. She hadn't managed a wink of sleep in the noisy hotel in Winchester where she and Ward had ended up last night. And now she felt ridiculously close to tears.

Oh God, she thought. I should have gone to Tunisia with Molly. That would have been so much less stressful.

But it was too late for that. Already they were crowding out to greet her. And suddenly she reminded herself what she had been through. Compared to standing in the middle of a field of vines pretending to be an Italian crone, fleeing through the streets of Toulon, or facing up to Hauptsturmführer Wessel, this was nothing. 'You're an actress, aren't you?' Molly would have said. 'Well then, act!'

So she turned her homecoming into a performance, acting out the role of the prodigal returned like the pro she was.

'Hello, Mum,' she said. 'Happy Christmas. I'm sorry if I stink, but I haven't had a bath in days.'

Her mother laughed with relief. 'Oh Jen,' she said, stepping forward to clasp her awkwardly in her arms. 'I'm so pleased you're all right.'

But facing up to Henry Keller wasn't quite so simple. It wasn't going to be so easy to pull the wool over his sharp eyes. She had forgotten his all-too-perceptive gaze, that watchful, contemplative regard.

She had already been hugged almost to death by Angie, kissed chastely on the cheek by Mr Lorenz, admonished for looking so thin by Sister Morris, heartily congratulated by Dr Goodacre, and told she smelt of sick by her brother Mick.

Now it was Henry's turn, and she wanted to get it over with as quickly and breezily as possible. This wasn't the time or the place for anything more than pleasantries. Already an expectant hush had fallen over the assembled company, punctuated only by Angie's excited giggle.

'Henry.' Jen smiled brightly. 'How lovely to see you.'

But true to form, Henry had sensed her discomfort. 'You don't have to put on a show for me,' he murmured, drawing her to one side. 'You must have had a terrible ordeal. And to find us all here is the last thing you probably want.'

'Well, I must admit I wasn't expecting to find *you* here,' Jen said.

He shrugged ruefully. 'I only called in for a quick drink. I'm not staying for lunch.' Catching the flicker of relief that crossed her face, he frowned. 'Don't look at me like that,' he murmured.

'Like what?'

'Like I'm some kind of ogre. I've been worried about you, Jen. You can't blame me for that. After all, it is my fault that you were on that damn ship in the first place.'

Jen had never seen him like this. So serious. So concerned. So intense. So preoccupied. Perhaps the last few months had changed him more than it had changed her.

But before she could answer, he swore softly under his breath. Then he took her elbow and, with a polite murmur of apology to the others, steered her out into the passage.

'I'm sorry,' he said, as she looked at him in surprise. 'But I can't say what I want to say with everyone pretending not to listen.'

Jen felt her heart start to beat uncomfortably hard and it irritated her. This was her first day back. She had been travelling all night. She had barely had a wink of sleep. She certainly wasn't looking her best. Now it seemed as though he was going to try to carry on where he had left off, and she really didn't want to have to go through all that again. All that being on her best behaviour and worrying about what he really thought about her.

She wasn't ready for it. All she wanted was to be left alone.

He put his hands on her shoulders. 'Jen, I—'

'No,' she interrupted. She backed away and held up her own hands in front of her as though to ward him off. 'I don't want you to say anything. Not just now. Not today. Maybe not ever. You are far too grand for me, Henry. I'm simply not in your league.' She waved a hand towards the front room, where she could hear Mr Lorenz and her mother making deliberately loud, self-conscious conversation. 'We live in completely different worlds.'

Henry shook his head. 'Jen, please …' He paused for a beat and his eyes narrowed slightly. 'I hardly dare ask,' he said. 'But this isn't about Conrad, is it? I know you were with him when the ship went down.'

'Conrad?' Jen almost laughed. She hadn't thought about poor old Conrad for weeks. 'No, of course not,' she said. 'It's to do with me.' She opened her hands expressively. 'I don't want to be always trying to be something I'm not. I want to be me. Yes, Molly and I did have a tough time. But we coped. We survived. We escaped. And we did it all on our own. In our own way.'

She took a breath, and glanced at him, willing him to understand. 'And now, as of last week, we are free again. I don't want to get trapped into something else. Not yet. However glamorous it might be. I just want to be me.'

Henry looked at her for a long moment. Then he smiled regretfully and took her hand and lifted it to his lips. 'I want you to be you too,' he said. 'I'm disappointed, but I understand.'

At the touch of his lips on her fingers, Jen almost melted. But she steeled herself. 'And I'll understand if you don't want me to work for you any more,' she said.

He looked shocked. 'Good God, what do you think I am? I'd be mad to turn down one of the most promising young actresses I know just because she doesn't want to marry me.'

Jen stared at him. Marry him? *Marry him?*

She heard a noise behind her. 'It's Jen that's mad,' Angie said. 'I'd marry you like a shot.'

And then Joyce was there too, squeezing past them self-consciously. 'I'm so sorry,' she muttered. 'But I must just go and check on the turkey.'

Jen glared at her wrathfully, but turning back to Henry, she saw the sparkle of appreciative humour in his eyes. And then suddenly she was laughing. And then everyone else was laughing too.

They were all laughing so hard, it was only Jen who heard the knock on the front door behind her.

Opening it, she found herself staring at a short, plump young man with a weather-beaten olive complexion and very dark, rather greasy hair.

'Good Lord,' Jen said. 'Who the hell are you?'

The young man took a careful breath. He had clearly been rehearsing his opening gambit carefully. 'I Gino,' he said, pointing at his own chest. 'I come for to claiming my bride. I come for Angela.'

Jen started at him in utter amazement. She simply couldn't believe it. After all Angie's romantic talk. All her pining. All her other admirers. And this, this miserable specimen, was the man she had been waiting for? *I Gino?* Good God, he'd been in England for well over a year. Was that really the best he could manage?

But before Jen could think of how to respond, an ear-piercing scream sounded behind her, and the next moment Angie was barging out of the door and flinging herself into the poor young man's arms, almost knocking him off his feet.

'Gino!' she shouted. 'Gino! My beautiful Gino! I knew you would come.'

Jen turned to Henry. 'Do you think she needs spectacles?' she asked.

Henry's eyes were once again brimming with laughter. 'I wonder how they are going to communicate,' he murmured.

Jen glanced at her sister. 'Body language, by the look of it,' she said sourly. And then she was laughing again. It was too ridiculous. The whole thing was ridiculous. She wondered what her mother would say. But her mother wasn't there. Glancing up the passage, Jen spotted her in the smoke-filled kitchen with Mr Lorenz, inspecting an enormous steaming turkey. They seemed to be standing very close together. Was it possible that they were even holding hands?

Good God, Jen thought. So that's the way the wind is blowing, is it? How come I am the only one to say no? But she was glad she had. There was plenty of time. Henry would just have to wait.

'It's a girl,' the midwife said. 'A lovely, bonny little girl.'

Katy opened her eyes and stared at the wrinkled creature in the midwife's arms. 'I knew it would be,' she said. 'My husband always gets exactly what he wants. That's one of the most annoying things about him.'

The midwife glanced warily at Ward. 'She is still suffering the effects of the gas and air,' she said.

Ward laughed. 'I'm not so sure about that.' He took the tiny bundle from the midwife and offered it to Katy. Then, easing himself on to the bed beside her, he pulled them both gently into his arms.

'Now I have two beautiful girls to love,' he said.

Katy felt tears of joy prickling her eyes. She could feel his heart beating strongly against her cheek. I love him too, she thought. I love him for coming back to me. For staying with me through the hideous birth. For holding the bossy midwife at bay. For caring. And for knowing that all I want now is to lie here in his embrace for ever and ever.

Wrapped in the tranquil, gently throbbing depths of the Wilhelmina, insulated from the havoc of the outside world, with her tiny daughter nestled on her chest, Katy felt a sudden profound sense of peace. Later she would suggest calling the baby Caroline after Ward's mother. But not yet.

462

Not now. This moment was too precious to spoil with talk of his parents.

Even as they lay cuddled comfortably together, somewhere in the distance Katy heard a shout and the sound of running feet. Smiling, she closed her eyes. It was nothing to do with her. For once it was someone else's problem. Her ordeal was over. She and her new little baby were safe in Ward's arms.

'Was everything all right at the pub this morning?' she murmured. 'I suppose you went there first.'

'Everything seemed fine,' he said. 'Kind of busy, but Louise and your new girl Elsa seemed to have it all under control.'

'What about Malcolm? I left him at the Nelsons'.'

'Malcolm was fine too,' he said.

The clatter of footsteps seemed to be closer now. Katy heard another shout, a female voice this time.

'Tell me about Molly and Jen,' she said. 'Are they both all right?'

'They are both fine,' Ward said. But Katy could tell he wasn't really concentrating. He was listening to what was happening outside in the corridor.

It sounded as though some kind of scuffle was under way. She could hear muttering voices and something scratching on the lino. And then a loud, repetitive puffing, snuffling sound, as though someone was operating a small pair of bellows. She saw the midwife glance at the door.

Trying to ignore the disruption, Katy snuggled closer into Ward's arms. She didn't want any distractions. She wanted this moment to last for ever. This sense of security. Of calm. Of total happiness.

'I want to know everything,' she said. 'Every detail.'

But Ward was already easing away. To her surprise, she heard him give a slight choke of laughter. 'I will tell you everything,' he said. He stood up, then turned back and kissed her. 'I promise I will. And there are things I want to know too, like why everyone is saying that you killed Barry Fish. And why there's a catapult on the bedside table. But first I have to go check what's making that noise. I brought a puppy back with me for Malcolm for Christmas. I left him in the back yard of the pub. But it sounds like he might have escaped and followed me down here. If so, I guess I'd better let him in before someone shoots him.'

Katy stared at him in amazement. She couldn't take it in. A puppy? From Corsica?

But the midwife took it in quick enough. Like a demented witch she flew across the room to bar the door. 'Oh no,' she said. 'Absolutely not. A husband is one thing. A dog is quite another.'

But she was too late. Ward's hand was already on the handle, and a second later, an enormous animal bounded into the room, followed by Sister Parkes and two porters, one armed with a broomstick.

As soon as the dog saw Ward, it leaped up at his chest, whimpering delightedly.

Katy could hardly believe her eyes. A puppy? He called that enormous brute a puppy? Its front legs reached almost up to his shoulders.

Apparently feeling that the situation had gone beyond their control, the two porters were already edging away. But Sister Parkes was almost incandescent with rage. 'Get that thing out of here at once,' she screamed.

Taking exception to her tone, the dog dropped back to all fours, flattened its ears and let out a low, ominous growl.

Sister Parkes was made of stern stuff, but not that stern. She took one look at the animal's enormous bared fangs and backed hastily out of the door.

Katy stared in disbelief. If only Molly was here, she thought. Oh, how I wish Molly had been here to see that. I can't wait to tell her that Sister Parkes was routed by a puppy.

Ward closed the door and calmly turned to the midwife, who was standing with her mouth hanging open and her eyes popping out of her head.

'I'm sorry about that,' he said, with one of his most charming smiles. 'I'll take him home in a minute.'

Then he glanced over at Katy. 'What do you think?' he asked. He nodded proudly to the dog, who was now sniffing with interest at the bloody towels on the floor. 'He's kind of cute, isn't he? I thought he'd be a nice addition to the family.'

'Cute?' Katy almost laughed out loud. But then she realised what he had said. So casually. So instinctively. *The family*. He thought of them as a family. His family. She felt a bubble of joy course through her.

She knew he would always be looking for excitement. For adventure. That was the kind of man he was. Life was never going to be boring with Ward Frazer. She knew he would go away again. Of course he would. He would never refuse the call of duty. But for now he was here. Here for Christmas, just as he had promised. Here with her. Here with his family. And she couldn't ask for more than that.

Lord de Burrel had invited Molly and Helen to a Christmas service at La Maison Blanche. As it turned out, it was quite a momentous day. It had been announced on the wireless the previous evening that General Eisenhower had been selected to lead an invasion of western Europe next year, with General Montgomery as his field commander. It was now clear

464

to everyone why Winston Churchill had come to Eisenhower's villa. To meet with the new Allied Supreme Commander.

It was only the second time Molly had been to La Maison Blanche. She felt rather more confident this time, dressed in one of her new little suits, her hand-made shoes, and a jaunty hat of Helen's. But she was disappointed to discover that Douglas was not on guard at the gate to see her arrive for the church service.

A small barn in the grounds of the villa had been converted into a chapel especially for the occasion. It was as she and Helen walked down through an avenue of palm trees to the makeshift church that they encountered Lord Moran.

'Ah, Miss Coogan,' he said, raising his hat and nodding politely to Helen. 'You've probably heard that the Prime Minister has made a good recovery?'

Molly nodded, irritated by the smug little smile that accompanied his words. 'I'm glad the sulphapyridine did the trick,' she said sweetly.

His eyes narrowed slightly as he fell into step beside them. 'I gather from de Burrel that you are considering applying for medical school?' he said.

He spoke rather sharply, and Molly cringed. Oh no, she thought. My big mouth. Why did I have to choose that moment to be facetious?

'Well, yes,' she stammered. She had mentioned something about it to Helen's father one evening at dinner, as a bit of a joke, but she hadn't expected him to take her seriously, let alone tell anyone else. Now, as she felt Lord Moran's cold, assessing eyes on her, she wondered how on earth she could have been so presumptuous. The thought of someone like her aspiring to become a doctor was ludicrous. And Lord Moran was clearly about to put her out of her misery by telling her so in no uncertain terms.

But he merely inclined his head. 'I wish you luck,' he said. 'We need more women in the profession. I shall look out for you. And if you need a letter of recommendation or anything of that nature, please feel free to come and see me when you get back to England. There may well be grants and scholarships available, and it can help if someone puts in a good word.' And with that, he raised his hat and moved away.

'You can be damn sure it helps,' Helen remarked with considerable satisfaction when he was out of earshot. 'They always say it's not what you know, but who you know. And now you know the top man.'

Molly spun round to face her. 'This is your doing, isn't it?'

Helen laughed at her accusatory tone. 'Not at all,' she said. 'Dr Florey told Daddy ages ago that you would make a good doctor. I only had to give him a little nudge in the right direction.'

When they reached the chapel, they found everyone standing about outside.

465

They were waiting for the Prime Minister, who was walking arm in arm with Mrs Churchill across the lawn. He was leaning on a stick and taking his time, but he looked a lot better than he had last time Molly had seen him.

As the small congregation stood back politely to make room for him to enter first, he nodded at them absent-mindedly, wishing them all a happy Christmas. But as he passed Molly, he paused. 'Ah yes, the little penicillin expert,' he said.

'I am glad to see you back on your feet, sir,' Molly murmured, flushing.

He looked at her from under his heavy brows. 'De Burrel has told me some of your story,' he said.

Molly already knew that Helen's father had told him about her recent experiences. Having escaped from a prisoner of war camp himself during the Boer War, Churchill had apparently taken an interest in her adventures. But she hadn't expected the great man to single her out.

But now he reached out and shook her hand. 'You are a credit to your country,' he said in his emphatic, booming voice. 'It is the kind of pluck and determination such as you have shown that will eventually bring us to victory.'

Molly was too overcome to reply. But as he passed on, she noticed Douglas Rutherford standing to attention outside the makeshift church with a small guard of honour, and knew he must have heard every word. She couldn't believe her luck. Ha, she thought gleefully as they shuffled in and took their seats in the little barn, that'll teach the cocky little blighter what's what.

Or was it really luck? She had a sneaky feeling that it was actually all down to some kind of magic. Ever since she had bumped into that blind man outside the hospital all those months ago, she had felt as if some kind of spell had been cast over her. She remembered the sympathetic amusement in his voice. He had known she wasn't destined to start midwifery training at Croydon.

Or perhaps it had been something to do with Romany Rose at the potato fair. Or the lucky charm Ward had given her.

She thought back to all the dangers she had been through, all the close shaves, all the difficult decisions she and Jen had had to make. Somehow she had come through it all, with only a small chip off her tooth to show for it.

And now here she was, sitting across from the Prime Minister himself, still glowing from his acclaim.

Hearing a soft flurry of activity above her, she tilted back her head to see what it was. Two white doves had flown into the barn, and were now perched, cooing gently, on one of the rafters.

'Oh Molly,' Helen breathed beside her. 'Surely it's a sign. A sign that peace is on the way.'

Molly felt a sudden welling of emotion. She had come such a long way since last Christmas, when she had been stuck in the Nelsons' house, miserably covered in spots. Now she had new friends. New supporters. New hopes and ambitions. A completely new life ahead. She even had a date with Callum Frazer for tomorrow night.

The blind man knew this would happen, she thought. He said my moment would come. And he was right. This is my moment.

Author's note:

The original inspiration for LONDON CALLING came to me during a holiday to Sicily. My aunt had asked us to visit the grave of her brother (my uncle, Basil Beazley,) who was killed during the airborne invasion of 1943.

As it happened we were staying with friends near Palermo and we knew it was going to take hours to drive the whole length of the island down to the military cemetery at Syracuse. We very nearly didn't go, and then we woke up one morning and thought that if my uncle had given his life for our freedom the very least we could do was make the effort to visit his grave.

It took us seven hours to get there. The cemetery was beautifully maintained. The lines of white memorial stones stretched in all directions. Uncle Basil was in the front row. He was twenty nine when he died. Amazingly he had survived the disastrous glider landings but died later defending a bridge. We put flowers on his grave, cried for twenty minutes, and then we drove the seven hours back again. And that night I decided I wanted to write a novel which in some small way would touch on his story.

So many people helped me in so many ways during the research and writing of London Calling. It is impossible to mention everyone by name but I want to give special thanks to a few people whose input made a specific impact on my story. To Antony Jefferson for his wry recollections of a torpedo attack on his ship in the Atlantic and for his casual mention of once visiting Howard Florey's penicillin laboratory. To Brenda Joughin, Billie Cullen and Jo Howe for their descriptions of hospital life in wartime Oxford and London. To Val and Pat Ripley for their reminiscences of growing up in the 1940s and the ENSA shows they attended. To Gordon Quarendon for his childhood memories of North Africa. To James Parker for bamboozling me with his magic tricks. To James Stone, Albert Berry, Alan Drayton and George Tones for their various accounts of war-torn London and of life in the forces, both in North Africa and Italy. To Janet Smith of the Wandsworth Historical Society and to the staff of Battersea Library Archive for their continuing support. And to Ian James for his advice on storing unrefrigerated turkeys!

As always, I have tried to be as accurate as possible with the information they have given me, and with the historical facts. But it is, in the end, a story and I hope they, and my readers, will forgive me any small adjustments I have made.

Most of all I want to thank my wonderful husband, Marc, for his constant, unstinting help and encouragement, and for not minding (too much) when for weeks on end I mentally disappeared into 1943.

Thank you so much for taking the time to read this novel. If you have enjoyed it please do tell your friends or write a review! LONDON CALLING is the fourth novel in my Lavender Road series. If you would like to find out about its predecessors, or about my other books, or if you would like to contact me, please do visit my website.

Helen Carey
www.helencareybooks.co.uk
Twitter: @helencareybooks
Facebook: /helencareybooks

Next in the Lavender Road series:

HELEN CAREY
The Other Side of the Street

It's January 1944. The British are weary of air raids and rationing. But now there are rumours of an Allied invasion of France. The tide of the Second World War finally seems to be turning.

For the residents of London's Lavender Road, however, the war seems determined to thwart their plans for future happiness.

When an attractive American officer arrives at her factory to recruit volunteers for a secret project, Louise Rutherford leaps at the opportunity, but soon discovers that things aren't going to be anywhere near as easy as she thought.

Actress Jen Carter's relationship with theatrical producer Henry Keller hits a hurdle when a former boyfriend unexpectedly reappears, and when V1 retaliation rockets start hitting London, even Jen's mother's tentative romantic dreams come under threat.

Praise for THE OTHER SIDE OF THE STREET:

'My return to Lavender Road was a delightful experience. The memorable characters and the great sense of time and place are a credit to the author. I can thoroughly recommend it.' *Ellie Dean*
'Superb London wartime saga.' *Natalie Meg Evans*
'Awesome book. Felt like I was there.' *Amazon reviewer*

Also by Helen Carey:

Lavender Road
Some Sunny Day
On a Wing and a Prayer
London Calling
The Other Side of the Street
Victory Girls

Slick Deals
The Art of Loving

http://www.helencareybooks.co.uk

BRIDGEPORT
PUBLIC LIBRARY

1230279150

CPSIA information can be obtained
at www.ICGtesting.com
Printed in the USA
LVHW01s1808251018
594823LV00013B/321/P